PAX BRITANNIA

The ULYSSES QUICKSILVER Omnibus

By
Jonathan Green

Abaddon Books

WWW.ABADDONBOOKS.COM

An Abaddon Books™ Publication
www.abaddonbooks.com
abaddon@rebellion.co.uk

This omnibus first published in 2010 by Abaddon Books™,
Rebellion Intellectual Property Limited, Riverside House,
Osney Mead, Oxford, OX2 0ES, UK.

10 9 8 7 6 5 4 3 2 1

Editor-in-Chief: Jonathan Oliver
Desk Editor: David Moore
Junior Editor: Jenni Hill
Cover: Pye Parr
Original series covers: Mark Harrison
Design: Simon Parr & Luke Preece
Marketing and PR: Keith Richardson
Creative Director and CEO: Jason Kingsley
Chief Technical Officer: Chris Kingsley
Pax Britannia™ created by Jonathan Green

ISBN (UK): 978-1-907519-36-9
ISBN (US): 978-1-907519-56-7

Printed in the US

INTRODUCTION

Unnatural Origins

Being a Treatise on the Origins of the World of Pax Britannia,

or,

Where Ideas Come From

by Jonathan Green

WHAT YOU ARE holding in your hands is the culmination of nearly three years work and something of which I am very proud. But if you're new to the world of *Pax Britannia*, the steampunk setting in which the three novels in this collection are all set, now would seem to be an appropriate juncture to bring you up to speed.

In the closing years of the 20th century the British Empire's rule is still going strong. Queen Victoria is about to celebrate her 160th jubilee, as she has been kept alive by advanced steam technology. London is a fantastical sprawling metropolis where dirigibles roam the skies, robot Bobbies enforce the law and dinosaurs are on display in London Zoo. Welcome to Magna Britannia, a steam-driven world full of fantastical creations and shady villains. Here dashing dandies and moustachioed villains battle for supremacy while below the city strange things stir in the flooded tunnels of the old London Underground.

I was recently asked how long the idea for the *Pax Britannia* series had been knocking around inside my head before I pitched it to Abaddon Books. My initial reply was that it was somewhere in the region of five or ten minutes. I remember stumbling upon the original press release from Abaddon calling for contributors to the four series they had in development at the time. But what I latched onto was the comment that this nascent publisher would be willing to consider pitches for new series. It was the whole idea of anachronisms that appealed to me at the time and so I sat down and composed the following email, which I reproduce here for the first time:

It's the end of the 20th Century and Queen Victoria still reigns supreme, maintained by a Babbage-esque creation. The British Empire still covers most of the known world as well as the Moon and the nearer planets. However, on these worlds sedition and discontent are growing with the Martian separatist movement gaining in power and influence all the time. Everything you have read in Victorian gothic novels is true. People can be brought back from the dead, there are dinosaurs still living in remote parts of the world (and London Zoo!), and Darwin's theory of evolution has been proved correct by a number of unstable, experimental scientists. Aristocratic vampire bloodlines hold sway over Eastern Europe and have sunk their claws into the Russian royal family (Russia being a princeling state of Magna Britannia), steam and clockwork robot-drudges work alongside the down-trodden under classes, whilst reasoning engines help the ruling classes maintain governance of this over-populated world. Railways bestride the world and there are cities on the ocean-bed. With much of the world united under British rule scientific advances have continued, in a retro-scientific fashion, beyond what we have achieved in our own world. Having mastered space-travel mankind is now tinkering with temporal-travel.

Into this setting we throw suave dandy and rogue Ulysses Lucian Quicksilver, sometime adventurer and agent of the throne, who works for shadowy masters desperately trying to maintain a regime that has lasted for over 150 years and which is falling apart from within, and who may not be all that they seem. He fights the arch-felons of the underworld... assisted by his unshakeable manservant Nimrod, as the clock of Big Ben counts down to the year 2000, and the end of the world.

As fans of the series will see, very little changed from this initial premise; rather, it is a case of more having been added since then rather than anything being taken away from the original outline.

However, as I have realised myself since being asked the question of *Pax Britannia's* origins, in truth the idea had been hidden away, gestating in some dark corner of my mind, for a long time, not quite entirely forgotten about, so that when I started to write the first *Pax Britannia* novel proposal all these ideas suddenly burst forth and simply wouldn't stop coming.

I stumbled across some notes the other day that I had not seen since I wrote them down ten years ago. Amongst them there was a page of barely legible scrawl about a character called 'Mandeville Sachs, Gentleman Adventurer'. The dinosaurs in the Challenger Enclosure at Regent's Park Zoo get a mention, as does Queen Victoria in a life support throne. There's a line about bases on the Moon and Mars, and there's even a paragraph about a scientist teasing out the strands of DNA, or, as he called it, 'the stuff of life'. Five years later, these ideas fought their way back into my conscious mind as I composed my initial email to Abaddon. Mandeville Sachs managed to escape from my subconscious on this occasion as well, only now he was called Ulysses Quicksilver.

I don't know where the name came from. I remember thinking at the time that it would do for now and that I could always change it later, only I never did.

But Ulysses didn't really come together properly as a character until I sat down to write the pitch for the first *Pax Britannia* book *Unnatural History*. He was finally crystallised during the writing of the prologue to that story, which can also be seen as a prologue to the series as a whole. So who is he?

Ulysses Quicksilver is a patriot, a lady's man, a toff, a show-off, an expert swordsman, a damn fine shot, an epicure, a dedicated follower of fashion, a thrill-seeker, a man of the people, a lover, a fighter, a habitual challenger of authority, a man of action, an incisive mind, a mass of contradictions, a playboy – but most importantly of all, he is a hero. But who is he *really*?

Well, inevitably, as he is a creation of my imagination, in some ways he is, in fact, me. However, there's some James Bond in there too, a dash of Sherlock Holmes and a soupcon of Oscar Wilde. But, at the end of the day, with nearly half a million words published about him and his adventures, he is his own man; just as *Pax Britannia* has become something that is more than the sum of its parts.

Pax Britannia wears its influences on its sleeve. Yes, it's steampunk – which for me means that it has a recognisably Victorian setting in which late nineteenth century technologies have formed the basis for all developments since, so that we have clockwork computers and robots, alongside steam-powered vehicles, married with that no-holds-barred attitude of the Victorian mind, the idea that there was nothing science couldn't achieve and that there were no real limits to Man's endeavours, with everything finished in teak and brass. (You can never have too much teak and brass in my book.)

But within *Pax Britannia's* wide-ranging bounds you'll also find the War on Terror, Agatha Christie, James Bond, *The League of Extraordinary Gentlemen*, dinosaurs, Darwinism, Sir Arthur Conon Doyle, penny dreadfuls, 1950s B-movies, Jules Verne, H G Wells and even a little *Doctor Who* (which, it could be argued, is becoming more and more steampunk itself in its latest incarnation).

And it is a whole world, a backdrop so vast that practically any tale you could ever want to tell can be accommodated within it, from spy thrillers and murder mysteries, to love stories and tales of unadulterated horror.

At the time of writing, I am actually working on my sixth Ulysses Quicksilver *Pax Britannia* novel, entitled *Dark Side*, in which our hero is going to take his own personal style of derring-do to the Moon. A seventh has already been commissioned as well, and I have ideas for several others. There's certainly plenty of life left in the old dog yet.

So, charge your brandy glasses and join me in a toast to Magna Britannia and Ulysses Quicksilver, Hero of the Empire!

Long live the Queen!

Jonathan Green
London, MMX

PAX BRITANNIA

UNNATURAL HISTORY

JONATHAN GREEN

For Mattie

for being late

PROLOGUE

The Return

THE JANGLING OF the doorbell rang through the echoing space of the entrance hall. It rang through rooms of shrouded furniture and echoed from marble and alabaster columns. It rebounded from ancient family heirlooms and antique vases. It did nothing to disturb the eternal sleep of the ancestors who were depicted in the portraits adorning the dark, papered walls. Eventually the sound was lost along the tiled passageway leading to the kitchen and the servants' quarters, no longer an echo but merely the memory of one.

Peace returned again to the London town house, the only sound in the otherwise silent rooms the regular mechanical ticking of the grandfather clock standing in the hollow of the stairwell. It was unshrouded, the motto 'Tempus Fugit' clearly visible on its peeling face. The gentle ticking marking time in a house where time no longer had any meaning.

A tapping joined the steady count of the clock; that of leather soles on glazed white tiles. The house's guardian strode purposefully, and yet unhurriedly, towards the front door. He passed along the corridor from his retreat beyond the kitchen, back straight, head upright, the aquiline features of his face cold and unsmiling as he stared straight ahead of him with piercing sapphire eyes.

The portraits watched him with their impassive canvas eyes as he passed. Electric light bathed everything in its yellow luminescence.

He walked past a huge gilt-framed mirror that dominated one wall but did not even glance at his reflection to check the starched collar, the knot of his cravat or the set of his grey hair, swept back from a widow's peak.

The bell rang again as he put his hand to the doorknob and pulled the front door of the London town house open. The shorter, stouter man waiting impatiently on the step physically jerked back, startled by the suddenness of the manservant's appearance.

The stout man looked up at the servant looming over him and into the flinty eyes glaring down from beneath darkly shadowed brows. Breaking eye contact, uncomfortable beneath the piercing stare, he looked the butler up and down, taking in the rest of his intimidating figure. The butler was a man of indiscernible age although he could not be younger than forty-five and could even be into his sixties. His expression of aloof disdain and his chiselled features gave him an aristocratic air. However, the butler's nose had clearly been broken on more than one occasion. It gave him the look of an aging prize-fighter carried off with the bearing of a gentleman's loyal retainer.

"Ah, Nimrod."

"Mr Screwtape, sir," the manservant replied. His accent was as polished and refined as his collar was starched crisp and white. "You are expected. Please come in."

There was nothing in Nimrod's tone and his impassive expression that suggested the lawyer was welcome. In fact the invitation made Screwtape feel as if he were trespassing.

"Mr Quicksilver awaits you in the study."

The butler stepped to one side and then shut the door on the chill of the night outside. Screwtape removed his bowler hat with one hand – a briefcase held in the other – revealing his feeble attempts to brush his thinning, obviously dyed black hair over the balding dome of his head. Small piggy eyes, set amidst flabby features, peered out from the lenses of a pair of pince-nez spectacles beneath which nestled a short, bushy moustache.

"May I take your coat, sir?"

"N-No, it's all right. I'll keep it with me." Nimrod was making him feel nervous.

"Very well, sir." Nimrod's tone was almost wearisome. "If you would care to follow me."

The butler led the lawyer through rooms of dust sheet shrouded furniture and glowering ancestral portraits, through a musty-smelling formal library and to a single oak-panelled door. There he stopped and gave the door a gentle knock.

"Come in," came an aristocratic voice from beyond. The butler opened the door, allowing the visitor to enter before him.

Screwtape found himself in a spacious study. The walls were lined with cases of books and, where the paisley-print wallpaper still showed, there were walnut-framed aquatints and spectrum-tinted photographs of exotic locations from around the globe. There were also curious artefacts no doubt collected from those self-same destinations. Amongst them Screwtape could see a Masai warrior's spear and antelope-hide shield, a Burmese demon-mask and, most disturbing of all, a dark, stained human skull stuck with flints and the plumage of a bird of paradise. The lawyer had no idea where that particular item had come from, nor did he want to.

Several pieces of furniture were well accommodated within the study also. A large mahogany desk stood before him, behind it a rich leather chair. There was also another chair and a chaise longue. In one corner an effort had been made at horticulture where a potted aspidistra stood on a turned ebony plant-stand.

The room was finished in mahogany and wine-dark velvet. Behind the desk, heavy drapes concealed tall windows and above the black iron mantle of a fireplace was the imposing portrait of a grey haired and moustachioed man. The subject of the painting was dressed in a tweed jacket, mustard-yellow waistcoat and hunting britches, looking every part the English country gent out enjoying an afternoon's grousing. He even had a rifle in his right hand; only the scene behind him was that of the African savannah and one booted foot rested on the carcass of a savage lion.

Screwtape looked from the heroic portrait to the young man standing beneath it. The family resemblance was remarkable.

Covering much of the scuffed green leather of the desk were clippings from *The Times*. A number of articles were of particular interest to the young man, which he was re-reading while he swirled the contents of a cut crystal glass in his right hand. As the lawyer peered through his pince-nez at the papers he saw from the larger print of the headlines that they appeared to concern the same matter. One headline read, 'Millionaire Playboy Missing over Himalayas,' another, 'Hot Air Balloon Adventure Ends in Tragedy.' The most recent report carried the banner, 'Quicksilver Missing, Presumed Dead.' The date on this newspaper read 3rd April 1996.

The ornate ormolu clock on the mantelpiece chimed ten. Seconds later the echoing chime of the grandfather clock sounded elsewhere in the house. There was something clandestine about the timing of this meeting and, along with Nimrod's lingering presence, it made Screwtape feel uncomfortable. Why meet at such an hour to seal the deal if there were not something nefarious about this venture? The hours of darkness were when the criminal fraternity went about their unlawful business. Not that such things would have normally bothered the lawyer. Every day it was his job to work with the law, around the law, to bend the rules, counteract conventions, confuse and bewilder with clauses, quoting obscure sub-articles. The firm of Mephisto, Fanshaw and Screwtape had been in the employ of the Quicksilver family for the last five generations, since the time of the Crimean War. They had a long-shared history and heritage.

"Screwtape, do have a seat won't you?" the young man said, gesturing to the padded leather chair.

The lawyer regarded the armchair uncomfortably, playing the rim of his bowler hat through his restless hands as he did so.

"No, it's all right. I'd prefer to stand."

The younger man cast his eyes towards the chair for the first time since the lawyer had entered the study. A distant, wistful look misted his eyes. "Yes, I know what you mean."

The empty seat seemed to exude an unsettling dominance.

"A drink then?" Quicksilver said, raising his glass as if in a toast.

"Yes, very well then," the lawyer said with some relief. A stiff drink was just what he needed. "Whisky."

"It'll have to be cognac I'm afraid. My brother's drinks cabinet appears to be a little poorly stocked of late." He cast a withering glance at the manservant, who still stood in the open doorway of the study, and handed Screwtape a brandy glass. Placing his hat and briefcase carefully on the desk, Screwtape took the proffered drink.

"The future," Quicksilver suddenly announced, chinking glasses.

The young man downed the contents of his glass in one gulp. Screwtape merely sipped at his. The warm fumes of the cognac filled his mouth and coursed down his throat to soothe his knotted stomach. "Indeed," he muttered.

"So, the papers?"

"Y-yes, of course," the lawyer said dragging his eyes away from the empty chair with some effort. "I have them here."

After some fumbling with catches, the lawyer eventually managed to extract the precious documents from his case. He passed them across the desk and Quicksilver grasped them eagerly. But Screwtape did not let go.

"Once these papers are signed," he said, his voice suddenly calm and laden with the gravitas of the moment, "your elder brother Ulysses will be declared legally dead. All this will be yours," he took in the study, and by inference the rest of the house with one sweeping gesture of his hand. "You will inherit everything as your brother's sole heir. You do understand that, don't you?"

"Yes. Of course I understand," Quicksilver said tugging at the papers. Screwtape at last relaxed his grip. "Much as it saddens me to do this," the young man said, without any hint of genuine emotion, "my brother has been missing for over a year. There has been no word from him since he set out on that fateful adventure. The wreckage of his balloon has been found on the lower slopes of Mount Manaslu. At those altitudes, even if he survived the crash, a man could not last more than a night in those sub-zero temperatures. I am sorry to say that those icy slopes must now be his final resting place."

Silence hung in the air between the two men, heavy with a dozen discomforting thoughts.

The doorbell clanged again, its jangling shattering the tense atmosphere. Both the lawyer and heir looked to the open door of the study and the shadows of the furniture-haunted library beyond.

"Who can be calling at this time of night?" Screwtape said, half to himself.

"Who indeed?" Quicksilver wondered, casting a suspicious eye in the lawyer's direction.

"If you will excuse me, sirs, I shall endeavour to find out," the butler said, the rich baritone of his voice unencumbered by the inflection of any emotion.

"Gladly," Quicksilver said, ushering him on his way with a wave of his empty glass, his eyes now fixed on the paperwork.

The lawyer's gaze returned to the pictures and curious paraphernalia that adorned the walls, the personal effects of a man they were about to condemn to the grave. Screwtape was drawn to a number of framed photographs. The same man could be seen in many of them; the only one who appeared more than once in any of the captured images, in fact. Moments of history preserved for posterity.

Here he stood with a half-naked tribe of pygmies from equatorial Africa, there he was shaking hands with a turbaned maharajah and in another he was dressed in the attire of an American frontiersman, standing arm-in-arm with an exuberantly over-dressed peacock of a woman at a poker table on board a Mississippi paddle steamer. This was not the same great white hunter depicted in the portrait over the fireplace – it was a younger man – but he bore more than a passing resemblance to the lawyer's client.

"He certainly travelled the world, your brother," the lawyer commented.

"Yes," the other man replied, "and look where it got him."

Quicksilver continued to scan the tightly typed pages of sub-clauses and legal jargon that, in no uncertain terms, stated that on declaration of the death of Ulysses Lucian Quicksilver everything in the family estate would pass to him.

"These artefacts," the lawyer said, taking in the curios, "they must be worth something to a collector."

"Mementos, bric-a-brac, nothing more. I'll bequeath them to the Pitt Rivers Museum in Oxford. Why not? It's the house that's the only real asset my brother has left me."

"And what will you do with the proceeds of the sale?"

"Move to one of the lunar cities. I have grown tired of London and I feel that London has grown rather tired of me. There is nothing to keep me here now."

"I hear that Tranquillity is nice," Screwtape offered, "or Luna Prime. That is supposed to have a pleasant atmosphere."

"Look, Screwtape, I think we have exchanged enough niceties so let's just get on with the matter in hand, shall we?"

A minute later and Quicksilver had completed his assessment of the documentation. "So, I sign here and here," he indicated with a finger, "and the deed is done?"

"Yes, sir. Done indeed," the lawyer said wearily.

"You do not approve?"

"You mean of what you do, Mr Quicksilver?"

"Oh you have played your part fully and with a complete understanding of the consequences, Screwtape. Don't tell me you've developed a conscience. That's hardly healthy for a man in your profession."

"Your brother was well respected. So is your family name and has been for many years. I would not wish it to become otherwise."

"Oh, neither do I, Screwtape. Neither do I. You speak of it as if it were not *my* family name."

"I-I mean no disrespect, Mr Quicksilver, I assure you."

"And I assure you that my precious family's name and that of my brother will be remembered for many years to come. I promise you that once we are done here, the first thing I shall do in the morning is commission a headstone to be raised in the family tomb at Highgate Cemetery and arrange for a memorial service to be held in his honour at St Paul's Cathedral."

"St Paul's, eh? Very grand. And what have I done to deserve such a display of public mourning?" asked a voice as rich as claret and as cutting as a rapier's blade.

Quicksilver looked up from the mess of newspaper clippings and legal documentation, the colour draining from his cheeks as he stared in stunned horror at the figure standing at the threshold of the study. Screwtape turned to face the new arrival, his mouth agape. The sound of glass smashing on the polished oak floorboards of the study shattered the silence as the solicitor's cognac slipped from his sweaty fingers.

"U-Ulysses?" The young man was supporting himself with one hand against the desk. He looked like he was going to be sick. "Ulysses... Thank God, you're safe and well! M-my prayers have been answered."

"I didn't realise that you and the Good Lord were on such amicable terms, Barty."

The man now standing in the doorway had the appearance of a taller and more strongly built version of the young man propping himself up against the large, mahogany desk. From his well-defined jaw-line to his thick head of hair, greying at the temples, and the sparkling glint in his deep brown eyes he was also the more handsome of the two. He looked every part the debonair gent, wearing a brown velvet frock coat, a paisley-patterned waistcoat with an emphasis on autumnal colours and moleskin trousers of the latest cut. A silk mustard-yellow cravat was set with a diamond pin at his neck and he was leaning jauntily on a black cane, set with a bloodstone at its hilt.

The manservant stood at his shoulder, his lined face still a cold mask of indifference, but now with a rumour of a smile about his eyes.

"This would seem to be rather a late hour for a meeting with the family solicitor, brother," Ulysses Quicksilver remarked.

"Ulysses, I still can't believe it's you," Bartholomew Quicksilver spluttered, colour returning to his cheeks in a flush of red-faced embarrassment.

"And what's this?" Ulysses said, striding over to the desk and snatching the papers from Bartholomew's hands. A wry smile on his lips, he began casually flicking through them. "So, the two of you were about to have me declared legally dead? Looks like I arrived just in the nick of time, as ever."

Ulysses calmly paced his way around the desk and lent against the mantelpiece, he glanced once at the painting of his father on the wall above him and then tossed the papers casually into the fire. The solicitor gasped and Bartholomew took a sudden step forward and then remembered himself.

"Well, I'm still alive and that's that. This residence is still the property of Ulysses Lucian Quicksilver, until I deem otherwise, and if I choose to leave it to the Cats Protection League in my will for when I really am dead and gone then that is my business."

Bartholomew opened his mouth as if to speak.

"And if you want to keep your allowance from our late father's estate, Barty," Ulysses said, silencing him with a glare, "then I suggest you don't say another word. Understood?" The younger man nodded, a look of defeat on his sallow face. "Nimrod, my brother will be leaving now. If you would kindly find him his coat?"

"At once, sir." The manservant bowed his head and then with an outstretched hand motioned Bartholomew Quicksilver to leave.

"Mr Screwtape will also be leaving now," Ulysses added, scowling darkly.

"M-Mr Quicksilver," Screwtape said, finding his voice at last, "you understand that I was working to help the Quicksilver family to the best of my ability and that if I had known..."

"Known what? That I was still alive?"

"Why, yes, sir. If I had but had word..."

"What are you trying to say, Screwtape? If you had known I was still alive you would have acted more quickly to bring this nefarious scheme to its conclusion for the benefit of my brother and yourself?"

"No, sir. Not at all."

"Nimrod?"

"Yes sir?" the manservant said, still waiting in the shadows at the threshold of the study.

"It has been a long day and I have travelled far. I am going to retire for the night very soon. If you would be so kind as to bring me up a nightcap – cognac, I think – once you have escorted my brother and our *ex*-family solicitor from my property."

"With pleasure, sir." Nimrod now ushered both Bartholomew and Screwtape from the room.

"Mr Quicksilver, I must *protest*," the lawyer persisted in foolish desperation.

"Yes, Mr Screwtape, so it would seem. But I insist, and I can be *very* insistent, as can Nimrod here, so I suggest you just go before my goodwill runs out. Do not think for one second that I would extend to you the same clemency as I do towards my wayward brother, which he has earned by dint of being my blood relative, heaven help me. So, I say again, *goodnight*, Mr Screwtape."

"Goodnight, Mr Quicksilver," the lawyer managed to bluster before a strong hand on his arm encouraged him to exit the study, leaving Ulysses Quicksilver alone, at last, for the first time since he had left over a year before to venture into the Himalayas and beyond on an endeavour that had nearly cost him his life.

Laying his cane on the desk Ulysses eased himself into the padded leather chair behind it and smiled as his eyes alighted on the same cuttings his brother Barty had been perusing earlier. 'Himalayan Adventure Ends In Double Death' one read. Certainly it had cost Davenport his life, the poor wretch. 'Search For Missing Millionaire Suspended' read another and 'Quicksilver: the Quick or the Dead?'

Well, the question had been answered now. Ulysses Quicksilver was back and tomorrow London would be reminded of what it had been missing.

ACT ONE

The Darwin Code

April 1997

CHAPTER ONE

On the Origin of Species

THE NIGHT ALFRED Wentwhistle died began just like any other.

The cold orb of the moon shone through the arched windows of the museum, bathing the myriad display cases in its wan blue light. The electric street lamps on Cromwell Road were a mere flicker of orange beyond the windows.

Alfred Wentwhistle, night watchman at the museum for the last thirty-six years, swept the polished cabinets with the beam of his spotlight. Gleaming eyes, hooked beaks and outstretched wings materialised momentarily under the harsh white attentions of its light. The beam's path was a familiar one, the repeated motions of a never-ending ballet of strobing light. The winding path Alfred took through the miles of corridors, halls and galleries was a familiar one also, the same route taken every night for the last thirty-six years. It was the course Shuttleworth had taught him when he was a boy of barely sixteen and when old Shuttleworth had just two months to retirement, having trod the same path himself for fifty-four years.

There was never any need to change the route. Night watchman of the Natural History Museum at South Kensington was not a demanding role. Alfred carried his truncheon and torch every night but he had never had need of the former in all his years in the post, and he no longer really needed the latter either. He could have found his way around the galleries on a moonless night in the middle of a blackout with his eyes closed, as he used to like to tell Mrs Wentwhistle with a chuckle. He simply carried the torch through force of habit. There had not been one break-in in all his thirty-six years at the museum. And apart from the infrequent change of the odd cabinet here and there or the moving of an artefact every once in a while, the familiar layout of the museum had changed little in any significant way since the arrival of the *Diplodocus carnegii*, ninety-two years before in 1905.

Alfred Wentwhistle enjoyed his job. He delighted in spending hours amongst the exhibits of stuffed beasts and dinosaur bones. Of course, you could experience the real thing now with the opening of the Challenger Enclosure at London Zoo, but there was something timeless and magical about the fossil casts of creatures that amateur archaeologists, who had effectively been the first palaeontologists, had taken to be evidence of the existence of the leviathans of legend such as the dragon or the Cyclops.

Every now and then, undisturbed by the presence of the public, Alfred took pleasure from reading the hand-written labels explaining what any particular item was, where it had been collected, who had recovered it and any other pertinent information the creator of the exhibit had seen fit to share. After thirty-six years there were not many labels that Alfred had not read.

He took great satisfaction from knowing that he was playing his part to keep secure the nation's – and by extension the Empire's and hence, in effect, the world's – greatest museum of natural history. Even though there had been no challenge to its peaceful guardianship of Mother Nature's myriad treasures since he took up his tenure, Alfred Wentwhistle was there, every night of the year – save Christmas Night itself – just in case the museum should ever need him.

Every now and again he would come upon one of the museum's research scientists working late into the night. They would exchange pleasantries and perhaps offer him a warming drink. They all knew old, reliable Alfred and he knew all of them by name. Over the years Alfred had seen professors come and go – botanists, zoologists, naturalists and cryptozoologists – but some things stayed the same, like the Waterhouse building itself and its night-time guardian. Alfred knew his place. The scientists were highly intelligent and erudite luminaries of the museum foundation and he was merely a night watchman. It was enough for him that he was allowed to spend hours enjoying the exhibits on display within. 'Nature's Treasure House' was what they called it; Sir Richard Owen's lasting legacy to the world.

Alfred's slow, steady steps inexorably brought him back into the central hall and to the museum entrance. He paused beneath the outstretched head of the skeletal diplodocus to shine his torch on the face of his pocket watch. Five minutes past, just like every other night; regular as clockwork.

He looked up, shining the beam of his torch into the hollow orbits of the giant's eye sockets. It stared ahead impassively at the entrance to the museum and saw 20,000 visitors pass beneath its archways practically every day.

Alfred heard the tap of metal against metal, caught the glimmer of light on glass out of the corner of his eye, and it was then that he realised one of the doors was open.

There was no doubt in his mind that the door had been locked. It was the first thing he did when he came on duty. Should any of the scientists or cataloguers be working late and need to leave after this time, Alfred himself had to let them out and then he would always lock the door again after them.

No, there was no doubt in his mind that something was awry. Pacing towards the doors he could see where the lock had been forced.

The sound of breaking glass echoed through the halls of the museum from an upper gallery.

There was something most definitely awry. For the first time in thirty-six years his museum needed him.

Turning from the main doors the night watchman jogged across the central hall, his shambling steps marking the full eighty-five foot length of the diplodocus to the foot of the main staircase.

Once there he glanced back over his shoulder and up at the grand arch of the first floor staircase. Above him carved monkeys scampered up the curving arches of the roof into the darkness, amidst the leaf-scrolled iron span-beams. The sound had definitely come from the gallery where the museum staff's private offices were located.

Putting a hand to the polished stone balustrade and taking a deep breath, Alfred Wentwhistle started to take the steps two at a time. At the first landing, where the staircase split beneath the austere bronze-eyed gaze of Sir Richard Owen, he turned right. Hurrying along the gallery overlooking the central hall and running parallel to it, past stuffed sloths and the mounted skeletons of prehistoric marine reptiles, brought him to the second flight of stairs.

Here he paused, out of breath and ears straining, as he tried to work out more precisely where the sound had come from. In the comparative quiet of the sleeping museum he heard a crash, like the sound of a table being overturned. The noise had come from somewhere on this floor, away to his right, from within the western Darwin wing.

Alfred turned into this series of galleries, passing beneath the carved archway that read 'The Ascent of Man'. He quickened his pace as he came into a moonlit gallery of cases containing wax replicas of man's ancestors. They stood frozen in time, in various hunched poses, every kind of hominid from *Australopithecus* to *Homo neanderthalensis*. His sweeping beam shone from bared, snarling teeth, glass eyes and the black-edged blades of flint tools.

On any other night Alfred would have paused to examine the specimens and their accompanying explanations, telling of the evolution of Man from primitive ape. He would have been just as fascinated and amazed as he had been the first time he had read *The Origin of Species* and learnt of the incredible story of the human race's rise to become the most powerful and widely proliferated species on Earth, and beyond.

When Charles Darwin had first proposed his hypothesis of the origin of species, natural selection and the survival of the fittest, he had been derided by the greatest scientific minds of his day and denounced as a charlatan and a heretic. For he had spoken out against the worldwide Christian Church and its core belief that God had created all life on the planet in its final form from the beginning of time.

With the rediscovery of the lost worlds hidden within the jungles of the Congo, atop the mesa-plateaus of the South American interior and on lost islands within the Indian Ocean, others – many of them churchmen – had come forward to challenge Darwin's claims again, vociferously supporting the supposition that because dinosaurs and other prehistoric creatures still existed on the Earth in the present day, the idea of one species evolving into another was ludicrous. And the debate still raged in some persistent, unremitting quarters.

But over a hundred years after his death, Darwin had been posthumously exonerated of all accusations of bestial heresy and scientific idiocy to the point where he was practically idolised as the father of the new branch of science of Evolutionary Biology, and had an entire wing of the Natural History Museum dedicated to the advances made since he first proposed his radical ideas in 1859. In fact there were scientists working within that field now; men like Professors Galapagos and Crichton.

On many previous occasions Alfred Wentwhistle had found himself wiling away time gazing into the faces of his evolutionary ancestors, his reflection in the glass of the cabinets overlaid on top of the pronounced brows and sunken eyes beneath. On such occasions he had wondered upon Darwin's legacy for the human race and what implications such an accepted theory might have for Her Majesty Queen Victoria, in that it presumed that the British monarch was descended from the apes of aeons past.

The familiar smell of camphor and floor polish assailed Alfred's nostrils. Moonlight bathed the gallery with its monochrome light. He found himself in a gallery displaying mammalia, reptilia and amphibia ordered so as to clearly show man's evolutionary path, from the moment he had first crawled out of the primeval swamps, to the present day when he bestrode the globe like a colossus, the human race covering the Earth and the nearer planets of the solar system.

It was off this gallery that some of the scientists had their private workspaces. A number of doors on either side stretched away from Alfred bearing the brass name plaques of the great and the good.

Alfred could hear clear sounds of a struggle now. In the beam of his torch fragments of glass glittered on the floor before one of the doors, looking like a diamond frost on the first morning of winter. The flickering glow of an electric lamp cast its light into the gallery from inside the office before suddenly going out. There was a violent crash of more breaking glass and furniture being overturned.

He would certainly have a dramatic tale to tell Mrs Wentwhistle over bacon and eggs the next morning, Alfred suddenly, incongruously, found himself thinking.

As the watchman neared the invaded office he noticed wisps of smoke or some sort of gas seeping under the door and a new smell – like aniseed, with an unpleasant undertone of rotten meat – that made his nose wrinkle.

The door suddenly burst open, sending more shards of glass spinning into the gallery, clattering against the display cases. The figure of a man burst out of the office and collided with the ageing night watchman. Alfred reeled backwards as the man barged past him. He couldn't stop himself from stumbling into a case containing a family of Neanderthal waxworks posed around an inanimate fire. The torch fell from Alfred's hand and its bulb died.

"Here, what do you think you're doing?" Alfred managed, calling after the intruder as he sprinted from the gallery. He was holding something about the shape and size of a packing box in his arms. But the thief did not stop and before Alfred had even managed to regain his balance, he was gone.

Alfred's heart was racing, beating a tattoo of nervous excitement against his ribs. In all his thirty-six years he had never known anything like it. Adrenalin flooded his system and he was about to give chase when something reminded him that the thief had not been alone in the office. Alfred had heard more than one voice raised in anger as he had approached and there had been definite signs of a struggle.

Cautiously, he approached the doorway of the office. The rancid mist was beginning to dissipate. The soles of his boots crunched on the fractured diamonds of glass.

Inside the pitch black office-cum-laboratory he could hear a ragged breathing that reminded him of an animal snuffling. Then, suddenly, there was silence.

Alfred took another step forward.

"What the devil?" was all he could manage as, in an explosion of glass and splintered wood something burst out of the office, ripping the door from its sundered frame. The night watchman barely had time to yelp out in pain as slivers of glass sliced his face and hands as he raised them to protect himself, before a hulking shadow of solid black muscle was on top of him.

Alfred had a momentary impression of thick, matted hair, a sharp bestial odour – a rank animal smell mixed in with the aniseed and rancid meat – broad shoulders and a blunt-nosed head slung low between them. There was a flash of silver as the moonlight caught something swinging from around the thing's neck.

He had never known anything like it, never in thirty-six years.

And then, teeth bared in an animal scream, its hollering cry deafening in his ears, fists flailing like sledgehammers, the ape-like creature attacked. Feebly Alfred put up his arms to defend himself but there was nothing he could do against the brute animal strength of his assailant.

It grabbed Alfred's head by the hair so violently he could feel clumps of it being ripped from his scalp. Then, in one savage action, the enraged beast smashed his skull into display case. With the second blow the glass of the cabinet shattered and Alfred Wentwhistle's world exploded into dark oblivion.

CHAPTER TWO

The Inferno Club

ULYSSES QUICKSILVER WOKE with the midday sun streaming in through the crack in the heavy velvet drapes of his bedchamber. The warm light reached his sleeping form, bringing to an end a night of vivid, almost feverish, dreaming. It banished the transitory memories of unsettling dreams and replaced them with physical reminders of a host of old injuries, his worn body aching.

He stretched beneath the crisp sheets of the grand four-poster and immediately regretted doing so. There was the sharp twinge in his right shoulder, the stab of cramp in his left leg and the dull throb in his left side.

He had slept long and deeply, his dreams overflowing with half-real recollections of the events of the past eighteen months. There was the rapid descent through the freezing fog above the snow-clad peaks, the violent lurch of collision as the gondola broke up on contact with the pitiless rocks. Then he was lying in the snow, teeth chattering hard enough to break, Davenport's body lying there next to his, his blood freezing black in the sub-zero hell.

Then his sleep had been filled with the sonorous chanting that had filled the monastery, the sensation of returning warmth, air thick with the smell of tallow fat and jasmine flowers. In another moment he had found himself training again with the masters of the temple, his still-healing body being subjected to a beating with bamboo poles and blunt wooden weapons. There had also been the mental challenges as he strove to acquire mastery over his body through strength of will alone. Then there had been the final test, the duel with the snow beast, his body suspended in the air above the arena before he had brought physical form and mind back as one and, incredibly, bested the creature.

His memories of what had followed since that time had been replayed in his sleeping mind in a time-lapsed blur, a hallucinatory haze of images. The journey back from Xigaze to Bombay, traversing the continents by train until, at last, Brunel's Trans-Channel tunnel had brought him back to England, London and home.

And now here he was lying in a bed in which he had not slept in over a year.

But was it really home for him anymore, he found himself wondering as he stared at the cracks criss-crossing the plaster of the ceiling above him. He kept telling himself that he was pleased to be back but for all the comfort of the goose-down pillows behind his head and the sprung mattress beneath him, part of him hankered for his hard wooden pallet back at the monastery and the ridged feel of the bamboo canes against his back.

A discreet tap at the door roused Ulysses from his reverie.

"Enter," he replied.

The handle turned and the door swung open as Nimrod entered the room. His manservant looked immaculate as ever, dressed in his grey butler's attire, not a hair out of place. Balanced perfectly on the splayed fingers of one hand was a silver tray. There was a starched linen cloth draped carefully over his other arm.

"Good afternoon, sir."

"Good afternoon Nimrod."

"It being past noon I took the liberty of asking Mrs Prufrock to prepare you some breakfast."

"Why, thank you, Nimrod."

"Not at all, sir," his manservant replied, placing the tray across Ulysses' lap and laying the white linen napkin open in front of him.

As well as a silver dish cover there was a slim cut crystal vase containing a single crimson carnation, a cafetiére of hot coffee and accompanying coffee cup, a silver toast rack containing four triangles of both white and brown toasted bread, and a copy of the day's edition of *The Times*.

Nimrod lifted the platter's cover with a flourish. Ulysses' nostrils were assailed by a bloom of steam smelling richly of the griddled eggs, smoked back bacon, Cumberland sausage, black pudding, grilled tomatoes, sautéed mushrooms and hash browns.

"I thought you would be hungry after your journey last night."

Ulysses heartily tucked into the meal in front of him. Eschewing good manners, through a half-chewed mouthful of sausage he spluttered, "Give Mrs Prufrock my compliments on what is, I think, the most wonderful meal I have ever eaten."

"With pleasure, sir."

Ulysses felt a warm glow well up within him and knew that it wasn't merely from having hot home-cooked food in his belly again. This was what it meant to be home, to be surrounded by those people who mattered to you and to whom you mattered also. It was all suddenly very familiar and he found that comforting.

"It's good to be back, Nimrod."

"And, if I might say so sir, it is good to have you back. If you will excuse me?" And with that he left, pulling the door to carefully behind him.

As he tucked into his breakfast, Ulysses spread out *The Times* on the bedspread beside him. It was time to get back up to speed with what was happening in the so-called civilised world. The copies of *The Times* he had been able to get hold of on the Orient Express had been woefully out of date, by as much as a week in most cases.

The headline on this edition, however – dated April 16th 1997, the paper still warm from where Nimrod had pressed the pages with an iron – was very topical indeed. It read 'Buckingham Palace Confirms Jubilee Celebrations' and concerned the celebrations planned to mark the 160th year of Queen Victoria's reign. The occasion was to be marked by the unveiling of a colossal statue of Britannia in Hyde Park, outside Paxton's glorious construction of the second Crystal Palace. All this was to occur on the twenty-third of June, in a little over two months time. The politicians, toadies, toffs and royal historians were calling it the most glorious time in the British Empire's entire history.

Indeed it had been a most incredible century and a half, during which time man had risen from the dawn of the industrial age and the inventive uses of steam power to tame much of the world around him and even conquer the stars. Space travel, now an everyday occurrence, was once the preserve of science-fiction, conjured up by the writings of authors such as H. G. Wells and Jules Verne. With interplanetary travel mastered, and with regular launches from the space terminus at Gatwick south of the capital carrying all classes of citizen to Her Majesty's Imperial colonies on the moon and the nearer planets, there was now talk in certain secretive circles of attempts to break the only frontier remaining to mankind – time travel. What once had seemed preposterous was now the everyday, the impossible simply tomorrow's breakthrough.

There had been unparalleled advances made in the medical sciences, difference engines and the newer field of cybernetics. The empire of Magna Britannia – once rather apologetically known simply as Great Britain – would not be what it was without the advances made in those areas. The Widow of Windsor would not be where she was without them and the nation was now policed thanks in part to the quantum developments made in clockwork-cybernetics, since Charles Babbage had accomplished the astonishing achievement of constructing the first fully automated analytical engine.

But whilst much of the world had moved on, as mankind's achievements had exploded exponentially, so the more shameful aspects of Imperial life had continued to deteriorate. At this time London's slums were darker, dirtier and more over-crowded than even the visionary Charles Dickens could have imagined in his most despairing hour, its streets filled with the dissolute and the destitute, the gin-sodden inheritors of the darkest days of the Empire.

Many were slaves to the machine, forced to work tirelessly in the great gothic factories built by their suffering ancestors, or had been overlooked in favour of the machine, robot-drudges taking their place in those same industrial workshops.

The consequences of being the 'Workshop of the World' had come at a high price too. Great swathes of the British Isles were now nothing but blighted wasteland, its flora and fauna mutated or destroyed by the pollution vomited out of its many thousands of factories.

While the great and the good enjoyed the benefits of electric light, automobiles and the thinking machines that were Babbage's legacy, dreadfully high infant-mortality, prostitution, malnutrition, cholera and syphilis still blighted the lives of the poor underclass that riddled London's streets.

As Ulysses laid his knife and fork across a practically polished plate, there was another tap at the door. At his beckoning Nimrod entered once again.

"Sir, when you are ready there is a cab waiting to take you to the Inferno Club."

"Really?" Ulysses commented. "Already? It didn't take long for Wormwood to find out that I was back in town, did it?"

"No, sir."

"I suppose he'll be wanting a debrief. I'd best not keep him waiting," Ulysses said with a sigh, running a hand through his sleep-ruffled hair, "it only makes him irritable. Spending any period of time with him is a chore at best, and when he's irritable it only makes it ten times worse. Some warning would have been nice though; perhaps a welcome home card, or a bouquet of chrysanthemums."

WITHIN HALF AN hour Ulysses Quicksilver had made his ablutions, dressed and, cane in hand, was on his way to the Inferno Club in the back of the jolting hansom cab, enduring the worldly banter of the cabbie. The cab turned into St James's Square and pulled up outside number 16A, next door to the East India club and its pillared frontage. Number 16A itself was an otherwise unassuming Regency period façade that did nothing to belie what lay beyond its closed doors.

Somewhat disgruntled at not only having been disturbed so soon on his first day back in the capital but also finding that the cab had not already been paid for, Ulysses ascended the steps to the rosewood doors as the smoke-belching hansom chugged away. He rapped on the door with the head of his cane three times.

The door opened a crack. Standing behind it was a squat, liveried doorman with a face like a battle-tested mastiff and who, even with the added height of his top hat, still only came up to Ulysses' shoulder. Thanks in part to his diminutive size many a roustabout had misjudged Max Grendel, former carnival performer known as 'Grendel the Man-Monster, The Strongest Dwarf in the World'.

"Good afternoon, Mr Quicksilver, sir," the doorman said, his accent distinctly that of the lower classes; there was no hiding the fact that he had been born within the sound of Bow Bells. He gave Ulysses a broad, broken smile full of missing teeth. "It's been a long time."

"Hello, Max, old chap. How are you?"

"Oh, mustn't grumble. You here for business or pleasure today, sir?"

"Most definitely business. If I was after the latter I'd be asking you for a recommendation, wouldn't I Max?"

The doorman chuckled filthily. "Right you are, sir. If you'd like to step this way then?"

Ulysses passed the doorman half a crown and proceeded through a second set of double doors. Above these, carved into the doorframe and picked out in gold leaf, was Dante's doom-laden motto *Lasciate ogni speranza voi ch'entrate*, the original Italian seeming incongruously out of place in this bastion of Englishness.

Uriah Wormwood was seated in one of two huge leather armchairs set before a crackling fire in the Quartermain Room. Despite the time of year and his proximity to the fire, the thin rake of a man still looked pinched with cold, his long hands and fingers pale, the blue network of veins visible through his porcelain skin. The hair on his head was thin and greying, swept back from the top of his balding pate and hanging down to his shoulders in greasy lank cords. In his dated frock-tailed black suit, starched white shirt and unassuming black silk cravat he looked every part the elder statesman.

Standing behind him was a silent, unsmiling aide, who looked as capable of handling himself in a fight as Max Grendel.

Ulysses took the seat opposite Wormwood. The older man fixed him with a needling stare. "I'd heard you were dead," he said.

"Well as you can see, minister, reports of my death have been greatly exaggerated."

A starched footman appeared and delivered a glass of whisky to Wormwood. "Sir?" he asked, turning to Ulysses.

"A brandy – cognac," he said and Wormwood waved the flunky away imperiously.

Ulysses took a moment to take in his surroundings. It had been some time since he had been here last but in all those months nothing appeared to have really changed.

The room was enveloped in a fug of blue smoke from the many pipes and cigars being enjoyed by the club's members. To the casual observer it would appear that this place was nothing more than a club full of aging peers, retired officers of Her Majesty's Armed Forces and directors of the board of a whole host of multinational companies. There was also a sprinkling of younger men thrown in, taking on the affectations of their elders, ready to take up the reins of power when they were offered.

Ulysses Quicksilver knew that such bastions of English misogyny – and the Inferno Club more truly and more covertly than any other – were where the real power lay. This was where the really important decisions were made, those that influenced the fate of nations. This was where the agents of all manner of organisations made their deals, were given their frequently unpalatable orders and reported back to their shadowy masters. Ulysses Quicksilver knew this better than most for he was such a man.

"So," Wormwood said, peering at Ulysses over steepling fingers, "niceties done with... your report. What happened? Do you have the artefact?"

"There's really no better way of putting this," Ulysses said, taking his brandy from the footman. "No."

"As I suspected," Wormwood said witheringly, that one simple phrase dripping with disdain.

"And our Oriental... friend? What of him?"

"His vessel went down along with mine," Ulysses recalled, images of their terrible, dramatic, and near-fatal descent flashing behind his eyes as he did so. "He tried to board our gondola. We fought. He fell. I have not seen him, nor the green-eyed monkey god of Sumatra, since."

"You should have informed us of your return."

"It was too risky. I still hoped to track down the Black Mamba myself. I take it that none of your other agents have reported his reappearance at any of his usual haunts?"

"No. We can only hope that he is lying there still on the southern slopes of Mount Manaslu, frozen like some relic of the ice age. But somehow I doubt it. And besides, the matter is out of your hands."

"What?" Ulysses said, taken aback.

"There is another more pressing matter I wish you to deal with."

"And what precisely is this new undertaking?"

"There was a break-in at the Natural History Museum last night."

"On Cromwell Road?"

"You know of another? A night watchman was killed. A lab was ransacked. You are to... investigate."

Ulysses took another casual swig from his glass. "Surely burglary and murder is the province of Scotland Yard."

"And your province is to serve your Queen and country as the representatives of Her Majesty's government see fit. Besides, there may well be more to this than there at first appears. You will, of course, be paid your usual retainer."

"Welcome home, Ulysses," the younger man muttered under his breath as he downed the rest of his drink.

"Is there a problem?"

"It's just that some things never change, do they, minister?"

Ulysses' governmental contact glowered at him, his knife-edge features becoming even sharper, even more threatening.

"I do not like you, Quicksilver, but then in my line of work I don't have to. I am, however, an... admirer of what you do and you are most accomplished, most of the time. But there are all manner of things afoot in the world. We are scant years away from a new millennium and Magna Britannia has never been in a stronger position. And neither have her enemies ever been more eager to see her fall so that they might feast richly upon the spoils.

"The Chinese Empire is an ever-increasing threat, looking to space to solve its own overpopulation problem. We can no longer rely on Russia being the surety it once was, even if it is still a princeling state of Britain. There is talk of ancient bloodlines asserting their self-professed ancestral rights in Eastern Europe. And then there are the unruly ambitions of the Germans and their National Socialist masters.

"There are even those within the empire who have their reasons for destabilising Her Majesty's most glorious realm, as well you know. Then there is the ongoing situation on Mars. The separatist-secessionist movement is gaining in strength and popularity daily.

"Of themselves, none of these are major threats to our stability or the stability of Her Majesty's throne. But together? The sharks are circling, Quicksilver, and there are precious few of us able to do anything about it. Mark my words. The sharks are circling... and they are hungry."

"Come on in, the water's lovely."

"What?" Wormwood asked sharply.

"Nothing minister," Ulysses replied with a sigh.

"What are you waiting for then? Be on your way."

"What indeed? The scene of the crime awaits and the game is surely afoot."

CHAPTER THREE

The Scene of the Crime

THE CAB TURNED onto Cromwell Road and pulled up outside the grand frontage of the Natural History Museum. The building's gothic façade was an awesomely impressive sight, although it was now dwarfed by other more recent edifices and the sprawling network of the Overground that filled the sky above it. The great pillar of the South Kensington stop rose from the right-hand corner of the Museum's grounds. The architectural design and execution of the Museum – that was Sir Richard Owen's cathedral to nature and his legacy to naturalists the world over – still took Ulysses' breath away every time he saw it, even after all the wonders and all the horrors he had witnessed in his life as an agent of the throne. Stone-locked monsters of a bygone age, pterosaurs, coelacanths, cats and primates gazed down at him through the sooty grime that sullied the face of the otherwise beautiful building.

Crossing the road Ulysses made his way up the steps that led into the Museum. There were already signs of the police presence that he would find inside. An automaton constable was tapping his truncheon rhythmically into the palm of his artificially manufactured hand. Passing through the main doors Ulysses entered the central hall of the museum to find a bustle of concerned staff, Scotland Yard's finest incompetents and bewildered museum visitors milling around beneath the impassive stare of the diplodocus skeleton that dominated the vaulted nave-like space.

Considering what had come to pass there the previous night it was amazing that the museum was even open to the public, Ulysses mused as he made his way up the central staircase, heading for the Darwin Wing. He hoped that once there it would reveal its secrets to him, such as why he had been sent to investigate a break-in and murder at the Natural History Museum in the first place.

Ulysses could see that the police had been there before him, marching in and trampling all over the crime scene. They had marked the entire Darwin Wing as theirs with strips of yellow and black tape bearing the legend, 'Crime Scene – Do Not Cross'.

Two constables stood either side of the entrance, their black bodies gleaming dully in the light cascading from the high windows. Ulysses approached the nearest of the Peeler-drones. The constable turned at his approach. "I am sorry, sir. This area is closed to the public," its voice crackled from somewhere behind its chestplate in an imitation of a cockney accent.

Ulysses deftly put a hand inside a jacket pocket and pulled out a leather cardholder with a flourish, flipping the case open. "I'm not the public," he said, the wry smile curling the corners of his mouth, "Constable Palmerston," he added, reading the badge plate on the automaton's breast. There was a curious habit amongst the Metropolitan Police of naming their cybernetic officers after the famous dead. Was there something that Scotland Yard's cyberneticists knew that the rest of the world didn't?

The constable scanned the card revealed inside the wallet with its visual receptors, the red glow behind its eye-visor panning from left to right. "I am sorry, sir," the drone apologised. "What can I do for you, Mr Quicksilver?"

"I wish to inspect the scene of the crime."

"Certainly, sir."

The constable unhooked the tape, allowing Ulysses into the wing.

"This way, sir. If there is anything else I can do to help..." the robot began.

"I'll be sure to find you," Ulysses interrupted, finishing the constable's sentence.

In the main hall of the wing Ulysses found more policemen – both mechanical and human – as well as other men not in uniform. A team of these, dressed in starched white lab coats, were dusting various cabinets and wooden benches.

Ulysses ignored them and made for the entrance to one of the secondary galleries, again flanked by automata-constables, through which a steady stream of forensics staff were flowing. Mote-shot beams of afternoon sunlight entered through skylights high in the ceiling.

Ulysses took in the display cases, the doors to offices and workspaces beyond and the cluster of men working in the centre of the room. He could just make out a figure, lying awkwardly within the ruins of a glass cabinet.

"Oi! Stop right there!" came a shout from behind him.

Ulysses turned to see a look of shock seize the approaching man's face.

"Bloody hell! I thought you were dead."

"And I've missed you too," Ulysses said, regarding the pale-faced, weasel of a man before him, his ginger mop of hair an unruly riot as always. "You shouldn't believe everything you read in the papers, Inspector," he added with a smile.

For a moment the trench-coated policeman said nothing. The human sergeant accompanying him looked from his superior to the dandy in bewilderment.

"Inspector Allardyce, shall I have this man removed?"

"W-what?" the inspector managed. "Yes. No. Not yet," he snapped, never taking his eyes off Ulysses. "What are you doing here Quicksilver?"

"Oh, you know how it is. I've not been in town for a while and someone said that I simply must see the Ascent of Man exhibit in the Darwin Wing at the Natural History Museum."

"Don't give me that bullshit!" Allardyce snarled. "What are you *really* doing here?"

"I'm here to investigate a murder," Ulysses said darkly, his face suddenly an impassive mask. "What are you doing here?"

"Oh, ha ha, very funny. And what the hell do you think you're doing investigating *my* murder?"

"*Your* murder? Oh, I'm sorry, no one told me. My commiserations. Where shall I send the flowers?"

"You know what I mean you arrogant bastard."

"You know how it is. Orders are orders."

"Well you're too late. We've practically finished here. You want to try getting up before midday occasionally. There's *nothing* for you here."

"I think I'll be the judge of that if you don't mind."

"Well I do mind. The forensics boys have already been over the place with a fine-toothed comb," Inspector Allardyce sneered. "If there's anything to find, they'll have found it. I doubt there's anything you can add. Like I said, there's nothing for you here."

"Yes, and we all know how thorough your lads can be, don't we, Allardyce?"

The policeman flashed Ulysses a look of volcanic anger. "I don't like your tone! I could have you arrested for wasting police time, you know that?"

"I thought it was *you* who was wasting *my* time," Ulysses goaded.

"Look, Quicksilver, do I have to remind you that I am an Inspector of Her Majesty's Metropolitan police force? I won't be spoken to like this!"

"And do I have to remind you of whose authority I am here under?" Ulysses said, reaching inside his jacket again. He pulled out the leather wallet for a second time and flipped it open. "My card. It certainly impressed your constable enough to let me in here in the first place."

"Yes, all right. You can put that away. You've got five minutes, then I want you out of here, never mind who pulls the strings."

"That should be more than enough time," Ulysses said, and strode past the inspector leaving the policeman grumbling to his sergeant.

Ulysses approached the men clustered around the body. The corpse was that of a man who had been enjoying portly middle age until the events of the previous night had resulted in his untimely death. He lay sprawled amidst the ruin of a shattered display case. The waxwork reconstructions that had been housed inside the cabinet had been removed and were now leaning against a gallery wall, baring their plaster teeth at anyone approaching the crime scene.

"Excuse me please, gentlemen," Ulysses said as he nudged his way between the white-coated men, waving his open cardholder casually at them. In the face of such superiority and upper class confidence the forensic technicians moved aside.

Blood, most of it dried, covered the jagged glass shards beneath the dead man's head and Ulysses could see that the victim's hair and scalp were matted with it too. Tiny slivers of glass, some of which were still embedded in the clay-like flesh, had cut the dead man's face and hands. But worse than the blood and mess of gore oozing from the back of his head, was the expression on his face. The night watchman had died in utter terror. His rigor-frozen features were a mask of dread, his lips pulled back from his teeth, his mouth open in horror.

"How did he die?" Ulysses asked, already suspecting the answer.

"A blow to the head; several in fact," one of the white coats said.

"Indeed," Ulysses mused.

But who, or what, had killed him? Ulysses wondered. What could have caused the poor wretch to die with such an expression of horror on his face?

"What time did he die?"

"From the onset of rigor mortis I would say... sometime around midnight," the pathologist examining the body replied. "Probably just after."

"Was anything taken from the body?"

"No," another technician said. "It doesn't appear so."

Ulysses stepped back, leaving the white coats to finish their work. He had his murder victim but Wormwood had said that there had been a burglary as well. So what had been taken?

Behind him a ransacked office gaped open, the shattered door wrenched from its frame. Policemen were busying themselves around the area. With cautious steps Ulysses approached, crunching tiny pieces of glass beneath the soles of his shoes. He paused at the entrance to look more closely at the splintered mess of the door frame. Then, in the muted sunlight spilling into the gallery Ulysses caught sight of no more than a thread of something, something all of Inspector Allardyce's forensic team had missed. Snagged in the splintered wood were three reddish-brown hairs. At first glance they made Ulysses think of coarse animal hairs. They certainly hadn't belonged to the murdered night watchman; they were the wrong colour.

The policemen and scientists around him were so caught up in their own work that none of them paid any heed as Ulysses took a small evidence bag from a jacket pocket, a pair of tweezers from another and, without touching them with his bare hands, extracted the hairs from the door frame, sealing them safely within the bag before returning it to his pocket. Then he entered the office-lab itself.

The place was a mess. The level of destruction suggested that more than a mere robbery had taken place here. There had been a struggle as well.

From the detritus now filling the office space and covering the floor, Ulysses was able to build a picture in his mind of what the laboratory had looked like before it had been invaded. There had been bookcases and shelves containing all manner of scientific journals and reference books, which now littered the floor, and tables covered with distillation apparatus that was now just so much broken glass. One of these tables had been overturned and a leg broken off it. A framed print of a classic cartoon from *Punch* magazine disparaging Darwin hung lopsidedly. There were stains across some of the furniture and even the walls, suggesting a vessel containing water or some other liquid had been smashed, spraying the room with its contents.

To Ulysses' trained eyes, amidst all this chaotic mess it was quite clear that something was indeed missing. Careful not to lose his footing on any of the detritus covering the floor he made his way to the far corner of the room. Here there was a desk, a jar of upended ink, its blue-black contents covering most of the papers spilled across the top. Amongst the mess of papers there was a curiously clear space, as if something had been resting on the desk and had only been removed after the papers had fallen into disarray. Ulysses moved the papers out of the way altogether. There, in the green cracked leather of the desktop was a clear indentation, where something square and relatively heavy had sat. And there was more evidence on the wall itself, a discoloration of the paint, suggesting something hot had marked it over time. Ulysses considered the size and position of the marks. Something hot, something box-shaped; something like a small difference engine. That was what the mysterious thief had claimed from this sanctuary of peaceful scientific enquiry.

Ulysses glanced around the room one more time but he was certain he had seen enough. Besides he wanted to get a private opinion about the contents of his pocket. He began to pick his way carefully across the office-lab again.

But there was something else, gnawing away at the edge of his conscious mind. It was not something seen but something he had smelt, a rancid odour that caught at the back of his throat and which left his mind buzzing with more questions. Ulysses sniffed and caught for a moment the trace of a smell like beef and fennel stew past its best. That was it – aniseed and spoiled meat; a truly unsavoury and unusual combination, certainly not the usual aroma of a musty old museum.

Ulysses paused in the doorway and looked more closely at the broken door, now propped against the wall. Its brass plaque was still attached. It read, 'Professor Ignatius Galapagos's and underneath, 'Evolutionary Biology Department'.

Leaving Scotland Yard's finest to it, Ulysses made his way out of the gallery. He was pretty certain that there was nothing else for him to see. It was time he pursued his investigation elsewhere.

Inspector Allardyce was at the entrance to the gallery talking to an anxious-looking member of the museum staff. There was no way Ulysses could avoid him.

"I thought I said you had five minutes. I make that seven," he said looking at his pocket watch.

"I'm sorry if I've outstayed my welcome."

"You always outstay your welcome. As soon as you turn up you've outstayed your welcome. So, what do you make of it all then, Quicksilver? Do you have anything new to shed on the case?"

"Oh, I'm sure you already have a theory or two of your own. You don't need me complicating matters."

"Indeed I do, and I certainly don't," Allardyce confirmed. "It's actually very straightforward if you know what you're looking for and how to read the signs."

"Really?" Ulysses said. He had been ready to leave but the opportunity to provoke the pompous inspector again – having had so few opportunities in the last year or so – was just too tempting. "Would you care to elaborate?"

Inspector Allardyce could not resist the opportunity to expound on his masterly skills of deduction and chalk one up against the aristocratic know-it-all.

"It's very simple really. All the evidence is there for those who have eyes to see it." *Indeed*, thought Ulysses. "Our thief was disturbed by the night watchman and then killed the poor bugger so he could make his getaway."

"And do you know what was taken?"

"Not yet, but we will do, once we have tracked down Professor Gapalago and got a complete inventory of the room from him."

"Galapagos," the museum staffer corrected.

"What?"

"It's Professor Galapagos."

"Does it matter?" Allardyce bit back.

"Yes, I rather think it does," Ulysses muttered under his breath. And then, so that Allardyce could hear him quite clearly, "If you don't have a full inventory of the contents of the room, how do you know that anything's been taken at all?"

"Isn't it obvious?" Allardyce asked incredulously. "Why else would someone break in here? It obviously wasn't to bump off that poor bastard lying over there with his head smashed in."

"Indeed," said Ulysses, "which brings me to another point. The injuries sustained by the victim look like the result of a frenzied attack. Why would a thief stop to make such a brutal job of doing away with one, aging, overweight security guard? And what of this Professor *Galapagos*" – he made a point of annunciating the name with added emphasis – "the man whose office was broken into?"

"Look, I told you, he's not turned up yet. You know what these academic types are like."

"Better than you, I'll warrant."

"Are you lecturing me on bloody police procedure?" Allardyce challenged, stabbing his index finger at Ulysses' chest. "Because that's exactly how things got out of hand last time."

"Heaven forbid, Inspector."

"I'll get round to this Gapalogo soon enough. But it's quite clear what happened here last night. I told you there was nothing to see here, Quicksilver," he spat, his voice dripping with undisguised contempt. "Unless you've got any other amazing insights to offer then I rather think you're done here, don't you?"

Ulysses paused. Should he share his own theory with Allardyce, that he thought the inspector should be looking for two culprits, connected certainly but not as he might at first suspect? It was tempting, if only to see the look of exasperation on Allardyce's red face. But as long as the police were following up red herrings of their own making it would at least keep them out of the way while he continued his investigation and allow him to get to bottom of things, such as why Wormwood had set him on this case in the first place. And, Ulysses had to admit, he was hooked. There was far more to this mystery than merely a break-in and incidental murder. There was something else afoot, he was sure of it.

"I couldn't agree more, Inspector. Good day."

"And don't come snooping around my murder scene again, you hear?"

"*Your* murder scene?"

"Look, just piss off!"

"With pleasure."

As he made his way out of the gallery, Ulysses halted again. He felt someone's eyes on him. He looked around and then the feeling was gone.

Putting it from his mind Ulysses made his way out of the museum, cane in hand, evidence in his pocket. He would need to pay Methuselah a call but he decided that it could wait until after he had dined. It had been too long since he had last visited the Ritz.

Another thought distracted Ulysses as he exited the museum and hailed a hansom. There were many unexplained mysteries in the world – such as who built the giant heads of Easter Island and the mystery of the Whitby mermaid – and Ulysses had even solved some of them in his time, but how Maurice Allardyce had ever made it to inspector he would never know.

FROM A DARK recess behind a roof strut, unseen eyes watched the exchange between the fair-skinned red-haired man and the taller, more confident interloper. The watcher had found sanctuary here in the darkened, elevated tunnels of the museum's ventilation system following the events of the previous night. After the attack it had become confused. Its mind was a fractured collection of half-recalled memories that made less and less sense as instinct gradually overtook rational thought.

It had wanted to flee but there had been something familiar and safe about the vaulted, hallowed halls that had made it stay. It felt curiously comfortable here. Besides, there were too many people around at the moment. There would only be more upset if it revealed itself now, more shouting, more panic, more fear.

No, the watcher would wait. It was safe here. It was secure. This was its home.

CHAPTER FOUR

An Unexpected Visitor

HAVING ENJOYED AN exquisitely prepared dinner of roast pheasant, seasonal vegetables and dauphinoise potatoes, all washed down with a half bottle of finest claret, Ulysses Quicksilver exited the Ritz, fully intending to hail a cab to convey him back to his house in Mayfair. Outside the hotel the gas lamps and sodium lights were glowing into life, the buildings of Piccadilly were dark monoliths against the russet and mauve sky.

Ulysses took a deep breath. The full-bodied scents of the fruity aftertaste of that last glass of claret mixed with the fumy air of the city, the bitter reek of the gas lamps and the smell of horse manure. London might have had combustion-driven automobiles for the last ninety years or so, and trams and trains for even longer than that, but there were still companies and private individuals who employed horses to carry them to and fro.

Cane in hand he paused for a moment as he savoured the familiar – even comforting – smells of the city and listened to the endless background noise that told him London was as alive as it had ever been. There were the unintelligible cries of the newspaper vendors, trying to shift the last of the late editions and the shouts of street sellers. There was the clatter of hooves and wheels on cobbles and the rumbling of petrol engines. There was the clamour of bells and whistles of the

Overground as the trains rumbled past overhead, the cross-town railway network a black spider's web of seemingly infinite complexity with London ensnared beneath it.

Turning left out of the Ritz, rather than hail a cab, Ulysses followed the railings about Green Park as he made his way past the thinning crowds walking along Piccadilly in the dusky half-light. It felt good to have the London streets beneath his feet again. It reminded him of where home was and what it meant.

It was that curious time after the sun had set and the working day, for most, had come to an end but the revelries of the night were yet to truly begin. It would not be long, though, before others claimed the city as theirs. Not so very long ago Ulysses would have been one of them. He briefly considered returning to the Inferno Club to while away the evening over port and cigars but almost as quickly thought better of it. His body still ached and he suddenly found himself stifling a yawn. It would still take him some time to fully recover from his journey back to civilisation and, besides, his mind was awhirl with questions. Keeping his own company over dinner had only allowed him to go over and over all that he had seen at the Natural History Museum and ponder the nature of the crimes that had been committed there.

There were a number of questions that demanded answering. Why would a disturbed thief do away with the night watchman so brutally, using only his bare hands? And what would such a savage killer want with a laboratory difference engine belonging to a professor of evolutionary biology?

The more he thought about it, the more convinced he became that he had been sent to investigate two different crimes committed by two different culprits. But who were they and where were they hiding? Were they acting in league with one another? And what of Professor Ignatius Galapagos? What part did he have to play in all this? And where was he anyway?

His mind a jumble of questions and unsettling thoughts, Ulysses found himself at the top of the steps before the front door of his own house. He knocked and was admitted by the ever-faithful Nimrod.

"A good afternoon, sir?" the manservant enquired politely.

"Intriguing is the word I would use, Nimrod."

"Am I to take it that you are working again, sir?"

"Indeed. A most curious case."

"And how was Mr Wormwood?"

"Acidic as ever," Ulysses admitted. "And then, to top it all, I had a run-in with Inspector Allardyce of Scotland Yard."

"How unpleasant for you, sir."

"Indeed."

"Shall I ask Mrs Prufrock to prepare you a light supper? I believe that there is a hock of ham or some smoked salmon in the larder."

"No thank you, Nimrod, I've already eaten. You can let Mrs Prufrock go for the night," he added, only then realising that he had not been to see his cook and housekeeper since his return. But then he hadn't been back twenty-four hours yet, after having been away for over a year. Right now what he really wanted was a moment to himself with a glass of warming brandy in the familiar surroundings of his study to consider what he had discovered so far.

"Very good, sir. Then I should inform you that you have a visitor waiting to see you."

"Really, Nimrod?" Ulysses did a double take, giving the butler a look of genuine surprise. Who else knew he was back so soon? Once the news got out of his return he had expected the information to travel like wildfire but who would have come calling so openly, so early? "It's rather late to be having visitors call isn't it?"

"Precisely what I thought, sir. I suggested she return in the morning but she was adamant that she had to see you this evening, even if it meant waiting."

"She?"

"A Miss Genevieve Galapagos," Nimrod said, his haughty expression having never looked more unimpressed. From his manservant's tone Ulysses could tell that his female visitor was probably young and certainly attractive. What London's most eligible bachelor got up to with the ladies was his own affair – or more usually several ongoing affairs – but it was one area that the otherwise ever-faithful and accepting butler did not welcome being so openly flaunted within the Quicksilver family seat.

"Galapagos?"

"An unusual name certainly, sir."

"And one I have already come across today in another context. How long has she been waiting?"

"I believe it has been about half an hour, sir."

"Then let us not keep Miss Galapagos waiting any longer."

"I took the liberty of asking her to wait in the drawing room, sir."

"Very good, Nimrod."

With that, Ulysses made his way through the dustsheet-shrouded rooms to the sterile, forced informality of the drawing room. Other than the familiar space of his study, and possibly his bedroom, the house still didn't seem fully like home yet. He had been away for too long and in that time too much had happened. It would still take him some time to adjust and the best way for that to happen was for him to throw himself back into London life and involve himself in a mystery he could really get his teeth into. And it appeared that Wormwood had given him just what he needed.

Sweeping into the room in his frock coat, cane in hand, Ulysses startled the young lady who was perched uncomfortably on the edge of the one unshrouded chair, a teacup held in her lap.

There was no doubting that Ulysses Quicksilver knew how to make an entrance. Last night had proved that. It disarmed his enemies and potential allies alike and put him in control of almost any situation.

"Miss Galapagos, I presume," he said, his voice like velvet, and put out a hand.

"You must be Mr Quicksilver," she regarded him shyly through the veil of her fringe. Her expression made it look like she had the weight of the world resting on her shoulders, worry creasing her otherwise flawless features.

She was certainly attractive, still in the prime of her youth – Ulysses judged still in her early twenties. Her ivory features were clearly defined, her almond eyes large and a rich russet. Her rosebud lips were pursed. What little make-up she had applied – a little powder around her eyes, a little rouge on her cheeks and a touch of gloss on her lips – merely enhanced her natural beauty. Her hair was long and a rich auburn that caught the light from the electric chandelier, returning it as a shimmering golden sheen. Her apparel was striking too. She was wearing a tweed suit of the latest cut, the trousers plus fours that ended at the knee, where well-cut suede leather boots that accentuated the toned curve of her calves began, the jacket open enough to reveal the frill collars of the white blouse she wore beneath. Even though she was seated, it was clear that the suit was cut to accentuate the curve of her hips and the swell of her bosom, even though her figure was carefully covered up. The whole was finished with a crimson scarf tied loosely around her neck.

"At your service and please, call me Ulysses. All my friends do."

The young woman broke eye contact, looking down at the cup in her lap, the red of her rouged cheeks deepening and the rumours of a smile curling the corners of her mouth. Ulysses thought he heard a tut of disapproval from Nimrod behind him.

"I am not sure that would be appropriate, Mr Quicksilver," she said coyly.

"Oh, but I insist."

Cautiously his unexpected visitor took his hand. "Then you must call me Genevieve," she said, returning her gaze to his. For a moment Ulysses was lost in those depthless orbs that swam with colour like precious tiger's eye stones.

"Very well, Genevieve. It is an absolute pleasure to make your acquaintance."

"Likewise, Ulysses."

She was his now, he was sure of it.

"Now, Genevieve, what can I do for you at this late hour?"

The young woman's face was suddenly serious again. "I do not believe in beating about the bush so I will come straight to the point, Mr Quicksilver," she said nervously. "I mean, Ulysses."

She paused. It seemed to Ulysses that her eyes were glistening with barely suppressed tears. "Go on," he said.

"It's my father. I am dreadfully worried about him. I heard today that there had been an attack at the Natural History Museum."

"And your father is Professor Galapagos?" Ulysses offered. "Professor Ignatius Galapagos?"

"That's right," Genevieve said, surprise replacing concern. "Do you know him, Mr Quicksilver?"

"Ulysses, please," he chided gently. "I have come across his name in my... work. He is a member of staff at the museum?"

"Yes. He works in the Evolutionary Biology department. He often works late, sometimes well into the night, even the early hours of the morning. On occasion he has been known to spend the entire night at the museum."

"He is dedicated to his work then."

"Yes, like no other. It is his passion."

So where was he today? If he was so passionate about his work why not turn up for work on this particular day?

"And was he working late there last night?"

"He was and I haven't seen him since." At that admission Genevieve's shoulders sagged and she returned her tearful gaze to the empty teacup in her lap.

"But, if you will beg my pardon, Miss Galapagos – I mean, Genevieve – you have just said yourself that it is not unheard of for him to spend the whole night in his office."

"Yes, but I eventually went to look for him there today and was turned away by the police. The museum staff said that there had been no sign of him all day – not since the police were alerted to the attack on the night watchman – and then someone told me that it was his office that had been broken into..."

She broke off again, as grief and anxiety overwhelmed her. Ulysses put a comforting hand on her arm.

"I am worried that my father may have been abducted!" Genevieve sobbed.

"Did you relay your concerns to the police?"

"I tried to, but they weren't interested." That sounded about right. "There was an Inspector Alla... Allardiss?"

"Allardyce."

"Yes, that was it. You know him?"

"You could say that."

"I thought so. He said that I should wait twenty-four hours before filing a missing persons report. The inspector mentioned your name though." Genevieve suddenly seemed tense, flexing her shoulders and shifting uncomfortably in the chair.

"Go on, you can say what you like. I won't be offended; not if it's what Allardyce told you."

"Well," Genevieve went on, still struggling with both anxiety and embarrassment, "he was rather... disparaging. But I didn't really like what I saw of him so I decided that if he didn't like you, you might actually be more willing to listen and help me. I understand that I can hire your services, for a suitable fee. I have some money saved..."

"Don't worry about recompense just at the moment," Ulysses said, interrupting her.

She suddenly smiled through the tears. Genevieve took both Ulysses' hands in hers and he was suddenly aware of the heady scent of jasmine flowers as she moved.

"Oh, Ulysses! You will help me then?"

Maybe it was something about being a Quicksilver, but Ulysses simply couldn't resist a pretty face, and when that pretty face belonged to a damsel in distress it made any attempt at resistance even more futile.

"I will do what I can."

"When can you start?"

"Well, as the saying goes, there's no time like the present." Ulysses turned to his manservant. "Nimrod, we're going out."

"You would like me to fire up the Phantom, sir?"

"Yes, I think our guest deserves better than a hansom at this time of night, don't you?"

"Will Miss Galapagos be joining us, sir?"

Ulysses looked to Genevieve. She smiled at him weakly, looking at him from beneath long luscious lashes. She nodded almost imperceptibly.

"Yes, she will."

As he guided Genevieve from the room, Ulysses turned to his dour-faced manservant and gave him a manic grin. "The game is afoot, Nimrod."

"So it would seem, sir."

"Oh yes, the game is most definitely afoot. It feels good to be a player again. This is just what my life has been missing."

CHAPTER FIVE

Galapagos

THE AUTOMOBILE PURRED through the sodium-lit streets, passing flickering broadcast screens on every street corner and the massive advertising hoardings of the mega-corporations. The spider's web of the Overground was black against the smog-laden velvet blue of the night above them. The vehicle passed chugging hansoms, its sleek silvered chassis glittering with the reflected lights of the city. Its engine running almost soundlessly, the car turned into Queen's Gate gliding past the wrought-iron railings that enclosed the Royal College of Music, the bold beams of its headlamps washing over the beggars and streetwalkers that lined the road before sweeping past them.

There was little traffic at this time of night. It would get busier again when the night owls were done with their revels. Nimrod turned the Mark IV Silver Phantom onto Cromwell Road. Ulysses looked out of the window at the cathedral-like towers of the museum, a shadow cut-out of the backdrop of South Kensington behind it.

The car pulled up smoothly outside the main gates and Nimrod turned off the engine. Ulysses opened his door and stepped out before helping Genevieve from the car, taking her hand gently in his. He could not help but take a lingering look at her legs as she climbed gracefully out of the Silver Phantom.

Genevieve looked up at him and, for a moment, their eyes met. He smiled confidently. The smile she returned was somewhat more demure and a moment later, she was the one to break eye contact.

As Genevieve adjusted her jacket Ulysses bent down through the open car door to speak to his manservant. "Nimrod, I want you to wait here just in case our investigation flushes something out."

"You think the killer could still be inside?"

"It's just a hunch – a feeling I have."

"Are you sure this is a good idea, sir?"

"Nimrod, you sound like someone's dear old nanny," Ulysses chided. "We'll be all right. I'm carrying protection," he added, patting the breast of his frock coat. "And besides, Her Majesty's finest Metropolitan Police will be able to keep an eye on us too."

Two robot-bobbies stood before the entrance. Nimrod looked at Ulysses, saying nothing but raising an eyebrow in undisguised disdain.

"Stop fussing, old chap," Ulysses said with a smile. "If I can survive the horrors of Kathmandu and the slopes of Mount Manaslu then I think there's little the Natural History Museum of South Kensington can throw at me that I won't be able to deal with."

"Is there a problem, Mr Quicksilver?" His new client was at his shoulder.

"No not at all, Miss Galapagos," he said, turning away from the driver's window with a dramatic swirl of his coat tails. "And please, call me Ulysses. I insist."

"Of course. Is there a problem then, Ulysses?"

"You know how it is, you just can't get the staff," he said, guiding her towards the entrance.

As they climbed the slope that led to the stepped entrance Genevieve suddenly hung back. "What are we doing here, at this hour?" she asked.

"What?" Ulysses asked, genuinely taken by surprise. "I thought it was because you had just hired me to find your missing father. And seeing as how you say he was last seen here it seemed like the logical place to begin our investigation. As to why at this late hour, it also seemed pertinent to be about our search straightaway."

Genevieve looked at him. There was a glistening sheen in her eyes, the rumour of tears. "That's not what I meant."

Ulysses stopped and took both her hands in his. "If anyone can find your father, I can. I assure you."

"That's what I'm afraid of."

"You have come here to find the truth," he said quietly, his words heavy with meaning.

"Yes, I have," Genevieve agreed.

"Then just remember that the truth is not always the same as what is good or for the best."

Genevieve squeezed Ulysses' fingers tightly.

"It will be all right."

"Will it?" she challenged.

Now it was Ulysses who said nothing.

Genevieve smiled at him, her eyes still wet. "Thank you," she said.

"For what?"

"For trying to spare my emotions."

"Come on," he said, "the truth awaits."

Ulysses mounted the steps at a jog, whipping his cardholder out of his jacket even as one of the automata-peelers initiated its own challenge with the words, "'Ello, 'ello, 'ello. What can I do for you sir? The museum is closed to the public for the night."

In the ambient light of the street lamps Ulysses' sharp eyes could make out the drone's nameplate quite clearly, as the robot scanned the card revealed inside the small leather wallet. "Ah, Constable Palmerston. We meet again."

The second drone – one Constable Disraeli – said nothing, but merely kept its ruby gaze fixed on Genevieve who stood a step or two below Ulysses.

"Indeed we do Mr Quicksilver, sir."

"And I think you will be able to recall from your memory-records your words to me at that juncture."

"Why, of course, sir," Constable Palmerston said in his synthesised voice. "I said that if there was anything else I could do to help..."

"And I said that I would be sure to find you. Well, here I am."

"What can I do to help, Mr Quicksilver?"

"My guest and I would like to examine the scene of the crime again."

"Inspector Allardyce ordered that you are not to be readmitted, sir," the constable reported without emotion.

For a moment Ulysses was taken aback. Genevieve looked at him anxiously. "Did he now?"

"Yes, sir."

"You scanned my card, constable. Then you will recognise whose authority I am here under."

"Yes, sir."

"Then you won't try to stop me if I enter this museum and examine the crime scene again, will you?"

"No, sir."

"Very good, constable. Keep up the good work," Ulysses said jovially as he marched past the two drones and pushed open the door. Genevieve followed, casting nervous glances at the two towering automata as she hurried after him. "Don't worry, they're ultimately on our side," Ulysses said, smiling darkly.

He might sound jovial, but inside he was fuming. How dare that little oik, Allardyce, try to stop him coming back here! What was he trying to hide?

Ulysses' steps rang on the polished stone floor of the entrance hall. Ahead of him the fossilised diplodocus gazed back across the millennia with its eyeless stare.

What *was* Allardyce trying to hide? Probably nothing. He didn't have the wits to. By now he would have decided that the wretched night watchman had been killed by his disturbed burglar and would have practically put the case to bed. Besides, in Allardyce's opinion, what could possibly have been worth stealing from an evolutionary biologist? Nothing that was worth him wasting any more police time over, that was for sure.

Passing the skeletal leviathan Ulysses climbed the grand staircase to the first floor and made his way to the Darwin Wing once again.

The place was deserted. There was no lingering police presence. There were no lights on anywhere in the museum either. Ulysses rather suspected that after the death of the watchman and the possible disappearance of one of their own, any other scientist who was in the habit of working late had decided that an early night was in order. Not that he needed any artificial light to see by. Here in the gallery, the monochrome light of the moon and the orange glow of the city's lights filtering in through the tall windows were quite enough.

Ulysses led the way into the gallery. The body of the night watchman had been removed by the police but dried blood still stained the floor beside the shattered display case. He stopped on reaching the ransacked office.

"This is your father's office, I believe," he said.

Genevieve gasped and put a hand to her mouth.

Allardyce's men had made little effort to secure the crime scene. The mangled door remained propped against the wall and a piece of black and yellow tape had been casually strung across the entrance. Ulysses took hold of the tape and tugged it free with a disdainful snarl.

"Should you be doing that?" Genevieve asked anxiously.

"Should the Metropolitan Police be sitting on their arses when your father has been reported missing?"

Taking out a flashlight from an inside pocket of his coat, Ulysses directed its hard white beam into the office. Light shone back at them from broken glass. Forensics must have been done with the place as some attempt had been made to clear the detritus that had littered the floor. Glass and smashed pieces of furniture had been swept into piles in either corner of the room.

Ulysses carefully stepped into Professor Galapagos's wrecked home away from home. There was still a lingering memory of an odour like aniseed and spoiled steak.

Genevieve paused at the threshold, her breathing rapid and shallow.

"It's all right," Ulysses said. "It'll be all right. Trust me."

Ulysses shone his torch into the far corner of the laboratory. He could still see where the professor's difference engine was missing from its place on the desk. It looked like someone had made some effort to tidy the papers that had been strewn across the work surface. Had any of them been taken away by the police for closer scrutiny? What secrets might they reveal?

But more importantly, what information had been stored on the Babbage machine?

"Your father used a difference engine in his work?" Ulysses asked, meticulously inspecting the walls and space around the desk.

"I believe so," Genevieve replied. "Doesn't everyone?"

"Indeed."

The sweeping beam struck upon several small, fractured display cases, each one holding a stuffed creature, preserved forever by the taxidermist's art. There was a coelacanth, a kaymen and some manner of small primate, its face frozen in either an aggressive or terrified teeth-baring shriek.

"Can you tell if my father was taken from here?" Genevieve asked.

"There are signs of a scuffle, that's for sure. But are they also signs of an abduction?"

Had the professor been abducted from this place at the same time as the thief was stealing away his difference engine? If so, there must have been more than one miscreant, and one of them prepared to kill to ensure their getaway as well as to take a hostage. What manner of men was he dealing with?

The lack of any inkling from his unerring sixth sense was informing him that there was nothing more that Galapagos's quarters could tell him. There were too many distractions there anyway; the mess of papers hinting at greater unsolved mysteries of the scientific world, the glassy-eyed specimens in their broken glass cases, Genevieve...

"Where is the answer? What am I missing here?" Ulysses was becoming frustrated. Was there really nothing more that he could deduce from this mess? The measure of a crime could always be traced back from the wreckage of evidence it left behind it. A crime always left its mark, a criminal his fingerprint even if those investigating the crime could not always see it. What was it that Ulysses was missing?

With a snarl of frustration he suddenly turned on his heel and strode out of the wrecked office again.

"Ulysses?" Genevieve's anxious voice followed him out of the room.

Then he felt it; an uncomfortable prickling sensation that made his skin goose pimple and the hairs on the back of his neck stand up. His hand tightened around his cane, his knuckles whitening.

It was the same sensation he had felt earlier when he had first visited the scene of the crime; the feeling of someone's eyes upon him, only intensified now in the silence and emptiness of the museum. Like fingernails scraping at the inside of his skull.

Was it the killer? Had he returned? Or had Ulysses' suspicions been right all along and had the killer never left?

"Ulysses, what is it?" He was staring blankly ahead of him, his flashlight held at his side, pointing at the floor. Genevieve was at his shoulder.

"Stay close," he whispered.

"There's someone else here, isn't there?"

"I rather think there is."

DARK EYES WATCHED as the two figures explored the gallery beyond the ruins of the ransacked room, the torch beam flicking into the darkened recesses of alcoves and behind glittering display cases. The watcher recognised the man; tall, confident, his stride purposeful, as if he owned the gallery and the museum. It remembered him from earlier that day.

It did not recognise the smaller female scurrying anxiously at his side. She smelt of fear and something else – something hidden.

The watcher pulled itself back behind a cast iron roof beam. It sensed, in its primitive way, that it was what they were searching for, and the interloper was persistent. He would not rest until he had found what he was looking for, until he had hunted the watcher down. It was only a matter of time before the sweeping beam uncovered its hiding place.

It was getting frustrated by its confinement in the museum. It was changing all the time. It wanted to stretch its limbs, test its new body, discover what it was capable of.

And its mind was changing too. It was no longer happy to watch whilst others trespassed within its territory. The desire was growing inside it to drive the interlopers from the gallery, to show them which was the dominant species here.

Lips pulled back from clenched teeth and a low growl issued from its altered throat.

SHADOWS FLICKERED AND writhed against the wall. Ulysses' sweeping torch beam suddenly picked out teeth bared in an angry snarl, eyes staring in open defiance. Genevieve gasped. The face that appeared in the cold white light was barely human, the expression contorting it one of bestial rage.

Ulysses leaned closer, pointing his torch directly into the subhuman's glassy-eyed stare. The creature didn't even blink.

"It's all right," he said. "*Homo neanderthalensis*, resident of the middle Paleolithic. Thought to have died out around 29,000 years ago until that inbred colony was found in the Urals in sixty-nine."

A hand on Ulysses' shoulder, Genevieve peered past him at the motionless figure in front of them. The waxwork replica of the Neanderthal, moved from its smashed display case earlier that day to lie propped against the wall of the gallery, continued to stare back, one arm raised, an antler held threateningly in its hand.

"This one isn't going to cause us any trouble," Ulysses said.

Awareness suddenly flared in his brain like a firework. Ulysses spun round, pushing Genevieve out of the way as something large swung out of the darkness and barrelled into him.

Ulysses was sent crashing to the ground, even as he reached inside his jacket for his pistol. His torch fell from his hand and went out. The wind was knocked from his lungs as the creature landed on top of him. He twisted, trying to free himself from the weight of the thing. As he did so he tugged his pistol free and aimed it at the shadow looming over him. A club-like fist smashed into his outstretched arm. In unexpected shock the muscles in his hand spasmed, releasing the weapon which skittered away across the floor of the gallery.

The beast let out a victorious roar. Genevieve screamed.

Disarmed, Ulysses would have to try a different approach.

In the eerie moonlit glow of the gallery the creature appeared as a ragged shadow above him. Ulysses could see nothing more than the glistening points of its eyes and the gleam of its bared fangs. The stench of its rancid breath made him gag as it came in hot gusts against his face.

He was suddenly back in Tibet as recollections of his struggle with the snow beast in the hidden monastery poured from his subconscious. He had survived that encounter and he would survive this one, thanks in part to the martial arts he had learned in the company of the Tibetan monks.

Ulysses kicked upwards sharply with his right leg. The toe of his shoe connected with the back of the creature's neck. The thing howled and arched its back, releasing Ulysses from the weight pressing down on his pelvis.

His leg swinging back down again he pendulummed his body forwards, raising his torso from the ground. As his arms came free he thrust them forwards, palms together. He struck the thing squarely in the sternum, the force of his blow pushing the creature from him.

But in a moment the creature was crouched on its haunches, ready to pounce again. Rising up on its muscular legs it towered over Ulysses, its hairy arms raised ready to pound him into the polished marble floor of the gallery. It bellowed its anger and beat its chest with its fists, declaring its claim to this place as its territory.

Without a moment's hesitation the creature sprang at Ulysses again. But this time Ulysses was ready. As the ape-like creature landed, grasping at him with leathery paws, he seized hold of the thing, grasping great tufts of hair in his fists as he let himself fall backwards beneath the creature's assault, pushing a foot into its midriff as he did so. He landed on his back again on the cold stone but this time the creature came with him, unbalanced by the change in its centre of gravity. As he felt the full weight of the thing above him Ulysses brought both his feet together and pushed upwards with all the strength in his legs, at the same time pulling the beast forward.

The creature sailed over Ulysses' head. He heard it howl in protest and then there was an almighty crash. Ulysses quickly got to his feet and turned, preparing to face his attacker again.

Shards of glass sparkled in the monochrome light bathing the hall. Unable to stop itself, the creature had smashed into one of the gallery's display cases. Snorting in annoyance the beast was trying to extricate itself from the shattered remains of the cabinet. Ulysses surmised that it must have been injured in the collision but whatever injuries it might have sustained did not seem to be slowing it down.

The creature was caught in the spotlight of his torch beam, pupils contracting against the sudden illumination. In that split second Ulysses saw his attacker clearly for the first time.

It was an apeman, dressed in a suit of ill-fitting clothes. What Ulysses could see of the creature beneath its curious garb was covered in reddish-brown hair, apart from its hands, feet and blunt-nosed face. The tweed jacket and trousers had torn where the beast's form was too large to be contained. A white shirt had popped its buttons, as had a formal paisley-patterned waistcoat.

Ulysses briefly wondered how anyone had managed to dress this savage in such a way, as he caught the glint of a silver chain hanging around its neck, until the only logical answer presented itself to him.

Ulysses pulled himself upright. Picking up his cane he took hold of the bloodstone at its end and gave it a twist. With one smooth movement Ulysses pulled a rapier from the middle of his cane. As the apeman's laboured breathing turned into a guttural growl Ulysses assumed the stance of an accomplished fencer. "En garde," he said with quiet purpose.

As the creature climbed free of the wreckage of the display case, Ulysses noted that its lumbering gait and low-slung head spoke of a kinship with the lower orders of primates. The semi-human features of the creature devolved into a bestial snarl and it knuckled forwards, using its forelimbs like another pair of legs, shrieking horribly. Rapier blade in hand, Ulysses prepared to meet its furious charge.

The shot rang out through the gallery like a cannon blast, the report of the pistol amplified by the acoustics of the hall. The apeman was suddenly hurled backwards, a welter of blood spraying from its left shoulder and a whimper of pain escaping its malformed lips. Then, as the blue pistol smoke cleared, the creature was back on its feet only now it was running to escape, rather than charging to attack.

Ulysses spun round. Genevieve stood behind him, the torch in one hand, his gun held rigidly in the other. "Nice shot," he said, the rumour of a smile inching itself onto his face, "but I had the situation fully under control."

Genevieve lowered the gun. "I thought that... thing was going to kill you."

"Your concern is touching, really it is," Ulysses said, sheathing his sword-cane and setting off at a run, back through the gallery, Genevieve trotting to keep up, "but I would rather we took that throwback alive."

They turned left into the main gallery of the Darwin Wing. In the dull monochrome light of the moon Ulysses could see black spots of blood speckling the polished floor, leaving them an obvious trail.

"Do you think that thing had anything to do with my father's disappearance?" Genevieve said.

They passed beneath the stone arch above which the words 'The Ascent of Man' were carved, Ulysses' shoes sliding on the polished stone floor. The slap of the ape-thing's leathery hands and feet could be heard ahead of them. "I would bet money on it. Which is why we can't let it get away."

Ulysses put on a turn of speed and, leaving Genevieve behind, sprinted onto the cloister-gallery that ran around the main entrance hall of the museum. Then he saw it, loping along on all fours like a dog. He swore sharply under his breath. He could have delivered a crippling shot to the creature, had Genevieve not still got his gun. He would have to try something else to halt the apeman's escape.

"Constable Palmerston!" he yelled at the top of his voice. "Constable Palmerston, if ever there was a time I needed your help that time is now! Palmerston!"

The apeman suddenly turned, its feet slipping momentarily on the polished stone, and then it leapt onto the ledge of the colonnaded walkway. Ulysses could see the chain around its neck more clearly now. Hanging from it was what looked like a silver locket.

The beast glanced momentarily at Ulysses, its eyes burning with animal fear and malign hatred, and then the creature hurled itself into empty space.

"Palmerston!" Ulysses screamed.

The apeman landed with a rattling crash on the spine of the diplodocus skeleton as the museum doors burst open and the two Peeler-drones marched into the building.

"Stop, in the name of the law!" Ulysses heard the Palmerston unit pronounce in its synthesised voice.

But the creature had no intention of stopping, in the name of the law or anything else. The diplodocus swayed precariously as the apeman bounded across it, grabbing at ribs and vertebrae to aid its flight across the hall.

Another shot rang out through the museum and a prehistoric shoulder blade exploded in a cloud of dust and bone fragments.

"We want to take it alive!" Ulysses shouted.

The two constables were beneath the diplodocus now, the apeman scrambling across the skeleton above them. Grabbing hold of the fossil's neck with one hand it swung over the heads of the automatons and launched itself at the main doors. It hit the floor as the cables holding the relic's head and neck gave way and the dinosaur's skull crashed to the ground, its jaw shattering on the hard stone floor.

In one bound the apeman was through the doors. A moment later Ulysses barged past the bewildered droids as he hurtled through the doors after the creature, only to see it swinging away into the night, using street lamps as a monkey would have swung through a jungle canopy. With a squeal of tyres the Silver Phantom sped off after the creature, swerving to avoid a crawling omnibus as Nimrod gave chase.

"Did we get it?" Genevieve gasped. She stood with her hands on her knees, panting for breath. There was a manic gleam in her eye that was so unlike the demure young woman he had met only a matter of an hour or so earlier.

"You certainly got it," Ulysses said in an almost disapproving tone.

"Yes, but where is it now?"

"What's going on 'ere then?" The two robot policemen had joined them at the top of the steps.

"I think we just spooked your murderer," Ulysses muttered.

There was the crackle of static as the Peeler unit used its internal radio to report the escape to its controllers back at Scotland Yard.

There was the sound of a horn and the Silver Phantom pulled up again outside the museum railings. Ulysses was halfway down the incline from the museum building by the time Nimrod had emerged from the car.

"I do apologise, sir, but I am afraid I lost the monkey."

Ulysses sighed. His first major lead in this case had just evaded him. But, he reminded himself, patting the pocket of his jacket, it wasn't his only lead.

"Don't worry, Nimrod old chap," he said. Genevieve had joined them, the drones following close on her heels. "Did you happen to see what that thing was wearing around its neck, along with the rest of its incongruous wardrobe?" Ulysses asked her.

"Why yes," she said, obviously somewhat shaken, the manic look gone from her eyes to be replaced by wide-eyed shock. "It was my locket."

"Your locket?"

"Well, I mean, it's my father's locket, but I gave it to him. It was a gift. That thing must have taken it from him. It must have had something to do with his disappearance."

Ulysses looked at Genevieve gravely and took her hands in his again. "Genevieve," he said, "I can't think of any other way to put this to you, but I don't believe that thing took the locket from your father. In fact I don't believe that your father has been abducted."

"What d-do mean? You're not saying that you think he's d..." She broke off, overcome with emotion. Her eyes were imploring him now, desperately wanting him to tell her anything that might help her make sense of what had happened.

"Don't ask me to explain how but I think that thing *is* – or rather, *was* – your father."

CHAPTER SIX

A Meeting with Methuselah

THE PARTIALLY RUSTED pull grated as Ulysses tugged on it and a moment later, somewhere deep within the house, he heard the clattering of an ancient bell. Then he waited. The old man didn't keep any servants; he preferred not to be disturbed even by domestic help while he worked, and his work was his life.

The debacle at the museum the previous night had prevented Ulysses from pursuing the most direct course of action regarding Professor Galapagos's disappearance. Despite taking off after the fleeing apeman in Ulysses' Silver Phantom, following the altered beast as it had swung from lamp post to lamp post down the Cromwell Road, Nimrod had had to give up the chase when the creature had scrambled up the side of a building and taken to the rooftops. There was no way he could have abandoned the car and still kept up with the apeman on foot.

After Ulysses had broken the tragic news to Genevieve Galapagos that her father had somehow become some kind of degenerate apeman, the girl had gone to pieces. She had refused the offer of something to eat, and a bed, at the Quicksilver residence – seemingly placing a portion of the blame for what had happened to her father at Ulysses' door – but Ulysses had insisted that Nimrod drive her home. He promised that he would contact her as soon as he knew anything more.

So it was that as the smog-laden sky over London began to lighten with the coming dawn, Ulysses found himself at the house of Dr Methuselah.

Although he was currently seen to be pursuing the Galapagos case, at the same time the mystery of the professor's transformation was inextricably linked to the mission that had been forced upon him by Uriah Wormwood. The more Ulysses could discover about what had happened to Professor Ignatius Galapagos, the more likely he was to find out what had really happened regarding the theft from the Natural History Museum. It seemed highly unlikely that the ape-like Galapagos – if it was truly he – would have had the wits to take his own difference engine, for some unfathomable reason. There had to be another felon involved, and somehow the two of them were connected. If he could track the errant professor down Ulysses Quicksilver was sure that he would eventually find his thief.

A clattering of bolts being drawn back and keys being turned stirred Ulysses from his reverie. The heavy black door creaked open a crack. It was still secured by a chain, and a wizened bespectacled face looked up at Ulysses.

"What do you want?" the old man snapped in a voice that was high-pitched and cracked with age.

"Dr Methuselah, it is so good to see you again," Ulysses said, smiling broadly.

"Is it?" Dr Methuselah blinked at him myopically from behind bottle-bottom lenses.

"It's me, doctor, Ulysses. Ulysses Quicksilver?"

The hunched figure looked Ulysses up and down, his face twisted into a scowl.

"I thought you were dead."

"Yes, I get that a lot."

"So, if you're not dead, what do you want?"

"Your help, doctor, as ever."

This request solicited the same response it always did. "You don't get something for nothing in this world. You can pay?"

"You can do this for me right away?"

"If you can pay me right now I can."

"You know I'm good for the cash," Ulysses said, feigning hurt. "At least I hope you do."

"You'd better come in then. You're letting in a draught."

The door closed, there was the rattle of the chain being unhooked, and then it opened fully to admit Ulysses to the house. Once he was over the threshold the stooped Dr Methuselah ushered him inside and shut the door behind him.

"Do you know what time it is?"

"I didn't think you kept conventional working hours."

"I don't, but that's not the point," the old man grumbled, and set off down the mahogany-panelled hallway. The musty smell of the place and the decaying décor all added to the character of the house.

As the ageing doctor shuffled down the corridor, Ulysses was better able to take in his appearance. Nothing had changed since the last time he had visited. Methuselah's clothes were filthy, covered in all manner of curious chemical stains. He had several days' growth of white stubble speckling his bony chin and hollow cheeks. He seemed to be permanently stooped and an unwashed odour hung about him like a mantle.

Ulysses followed Methuselah through the darkened house and into the back room that served as the curmudgeon's laboratory. Not that it looked or smelt like one. Floor to ceiling bookcases covered almost every available wall space, stuffed with yellowed tomes and rolls of parchment. More books were piled in tottering towers on the floor. There was no natural light in the room. Any windows that there might once have been were now barricaded by bookcases or covered by cork pinboards on which the doctor's meticulously ink-drawn autopsy studies were displayed. The air was thick with the unpleasant combination of formaldehyde, mothballs and tobacco smoke.

Along the length of the room was a timber-top workspace. All manner of curious, scientific or medical equipment cluttered its surface. There were jars with unnaturally shaped things floating in brackish liquid and Ulysses saw a half-dissected creature pinned out on a slab that might have been a deformed toad or could equally have been, even more horribly, a deformed human foetus. Another table was covered with a mess of electrical gadgetry.

"So what do you want me to look at?" the doctor asked.

Ulysses reached into the pocket of his frock coat and took out the evidence bag containing the sample he had taken from Galapagos's office. "I want you to take a look at this."

"Very well." Methuselah took the bag and peered at the reddish-brown hairs inside through his thick-lensed spectacles. Ulysses couldn't help noticing that the doctor's fingernails were black with grime.

Having scrabbled around within the clutter of his workspace to find a pair of tweezers, the doctor placed the hairs on a slide, which he then inserted beneath the rotating lenses of a brass microscope. Methuselah put one lens of his glasses to the viewing piece and, with no small amount of huffing and puffing and unintelligible muttering, twiddled a variety of brass wheels to focus the device and magnify what he saw.

The doctor paused while he pulled up a stool, so that he might continue his study of the specimen in relative comfort.

Ulysses looked for a seat himself, but there were no more available. It wasn't that there wasn't any furniture in the room it was just that every available surface was covered with the paraphernalia of the doctor's work. Instead he leant over the doctor's shoulder to watch what

Methuselah was doing. The doctor's malingering body odour assailed Ulysses' nostrils, catching in the back of his throat. Ulysses pulled back before the festering smell made him gag. He occupied himself instead by distractedly poking at piles of papers with his cane, examining some of the titles on Methuselah's bookshelves and taking a closer look at some of his Da Vinci-like anatomical drawings.

"Darwin's eyes!" the old man suddenly exclaimed.

"What is it, Dr Methuselah?" Despite the poor state of the old man's personal hygiene, Ulysses was back at his side again.

The doctor of forensics looked round sharply. "No, I'm not ready to present my findings yet," he snapped cantankerously.

"Very well, doctor," his client said soothingly, "take as long as you need."

With that the doctor went back to his work, which was now accompanied by him noisily sucking his teeth. He extracted a cogitator keypad from somewhere on his desk and it was only then that Ulysses realised that, amongst everything else crammed into the shelf space above Methuselah, was a cathode ray unit. As the doctor began to type sequences of numbers into the machine the screen began to warm up with a rising hum, turning from black to a glowing green.

After a few more minutes there was another gasp from the absorbed doctor.

"Where did you get these hairs?" Methuselah asked, unable to hide the astonishment and excitement in his voice.

"You know better than to ask that doctor," Ulysses chided.

Methuselah grunted and muttered something that Ulysses strongly suspected was either blasphemous or a personal slight against him.

There was now an image on the difference engine's view screen. Ulysses assumed it was a magnified cross-section of what Methuselah could see through his microscope. Streams of data scrolled up the side of the screen in a repeating pattern. Knowing a little about the science of biology he recognised what he was seeing in the flickering emerald lines as cells. To understand anymore he would need the expert to explain it to him.

"If we extrapolate the data back to the original source," the doctor said, thinking aloud rather than addressing Ulysses directly, "and if my hypothesis is correct," the doctor tapped something into the difference engine's brass-faced keypad, a series of confusing images now being relayed by the screen, "... we find... Yes!" he declared triumphantly. "An exact match!"

"With what, doctor?"

"Hmm?" Methuselah seemed to have become absorbed in his work to the point of practically forgetting that Ulysses was still there. "What?"

"An exact match with what?"

"Oh, an exact match with human DNA of course."

A feeling of self-satisfied vindication settled like a warm mist over Ulysses. "I love it when I'm right," he said, smiling to himself. He couldn't say he was surprised; it was what he had suspected ever since he had visited the scene of the crime and heard of the disappearance of Professor Galapagos. He had just needed someone with the scientific knowledge to prove that his hunch had been more than just that. He still had no idea, though, what could have caused such a degeneration in the evolutionary biologist.

"Doctor, I appreciate your candour but I would appreciate it if you could put what you have discovered into layman's terms. And start at the beginning."

Methuselah sighed in irritation at the thought of having to dumb down his findings for this dandy.

"Take a look at this," the doctor said in a weary tone, nodding at the thinking machine's monitor. He typed something else into the Babbage engine and the magnified image of cells appeared on the screen again. "What you are looking at here is one of the hairs you brought me but at the cellular level."

"I realise that, doctor," Ulysses interjected impatiently. "But what have they revealed to you?"

"If you let me finish I could tell you."

"Of course, doctor. I am sorry. Please continue."

"Very well," Methuselah said, almost grudgingly. "These are hair cells from a member of the primate family. There is nothing particularly remarkable about that until we observe them at a molecular level."

The image on the screen flickered and blurred, reforming to show Ulysses something he had never seen before in his life.

"What am I looking at now?" he asked, staring uncomprehendingly at the spiralling ribbons of bonded molecules.

"This," said Methuselah, unable to hide the tone of smugness from his own voice, "is the stuff of life itself. You are gazing upon the very building blocks of all life on this planet. This is the double helix of deoxyribonucleic acid. DNA."

"That's DNA?" Ulysses uttered incredulously.

"The very same. Chains of only four different nucleotides, combined in an infinite number of ways results in the vast biodiversity we witness on this planet. From snails to whales, from the lumbering leviathans of the Jurassic that are still with us today to the mosquito that feeds on its blood, every living thing is the result of strings of genetically coded information carried by the strands of DNA wrapped up inside its cells."

"But you said that you had found human DNA here and yet now you tell me that these are hairs from some kind of ape." It was not that Ulysses did not believe the doctor; it was just that he wanted to understand more completely what could possibly have happened for this to be the case.

"I was just getting to that. The DNA sample inside these hairs is unstable."

"Unstable? How do you mean?"

"It is unravelling, as it were."

"Doctor, I still don't fully under..."

"How can I put this any more plainly?" Methuselah said, the frustration he felt rising in his voice. "These are now the hairs of a primate but they once belonged to a man, a human being, like you or I. These hairs have somehow devolved into those belonging to one of Man's evolutionary ancestors. And the process is ongoing."

Now Ulysses felt genuine surprise. "It's still happening?"

"The genetic make-up of the sample is steadily reverting to previous evolutionary forms. Imagine it! The very essence of life unravelling, de-evolving, if you will, back into the amino acids and bacteria from which we were first formed. What we are looking at here is a veritable history lesson in the creation of the human race from baser forms of life on this planet. As each layer of history peels away, these cells here are changing into a prior evolutionary form, as the very DNA held inside each of them is continually re-written at a genetic level."

"So when will this metamorphosis reach its conclusion?"

"I won't know for sure without continued observation."

"Humour me. Give me a hypothesis."

"Well, looking at the sample I have here, there's no reason to suggest that it won't stop until it reaches the beginning."

"You might as well be speaking in riddles, doctor."

"I mean at what we understand to be the beginning of all life on this planet. These cells are already beginning to display characteristics of those of a reptile. There is no evidence to suggest that they will not continue to regress until the biological matter under this microscope has dissolved back into the component parts that make up all life on this planet, effectively into a protoplasmic soup."

For a moment neither man spoke as they both digested the import of the doctor's revelation.

"Quicksilver, where is the poor wretch these hairs came from?"

"I wish I knew," Ulysses said with a heartfelt sigh.

"He needs to be studied, quarantined perhaps."

"What, and dissected, doctor?" Ulysses challenged, putting a sarcastic emphasis on the word 'doctor'.

"No, for his own safety."

"Well, when I catch up with him again, I'll be sure to tell him to look you up. Now, what do I owe you for your services?"

Methuselah stared at Ulysses, mouth agape, until the mention of payment reminded him that morals were all very well for men of the cloth but they didn't cover gambling debts or keep a man in opium. "We'll call it ten guineas – cash."

Ulysses opened his wallet with a flourish, took out the agreed fee and handed it over to the old man, who was watching his every move with the avaricious hunger of a gold prospector.

"Thank you for your time, doctor." Placing his wallet back inside his jacket pocket Ulysses turned to go.

"What about the sample?" Methuselah asked.

"Keep it," Ulysses said, turning at the door to the workroom. "And I'll pay you for any other information you might be able to impart after further observation. I'll see myself out."

Back on the street Ulysses took a moment to clear his lungs of the acrid smell of preserving fluid and savour the honest tarry smell of the London streets. Delving deep into a pocket he pulled out the teak and brass handset of his personal communicator. He flicked it open and extended its aerial. He waited whilst a train clattered by overhead, then keyed in Genevieve's number.

It rang three times before there was the click of a receiver being lifted at the other end and he heard Genevieve's voice. "Hello?" was all she said, but even that one simple response made Ulysses' stomach flutter with a frisson of excitement. He surprised himself with such a psychosomatic reaction. He hadn't realised how sorry he had been to cause her so much distress only hours before and how unhappy he had felt at the abruptness of their parting.

"Genevieve, it's Ulysses. Please don't hang up."

"I have nothing to say to you."

"But I have more news," he gabbled.

There was no response from the other end of the line. Was she still there? "Genevieve?"

"What news?" Her tone was flat with suppressed emotion.

"I'd rather not discuss it over the phone. Let's meet up."

Again there was a pause. "Where?"

Ulysses thought fast. His mind was awhirl with their last encounter among the prehistoric exhibits and Dr Methuselah's talk of DNA and evolutionary genetic heritage. One place came immediately to mind, but he thought it best to avoid the Natural History Museum for the time being. He didn't want Scotland Yard getting in the way of his private business again and somewhere public and open was always best if you wanted to avoid arousing suspicion.

"London Zoo," he said, "the Challenger Enclosure. Then I can share with you what I have discovered."

"Very well." Her tone had softened. "I'll meet you there at ten o' clock tomorrow morning." The connection went dead.

Ulysses closed the communicator and stowed it back in his pocket. Soon he would have to convince Genevieve of the horrifying truth regarding her father's disappearance and no doubt batter her emotions once more.

CHAPTER SEVEN

Terrible Lizards

"THANK YOU FOR agreeing to meet with me," Ulysses said.

Breaking eye contact Genevieve redirected her gaze at the floor, demonstrating the same demure tendencies she had shown on their first meeting. "Well seeing as how I am your client and I am paying you to assist me in this matter it would be foolish not to. You said you had some news."

"That's right."

"I was surprised to hear from you so soon," she admitted. "In fact, I was surprised to hear from you again at all."

"Why? What do you mean?"

"After the way I... overreacted. I was overly emotional."

"That's hardly surprising when you consider all that you have experienced. I should have been more tactful."

"I may not have known you for very long, Mr Quicksilver, but I already know that you are a hopeless liar."

"Is that so?" The disarming smile came easily to Ulysses' lips.

Genevieve returned the expression, also returning the soul-searching gaze of her rich russet eyes to his.

"You are a champion of the truth. And no matter how painful that truth might be, it should be known and faced up to."

"But perhaps I did not choose the best moment to impart all I suspected, particularly without the evidence to back it up."

"But you have that evidence now." It wasn't a question. Genevieve Galapagos was no fool. The previous night's adventure had convinced Ulysses of that much.

"Walk with me," Ulysses said.

As she took his arm he caught the scent of her again carried on the warm breeze; the scent of jasmine flowers. For a moment he was transported back to Tibet and the Gardens of Sanctuary at Shangri-La. Then, in silence, the two of them joined the other promenaders in their wanderings of the Challenger Enclosure.

The Regent's Park menagerie was always popular with the leisured classes and it was busy now, the zoo having been open for over an hour. Chaperoned courting couples were making their promenade of the dinosaur pens. There were ladies at leisure carrying parasols against the glaring sun, and nannies pushing perambulators whilst trying to keep their slightly older and yet more unruly charges under control.

Genevieve had been late. Ulysses had waited half an hour, with only the lowing and farting of the goliath animals and the clattering of the Bakerloo line above him for company, before trying her again on his personal communicator. The phone had rung and rung without anyone answering. After an hour, and with the crowds steadily increasing, he had begun to wonder if she would come at all and whether he shouldn't just give up on the distraught Miss Galapagos and continue with his investigation.

And then she had appeared between the crowds of sauntering zoo-goers, dressed in a long green velvet coat with her luxurious auburn hair done up in a bun under a top hat, an anxious searching look in her eyes.

They joined the ambling throng of the general public as if enjoying the wonders of the Challenger Enclosure like any other curious couple, for a moment all their worries and the pressure of the mission put to one side. As they walked they caught snippets of conversation.

"In the wild they graze the low-growing vegetation of their savannah homes but here at the zoo they do just as well on a diet of hay and fresh fruit and vegetables," a keeper was explaining to an interested party of parvenus, describing the dietary habits of the stegosaurus. "Mabel here is particularly fond of bananas, aren't you girl?"

"Are they not dangerous?" a young woman asked.

"Only if they're frightened and you get in the way of a stampede. They're quite placid really. They're only really dangerous during the mating season when the males fight for the females' attention but old George over there is a bit past that sort of thing these days. He can only really manage a bit of bellowing now. But then we don't have any other younger males here at the zoo to threaten his position as top dog, as it were."

They moved on to where a party of school children were completely ignoring what their harassed teacher was trying to tell them about the styracosaurs they were supposed to be studying. "They produce as many as eight eggs in a clutch," the schoolmistress was saying. "Gregory Pike, will you stop that at once!"

"But what's to stop the animals escaping?" a concerned portly woman wearing a garish ostrich-feather hat was asking another attendant whilst her hunched and hen-pecked husband gazed distractedly at a younger man's more comely companion.

"Don't worry, madam," the zookeeper reassured her jovially. "Every pen is either surrounded by a moat or ditch, like this one here, so that the animals can't climb out, or they are kept behind six-inch thick reinforced steel bars, like the carnivores in the 'Prehistoric Killers' section. And if that weren't enough the fences are also electrified."

"Goodness me. Did you hear that, Stanley?" the woman asked her husband.

"What was that, my dear?" he replied distractedly, as though enjoying some lovely private dream.

"The fences are electricityfied. Oh I do wish you would listen!"

"Yes dear."

"So you have nothing to fear, madam. You are perfectly safe, as is the rest of London," the keeper said with a chuckle.

They walked on, leaving the herbivore pens behind, moving into the area the keeper had referred to as the 'Prehistoric Killers' section.

"Why, they're just like birds," a chinless fop with a monocle and an oiled moustache was saying to impress an equally inbred-looking pug-nosed girl.

"And of course the work we're doing here has an environmental aspect to it as well," a zoo employee dressed more like a clerk than a keeper was explaining to a group of broad-waisted venture capitalists. "In the wild these animals are either being hunted to extinction for sport or their natural environment is being steadily destroyed as a result of Man's continued, and utterly thoughtless, pillaging of the planet. Either to provide farmland to grow crops to feed an ever-increasing population, or to be strip mined in the incessant quest for coal for the monstrous machines on which we have all so come to depend. So you see, gentlemen, your investment is of vital importance to our continued good work here."

They passed a large domed enclosure that looked not unlike a giant birdcage, for that was effectively what it was. Perched on the branches of trees growing inside were a flock of leathery-winged pterosaurs.

"Look, Templeton Trench brought this specimen back from the Congo as an egg," a tanned, older man with a huge white handlebar moustache was bellowing to the two simpering girls hanging off his arms – both young enough to be his nieces but of no apparent familial connection. They ooh-ed and ah-ed and giggled in all the right places as he continued his monologue, casting only half-interested glances in the direction of the monstrous, red-skinned allosaurus devouring a pig's carcass in front of them.

"Of course the Megasaurus Rex is our finest specimen." The party of businessmen and their fund-raising guide had moved along with Genevieve and Ulysses. "A true king of the megasaurs, although of course ours is a female. The keepers call her Glenda. She eats up to three cows a day."

"How horrible!" Genevieve suddenly exclaimed and Ulysses felt her squeeze his arm more tightly. In the shade of a magnolia tree she pulled him to a halt. "You said you had some news." Suddenly he was abruptly back in the real world with all its attendant worries and inconclusive problems.

Ulysses looked Genevieve squarely in the eyes. He could have let himself drown in those limpid pools. "What was your father doing? What did his most recent work entail?"

An expression of guilt flickered across her face for a moment and she turned her eyes away. The croaking cries of the dinosaurs filled the silence.

"The truth is, I don't know," Genevieve admitted at last. "I hadn't actually seen him for some time. He had become totally absorbed by his work, whatever it was. And you think that whatever it was he was working on caused him to..."

"Change?" Ulysses finished for her. "Yes, I do."

Then she was staring intently into his eyes again with that imploring look of hers and Ulysses felt his heart leap inside his chest. "Help me find my father," she said, "I beg of you. Help me." There was a hand on his shoulder now, the other slipped from his arm around his waist. Above them an Overground train whistled as it approached the aerial platform of Albany Street station four storeys above.

She was beautiful, of that there was no doubt – her body athletically slim, accentuated with curves in all the right places – and she was no mean markswoman either. What more could a man look for in a girl?

But he was becoming distracted. Another part of his mind was musing upon the matter of where a rogue apeman would hide in London, if not the Natural History Museum or London Zoo? Except that the sample he had taken to the old curmudgeon Methuselah was now showing signs of turning into something more akin to lizard scales, so the supposition was that Professor Galapagos would be undergoing the same unspeakable transformation. So the question wasn't so much, where would an apeman hide in the overrun capital as, where would a lizard make its lair? And then, by extension, how on Earth would Ulysses Quicksilver, dandy adventurer and detecting intellect for hire, find it?

All the while that other part of his mind, the part ensnared by Genevieve's lustrous gaze, her cherry bud lips, her jasmine blossom aroma and the warmth of her breath on his cheek, was aware of how close the two of them were to one another now. He took her in his arms, lowering his head to meet hers. Her glistening lips parted to meet his.

Then another, almost subconscious, part of his mind, took over as his sixth sense screamed for his attention. And what it screamed was 'Danger!'

The thunderous roar of the explosion tore through the peace of the morning promenaders, the force of its shockwave throwing many to the ground. Ulysses instinctively threw himself on top of Genevieve as the two of them were bowled off their feet by the blast. Pieces of twisted metal and other debris rained down around them. One man went down with blood pouring from his head. Another cried out as a buckled spar speared his torso and then fell silent.

Ulysses turned to look up at the Overground line that crossed the sky above the zoo, his body taut, ready. Thick black smoke shot through with greasy orange flames rose into the sky over Regent's Park from a fifty foot wide span of the Bakerloo line. As Ulysses watched, with a tortured metal scream, a section of track broke free from a cast iron stanchion and fell, cantilevering under its own great weight. To Ulysses' adrenalin-heightened senses it seemed that the track was falling in slow motion, trailing oily smoke and charcoal-blackened railway sleepers as it swung down towards the crowded Challenger Enclosure. People were screaming. Some were running in an attempt to escape the catastrophe unfolding around them.

The descending track crashed into the side of the stegosaurus pit, crushing a keeper and the panicking woman he was trying to save as the pen wall crumbled. Other pieces of debris continued to rain down from the devastation of the Bakerloo Line above. Ulysses could hear the schoolmistress screaming hysterically, her wailing charges suddenly desperate to obey her instructions.

The animals were in uproar. Herbivores hooted and bellowed in fear. Carnivores paced their cages roaring, smelling the pheromone fear of their natural prey. The musky scent was sending them into a frustrated frenzy, desperate to get to the panicking animals – and desperate humans.

Keepers were running from other parts of the zoo, along with huddles of zoo-goers, eager to witness the escalating drama within the Challenger Enclosure as much as to aid those at the forefront of the disaster.

But it seemed that Ulysses alone realised that this was only the beginning and that a more terrible disaster was about to strike. The Overground was running still, the drivers of the trains on the Bakerloo Line as yet unaware of the accident, or act of sabotage, whatever it might be. And there was a train coming now.

There was the shriek of brakes being applied as the driver saw first the roiling column of smoke and then the gaping hole in the track, but with the train still travelling at speed there was no hope of it stopping in time. Instead, the fully laden passenger train careered off the broken span, following the track down into the zoo, the carriages being pulled violently off the rails as the lead engine hurtled down into the Challenger Enclosure. The engine hit the tarmac with deadly force, its boiler casing rupturing and its smokestack exploding into flame. Those within ten yards who were not crushed beneath the falling train were scalded to death by the superheated steam rushing from the broken boiler, or burned alive in the fiery inferno that followed.

But the train did not stop there. It ploughed on through the enclosure, carried forward under its own momentum as well as being shunted from behind by the ten carriages that clattered after it. Walls crumbled to dust before the hurtling comet of the burning engine, bars of cages crumpling and steel tearing like paper. Yet still the train hurtled on, sparks flying from the pathways and plazas, carriages keeled over onto their sides, the passengers trapped within screaming as fires took hold throughout the body of the wreck. Dinosaur pens were breached, carnivore cages torn down and the pterosaur enclosure smashed open.

Finally the devastated engine broke through into the apatasaurs' lake enclosure, killing a young female as the train wreck smashed through the electric barrier and into the animal's flank, ploughing a great furrow into the turf leading to the shore of the herd's watering hole. Carriages piled into the back of the engine, several breaking free at last. Ulysses watched as one of the carriages – its side scraped bare of its coat of paint – barrelled through the air over him and Genevieve. He momentarily glimpsed the faces of the carriage's terrified occupants pressed against the shattered windows as it spun in its hurtling airborne path. Then it crashed down into the high perimeter wall of the zoo and smashed through, breaching the one barrier that remained between the prehistoric bubble of the Challenger Enclosure and the outside world in a cloud of mortar and brick dust. Ulysses – his heart pounding from their dramatic escape – heard the blaring of car horns, the screech of more brakes and the inevitable collisions as the carriage ploughed onto the thoroughfare beyond the boundary of the zoo.

People fled in panic, as did the zoo's most prized exhibits; the dinosaurs breaking free from their long incarceration. There was a sobbing shout from one of the keepers that the electric fence was down.

"We have to get out of here!" Ulysses yelled at Genevieve over the screams of the fleeing crowd and the bellowing of the dinosaurs, pulling her to her feet. Genevieve was too shocked to answer but merely stumbled after Ulysses through the chaos as he pulled her onward, his hand in hers, the force of his desperate grip crushing her fingers.

Already velociraptors were running through the enclosure, instinct taking over, seizing the opportunity to hunt amidst the confusion of the crowd. Out of the corner of his eye Ulysses saw one of the lithe reptiles leap from the top of an ice-cream kiosk onto a nurse, snatching the child she was desperately clinging onto with its razor sharp jaws. Genevieve whimpered beside him.

They ran on. If they made it to the exit Ulysses knew Nimrod would be there waiting for them, ready to carry them clear of this present danger.

Then Ulysses stumbled as he heard a crunching thud behind him that he felt ripple through the ground beneath his feet. Genevieve tripped and, as she went down, her hand slipped from Ulysses' sweaty grip. He stumbled to a halt, turning in time to see the terrifying form of the zoo's Megasaurus Rex bearing down on them both.

It was as tall as a house, its bipedal saurian form built of slabs of muscle. Its hind legs were two massive pistons of bone and muscle, powerful enough to carry it at a speed of twenty-five miles an hour under the right conditions. By contrast its forelimbs were little more than tiny, grasping claws. But then the monster had little need for anything more when one considered its over-sized jaws, filled with teeth the size and sharpness of butchering hooks. Its eyes were tiny black orbs of pitiless, primeval savagery, and they were fixed on the fallen Genevieve.

Even as its head came down, its jaws hinging open, Ulysses grabbed Genevieve around the waist and pulled her clear as the megasaur's teeth snapped shut, the weight of its hard-nosed skull cracking the skin of the tarmac where Genevieve had been scant moments before.

And then they were running again, their legs given a new burst of energy by fear.

The zoo's ornately gated entrance appeared before them as they barged through the stumbling masses, Nimrod blaring the horn of the Silver Phantom even as he revved the engine, ready to make a speedy getaway. They hurdled the turnstiles as a pod of apatasaurs barged through the breach in the wall made by the crumpled carriage that now blocked the road outside.

Then, in the merest blinking of an eye, he caught sight of a face in the crowd ahead of him – an unpleasantly familiar face that made his blood boil in fury – and suddenly he understood what had happened here.

Ulysses slammed into the side of the car and pulled open the back door. "We ran into a little trouble," he panted, pushing Genevieve onto the back seat.

"Evidently, sir," Nimrod managed with barely any hint of emotion, despite their current predicament.

"And I think I know who's responsible."

Ulysses slammed the car door shut.

"What are you doing, sir?" Nimrod called through the open passenger window.

"Ulysses, get in the car!" Genevieve screamed.

Ulysses looked back into the fleeing crowd. One man stood still as an island amidst the panicked flow. Dressed all in black like a navvy, bald-headed, roguishly unshaven, his darkly handsome features twisted by the livid purple scar that bisected his face. The figure stared back at Ulysses, his expression set in a tight-lipped scowl, his narrowed eyes filled with a depthless hatred. It was a face from his past, one that he had believed he would never see again, that belonged to an enemy he thought he had put an end to long ago. It was Jago Kane: agitator, revolutionary, terrorist.

Then, as if suddenly shamed by what he had done under Ulysses' righteous glare, the reactionary turned and fled, running for the Albany Street stop elevator pillar.

"Nimrod, get Miss Galapagos out of here," Ulysses commanded.

"But what about you, sir?"

"Please, get in the car!" Genevieve was begging, pushing the rear door open.

"I can't, Genevieve," he said, flashing her a manic grin. "There's an old friend from the past who I really must catch up with."

"Now?"

"Well, there's no time like the present," he laughed mirthlessly, slamming the car door again. "Now, Nimrod, drive!"

With a screech of tyres the Silver Phantom hared away along Prince Albert Road leaving a cloud of burnt rubber in its wake. Ulysses sprinted across the road – men, women and children running, screaming in disarray all around him – towards the Overground pillar, and after Jago Kane.

CHAPTER EIGHT

Overground

Ulysses burst out of the elevator carriage and onto the Bakerloo Line aerial platform. The platform was packed, the people there milling around in confusion. Some were crying in fear, many were trying to barge past Ulysses and into the lift, while just as many were pushing their way towards the end of the platform to his left. Ulysses craned his head that way, trying to see over the heads of the crowd.

He could see the smoking void left by the explosion and the resultant train crash. The end of one carriage still poked above the visible portion of track. Overground staff and altruistic members of the public were helping shaken passengers out of the back door of the last carriage and onto the vertiginous track. Just as many were merely interested in peering over the edge of the precipice in morbid fascination at the devastation below. To his right the platform ended at a barrier another thirty yards away. What he could not see, in either direction, was his quarry, Jago Kane.

"Going up," came the tinny voice of the automaton lift attendant behind him. Ulysses turned and pushed his way urgently back into the box-cage of the elevator. "Next stop, Bakerloo Line southbound." Kane must have gone on up to the next level, another two storeys above the city streets. But of course, Ulysses inwardly chided himself, why would as experienced an agitator as Jago Kane leave himself trapped on the line he had already put out of action? He would already have his escape route planned. If he were planning to ironically escape via the Overground he would be heading for the southbound route.

"Here, what do you think you're doing?" a red-faced man protested as Ulysses pushed him out of the way to get inside the elevator.

"Careful, sir. Only twelve passengers are allowed to travel at any one time," the lift-droid told Ulysses.

"Yes, and I was here first, you blaggard," the red-faced man continued to complain officiously.

Cursing in frustration Ulysses pulled the leather cardholder from his jacket pocket. "You, scan that," he instructed the droid. "You," he said, turning to the protesting beetroot, "this is a matter of national security. If you don't get out of my way now the Lord High Chancellor himself will have you up on a charge of treason. Now, piss off!"

He had been back in London for less than forty-eight hours and already the red tape of its bureaucrats and the petty mindedness of its citizens was obstructing him for the second time in as many days.

"Well I never," Ulysses' challenger blustered, staggering back out of the lift. Several other passengers, having half-heard what Ulysses had said, followed him.

Ulysses turned back to the lift attendant. "Now, take this lift up to the next level or I'll see you melted down for scrap."

"Right away, sir," the automaton's synthesised voice said cheerily.

"Do you know what's going on down there?" another man was demanding of anyone who would listen. "The dinosaurs are loose! It's every man for himself." Men cursed in disbelief. Women gasped and one even swooned, her partner catching her in his arms.

It had been cramped enough inside the carriage to the first level as it filled with people already attempting to escape the confusion that had taken hold around the zoo. Kane had made it into a lift ahead of Ulysses, its doors shutting in his face, the carriage sailing up into the shaft of the Overground pillar, leaving him cursing in frustration.

For a second he had considered taking the maintenance stairs in the pillar to the next level, exhausting as that would have been. But then almost immediately the second elevator opened at ground level. Ulysses made sure that he was onboard, and readied himself to make a swift exit at the next level. But of course Kane had not stopped there.

Ulysses was sure that Kane had had a hand in the chaos that had been unleashed on the capital. It had all the hallmarks of his indiscriminate terrorism and revolutionary philosophy, whereby whatever warped end he was trying to achieve always justified the means, no matter how many innocent people died as a result. In fact, considering Ulysses' encounters with Kane in the past, it seemed quite possible that the more innocent victims who died the more effectively he felt he had made his reactionary point to the ruling classes of Magna Britannia and the supporters of the British throne.

Several people were now demanding to be let out of the ascending elevator, rumour and half-accurate information working its bewildering magic on them, as they started to believe that it was now as unsafe on the higher levels of the Overground as it was down on the streets with the dinosaurs.

The elevator clanked to a stop. "Alight here for Bakerloo Line southbound," the attendant announced jovially. The gate concertinaed open and Ulysses burst from the carriage onto the platform. Up here the Overground was level with the rooftops of the grand townhouses that lined the streets adjoining Regent's Park. However, the aerial railways were still dwarfed by the tallest skyscrapers at the heart of the City financial district further to the south.

Incredibly, the Bakerloo Line was still running. But then again, the train crash, the breakout from the zoo and Ulysses' subsequent pursuit of his old enemy had all taken place in less than five minutes. A train was waiting at the station, steam hissing from its wheel-pistons. Those who had just alighted looked in dazed confusion at the smoke rising from the ruined track below, or peered over the safety railings at the chaos unfolding beneath them on Prince Albert Road.

A whistle sounded. The train was ready to depart and then Ulysses saw his quarry dashing on board some three carriage lengths further down the platform.

"Stop!" Ulysses yelled just as the whistle sounded again and the train's driver released a great hissing cloud of steam from the boiler. He shouted again but only those travellers nearest him took any notice, looking at him in annoyance. The aural receptors of the automata station porters were deaf to his cries, his desperate shouts drowned out by the furious noise of the train itself. The flag was waved and the train began to pull away.

Barging startled travellers aside, Ulysses ran down the platform after the departing train, dodging his way through the obstructing masses to get at his quarry. He suddenly found himself unavoidably bowling into a large, matronly woman carrying two heavy bags and could only manage a snatched, "Pardon, madame!" as he sent the poor woman tumbling onto her well-padded behind, her shopping spilling out all around her.

Then he was past the last of the travellers, the platform a clear stretch of iron and concrete ahead of him as the distance between him and the train widened. With the matron's tirade haranguing the insolent fop – as she called him – Ulysses put on a turn of speed, the adrenalin still racing through his system as he sprinted after the Overground train.

The last carriage was still just parallel with the end of the platform as Ulysses caught up. Then it was past him and, without hesitation, Ulysses hurled himself at the train.

He hit the rear carriage, his feet finding purchase on the backplate as he grabbed hold of the bars either side of the door. Cane still in hand, he tugged open the door and swung himself into the train to be greeted by startled gasps and exclamations of surprise.

"Excuse me, ladies and gentlemen," he said, making his way between the seated passengers. "There's absolutely nothing to worry about but if you'd just like to clear the way, your compliance would be much appreciated."

He hustled his way through the passengers as the train got up to speed. He knew that Kane was at least three carriages closer to the front. At the far end of the carriage Ulysses reached forwards and opened the door into the next passenger compartment, the wind tugging at his hair and jacket. Making sure he maintained contact with at least one of the carriages at all times he stepped across the divide.

On reaching the end of the third carriage in this way, cane in hand and with the upper floors of tall apartment buildings speeding past beyond the train's windows, he paused with his hand on the handle of the next access door. Packed in with the rest of the passengers he saw Kane's unmistakable profile ahead of him.

Ulysses pressed on, now even more determined to catch up with his old enemy. Bursting into Kane's carriage he shouted, "Seize that man!"

Kane's head snapped round, his eyes locked onto Ulysses and gave him a sour look of pure hatred. Reacting immediately, Kane began forging his way through the throng. "Stop him!" Ulysses shouted.

His sixth sense suddenly flared and he ducked even as Kane swung round, gun in hand. The shot was painfully loud in the confines of the packed carriage. The passengers flinched as one as the glass pane in the door behind Ulysses exploded.

Then Kane was pushing his way through the carriage again, his progress less hindered by the people who whimpered as they strove to get out of his way. Not one of the passengers tried to stop him. *The great British public*, Ulysses thought, *as reliable as ever.*

His own pistol was in its holster beneath his jacket but he didn't want to risk using it in the packed train. He doubted he would be able to get a clear shot anyway and the continual jolting of the train as it sped over the high-rise tracks ruled out such rash behaviour altogether. It was one thing for uncaring revolutionary terrorists to carelessly gun down innocent members of the public, but it wasn't behaviour becoming of an agent of the throne of Magna Britannia. Besides, he wanted to finish this up close and personal. Kane had got away before. Ulysses was not about to let him do that again.

Although the terrified passengers were doing their level best to evade Kane's fury they were still slowing his progress and Ulysses was beginning to catch up. Kane reached the door to the next carriage as Ulysses reached the mid-section doors. Ulysses considered pulling the emergency cord, to get the driver to stop the train, but decided that such an action might merely aid the terrorist's escape.

And then Kane was gone anyway, not into the next carriage but up the ladder bolted to the end and onto the roof. Ulysses hurried to the banging door as the train sped on through the Upper City. In a matter of seconds he too was on the ladder, clambering up towards the roof of the hurtling train.

The hobnail heel of a boot came down on the top rung where Ulysses' fingers should have been, just as he had anticipated. Lurking one rung lower, he athletically pulled himself up in a sudden spring as his feet kicked off from their footing below. With one hand still on the ladder Ulysses swung with his cane at Kane's other leg, as his premature stamp unbalanced him for a moment. The ebony cane struck home as the train bumped over a join in the rails. Kane crashed down onto the roof of the carriage, landing hard on his backside. It was all Ulysses needed to finally make it onto the roof himself, no longer threatened.

He braced his legs against the rocking motion of the train as Kane slid himself backwards out of reach. Ulysses now stood between Kane and the front of the train, smoke from the engine stack whipping back over the carriage roofs around them like escaping wisps of cloud.

"I should have known you would cheat death. I just don't know how you managed it," Ulysses said, taking in the long scar that bisected Kane's face.

"You just can't keep a good man down," the revolutionary sneered, the scar twisting his lips into a grotesque sneer. Kane's educated accent seemed as at odds with his appearance as with his revolutionary politics.

"This little debacle we find ourselves caught up in has all the hallmarks of a Kane mutiny," Ulysses said, the words dripping with venomous bile.

"Prove it!" Kane spat back.

"And what do you know about the disappearance of one Professor Galapagos from the Natural History Museum?"

"More than you will ever know and more than I will ever tell you!"

"Oh, I'm so glad," Ulysses said with a cruel smile. Just for a moment doubt flickered in the terrorist's dark eyes. Ulysses smoothly pulled the sword blade from the sheath of his cane, the action culminating with a grandiose flourish. "Because that means I don't have to worry about bringing you in alive for questioning. So I rather feel that this concludes our brief reunion. You and I have nothing more to say to one another," Ulysses pronounced.

"Nothing you would want to hear, I'll warrant, fascist!" the revolutionary spat – his gun suddenly in his hand again – and fired.

NIMROD PULLED THE steering wheel hard to the right as another apatasaur lumbered into the path of the Silver Phantom, throwing Genevieve across the padded white leather upholstery. Horns blared as he crossed onto the other side of the road, narrowly avoiding an omnibus heading straight towards them, and then they heard the shattering crunch of collision as the double-decker collided with the column of the leviathan's pillar-like leg.

Beyond the comparative safety of the car the streets of Marylebone were in chaos as the unleashed dinosaurs stampeded down Portland Place.

"What are you doing?" Genevieve yelled at him, her hands gripping the back of the driver's seat. "Ulysses told you to get me out of here!"

"Yes, ma'am," Nimrod calmly agreed, swerving to avoid a man who had stumbled into the road to avoid a lumbering ankylosaur. "That is what I am attempting to do." He peered upwards at the distant winding course of the Bakerloo Line high above and the train speeding on its way towards the next station. This stretch of the Bakerloo Line followed the streets beneath quite closely and, despite the stampeding dinosaurs and the chaos they left in their wake, Nimrod was managing to keep up with Ulysses' progress above.

He brought the Phantom back onto the left side of the road. Genevieve yelped in surprise and Nimrod shot a glance out of the passenger window to see a velociraptor running along the pavement beside them, keeping pace with the car. For a moment the terrible lizard returned Nimrod's gaze with its cold-blooded reptilian stare. Its ophidian pupil dilated as if, in that moment, it recognised the car's occupants as potential prey. The tone of the car's engine rose as Nimrod floored the accelerator and the Silver Phantom powered away from the sprinting raptor.

They sped through Langham Place into Regent Street, Nimrod bouncing the vehicle over the corner of a pavement, pedestrians scattering before them. "Where did you learn to drive?" Genevieve gasped.

"On the streets of Calcutta," he replied, flatly. "It might be wise to fasten your seatbelt, ma'am."

There was the screech of brakes and a delivery van shot past them, colliding with another running dinosaur and sending the creature smashing through the plate glass window of a jewellers.

They were now right in the thick of the stampede as the city streets funnelled the animals into the bottleneck of Regent Street, towards Oxford Circus. Despite the alien nature of their surroundings, some of the dinosaurs were reverting to their natural instinctive behaviour. Apatasaurs charged past startled shoppers, crushing the unwary beneath their elephantine feet, running in fear of the pursuing carnivores.

Still some way ahead of Nimrod and Genevieve, the Megasaurus Rex turned into a packed Piccadilly Circus. A startled omnibus driver spun his steering wheel to avoid the prehistoric obstacle. The bus lurched violently to one side and into the path of a steam-belching hansom cab. The two vehicles collided with a dreadful inevitability, the bus toppling onto its side. The Megasaur put a huge clawed foot on top of the stricken omnibus, as though claiming its kill, and snapped the driver from his cab.

An old battle-scarred bull triceratops ran amok through Langham Place, dragging torn shop awnings behind it as its tiny, enraged brain translated every obstacle in front of it as a potential challenger to its position as alpha male. It didn't stop even when it hurtled into the front of the Langham Hilton Hotel, shattering the glass revolving doors with its battering ram horns.

The police had mobilised, the emergency services having been notified of the unfolding disaster, no doubt by the embarrassed zoo authorities. A pair of squad cars were now racing up the road towards Nimrod and Genevieve, blue lights flashing, sirens wailing.

With a metal buckling *crump* a clawed fiend landed on the bonnet of the Silver Phantom. Nimrod's first instinct was to brake, but the furiously working rational part of his brain told him that if he did, chances were the Phantom would be crushed beneath the hooves of the stampeding creatures behind it.

For a split second Nimrod looked up through the windscreen into the ophidian eyes of a velociraptor and, in that moment, was convinced it was the same creature that had kept pace with the car only seconds before. The monster opened its terribly fanged jaws – giving Nimrod a clear view right down its throat – screeching as it butted the glass of the windscreen, trying to get at the people within.

Nimrod worked the steering wheel, trying to unbalance the raptor whilst still remaining in control. The creature scrabbled for purchase on the automobile's bonnet, trying to hook its deadly talons into the thin metal. Nimrod gave a sharper pull on the wheel and the raptor was gone, tumbling onto the road and into the path of a police car. The squad car slammed into it, its radiator grille buckling, the whole vehicle bouncing over the top of the fatally injured predator. A smoke-belching coal-lorry hit the raptor's carcass after it and turned over into the path of the apatasaurs. One of the leviathan herbivores tripped, its front legs becoming entangled within the wreckage of the steam-lorry. As its forelegs buckled its momentum carried it forwards and the apatasaur came crashing down just metres from the Silver Phantom. The car sped on, leaving behind it the sounds of shop windows shattering, people screaming and one vehicle after another smashing into the stampeding dinosaurs.

A horse-drawn carriage suddenly came face to face with a hunting allosaurus. The horses whinnied in panic and reared. Then the carnivore was on them, crushing one of the terrified beasts under a massive clawed foot and ripping the head from the other with its steel-trap jaws.

Elsewhere Peeler-drones had surrounded an ankylosaur. One of the automata advanced confidently towards the tank-like brute, giving its default, "'Ello, 'ello, 'ello, what's going on 'ere then?" The ankylosaur gave a guttural bovine moan, feeling threatened by the Bobbies that were steadily tightening their cordon around it. Then the creature decided that it had had enough. With one deadly accurate swipe of its heavily armoured tail it took off the head of one advancing drone and sent another three tumbling like bowling pins. It would take more than Scotland Yard's finest to bring this situation to a satisfactory conclusion. At this rate, the authorities were going to have to call in the army.

Leaning forwards against the steering wheel, Nimrod looked up again at the top of the canyon formed by the buildings either side of Regents Street, moving a momentarily misplaced flick of hair out of his eyes as he did so. He had lost sight of the train he had been certain Ulysses was on, as the Bakerloo Line was replaced by the Victoria branch of the Overground. A family group of five pterosaurs flapped past above the rooftops, keeping clear of the carnage consuming the city streets below. Nimrod could only hope that his employer was having more success than they at evading danger.

Ahead of them lay Oxford Circus, beyond that the teeming hunting ground of Piccadilly Circus, and nothing that could stop the frenzied dinosaurs and the world of carnage that was surely to come.

ULYSSES ARCHED BACK, pulling his exposed midriff out of the path of Kane's bowie knife as the anarchist slashed at him. Kane pressed forwards, following up with a backhanded swipe.

The two combatants so far appeared to be evenly matched. Neither had managed to draw blood, although Ulysses had managed to lay a punch against Kane's chin, Kane in response having kicked Ulysses painfully in the shins. Incredibly both had managed to maintain their balance on the roof of the speeding train, in spite of its irregular rolling motion. Ulysses thanks, in part, to the skills the monks of Shangri-La had imparted to him. Kane through sheer luck or stubbornness. Yet both were putting their all into the duel and the energy they were expending was beginning to weary them.

But now, as Kane pressed home his attack with an angry snarl, Ulysses saw a way to break the exhausting impasse. He had to concede ground to escape the blade but did so by spinning on one heel and turning himself at a right angle, placing himself very close to the cambered edge of the carriage roof and with his back to the precipitous drop beyond the edge of the aerial railway. As Kane's blade nicked the lapel of Ulysses' jacket, Ulysses grabbed hold of his opponent's over-reaching arm and pulled him forwards with all the strength he had in his left arm, the rapier blade of his sword-cane still held tightly in his right.

The revolutionary stumbled forwards, losing his balance at last, sprawling onto his hands and knees on the roof of the rattling carriage.

Ulysses didn't waste a moment. But Kane was fast too. As Ulysses brought down his blade in what would otherwise have been a killing stroke, Kane twisted round, stopping the rapier with his bowie knife. Ulysses' blade slid free, turned by the knife, and as he tried to bring his weapon back under control, and not lose his own footing, he managed to snag its tip in Kane's wrist. The felon cried out in pain and astonishment, unable to stop his hand spasming, the knife falling from his open fingers onto the roof of the carriage.

Ulysses rocked backwards as the train clattered over an intersection. Kane, seeming to ignore his new injury, lunged after the knife. His fingertips scraped the carved horn handle, only for the motion of the train to send the knife over the edge. The weapon clattered down between the sleepers of the aerial track, to plummet towards the distant streets below.

Kane shot a savage look of pure hatred over his shoulder as Ulysses bore down on him. Then the sneer became a grin, more disconcerting than anything Ulysses had seen in a long time. Before he could stop the anarchist, Kane pulled himself forwards and threw himself off the edge of the train.

Ulysses made a grab for him, landing heavily on his stomach, his head and shoulders over the edge of the roof, one arm outstretched. He could not bear to lose Kane again now. From this position Ulysses was treated to a clear view of the fate of his enemy. Kane dropped, arms and legs flung out, his body flat, freefalling for a good twenty feet. Then, incredibly, the northbound Bakerloo train hurtled by beneath him and he landed on its roof, snatched from a certain death on the rails below. Ulysses watched, stunned, as Kane was carried away.

Without hesitation Ulysses swung down onto the side of the carriage, still clinging onto the lip of the roof with one hand and, breathing deeply, watched the carriages passing on the track below him, carefully timing his jump.

But the moment passed. The train was gone taking Jago Kane with it. His heart sank.

The ringing from his pocket took him completely by surprise.

He extracted his personal communicator and flipped it open. "Yes?" he barked into the handset.

"Sorry to trouble you, sir," his manservant's cultured tones came through. "I hope this isn't a bad time."

"No, now is fine," Ulysses said, his voice relaxing even as he did so. The train's passengers watched him through the windows in appalled fascination as he calmly conducted his call whilst clinging to the exterior of the carriage.

"I'm pleased to hear it, sir. I wish the same could be said of down here but we have a situation developing."

In his desperate determination to corner and finish his old adversary, Jago Kane, Ulysses had momentarily put from his mind the breakout from the zoo. Now, high above the city streets, the wind roaring in his ears, he was only too aware of the dinosaurs rampaging through the streets a hundred feet below.

"What's happened?" was all he could think to say. "Is Genevieve all right?"

"Yes sir, Miss Galapagos is with me."

Ulysses heard a muffled scream through his communicator accompanied by a primeval reptilian roar.

"What was that?"

"That was the situation I was telling you about, sir. It would appear that there is a Megasaurus Rex running amok down the Mall. It is all most perturbing. Something needs to be done, sir."

Ulysses looked beyond the engine ahead of him, trying to ascertain the train's precise location within the capital, peering at the architecture of the Upper City through the smoke belching from the chimneystack. Slowly he began to recognise particular buildings – the Regent Palace Hotel, the Criterion Theatre.

He was somewhere over Piccadilly. Distant guttural bellowing, hooting car horns and shrill human screams rose to his ears from the streets below. Ahead the Bakerloo Line curved round as it passed over Trafalgar Square.

"Where is the beast now?" Ulysses said into the communicator.

"It's passing under the Admiralty Arch. It's now moved into Trafalgar Square itself."

"Don't worry, Nimrod, I'm on it."

Quickly and carefully he stowed the communicator.

Peering over the edge of the blurred track speeding past a few feet below him he saw the domed roof of the National Gallery and the towering pillar of Nelson's Column as the Bakerloo Line began to descend towards the station at Trafalgar Square.

And then he saw the terror-inducing form of the colossal carnivore. People fled in waves of panic before the titan as it claimed dominion of its new territory.

His heart in his mouth, Ulysses judged that he would pass over Trafalgar Square as the Megasaurus lumbered under this stretch of the Overground.

He took a deep breath to steady his nerves, checking his grip on the roof of the train and adjusting his hold on his sword. Ulysses was about to attempt either the bravest or the most stupid stunt in his life.

"Well, here goes nothing," he said to himself.

And jumped.

CHAPTER NINE

Evolution Expects

ULYSSES DROPPED, THE wind whipping through his hair and pummelling his face. Just as he was beginning to wonder whether he had misjudged his fall and would not stop until he collided with the flagstones of Trafalgar Square, he came to an abrupt halt as he slammed onto the back of the dinosaur. He started to slide but then managed to get a grip on the knobbly exterior of the dinosaur's hide. Its scales were rough as sandpaper and one cheek was grazed from his collision with the creature.

But it seemed to Ulysses that as far as the Megasaurus Rex was concerned he might as well not be there at all. It continued to stalk between the leonine statues of the square and Ulysses took a moment to recover himself, feeling the creature's body moving beneath him, the curious texture of the dinosaur's hide uncomfortable against his skin. His cheek stung from the graze, but it was not the only part of his body now telling him that it was suffering. His fight with the revolutionary Kane had taken its toll more greatly than he had realised, so focused had he been on thwarting his foe, his bloodstream flooded with adrenalin. On top of the dramatic drop he had just made onto a surface almost as hard and resistant as tarmac, all his old injuries had come back to haunt him. The calf of his left leg ached, but that would pass and certainly wasn't debilitating. However, he knew for a fact that he had strained his shoulder again, and he had added a whole host of bruises to his battered body. The ribs of his left side in particular were protesting forcefully, wincing stabs of pains reacquainting him with past battles. But there would be time enough to worry about that later. For back in the present he had to see to bringing the matter in hand to conclusion.

Fortunately – incredibly even – he had managed to maintain his hold on his sword-cane. He also had his personal communicator about his person, as well as his Brabinger pistol.

He raised his head, all the while keeping the rest of his body flat, lest he dislodge himself from his precarious position. They were in the middle of Trafalgar Square. Lord Admiral Nelson and his attendant pigeons watched with, on one side, stony disinterest and, on the other, dumb avian curiosity as the Megasaur scattered the crowds. But still there were those who could not get out of the way in time, the monster scooping them up with its dredging jaws, gulping them down to satisfy its newly acquired appetite for human flesh.

"What did I think I was doing?" Ulysses asked himself aloud as the rational part of his brain took over, his gung-ho, thrill-seeking side evaporating in a cloud of logic.

But what he was doing now on the back of the dinosaur was academic. The more pressing question was, now that he was lying between the heaving shoulder blades of the dinosaur, how was he going to bring its bloodthirsty rampage to an end?

He felt the weight of his gun in its holster against his aching ribs. "That has to be the way, surely," he told himself, but he didn't sound too convinced, even to his own ears. But if he were going to be able to take a shot, he would have to get into a better position than the one he was in now. Somehow he was going to need to get up onto his feet, or at least his knees.

Pushing himself up with his left hand, his fingers clenched around a protruding scale, he was able to bring his sword to bear. With one powerful downward thrust, he plunged the tip of the blade into the creature's hide. It sank up to fully half its length. Now he knew for sure that he had got the monster's attention.

The dinosaur let out a primeval roar, redolent with pain and savage fury. Its jaws opened wide as it threw its head back in agony, the megasaur leaving the pram and its occupant that it was about to consume, the infant never knowing how close it had come to an early death.

The megasaur bucked. Ulysses kept a tight hold of his half-buried sword, riding the beast like some American rodeo rider. And then the enraged beast was off. With its massive piston legs of muscle and bone covering five yards with every bounding stride, the megasaur left off hunting the tiny, shrieking mammals and abandoned the abattoir it had made of Trafalgar Square, haring off at speed along Whitehall.

As he clung on to the hilt of his rapier-blade, his legs braced against the rolling gait of the running carnivore, Ulysses pulled his gun from its holster. There was no time to check the load, and certainly no way of reloading here and now. It was all he could do to maintain his position on the creature's back; it was like trying to keep his balance in a storm-tossed boat. He pointed the muzzle at the creature's heaving sides and let off five shots in quick succession.

The beast bellowed again and careered in front of a steam-driven omnibus – Ulysses was dimly aware of further cries of horror and surprise rising from the street, the screech of brakes and the dull crumps of collisions – but the megasaur showed no signs of slowing, let alone of actually dropping down dead.

The Admiralty passed by to the left in a blur. The plume-helmed guardsmen on sentry duty outside Horse Guards Parade were thrown into disarray, one terrified horse throwing its rider, the other galloping away back in the direction of Trafalgar Square.

It had been nothing more than dumb hope that had made Ulysses try shooting the creature, he realised now. If he had been able to get into a position whereby he was close enough to shoot the megasaur through the eye, at point-blank range then he might have been able to bring it down with a single shot. But chances were that he would die before he even managed to take aim, either eaten alive by the brute or by having his brains smashed out on the tarmac of Whitehall as he was thrown from his curious steed.

The megasaur sprinted past the entrance to Downing Street, a rattling fusillade of gunshots chasing after it from the armed sentries on duty there. Their bullets did nothing to stop the monster and fortunately missed the startled Ulysses as well.

"Bloody hell!" he swore as they swept past the Cenotaph.

The momentum of the charging beast beneath him swung Ulysses to the left so that he could see the pavement clearly beneath him, as the dinosaur cracked the dressed stones beneath its massive, pile-driving feet, forcing him to pull on the embedded sword. The megasaur roared again as the blade cut deeper into its flesh.

And then the jumble of desperate thoughts crowding Ulysses' mind resolved into something resembling a logical idea. The orbits of the eye were not the only weak point in an animal's skull; something as thin as a rapier blade thrust into the base of the skull, where it joined the neck, could find a way between vertebrae and sever the spinal cord, or even pierce the monster's diminutive brain.

"All very well in theory," Ulysses addressed himself again. Achieving such a feat would be another matter altogether. But there was no longer any time to think about how such a thing could be achieved. There was only time for action. The Palace of Westminster and the looming tower of Big Ben lay ahead. This had to stop now.

In one deft movement Ulysses pulled the sword-cane clear of the beast's flesh even as he used it to steady himself as he scaled the ridge of the megasaur's back. He flung himself forwards, bringing the sword in a high arc as he did so. As he landed on the neck of the creature so he landed his blow, the devilishly sharp tip of the rapier blade split scales as Ulysses put all his weight behind it, plunging the sword beneath vertebrae the size of ale casks, cutting cleanly through the cable-thick spinal cord they shielded and into the monster's cerebellum.

All muscle activity within the creature ceased. Its legs gave way beneath it and the dinosaur crashed to the ground, its massive jaw ploughing a trench through the scrubby grass in the middle of Parliament Square. Its glassy eyes closed and its jaws slammed shut, half severing the monster's huge purple tongue that lolled from the side of its mouth. The megasaur was dead.

Ulysses gratefully slid down from the back of the beast, stumbling to regain his balance now that he was back on terra firma after his hair-raising ride. He was bruised and battered, bloody from numerous cuts and grazes. The joint of his right shoulder had gone beyond pain to a dull throb that told him he had probably dislocated it.

Slowly, the sound of a city in heightened panic seeped its way back into his beleaguered senses. The megasaur's desperate charge and subsequent death had brought the streets around Parliament Square to a standstill. An expectant host of Londoners surrounded the square. Confident that the megasaur was dead, some of the bolder members of the public were approaching the fallen monster and the dino-killer, their faces slack with bewilderment, making them look like weird wandering lost souls as they tried to make sense of what had just happened. There were robo-Bobbies among the crowd too. The Northern Line branch of the Overground trundled on its way overhead as if nothing out of the ordinary had happened at all.

A stupefied tramp, sporting a filthy white beard and clutching a crumpled brown paper bag to his chest, cautiously approached the equally stunned Ulysses, an outstretched hand offering comfort. "Are you all right, son?" the old codger asked.

"A-Am I?" Ulysses stammered. "That's a very good question. Give me a swig of whatever you've got wrapped in that paper bag and I'll tell you."

As Ulysses put the fumy bottle to his lips, and felt the bite of the alcohol on his tongue, he saw the sleek silver shape of the Mark IV Phantom ease its way through the gathering crowd as Big Ben struck noon.

A discordant wail, like a hundred foghorns sounding in jarring synchronicity, suddenly filled the square. The crowd tensed and Ulysses, despite the sharp pain in his shoulder, tried to cover his ears.

With an epileptic flickering the kinema-sized broadcast screens around Parliament Square hummed into life. But rather than the usual propaganda messages or mega-corporation advertisements, grainy static soon resolved into the image of a rippling New Union Jack. Only rather than bearing the encircled silhouette of Britannia herself at the centre there was the silhouette of a dinosaur's skull.

"People of Britain and Londinium Maximum!" The voice boomed from the loudspeakers. No one could ignore it. Suddenly all eyes were drawn hypnotically to the massive broadcast screens. "This is the voice of the Darwinian Dawn!

"The British Empire of Magna Britannia is a dinosaur of a previous age and should have perished long ago. Our cities are over-populated and none more so than the jewel of the Empire that is Londinium Maximum. The filthy slums overflow with the poor, the unemployed, the destitute, and the downtrodden."

As the condemning voice continued in its tirade, like that of some vengeful deity passing judgement on the British Empire, the image of the defaced flag faded to be replaced by a relentless moving montage culled from newsreel footage and who knew what other media sources. There were starving, malnourished children begging in gutters clogged with filth. The automata armies of Magna Britannia marching against unarmed Indian villagers. Factories the size of towns pumping clouds of polluting toxins into the atmosphere from colossal chimney stacks. A pox-ridden prostitute kicked to death by a gang of thugs. Swathes of rainforest being cut down by monstrous harvesting machines to feed the hungry furnaces of the workshop of the world. Livestock being reared in appalling conditions in cathedral-sized factory barns to feed the rapacious appetites of the decadent elite while the poor starved only streets away in the same cities. But no matter what the image being broadcast – whether war, famine, poverty, moral decline or the heedless raping of the Earth's natural resources – they all had one thing in common; each and every image was a condemnation of the world-dominating super-power of Magna Britannia, the ravenous monster that was the British Empire in the dying days of the twentieth century.

"We have become slaves to the machine," the voice was saying now. "The workshop of the world has become the most heinous pillager of the planet. And now, the rulers of this Empire are prepared to make the same mistakes beneath the oceans and on other worlds beyond our own, condemning the rest of the solar system to death."

The images being broadcast changed accordingly, now including scenes from the lunar cities and the colonies on Mars.

"Every minute of every hour of every day, the Empire commits the most heinous crimes against the planet and its own people. The upper classes hunt animals they do not intend to eat whilst children starve on our own doorsteps. Magna Britannia is the most technologically advanced nation on the planet and yet disease is still rife among the abused lower classes.

"And what are these crimes perpetrated in aid of, in an endless cycle of abuse of this planet and its soon-to-be endangered indigenous species?"

At this point a picture of Victoria Regina, from her heyday during the last century, appeared on the multiple screens, and flames began to lick hungrily at the sepia-tint photograph.

"To maintain the intrinsically corrupt status quo. Magna Britannia is morally and ethically moribund. After 160 years under the yoke of the corrupt, bloated ogre that is the British Empire, it is time for a change, in order to beat the social and moral stagnation and corruption that has infested this nation like a life-stealing cancer, and to welcome in a new age of freedom from the shackles of industrialism and Imperial rule. The old must make way for the new, so that social evolution can pursue its natural course."

The last scraps of the photograph of the Queen burnt away to reveal a new flag that was entirely black other than for the white-stencilled dinosaur skull at its centre. This too was ultimately consumed by the flames.

The protests and even occasional cheers from the crowd could not drown out the voice of condemnation that damned a nation and a whole, world-spanning way of life. The voice blasted from every street corner across the capital, and could be heard throughout the cities of the United Kingdom, wherever the propaganda screens of Magna Britannia stood, so that every citizen of the British Empire – man, woman or child – who laboured under the dominion of the Empire might hear the Darwinian Dawn's brutal message of savage hope.

Ulysses Quicksilver, his manservant Nimrod and Genevieve Galapagos – emerging from the back of the battered Silver Phantom – simply stared dumbfounded at the burning screens before them.

"The time for change is now. We are the agents of that change, the Darwinian Dawn. It is time for the old way of life to be made extinct. Our terms are simple. We demand that the Queen abdicates her throne immediately and that the bloated glutton that is Magna Britannia be dissolved. Until such time as our demands are met we vow that such incidents as have been witnessed today will continue to escalate, and anarchy will reign."

As the booming echoes of the voice of the Darwinian Dawn died away two words – one simple alliterative phrase – swam into clarity on the screens amidst the crackling flames of anarchy, until they dominated every screen visible around the city and beyond. And in case any could not read the words, the same voice of thunder uttered the phrase over and over.

"Evolution expects!

"*Evolution expects!*

"EVOLUTION EXPECTS!"

ACT TWO

Survival of the Fittest

May 1997

CHAPTER TEN

Wormwood

URIAH WORMWOOD STEPPED into the Members' Lobby, beyond the Commons Chamber of the Palace of Westminster, and allowed himself a smile. His speech on the occasion of being elected to the position of Leader of the Conservative Party, and thereby Prime Minister of Her Majesty's government, had been particularly rousing.

Minister for Internal Affairs to leader of the Tories and First Lord of the Treasury in a few simple, yet cunning, moves that seemed to have taken everyone else, including the leader of the opposition and his own predecessor, totally by surprise. But then he was a chess player of grandmaster level, so the Machiavellian manoeuvrings and machinations of the British Parliament were easy enough for him to negotiate and twist to suit his own agenda.

His predecessor discredited, following the recent terror attacks on the capital, he was now the single most powerful politician in Magna Britannia and hence, effectively, the world. In light of his predecessor's perceived ineffectual action in the wake of the terrorist atrocities perpetrated by the Darwinian Dawn there had been no way that he could keep his position as head of the government. George Castlemayne had been forced to resign in the face of further terror attacks on the city. Following the Overground disaster at London Zoo, and the subsequent release of the dinosaurs from the Challenger Enclosure, there had been bombings at Marble Arch, Charing Cross and even during a concert at the Royal Albert Hall. All had resulted in loss of life and the Overground had been forced to close. It was still closed now and the situation was having a crippling effect on the city's economy.

"What we need now is a man of action as well as words, who will see Londinium Maximum, and hence this nation, put back on track. And Her Imperial Majesty's jubilee will not only be a celebration of 160 years of her noble reign and wise rule but will act as a starting point for a new Imperial age the like of which the world has never seen, as we approach the dawning of a new millennium." That bit in particular had made him smile wryly to himself.

He had made all the usual vapid promises – an end to poverty, jobs for all, better health care, a clearing of the slums, open formal discussions with the Martian Separatists – fully aware of the fact that if any such things ever did actually come to pass that it would, in reality, spell the end of the Empire. And that wasn't what he had in mind at all. No, not at all. He smiled his chilling crocodilian smile again at the thought.

"But how can you seriously countenance the idea of Her Majesty's jubilee celebrations going ahead at this time, in this climate of terror watched over by the spectre of the threat of violence? Would you, newly elected as First Lord, really make your first action to put our beloved monarch in mortal danger?"

"My Honourable Friend is labouring under a serious misapprehension," Wormwood had said, to chuckles from the commons benches behind him. "Of course not, but Magna Britannia will not kowtow to terrorists. This glorious Empire, of which I am proud to be a part, has endured for over one and a half centuries. It is the strongest and most profitable it has ever been. Fully two-thirds of the world's population, and two-thirds of its landmass, are fortunate enough to fall under the benevolent shadow of this great nation, enlightened by both its knowledge and power. We rule on land, and sea, and below it, and the skies are ours to command.

"No, I make my declaration now that the celebrations intended to mark Queen Victoria's 160th jubilee, along with the unveiling of the nearly-completed statue of Britannia in Hyde Park, will go ahead as planned, come hell or high water. And to ensure that this all comes to pass, as it should, I would take this opportunity to urge each and every honourable member here present to vote in favour of the new Anti-Terrorism Bill."

There were shouts of "Here, here!" from his own party and childish mutterings from the other side of the House.

"It will mean more police on the streets with more effective powers, tighter controls on those passing through our borders and, most importantly, a safe home for the good people of Britain. Britannia rules the waves – above and below – the land, the air. Even the worlds beyond our own submit to British rule. Britons never, never, shall be slaves!"

At that a great cheer had gone up from the Conservative benches and his rhetoric had even stirred some members of the opposition to raise their voices in support, before they realised what they had been duped into doing by his powerful oration. The public gallery had gone wild.

But it was all just words, telling his fellows what they wanted to hear. And yet Uriah Wormwood never underestimated the power of words. With armies, fleets and factories a man could rule all the peoples of the world. But with words you could own their thoughts, their hopes, their desires, their very souls. Magna Britannia's armies could bring a nation to its knees! Words could make those same nations give themselves willingly to the rapacious monster that was the British Empire without a single shot ever having to be fired. No, he never underestimated the power of words. The man who controlled them could reshape the world as he saw fit.

The Bill Against the Predations of Terrorism – devised by Wormwood himself – was as good as passed, he was sure of it. When the House of Commons voted in its favour there was no way, in light of the current situation, that the Lords would dare contest it. For the peers almost all had a vested interest in keeping London free from terror attacks. As well as having personal palatial residences within the capital, many of them were feeling the aftershock of the effects on the nation's economy, having great portions of their own fortunes tied to the success of various businesses throughout London and beyond. The sooner the Overground was open and running the sooner a number of the lords would see the money stop draining from their accounts.

And with the Anti-Terror Bill in place Wormwood would be in a position to personally do something about the current climate of fear and dread of imminent, and bloody, disaster. For, amongst other measures, such as allowing the police to arrest anyone suspected of terrorist activity, the bill would give the First Lord of the Treasury the power to declare martial law in cases of extreme emergency. Then all the resources of Magna Britannia would truly be at his disposal, to be used to reshape the Empire as he saw fit.

WORMWOOD MADE HIS way through the corridors of power – the civil servants he encountered on his way all bowing or congratulating him on his recent rise to power – until he reached his office.

He pushed open the door into the outer office where his personal secretary was rearranging the papers on her desk in a state of some agitation. She had only been with him for the last two weeks and was still having to adjust to his draconian ways.

"Oh, sir, thank goodness you're back."

"What is it, Blythe?" Wormwood demanded, his eyes narrowing and the unnatural smile disappearing from his lips.

"Y-you have a guest, Prime Minister."

"Where?"

"Well, that's the thing. He is waiting for you in your office."

Wormwood's face darkened to a scowl as he strode towards his private chambers, without waiting to hear any more.

"He said his name was Mr..." The rest of the sentence was lost as Wormwood flung open the door.

"Good afternoon, Prime Minister," came a voice from the high backed leather-upholstered chair in front of his desk. "Congratulations on your recent promotion."

"Quicksilver. What are you doing here?"

"Can't a friend drop by to congratulate you on your recent success? You've got it all now, haven't you?"

Wormwood rounded the desk and sat down. Ulysses Quicksilver grinned at him, glass of cognac in hand.

"I hope you don't mind. I helped myself," he said, raising the glass as if in a toast. "Anyway, here's to you."

"What do you want?"

"Like I said, I just wanted to come by now that I'm up and about again, pat you on the back and say well done! Perhaps you'll get a nicer office now. One with a little more natural light. A view of the river, maybe. By the way, when do you move into Number 10?"

"Quicksilver," Wormwood said, arching his fingers in front of his face, elbows on the edge of the desk, "my patience is like the spare time I have to conduct impromptu meetings such as this one, there is very little of it."

He stared into the smiling face before him. Ulysses looked a mess, despite his otherwise smartly turned out appearance. His cheek was grazed, there were the scabs and scratches across his forehead and he was still sporting the yellow and purple bruise of a black eye.

"I thought you might like an update, seeing as how I am currently engaged on a mission on behalf of the British throne."

"Then why not arrange a meeting at the usual venue, as protocol and good sense would dictate?"

"My time is precious too. I decided direct action would be the best approach. You are a man of action, aren't you, as well as words?"

"Why are you really here? Why risk exposing our unique... relationship."

"Very well," Ulysses said, putting the glass down on the desk, the smile vanishing from his own swollen lips. "I want some answers."

"So am I to take it that your mission is still ongoing, that you have not reached any conclusions? The murder remains unsolved, the item stolen from the museum... missing?"

"Indeed. That would be a fair assumption to make."

For a moment, Magna Britannia's new First Minister said nothing. Then he eased himself stiffly back in his chair. His face remained an impassive mask, his lips pursed.

"Then I shall do my best to answer your questions, if it means that you will then be able to pursue your mission without further assistance and you will leave me in peace."

"Very well. Why did you send me to investigate the incident at the Natural History Museum in the first place? Am I to take it that Internal Affairs was already aware of the work of one Professor Galapagos?"

"That might have been the case. I couldn't possibly comment."

"But what possible interest could it be to Whitehall?"

"Naturally everything that might be a threat to the security of this nation and its people is of interest to the powers that be."

"So what you're saying is that Galapagos was developing a biological weapon?"

"I am saying no such thing. That is an assumption that you have managed to come to all by yourself. You know what was taken from the museum?"

"You might choose to make that assumption."

"I see. Very well." Wormwood breathed in sharply. "But you have not rounded up a suspect?"

"Again, you might choose to assume that, but I have my suspicions." Ulysses picked up the glass and took another sip of the warming spirit. "Did you know that Jago Kane is back in town?"

A nervous tic tugged at the left side of Wormwood's face.

"Didn't you claim that he was dead?"

"It would seem that appearances can be deceiving. I think I recall reporting that he was missing, *presumed* dead. Happens all the time."

"And now you are claiming to have seen him again?"

"I've done more than that. I fought him, up close and personal. There's no doubt it was him."

"And you believe he was involved in the robbery at the museum?"

"I wouldn't be surprised, but I think he's up to his neck in more than just that."

"I assume you are talking about the attacks by the group calling themselves the... Darwinian Dawn?"

"You know I am. Couldn't have come at a better time for you either, could it?"

"I hope you are not suggesting that I would use the occasion of such a tragic loss of human life to further my own ends?" Wormwood snarled, rising to the bait despite himself.

"You might think that, I couldn't possibly comment," Ulysses said with a smile. "And, while we're about it, how did the Darwinian Dawn manage to take control of every broadcast screen in the capital?"

"That is being looked into."

"By whom?"

"All you need to know is that the matter is already being investigated."

"And Kane?"

"You can leave that matter with me as well. It too will be looked into. Do not worry about Kane. You already have a job to do. Focus on finding this Professor Galapagos."

"Did I say that he was missing?"

"Now, Quicksilver, you have tried my patience enough today. Do not come here again, do you understand?"

"Oh, I understand."

"Then this meeting is over. Good day to you."

Taking his cue, Ulysses rose stiffly from the chair and put the glass back on the desk. "Good day, minister," he said, turning towards the door. Then he paused, glancing back at the scowling Wormwood. "Sorry... Prime Minister."

Then he was gone.

CHAPTER ELEVEN

The Missing Link

FROM THE SHADOWS on the other side of the street Ulysses looked up at the façade of the town house. It looked as decrepit as its neighbours – all crumbling brickwork and paint-flaking window frames. It looked like the kind of place you might find an Oriental's opium den, or a back street abortionist's, rather than the home of an eminent professor of evolutionary biology.

After the Challenger Incident – as it was being referred to in the popular press – and the surfacing of the Darwinian Dawn, both the trails he had been pursuing had gone cold. Following the train-top battle and Kane's escape from his clutches, there had been no sign of the revolutionary. It would take all of Ulysses' underworld contacts for there to be any chance of him getting even a sniff of the anarchist's whereabouts. The Darwinian Dawn were a new group that, apparently, no one had ever heard of before, which would make tracking them down even harder. And besides, Wormwood had made it plain that Ulysses was not to pursue that particular line of investigation any further.

With regard to the missing Galapagos, as far as Ulysses was aware there had been neither hide nor hair seen of the apeman since the de-evolving professor's breakout from the Natural History Museum weeks before. London was a big place after all, a vast teeming metropolis, one of the largest cities – if not *the* largest city – in the world. It had a population that numbered in the millions and covered an area of hundreds of square miles, operating on several towering levels within that vast expanse of space. And in such a large warren of a city there were an uncountable number of places to disappear, if one had a mind to.

It was always possible that Galapagos was already dead, of course, having met his end in any one of a thousand ways – under the wheels of a train, drowned in the Thames, or even as a result of the morphological change taking place within his body. However, a niggling instinct, that wasn't often proved wrong, told Ulysses that this was not the case. He was almost certain that Professor Ignatius Galapagos was still at large, somewhere within the capital.

So it was that Ulysses and his trusty manservant now found themselves on a dilapidated street in Southwark, the Overground line that ran above its length holding it in almost perpetual shadow.

Both of the men were attired in dark, practical clothes, a world away from the sort of flamboyant attire Ulysses usually favoured. With their black roll-neck jumpers, and woollen hats – Ulysses lacking his trademark bloodstone cane – the two of them looked like a pair of cat burglars.

"Not much to look at is it, Nimrod?" Ulysses said.

"No, sir."

"Are we sure this is the right place?" Ulysses had managed to wheedle Professor Galapagos's address from a rather staid secretary at the Museum who at first had been wholly unhelpful, until Ulysses had confronted her with his irresistible charm.

"Quite sure, sir."

"Then we had better get on with it, hadn't we?"

"If I might be so bold sir?"

"Why of course, Nimrod. Be as bold as you like."

"Why didn't Miss Galapagos mention this place, sir?"

"I don't know, Nimrod. I don't know."

"How do you suggest we gain access, sir?"

"I thought I would leave you to solve that problem, Nimrod," Ulysses said, flashing his flunkey a devilish grin, "what with it being your area of expertise and all."

"Then follow me, sir," Nimrod said, his plummy accent never slipping for a second.

There did not seem to be anyone about at this time of the morning to see what they were about as the two of them strolled nonchalantly across the road, passed the front of the house without showing anything other than a passing awareness of it, and then ducked sharply down the narrow alley next to it.

It was dark and cold in the alleyway, the narrow space between the terraces being out of reach of the sun for all but about fifteen minutes a day. The only ones to observe their dubious actions, as Nimrod forced open a grimy window, were a pair of rats that were more interested in devouring the distinctly inedible-looking detritus of the alley. With no little amount of grunting and groaning, the two of them eventually managed to scramble through the window and into the near total darkness of the house.

Inside, Professor Galapagos's home festered under a pall of perpetual gloom. Every shutter and blind or curtain in the place must have been closed. What was it that Galapagos had been wanting to hide? What atrocities had been committed here in the name of evolutionary biology and scientific advancement?

The only sound was the slow, dull ticking of a grandfather clock in the hall.

Ulysses' skin crawled. The house felt empty, hollow – dead. What had gone on here? It was certainly not the sort of place he would have expected the delicate Genevieve to have had anything to do with. But then she had confessed that she had not seen her father for some time. Ulysses wondered how long 'some time' really meant.

"I don't mind telling you, Nimrod old chap," Ulysses hissed in barely more than a whisper, "that this place gives me the willies."

"I know what you mean sir," Nimrod replied, smacking the hooked end of a crowbar into the palm of his glove. "Where now?"

"I'll check this floor. You check upstairs," Ulysses instructed, and the two of them went their separate ways. Creeping like cats they tried not to make a sound as they moved over the creaking floorboards.

Ulysses found a drawing room darkened by heavy velvet drapes. It looked like any other drawing room, with a potted aspidistra on a plant stand and portraits of the professor's family above the fireplace. All of the pictures seemed to be of the older branches of the Galapagos family tree. The room had the air of a chamber that was never used, except on the most rare and formal of occasions.

Next he came across a dining room, similarly formal in its layout and similarly infrequently used. Everything was in order, if a somewhat clinical, dispassionate order. The only thing that gave the rooms any reflection of their owner's character were sinister stuffed birds and animals, masterpieces of the taxidermist's art. Hawks glared down from the tops of bookcases – which in turn contained the usual classics, most showing no signs of having been read at all – foxes snarled from beneath occasional tables and an owl, with wings outstretched menacingly, looked as if it might launch itself from the top of the grandfather clock at any moment.

When was the last time anyone had even been here? The house felt as though it had been unlived in for some time, possibly even before the Professor's disappearance. When *was* the last time Genevieve had visited her father?

In the kitchen Ulysses found a mess of unwashed plates and mouldering food. The room was thick with flies. They congregated in a black mass against the grimy panes of a window that looked out over a featureless back yard. Although this room was clearly the most lived in, no one had been here for a while either.

Ulysses and his manservant met again in the hall at the foot of the stairs. "Anything?" Ulysses asked.

"Nothing of note, sir, apart from one attic room that appears to have been used for the practice of taxidermy. The rest are just bedrooms. Most have dated décor and have probably not been used in years. The master bedroom shows no sign of having been used recently."

"As I suspected," Ulysses confided.

"So where do we go from here, sir?"

Ulysses nodded towards the door to the basement. "The only way we can go, down."

Ulysses led the way, cautiously. Neither of them had any idea what they might find in the stygian depths below.

What they found was what had evidently been Galapagos's workroom. Ulysses boldly flicked a switch and electric lamps around the walls crackled into life, casting jaundiced pools of light around the room. A little natural light crept uncomfortably into the long room from grime-obscured windows positioned at pavement level, adding its own insipid grey haze to the room.

There was a sharp intake of breath from Ulysses. "This could be the missing piece of the puzzle."

The basement ran the length of the house and had been divided into clearly defined sections. First there was the professor's workspace. This part of the room had been fitted in the style of a gentleman's study. There was a desk, bulging bookshelves and a small grate, set into one wall. Walnut-framed lithograph studies of animals had been tacked up, along with an authentic nineteenth century map of the Galapagos Islands and a watercolour of Darwin's exploratory vessel *The Beagle*. A pair of stuffed finches, frozen in the moment of taking wing from a branch, sat on the narrow mantelpiece above the cast iron hearth.

Curiously, the desk and tables were clear of papers. It looked as if someone had gone to some deal of trouble to clear up thoroughly before leaving. As he looked with more care Ulysses also saw that there were gaps, distinct gaps, within the bookshelves. He moved to the grate. The charred, fire-eaten remains of leather-bound notebooks and other papers lay in the cold hearth. He picked a few scraps of blackened paper out of the fireplace but was unable to read anything more than the odd word. Disparate snatches of scientific jargon, written in a well-formed copperplate, that made little or no sense to him anyway and were certainly nothing more than nonsense, their context destroyed by the illiterate flames.

"He was here," Ulysses thought out loud.

"I'm sorry, sir. By 'he' do you mean Professor Galapagos?"

"Indeed I do, Nimrod. These notes, they've been burnt. And there are no signs of anyone having been here before us. I think Galapagos burnt his notes himself and then left here to return to the museum."

"You think he was trying to wipe out any traces of his work?"

"Do I think he was trying to reverse what he had done? Yes, I do."

"But what has been done cannot be undone, sir."

"Yes, I know. However, it would appear that Professor Galapagos chose to ignore that particular metaphysical fact, in a moment of irrational desperation no doubt. And inventions cannot be uninvented, discoveries cannot be undiscovered again. And now it would appear that he fell foul of whatever he had been developing himself."

Ulysses had moved into the next part of the room. A series of scrubbed oak tables were covered with pieces of glass and brass apparatus – including crucibles, condensers and various Bunsen burners connected to the house gas supply – which formed a complex chemical still. A little liquid remained in some of the blown glass vessels and a furry grey coating of dust covered everything. Again, this equipment hadn't been touched for some time. Cruelly large syringes lay on the table, as well as neatly arranged scalpels and other operating tools.

Ulysses sniffed. There was the faintest trace of a lingering odour amidst the acrid aftertaste of burning that had been trapped in the airless basement. It spoke to his subconscious. It was said that the human sense of smell was the strongest trigger for memory, but Ulysses couldn't quite recollect where or when he had last come across the bittersweet aroma.

"And what have we here?"

Beyond the Heath Robinson laboratory were several rows of shelving racks. Filling the shelves, held suspended in glass jars of various shapes and sizes, was Professor Galapagos's private collection of biological specimens.

There were the usual subjects anyone might have expected to find in the lab of an obsessively driven evolutionary biologist such as deep sea angler fish, octopi, an aborted elephant foetus, a calf's head. But then there were other things as well, less identifiable things, all preserved in the same urine-coloured formaldehyde.

They were amorphous with barely recognisable protrusions of pallid malformed anatomy here and there; a vestigial limb, a lidless staring eye, half a dozen teeth where there was no mouth, flippers, fish-like tails. Whichever way Ulysses looked at it they were grotesque abominations that were an affront to God and Nature, half-evolved, or perhaps de-evolved, foetal things that should never have been brought into existence and that could never have naturally been given life. All were dead, floating in their preserving jars like the corpses of fish in a polluted river. Some looked as though they had been partially dissected and then returned to their containers. What had the eminent professor been up to in this house of the macabre?

Beyond the shelves of abominations, at the other end of the basement room was a heavy iron door, set into a sturdy frame in the bare stone of the unlimed wall. There was a key in the lock.

"Shall we go on, sir?" Nimrod asked.

"Well we've come this far, haven't we," Ulysses said, smiling grimly. "And after this morbid museum I have to confess that I am curious as to what could possibly lie beyond an iron door in an evolutionary biologist's house."

"Very good, sir. Shall I do the honours?"

"Why, thank you, Nimrod."

"Not at all, sir." The manservant turned the key and held the door open so that Ulysses could pass through.

A flight of stone steps had been cut into the foundations of the Southwark house descending to a narrow sub-basement corridor. Light filtered through another pavement-level slit, enough for Ulysses to see where he was going. The walls ran with moisture and there were patches of moss growing between the joins. There was a strong earthy smell, mixed with the tang of ammonia and damp straw.

The corridor ran off from the foot of the slime-slick steps and soon led to a T-junction. To the left was another iron door. To the right the stygian passageway opened out into a larger subterranean chamber.

"Flashlights on, I think," Ulysses said, taking out his own torch.

The door to the left had been locked from the outside and the key left in the lock. Ulysses turned the key and opened the door. Only then did his uncanny sixth sense alert him to danger. Instinctively he leapt backwards, away from the open door, the stink of ordure assaulting his senses in a potent wave, whilst the spot-beam of his torch pierced the lightless cell beyond.

"Careful now, old chap," Ulysses warned. "We're not alone."

There was a shuffling movement, the sound of straw rustling underfoot as something moved out of the way of the light. Nimrod and Ulysses both stood before the cell, flashlights penetrating the darkness. There was a whimper from inside and both men were rendered speechless by what they saw before them.

Pressed into the corner of the tiny stone walled cell was a hulking brute of a creature. It might well have been a good head taller than Ulysses but it held that head low, its posture that of an ape. It was naked apart from a loincloth. Its skin was pallid, its body heavily muscled, its head covered with lank hair that hung down to its shoulders. It had flung its hands in front of its face, blinded by the sudden invasion of torchlight. The heavy line of its brow and the blunt shape of its snout suggested that this creature was closer to Man's ape ancestors than *Homo sapiens.*

"Get down, sir!" Nimrod shouted, pushing Ulysses out of the way. The manservant barged into the cell, crowbar in hand. The creature flinched. Raising the improvised weapon above his head, Nimrod stared into the face of the half-human creature in front of him. Wholly human eyes looked back into his, welling with a deep sadness.

Nimrod hesitated. It was all the time Ulysses needed. He had seen the look in the cowering creature's eyes as well.

"Nimrod, old chap, thanks for your concern for my well-being, but I don't think you'll be needing to use that crowbar."

"But it's the apeman, sir."

Keeping his manservant at bay with one hand, Ulysses slowly but deliberately moved between Nimrod and the creature. Despite such an action of disarming trust his body remained tensed, ready to fight if he had to.

"Correction, old chap. It's *an* apeman, not *the* apeman, not Professor Galapagos." Boldly Ulysses took another step, his nose inadvertently wrinkling against the smell. He had seen its like before. "In fact I rather think it's an *Homo neanderthalensis.*"

"A what, sir?"

"A Neanderthal, Nimrod. An evolutionary dead-end but an ancestor of the human race nonetheless. I rather think that *this* is our missing link, so to speak."

"But it could still be dangerous, sir."

Ulysses took another step, lowering his torch and holding out a hand towards the creature. Slowly the Neanderthal lowered its hands from its face and reciprocated the gesture, reaching towards Ulysses with one meaty paw.

"It doesn't look like it so far, does it? Besides, have you not noticed the manacle around its ankle chaining it to the wall? I know it's a cliché – and this fellow here could probably snap both our necks like twigs – but I think he's more scared of us than we are of him."

For a moment their fingertips touched and Ulysses sensed a common ancestry – a shared humanity with the captive Neanderthal. At the back of his mind he wondered how someone who had sired such a magnanimous wonder as Genevieve Galapagos could have been so cruel to this creature. The Neanderthal was not so much the Professor's pet as the result of some inhuman and immoral experiment.

"Nimrod, pick the lock on that manacle."

"Are you sure, sir?"

"Trust me."

His sense of duty overcoming the persuasive voice of doubt in his mind, Nimrod approached the creature. It jerked away from him,

Nimrod's immediate reaction being to do the same. But slowly, with ever such cautious movements, the creature allowed Nimrod to free it from its chains.

A terrible reptilian roar rang through the echoing darkness of the cellar space, a crocodilian bellow of defiance and savage prehistoric fury. It was a roar redolent with the promise of a cruel death.

The Neanderthal howled in abject fear. Ulysses' blood ran cold.

"Now what was *that?*"

In the black hole of the basement chamber opposite the cell, stabbing their torch beams into the stygian gloom as if trying to drive it back into the bowels of the underworld, they found a single cast iron manhole cover.

The reptilian roar echoed through the chamber, emanating from beneath them through the slits in the iron plate. Was it the cry of some rogue saurian, still loose after the break out from London Zoo, or did it belong to something infinitely worse?

As the echoes died away the sound of running water could be heard coming up from below and a gust of foul air rose with it. Whatever had given voice to that terrible sound was lurking somewhere below, in the noxious labyrinth of the city's sewer system. So that was where Ulysses Quicksilver would have to go too. Destiny called. Whether the creature realised it or not, it was waiting for him.

CHAPTER TWELVE

Going Underground

THE WINDING, LOW-ROOFED tunnels stank, which was unsurprising considering Ulysses and Nimrod now found themselves exploring one of the largest sewer systems in the world. Human waste filled the sewers with its miasmic stink, as foetid brown water swirled around their ankles, and sometimes up to their knees, soaking through their trousers and boots as they trudged through the filth. Ulysses breathed in through his nose as much as he could, so as to avoid tasting the foul stench, concentrating hard on not letting his gorge rise. Nimrod simply advanced through the tunnels with a permanent, nose-wrinkled scowl distorting his aquiline features. They could feel solid lumps of waste swirling around their legs with every step; every time they placed a sodden boot down they felt the filth shift and ooze underfoot.

From the shaft leading down into the sewers the two explorers had found themselves in a cramped, brick-lined tunnel that ran away ahead and behind. Their torch beams illuminated about twenty yards of the tunnel in any one direction and revealed walls coated with glistening slime whilst unspeakable things slipped past them in the insistent current of the waste channel.

They trudged on, any efforts at stealth thwarted. Every dredging step they took sloshed in the filthy current, every word spoken – even whispered

– was amplified into uncomfortable clarity by the cavern-like acoustics of the place. Ulysses found himself wondering whether any of Professor Galapagos's aborted experiments had ended up down here. Although it looked like he had kept everything he had ever created in his unholy laboratory, perhaps other degenerate things had survived and escaped into the sewers beneath the city. There were certainly all manner of urban myths regarding what was living, hidden and undisturbed in the sewers of the Empire's largest city, from giant albino salamanders and ancient crocodiles to more far-fetched rumours of a tribe of cannibalistic troglodytes. It was not so far-fetched to believe that there could be other things living down there too, things like the offspring of an obsessive scientist's experiments.

They had left the maltreated Neanderthal in the basement room. It had appeared unwilling to follow them into the sewer; perhaps it knew what was waiting for them down there even if it couldn't communicate that fact to them directly.

At every junction they waited in anxious anticipation. Never quite sure of what they might meet. Sometimes the roars sounded as though they were coming from just around the next corner in the twisting tunnels and at other times they sounded more distant again. Then they would not hear anything at all for as much as a quarter of an hour.

Was the reptile or dinosaur, or whatever it was, hunting them, scenting their blood even over the overwhelming stink of the sewers? And there was another nagging thought at the back of Ulysses' mind that he almost didn't want to even consider. Were they in fact hunting the transformed Professor Galapagos altered even further, changed into a totally inhuman form by whatever degenerative disease he had contracted?

Then, at last, the tunnel began to widen, the roof becoming higher, so that they could walk two abreast without having to stoop. Another thirty yards further on and a walkway, raised from the stream of filth, appeared on the left hand side. It was a relief for them to get their feet out of the stinking sludge.

Ulysses paused at another parting of the ways. Four tunnels met at an intersection, the current becoming stronger at the confluence as three of the sewer passages emptied into the fourth – and largest. The roar of water suggested that a little way down this last tunnel the depth of the sewer increased, the current being carried over a precipitous waterfall into the even more unsavoury depths of the sewer network.

But Ulysses was not interested in any of these new tunnels, at least not for the time being. He was shining his torch down at the narrow walkway they were now on.

"What is it, sir?" Nimrod asked. "What have you found?"

"Something's last meal," Ulysses said, studying the half-eaten remains of a rat. It was missing its hindquarters, the spill of its pallid intestines a greasy purple-grey in the light of his torch.

"And here's another one." Something had clearly taken a bite out of the middle of this rodent. The rat's head, tail and legs were all intact but the flesh of its middle was completely gone, only a few stringy bits of gristle remaining attached to its gnawed spine. "Watch where you're stepping, old chap."

"Sir?" Nimrod's voice floated back up the tunnel. "I think you should see this."

Ulysses turned and looked back down the tunnel. His manservant had stopped a few yards behind on the walkway. He had his torch beam pointed down at the side of the ledge.

"What is it?" Ulysses asked, joining Nimrod where he was crouched at the channel's edge.

Whatever it was, it looked like a swatch of leather, discoloured almost beyond recognition by the filth of the effluent half-filling the tunnel. It had caught on a rusted pipe jutting out from the stonework. Nimrod pulled it free and carefully laid it out on the mouldering pathway.

Now that it was out of the muck both men could see quite clearly that the material was covered in coarse hair and had gathered in folds. In the light of the torches Nimrod began to tease out the folds, separating them in an attempt to stretch the object out.

"My God!" Ulysses gasped, as the shape of the object became unquestionable. The thing Nimrod had recovered from the sewer was undoubtedly a skin. It was not complete but both men could see arms, the outline of legs and a face.

"How vexing," Nimrod said, without any apparent emotion. "It would appear that something has eaten the wretched Professor Galapagos."

"I don't think so, old chap," Ulysses corrected, running his torch up and down the ape-skin. "I don't think that the errant professor has been skinned and eaten. These ruptures here don't look like talon marks, they look more like tears to me. There's no subcutaneous fat, blood and general mess on the skin. It's relatively clean, if you choose to ignore the fact that it's been soaking in sewer filth. I think that Professor Galapagos has shed his skin."

"I am no naturalist, sir, but as far as I am aware, mammalian species do not shed their skin."

"No, they don't, do they?"

"So," Nimrod said, seeking a better understanding so that he was clear as to what the two of them could expect to face down in the stinking darkness, "you believe that the cry we heard was not made by the professor's killer but by whatever he might have become."

"Something like that, yes."

A sense like precognition sent shockwaves skittering along tingling nerve endings. Ulysses threw himself backwards against the wall of the tunnel as the effluent stream exploded, showering the two men with filthy water. A hulking shape hurled itself at the crouching men. A sweeping claw struck the edge of the walkway, the rotten brickwork crumbling under the blow.

Mastering their shock at the abrupt appearance of the monster, Ulysses and Nimrod turned their torches on the creature. The thing roared in fury, its reptilian voice brimming with anger, and threw its arms up in front of its face. Its eyes had become used to the fetid darkness and so it was now blinded by the sudden sharp light of the torches.

It had used other senses to track the two hunters which, as well as a heightened sense of hearing and smell, included the ability to sense a creature by body heat alone.

The creature had found it easy to hunt the rats, the scrawny rodents appearing as scampering blurs of hot orange and yellow against the dull black of the bone-numbing slurry water. Then it had chanced upon the two men, sensing the heat of their bodies in the darkness, feeling an animal thrill of satisfaction that here at last was some more satisfying prey with which it could sate its ravenous hunger. It was only Ulysses' precognitive sense that had saved him from an instant death at the claws of the lizard man.

In the split second in which it was rendered incapable by the light of the torches, Ulysses' heightened mind took in every detail of the creature's unnatural anatomy. The trunk of its body was like that of a muscular human but covered with scales instead of skin. The scales of its belly were pale, the colour of ivory, but on the rest of its body the creature's rough hide became more like the colour and texture of tree bark. Its arms were again humanoid in form, but corded with muscles like ship's cables and ending in sharp-clawed talons.

The monster's face and head had lost all vestiges of its original form, showing no signs of its human origins. It looked more like that of a lizard. It was completely hairless and had a short crocodilian snout, strong jaws bristling with needle-sharp teeth, its tongue a stabbing spear of black muscle. But its eyes were the most chilling aspect of all; they had lost any sign of the humanity that might have once lingered within. Around the scales of its neck – so tight that it was cutting into the saurian flesh beneath – was a silvered chain and the curiously shaped locket Ulysses had seen before around the neck of the apeman in the Natural History Museum. There could be no doubt now as to the identity of the mutated half-lizard thing.

"Professor Galapagos, I presume."

The creature responded by issuing another blood-curdling roar from between gaping jaws, large enough to remove a man's head from his shoulders with a single bite.

The change that had come upon the professor was obviously not as straightforward as him simply transforming into other ancestral life forms as his body regressed. With every change he underwent his body maintained its overall human proportions as if he was actually becoming a hybrid of a human being and whatever other evolutionary form he might be regressing into. It was as if the damned Professor was creating new species, or sub-species, with every transformation. The form he was in right now the academics would give the name *homo lizardus* or *lizardus sapiens*. That was his divine punishment for the hubris he had demonstrated in meddling with the secrets of evolution, for cracking the Darwin Code. God alone knew what he would turn into next. It seemed to Ulysses that Galapagos's regression was accelerating.

The monster howled, its saurian voice like the shriek of a circular saw. It lashed out again, this time catching Ulysses' flashlight, smashing the torch from his hand and shattering the bulb. The light died, but with Nimrod's torch still dazzling the creature Ulysses sought a way to defend himself.

Before the pistol was even in his hand, the lizard-thing hurled itself back into the brown slurry and vanished beneath the surface.

Ulysses trained his gun on the spot where the lizardman had disappeared but it failed to resurface. "Come on, we can't let it get away!" He shouted, recklessly leaping into the sewer channel again.

"But which way, sir?" Nimrod asked, shining his torch after Ulysses.

Ulysses scoured the sewer intersection for any sign of where the Galapagos-lizard had gone, whether that sign be sight or sound of the lizardman or some precognitive clue from that extra-sensory part of his subconscious.

"This way," he declared, pointing at the pipe into which all the other channels emptied, and began dragging his legs through the water with heroic strides.

"Sir, wait!" Nimrod called after his reckless employer, but Ulysses' blood was up and he would not be held back.

Entering the gaping mouth of the main tunnel Ulysses instantly felt the pull of the stronger current. Only a few yards ahead the sewer passage emptied over the edge of an abyssal drop, the sound of the water a thunderous roar.

"Sir!"

Ulysses heard his flunkey's warning as his heightened sixth sense cut through the adrenalin. He spun round to see the monstrous saurian shadow rise behind him, filthy brown water running from its rugged hide.

He had been ready for the monster but turning cost him precious fractions of a second. Something lashed out of the darkness, whipping him across the forearm, smacking the gun from his hand and opening up the flesh of his wrist.

"A tail! A bloody tail!" Ulysses gasped, clutching a hand to the gash in his arm. Galapagos had become even more like one of humankind's prehistoric reptilian forebears than Ulysses had at first realised.

As the creature bore down on him, Ulysses realised that he had no choice but to fight the creature hand-to-hand. And then the time for calm, reasoned thought was gone and there was only time for brutal, instinctive action.

The lizardman reached for Ulysses with taloned hands and Ulysses grabbed hold of both the creature's wrists, feeling the scales scrape against the softer skin of his palms. The Galapagos-lizard was taller than he and had the greater body mass. But Ulysses was lithely strong too, more so than might at first have appeared to the casual observer. And in his months away from the rest of civilisation he had learnt how to use an opponent's own strength and weight against them. He did so now, pulling the lizardman towards him whilst deftly sidestepping. As the scaly creature stumbled past him, Ulysses delivered a strong, straight-legged kick into the base of the lizard's spine.

The beast stumbled but retained its balance, the taloned claws of its feet anchoring it to the floor of the tunnel beneath the rushing effluent. Without even looking back over its shoulder, the Galapagos-lizard delivered another unavoidable whip-cracking stinging blow with its tail, this time catching Ulysses across the chest. He stumbled backwards, desperate to keep his balance, fearing what might happen should he become submerged.

Then the beast was on him, Ulysses and the lizardman wrestling one another at the very edge of the subterranean waterfall.

Ulysses looked up into the elongated face of what had once been Genevieve Galapagos's father and into the eyes of what had become *Lacerta erectus*. Those eyes were now a chilling ophidian yellow, the pupils cruel crescent slits. The monster stared back, nictitating eyelids blinking rapidly.

There was the crack of a pistol shot and a bullet buried itself in the wall of the tunnel next to them.

"Try to hold it still, sir!" Nimrod called over the roar of the lizard and the furious crashing of the cascading sewage.

Ulysses felt his shoulder cry out as he tried to resist the weight of the beast bearing down on top of him.

"All right," Ulysses spluttered, closing his eyes against the torch beam as it swept into his eyes, "and while I'm at it, I'll ask the dear Professor Galapagos to pose for his portrait for the National Geographic Magazine."

Nimrod's aim was compromised by the disorienting shadows cast by his small torch and also by the fact that he did not want to hit Ulysses. To kill one's own employer would not look good on his curriculum vitae should he have to look for other gainful employment following this incident.

There was another crack and this time the lizardman cried out in pained surprise. For a moment it turned, as if considering this new threat.

"A hit, Nimrod, a very palpable hit!"

"Thank you, sir!"

"Not that it seems to have made any difference," Ulysses added to himself.

Driven on by its rage at having been shot, the lizardman grappled with Ulysses, snapping at him with its alligator mouth, forcing him closer and closer towards the edge of the pitch-black precipice. Ulysses lashed out with kicks and punches, but the creature's hide protected it from his pummelling. Where he landed punches with his fists he winced as he took the skin off his knuckles.

There was a splash as Nimrod entered the channel after them. The manservant's torch beam wavered as he did his best to run to the aid of his master. "Watch out, sir! I'll get the blighter!"

There were two more pistol shots. It sounded like one of them *spanged* off the bony ridges of the lizard's back. The other hit home.

The creature roared, enraged by the manservant's constant goading. It spun round savagely, delivering Ulysses a reeling blow to the head with one club-like fist as it did so.

For a moment grey supernovae exploded across Ulysses' vision. He reeled backwards, grabbing out at anything that might arrest his fall. His fingers closed around something small, sharp and hard. There was the ping of a chain snapping and then the mighty pendulum weight of the monster's tail connected with the back of his legs.

There was no way he could have avoided the tail attack. His legs swept out from under him, his feet slipping in the rancid silt covering the floor of the sewer passage, Ulysses felt the surging current catch him and pull him with it into the void.

The flickering light of Nimrod's torch illuminating the circular mouth of the tunnel disappeared rapidly upwards, receding gunshots echoing from the sewer pipe.

He could feel nothing but air beneath him, his ears deaf to all but the roar of the effluent-fall. And the hungry darkness of the sewer swallowed him up.

CHAPTER THIRTEEN

His Waterloo

ULYSSES SURFACED, COUGHING violently, the surging current of the sewer channel bringing him to a stone ledge in the septic darkness. He scrabbled for a hold, trying to pull himself out of the vile water. His stomach heaved and before he was fully aware of what was happening he vomited, his body's reaction to the presence of the noxious effluent that had suddenly flooded his digestive system. He spluttered, spitting in an attempt to rid his mouth of the ordure, and his stomach heaved again.

Eventually Ulysses managed to pull himself onto the ledge and then could do nothing but sit with his head hung low, weakened by the experience and disorientated by his plunge into the deeper sewer tunnels. Taking in heaving lungfuls of air he retched again, unable to rid himself of the nauseous taste. This time nothing more came up; there was nothing left inside him. There was a dull throbbing ache in his skull from the resounding blow the lizardman had laid against him during their struggle.

As he sat there, leaning over the sewer channel in the darkness, he became uncomfortably aware of his own ragged breathing. Ears straining to hear anything else, he searched for any clues as to his surroundings using sound alone. Down there in the darkness, soaked to the skin in malodorous sewer water, without a light source to see by and minus his gun, Ulysses felt horribly vulnerable.

He could hear the ever-present gurgle of the steady stream coursing through the sewer pipe. There was also the slow drip of moisture from the ceiling and the small splashes of the drips falling into puddles collecting on the pitted stone of the ledge. And then there was the occasional scampering patter of tiny feet as the rats went about their disgusting business.

He could see nothing and smell far too much. It was as if the fetid stench had taken on physical form and was trying to smother him as well as take away his sight.

Ulysses couldn't hear the sound of gunfire anymore, but then he wasn't sure how far he had been carried following his plunge. He wondered what had become of the ever-loyal Nimrod. Had he bested the lizardman or had he simply become Professor Galapagos's latest victim? There was no time for mourning now, though. Besides, he had no idea really as to his manservant's fate one way or the other – Nimrod had been armed, as had the lizard in its own way. His priority was to get out of the sewers alive so that he could pursue his investigation to its conclusion, and if that meant avenging Nimrod's death, then so be it.

Ulysses could still feel the professor's curious locket gripped tightly in his fist. Incredibly, he had managed to hold onto it after his fall and all the time he was being carried along through the miasmic dark.

He couldn't hear anything that might hint at the approach of the inhuman lizard-thing – either the sound of something breaking the surface or surging towards him through the foul water – but then he had barely been given any warning the last time that the monster had attacked. Was the lizardman hunting him even now through the cloying, fetid darkness? Or was its corpse floating through the tunnels, on its way to the Thames, shot dead by his butler?

As he sat there in the gloom, the nausea slowly subsiding, he realised that he was not actually in total darkness. As his eyes adjusted to the gloom, eking every scrap of light from his surroundings, he saw that the curved walls and ceiling of the brick-built tunnel were covered with patches of luminescent moss that appeared to thrive in the putrid, methane-rich atmosphere.

It was as nothing in comparison to having a halogen beam or storm lantern but it was enough to help him discern one shadowy form from another. It was enough for him to make his way without braining himself against a low arch or stepping off the edge of a precipice, but he would still need to proceed with caution. The darkness could hide a hundred hazards.

Rising to his feet carefully, using the crumbling, slime-encrusted wall for support, Ulysses set off, following the same course as the brackish water through this stinking subterranean world. He saw little point in trying to return to where he had begun his frightful journey.

He didn't fancy his chances of trying to scale the precipice he had been thrown from. And besides, the water in the tunnel would ultimately end up pouring into the Thames and lead him to a way out.

So, in almost total darkness, save for the dull green glow of the bioluminescent vegetation, feeling weak and nauseous, as well as wet and cold, with barely any awareness of time passing, Ulysses Quicksilver continued to navigate the labyrinthine tunnels, every sense straining to make sense of this disorientating world.

He had no idea for how long he had been exploring the dark tunnels. His watch had a luminous dial but it had rather uncharacteristically stopped working. He suspected that his dunking hadn't done the usually reliable timepiece much good. It hadn't done much for his communicator either.

Steadily, through the nigh on impenetrable black murk, the broken edges of a patch of deeper darkness could be discerned in the gloom. It was ahead of Ulysses and slightly to the right. Cautiously he made this his focus and approached the hole in the darkness. As he neared the space his straining eyes were able to discern depth to the darkness too. Reaching out a hand, he ran his fingers over the broken, angular edges of bricks. Something in the past had caused part of the sewer wall to collapse. The current diverged at this juncture. Most of the stinking water continued on its way along the brick pipe, but some swirled out through the hole mixing with a second subterranean watercourse.

Ulysses paused, listening. At first he could hear nothing beyond the rush and churn of the sewer and the ripple of water lapping against the wall. There was an echoing quality to the watery sounds coming from the other side of the hole, suggesting that the dimensions of the space beyond were of more cavernous proportions than the tunnel in which he now stood.

Then he heard another sound, muffled by distance. It sounded like the clanking of machinery, a rhythmic tattoo, the beating of a mechanical heart.

For a moment Ulysses considered the sewer passage ahead of him but then felt compelled to enter the larger tunnel, beyond the hole, and follow the sound to its source. With no other beacon to direct his way through the fetid darkness, Ulysses concentrated on the distant, echoed clanking.

Clambering through the half-submerged rupture in the tunnel wall, Ulysses immediately felt the floor drop away beneath him and started treading water. The water filling this new tunnel was just as bone numbing as that of the sewer but, although it smelt old and stale, it was like the scent of roses compared to the stench that he had just had to wade through.

Ulysses let his senses adjust to this new space, hearing the rippling waves his swimming sent out rebound from a barrier only a matter of a few feet away. Light-excreting blankets of moss grew in irregular patches on the curving walls and ceiling here too, so that gradually Ulysses was able to make sense of the puzzle and realised that the space he was in now was much larger, but just as tube-like, as the sewer passage he had emerged from.

The tunnel was flooded but the water here was more or less still; there was no restless current pulling him one way or another. Instead he directed himself towards the distant, rhythmic clanking that sounded like the echoing hubbub of a factory production line. He moved with a strong breaststroke. Ulysses followed the gradual bend of the tunnel, the sounds of the relentless machinery becoming clearer and being joined by other noises now – the wheeze of steam being released under pressure, the regular *thud-thud-thud* of a hammer, the wail of a klaxon, even human voices.

The sounds were so clear now that Ulysses felt that he was on the verge of making out recognisable words, snatches of conversation, between the loud thumping, pounding and rattling of the hidden production line. As he rounded the bend, the architecture of the tunnel changed, as the roof seemed to rise away above Ulysses' head, an oblong shape emerged from the gloom to his left. At the same time his feet kicked against the bottom of the tunnel floor. His foot slipped on a submerged obstruction. It felt like the floor was cut with grooved channels or... set with rails.

Then the pieces of the puzzle finally fell into place.

The oblong was a ledged walkway. He pushed his way through the sludgy water and there hauled himself out of the chill, oily lake. He sat for a moment listening to the *clank-clunk* that seemed to come from above as well as beyond now, feeling the slight tremor of a vibration pass through the stone beneath him.

Ulysses reached out a hand to the wall. The surface his fingertips came into contact with was cold and slick with moisture, but it was smooth. In fact it felt like glazed ceramic.

"Tiles," Ulysses said to himself. Leaving the collapsed sewer he had entered the flooded tunnels of the old, abandoned Underground railway system. It explained much – the increased size of the tunnel, the materials from which it had been constructed. He was sitting on a station platform.

The Underground had been abandoned for more than sixty years, ever since the Kingdom Incident, as it had since become known. The capital's subterranean rail network had been replaced by the far superior Overground in the intervening years. Ulysses had believed most of the Tube tunnels to be completely flooded, but it would appear from the evidence of his own eyes that this was only partly the case.

He got to his feet. Fetid water ran from his body and clothes, pooling on the slime-coated platform under the soles of his sodden shoes.

Taking a moment to gather himself, he pushed his wet hair out of his face, slicking it down with a greasy palm.

He was lost within the forgotten tunnels of the London Underground which had once been the pride of the nation, having been thwarted by the lizard-beast that the missing – not to mention, evolutionarily-degenerating – Professor Galapagos had become. Whatever awaited him within the supposedly abandoned labyrinth of the subterranean railway system could not possibly surprise him – not now. It was all in a day's work for Ulysses Quicksilver, dandy adventurer and servant of the crown.

"You couldn't make it up," he said to himself, smiling inwardly, despite the dire state of his personal attire and the nature of his current predicament.

Further along the platform he found himself at the opening of a side passage, which connected to a flight of steps. A flickering orange glow came from above, illuminating the top of the steps. Ulysses blinked, his eyes taking a moment to adjust. Then, taking a firm hold of the rusted handrail next to him, he began to ascend.

PRESSING HIMSELF FLAT against the smooth tiled wall, Ulysses took several measured breaths and then peered warily around the edge of the archway.

The place might once have been the warren of gleaming tiled tunnels that made up an Underground station concourse but it had now been filled with machinery and transformed into an underground factory. Ulysses was looking down on a veritable production line, which would not have been out of place in one of the steam-driven mills of the Black Country. The whole place lay under a fug of steam and coal smoke, whilst caged sodium lights pierced the smoggy murk, looking like fog-distorted ship's lanterns. The factory was also pervaded by the noise and vibration of the working machinery.

To Ulysses' left, at the far end of the concourse, massive machines – all spinning flywheels, thumping hammers and crushing compressors – produced shell-like spherical steel cases, from which protruded sea urchin-like spines. Steam and clockwork powered automata-drudges separated each steel globe into two equal halves, and half of these hemispherical cases were then heaved onto a rattling conveyor system. These shell casings then passed along the production line to have other components fitted inside them by other robot-drones. The air reeked of lubricating oil and hot metal, accompanied by an all-pervading acrid chemical smell.

To the far right, in the shadow of a broad archway at the end of the relentless production line, yet more drones put the two halves of the metal spheres back together and from there they were ferried away into the darkness of a side passage on great wheeled frames.

On the wall above it all, through the smoke and steam, Ulysses could make out the rusted Underground sign that signified which station it was he now found himself in. The name on the banner read: Waterloo. It somehow seemed apt.

There was no doubt in Ulysses' mind that this place was a bomb factory. But how long had production been in operation on this spot, hidden from the prying eyes of the world above?

Carrying out all manner of unskilled labouring jobs around the automatons, so that the man-machines might complete their work without hindrance, were the kind of dregs of society that made the beggars on the city streets above look fortunate. These troglodyte workers might once have been human but they were now barely more than warped wretches, their bodies afflicted by all manner of hideous mutations.

They all wore the same, shapeless, grubby overalls and shambled about the place with their ankles shackled together. They were prisoners here, as much as they were workers, employed to do the jobs deemed too lowly even for the automated workforce. Not one of them would have looked out of place in a circus freak show. They all looked as if they could be descendants of Joseph Merrick, the Elephant Man. These people were either losing their hair, or their teeth, no doubt as a result of the terrible conditions in which they were forced to work, their faces and bodies misshapen by hideous growths of pallid, purple-veined flesh. In some cases, their disfigurements were so extreme that it was impossible for Ulysses to determine the gender of the limping creatures that had been enslaved to the production of the evil devices.

It was these same wretches who were spooning a noxious, bubbling green gunk from a crusted iron vat into each of the shell casings. Wisps of malodorous vapour rose from the patently toxic goo. Ulysses' eyes stung and he was in no doubt that it was as a result of this poisonous stuff diffusing through the atmosphere of the factory.

Watching over the production line from gantry walkways and the openings of side passages were armed men, dressed in plain black uniforms. The only distinguishing mark on any of them was the insignia of their clandestine organisation that until, only a few weeks ago, Ulysses had never even known existed. They each wore the badge of an encircled dinosaur skull on their arms. Each of them was armed with a sub-automatic machine pistol, their faces hidden by the rubber snouts of gas masks.

Ulysses' rage at witnessing first-hand the fate that had been forced upon the poor mutant work force seethed and simmered just beneath the surface, ready to explode with volcanic fury. He would dearly have liked to vent that fury against any one of the armed guards but such recourse would merely lead to his own demise. He was still unarmed, and no matter how skilled he might be, in unarmed combat the odds did not appear to be in his favour.

No, he would have to bide his time and wait, and perhaps then a more practical course of action would present itself to him.

Watching the factory floor, Ulysses saw a figure unlike any other he had so far seen. He was wearing a grubby lab coat that might once have been white. His eyes were hidden by a pair of thick goggles. His hair was matted and spiked with filth. His hands were encased within heavy rubber gloves. He grasped a stained clipboard on which he was scrawling notes as he monitored progress on the production line. He was followed by a gaggle of similarly garbed assistants, but there was no doubt that this tech-engineer scientist was their senior.

Ulysses watched the scientist as he made his way through the converted station concourse. There was little he could do directly to counteract whatever the Darwinian Dawn were doing here, but if he stealthily shadowed this individual he might be able to get one step closer to the heart of the group's operations. They were obviously planning a bombing campaign on a scale undreamt of before by those in power in Whitehall. Quietly, Ulysses ducked out from behind the pillar and in two long strides was hunkered down behind one of the supports that held up the clanking conveyor.

He was suddenly distracted by a shout from the other side of the factory. He glanced to his left, peering between cast iron spars and his heart was suddenly in his mouth.

A figure dressed in practical black clothes had emerged from a passageway on the other side of the concourse, accompanied by two of the armed guards. It was Kane – Jago Kane – here! He was instantly recognisable, thanks to the distinguishing mark of the livid scar that bisected his face. It was all Ulysses could do to stop himself gasping in surprise. So the blackguard *was* at the centre of the Darwinian Dawn's operations. Ulysses had *known* it!

The vile revolutionary joined the scientist-supervisor and his lackeys on the factory floor. The two of them immediately engaged in what appeared to be an intense discussion. If only Ulysses could discover what it was they were talking about, the information he could then provide to his masters in Whitehall would be all the more valuable, but to achieve such a thing he would have to get closer.

Keeping himself crouched down behind the conveyor production line, obscured by the steam, any sound he might make drowned out by the roar of the bomb-making construction, Ulysses crept towards the plotters' position, at the same time assiduously avoiding the human slaves and their masked overseers. Gradually he began to pick up snippets of conversation.

The scientist was assuring Kane that they would be ready, as planned, and on schedule. Kane pressed on about having the devices in position by... but then Ulysses missed the rest as an automatic valve released a burst of steam from a pipe above his head.

The snatches of conversation didn't make any real sense out of context, and merely added to Ulysses' frustration and determination to find out more.

Concentrating intently he pressed on. Kane seemed almost close enough for Ulysses to reach out and touch. Ulysses was concentrating so hard that he only became aware of the tingling at the back of his brain at the last second, when it was too late to do anything to save himself.

With a sharp jab, the cold metal of a rifle muzzle was shoved against the back of his neck. He had been in such a hurry to catch up with his nemesis that he had thrown all caution to the wind and acted like some reckless youth.

"Don't get up," came a gruff, uncultured voice from behind him, "unless you want me to put a bullet through the back of your skull."

He was prodded in the ribs by a second gun muzzle and another voice declared, "At this time of social civil war you can consider yourself a hostage of the Darwinian Dawn."

CHAPTER FOURTEEN

A Bad Day to Die

"So, Ulysses Quicksilver, we meet again."

Ulysses looked up into the sneering scowl that was Jago Kane's face. Ulysses had been roughly searched, dragged in front of his nemesis and the scientist and then forced to kneel before them, his hands behind his head. "The pleasure's all yours."

The punch snapped Ulysses' head sharply to the right.

"Always there with the snappy, oh-so-clever retorts and hilarious one-liners," Kane snarled.

Before Ulysses could come back at the revolutionary with another of his trademark verbal ripostes, Kane's fist descended again. Something cracked and Ulysses spat a gobbet of bloody saliva from between bruised lips. His head sagged.

"Not so quick with the witty ripostes now, are you?"

"I see falling from a train hasn't dampened your eternally optimistic spirit, more's the pity."

Fury seething in his eyes Kane said nothing, simply delivering a sharp kick to Ulysses midriff. Ulysses could not stop himself howling in pain and doubled up, his forehead practically touching the floor.

"I won't ask how you stumbled upon our operation or how you got past the guards."

"What, aren't you even a little bit interested?" Ulysses managed between agonised gasps.

"No. Such details are irrelevant now because you're never going to get out of here alive."

Eyes watering from the pain of the kick to his stomach Ulysses nonetheless managed to raise himself enough to fix the terrorist with a withering stare.

"I know exactly what's been going on down here, you traitorous bastard." His voice was a strained snarl of contempt. "And when the authorities pick up my message..."

"Again, irrelevant. You're never going to get the chance to report back to those self-serving idiots who so desperately hang on to the failing status quo. You're too late."

"Too late?" Ulysses coughed. "I would think that a handful of Special Forces strike teams are on their way down here as we speak."

"But your masters in Whitehall have no idea what is right beneath their feet."

"Oh no?" Ulysses purred. "Before your goons here picked me up I sent a coded message to those in the know."

"What on this?" Kane held out a hand. One of those same goons who had searched Ulysses passed the terrorist his waterlogged personal communicator.

"I doubt very much that this is working after its dunking in God knows what."

At least they hadn't found where he had hidden Galapagos's locket.

"Well, it was worth a try."

Kane hit him again.

"Will you stop doing that?" Ulysses screamed, his nerve suddenly snapping.

Kane looked down at him, eyes narrowing.

"No one's coming down here to look for you. There are no strike teams on their way. And there is nothing to stop us proceeding according to schedule. But what should we do with you?"

"I expect your mother asks the same question on a daily basis," Ulysses threw back.

"What shall we do with him, Mr Tesla? Any ideas?" Kane mused, feigning indecision.

"We could use him as a test subject, Agent Kane," the goggled scientist suggested. "Strap him to one of the devices, set it off in one of the lower tunnels. See what happens."

"Hmm, fun as that sounds I don't think so. It would be a waste of resources. No, but I do like the sound of the lower tunnels. Bring the bastard with you and follow me," Kane said addressing the two guards, "and bring some rope as well."

Ulysses was dragged back down the steps by which he had entered and back to the flooded Underground tunnels. The two guards heaved him into the numbing, fetid water and, at Kane's direction, forced him down into the chill subterranean canal. But he was not prepared to go willingly to his doom. In desperation he struggled to free himself until, eventually, Kane put an end to his thrashing by giving him a kick to the head.

Barely conscious, Ulysses could do nothing as the guards tied both his hands and feet to the rusted rails submerged beneath the water, leaving only his head above the filmy surface. Once he was secured Kane crouched at the edge of the platform and looked down at his prisoner, shining a flashlight into Ulysses' eyes.

"You want to know something interesting about these tunnels?" he said with a dark smile. "The water that fills this flooded labyrinth comes straight from the Thames, and just as the Thames is a tidal river, so these channels too are tidal. Only, because the water's forced into such constricted passageways, as the river rises the water level in these tunnels can change dramatically. The water in here can come right up to the top of those stairs we came down by and the tide's on the turn. I'll let you work the rest of it out for yourself."

Kane rose, ignoring Ulysses – who made to shift the ropes by pulling with his arms and trying to bring his knees up – and spoke to his fellow conspirators. "Fun's over. Get back to work. The clock is ticking. The new dawn is coming."

As the scientist and guards left, Kane hung back, looking down at the futilely struggling Ulysses once more. "Any last words? Any snappy retorts? A last clever one-liner by which you would like to be remembered?"

"I hope you burn in the hell of your own making!"

"Oh yes, very witty. Very clever. Say hello to eternity for me."

With that Jago Kane turned on his heel and left.

Alone in the cold and the dark Ulysses contemplated his fate. If he could loosen his bonds even just a little he might be able to create enough friction between them and the rusted rails to break through. Muscles bunching he pulled, feeling the rough hemp of the rope rubbing the flesh of his wrists raw. Similar agonies were being suffered by his ankles.

Was it his imagination or was the water level in the tunnel already beginning to rise? As Ulysses thrashed against his bonds, his head aching from the cruel blows he had received, the water splashed against his face and he spluttered to keep it out of his mouth.

Ulysses did not consider himself a particularly godly man but now seemed like an ideal occasion to become better acquainted with the Almighty before they actually met face-to-face. Closing his eyes, arms and legs still straining, he prayed for a miracle.

His constant struggling was beginning to take its toll. The throbbing in his head was worsening and white-hot pokers of lightning pain shot through his muscles. Gritting his teeth he let out a great howl of rage, frustration and exhaustion. Filthy black water poured into his mouth. Ulysses coughed, gagging on the brackish liquid, and cleared it from his mouth with a gob of oily phlegm.

For a moment he stopped struggling, submerged up to his neck, muscles straining to keep his head back out of the water. It was in that moment that he heard a tiny splash – little more than a ripple – as something lithe and sinuous broke the surface of the water.

In the meagre luminosity of the moss patches Ulysses could not see what it was that was approaching him, but he could see it in his mind's eye all too clearly. His desperate sixth sense, scratching furiously at the inside of his skull, wailed at him from his subconscious.

Something touched his leg and Ulysses kicked out. A wall of water suddenly rose out of the murky flood in front of him. Then, as it cascaded away, the hulking, hideously changed shape was revealed to him, a dark shadow that glistened in the near-impenetrable gloom. Ulysses could make out the outline of its broad, curving shoulders, muscular arms and barrel-like torso. But there was something else, the impression of an equally broad toad-like head, a wide mouth bristling with needle-like teeth. Smooth skin glistened. A hand – fingers more like sucker-tipped tentacles than shredding talons – reached out and stroked Ulysses' face, the languid touch making him shudder in revulsion. He felt the caress of a finned tail against his legs.

Part of Ulysses' subconscious mind, disconnected by the horror and desperation of the moment, reasoned that Professor Galapagos had tracked him down at last, and yet that this was not the same Professor Galapagos he had battled at the edge of the sewer precipice. The damned biologist had changed again, into something soft-bodied, amphibian, newt-like.

But no matter what the truth of the weird science behind it all, Ulysses knew that he was still going to die and resigned himself to his fate.

However, God had clearly decided that it was not yet time for his meeting with the dandy, for it was then that the longed-for miracle came.

A shot rang out through the flooded tunnel, the unreal acoustics of the place giving its echo a strange, otherworldly quality. The amphibian-Galapagos turned, distracted.

There was a second shot. The creature howled – a grotesque wailing hiss, a grisly parody of a voice – and suddenly the Underground station was filled with the noise of splashing, human shouts and half-human yelping.

Something bounded out of the darkness, leaping through the water towards Ulysses, yowling as it did so, all pallid flesh and lank hair flapping around its shoulders. This new arrival sounded as though it was trying to scare the amphibian away, and it was working. The amphibian recoiled, hissing in annoyed retaliation. Then the Neanderthal was on top of it, fists flailing. The toad-creature fought back but the proto-human soon proved itself to be stronger. The Galapagos-amphibian freed itself from the Neanderthal's clutches and, as its attacker lunged again, the apeman determined to trap the huge newt in a crushing bear hug, the creature slipped back under the water and was gone.

Torchlight flickered across the tunnel walls. There was more splashing as another figure strode through the water towards Ulysses.

"Sir," came an acutely cultured voice, the sound of which filled Ulysses with unadulterated relief. "It looks like you could do with a hand."

Ulysses opened his mouth to speak but water rushed in before he could say a word. The tide was still rising.

His faithful manservant reached him in four more strides and, attempting to haul him up out of the water, immediately made an accurate assessment of the situation. It took Nimrod no time at all to take a knife to the knots and free his master, lifting him under his arms and up onto the station platform.

"Just in the nick of time, eh, Nimrod?" Ulysses managed before his body was wracked again by hacking coughs.

"It is a batman's duty, sir. After all, look what happens when you're left to your own devices," Nimrod added, rolling Ulysses onto his side on the cold, wet platform.

The last of the oily water dribbled from the side of Ulysses' mouth. He lay there for a moment, gathering his reserves of strength. "Are you alright Nimrod?"

"Apart from smelling like a blocked drain," the manservant replied, his nose wrinkling, "I suppose so." Nimrod looked as dishevelled and unkempt as Ulysses felt, quite a contrast to his usual impeccable appearance. "A few more shots from my pistol soon sent that despicable lizard-thing running for cover."

"They've got a factory down here, Nimrod. A bloody bomb factory!" Ulysses spluttered between hacking coughs, as his body expelled the rancid water from his lungs, trying to push himself up on his hands. "We've got to shut it down."

"All in good time, sir. You've just narrowly escaped drowning."

Ulysses gave in to the coughing fit seizing his body, and closed his eyes against the pain for a moment. Nimrod was right. The Waterloo operation could wait five minutes. Kane and the Darwinian Dawn wouldn't be going anywhere in a hurry.

There was more splashing and Ulysses opened his eyes to be greeted by a guttural grunt and the lumpen face of the Neanderthal peering at him from the edge of the water channel. He blinked. Its face a gormless mask, the proto-human blinked earnestly back.

"Nimrod," Ulysses croaked, "you appear to have found yourself a friend."

"Yes, sir." Nimrod glanced at the Neanderthal, making no effort to hide his expression of disdain. "It would appear that he – it – followed us down into the sewers after all. I bumped into him – *it!* – again after driving off the saurian, sir. Couldn't get rid of the bally thing after that, and believe me, I tried."

"Why didn't you shoot it then?" Ulysses said, managing a tired smile.

"It would seem that I simply hadn't the heart, sir."

"Fortunately for me, as it would transpire."

"As you say, sir, fortunately for you. It was the brute that tracked you down here. I think it somehow managed to follow your scent, despite the hellish stench of these tunnels."

"And now he's saved me from poor Professor Galapagos's attentions again. Did you see what he's become now, Nimrod?"

"Barely, sir."

"He looks like a ruddy great toad, or a newt or something. There can't be much further for him to travel back down the evolutionary ladder before he's just pond slime."

"So it would seem, sir."

"But anyway," Ulysses said, sitting up and starting to rise to his feet, "back to more pressing matters. The bomb factory."

"Very well, sir."

BY THE TIME Ulysses had led Nimrod back to the station concourse and its wheezing, rattling production line, there was no longer any sign of Jago Kane or the scientist-engineer, Tesla.

"What now, sir?" Nimrod whispered as the two of them peered around a tiled pillar.

"The devices come off that conveyor over there," he said, pointing through the clouds of filthy steam. "If we can find where they're storing them, I think from that point on it would be a relatively straightforward thing to bring an end to this terrorist facility."

"What did you have in mind, sir?" Nimrod asked guardedly.

"Just a few fireworks. Nothing spectacular."

"And how do you suggest we achieve the initial part of your plan?"

"Oh, you know me, Nimrod. I'm making this up as I go along. We need a distraction. Something that will keep those guards off our backs."

There was a grunt from the shadows behind them. The Neanderthal knuckled over to the two men.

"By Jove, Nimrod, I think this fellow here's got the right idea. I think he understands just what we've got in mind."

"You think he can understand more than a few simple phrases?"

"You shouldn't have such low expectations of your new friend. He's not a dog, you know? What do you say, boy?" Ulysses said, turning to the Neanderthal. "Do you think you could cause a bit of a rumpus in there for us?"

The hulking subhuman nodded excitedly, his tongue lolling from his mouth like that of a happy hound.

"Off you go then."

Scampering forwards on all fours the Neanderthal disappeared into the obscuring smog of the factory floor.

"And good luck, eh, old chap?"

It was only a matter of moments before startled shouts of surprise came to their ears followed rapidly by the chatter of sub-automatic gunfire as the Neanderthal swung out of the roiling smoke right into the midst of the Dawn's guards, only to disappear back into the obscuring clouds a moment later.

It was exactly what Ulysses had hoped for.

"Come on, Nimrod. Let's get this party going with a bang!"

"ARE YOU SURE this is a good idea, sir?" Nimrod asked, with the tone of a disapproving schoolmaster, as Ulysses ran his hands over the explosive device on the gurney in front of him. Its hard metal body was a full metre in diameter.

"Don't worry, Nimrod," Ulysses said, flashing a devilish grin. "Remember, I've seen how these things were constructed. Now if I turn this knob here, and then depress this switch here..."

The bomb on the rack in front of him had been silent all the while Ulysses had been examining it. But with the depression of the button an ominous ticking commenced somewhere inside the spiked steel ball.

"Ah, I think it's time we weren't here, Nimrod." Ulysses jumped to his feet.

"I couldn't agree more, sir."

The two men sprinted out of the side passage and back across the concourse, not caring now whether they were seen or not.

Explosions ripped through the station, shaking its very foundations, as one detonation after another tore through the factory, bringing the great conveyor production line to a standstill before blasting the machinery to smithereens. The wreckage of monstrous steam presses was hurled about, along with the shattered remains of automata-workers. The mutant workforce died or fled in panic, Darwinian Dawn troopers and scientists suddenly made equal by the threat of sudden, violent death.

"This way!" Ulysses yelled over the sounds of destruction ringing in their ears. They ran hell-for-leather across the concourse and through the archway underneath the Waterloo sign. They found themselves in a broader exit tunnel. There was another concussive blast behind them and dust and fractured tiles fell from the roof.

It was then that Ulysses' sixth sense screamed a warning. He skidded to a halt. "Nimrod, back!" he shouted. "The roof's about to-" before he could finish his warning, with a yawning heave the roof of the tunnel came down ahead of them.

The two men turned tail, running back the way they had come, back towards the inferno that had taken hold of the factory.

"Bloody hellfire!" Ulysses exclaimed. "Now where?"

"Over there, sir!" Nimrod shouted, pointing back to the archway through which they had entered the factory. The Neanderthal was hunched there, its body smeared with soot, blood running from a number of gashes, but otherwise alive.

Ulysses didn't need any further encouragement. The dandy gentleman investigator and his manservant legged it back across the concourse – dodging falling masonry, throwing up their arms to protect their faces from the fierce heat and flying shrapnel of shattered machines.

As Nimrod joined the Neanderthal beyond the archway, Ulysses stumbled, his foot catching against a fallen scientist. In one hand the man – who was either dead or unconscious – clutched a clipboard, the notes it held sullied with stone dust and soot.

"What have we here?" Ulysses wondered.

"Sir, you must hurry!" Nimrod shouted back over the thunderous rumble of destruction.

"Don't worry about me," he called back, snatching up the clipboard in one hand, "you get yourselves out. I'm right behind you."

And then the three of them – master, servant and Neanderthal – were stumbling back down the steps to the flooded station platform. Their feet splashed into several inches of water, the tidal Thames having risen the level as Jago Kane had said it would. Had the Neanderthal not tracked him down here, Ulysses would have drowned in that same stinking tunnel.

There was another shuddering blast and a fireball of intense ferocity rushed down the stairs after them.

"Into the water!" Ulysses screamed, throwing himself forwards, pushing the subhuman and his manservant into the water ahead of him.

As the water closed over their heads, the flames ignited the pollutant film on its surface.

Ulysses surfaced again, some way further down the tunnel, amidst patches of flame. Nimrod and the Neanderthal both surfaced nearby.

"Nimrod, are you alright?"

His manservant gave him a wet, disgruntled look. "Again, apart from being soaked to the skin and smelling like a petrol sump, yes, sir."

A strong rubbery hand grabbed hold of Ulysses' leg and yanked him sharply back under the water. Lit by the burning pollution on its surface, through the filthy murk Ulysses could see the fish-like features of the amphibian-Galapagos. The professor was persistent, he'd give him that.

For a moment his eyes met the lidless jellied orbs of the altered thing and a startled cry escaped his mouth in a rush of bubbles. Then he was kicking furiously at the creature. He planted a foot squarely between the fish-thing's eyes and the creature's grip went slack.

Ulysses surfaced again, gasping for air, followed almost immediately by the Galapagos thing, breaking the surface in an impressive salmon leap. The monster landed on top of him. Nimrod was shouting behind him, the Neanderthal splashing through the water towards him too, but Ulysses had the creature by the throat now. The tables had been turned.

Another explosion ripped through the tunnel and a fiery wind swept over the water's surface. Shielded from the blast by the creature in front of him, Ulysses witnessed something the like of which he had never known despite all he had seen in his curious life.

With a hideous gulping gasp, like a fishy death-sigh, the creature stopped fighting him and went limp. He could feel his hands sinking into its unnatural flesh as it went soft around them. It felt like he was putting his hands into buckets of cold semolina pudding. And then, quite simply, Professor Galapagos's body collapsed in on itself, the flesh dissolved into slime. Its fish-face mere inches from his own, Ulysses stared into its horrible liquid eyes, unable to tear his gaze away, as those same eyes melted like hot wax.

In mere moments all that was left of the transformed professor were strings of glutinous protoplasmic slime, cooking like frogspawn amidst the burning residue all around them.

Professor Galapagos – or rather the evolutionary-regressing freak that he had become – was gone.

CHAPTER FIFTEEN

On Evolution and the Modern Man

"So, DOCTOR," ULYSSES said, entering the hallway of the old man's house, "how are you?"

Doctor Methuselah blinked from behind the bottle-bottom lenses of his spectacles. Despite having obviously made a supreme effort to uphold his usual high standards of dress, being attired in a crushed blue velvet frock coat, moss green satin waistcoat and lilac cravat, with charcoal grey moleskin trousers, the gentleman adventurer did not seem to be quite the same man who had visited him the previous month. He appeared drawn and tired, his cheeks hollow, his eyes sunken and grey. His skin had a waxy sheen to it.

"Better than you, by the looks of things."

The old man shuffled off along the hallway towards the back of the crumbling house, as decrepit in appearance as its badly aging owner. Ulysses followed. After his sojourn in the sewers he was barely even aware of the malingering odour of stale tobacco smoke. Half the time he still thought he could smell the cesspit-stink of the effluent tunnels.

He might look like death warmed up but it was better than *feeling* like death, which was precisely how he had felt for the last week. His days and nights had been spent vomiting every few hours, reduced to a shaking wreck following relentless barrages of diarrhoea. For all the mental training and physical healing he had received in the highlands of the Himalayas, they did nothing to alleviate the gut-knotting agony this bout of sickness brought. There was nothing he had been able to do but wait it out.

On top of that it had taken half a dozen baths since returning to his Mayfair home, scrubbing himself with industrial cleaner to rid himself of the stink of the sewers, and even now he could still sometimes catch the acrid, bile-taste of the chem-polluted water in the back of his throat.

But on this morning he had actually managed to get out of bed and so, having carried out his ablutions and dressed to impress, bloodstone cane in hand, he had set out to pay a visit to the curmudgeonly Dr Methuselah. And although he didn't want to admit it – least of all to himself – even that simple effort had weakened him.

"So enough of this small talk, what news?"

"I take it you mean the sample."

"Of course." Ulysses tapped the end of his cane impatiently against an overburdened worktable.

"That was a very interesting little project you set me," Methuselah said, powering up his difference engine. There was a hum as the cathode ray tube came to life. "Look at this." He pointed at the grainy, green and black image coming into focus on the screen.

Ulysses realised that there was a Petri dish already in place under the magnifying lenses of Methuselah's brass microscope. The image on the screen was obviously a significantly enlarged image of the contents of that dish. At his last visit Ulysses had at least been able to determine that he was looking at the image of cells projected on the screen. This time, however, he couldn't make out a thing.

"What am I supposed to be looking at, doctor? I can't see anything."

"Precisely."

"What do you mean?"

"There's nothing there to look at."

"But isn't that the sample I gave you?"

"Yes, but that's the point."

"What's the point?" Ulysses suddenly felt incredibly weary. The effort of being up and about was taking its toll more than he had expected. "Doctor, I am tired. Please explain."

The old man grunted, hawking phlegm into the back of his mouth, and pushed his glasses back up his nose with an index finger ingrained with dirt.

"It's like this. I maintained close observation of the tissue sample, as requested. And my initial hypothesis proved, in time, to be correct. What started out as a few hairs first took on the qualities of lizard scales, then the cells mutated into those I would expect to find in an amphibian – the Central American axolotl was the closest match I could find. Towards the end of my observations it became apparent that the process of cellular degradation was accelerating. The sample briefly exhibited piscine characteristics and then it simply dissolved into slime. Look."

Methuselah removed the Petri dish from beneath the microscope and passed it to Ulysses. Where there had once been three reddish-brown hairs there was now what looked like nothing more than a blob of snot.

"What you're looking at is now just so much biological detritus. The only cells in there belong to the bacteria no doubt feasting on that gunk. It's not even protoplasmic slime anymore. Total cellular collapse."

"Do you know what could have caused it?"

"Why, yes." Ulysses looked at the doctor in excited anticipation. "Acute genetic-regression. And I would extrapolate that precisely the same thing happened to the subject the original sample came from. Is that not the case?"

"Evolution and the modern man, eh?"

"You're sure you don't want to tell me where these came from?"

"You know better than to ask," Ulysses chided, remaining tight-lipped. Professor Galapagos might now be dead, having literally turned to slime in Ulysses' hands but this case still qualified as one that was a potential threat to national security.

"Have it your way," Methuselah grumbled. "So, what happened to you? Did you find the errant professor?"

"How do you know about that?" Ulysses said sharply, alarm bells ringing in his mind, suddenly suspicious.

"Don't get your knickers in a twist. You're not the only one with contacts, you know. So, did you?"

"After a fashion."

"What was it like? How did it happen?" Methuselah said, almost slavering at the prospect, his interest having been piqued, his eyes alight with eager, almost boyish, excitement.

Ulysses paused, considering his next words very carefully.

"It was... messy."

"Is that all you're going to give me?"

"That's probably more than I should have told you already," Ulysses muttered, unable to get the image of the overgrown trout-face bearing down on him before turning to milky frogspawn out of his mind. "Now," he said, reaching into a coat pocket and pulling out the curious barbed locket he had recovered from the Galapagos-lizard, "what can you tell me about this?"

GENEVIEVE GALAPAGOS WAS standing in the shadow cast by the gleaming golden Albert Memorial. Ulysses realised, with momentary surprise, that she was wearing a full-length dress, pale cream with a lilac flowery pattern. It was the first time he had ever seen her wear anything other than trousers or jodhpurs. Her luxuriant auburn tresses were gathered together beneath a small bonnet. He felt a rush of warm adrenalin in his chest and let out a sigh. She was strikingly beautiful. And then her eyes met his. She looked so... womanly. Not that she had not looked so before, but her appearance now leant her a vulnerable, feminine quality.

"Ulysses!" she gasped and, despite the restricting nature of the dress, trotted over and flung her arms around him, trapping him in a heartfelt hug. "It's wonderful to see you again." She squeezed him again and then, as if suddenly remembering herself, held him back at arm's length. "Um, I did call but your butler sent me away."

"Yes he did say. I was sorry not to be able to see you, my dear," Ulysses felt an earnest need to apologise, "but I was... indisposed."

"So I understand. Nimrod said that you had been through quite an ordeal."

"Yes, you could say that. But it's in the hands of the police now."

Much as he resented having to pass the operation into the hands of Inspector Allardyce, Ulysses knew when a situation demanded more than merely he was capable of. He was still intermittently suffering from the dysentery that he had picked up following his foray into London's murky underworld. But the escapade had brought its own benefits as well; the paperwork he had been able to salvage from the clipboard he had rescued from the burning factory, for one thing.

It was amazing that he had been able to salvage anything at all, considering that the papers had been scorched and then submerged in water as Ulysses, Nimrod and the Neanderthal had made their escape from the flooded Underground, which had necessitated allowing themselves to be sucked through an overflow pipe that ejected them into the Thames.

After some careful scrutiny, the documents had revealed a crucial part of the terrible plan the Darwinian Dawn had for the capital. They had been intending to use the old Underground network to position the deadly explosive devices they had been developing throughout the city. Had they succeeded in completing their task the cost to the city in terms of collateral damage, as well as the cost in human life, would have been catastrophic. The death toll could easily have been in the thousands, if not the tens of thousands.

But thanks to Ulysses' timely discovery, their plans had been irrevocably set back and even though it was suspected that a number of the devices had already been put in place, so far none had detonated. With the authorities now in possession of information as useful as a map, having reluctantly already reported his findings regarding the bomb plot to Inspector Allardyce, Scotland Yard had raced to mount a top priority security operation to recover all of the devices. It looked like matters would be brought to a resolution in time for the Queen's jubilee.

"To think what you went through!" Genevieve exclaimed.

Ulysses smiled. Despite being every inch the ladies' man, there was something innocent and disarming about the genuine affection and concern Genevieve was showing him. It made what he had to tell her all the harder.

"I'm all the better for seeing you. Walk with me?"

"But of course," Genevieve took his proffered arm. "What is it, Ulysses? Your manner is causing me concern."

The two of them set off, strolling along beneath the beech trees, joining other promenaders, dog-walkers and penny-farthing enthusiasts in their tour of Hyde Park.

"I have news concerning your father."

Genevieve stopped. "I knew you would have. I was too afraid to ask." She looked at him again, her eyes shaded beneath the rim of her parasol. "It's not good news, is it?"

"No, I'm afraid not."

Genevieve's chin dropped and she gave a sob of heartfelt sorrow.

"I'm so sorry, Genevieve, I really am. If there had been anything I could have done I would have, you have to believe that. We found him in..."

"No, don't tell me. I don't want to know. My father died that night at the museum, the night of the robbery. Whatever he had become after that, it was not my father. Not anymore."

And then she gave in to her tears. Ulysses held her close, Genevieve sobbing into the lapel of his frock coat.

It had not been so hard in the end. As Genevieve herself had once told him, he was a champion of the truth and no matter how painful the truth might be, it should be known so that it could be faced up to.

Neither of them cared that the eyes of half the promenaders in the park were on them. For them there was only their shared grief. Genevieve mourning the loss of the father she had never really known, and for Ulysses the knowledge that he had been responsible for causing her such heart-rending sadness.

Eventually she eased herself away from him, blinking the tears from her reddened, puffy eyes. She could not look him in the face.

"Here," he said, putting his hand into his coat and removing something from a pocket. "I have this for you."

He opened his hand. There lay the locket Genevieve had told him she had once given to her father as a gift. A smile of incongruous delight broke through her sorrow-spoiled features. Her bottom lip started to quiver as she took the silvered object, clean now of the muck that had tarnished it on its journey through the sewers.

She reached up, putting a soft hand to Ulysses' face, caressing his cheek with delicate fingers. "Thank you," she whispered.

And then, before Ulysses really knew it, they were closer than they had ever been before, her lips only inches from his, her breath warm on his face. The air was heady with the scent of jasmine flowers, the ground beneath their feet dappled with the golden light filtering through the leafy branches, despite the ever-present smog over the city.

He held that moment in his head, that perfect moment when nothing else but the anticipation of the kiss to come mattered.

"We aren't close to any Overground lines here are we? Or dinosaurs?"

Genevieve smiled, her tear-stained cheeks flushed red, and she pulled him closer.

"Now, now, Mr Quicksilver," she chided. "Do you always put work before pleasure?"

And then they kissed.

CHAPTER SIXTEEN

A Night at the Opera

"So, DO YOU think you'll see this woman again?" Bartholomew Quicksilver asked, tucking into his plate of roast pheasant with such gusto that it rather implied that this was the first decent meal he had enjoyed for some time.

"I don't know," Ulysses mused, looking up from his plate. "I would certainly like to, at least I think I would, but I rather suspect that the ball, as they say, is now in her court. But enough about me. How have you been since I last saw you, dear brother?" This last acerbic comment did not sound quite like the enquiry after his brother's health as the wording of it might have suggested.

"About that," Bartholomew said, his face reddening.

"And what would *that* be?"

"Look, don't make this harder than it already is."

"Why not? You were certainly planning on making it quite hard for me, all things considered."

"Look, you have to believe me. I didn't know you were still alive."

"Patently."

There was silence between the two of them for a minute.

"Go on, then. With your excuse, I mean." Ulysses had to admit that part of him was enjoying watching his brother squirm.

For a moment Bartholomew struggled to find the words he needed to express himself. The hubbub of the Savoy rushed in to fill the vacuum left by his reticence.

The dining room was a sea of hazy lamplight, interspersed with the circular tables of the diners. For a moment Ulysses could almost believe that he had returned to his former life of evening revels and outrageous parties.

He shook the memory from his mind. That seemed a lifetime away now. Besides, he felt an ambivalent mix of rival emotions, both purposeful resolve and nervous anticipation at the same time. Resolve at needing to confront his brother and nervous as to the effect the rich food in front of him might have on his body. It was the first full meal he had eaten since rising from his sick bed.

"Look, I acted too hastily. I know that now. But you have to realise that there had been no word from you or any sign of you for eighteen months. I thought you were dead. The *world* thought you were dead. Would you have had me wait indefinitely for you to return?"

"And what would you say if I answered your obviously rhetorical question with a 'yes'?"

"I'd say you were being pig-headed, just like you always were when we were boys and Nanny wouldn't let you get your own way."

For a moment both of them sat in seething silence again.

"But look, let's put all that in the past now, shall we?' Bartholomew ventured, at last facing up to the fact that it was going to have to be up to him to proffer the olive branch. For all the grovelling he was being made to do, Bartholomew might as well have been eating humble pie rather than roast pheasant. Taking up his wine glass, he gestured as if to make a toast.

"To you, eh, Ulysses? No hard feelings?"

Almost reluctantly Ulysses picked up his own glass.

"No, to us, Barty, heirs to the Quicksilver name," he said, and knocked back the last of the Pinot Grigio.

The hubbub of the Savoy returned and the two brothers finished the rest of their main course in a tolerable silence.

"How's business?" the younger asked at last.

"Oh, you know, a matter of life and death on a daily basis. How's the world of profit and loss, and fund management?"

Bartholomew eyed his elder brother coldly. 'Fund management' was a coy euphemism for a compulsive gambling habit of which Ulysses was fully aware. He also knew what sort of situations his brother had gambled himself into over the years, which was why he guarded the rest of his family's fortune with such care.

Ulysses met the younger man's stare, his brother quickly wilting under the sun-fierce gaze and suddenly finding something to occupy his attention on the tablecloth in front of him.

"Well?"

"Oh, you know how it is."

"Yes, I rather think I do. Still planning on leaving the capital, or even the planet, anytime soon?"

"Hmm. Funds won't stretch that far."

"Now why doesn't that surprise me I wonder," Ulysses said witheringly, shaking his head in disappointment at his feckless brother's mismanagement of his share of their father's legacy.

"I wasn't going to bring it up," Barty said, an uncomfortably familiar wheedling whine entering his voice, "but as you've seen fit to raise the matter yourself, if you could shout me some cash – consider it a loan – I could purchase my passage on a lunar liner and be out of your way at last, dear brother."

"And what would you do once you got to the moon?"

"I've got a few job prospects lined up there, one out at Serenity, another couple of possibles in Luna Prime. You know, friend of a friend kind of things."

"Yes, I know the kind of thing. And I know the sort of people you curiously choose to call friends."

"Now, don't start, Ulysses."

"Well, you said it. If you're not going to look out for yourself, who else will, if not me?"

"You're not father, you know."

Ulysses was quiet for a moment, as if wrong-footed by his brother's riposte. "Yes, I know."

"How's your dinner?" Bartholomew said, obviously uncomfortable and trying to change the topic.

"Well, the warm roasted wood pigeon salad with black truffle sauce was barely warm and the pigeon not as tender as I would have liked. The wine is not to my palate, the company tolerable. Let's hope the dessert is something more worthy of writing home about. Although, whatever the final outcome of this entire dining experience, I rather suspect that I'll be made to suffer for my excess in the morning."

"I'm sorry I asked," Barty said miserably.

The awkward silence returned.

Neither of them said anything as a waiter cleared their plates away, topped up their wine glasses and then brought them their desserts. Ulysses' chocolate torte was more to his liking, although even as he savoured the last mouthful he rather regretted such a rich choice of dessert.

He put down his fork and looked at his forlorn brother. Despite being the younger of the two of them, and despite all that Ulysses had been through, Barty looked to be the more harassed and careworn by life. A curl of hair had come free and hung in front of his eyes. His shoulders looked bowed as if the weight of the world rested upon them. His skin had an unhealthy pallor to it and his red-rimmed eyes belied a lack of sleep. "When was the last time you ate a meal like that? Come to think of it, when did you last get a decent night's sleep?" he asked.

"What do you care?" Barty riled at his brother's condescending tone.

"Of course I care, you ungrateful wretch," Ulysses sighed. "Anyway, this dinner was supposed to be a reconciliation. Let's not fight anymore. I have enough enemies in this world without my brother being one of them. What's done is done, and there's been no real harm as a result either. Pax?"

Ulysses offered his hand across the table. Bartholomew maintained his grumpy demeanour for a few moments more before relenting.

"Pax," he agreed and the two brothers shook.

"Now let's settle up here or we're going to be late for curtain up."

Ulysses summoned a waiter. "Can I get you anything else, sir? Coffee? Liqueurs?"

"Just the bill," Ulysses said.

"Ah, about that too."

Ulysses gave his brother a withering look. "It's on me, as usual," Bartholomew visibly relaxed, "as is tonight's performance of Puccini. Now let's get out of here."

DINNER PAID FOR, the Quicksilver brothers left the Savoy and made their way to the Covent Garden Opera House, there to join the expectant throng awaiting that night's performance of Madame Butterfly. The opera lasted a barely tolerable three hours, at the end of which the two brothers departed the auditorium, with a feeling akin to what it must be like to be released from a stay in prison.

"How did you find it?" Barty asked as the two of them made their way across the cobbled forecourt in front of the Opera House.

"About as good as the meal beforehand," Ulysses said cuttingly.

"That bad?" Bartholomew laughed. He appeared significantly more relaxed than he had during dinner. The two double whiskys during the interval had helped, of course.

"Perhaps not that bad. Although, to my mind, the character of a nubile, teenage Japanese *geisha* girl should not really be played by a middle-aged soprano with a figure like a circus wrestler, and the body hair to match."

His brother laughed heartily. "I know what you mean. And the dashing young lieutenant looked like he'd be out of breath dashing for an omnibus!"

"You're right there, Barty, old chap."

"Is one supposed to *enjoy* opera?"

"No, I don't think so. It's just one of those tiresome things one must be seen to do if one is to be received into polite society – rather like plucking one's eyebrows or visiting the dentist. I only partake myself because it is part of the social high life and it is good for one to be seen to be doing such things. I just wanted to go – having not been for so long – to confirm to myself how bad it is. And, of course, the ladies love it! Now then, back to mine for a nightcap? Nimrod should have the Phantom parked around here somewhere."

"Yes, why not?"

The subconscious warning came like a burst of lightning in his brain even as the shot rang out, echoing like a thunderclap from the close-packed buildings that lined the square. He had no conscious idea of where the threat lay, only that he must move.

Ulysses lurched sideways. There was the report of a second shot. Barty gasped as if he had been plunged into an ice cold bath. He slumped forwards, Ulysses caught him, stopping him from falling flat on his face on the cobbles.

"Barty? Barty!" he cried, easing his brother down onto the ground. He was barely aware of the cries of panic around him.

"I-I've been shot," Bartholomew gasped. "Bloody hell, I've been shot!"

Ulysses carried out a hasty assessment, fully aware of the fact that there was a sniper still scoping their position from somewhere on the rooftops nearby. His brother was shaking whilst blood oozed from the newly made hole in the shoulder of his jacket.

"Try to stay calm," Ulysses said, keeping his voice low so as not to heighten his brother's state of anxiety.

"Stay calm? I've been bloody shot!"

"Look, you're in shock." Ulysses whipped off his jacket and draped it over his brother's prone body.

"Of course I'm in shock. I keep trying to tell you, I've bloody well been shot!"

"If you don't shut up, I'll shoot you myself!"

Ulysses scanned the tops of the surrounding buildings, trying to glimpse anything that might reveal the position of the would-be assassin – the reflection of a streetlamp from a gun barrel, a shudder of movement as the gunman adjusted his position – anything at all.

The bullet had been meant for him, he was sure of it. Of course, when he considered the sort of company his brother kept and factored in the debts he doubtless owed, it was possible that the gunman had really been targeting him but Ulysses' sixth sense had warned him of the danger *he* had been about to face.

Two shots. Anyone attempting an assassination would like as not be using a rifle with two cartridges in the chamber. They would not risk reloading unless they were prepared to give their position away. Right now, the sniper would be putting a previously prepared getaway plan into operation.

There was the sound of someone running across the cobbles towards them. It was Nimrod.

"I heard the gunshots, sir. Are you alright?"

"I am but Barty's been hit. Will you take care of things here?"

"Of course, sir."

"I have a gunman to catch."

As Nimrod rested Bartholomew's head against his knees, Ulysses patted his brother gently on his shoulder. "No hard feelings, eh, Barty?" And with that he hared off across the plaza.

After hearing the second shot, and considering the angle of trajectory of the bullet that had hit Bartholomew, Ulysses judged that the gunman had been hunkered down on the rooftops of the buildings on the south side of the square.

He sprinted across the cobbles, barging past drunken fops and London's social elite making their way home. As he ran, senses straining for any clues as to where the gunman might have gone, Ulysses' mind was awhirl as he considered the identity of the would-be assassin. Who could it be, and how long had the marksman been trailing him? Was it Jago Kane, surfacing again to put paid to his old adversary once and for all? Ulysses had his doubts about that; it wasn't Kane's style. And although Ulysses had made a fair few enemies in his somewhat chequered career as a soldier of fortune and agent of the crown, he was pretty certain that whoever the gunman was, he was like as not working for the Darwinian Dawn. Whether he was an agent of the terrorist organisation or simply a hit man hired to off the dandy adventurer after he had set back their plans, Ulysses was sure of his connection with the enemy.

But in the end, as he ran down an adjoining street towards the Strand, he had to admit that his pursuit was futile. He didn't even know if he *was* pursuing anyone. He could have been haring off in completely the wrong direction. The cowardly gunman had both the city and the night on his side. The two working together to swallow him up and hide him in mundane normality.

Ulysses was aware that his footsteps sounded incongruously loud as they rang from the pavement, passers-by watching his mad dash with incredulous, slack-jawed curiosity. With a snarl of frustration he came to a stop in a pool of wan light cast by a crackling street light. His acute sixth sense was quiet again. The danger had passed, for the time being, but Ulysses knew that it would not be long before jeopardy and peril came calling again.

His blood boiled in his veins, becoming the bitter bile of rage in his stomach. His brother might be a useless, good-for-nothing compulsive gambler with an unlucky streak a mile long, but he was Ulysses' little brother nonetheless, and, as such, his responsibility.

Whoever the secret assassin had been, he had failed in his mission. Ulysses was still alive. And for as long as that was the case there would inevitably be another attempt on his life. He would have to remain vigilant at all times, or pay the ultimate price.

CHAPTER SEVENTEEN

Revelations

"Excuse me, sir, but will there be anything else?"

Ulysses Quicksilver looked up from the copy of *The Times* he was perusing. Nimrod was standing in the doorway to the mahogany-panelled study. Standing there so rigid and so formal. Back in his grey suit, with his sharp, aquiline features he bore all the characteristics of the grandfather clock that was tolling hauntingly in the atrium hallway behind him.

Ulysses glanced at the brandy glass on the desk in front of him, a slosh of the amber fire still in the bottom of it. He checked his pocket watch despite there being the ormolu clock ticking on the mantelpiece behind him.

"No, it's alright, thank you, Nimrod."

"If you don't mind, then sir, I think I shall retire for the night. It feels like it has been a particularly long day."

"I know what you mean, old chap. I know what you mean."

It was not only Ulysses who had been beset by illness following their escapades through the sewers. Although they had both now been given a clean bill of health they had been left fatigued by their bout of sickness. Nimrod was never one to make a fuss about his own state of health but Ulysses could see the weariness in his eyes, even though his posture was as upright and unbending as ever. Of course the faithful family retainer wasn't a young man anymore. In fact, the silver-haired butler had never been a young man in Ulysses' eyes, ever since he was a young boy growing up in the Mayfair townhouse.

"Oh, Nimrod," Ulysses said suddenly, causing his butler to turn. "Is Barty asleep?"

"Yes, sir. I had his old room made up."

"Yes, I think it better that he remain with us for the time being. Just until we sort this mess out. For his own safety, you understand."

"As you wish. Now, if you don't mind, sir?"

"No, not at all, Nimrod. You get off to bed."

Ulysses returned his attention to the broadsheet in front of him. The butler turned to leave again.

"Oh, I meant to ask," Ulysses said, looking up from his paper again. Nimrod paused once more, a nasal sigh escaping his flaring nostrils. "How's Simeon finding the boot room?"

"You mean the apeman, sir?"

"Yes, Nimrod, our guest. Has he stopped eating the shoe polish yet?"

"I've confiscated the last few tins so that I can maintain standards, sir, and keep the footwear in good order. But yes, the monkey has made himself quite at home in the boot room, sir."

"Now now, Nimrod, he's not a monkey. He's merely an ancestor of the human race. The boot room is opposite your room, is it not?"

"Precisely, sir. It would appear that the coach house was not to his liking, despite being a far superior habitat than the one we originally found him in."

"I think you've made a friend there, Nimrod."

"Hmm," Nimrod replied non-committally. "I thought one was supposed to be able to choose one's friends, sir. It's one's family that one has no say in."

"Well I suppose he is family, after a fashion. Think of him as a very distant relation," Ulysses said with a smile.

"Yes, very amusing, sir. Do you know how long our house guests will be staying, sir?"

"For the foreseeable future, I would say."

"Very well, sir," Nimrod conceded morosely. "Might I ask why you insist on calling the apeman Simeon, sir?"

"The name seemed to suit him, that's all. And besides, if he's going to be part of polite society he needs a name, doesn't he. It will help him appear more – what's the word I'm looking for? – civilised."

"I would suggest that he might appear more civilised, sir, if I could persuade him to wear some clothes. Mrs Prufrock has altered an old suit of her husband's especially. Now, if there's nothing else?" Nimrod said tartly.

"No, I don't think so. Sorry to have kept you. You should turn in for the night. I won't be up much longer myself. I just need to wind down after our rather exciting night at the opera."

"I understand, sir. Good night."

"Good night, Nimrod."

The manservant hesitated. He was quite clearly looking at the large portrait hanging above the mantelpiece and yet there was a far away look in his piercing sapphire eyes. Ulysses couldn't remember ever seeing Nimrod look so vulnerable and open.

"Something troubling you, Nimrod?"

"I was just thinking, sir. You look so like your father."

"Indeed, it has been said before."

Nimrod turned and left the study.

Ulysses returned to the papers arrayed before him on the desk. But he was distracted, considering Simeon's nature once again and, by extension, the nature of mankind in an evolutionary context. It was humbling indeed to be in such close proximity to one's ancestors.

Had Simeon always been as he was now, an example of one of the previously thought lost tribes of proto-humans that had been found to still exist in some of the most remote parts of the world? Or had he been the unfortunate subject of one of Galapagos's sinister experiments, considering what had befallen the evolutionary biologist himself? It appeared that there was no way of knowing and, if the latter was the case, it was highly unlikely that they would ever discover the real identity of the poor wretch who had somehow devolved into the creature that was now Ulysses' house guest. Professor Ignatius Galapagos had turned out to be a very different man to the dedicated scholar and devoted father Ulysses had at first taken him to be. Very different indeed.

The sound of Nimrod's leather heels on the polished floors of the house receded into its shadowy depths. Ulysses listened to the *tap, tap, tapping* of his servant's footfalls whilst the subconscious part of his mind turned over the myriad thoughts that rose from the fathomless depths like great leviathans, immeasurable, terrifying and dark.

Ulysses finished off the last drop of his cognac, closed his eyes and savoured the fumy tang on his tongue before swallowing. Dreamily he opened his eyes, his gaze falling on the pages of *The Times* spread out in front of him. Scattered across the desk, amidst the carefully selected articles, were various pieces of the last few days' post, some as yet unopened. They included a letter from the firm of Mephisto, Fanshaw and Screwtape, an invitation to join the maiden voyage of a new sub-ocean liner, and something from the Cats Protection League asking for his support.

Ulysses ran his eyes over the articles, his attention flitting from one set of column inches to another, as he absent-mindedly ran the blade of his letter-opener under the sealed tab of a crisp, white envelope.

One bold banner headline read, 'Wormwood Wins Terror Debate' and another, 'Anti-Terror Bill Passed'. So, mused Ulysses as he extracted the folded piece of headed paper from the envelope, Wormwood had got his way. The bill that he had championed and pushed through Parliament had been passed by both the Commons and the House of Lords. But, Ulysses wondered, did those who had voted in its favour realise fully the implications of the new law that effectively permitted one man to take charge of not only the government, but also the country and hence the Empire, should a state of emergency arise?

But of course the politicians must have realised. So in that case, what was in it for them? Ulysses was fully cognisant of the Machiavellian workings of the British Government and the nature of those who sought election to that exclusive gentleman's club. They must have good reason to believe that the intentions of the man into whose control that self-same bill would put the whole country were honourable. But then perhaps they didn't know Uriah Wormwood like Ulysses Quicksilver did. Or maybe they did, and their votes had simply been secured by other, uncomplicated means, such as threatening their lives, the lives of their loved ones or by threatening to air their dirty laundry for them in public.

Ulysses glanced at the letter now in his hands. It was another begging letter from the Chelsea branch of the Women's Institute – who were obviously aware of his existence again following his very public David and Goliath struggle with the rampaging megasaur – asking him to speak about his adventures in the Himalayas at one of their forthcoming tea and cake get-togethers.

He turned a few pages of the paper in front of him, skimming them for anything of particular interest. With the Galapagos case tied up, he would have to start looking for another paying job soon. He doubted Wormwood would be in need of his services in quite the same way as he previously had.

The news items he gleaned from the papers gave him a curious snapshot of the capital of the Magna Britannian empire in the dying days of the twentieth century. Apparently some of the escaped dinosaurs from the Challenger Enclosure were still managing to evade capture. A petition had been sent to 10 Downing Street, and copied to Scotland Yard, asking what the new Prime Minister was going to do about the reptilians' anti-social behaviour. Ulysses wondered for a moment whether he should consider branching out into big game hunting, but then quickly dismissed the idea.

There was also a piece about the luxury passenger liner *The Neptune*, which would be setting off on its inaugural cruise around the world from Southampton that summer – Ulysses glanced again at the invitation he had been sent, it was the same vessel – and another article regarding the health of the industrialist and amateur naturalist, Josiah Umbridge.

'Jubilee to go ahead as planned' a spokesman for Buckingham Palace had apparently told a reporter. The preparations for the extravaganza appeared to have been upped a notch or two, since Wormwood had come to the office of Prime Minister and following the Darwinian Dawn's terror attacks. Funnily enough, Ulysses thought, with a wry smile, there had been no further broadcasts or public announcements from the terrorist group or any further attacks on London since Ulysses had brought about the destruction of their bomb production plant. Apparently the jubilee celebration and day-long parades were to conclude with a gala dinner, to be held in the re-built Crystal Palace in Hyde Park.

Beneath the article detailing the arrangements for the celebrations, which marked another decade in Victoria's long reign of more than a century and a half, Ulysses' eyes alighted on a much less obvious, almost secondary consideration of an article title. In fact, it was not so much a headline as a question:

'Anti-social behaviour a thing of the past?'

Ulysses read on. Apparently 'an eminent scientist' was conducting 'exciting and ground-breaking experiments' into 'behaviour adjustment' on inmates at London's maximum-security prison, the Tower of London.

"Not another one," Ulysses found himself saying out loud. He was sure that Professor Galapagos's experiments would have been considered 'exciting' and 'ground-breaking' as opposed to 'unnecessary' and 'cruel'. He was certain the moniker 'eminent scientist' would have been used as well, rather than 'malicious misguided genius' or 'sinister sadist'.

There was a box-shaped package amongst the post. Ulysses took up this item now. At the same time his eye caught a small piece at the bottom of the page – his subconscious having made the connection – no more than three column inches. 'Eminent Evolutionary Biologist Still Missing' the title read. There was that word again, 'eminent'. It appeared that the reporters at *The Times* were in need of a new thesaurus.

The package was approximately eight inches along every vertex and wrapped in unassuming brown paper. His name and address had been written on one face but there was no stamp. It must have been hand delivered. He would have to ask Nimrod who had visited that morning.

Ulysses gave the box a gentle shake. There was a muffled rattle inside. The weight of it in his hands made him think that the enclosed object must be made of metal. Placing the package carefully back on top of his desk he began to undo the brown paper, glancing back to the article as his fingers worked on the package.

The piece reported that Professor Ignatius Galapagos had been missing since his office at the Natural History Museum had been broken into and ransacked weeks ago. It also mentioned – without shedding any more light on the true extent of his work – that he had been carrying out research into the evolutionary path that connected man with his distant, primitive forebears.

The article reported some of the facts but, Ulysses thought – a wry smile on his lips as he did so – it didn't report the whole story. One day he would have to write his memoirs chronicling his weird and wonderful adventures, revealing the truth behind dozens of allegedly 'unsolved' mysteries. It would be a best seller, if anyone were prepared to believe that the stories he had to tell were true. Would any editor ever believe half of what he had experienced? Perhaps it would be better to publicise his tales as a work of fiction, just in case. But some of the people Ulysses worked for might not appreciate such candour from one of their employees. He wondered how much more his clandestine masters in Whitehall knew than he did himself.

Ulysses folded back a flap of paper. A card had been slipped in between the folds of the package. The message on it had been written in a delicate, feminine hand. Ulysses' cheeks reddened as he read the four simple words.

'From Genevieve, with love.'

Carefully, he put the card to one side. As he did so, his eyes momentarily focused on a particular sentence towards the bottom of the article about the 'missing' professor.

In the event of confirmation of Galapagos's death, his estate will be sold and the monies raised given to trustees of the Natural History Museum, that his ground-breaking work might continue, Galapagos being unmarried and having no heirs to follow after him.

He was suddenly sharply aware of the ticking of the ormolu clock on the mantelpiece behind him. It was answered by a ticking from the package on the desk.

IN THE MOMENT before the explosion it was as if there was a sudden absence of noise. Then a horrendous cacophony rushed into the vacuum, as the windows at the southeast corner of the house blew out in a hurricane of flame. Curtains were blown outwards by the blast, wooden casements splintered and the ground shook, as millions of tiny shards of glass rained down into the street like diamond shrapnel.

Obscured by the shadows of a darkened alleyway on the opposite side of the road a lone figure watched, unmoving, as the explosion tore through the dandy's study.

As the echoing roar faded it was replaced by the plink of cooling stone, the sound of glass cracking under the heat of the flames and the hungry snarling of the fire itself.

A limousine – no registration and ministerial black – pulled up in the street opposite the alley and the figure stepped out of the shadows. A tress of auburn hair shook loose from the tight bun at the back of her head. A tweed suit that was all the rage amongst London's younger, more daring, fashionable circles, accentuated the curves of a toned, womanly body.

The front passenger door of the car opened and the woman climbed inside, plus fours and suede leather boots giving definition to shapely, athletic legs.

The young woman closed the door. In the darkness of the car's interior she turned to the driver and flashed him her winning smile. Jago Kane smiled back, the bisecting scar turning the expression into a savage sneer.

"Mission accomplished, my dear Genevieve?" a refined voice said from the back seat of the car, oozing self-satisfaction. "Or should I say, Kitty?"

Somewhere, away across London, sirens were sounding. London's fire brigade was already on its way.

Genevieve Galapagos turned round in the leather-upholstered seat and fixed the elder statesman behind her with her striking gaze.

"But of course, Mr Wormwood," she said, her tone flirtatious, soft as velvet, rich as chocolate. "Kitty Hawke always gets her man."

With that the car pulled out into the street and away from the burning town house.

ACT THREE

Theories of De-Evolution

June 1997

CHAPTER EIGHTEEN

Death of a Dandy

PHILANTHROPIST ADVENTURER DIES IN HOUSE FIRE

IT IS WITH *great regret that we report the death of philanthropist Ulysses Lucian Quicksilver, following a freak gas explosion at his home on Thursday night. Quicksilver recently returned to the headlines after an absence of almost a year and a half following the catastrophic break-out of prehistoric monsters from the Challenger Enclosure at London Zoo last May. This the first in a series of terrorist attacks by the self-styled evolutionary revolutionaries, the Darwinian Dawn. During the dinosaur debacle Quicksilver played a significant role in the suppression of the stampede, bringing down a fully-grown adult megasaur single-handedly.*

Ulysses Quicksilver had been missing presumed dead since October 1995, following his disappearance during an attempt to cross the Himalayan mountain range by hot air balloon. Only a few days before the Challenger Incident, as the authorities have now labelled the first of the many atrocities perpetrated by the Darwinian Dawn, Quicksilver turned up alive and well at his London residence.

Sources with connections to Scotland Yard have reported that Quicksilver had been helping the authorities with their investigation into the death of a watchman at the Natural History Museum during the break-in there, as previously reported by this paper. A spokesman for the Metropolitan Police, one Inspector Allardyce, told our reporter that there were no suspicious circumstances surrounding Quicksilver's tragic death and that Scotland Yard do not believe it is in any way connected to the Natural History Museum case. The inspector also said that an inquiry would not be held into the circumstances surrounding the accident.

Quicksilver was at his Mayfair home on Thursday night, having enjoyed dinner at the Savoy earlier that same evening followed by a visit to the Covent Garden Opera House to see Webber's production of Puccini's Madame Butterfly. No one else was injured as a result of the explosion or the subsequent fire, despite there being several other people in the house at the time, including Quicksilver's own brother.

Ulysses Quicksilver, eldest son of the late, great colonial hero Hercules Quicksilver and Lady Amelia Quicksilver, daughter of the Marquis of Malhembury, made regular appearances on the London social scene before his disappearance over the Himalayas and had been connected with many of London society's most eligible heiresses, although he never married.

Quicksilver was educated first at Eton, then Oxford University, where he studied social anthropology, following in the footsteps of many of his family before him, including both his father and grandfather. On graduating from Oxford he joined the Royal Dragoons, during which time he saw action in both India and the Crimea, and having completed a three-year Grand Tour of the Solar System he became better known for his socialising and womanising ways than for the heroic deeds of derring-do.

Following the death of his father in 1975 he inherited the entirety of the Quicksilver estate, which, as well as the town house in Mayfair where he met his death, included residences in the Warwickshire countryside, the Highlands of Scotland, and villas in Tuscany and the south of France. He also took on the mantle of philanthropist adventurer and was the most recent in a long line of famous supporters of the British crown from his celebrated family, amongst them his great-great-uncle who was involved in the creation of the Empress Engine.

His many achievements include holding the record for the Paris-Dakar rally for eight years running and re-discovering the lost civilisation of the Kuwato in Indonesia.

Ulysses Quicksilver, who was thirty-seven when he died, leaves no issue and is survived by his brother Bartholomew who stands to inherit the entirety of the substantial Quicksilver estate.

URIAH WORMWOOD CAREFULLY folded the newspaper shut and placed it with precision on the desk in front of him. He sat back in his leather-upholstered chair, steepling his bony fingers before his face, and breathed in sharply through his nose. A languid lizard's smile creased his lips as his eyes took in the décor of his private chambers at Number 10 Downing Street, his thoughts on Quicksilver's untimely demise.

Well at least that was one less fly in the ointment. Quicksilver had started to become an uncomfortable thorn in the newly appointed Prime Minister's side.

Wormwood picked up his whisky, sniffing it with all the finesse of a connoisseur of the finer things in life as he put the rim of the glass to his lips. He glanced down at the paper again.

Towards the bottom of the lead article, regarding the growing excitement centring on the preparations for the Queen's Jubilee, a source from within the Queen's household had stated that the monarch herself would be making an uncommon public appearance.

The Times had made a great deal of fuss regarding Quicksilver's part in the Challenger Incident. That was one of the things he would put right, as soon as the opportunity arose. He couldn't stand such hero-worship and glory-mongering by the press. *The Times* was supposed to be one of the pillars of British society, along with high tea and cricket, and therefore was one of the benchmarks by which the rest of the world assessed their own achievements. Yet, of late it seemed to Wormwood that it was fast going downmarket, until it was little better than the rest of the gutter press of Fleet Street. But that would all change once the final act in this play of Machiavellian machinations – of which he was playwright, director and principal actor – was put into action.

The aftermath of the Challenger Incident was still lingering within the column inches, like the smell of festering dino-flesh. Some of the smaller saurians released by the Darwinian Dawn's attack were still at large within the capital. The latest press on the matter regarded the breeding colony of pterodactyls that had broken free of the Roxton Aviary. The flying reptiles had since taken to roosting on Tower Bridge and harassing passers-by. Questions had been raised in the House, as well as in the broadsheets, as to what the authorities were going to do about the problem.

It was also reported that it would take months for essential repairs at the zoo to be completed, as many of the animal pens and cages would have to be entirely rebuilt. There were some doom-mongers who were spreading the rumour that the whole debacle would bankrupt the zoo and that it would have to close permanently unless the government baled out its owners. In the meantime many of the animals, including certain prehistoric exhibits, had been moved to other zoological gardens around the country including Whipsnade and Longleat.

There were three precise knocks on Wormwood's office door.

"Come," the Prime Minister said imperiously.

A robotic servant, its metal chassis sculpted and painted to make it look like it was wearing a butler's black suit and starched, white wing-collar shirt, entered at his behest.

"Yes, Harcourt?"

"Your guests have arrived, Mr Wormwood sir," the automaton-flunkey said with a mechanical wheeze.

"Then show them in."

The robo-servant exited again, pulling the door to behind him. Wormwood leant forward in his chair, gripping the arms with his porcelain-fine fingers so that the knuckles showed hard and white. His released his grip, only for a moment, to tuck a stray strand of lank grey hair behind one ear.

The door opened and the servile Harcourt-droid admitted the two visitors.

"Kitty, my dear," Wormwood said. "You are – how can I put this tactfully – late. I do hope that you are not in the habit of being tardy. Kane," he nodded at the revolutionary who acknowledged the Prime Minister with a sneer.

Kitty Hawke, until only recently Miss Genevieve Galapagos the imaginary daughter of Professor Ignatius Galapagos, fixed Wormwood with the dark orbs of her eyes, her lips pinching into an aggressive pout. "In case you hadn't noticed from here in your ivory tower, I have been immensely busy making sure that our mutual plans come to fruition," Kitty protested petulantly.

"Small cogs, my dear... mere cogs in the machine. And I would have you show me some respect." Wormwood snarled. "I had enough of that sort of... defiance from that imperious upstart Quicksilver."

"I would have thought that you would have at least been a little more understanding considering that Quicksilver is now dead."

"Don't get me wrong, my dear. I am delighted at the demise of that dandy adventurer. I had grown tired of his insolent attempts at witty repartee. But I cannot forget that, thanks to his meddling, he has forced us to modify our plans at this late stage in... proceedings. Talking of cogs in the machine and being ready in time, how are things progressing at the Tower? Is the good doctor ready to advance to the next stage of the plan?"

"I am pleased to inform you that the formula has been successfully reproduced by the team at the secondary facility," Kitty said, trying to recover some of her lost composure, hoping that the good news she brought might help her save some face following Wormwood's patriarchal chiding, "now that we have been able to access data stored within the late professor's difference engine."

"So, as I understand it, the locket was the key all along," Wormwood said, looking pointedly at the gruff-looking Kane.

Jago Kane, his expression one of disgruntled annoyance, at having his initial failure pointed out to him once again, did not meet the Prime Minister's gaze, instead studying the pattern woven into the carpet that covered the floor of the PM's private chambers. "Yes. It was."

"Then we have something to thank the late Mr Quicksilver for after all. I wonder how he would feel if he knew that he had inadvertently helped us achieve our goal, despite our initial ... problems."

Kitty Hawke smiled in self-satisfaction at this slight against Kane.

Wormwood could not forget that it was because of Kane's failure to retrieve this item at the beginning of their endeavour that their plans had been forced to change so drastically and had almost been scuppered entirely by the subsequent – yet necessary, as it turned out – involvement of Ulysses Quicksilver. It had been a dangerous hand Wormwood had played, yet one that had seemed to pay off at first, until the somewhat upsetting incident at Waterloo Underground Station.

As a consequence Wormwood could not forgive Kane for his previous failure. Once their scheme had been seen through to its conclusion, the revolutionary would be made to pay for that careless mistake, for his haphazard handling of the simple mission to recover the Galapagos formula from the Natural History Museum.

But there was no doubting the fact that now the professor's difference engine and the locket – in reality the engine's access key – had been reunited. Wormwood's laboratory technicians had been able to open Galapagos's private data files in which was stored the chemical breakdown of his evolution-reversing formula – or his de-evolution formula, as Dr Wilde preferred to call it.

"Dr Wilde is preparing his subjects even as we speak," Kitty went on. "He has assured me that all will be ready in time for the main event."

"Good, good," Wormwood said, nodding approvingly. "You have redeemed yourself, my dear."

"And what of the remaining devices, Mr Kane?"

"Allardyce and his lackeys at Scotland Yard have unfortunately managed to recover most of them."

"That is indeed unfortunate." Wormwood's knuckles whitened as he took hold of the whisky glass, betraying that which his emotionless tone kept hidden. "Now tell me something that will be more appealing to my ear."

"We are still in possession of a number of the devices, certainly enough to achieve our modified mission objectives."

"Well, that is better news. Have you anything more to further cheer me?"

"They are now at the Limehouse facility being fitted with canisters of the formula. The last phase of the plan is almost ready to be put into action."

"Even better. Then we can progress in a satisfactory manner."

Uriah Wormwood fixed each of his lieutenants with his needling stare, both meeting his intense gaze.

"Miss Hawke, Mr Kane, we are about to make our mark on history." He toasted them with the glass in his hand. "Let us not delay any longer; for we have a date with destiny."

CHAPTER NINETEEN

Prisoners of the Tower

"And now, gentlemen, we come to the point in our tour where you can see how your money can help us with the good work we do here for, and on behalf of, the Empire," Governor Colesworth said, with some small measure of genuine enthusiasm colouring his voice.

He paused before the solid steel door sunk into the three-foot deep wall behind him. The party of industrialists, steel mill owners, landed gentry and money men leant forwards in anticipation, tightly-buttoned waistcoats straining against bulging stomachs recently filled from the lavish buffet laid on for their visit. "At this juncture I would like to remind you that a number of the inmates you will encounter here, and some of the techniques that we use to control them, can cause some distress to upstanding, god-fearing men of a sensitive disposition. But do not worry, you are not in any danger yourselves. Orderlies and wardens will be on hand at all times keeping our experimental subjects in their place."

Colesworth turned the large round wheel-handle and with a squeaking groan the heavy vault door swung open. Two orderlies, both armed with electric goads – the associated battery packs needed to power them strapped to their backs – stood to either side of the entrance. The governor proudly ushered his guests into the vaulted space beyond.

It was a huge room at the base of the White Tower, bustling with inmates and orderlies alike, although at first it was hard to tell the two groups apart. The prisoners all wore the same, drab, shapeless coveralls, grey and stained with God alone knew what. The orderlies' uniforms weren't much better. The prison warders looked just as brutal and violent as those they had been tasked with guarding.

The party of visitors was standing at the edge of a balcony that ran around the circumference of the cell-vault. An iron-railed staircase descended to the dungeon floor ten feet below and a second rose up again to the walkway on the far side. Opposite stood another solid iron door. During the early years of Queen Victoria's reign, when the Tower had been open to public visitors, this space had been used to store elaborate displays of weaponry. Now its purpose was more like that for which it had originally been intended.

Several of the governors' guests wrinkled their noses at the fusty damp and ammonia smell of the dungeon but all stared, transfixed by the shambling monstrosities before them. The longer they looked the easier it was for them to tell the incarcerated and incarcerators apart. For one thing, all of the prisoners had at some stage had their heads shaved. Some inmates still bore the nicks and scabs on their pallid white pates of the more recent attentions of a barber.

And there was another distinguishing mark that all the prisoners here bore. Each man had a sturdy iron collar fitted around his neck. These metal braces held their heads up and the more observant amongst the group saw that the thin flesh at the base of the prisoners' skulls was pink and raw. As yet the governor's guests could not see a reason for these devices. Were they some form of punishment, identity markers, or did they serve some other, more sinister, purpose?

Every now and again orderlies turned high-pressure hoses on the mewling and moaning inmates, dousing them with ice-cold water. This action provoked mixed responses from the party of visitors.

"Is that really necessary?" one woman asked the governor.

"Oh yes, madam," Colesworth replied, matter-of-factly.

"But as far as I could see that poor soaked wretch there hadn't done anything to incur the guard's wrath."

"Madam, if they are imprisoned here at her majesty's pleasure, then they have all done something and deserve whatever punishment is meted out to them. Would you not agree?" There were murmurs and nods of assent from the rest of the party and the woman said nothing more.

"Besides, a regular dousing reminds the prisoners of their place and of the price they must pay society in recompense for their misdeeds," Colesworth went on, warming to his subject. "These you see before you are amongst some of our most recalcitrant offenders, murderers and rapists – excuse me, ladies! – who, it has been deemed, can never be rehabilitated. It is the judgement of the courts that they should remain here for the rest of their natural lives. Just as it is our penance to care for them for that time." What the investors saw before them now did not look very much like care.

"Excuse me, Governor Colesworth," a haughty-sounding gentleman said, "but might some of these godforsaken souls be classed as retards?"

"Indeed, some of them are," Colesworth agreed, "which is why they have ultimately found themselves here. Gentlemen and ladies, there, but for the grace of God, go us all."

Several of the party crossed themselves and again potential dissenters were hushed.

"And it is the very nature of those incarcerated here that makes them such ideal subjects for Dr Wilde's work." The governor indicated a tall, stick-thin, lab-coated figure striding imperiously through the cavernous space beneath them; very obviously presiding demon lord of this outer circle of hell. Dr Wilde caught the eye of the governor and threw him a jovial salute. He bounded up the stairs to the balcony two at a time. Next to Colesworth he made the governor appear even shorter of stature and wider of girth.

"Ladies and gentlemen, it is with great pleasure that I introduce Dr Cornelius Wilde."

The looming doctor bowed at the middle, looking like a wheat stalk bending in a strong wind, and then sprang back up again. He looked every bit an experimental brain medicine specialist. His thinning blond hair was swept back from a widow's peak and he wore thin-framed round spectacles, which gave his eyes a slightly discomforting magnified appearance. The lengthened features of his face were all the more clearly defined by his gaunt, hungrily thin physique.

"Good afternoon, ladies and gentlemen," he said, with all the manner of a ringmaster about to introduce the star act. "Welcome to what I like to call our little *cirque du freak*." A titter of nervous laughter passed among the investors.

"It is here that Dr Wilde is carrying out some of the most exciting research into behavioural adjustment taking place at this time," Governor Colesworth said proudly, beaming his ingratiating smile at the party. "Would you care to explain the purpose of your work here, Dr Wilde? I'm afraid the science of it baffles me."

"It would be my pleasure," Wilde beamed. "Basically, ladies and gentlemen, here at the Tower of London maximum security prison facility, we have long been involved in finding a way to best rehabilitate those who find themselves on the wrong side of the law. But undeniably, for some, there has never been any hope of rehabilitation within normal, decent human society. That is, until now."

Colesworth looked from the doctor to his guests and back again, simpering all the while. The ringmaster had his audience hooked.

"You see that each of the inmates here is wearing a special collar?"

The party nodded. "I am sure that intelligent men and women like yourselves will have wondered what they are for." More nods. "What you see before you is the most exciting advance in social rehabilitation and behavioural improvement this century. Those collars represent a quantum leap forwards in our understanding of the human brain." Here Wilde paused for dramatic effect. "And how it can be controlled."

There were a number of audible gasps from the assembled economic elite.

"At this present time we are carrying out final tests on the patented Wilde Mind Control Collar."

"Can you elaborate as to how the collars work?" an industrialist asked, his eyes twinkling as he imagined the profit to be made from investing in this new project and securing sole manufacturing rights.

"Well, obviously the technical details will only become available to the highest bidder," Wilde smiled, "but the principle of it is really quite simple."

"But then aren't all the best ideas?" Colesworth simpered.

His eyes aglow with unhealthy enthusiasm, Wilde attempted to explain to the group of laymen how the complex collar worked. "Most of what you see locked around each subject's neck is actually a battery power pack. The clever bit, the mould-breaking technical gubbins, is at the back. There an electrode enters the base of the skull, allowing electrical impulses to be sent directly into the cerebral cortex, thereby modifying the subject's behaviour. But I can see that I am losing you. As you said, Governor, the science of it baffles most people so I have prepared a brief demonstration."

"Excellent, excellent."

"If you would care to follow me?"

Wilde led the party around the edge of the chamber to the sturdy door on the opposite side.

A warder armed with an electric prod prepared to open this second door but Wilde paused before it, halting the man's hand on the wheel lock.

"What is it, Dr Wilde?" one of Colesworth's guests asked.

"I should warn you, honoured guests, that some of you – if not all – may find what I am about to reveal a little, how should I put it, unsettling? I would completely understand – and I am sure that Governor Colesworth would as well – if anyone of you felt that they would rather leave the tour at this juncture."

Colesworth looked anxiously from the trailing crocodile of investors to the charismatic doctor and back again, uncertainty writ large upon his face.

The huddle of investors all stared at Wilde, transfixed in nervous, hollow-eyed anticipation, but not one of them asked to leave.

"Very well then. I applaud your courage and tenacity. If you would step this way?"

The party entered a much smaller, white-tiled room. An overpowering clinical smell of disinfectant masked a more deeply ingrained odour of bodily excretions and raw fear.

At the centre of the doctor's lab was an upended steel gurney. Secured to it by thick buckle-locked leather straps so that he was almost vertical, arms held tight to his sides, was an ox of a man. The doctor's latest clinical subject had been stripped to the waist, revealing a torso that was a veritable historical account of his wanton life, a patchwork of livid bruises, tattoos and old scars. The restrained prisoner was being attended to by a pair of lab assistants and watched over by two more of the brutal-looking orderlies.

As soon as Wilde entered the room, the inmate's muscles bulged as he fought against the leather straps and embarked on a blasphemous tirade of expletives that made the more sensitive among the governor's guests gasp in horror. One woman was on the verge of swooning in shock. "I'm going to rip your throat out and eat your heart, Wilde you bastard! Do you hear me?" the inmate screamed in a strong Glaswegian accent.

"Gag him!" the doctor ordered sharply.

As two orderlies pushed a thick padded gag between the prisoner's jaws, the startled investors could quite clearly see that the savage's teeth had been filed to a point so that they looked like sharp arrowhead flints.

"Ladies and gentlemen, let me apologise for our subject's outburst. Unfortunately not all can appreciate the benefits of the good work we do here, least of all those of a criminal bent."

Wilde strode past the captive inmate and, taking the goad from the orderly standing there, rammed the prongs of the device into the prisoner's ribs. The man's whole body jerked violently and the ammonia-stink of urine permeated the close atmosphere of the chamber.

"Honoured guests, let me introduce Ramsey 'The Shark' McCabe. Serial killer, cannibal and downright nasty piece of work. A recalcitrant sociopath, with twenty-six murders, dismemberings and devourings to his name."

The morbidly fascinated group fanned out in front of the gurney, so that all could see more clearly. 'The Shark' McCabe continued to thrash and fight against his restraints, causing the gaggle of investors to flinch and take a step back. But there was no way that he could free himself from the steel slab, and neither was there any chance of any of the party leaving now, for fear of missing what might happen to the brute next.

"As you can quite clearly see, Mr McCabe is a brutal and violent man, who is serving multiple life sentences at this institution, with no chance of a reduction to his sentence and most definitely no chance of a reprieve. Isn't that right, Mr McCabe?"

Wilde stepped up to the restraining table and indicated the collar fitted around the prisoner's neck. As he did so, McCabe twisted his head sideways, veins bulging in his neck as if he would dearly like to bite the doctor's face off.

"You can also see that he has recently been fitted with a collar. Now, ladies and gentlemen, for the purposes of this experiment I am afraid that we must ungag the subject once more. You may want to cover your ears."

Some kind of metal box of tricks, all dials and switches, and sporting a long aerial, had appeared in Wilde's hands.

"Remove the gag," Wilde commanded. The governor's party watched in horrified fascination.

As soon as the gag was off, the tirade began again.

"Wilde, you shit, when I get out of here I'm going to rip off your head and sh..."

Dr Wilde flicked a switch on his handheld device. The torrent of verbal abuse ceased immediately as McCabe fell silent, the inmate's eyes glazing over and his face taking on a slack-jawed, moronic, almost zombie-like expression. The assembled onlookers gasped.

"Wh-What happened?" someone spluttered in disbelief.

"Ladies and gentlemen," the ringmaster declared, as he came to the highlight of the performance, "the subject is now totally under my control. Isn't that right, Mr McCabe?"

A frown flickered across the prisoner's face and then, his voice as emotionless as his expression, the Shark replied, "Yes, Dr Wilde."

The party gasped again.

"By using this handheld remote I can now coerce Mr McCabe into performing any action I ask of him. It is easier to control less developed brains, of course. Our initial experiments with dogs and monkeys paved the way for developing a mind control device that could be used on humans. Some of our more retarded subjects have proved most susceptible to control, and, believe me, gentlemen, in a place crammed full of backward hoodlums, subnormal rapists and psychotic murderers, we have plenty of those here."

A nervous titter of laughter passed through the assembled group.

"I don't believe it!" a rotund industrialist muttered, jowls quivering as he shook his head in disbelief.

"Believe it, sir," Wilde countered. "In fact, let me prove it to you. What would you like to see Mr McCabe do?"

There was a smattering of 'um's and 'ah's as the gathered voyeurs tried to come up with a suitable test now that the doctor had set his challenge.

"Have him recite *Mary Had a Little Lamb*," a voice came from the back of the group.

"Very well." The doctor turned to his docile subject. "Mr McCabe, do you know the children's rhyme *Mary Had a Little Lamb*?"

"Yes, Dr Wilde."

"Then recite it for our guests."

"Mary had a little lamb, its fleece was white as snow," McCabe drawled, his Scots accent monotone and lacking any expression whatsoever, "and everywhere that Mary went, the lamb was sure to go."

"Very good, Mr McCabe."

The party of visitors offered a polite round of applause.

"Make him stand on one foot," another man suggested.

"Very well, but we shall have to release him from his restraints first," Wilde pointed out.

There was a hesitant murmur of uncertainty from the group and some of the party took a step back as Wilde directed his assistants to undo the buckled straps.

"Are you sure about this?" Colesworth hissed, suddenly at Wilde's side.

"But of course I am, Governor. Have faith."

Colesworth swallowed hard and took a step back, wringing his hands in anxiety.

One by one the leather restraints were undone. The doctor's assistants moved aside, prison orderlies moving up to take their place, electro-goads ready just in case. McCabe just stood there, a good head taller than anyone else in the room, his great wrestler's form terrifying to behold.

"Mr McCabe," Wilde said, turning a dial on his control box and depressing another switch, "if you would be so kind, stand on one foot."

The prisoner robotically raised one foot so that he remained balanced on the other.

Suggestion followed suggestion from the increasingly impressed investors. They watched as the cannibal serial killer rubbed his stomach whilst patting his head, childishly recited his ABC and the routine ending with a rendition of 'I'm a Little Teapot'. All the while the Shark remained as docile as a kitten.

A spontaneous round of applause erupted from amongst the investors. Colesworth beamed like a Cheshire cat. Dr Wilde, one eyebrow raised in acknowledgement, kept his own counsel.

"Thank you, thank you," Wilde said, taking a bow as he luxuriated in his audience's adulation. "But now, if you will excuse me, I have vital work to attend to."

The show over and Colesworth assured of the investment he had so desperately been seeking, the ringmaster bid the audience of investors farewell. The party filed out of the clinical white laboratory, the governor asking if any of his esteemed guests would be attending the jubilee celebrations in Hyde Park the following day.

Dr Wilde stayed where he was. He turned to one of his assistants.

"Nash, have this one taken back to his cell," he said, throwing a sidelong glance at the subdued psychopath, "shock him hard enough to knock him unconscious and then you can turn this off." He tossed the collar controller to the man.

"Yes, Dr Wilde."

"And remember, Nash, I want the rest of the collars fitted by tonight." His previously crowd-pleasing tone had become pointedly instructional.

"Yes, Dr Wilde," Nash acceded.

Leaving his underlings to put everything into operation in his absence, Wilde left the lab through another steel door and entered his private office lit by one, lonely, naked light bulb. He shut the door securely behind him and sat down at an unassuming grey metal desk. The only thing remotely interesting about the desk was the teak and brass-finished box that sat on top of it. It looked like a considerably larger version of the control box he had used to demonstrate how the mind control collars worked.

Wilde looked at the clock on the wall and then at his pocket watch, then at the clock again.

Drumming his fingers in distraction on the desktop he gazed out at the smog-laden sky beyond the small barred window. The mauve and mustard clouds were criss-crossed by the sweeping beams of the Tower's searchlights.

The Tower had been many things in its time – a royal palace, a menagerie, a museum, a treasure house and a tourist attraction – but now it was back to being a prison once more. As a prison it had put up many famous 'guests' including queens, kings and traitors. Now it was home to some of the most violent and brutal villains the empire had ever known – murderers, rapists and compulsive criminals the lot of them. In one wing were kept the most dangerous inmates, the clinically deranged psychopaths, the abusers, the schizophrenics, the mentally ill, those who, by rights, should not have been permitted to continue their godless lives. But that would all change soon enough, when the new order was in place. And for the time being, these very wretches were to form the vanguard of the most exciting scientific experiment in the last fifteen years.

A tinny buzzing disturbed the doctor's reverie, forcing him to answer his personal communicator.

"Wilde," he said simply.

"Dr Wilde, the hour is upon us," a voice said at the other end of the line. "The plan is to proceed at the agreed time. Will you be ready?"

"I am ready, Agent Kane," Wilde confirmed.

"The Dawn is coming, brother."

Then the line went dead.

Cornelius Wilde felt a tingling surge of adrenalin and became aware of his heart jumping in his chest.

It was time, the Dawn was coming, and with it a glorious new epoch in the history of human kind. It was time that the social order be overturned and the masters of the sciences given the opportunity to stretch their wings, rather than remain bound to outdated and outmoded scientific principles. The age of steam was coming to an end and ahead lay a glorious era of opportunity. Such an age would need its pioneers, its scientific heroes, its leaders.

The ringmaster smiled. All that had come before was merely the warm-up act, the precursor to the main event. The three-ring finale was about to begin.

"Show time!" Wilde said to himself, as he watched the silhouette-black shapes of ravens clear the barbed wire battlements of the Tower and fly into the storm-dark sky.

CHAPTER TWENTY

The Limehouse Connection

THE SILVER PHANTOM Mark IV rolled to a halt in the gathering gloom beside the warehouse, headlamps already doused, its tyres making almost no noise on the harbour side.

Nimrod peered out through the windscreen at the dusk-shadowed buildings of the Limehouse Basin. The smog-clouds, thicker and more cloying thanks to the summer heat, had helped accelerate the onset of night.

This run-down stretch of dockland appeared to be deserted. There was no sign of anyone about but then everyone, from the lowest of the low to the great and the good, would either be taking part in the Queen's jubilee celebrations in person or observing the proceedings as they were relayed via the huge broadcast screens on every street corner and through cathode ray sets in homes across the nation.

"You're sure this is the place, sir?" Nimrod turned to the man sitting in the passenger seat next to him.

"Absolutely," Ulysses Quicksilver assured him, a wicked gleam in his eye, as he checked the scanner he was holding in his lap. A red blip was repeatedly pinging at the centre of a lambently glowing green wire-frame image.

"So that Heath Robinson invention of Dr Methuselah's really works," Nimrod said with a hint of scorn.

"Yes. I have to say I'm rather impressed. Who'd have thought that old Methuselah was as handy with electronic trickery as he is with medical mumbo-jumbo?"

"You think Miss Galapagos is here?"

"Indeed I do," Ulysses said, his face suddenly grim again. "Genevieve Galapagos, my arse! She and I have unfinished business. The key is certainly here."

Ulysses stared out of the windscreen and back into the night of the explosion, when he had discovered Genevieve's betrayal. One good betrayal deserved another and so he had faked his own death, allowing Genevieve's parting gift to explode with dramatic consequences whilst making sure that he, and anyone else who mattered to him, was out of range of the blast.

With the parcel-bomb counting down the last seconds until destruction, it had been necessary for Ulysses to make a snap decision. He had decided that if he were considered to be dead, it would be much more straightforward for him to discover who was truly behind this conspiracy. Once he was in the grave, as it were, he would have the precious time and anonymity he needed to make a more careful assessment of what was really going on and what needed to be done to put an end to such devilish schemes.

He would be eternally glad that he had asked Dr Methuselah to examine Galapagos's locket before returning it to its allegedly rightful owner. The old curmudgeon had almost instantly identified it as an encoded access key. Seeing as how Ulysses had already worked out that it was a difference engine that had been stolen from the Natural History Museum it did not take a genius to deduce the connection and realise that, whatever it was that Professor Galapagos had created in his lab, the means to recreating it was locked inside that same data storage engine.

It had been Methuselah's idea to fit Galapagos's 'locket' with a tracking device. By means of the accompanying scanner, Ulysses had been able to follow the mysterious and capricious Genevieve Galapagos's movements as she went about her business. Meanwhile Ulysses had put his own spy network into operation through his ever-loyal manservant Nimrod who, himself, had most useful connections to the darker side of the capital.

Since the counterfeit Miss Galapagos had made such an unsubtle attempt on his life, Ulysses had managed to implicate her in the workings of the Darwinian Dawn, which, as it turned out, were not quite as done for as he might have hoped following his own personal Waterloo.

Had it been she who had tried to assassinate him with a bullet earlier on the same night as the explosion? She had certainly demonstrated a marksman's eye on the evening of their first meeting. Ulysses had also managed to uncover her true identity. She was, in reality, Kitty

Hawke. Cat burglar, hustler, and consummate actress with her own revolutionary tendencies.

He wondered whether he had found himself his mysterious thief at last and that when she had been so insistent about accompanying him to the Natural History Museum the night they first met, whether she had not, in fact, been returning to the scene of the crime, hoping to bring to a conclusion what she had started by recovering the missing code-key.

It had been a gamble allowing Kitty Hawke and the Darwinian Dawn access to Galapagos's encrypted data files, but he had considered it a calculated risk. He had hoped to bring matters to a halt before they could reach their deadly conclusion.

"What time do you make it, Nimrod?" Ulysses asked, taking out his pocket watch. "Synchronise watches and all that, what?"

"Nine o'clock, sir," his manservant replied, checking the clock built into the automobile's dashboard.

"Good. Dead on. Same as me." Ulysses gazed out at the purpling sky. "I should think that the great and the good will be sitting down to their aperitifs about now," Ulysses said with a heartfelt sigh.

"Weren't you invited to the Hyde Park celebrations, sir?"

"I would be there right now myself if it weren't for the fact that I'm supposed to be dead. But then I'd have to miss out on all this, wouldn't I?" he said, turning to look over his shoulder into the back of the Phantom. The Neanderthal squatting on the back seat grunted, an amiable grin splitting the lumpen features of his subhuman face. "And besides, now the fun can really start!"

"Sir, I must protest. It should be I who attends you on this escapade. You know what happened the last time I left you to your own devices. You were nearly drowned, blown up and eaten by a de-evolving professor of evolutionary biology."

"But you're my getaway driver," Ulysses said. "You're my Plan B."

"I really don't know why you insisted on bringing him along," Nimrod grumbled.

"Think how useful he proved to be at the Waterloo bomb-making facility," Ulysses pointed out. "I thought he might help to – you know – mix things up a bit. It always pays to walk into a criminal HQ with a bit of muscle and a back-up plan."

Nimrod said nothing more but simply shot his employer a withering look.

"Besides, you've done very well with him. You should be pleased with yourself, Nimrod. I think our friend here looks very dashing in a suit and tie."

"Well..."

"You'll have him drinking Earl Grey out of a cup and not the saucer in no time."

Nimrod sighed tiredly. Ulysses carefully opened his door.

"It's time I returned to the land of the living!" Ulysses declared, with overly exuberant showmanship. "Keep the engine ticking over. We'll be back in a jiffy, just you wait and see."

"KEEP BEHIND ME and try not to knock into anything," Ulysses told his Neanderthal companion in a hissed whisper.

They were inside the gloomy confines of the warehouse, access gained with the aid of a crowbar through an abandoned foreman's office. The hulking, rusted carcasses of dead machinery surrounded them. According to the blip on the scanner their target was only a matter of a hundred yards further inside.

Simeon looked like a most curious beast, dressed in an altered suit of Mr Prufrock's, buttons pulling against the stitching across the Neanderthal's barrel chest. He crouched behind a rusted iron cargo crane, hairy knuckles dragging on the ground. His feet were bare, his toes gripping the floor almost as fingers might. He was wearing a clean white shirt and one of Nimrod's black ties that the butler had tied for him. His lank dreadlocks had been trimmed and a comb run through his hair before it was slicked down in the same manner that Nimrod favoured.

Ulysses smiled. It looked like Nimrod would soon have an assistant to unburden him of some of his chores about the Quicksilver household.

Ulysses himself had decided to go with flamboyance over subtlety on this occasion. He was wearing a House of Leoparde waistcoat all in chartreuse and crimson thread, his cravat was held in place with a diamond pin, and his bloodstone cane was in his hand. He wanted to make an impact when he returned from the dead for a second time. He had set himself a tough act to follow after his last resurrection from the grave – although at least he had been reported dead this time rather than just having been missing *presumed* dead.

"Ready?" he asked the apeman.

Simeon nodded, his tongue lolling from his mouth like a happy dog.

Cautiously Ulysses led the way through the dead monoliths of the fish-packer's machinery. It might still only be dusk outside but in the warehouse it was dark as night, the skylights above merely grey panes of opacity, their translucence gone with the failing of the light.

Even now that his eyes had become more accustomed to the preternatural darkness, objects merely appeared to Ulysses as amorphous black clots against the only slightly lesser gloom of the warehouse's interior. And although he had a flashlight about his person, he did not want to use it here and draw unwanted attention to their presence.

Simeon didn't seem bothered by the lack of light at all, proving surprisingly nimble at negotiating the various obstacles that the gloom seemed to throw into their path. Ulysses wondered whether there were still some things that the more primitive evolutionary forms were better at coping with than the more sophisticated *Homo sapiens.*

The warehouse smelt dusty and dank, of dirt and mouldering wood. But there was something else – something acrid and unpleasantly familiar – almost subsumed by the smell of old oil and rust-eaten metal. Ulysses suspected that Simeon could smell it too, and probably more clearly than he could himself, for he kept sniffing and then holding back almost nervously after each intense inhalation. What did the aroma remind him of? Where had the Neanderthal experienced the smell before? And where had Ulysses? He could almost taste its sickly sweetness.

Then there were the sounds too. As they advanced across the warehouse they became steadily more distinct – muffled human voices, the rattle and thud of machinery, reminiscent of the Darwinian Dawn's Waterloo Station facility.

Ulysses could feel heat prickling his forehead. Was the closeness of the air and the heat a consequence of the early summer climate or a result of the industrial processes taking place elsewhere within the warehouse?

The outline of a door became visible ahead of them. The glass pane set into it was so smeared with grime as to be almost entirely blacked out, but for tiny scrapes in the obscuring dirt. Slivers of muted light broke through into the darkness that enveloped them, turning swirls of dust into cascades of golden motes.

Ulysses put a hand to the door and held it there for a moment. Then, with a confident motion, he pulled it open and a waft of something hit him, immediately carrying him back to both Professor Galapagos's ransacked office and the macabre workroom beneath the house in Southwark. It was the lingering odour of meat on the turn and aniseed, like spoiled fennel and beef casserole.

Simeon flinched but the two of them ducked through the door, Ulysses shutting it swiftly behind them. Everything that they had sensed in the outer warehouse space was amplified here – the heat, the noise, the smells – but they still weren't at the heart of operations. Although there was light here and the condition of the machinery told of its recent use, the place was still devoid of any human or even robot presence.

It didn't take long for Ulysses to ascertain the purpose of this part of the complex. It was the still-wet vats, the lengths of glass piping and the all-pervading smell of aniseed and rancid meat that gave it away. Whatever it was that Professor Galapagos had been brewing in his Southwark workshop, the same stuff had been reproduced here but on a noticeably more grand and terrifying scale.

Confident that there was no one to observe their progress Ulysses darted between the distillation tanks and workbenches, always following the lure of the blip on the scanner.

He paused, realising that Simeon was no longer at his heel. Turning he saw the Neanderthal rocking from side to side where he stood between the benches of apparatus. He was whimpering to himself, almost overwhelmed by the now oh-so-familiar and disturbing aroma.

"Come on!" Ulysses hissed. The Neanderthal didn't budge. "Simeon, come here now!"

A grimace of anxiety contorted the primitive's ugly features, obviously torn between his fearful recollections and his desire to please his new master.

"Oh, have it your own way," Ulysses sighed, giving in to exasperation, and continued towards the other side of the workroom, following the thumping of machinery and what sounded like the purr of an engine running up to speed.

Simeon gave a little yelp and then, having overcome his demons – whatever they might have been – knuckled after Ulysses.

IT HAD BEEN a long time since Ulysses had seen anything like it and he froze for a moment in genuine, awestruck wonder. He found recollections of his hair-raising flight over the Himalayas springing to mind, but the balloon on which he had been a passenger was as nothing compared to this Leviathan.

Lit by flickering running lights, the zeppelin was huge – at least two hundred yards from nose to tail. The massive balloon of its inflated gas envelope was barely contained within the converted warehouse-hangar. From the locking clamps and iron cables beneath it hung an armoured gondola, itself as big as two railway carriages strung together. The whole thing was kept anchored in place by sturdy guy ropes.

The rear loading ramp of the dirigible's gondola was down and robot-drudges were loading the last of the Dawn's mine-bombs on board. Close to where Ulysses and the panting Simeon were hunkered down behind the hangar's fuel dump, there had also been discarded the straw-packed crates that had been used to transport the terrorists' surviving devices from the bomb factory. Ulysses had no idea how many the Darwinian Dawn had managed to recover but judging from the number of robots trudging up the ramp into the bomb bay it was enough to do some serious damage.

And right at that moment, across London, thousands of people were crowded into and around Hyde Park and the newly-reconstructed Crystal Palace for a chance to be a part of Queen Victoria's 160th jubilee celebrations and perhaps even catch a rare glimpse of the monarch herself.

And there was not only the devastation that might be caused by the initial detonation of the devices, considering the level of destruction they had wrought inside the confines of the Waterloo facility. If Ulysses' suspicions were correct – and with all the evidence he had seen with his own eyes within the Limehouse complex, how could they not be? – those remaining devices now carried an added ingredient, an extra surprise for the beleaguered populace of London: Professor Galapagos's de-evolution formula.

Whatever else the Darwinian Dawn might have planned to help the Queen's jubilee go with a bang, Ulysses knew that he had to stop that zeppelin from leaving its warehouse-hangar. But for that he needed a distraction, and time was truly against him.

He cast the Neanderthal an anxious look. "For Queen and country, eh, old boy? You didn't know you were signing up for a suicide mission, did you?" Simeon grinned back amiably, ridiculous in his strangely fitted suit. "That's the spirit."

Ulysses' pistol was out of its underarm holster and in his hand. He snapped off two precisely aimed shots. Two men fell.

There was a burst of furious shouting, a flurry of sudden, instinct-driven activity, as the guards' hours of brainwashed training kicked in and they took up firing positions of their own. A tattoo of gun reports resounded around the warehouse-hangar as the pitch of the airship's engines rose, its pilot preparing the craft for immediate take-off. If a stray bullet ruptured the zeppelin balloon the results could be catastrophic.

A bullet ricocheted from the ground in front of the fuel dump throwing off sparks as it did so. Ulysses was aware of the gentle *whoomph* as a single spark ignited a pool of oil that had collected in the uneven, rutted surface of the concrete floor. He also heard the shout from one of the guards that followed. However much it might gall the terrorists they realised that it they continued to fire on Ulysses' position they risked starting a conflagration, which would in turn jeopardise the safety of the airship.

It soon became apparent to those few armed guards left to oversee the loading of the zeppelin that they were not going to be able to put an end to the interlopers' attack by force of arms alone. Some other means of defence was needed now, something that was no longer required to fulfil any other duties, something entirely dispensable.

The gunfire stopped, rattling into echoing silence. Hearing the clank-clank-clank of pistoning legs and the ringing of metal heels on concrete, Ulysses risked a glance.

The automata-drudges employed by the Darwinian Dawn were running and leaping across the hangar towards the fuel dump behind which Ulysses and Simeon were sheltering. Ulysses counted a dozen, maybe more.

He fired off two more shots, despite knowing that they would make little impact against the droids' armoured chest plates. Perhaps if he had been armed with one of the guards' sub-machine pistols he might have been able to defend himself more effectively.

Something spun over his head and crashed into one of the bounding robots with a resounding clang. A mechanical man was torn off as a heavy engine part collided with it. There was the whickering of more spare parts scything through the air followed by clattering crashes and rattling collisions as Simeon hurled more of his improvised arsenal at the advancing robots. However, although his efforts were making a small difference, they weren't going to be enough to save the two of them for much longer.

Ulysses tugged his communicator from his pocket. "Nimrod!" he shouted into the comm. "It's time for Plan B!"

His voice was drowned out by the roar of the zeppelin's engines and the rich, gagging stink of exhaust fumes washed over them.

With a loud grinding of gears and the clanking of chains, the panels of the roof above them pulled back, exposing the laden airship to the polluted London skies.

The engines whirring at take-off velocity, the zeppelin, with its deadly payload, lifted off, pulling free of its mooring hawsers, like some great whale rising from the ocean depths.

The robots braving Simeon's barrage were nearly on them now.

Ulysses was abruptly aware of the scream of a revving engine. With a splintering crash, the Silver Phantom smashed through a wall, headlights flaring in the exhaust-smogged gloom of the hangar. It crashed down on the hard floor of the building, bouncing on its tyres and colliding with the two robots bearing down on Ulysses and Simeon. The automata-drudges were sent flying, arms and legs windmilling wildly as the automobile skidded to a halt side-on, less than a foot from Ulysses' position.

The front and rear passenger doors flew open. "Get in!" Nimrod shouted from behind the cracked windscreen.

Ulysses didn't need to be told twice. He threw himself into the front of the Phantom as Simeon bounded into the back, slamming the door shut behind him. "Just in the nick of time, eh, Nimrod?"

There was a metallic crash above them and a dent appeared in the roof of the car.

"Get us out of here!" Ulysses commanded, eyes wide with the adrenalin rushing through his system.

Nimrod floored the accelerator. Wheels spun, there was the stink of burning rubber, then the tyres gripped and the Phantom took off like a rocket. The car had suffered a fair amount of damage to its pristine bodywork during the Challenger Incident, particularly when the velociraptor had crashed onto the bonnet. However, it had since been repaired so that it looked as good as the day it had left the showroom but all that careful work was now being undone in another pulse-pounding escape.

Reaching the far end of the hangar Nimrod swung the car round sharply, dislodging the droid on its roof. The automaton was sent barrelling across the concrete – sparks flying from its steel body – and into a pile of discarded packing boxes. The drudge lay there, like a marionette with its strings cut, flames dancing within the bone-dry tinder around it.

All they could see of the rising airship, through the windscreen of the Phantom, were the swinging ropes and cables of its freed tethers. The abandoned automata, caring nothing for their own well-being, strove to carry out the last command they had been given, dashing and leaping towards the car, their movements jerky and insect-like.

Gunning the engine, Nimrod sent the Phantom hurtling forwards. Droids bounced off the bonnet, were smashed aside by its radiator grill or sent under its wheels as the automobile's engine flung it forwards with all the force of a steam-hammer.

The fire had now taken over the pile of packing cases and was licking at one wall of the warehouse. A trail of flames slithered across the floor of the hangar behind the Phantom, following the rainbow-sheen of leaked fuel leading back to the fuel dump.

Then the automobile was through the barricade formed by the charging robots and the smoggy dusk beyond the sundered wall of the hangar was beckoning them.

The Silver Phantom, its battered bodywork reflecting the fury of the flames in shimmering crimson and orange, launched through the hole it had made, as the last few barrels of the fuel dump exploded. The car flew through the side of the building chased by a volcanic explosion of greasy smoke and flames as windows blew out above it. The shattered body parts of destroyed automata winnowed through the walls and windows and clattered off the back of the vehicle in a shower of bullet-hard shrapnel. The rear window shattered.

The car crashed down onto the harbour side, Simeon tumbling across the back seat as Nimrod swung into a tight turn, stopping them hurtling into the oily, black waters of the Thames.

Through his window, Ulysses could see the zeppelin rise clear of the Limehouse complex, flood-lit by the conflagration consuming the warehouse-hangar. The airship was turning west, manoeuvring itself in the direction of the centre of the capital, continuing to climb, to soar above the elevated trackways of the Overground.

He turned to Nimrod, his eyes wild. "We have to stop that zeppelin!"

"Yes, sir," his manservant agreed, his expression as stoical as ever, and put the pedal to the metal.

With a screech of tyres and a leonine roar from its engine, the Silver Phantom sped off into the darkening night, leaving the blazing docklands of Limehouse behind.

CHAPTER TWENTY-ONE

Unnatural Selection

THE ZEPPELIN FLEW slowly through the smog-bound skies over London. It passed over towering tenement buildings and the spider's web of the Overground network, following the course of the Thames, a darkly glistening amethyst in the last light of dusk and the first hour of darkness. Aero-engines purring at cruising speed, it soared majestically through the encroaching night, caught in the staccato flicker of the city's rainbow display of lights, their ever-changing colours giving the envelope of its balloon the illusion of shimmering scales.

Slung beneath it was the heavily-armoured gondola, looking not-unlike the hull of a battle-cruiser, inside which was carried the vessel's deadly payload, as well as a squad of armed and dangerous Darwinian Dawn guardsmen. These men were fanatics, prepared to lay down their lives for what they believed to be the good of mankind, to bring about a violent social revolution at the very heart of the world-spanning empire of Magna Britannia. Positioned towards the aft of the gondola the twin engines directed the dirigible onwards over the labyrinthine streets beneath, over the crumbling docklands of Limehouse, past Ratcliff, above the thoroughfares of Shadwell, skirting the wharfs of Wapping, and on towards its target.

Beneath the great behemoth of the skies, but still a good half a mile behind it, the sleek, darkly gleaming shape of the Mark IV Silver Phantom sped through the celebration-emptied streets, pursuing the dirigible on what its driver hoped would be an interception course.

DR CORNELIUS WILDE gazed out over the fenced compound beyond the rooftops of the Waterloo Barracks, past the rolls of razor wire that topped the towers of the Outer Ward and into the deepening darkness to the east.

The air was still and close with the heat of summer, intensified by the smothering layers of pollution-troubled cloud that hung over the city like a funeral shroud. The usual long white lab coat hung from his bony shoulders as if still on its hanger. A large teak and brass-finished mind box was harnessed to his chest and shoulders with leather straps. A deep pocket bulged.

Beneath his lonely position, high on the battlements of the White Tower, his test subjects trudged around the perimeter of the cobbled Inner Ward as they were coerced into enduring yet another hour of enforced exercise, under the ever-attentive optical sensors of the 'Beefeater' model automata-guards.

It was unusual for the inmates to have a drill period when they would normally be back in their cells, doors locked for the night, but then there had been many out of the ordinary arrangements during Dr Wilde's work to develop the mind control collars, that one more aberration was not really that much of a surprise to anyone. As far as the robo-guards were concerned, Dr Wilde's command clearance was second only to that of Governor Colesworth himself. The governor was among those invited to attend the gala dinner at the recently reconstructed Crystal Palace, to conclude the day's jubilee celebrations. So, as far as the droids were concerned, Dr Wilde's word was the highest-ranking authority left in the complex.

The inmates trudged on round the stark floodlit ward, begrudging every step but knowing no other life. Any sense of individuality his subjects might have once have had had been stripped from them. Fading blue tattoos, rough scars and other bodily disfigurements, such as broken noses and missing teeth, the only remaining reference to them ever having had a savage and down-trodden life of their own. Their heads were shaved, they all wore the same drab, one-size-fits-none coveralls and each man had his neck trapped in the vice of one of the good doctor's behaviour modification devices.

And then, there it was, a flicker of reflected light from one of the sweeping arc-beams. Peering even harder through his round-rimmed spectacles at the blanket of smog smothering the city, Wilde could make out the piscine shape of the airship as it hove into view over the Thames, framed between the ornamental barbican of Tower Bridge.

His heart leapt in excitement, the dour expression on his face becoming a grin of adrenalin-fuelled excitement. The hour had come.

He could see the running lights as well now. The movement of its tailfin suddenly side on, starkly visible in the sweep of a searchlight, as with a shift of its rudder, the zeppelin angled in over the river, heading directly towards the maximum security prison facility. Wilde could almost make out the distant purr of its engines. It was no distance away at all now, three hundred yards at most. The doctor was not the only one aware of the zeppelin's approach now. The prisoners paused in their tracks, looking up at the great grey belly of the dirigible as it hove into view over the turrets of the White Tower.

Even the Beefeater-drones, their clockwork craniums processing the overwhelming sensory input and calculating that this was a possible threat to the security of the facility, turned their glowing bulb eyes towards the airship – and promptly shutdown.

Wilde smiled, taking his finger off the nondescript brass switch on the control panel in front of him. Command clearance was a wonderful thing.

A klaxon wail began somewhere within the prison compound. Ignoring the clamour and commotion welling up within the cordoned exercise yard, Wilde turned his full attention back to the approaching leviathan. It was preparing to cross the outer curtain wall of the Tower complex, having steadily descended to a height nearing only one hundred feet.

There was a barely-heard whining mechanical noise and the bottom of the steel gondola's hull cracked open, ready to deploy the airship's deadly cargo.

"They're getting ready to deploy!" Ulysses gasped, watching through the windshield as the zeppelin's bomb bay doors eased open. He had assumed that the jubilee celebrations in Hyde Park would be the Darwinian Dawn's target but it seemed that he had been wrong.

The dirigible had moved ahead of them with ease, unimpeded by the need to follow the maze of city streets beneath it, able to travel where it pleased over and among the great canyons of the capital's towering skyscrapers and tenement buildings.

"Don't worry, sir, we're nearly on them," Nimrod said, disregarding a set of traffic lights and steering the speeding automobile over onto the other side of the thoroughfare.

Simeon hooted in wild abandon at the adrenalin-rush of the ride as Nimrod accelerated away from Jamaica Road and onto Tooley Street.

In their journey from the decrepit Limehouse docks they had already crossed the river once at the Rotherhithe Bridge to avoid a road closure, and now they were going to have to do so again if they were to have any chance of catching up with the zeppelin.

The Silver Phantom roared up the road and towards the floodlit bastions of Tower Bridge.

"Oh, I don't bloody believe it!" Ulysses exclaimed.

The bridge was closing to traffic, beginning to rise to allow a steam ship to pass through. Nimrod had to slam on the brakes to stop them from running into the back of the vehicle in front. There was a short queue waiting for the barriers to rise again.

"Don't worry, sir, a little obstacle like this won't stop us," Nimrod declared, pulling out from behind a cab and gunning the throttle. "I have long had a healthy disregard for the rules of the road."

He slammed his foot down. Wheels spun and the stink of burning rubber assailed them. Then the tyres found purchase and the car rocketed forward.

The red and white-painted barrier splintered like matchwood across the front of the Phantom. The front bumper crunched as it hit the rising section of roadway. The automobile hurtled on up the incline. The edge of the bridge section appeared ahead of them – the clear air between it and its counterpart steadily increasing as the bridge continued to rise.

"Nimrod, are you sure we can make it?" Ulysses said, overcome by a sudden moment of doubt.

"Have no fear, sir," Nimrod replied, voice raised over the protesting scream of the engine. "Of course we ca..."

Ulysses' prescient sense flashed like a camera bulb in the darkness. A dark shape swooped at them out of the enclosing night.

"Bloody hellfire," the unflappable butler suddenly exclaimed, "what was that?"

"Pterodactyl I believe, old chap," Ulysses replied, equally startled. "They're getting bold."

The unexpected appearance of the dinosaur had caused Nimrod to swerve instinctively.

And then the car hit the end of the rising bridge-section.

WITH A CLATTER the first of the huge spined devices was ejected from the bomb bay of the zeppelin. Looking like some massive steel-skinned sea urchin it dropped like a stone into the drained moat, detonating on impact with the sludgy mud at the bottom of the ditch. The explosion peppered the bastion's outer wall with deadly steel shrapnel that impaled itself in the stonework, smashing windows. Although it had missed the inner curtain wall by only a matter of a few feet, the sudden heat generated by the explosion vaporised the contents of the device's secondary compartment. The steam produced by the exothermic reaction washed across the moat and over the curtain wall of the Tower's original medieval fortifications as a heavy, low-hanging mist.

Alarms bells were set ringing inside the prison, the cacophonous sound of them joining the wailing of sirens, throwing those trapped inside the Tower into a state of panic.

The second bomb smashed through the roof of the hospital block, blowing out every window in the building as it exploded somewhere between the second and first floors, killing or maiming many of those recovering there as they lay helpless in their beds.

A third device – fully four feet in diameter – was launched into the wailing air and bounced off the north-east turret of the White Tower, crushing the lead-covered cupola and tearing down the seventeenth century weathervane, landing in front of the sturdy, reinforced doors of W block. The solid construction of the stone archway at the entrance to the old barracks directed the force of the blast. It shredded the prison-block doors, hurling what remained of them inwards, chased by a devastating fireball. The concussive force of the blast swept across the courtyard compound, bowling prisoners before it, several men being impaled by the spiny shrapnel of the cruel device.

Inmates were fleeing in all directions, some in panic but just as many having clocked that their robotic guards were failing to react and seizing on the chance to escape, scaling the chain-link fence or throwing themselves through the now unprotected gateways.

Mist was pouring out of the shattered frontage of the hospital block, drifting inexorably across the inner ward and through the chain-link fence surrounding the exercise yard. The choking clouds smothered the desperate prisoners like a thick sea-fog until they could hardly see their own hands in front of their faces, their fellow inmates appearing as blurred grey figures amidst the searchlight-shot whiteout.

There were prison warders amongst them too, unimpeded as their robot counterparts mysteriously appeared to be, but the acrid, obscuring steam took away identities and made one man like another – a new status quo achieved through one simple, violent action – incarcerated and incarcerator truly one at last. The mist smelled unpleasantly of spoiled meat combined with the sickly sweetness of aniseed.

Men were coughing now, choking as they inhaled the vapour, the mist hot and wet in their throats. Then the wracking coughs gave way to a palsied shaking, the bodies of prisoners and prison guards alike gripped by agonising seizures, hands forming into rigid talons, eyes bulging from faces turned near purple with the strain, veins writhing beneath the skin.

As they struggled for air, drawing in yet more of the poisoned air, a terrifying transformation took hold.

Dr Wilde watched the chaos consuming the Tower of London through the thick lenses of a gas mask.

The walls of London's maximum security prison and correctional facility had been breached and those interred within it were being transformed into a berserk fighting force that would bring the capital to its knees.

"Dr Wilde!" It was Nash, running onto the battlements. "The Tower's under attack."

Wilde turned. "Really?" he said, his voice muffled by the rubber snout of the gas mask.

Nash looked back at him stunned, the assistant's face ashen with fear. "It's a breakout, sir! A full scale prison break!"

"I would call it a liberation."

"What do you mean? Dr Wilde..." but the rest of Nash's words were drowned out by the roar of engines. The appalled young man looked up, his face paling still further as he took in the enormity of the airship above him.

There was the clatter of metal on stone as a rope ladder was dropped down, a black-garbed soldier visible in the open hatchway of the docking port above. As the ladder swept past him, the end of it trailing across the lead panes of the roof, Dr Wilde put one arm between a pair of rungs, a foot on another and held on as the airship moved on over the Tower keep.

With the doctor on board, the zeppelin began to rise. Nash looked on in disbelief as it climbed five, ten, fifteen feet. Then the trailing end of the ladder was in front of him and, without really thinking about what he was doing, he grabbed hold.

"I can't be a party to this!" he screamed into the rushing air over the deafening roar of the engines. Dr Wilde ignored him – probably not even aware of the insane actions of his underling – and continued to climb as the airship rose higher.

Not daring to look down, the downwash of the zeppelin's engines forcing him to narrow his eyes, Nash began to climb. He caught up with Wilde at last and clamped a hand around his ankle.

Then the doctor knew he was there and was not pleased by the discovery. "What are you doing, you idiot?" Wilde shouted through the mask, shaking his leg violently. But Nash would not budge willingly. In fact, now that he had caught up with Wilde, he didn't know what to do next.

Clinging on to the rung before him with both hands, Dr Wilde risked lifting a foot off the ladder. Taking the strain with his arms he kicked out at the poor man beneath him.

"Get off!" he screamed as the heel of his shoe slammed into his assistant's cheek. "Get off!" He struck out again.

Nash's nose broke with a wet crack and he reeled, his vision blurring. His grip on the doctor's ankle slackened.

"Get! Off!"

Wilde's foot slammed down on the fingers of Nash's hand and the man let go. His intentions had been insanely courageous, but ultimately suicidal.

No scream escaped his lips as, only barely conscious, Abelard Nash dropped one hundred and thirty feet, only just missing the crenulations of the White Tower. The vaporous billows of the Galapagos serum swallowed his body and deadened the sound of his impact on the cobbles below.

Amazingly the fall did not kill the valiant, yet wretched, man instantly. Even as the de-evolved things that had once been the criminal inhabitants of the Tower of London tore his broken body apart, Abelard Nash was already beginning to resemble something less than human himself.

AND ALL THE while the bombs continued to fall. Only someone on board the airship was getting his eye in now.

A fourth bomb smashed into the roof of the Bloody Tower checkpoint, obliterating it entirely in a sheet of flame and concussive white noise. A fifth device thudded into the cobbled alleyway of Mint Street and remained there for a moment, buried up to its mid-line in the foundations of the roadway, before detonating seconds later. A sixth bomb demolished the riverside wall of Water Lane.

The seventh device shunted out through the belly of the gondola missed the gatehouse of the Byward Tower but hit the ground in the culvert beneath the bridge connecting the structure to the outer Middle Tower. The explosion brought down part of the bridge and shattered the foundations of Byward, the tower falling in on itself and breaching the outer defences of the facility.

Somewhere in the distance the wails of approaching emergency vehicles could be heard, although what they would be able to do to help now was anybody's guess. The greatest concentration of emergency services was on standby around Hyde Park and the surrounding streets that night. Those few that would be spared to rush to the beleaguered Tower would be too little and too late to contain the situation.

With a great hooting and caterwauling Dr Wilde's test subjects – no longer men but changed into something more degenerate and primitive – broke free of their prison. The brutal ape-like creatures that emerged from the shattered gatehouse of the Middle Tower wore the garb of prisoners and prison officers alike, burst and torn by the warping bodies trapped within them.

A hairy beast at the front of the brawling pack – stripped to the waist with the faded blue tattoo of a death's-head just visible beneath the thick matting of orange fur covering its torso – rose up on its hind legs and bellowed its savage intent at the sprawling capital. A small red light winking on the iron collar fastened around its neck, with a bellow of primeval fury, the apeman with the shark-like teeth led the rambling degenerate tribe west and into the city.

* * *

THE SILVER PHANTOM rounded the corner of the Tower and sped away along Byward Road. Having cleared the gap between the separating sections of the bridge and smashed through the barriers on the other side, the car and its three jolted passengers had pulled up outside the Tower as the zeppelin passed over the prison complex.

It had been immediately apparent that there was nothing they could do that would make any real difference to the catastrophe engulfing the prison. Instead they pulled away, Ulysses seizing the opportunity to get ahead and warn the authorities at Hyde Park of the impending danger. Then, suddenly, he had a novel idea.

"Nimrod, stop the car!" he commanded. His manservant reacted in an instant, slamming on the brakes hard.

The Phantom slewed to a halt on Byward Street, west of the Tower, a steam-powered vegetable delivery van honking its horn as Nimrod blocked the road. Ulysses leapt out and ran round to the boot of the car.

"Sir, is this really the time?" Nimrod shouted from the driver's window.

Simeon was bouncing up and down on the back seat in unrestrained excitement.

Ulysses had opened the boot and was rummaging through the eclectic mix of objects that cluttered the back of his car.

"Trying to win us an advantage," Ulysses called back, tugging aside a tarpaulin and rooting around in the compartment next to the spare wheel.

The airship was heading towards their position now, pulling away from the Tower as it continued on its inexorable journey westwards across the capital.

"Sir, I don't think we have anything that can bring down a zeppelin," Nimrod stated with grim finality.

"I'm not planning on bringing it down." He said, and then he found what he was looking for. "Yes! I knew that this was still in here!" he lifted out a heavy metal cylinder.

"Oh no, sir, you don't mean..."

"Look, don't worry about me," Ulysses said, slamming the boot shut and flashing Nimrod a devilish grin. "I've told you before; I'm making this up as I go along. You just worry about getting to Hyde Park before that dirigible does. Find Allardyce, or whoever's in charge there. Warn him. Tell him the Queen is in danger. Here," he said reaching into a jacket pocket and taking out a slim leather card case. "You'll probably need this. Now go!"

Nimrod didn't question the command but, trusting to his employer's instincts, drove off at speed, leaving a fumy cloud of exhaust in his wake.

With Nimrod, Simeon and the Phantom speeding away in the direction of Hyde Park and the festivities being held there, and with the armoured zeppelin of the Darwinian Dawn heading towards him at cruising speed, Ulysses secured his cane in the belt of his trousers before hefting the dull grey barrel of the launcher onto his shoulder. Jerking his shoulders to adjust its position, he sighted the approaching airship.

Ulysses closed his eyes and breathed in deeply. Letting the breath out again in a controlled manner, he focused. It was a conscious effort to slow his heart rate and calm his adrenalin-agitated system, a technique he had learnt from the monks of Shangri-La. All the while his extra-sensory awareness screamed, his heightened fight or flight response setting every nerve ending tingling, trying to prepare him for whatever might befall him next.

Ulysses had the aft section of the airship's gondola caught in the cross hairs.

"Steady," he told himself, letting the dirigible come even closer still. "Steady."

He tracked a spot on the gondola's hull, moving with it, until the airship was directly above him. And only then did he pull the trigger.

With a firework *whoosh* the rocket-grapple launched, the claw hurtling skyward, a high-tensile cable uncoiling from the chamber behind it in a spinning whirl. Through the cross hairs of the launcher's sights, Ulysses watched as the grapple struck the side of the gondola and snagged around an engine mounting, locking shut like a gin-trap.

With the grapple locked tight, the winding mechanism inside the launcher kicked in, motor screaming as it wound in the slack on the cable. Hanging onto the launcher handle, muscles tensed, Ulysses' feet left the ground and the breath was snatched from his lungs as he was carried upwards into the smoggy London night sky. The winch continued to wind him in as the zeppelin continued on its inexorable flight across the capital towards Hyde Park and the downfall of the British Empire.

CHAPTER TWENTY-TWO

State of Emergency

THE TORNADO HOWL of the engine in his ears, Ulysses clung on as the grapple-winch wound in the last few feet of cable bringing him within reach of one of the gondola's landing struts. Buffeted by the wind, with London spread out below him like an illuminated street map, he reached up with his left hand and grasped hold of the strut. Now, how was he to get inside?

Ulysses looked around him, scanning the exterior of the armoured gondola for an easy access point. An arm's reach away, in front of the undercarriage was an emergency release handle.

Adjusting his grip around the landing strut, his eardrums aching at the pressure of the whirling propeller roar, he released the grapple-launcher and swung himself under the hull of the gondola, grabbing hold of the pull-release. He pulled the handle away from the riveted hull and, with a hiss of escaping air, a panel swung open.

He hung there for a moment, feeling a twinge in his right shoulder, the wind whipping around him, tugging at his jacket, as he considered the precipitous drop beneath him. Then, with a supreme effort, he swung out beneath the gondola, letting go of the landing strut and grasped the lip of the open hatchway. Fingertips scrabbling for a better purchase, he seized hold of a cable bundle, just as the sweaty fingers of his left hand lost their grip on the release handle. He winced, gritting his teeth against the pain flaring in his right shoulder and, for a moment, Ulysses swung from the open hatchway by one arm, the fatal drop waiting below him.

Then, at last, his left hand found a hold and he hauled himself up into the belly of the gondola, puling the hatch shut after him.

Crouched next to the access panel, Ulysses quickly took in the criss-crossing girders ahead and behind him. He was in some kind of service and maintenance sub-deck. Knotted cabling ran the length of the space and the roof was too low for him to stand upright.

Inside the roar of the engines became a background thrumming that he could feel vibrating through his body. The tight space was hot with the smell of rubber glue and oil. To his right a metal ladder led up to a hatch. This, he deduced, must lead into the main body of the airship's gondola carriage. He listened at the hatchway, trying to filter out the background noise of the engines. He could hear nothing out of the ordinary so, pistol in hand, he opened the hatch. Poking his head through he found himself looking at a narrow corridor, with a wheel-locked door at the far end. Without further hesitation, Ulysses pulled himself up and into the main body of the zeppelin.

His sixth sense flared even as he heard the metallic click of a door opening.

INSPECTOR MAURICE ALLARDYCE surveyed the great and the good of the empire of Magna Britannia. Minor royalty, nobility, politicians, philosophers, academics, scientists, industrialists, philanthropists and self-made millionaires of one kind or another, all gathered together under the glass roof in the second Crystal Palace.

The Bolshevik in him wanted to rise up and overthrow the bourgeoisie oppressor. This part of him despised them all. In his eyes they had all got to where they were, and continued to enjoy the position they were in, by taking advantage of the downtrodden working classes. Men like that were the bane of his life, just like Ulysses Quicksilver had been. Allardyce prided himself on being a 'common man', rising from a humble working class background, his father a navvy at the cavorite works at Greenwich, to become an Inspector of Her Majesty's Metropolitan Police. He had not taken advantage of anyone to get where he was today.

But cut Maurice Allardyce in half and you would have seen the words 'Royalist' and 'Patriot' running right the way through. Again, it was Allardyce's working class roots that had bred in him a fierce devotion to the crowned head of Magna Britannia. He had been brought up to respect the throne of England and all that it stood for even though, ironically, it was the House of Hanover that had taken advantage of and kept entire nations – and now most of the globe – downtrodden beneath its colossal heel. But then Allardyce's logic gave up long before ever reaching such conclusions. He liked to keep things simple – black and white, right and wrong – which was one of the reasons why he had become a policeman and another reason why he despised men like Ulysses Quicksilver.

As a servant of Her Majesty's police force it was his duty to protect the Queen and all Her Majesty's guests. On this most grand and important of occasions, the responsibility for seeing that the monarch came to no harm had been laid directly upon him. When he had been given the news of this latest assignment he had almost burst with pride.

Pride that he felt now as he looked across the vast expanse of the Crystal Palace's interior. It was bedecked with glittering chandeliers strung with the lights of thousands of candles, and was laid end to end with tables covered with miles of cloth, hundreds of floral arrangements, ice sculptures, and thousands of pieces of cutlery and crockery. All this to feed twelve hundred guests at a gala dinner that was the culmination of a day of empire-wide festivities, parades and celebrations. In London alone these had included a fly-by by Her Majesty's Royal Airship *The Empress*, and the unveiling of the colossal statue of Britannia. Ninety feet tall and wearing draped white robes with her traditional regalia of Corinthian helmet, trident, spear and Union flag-bearing the hoplon shield, this striking statue had been designed by the world-renowned Italian sculptor and artist Eduardo Michelangelo.

As he was checking on the positions of the Peeler-drones and their human counterparts stationed around the perimeter of the palatial dining room, Inspector Allardyce became aware of the commotion halfway down the hall to his right. The guests seated close to this spot were turning round in confusion and annoyance. Swearing like the navvy's son he was Allardyce hurried to intercept the constable-droid now approaching him. The Peeler-drone's black carapace had been polished especially for the occasion to give it that 'just off the production line' look.

"What is going on, Palmerston?" Allardyce demanded.

"Is that Allardyce?" an imposing, grey-haired older man was asking as he pushed his way out from behind the constable-droid. "It is imperative that I speak with you, sir."

"And who the bloody hell is this? Did you let him in here? What's wrong with you? Is your Babbage unit on the blink, you useless piece of scrap?"

"I have a dire warning to impart, Inspector," the man was insisting. He was wearing an outfit befitting a gentleman's butler.

"How did you get in here?" Allardyce demanded. The butler flipped open a leather cardholder. "You're not sodding Ulysses Quicksilver that's for sure!"

"No, inspector. My name is Nimrod."

"Somebody take that off him at once!" Allardyce snapped. No one had thought to revoke Ulysses' security clearance since his widely reported demise, and the slowly chugging administrative machine was yet to deal with the aberration.

As a Peeler-drone moved to obey, something that looked like a gorilla in a dinner jacket flung out an arm and lifted Constable Palmerston off the ground, one meaty hand gripping the robot's neck.

"And what the bloody hell is *that*?" Allardyce shrieked, pointing at the man-beast lurking at Nimrod's shoulder. Fully half the diners were looking in the direction of the rumpus now.

"*He*," Nimrod stated pointedly, "is my associate, Simeon." Curiously, the Neanderthal didn't look entirely out of place in his black suit, shirt and tie.

"And for the umpteenth time, who exactly are you, Mr Nimrod?"

"I am Mr Quicksilver's personal manservant."

"Well, you are incredibly poorly informed for someone who was once in that dandy's employ. Hadn't you heard? Quicksilver's dead!"

"Look, we haven't got time for this, Inspector. The queen is in terrible danger. There has been a mass breakout from the Tower."

"The Tower? Are you mad as well as stupid? That's a maximum-security facility. The only way anyone could break out of there would be if someone on the outside blasted a hole in the wall."

"Such as someone with a zeppelin carrying a payload of explosives like the ones that you and your men recovered from the Underground, you mean?"

Doubt suddenly seized hold of Allardyce then.

"Mr Nimrod, you are under arrest. Constable Palmerston, would you..."

"Is there a... problem, Inspector?"

Allardyce froze, hearing the icily calm voice behind him. He turned, suddenly flustered. "No, Prime Minister, no problem at all."

Uriah Wormwood peered down his nose at Allardyce from behind steepling, porcelain-fine fingers and arched a quizzical eyebrow in the Neanderthal's direction. "Only her majesty is preparing to address her loyal subjects."

"Yes, Mr Wormwood sir, of course, sir. I was just about to have this felon and his monkey escorted from the premises."

"Very good, Inspector. Carry on."

"Prime Minister!" the belligerent butler suddenly shouted, the carefully judged tone of his voice cutting through the hubbub of the excited diners. "Mr Wormwood, sir! I have a message from Mr Ulysses Quicksilver."

The Prime Minister suddenly froze and then turned quick as a striking snake.

"What message?" he asked in an icy hiss that dropped even a few degrees more.

"Her Majesty is in terrible danger, sir. The Darwinian Dawn are on their way here now in an armoured airship having engineered the release of the maniacs from the Tower of London. They also have a payload of explosives like those used in their earlier bombing campaigns, only ten times more powerful. You have to get the Queen to safety, sir!"

The Prime Minister listened to the butler's outburst with consternation knitting his brow. Then a slow, reptilian smile spread across his face and he leapt onto the dais from which the speeches were to be made, with almost balletic joy. Not once did he question the veracity of the butler's words.

"Your Majesty, honoured guests, lords, ladies and gentlemen," he said into the microphone, his voice reverberating from speakers positioned throughout the Crystal Palace and being relayed to those enjoying the spectacle via the giant broadcast screens around Hyde Park, "I am sorry to interrupt these celebrations but it has come to my attention that those who traitorously seek to overthrow our glorious empire are making one last desperate move at the very heart of our nation, within the capital itself!"

Cries of disbelief erupted from the assembled throng.

"Even as I speak the most violent and dangerous criminals this nation has ever known are running amok through the streets of our capital and all reports suggest that they are bringing their wanton orgy of carnage and destruction to our very gates, whilst the self-styled evolutionary revolutionaries of the Darwinian Dawn are heading this way, intending to depose our most beneficent and dearly loved monarch!"

There were screams now, the clatter and crash of tables overturning as the guests rushed to escape the oncoming chaos. Outside, in the shadow of the newly unveiled monolithic statue of Britannia, the crowds of gathered patriots and well wishers panicked, jostling one another to get away from the approaching menace, not caring who they trampled beneath their feet. It was truly every man for himself, as the animal instinct to fight or flee took over.

Back inside the rapidly emptying Crystal Palace Wormwood went on with his address to the nation. "Magna Britannia is facing the greatest threat it has known in over fifty years. And so, by the powers invested in me by the Anti-Terror Bill I declare that this nation is facing a state of emergency and do submit myself to take full control of our proud nation's resources to put down this insurrection and bring an end to this crisis. Londinium Maximum is now under martial law.

"Inspector Allardyce, have your men ready to repel an attack from the ground and the air. And somebody turn off those cameras. This broadcast is over!"

* * *

LETTING THE GUARD'S unconscious body slide to the floor of the corridor, Ulysses paused at the door to the zeppelin's flight deck to check the load of his pistol and unsheathe his sword-cane. It hadn't been hard for him to outwit a bunch of rank amateurs like those employed as guards by the Darwinian Dawn. What they lacked in ability and awareness they made up for in quasi-religious revolutionary zeal.

He paused with his hand on the door. As he was so fond of telling Nimrod, he was really just making this up as he went along. He wasn't sure who or what he would find waiting for him on the other side, or what he was going to do about it once he found out. But in all honesty anything that could be done to slow the approach of the airship or change its flight path would be better than nothing and would give the authorities the time they needed to neutralise the threat the zeppelin and the escaped prisoners posed.

With a bold move he pushed open the door and burst onto the flight deck of the lumbering craft. "Nobody move!" he shouted. "I am taking control of this airship in the name of the empire and Her Majesty Queen Victoria. Anyone who has a problem with that will be the first to get a bullet in the gut. Got that?"

Ulysses Quicksilver panned his outstretched pistol arm across the surprised faces of those on the flight deck. There was the scar-faced blackguard Jago Kane – turning up once again like a very bad penny indeed – an older man wearing a peaked cap and the innocuous plain black uniform of the Dawn at the helm whom Ulysses took to be its pilot and a tall, blond-haired gangling figure in lab coat and glasses.

"You're a harder man to kill than I gave you credit for, Quicksilver," Kane said with unsmiling humour.

"Let's hope the same doesn't prove to be the case with you," Ulysses threw back.

Ulysses' attention was momentarily drawn to the conglomeration of lights to the fore and below the still advancing airship. Through the glass bubble at the prow of the zeppelin's gondola he could see Hyde Park spread out beneath them.

"You've failed, Kane. You and your evolutionary revolutionaries," Ulysses sneered, savouring the moment. "It's over. Your little schemes for this great sceptre'd isle have all come to naught."

"Oh, I wouldn't be so sure of that," came a voice like honeyed silk, and suddenly Genevieve Galapagos – or rather Kitty Hawke – was behind him, the cold snub nose of a gun pressed to the back of his head. "And I won't miss this time, lover-boy."

CHAPTER TWENTY-THREE

The Importance of Being Simeon

"GOODBYE, LOVER," KITTY said.

There was a sharp crack. Ulysses flinched whilst Jago Kane gave a stifled groan, his scarred face twisting into an even more ugly grimace as he crumpled to the floor of the flight deck.

Momentarily deafened Ulysses spun round, instinct taking over, bringing both pistol and sword to bear.

"Don't look so shocked," Kitty said, levelling her gun at Ulysses. "He had served his purpose. As have you, Ulysses darling."

In the split second that followed it seemed to Ulysses as if time had slowed and yet, despite his state of heightened awareness, he could not move any more quickly himself. It was like he was trying to run through treacle. He could see Kitty's finger tightening on the trigger of the gun, see the barrel rotating to bring the next chambered round into the breach, see the sinister glint in her eye, the lascivious smile on her perfect rosebud lips. He was aware of the distant chatter of what he thought was gunfire. He could feel the thrumming of the airship's engines through the metal panels of the floor beneath his feet; smell the weird mixture of combusted fuel and hot rubber.

And then time sped up again as an almighty explosion shook the gondola. Kitty's shot went wide, the high velocity round striking one of the floor-to-ceiling windows at the nose of the craft. There was a sharp *plink*. All eyes focused on the perfectly round hole in the glass and Ulysses felt the rush of air being sucked out of the cabin. A spider's web of cracks skittered across the glass and then the window exploded, a sudden strong wind howling through the cockpit.

The airship lurched and its course altered dramatically as the pilot fought to regain control. Then the zeppelin nose-dived, the floor dropping away beneath their feet. Ulysses smacked into the observation bubble at the front of the flight deck, landing facedown on the glass, his cheekbone and jaw receiving a nasty smack. His right shoulder clenched in pain and his ribs felt bruised and sore.

The blond-haired gangling scientist was not so lucky.

Dr Cornelius Wilde felt the rush of air as the window blew out and looked around in frantic panic at the chaos consuming the cockpit. What was going on? Who was the interloper who had just burst onto the flight deck at this crucial moment? And what exactly did he think he was going to achieve? For that matter why were fellow agents of the Darwinian Dawn suddenly shooting at each another?

Before any of his questions could be answered the gondola lurched sharply. The floor dropped away and suddenly he was falling through the cockpit cabin. He flung out an arm to arrest his fall but cried out in pain as it struck the iron girder of an exposed structural beam. And then he was pitched sideways out of the shattered hole where only moments before there had been a floor to ceiling window.

With a shrill scream Dr Cornelius Wilde plunged groundward, dropping through the unresisting air, the cigar of the dirigible seeming to fall away from him into the night sky.

As he hit the ground pain so fierce and shocking, that it would have taken his breath away even if it had not already been forced from him, seized his body in its bone-wrenching grip. He tried to move but a dislocated part of his mind told him that he had broken both legs, his right arm and probably his back, whilst various ruptured organs were even now filling his internal spaces with blood and other bodily fluids.

He suddenly felt so inexplicably tired that he decided he would just stay where he was and let sleep take him. The police would doubtless pick him up soon – the prospect seemed quite appealing – but until then he would just close his eyes for a few moments...

Hearing a savage grunt, Dr Wilde forced his drooping eyes open again. Standing over him was a colossal brute of a creature. It looked almost like a man in shape and form but there were some distinct differences, which that same detached part of his mind now focused on. The creature had the pronounced brow of a Neanderthal and its bruised and battered features looked like those of the lower orders of primates. Its shoulders were broad, its arms long and muscular and much of its exposed skin was covered with thick, wiry hair. From the waist down it was still wearing its grubby prison fatigues.

Wilde was gripped by a sudden and fearful realisation, just as a glimmer of what could almost have been recognition entered the apeman's eyes. Then he took in the collar clamped around the creature's bulging neck and the improvised club – what looked like part of a drainpipe – clenched in one curled fist.

A low growl issued from deep within the chest of the creature and Wilde felt what little blood there was left in his cheeks drain from them, the perspiration of shock and horror beading on his forehead. His blurring vision was drawn to a smudge of blue ink that was the mark of something on the flesh of the creature's chest under the fur that now covered much of it. The image had been stretched and distorted by the physiological changes that the creature's body had undergone, but it was still recognisable as a death's-head tattoo.

"M-McCabe?"

The apeman growled again, baring sharp yellow teeth in a grimace of simian aggression. Suddenly Wilde found himself surrounded by more of the de-evolved prisoners, all displaying the same stooping gait, arms pent up with furious muscular strength.

Shock forcing any desire for sleep from his mind, Wilde scrabbled for the control box with his shaking left hand. It lay at his side, the leather harness broken. He was dimly aware of buckled metal beneath his fingertips. Then they found purchase on the controls and Wilde furiously flicked at the switches and twisted the dials. But no matter what he did, it made no difference to the behaviour of the creature looming over him now. A high-pitched mewling whimper escaped Wilde's lips as he realised what was going to happen to him.

Wilde's degenerate army of psychotic apemen had reached Hyde Park. And now there was no one capable of controlling them.

The ape-beast that had once been the serial killer and cannibal, Ramsey 'The Shark' McCabe, felt a murmur of something in its primitive brain, an emotion that a more intelligent species might have called satisfaction, a feeling that justice had at last been served. Was there even a hint of something that a creature which could still articulate would have named, 'revenge'? Whatever the truth, it was its own creature again, with a mind of its own – with a mind to kill.

THE AIRSHIP JOLTED slightly as the shots hit home.

"That was a lucky hit," Nimrod muttered, slighting the Met's efforts.

"Lucky or not we got them!' Allardyce declared with grim triumph.

"All units!" he called into his communicator. "Hit them again with everything we've got!"

At his command, the armed officers and droids of the Metropolitan Police Force opened fire once more on the zeppelin, which was even now dropping lower over the park, as if making a final strafing attack run. Truth be told, no one quite knew how they had managed to hit the zeppelin and take out an engine but they were certainly going to try to do the same again.

THE ZEPPELIN PULLED out of its nose-dive and, hearing a cat-like shriek, Ulysses uncanny prescience flared and he rolled quickly onto his back. Then Kitty Hawke was on him. Carefully manicured nails clawed at his face, drawing blood. Her toned thighs gripped him around the waist, painfully squeezing his kidneys.

Pistol and sword abandoned, Ulysses grabbed Kitty's wrists and pushed her back up off him.

"Oh, Mr Quicksilver," she purred, her eyes those of some feral creature, mad and staring beneath the loosened fringe of her auburn hair, "are you always so rough on a first date?"

Swinging from the hips, pushing with his legs and pulling at the same time with his arms, Ulysses rolled onto his side again only this time trapping the coquettish Miss Hawke beneath him.

"First date?" he queried. "I thought this was the break-up!"

The two of them wrestled across the steel plate of the flight deck, the rattle of gunfire besetting the zeppelin and shattering windows around them. Until only recently, the thought of enjoying such vigorous physical contact with the erstwhile Genevieve Galapagos would have brought a twinkle to his eye and a yearning to his loins.

"I bet you never thought Genevieve Galapagos could be so frisky," Kitty teased, as if reading his mind.

Part of Ulysses still couldn't help finding the tousle-haired beauty beneath him attractive, the heave of her bosom in danger of escaping from her low-cut blouse, her lithe legs wrapped tight around his waist, hugging his flat stomach against hers. Only it wasn't Genevieve Galapagos, and although it had been Kitty Hawke's physique he had found arousing, it had been Genevieve's demure vulnerability he had been smitten by.

"Nothing but lies and deception, my dear, that's all it was," Ulysses stated accusingly. "I wanted to believe you. I wanted all my suspicions to be proved wrong. Genevieve Galapagos was such a charming, demure and sensitive young woman, whereas it would appear that Miss Kitty Hawke – streetwalker and gun-for-hire – is another manner of creature altogether. A complete and utter – how shall I put this? – bitch!"

With that Kitty Hawke spat at Ulysses, making him jerk back as the gobbet of saliva hit him squarely in the face. "You bastard!" she snarled.

Ulysses winced as she raised a knee, ramming it into his groin. As his own grip slackened in reaction to the sickening pain, the gorge rising in his throat, Kitty seized her chance. Managing to free one hand from Ulysses' grip, she grabbed his left arm, pulled her head up and sank her teeth into his wrist. Ulysses couldn't help but cry out in pain.

"I don't normally make a habit of hitting women," Ulysses gasped as Kitty hung on with her teeth, "but in your case I think I'll make an exception!"

His own right hand was free now and bunched into a fist. The punch descended, delivering a resounding blow to the side of Kitty's head. Her grip slackened and the hellcat slumped unconscious to the deck.

Wind howled around the cabin-cockpit, smoke boiling in from the burning engine. The remainder of the Darwinian Dawn were dead, unconscious or missing. The pilot lay broken at the helm. There was no one controlling the course of the zeppelin now.

Wrapping a handkerchief around his wrist to stem the flow of blood, Ulysses got rather unsteadily to his feet. He glanced down at the beaten beauty who looked so peaceful and innocent now, as if merely sleeping.

"Consider our relationship over," he said snidely, carefully probing his groin with one hand. And then, to no one in particular, "Now, let's see about stopping this thing."

"What's the situation on the ground, Nimrod?" his employer's voice crackled over the comm.

"In a word, chaos, sir," Nimrod replied matter-of-factly. "It's madness down here. The fugitives from the Tower have reached the park and are going on a bloody rampage. There are hundreds of them, sir and they're all..." Nimrod broke off, suddenly lost for words as he gazed upon the scene of carnage before him.

He stood at one of the entrances to the New Crystal Palace looking out across the darkened lawns of Hyde Park. Everywhere he saw the public fleeing as the savage subhumans slaughtered policemen and fleeing dinner guests in an orgy of violence.

Simeon loitered at Nimrod's side, rocking from one foot to the other, as if just waiting for the command to join the fray.

The officers of the Met were fighting back but the savage brutes seemed able to sustain endless injuries, some unnatural vigour keeping them going even after they had been shot. The automata-policemen were faring little better, the ape-like creatures tearing them limb-from-robotic-limb, twisting off the droids' heads as if unstoppering bottles of beer.

"Nimrod, please repeat, I missed that last bit," Ulysses' voice came back.

"It's as you feared, sir. They're de-evolving. They're apemen, primitive savages with a taste for blood that delight in killing."

"Just as I suspected. Then I have a solution. Nimrod, get everyone out of the Crystal Palace: the Queen, Prime Minister Wormwood, everyone. And then get the apemen contained within it."

"And how do you suggest I do that, sir?" he asked, letting off a shot from his pistol as a tattooed ape smashed a droid-constable into the ground not ten feet away from him.

"There was some hare-brained scientist fellow on board using some kind of device to control them. He took it with him when he made his unexpected exit from the zeppelin through a window."

"I don't think anyone's controlling them now..." Nimrod broke off again as his eyes focused on the massive brute at the centre of the ape-pack. The creature was bellowing whilst holding something above its head.

"Nimrod? Come again old chap. I lost you again there."

The manservant said nothing as he stared at the mangled, blood-splattered wreckage of what could very well have been the device that Ulysses was talking about. Then the roar of aero-engines filled his ears and he looked up to see the zeppelin bearing down on the New Crystal Palace out of the flickering night's sky.

"Get them inside!" Ulysses was shouting. "I can't keep this thing airborne much longer. Ready or not, I'm coming!"

Nimrod jumped as Simeon gave a great bellowing hoot beside him and then leapt into the fray, barging policemen, party-goers and apemen out of the way as he made for his target.

He might only be a primitive imitation of a man but he understood enough to know that his new masters needed his help and he knew an alpha male of a pack when he saw one too.

Simeon's sudden outburst shook Nimrod into action. Turning, he ran back into the palace behind him. "Your attention ladies and gentlemen, if you would be so good as to make your way to the nearest exit? Everybody out! Move!"

BATTING A SHAMBLING prisoner-ape aside with a double-fisted swipe, Simeon landed in front of the pack leader, the towering, collared, half-naked creature holding the ruined control box in its massive paws. The ape-thing fixed him with its beady yellow eyes from beneath beetling black brows.

Simeon rose up and then, ripping open his jacket and the shirt beneath, beat a tattoo of challenge upon his chest.

Lips pulled back from yellow teeth as the apeman displayed its response to Simeon's threat. It knew that its position as head of the pack was being challenged. And it seemed that the other apemen sensed it too. With a roar it returned the gesture, hurling the metal box aside. With barely a moment's hesitation, it threw itself at the Neanderthal.

Simeon was braced, ready for the tattooed ape's attack. As the brutal savage grabbed him round the middle, he trapped the brute in a headlock.

Toes gripping the turf beneath its feet the alpha apeman pushed up with its legs. Eyes bulging and face turning purple as Simeon tightened his grip around its neck, the apeman lifted its challenger off the ground. With a guttural, half-choked growl of effort it threw itself backwards, hurling Simeon over its shoulders. The two of them crashed to the ground, the action loosening Simeon's hold. But in the next instant the two battling primitives were on their feet again, a circle clearing around them – as the other apemen moved back or paused to watch – like a pair of roustabout prize-fighters ready for round two.

With mutual roars of aggression the Neanderthal and the apeman threw themselves at each other. Kicking, punching, gouging and biting, the two brute wrestlers fought on. They appeared equally well matched – one a de-evolving serial killer and cannibal, the other the semi-tamed product of a mad professor's dark ambition.

Getting in under Simeon's guard, the apeman sank its teeth into the Neanderthal's side. In response Simeon clubbed the savage around the head with both huge hands locked into one fist. The Neanderthal twisted a red-furred arm behind the monster's back until something snapped, the ape planted a foot into Simeon's midriff and kicked him clear with a roar of shrieking baboon rage.

Simeon crashed to the ground on his rump and felt something sharp dig painfully into his back. He reached behind him, hands closing around the roughly cuboid object, as the apeman, blood streaming from various cuts and grazes, bounded towards Simeon, ready to finish him once and for all.

The Neanderthal brought his arm back round, smacking the ape-savage around the head with the mangled control box. The blow sent the apeman tumbling sideways, stunned. Before it could recover itself, Simeon was on his feet again, the metal box now held in both hands above his head. With one powerful motion he brought the lump of metal and electronics down on top of the apeman's skull. There was a wet crack and the de-evolved convict slumped motionless onto the churned turf, but just to be sure, Simeon did the same again.

Ripping the torn remnants of the soiled shirt from his back, filled with his own feelings of savage satisfaction, Simeon planted one foot on the corpse of the apemen's bested quasi-leader. Howling with barely restrained feral joy he beat his chest again, his bellow ringing across the darkened park. The rest of the ape-pack seemed to freeze and then the regressed fugitives answered Simeon with a hooting cry of their own as they saluted their new leader.

With a sweep of his arm Simeon beckoned his tribe towards the glittering structure of the New Crystal Palace.

ULYSSES DUCKED AS another pane of glass was blown to smithereens by gunfire. Gripping the wheel tightly in both hands – so tightly in fact that he could feel the nagging pain in his right shoulder grumble again – he braced himself against the floor of the flight deck as the zeppelin closed on the New Crystal Palace.

He felt a sudden tug on his leg and started. It was Jago Kane.

"We're going to die, aren't we?" he gasped, spluttering through bloody lips.

"You might be planning on doing so," Ulysses remarked sourly, "I, however, do not intend to go down with this particular sinking ship."

"Look, I know what you think of me," Kane coughed, bringing up more blood, "and you know what I think of you. You might say that our moral codes are... incompatible."

"Moral code? You?" Ulysses almost laughed.

"Look, just listen you arrogant shit," Kane's voice was as cold and clear as ice. "If you do get out of this alive the one you really want is Uriah Wormwood."

"Wormwood? What do you mean?"

"He's the one behind all this. Who else would have the power and influence to set something like this up, undetected?"

"How can I believe anything you tell me?"

"Can you afford not to?"

"Wormwood," Ulysses mused, half-forgotten suspicions reawakened. "But why are you telling me this now?"

"Because that slimy bastard betrayed me. He sold me out, me and my men, the ones who trusted his intentions." His increasing ire instigated another bout of cruel coughing. "Because if I'm going to die I want him to pay." Kane fixed Ulysses with a steely stare. "Swear it! Swear you'll get the bastard!"

"I... I swear it," Ulysses replied, dumbfounded, the words feeling strange on his tongue as he swore an oath to the man who had long been his nemesis.

The glittering glasshouse structure now filled the view from the shattered cockpit. There was no doubt that the airship was set on a collision course. Sprinting back up the slope of the flight deck, as the zeppelin dived towards the Crystal Palace, he hurled himself back through the door by which he had entered.

Its one remaining engine emitting a high-pitched whine, the zeppelin hit the Crystal Palace. Iron bracing struts buckled, glass shattered and the flight deck was filled with whickering diamond shards.

The deafening scream of shearing metal and the cacophonous blast of hundreds of panes of glass shattering rang throughout the juddering gondola as Ulysses half-ran and half-fell through the airship as he made his way to the zeppelin's bomb bay.

There, in their steel cradles, hung the last of the Darwinian Dawn's deadly devices. Each carried a portion of Professor Galapagos's deadly regression formula.

Tugging the gas mask from the corpse of a black-clad guard Ulysses put it on, the smell of warm rubber and human sweat assaulting his nostrils.

He pulled hard on the first of a series of large metal levers in front of him. With a yawning groan the bomb bay doors swung open. Looking down, through the hole in the bottom of the airship, Ulysses could see the red-haired ape-things capering about inside the Crystal Palace. Shards of glass had rained down on top of them as the gondola collided with the palace and some lay either dead or mortally wounded as a result. Others were running amok, overturning dining tables and throwing gilt candlesticks, fine bone china and silver-plate cutlery at one another whilst others tried to eat the table decorations.

Ulysses grabbed hold of the second lever and then paused. Keying a number into his personal communicator he put the device to his ear. When the call was picked up he said, "Nimrod, are you clear?"

"Yes, sir. Everyone is out."

"Then keep going. This is one grand finale that's guaranteed to bring the house down."

"Yes, sir. Good luck. Nimrod out."

Ulysses took hold of the lever and pulled hard. Released from its harness the first of the Galapagos-bombs rolled forwards and off the end of the tilting cradle. Locking the lever in place, Ulysses got clear of the bomb bay as the rest of the devices followed the first, dropping towards the half-destroyed palace.

The airship had become wedged within the roof of the Crystal Palace, so that its gondola now hung amidst crumpled roof joists, its dirigible balloon still above it and undamaged outside of the stricken structure. For a moment Ulysses' world was wonderfully still, and then the first of the devices made groundfall.

Sheets of flame burst from the shattered glasshouse, consuming what had, only a matter of hours before, been a grand dining hall in a raging firestorm. The limp bodies of apemen were tossed into the air. The series of detonations rocked the gondola. Then, after the initial explosions, came the transmuting chemical clouds.

Having already been exposed to the weaponised gas of the formula, the Galapagos transformation was accelerated within the bodies of those convict-apemen not killed by the explosions. Stricken by a terrible palsy, their warping bodies spasmed as their entire physiological structure regressed at an unimaginable rate. Savagely snarling ape-features became as fluid as melting wax, mutating into lizard-like visages. Fur fell away to reveal scales or pliable amphibian skin.

Grotesque abominations were born as entire cell structures collapsed under the incessant changes they were being subjected to. Things that were half-mammalian and half-reptilian gurgled and hissed in their death-throes. Things with the blunt snouts of primitive men slithered through the coiling, rancid mists, limbs uncertain as to whether they should be claws or fins. Fish eyes blinked from quivering mounds of amorphous flesh, bones dissolved into the fluid flesh of invertebrates.

The process of accelerated de-evolution continued to a chorus of mewling moans and croaking cries until the warping bodies could no longer support themselves. Every last one of them ultimately collapsed into a morass of protoplasmic ooze that covered the carpeted floor of the New Crystal Palace in sticky mucus-like slime.

And at the far end of the hall, amidst the pooling slime, lay the remains of an altered suit of clothes.

CHAPTER TWENTY-FOUR

Unnatural History

FLINGING OPEN THE door to the flight deck Ulysses surveyed the devastation. Glass littered the floor in myriad glittering shards. The bodies of the airship's pilot and the guardsmen lay where they had fallen. Kitty Hawke lay unconscious, face down, her body a pincushion for stiletto blade slivers of glass. But Jago Kane was gone.

Ulysses Quicksilver swore. Still his nemesis had managed to evade him. He had more lives than a cat! But wherever the murdering revolutionary had got to, he couldn't have gone far. He wouldn't have been able to make much of a head start with all his injuries. But, if Kane had been telling the truth – and Ulysses' own niggling suspicions made him believe that, incredibly, the terrorist might have been – the real villain of the piece could be making his getaway right now.

Leaning against a buckled strut Ulysses gazed down at the floor of the devastated Crystal Palace. Even through the gas mask he could smell the rancid meat and aniseed stench of the dissipating formula-gas. Amidst the bomb craters and burning piles of debris a thick ooze covered the floor of the building. From it rose wisps of a jaundice-yellow vapour. Nothing was moving down there, other than the occasional pop of a bubble in the seething slime.

Ulysses thought he heard the sound of footfalls. Looking to his left he could just see that where the gondola had come to rest. One of several maintenance walkways was accessible. From there his fugitive could easily make it to the ground and escape. That was the way Kane would doubtless be heading and it was where Ulysses needed to go now. For, even if his old nemesis had evaded him again, somewhere below, amidst all the chaos and confusion, Uriah Wormwood was in danger of getting away.

WORMWOOD CAST FITFUL glances around whilst striving to maintain an outward appearance of calm, self-assured superiority. He had allowed himself to be evacuated from the dining room, along with the Queen and her dinner guests, and stood now at the side of the contraption-bound monarch, along with Victoria's personal attendants – her ladies-in-waiting and personal physician, the French surgeon Dr Mabuse – the entire party being surrounded by a bodyguard of armed police officers. Fifty yards away stood the smouldering wreckage of the New Crystal Palace, the Darwinian Dawn's airship still locked within its steely embrace.

Wormwood glanced at the ruler of the greatest empire the world had ever known, the merest arching of an eyebrow betraying his true feelings of disgust and disdain. She was a far cry from the public image of the noble, determined woman who had ruled a quarter of the world during the greater part of the last century. There was more machine than monarch now, the physical husk the old woman had become was trapped inside the Empress Engine, a Babbage difference unit of the greatest complexity that provided life support and a basic level of steam-powered mobility for the Queen. The Widow of Windsor was just a withered creature kept alive long beyond her natural span and far longer than was good for her deteriorating mind. The scurrilous voice of rumour suggested that the encoded intelligence of the Babbage unit spoke on behalf of Her Majesty these days, mimicking the Queen's own voice by manipulating a bank of sound recordings made when Victoria was still able to speak for herself.

For many people the world over, Queen Victoria, Empress of India, Monarch of Mars and Ruler de facto of the Lunar colonies *was* the empire of Magna Britannia and Wormwood felt that too. She was the perfect embodiment of a decaying, outdated system maintained for much longer than was healthy for the benefit of the privileged few. But all that was about to change. When the sun rose the following morning, it would mark the dawning of a new age for Magna Britannia, its citizens and all the peoples of the world. The age of dinosaurs was over.

Thoughts of the future returned Wormwood to the upheavals taking place in the present. Things had not proceeded exactly according to plan, but he had his state of emergency nonetheless and had been able to put into play the special powers he was granted under the terms of the recently passed Anti-Terror Bill. This could still all turn out to his advantage. He just needed to make sure that he didn't let his mask of calm composure slip.

"Prime Minister, a word!" came a shout from behind him. Wormwood froze, feeling the trickle of ice water down his spine. It was the voice of Ulysses Quicksilver.

There was a gasp of wonderment from the gathered throng as Ulysses approached. Wormwood took a moment to compose himself and then turned to face the approaching dandy.

So it was confirmed. Ulysses had somehow survived Genevieve Galapagos's parting gift but he didn't look any the better for it. His once impeccable outfit was now in disarray as was the rest of him. His face was a mess of contusions, swollen lips and bleeding gashes. His left forearm was bound with a red-soaked handkerchief and one eye was half shut by a swelling black bruise.

"Greetings, Prime Minister," the rogue said, combing a hand through the tousled mess of his hair. "I am here to report the successful resolution of the case you yourself charged me with two months ago."

"You are?" Wormwood said warily.

"I am, Prime Minister."

"Did I miss something? Aren't you supposed to be dead?" the astounded Inspector Allardyce interjected, forgetting himself for a moment.

"And good evening to you, Inspector," Quicksilver said with a sideways glance, flashing the bemused trench-coated policeman a wry smile, wincing as he did so. "You just can't keep a good man down I suppose. Aren't you keen to hear my conclusions?" He said, addressing Wormwood again.

"As I understood it that matter had already been brought to a conclusion weeks ago," Wormwood said, a frown of annoyance lining his face.

"Indeed. And that was my own opinion on the matter – although I had some lingering doubts – until you tried to have me blown up."

A gasp passed around the gathered group.

"Are you out of your bloody mind?" Allardyce challenged. It had been a long day and everything had just gone tits up in the most spectacular way possible. He just felt lucky that the Queen herself wasn't dead. "Have you recently received a bang on the head? Cos if you haven't I'll happily give you one if you carry on like this."

"No, Inspector, I am in full command of my faculties, thank you," Ulysses bit back. He was aware of Nimrod joining him at his shoulder.

"Is everything all right, Prime Minister?" the recording-synthesised voice of the monarch herself crackled from the speaker-horn of her mobile throne.

"I do apologise, your majesty," Wormwood said, a quiver of uncertainty entering his voice for the first time. "This will only take a minute. I shall be with you shortly."

"I was about to say the same thing myself, your majesty," Ulysses called out.

Around the park and the streets of the capital beyond, a thousand broadcast screens – that had relayed the apeman attack to the nation as the cameras continued to roll – now relayed the intrigue unfolding before the burning glasshouse ruins to an eager and anxious public.

"Arrest that man," Allardyce ordered a pair of robo-constables. "And turn those bloody cameras off!"

"Hold that order!" Nimrod commanded, stepping in front of the two drones, leather wallet card-case held open in front of their visual sensors.

"On whose authority, sir?" one of the constables asked affably.

"By the authority stated here on this card, Constable Palmerston," Nimrod said, reading the drone's name off the badge on its chestplate.

"I don't bloody believe this," Allardyce fumed, in exasperation. "You're supposed to be under arrest!"

"Inspector, if you would be so kind as to actually do something!" snapped Wormwood.

"Yes, of course, sir." The inspector moved to take hold of Ulysses himself. "I'll have this tosser out of your hair in no time, sir, if you'll pardon my French."

"But aren't you intrigued to know who's been behind the Darwinian Dawn and their attacks on our glorious capital all along, Inspector?" Ulysses asked, turning his attention to Allardyce.

"Scotland Yard are looking into it."

"It was you, wasn't it, *Mr Prime Minister Wormwood*?"

The nation took a sharp collective breath as the dramatic confrontation played out across the empire, courtesy of the Magna Britannia Broadcasting Company's continuous coverage of the jubilee event.

All eyes now turned in startled disbelief to the Prime Minister. Nimrod threw Ulysses an uncertain look as much to say, "Do you realise what you are saying?" Then the merest rumour of a tick rippled across Wormwood's face and Nimrod's moment of doubt was gone; he was convinced. The world held its breath.

"Where's your evidence?" Allardyce demanded.

"Do you want to tell them, Prime Minister, or shall I?"

Wormwood appeared not to have an answer for the dandy, for a moment. That in itself was unusual for the Prime Minister, who was used to verbal sparring on a daily basis in the House of Commons.

"You have wasted enough of my time already," Wormwood said at last and then, changing the subject: "Her majesty must return to Buckingham Palace at once."

"No? Shall I then? It was a dangerous game you were playing, involving me in your schemes. Arrogantly dangerous in fact, but then you had your get out clause planned from the start, didn't you?"

Ulysses began to pace between the frozen constables, making expansive gestures with his hands as if giving an after dinner presentation.

"I don't know what really happened at the Natural History Museum that first fateful night – I suspect only two people really do, and one of them is dead – but I think I have a pretty good idea."

"The Natural History Museum? What's that got to do with anything?" Allardyce asked, incredulously. He was seriously out of his depth now.

"Everything," Ulysses stated simply.

"Would you care to enlighten us then, Mr Quicksilver?" It was Wormwood who spoke now, his voice like the hissing of a viper.

"Inspector, tell me, did you ever discover what was taken the evening the night watchman died?"

"Well..." Ulysses had caught him off guard.

"You must have realised that the late Professor Galapagos's difference engine had been stolen. And who would go to all the trouble of stealing a very specific difference engine from the professor's lab at the museum, other than our mutual friend Jago Kane – eh, Prime Minister? – working on behalf of your good self, of course.

"I can only surmise what happened. Kane broke in but was surprised by the professor who was working late that night. There was a scuffle, things got broken, including a beaker of Galapagos's regression formula, which splashed onto the professor. Kane was untouched and made his getaway but the doomed professor underwent a sudden and violent transformation, becoming the apeman that later escaped from the Museum."

Ulysses was well into his stride now.

"It wasn't the engine itself that you wanted as such, but the formula for the serum that was contained within its data files."

"So who killed the night watchman?" Allardyce asked, having been so sure that it had been the same mysterious thief up until that point.

"Ah, that would be Professor Ignatius Galapagos, or what had once been one of the world's leading evolutionary biologists before the formula changed him. But there's no point looking for him now, he's dead."

"So you said. What happened to him? And how do you know so much about it?" the bewildered Allardyce pressed on. "Did you kill him, Quicksilver?"

"Oh no, it wasn't me. You might say he was 'hoist by his own petard'."

"You what?"

"He got a taste of his own nasty medicine."

"You've lost me."

"Yes, I rather thought I had."

"But how does all this rumour and supposition allegedly link the Prime Minister with the Darwinian Dawn?" Allardyce threw in, smiling proudly to himself as if he had just played his trump card.

"Because Galapagos's difference engine contained the chemical breakdown of his regression formula, and the man who had that could reproduce as much of the stuff as he needed."

"Needed? For what?"

"For what you witnessed tonight: to create a suitably direct and dramatically devastating attack on the monarch, which would put his newly-introduced Anti-Terror Bill into action, thereby ensuring that he was given total control of the country and, by default, the entire empire. And all this would have been achieved perfectly legally, mind.

"But to access the difference engine's data files first he needed the unit's coded decryption key, and that was where his agent Jago Kane had fouled up. The now transformed Galapagos still had it about his person and that was where I came in, to search for the missing professor.

"If you hadn't given me that particular mission, I would never have stumbled upon the Dawn's secret bomb-making facility, but then you already know about that, don't you, inspector?"

Both Ulysses and Wormwood could see that the resolute Allardyce was wavering. His black and white view of the world was rapidly turning into a messy, confusing grey.

"You would trust the word of a known terrorist over that of your Prime Minister?" Wormwood yelled, his voice rising in pitch, his porcelain-pale skin flushing a deep crimson.

"But I still don't see how this all connects to the Prime Minister!" Allardyce was floundering

"I'm getting to that," Ulysses said darkly. "Two individuals have kept making regular appearances during the course of my investigations, either keeping me on track – giving me new clues, guiding me onwards – or alternatively attempting to frustrate my successful completion of the mission. Your accomplices, Prime Minister. You might call them your partners in crime. Jago Kane and Miss Genevieve Galapagos, the errant professor's lovely daughter."

No one passed comment now. Ulysses had his audience enthralled.

"The former a known terrorist now linked to the Darwinian Dawn, the latter, a fiction. There is no such person as Genevieve Galapagos is there, Prime Minister? This femme fatale goes by another name, does she not? Miss Kitty Hawke, assassin and strumpet extraordinaire!

"And before the good Inspector asks me once again what all this has to do with you, I have the evidence that you have had direct dealings with both these individuals, thanks to hearing it straight from the horse's mouth – the nag in this case being a very ill-humoured and embittered Kane – and secondly because the professor's code-key, which I returned to his oh-so loving 'daughter', was fitted with a tracking device. Wherever your little kitten and her imagined father's locket went, I went too."

Ulysses was interrupted by the abrupt roar of an aero-engine. All attention was diverted away from him and back to the ensnared zeppelin. The craft's remaining engine was firing back into life. Accompanied by a terrible screeching of tortured metal, the airship freed itself from the palace roof.

All eyes in the park watched as the dirigible came about, yawing heavily to port with only one engine still in operation.

There was a sudden shriek from one of the Queen's ladies-in-waiting and a cry of, "Mon dieu!" from Dr Mabuse. Ulysses turned.

"You argue a very convincing case, Quicksilver. Well done, very clever. Consider your mission successfully... concluded."

Wormwood was standing beside the Queen's steam-powered throne, the cold grey muzzle of a gun pushed up against the forehead of the withered old woman smothered beneath her heavily-embroidered mourning clothes.

"Mr Wormwood, we are not amused. What is going on?" an incongruously chiding voice issued from the throne's speaker-horn.

"I am very sorry, Ma'am, but unfortunately it would appear that everything is unravelling around me. The best laid plans, as they say. Consider yourself my... hostage."

A dumbstruck Inspector Allardyce made as if to direct his officers to act.

"And before anybody does anything rash, Inspector, need I point out that a man who was prepared to accept the deaths of hundreds, if not thousands, of innocent Londoners, for the greater good, whose plans have fallen down about his ears and who has nothing at all left to lose, would not hesitate to put a bullet through your dear monarch's head?" Wormwood said.

"Allardyce, stop!" Ulysses commanded. A horrible smile spread across Wormwood's lips as he saw a glint of panic in Ulysses eyes. "Just tell me this. Why would a man in your position, with your power, be interested in destabilising the status quo and throw in his lot with a group of zealous, quasi-religious revolutionaries?"

"The Darwinian Dawn? A mere fabrication, an invention of mine. Oh, of course, those who pledged their all to the cause believed it was for real, but it was merely a tool. But the core tenet behind it all is still sound."

"And that is?"

"Look around you, Quicksilver. Are you so blinkered by your own accepted worldview? Can you not see that there is so much wrong with London and, by extension, Magna Britannia itself? I could make it all so much better."

"So the Darwinian Dawn and its actions were merely a means to an end for you?" Ulysses said with growing realisation. "Engineer a suitably threatening state of emergency and then, with the powers granted you by your Anti-Terror Bill invoked you would..." Ulysses trailed off.

"Have the power to do what I wanted. To go back to beginning, to start from scratch. I would have brought an end to slum-living, overcrowding and endemic disease and re-built London."

"In your own image."

"I had a great master plan for this city. The greatest advances this nation has ever known have followed times of trial and tribulation, times of enforced evolution, if you will. Consider the Great Fire of 1666. From the ashes rose a greater city, a better city for all. From the ashes of Londinium Maximum a still greater metropolis could have arisen, like a phoenix from the flames.

"And change is always difficult and traumatic, I understand that, but I could have coaxed the nation through that time until it fulfilled its true potential. Magna Britannia is an out-moded dinosaur, a creature of a bygone age that should have become extinct long ago. Just think of me as the agent of evolution."

"By Jingo! Finally I see what all this has been about," Ulysses declared.

"Of course, I have just told you what it is all about you idiot!" Wormwood said.

"Well yes, but you have given us the politician's answer. It is when we read between the lines that we see the truth. This is all about power. That's all it's ever been about from the start. Absolute power... corrupts absolutely."

"The opinion of fearful fools."

"You would have effectively re-written history according to your own warped view of how you think the world should be, your own unnatural history of the British Empire. But history is written by the victors. And you just lost!"

"Sir!"

Ulysses heard his manservant's shout at the same time as he became aware of the swelling sound of the zeppelin's straining engine and felt the howling gale of its downwash tugging at his clothes and hair.

Nose angled towards the ground, the zeppelin powered across the spoiled lawns of the park on an apparent collision course with the royal party. Gunfire chattered and ricocheted from the body of the armoured shell of the airship as Victoria's personal guard opened fire.

And then the dirigible was passing directly over them. Something swung out of the darkness beneath it. Ulysses ducked, the rattling rope ladder sweeping past him. As Ulysses rose again, following the airship's passing, his sixth sense flashing him a warning, he already knew what was going to happen. Time seeming to slow around him, he reacted without thinking, operating on instinct alone.

Then the zeppelin was rising and the Queen stood alone again, Wormwood scrambling up the ladder as the airship climbed to move out of range of fire.

Ulysses sprinted across the grass, paying no heed to how Allardyce and his robo-Bobbies might react, and then the last rung of the ladder soared away out of reach. The moment had passed. He had missed that vital window of opportunity.

Prescience flared again and one of the craft's mooring cables swung out of the darkness behind him. Suddenly fate had presented him with a second chance, and Ulysses leapt.

"Do you think he knows what's he's bloody well doing?" Allardyce asked the manservant.

"Oh, I expect he's making it up as he goes along, sir. That's his usual strategy," Nimrod replied.

Arms and legs aching, lungs heaving, heart pounding fit to burst, Uriah Wormwood staggered onto the flight deck of the airship. Air howled in through the shattered hemisphere of the gondola's burst glass bubble.

Amidst the wreckage of the cockpit Kitty Hawke, clothes and skin cut by splinters of glass, clung to the ship's wheel, her half-leaning stance making it hard to discern whether she was struggling to maintain control of the craft or whether she was clinging tightly to the steering mechanism to hold herself up.

Wormwood joined the young woman at the controls. Kitty turned, glaring at him in petulant, frustrated fury. Her hair hung down about her shoulders, in a wind-swept mess. Her perfectly-sculptured features were criss-crossed by the surgeon-fine red lines of myriad glass cuts and a bruise darkened the flesh above her right cheekbone.

"We failed," she said, the fire suddenly gone from her.

"No, my dear. This is not a failure. It is merely a... setback," Wormwood said, pulling himself up tall, staring into the distance. "We have merely lost the battle, not the war. I am not done with Londinium Maximum yet. No, this is not the end. The world has not heard the last of Uriah Wormwood. Or Kitty Hawke." Stiffly the elder statesman stretched out an arm and placed a hand on Kitty's shoulder.

"No, father."

Wormwood continued to stare out of the shattered cockpit, eyes narrowing against the rush of air. Below them the Victoria Embankment gave way to the rippling black mirror of the Thames, glistening with the lights of the sleepless city.

"We appear to be losing height, my dear," he said at last, as the floodlit barbican of Tower Bridge filled more and more of his field of vision.

"It's the balloon," Kitty said, sounding exhausted. "We've taken too much damage. I've lost rudder control and we're going down."

"How vexing. Then it is time to take evasive action, my dear, would you not agree?"

"Yes, father, only I think it might be too late for that."

"It's never too late, my dear. Remember that. It's never too late."

ULYSSES CLUNG ON. His arms ached, his right shoulder numb with pain. He only wished he knew what he was supposed to do next. All he could do, it seemed, was hold on and hope to finally catch up with the errant Prime Minister when the airship finally came to ground, wherever that might be. But it seemed that the craft might be making its descent sooner rather than later.

Tower Bridge loomed before it and, rather than rising to pass over the rather obvious obstacle the edifice presented, the zeppelin was dropping towards it. A hundred feet below the dark waters of the Thames swept on towards the sea.

Ulysses considered his options and soon surmised that he didn't really have any. A fall into those turgid waters from this height would like as not prove just as fatal as a collision with the stone pylons of the bridge.

Let go or hang on. "Damned if you do and damned if you don't," he found himself pondering aloud. "Come on, Quicksilver, you've got out of worse scrapes than this in the past." His mind suddenly rushed back to his plummeting descent through the freezing air over Mount Manaslu. He had escaped death then – thanks to the fickle whim of fate and the beneficent monks of Shangri-La – but could he again? Had he finally run out of last chances?

And then the decision was taken out of his hands.

The nose of the zeppelin struck the north tower of the bridge and crumpled. Moments later the gondola collided with the crenulated turret tops. There was the sound of metal scraping against ornately carved stonework as chunks of masonry came away from the towers. Then there was a spark.

The balloon erupted into flame, a series of explosions blowing it apart as one gas compartment ignited after another. The zeppelin's final blaze of glory lit the City district and the tenements of Southwark for miles in every direction.

Ulysses fell, the rope suddenly slack in his hands, eyebrows scorched by the explosion, the blazing carcass of the dirigible dropping after him.

Then there was a stabbing pain in his right shoulder, as talons seized hold of him. The thump of leathery wings beat the air and Ulysses was suddenly pulled away over the water, away from the plummeting zeppelin.

Ulysses looked up. Above him the pterodactyl that had decided that he would make a tasty snack was struggling to maintain height itself.

A moment longer, Ulysses realised, and the flying reptile would let go again, abandoning him to his original fate.

Now it was Ulysses' turn to hang on, grabbing hold of the pterodactyl's scaly legs even as it released its grip on his protesting shoulder. Ulysses' descent continued, only now in a more bizarrely controlled manner. It was only when his feet were practically dragging through the muddy waters of the river that Ulysses let go, the pterodactyl flapping away, back to its roost on the bridge.

He pulled himself from the river and climbed the iron rungs set into the embankment as the battered Silver Phantom pulled up on the road adjacent.

"It would appear that you have prevailed once again, sir," his butler said stoically as he emerged from the car and opened the rear passenger door.

"Indeed," Ulysses replied.

"If you don't mind me remarking, sir, you appear to be a little worse for wear."

"There's nothing quite like a night-time dip in the Thames is there Nimrod?"

"I wouldn't know, sir."

Nimrod shut the door after him and got back into the driver's seat. Ulysses gazed out through the darkened window.

"How is her majesty?"

"Returning to Buckingham Palace as we speak, sir."

"Good. Then the status quo is maintained. Everything is as it should be."

"I wouldn't say that, sir."

"No, I suppose you're right, now you mention it. Wormwood has made a change after all," he said, watching the burning wreckage of the zeppelin slowly being carried away on the surface of the restless river. "It is how those of us who are left deal with it that will make all the difference."

"Yes, sir."

"But we can worry about that later. Magna Britannia will still be there, waiting for us, in the morning won't it, old chap?"

"Thanks to you, sir."

"Bully for me."

And with that, the Silver Phantom slid away into the remains of the night and towards the dawning of a new day.

EPILOGUE

Queen and Country

"HER MAJESTY WILL see you now," a lady-in-waiting said and Ulysses Quicksilver was admitted to the high-ceilinged Throne Room.

Ulysses kept his head bowed as he approached the dais at the end of the ornately decorated audience chamber. Everything gleamed or sparkled, the crystalline light of the Throne Room's magnificent chandeliers reflecting from the gold leafed surfaces and polished marble.

The top tier of the dais, from where Queen Victoria had once received royal guests in person was now cordoned off from the rest of the room, surrounded by a curtain of scarlet velvet drapes.

There was a hazy quality to the air of the chamber and an all-pervading smell of pomanders and lubricating oil. Flunkies stood to either side of the dais, each of the automata-drones decked out in a footman's finery.

Ulysses looked up at the dais. The lady in waiting ushered him forwards and then disappeared behind the curtains herself, before emerging again and returning to Ulysses' side without saying a word.

Ulysses waited, standing to attention. He certainly didn't look out of place in top hat and tails, the sombre tones of the suit set off by a striking gold silk cravat embellished with a diamond pin and a red carnation buttonhole. In his right hand he held his bloodstone cane. His left arm was held tight to his chest in a black satin sling.

He cleared his throat nervously, recalling the last time he had met his monarch. A week had passed since the dramatic events surrounding the celebrations to mark the Queen's 160th jubilee year. If a week was a long time in politics, the political world had never known a week like the one just passed. Despite the Thames being trawled Jago Kane's body had not yet been recovered and he appeared to have disappeared from the face of the planet once again. At least the breakout from the Tower of London had been contained and work crews were already affecting repairs to the aging prison facility.

"Good morning, Mr Quicksilver," a voice like an old gramophone recording crackled from speakers standing either side of the drapes.

"Good morning, your majesty," he replied.

"Mr Quicksilver, we are informed that we have you to thank for the happy resolution of Prime Minister Wormwood's disgraceful rebellion."

Ulysses considered the hundreds who had died during the course of the Queen's jubilee and the terror attacks on the capital leading up to it. He would hardly have called it a happy resolution himself. But, "Thank you, Ma'am," was all he said.

"It would appear that you are following in a long-established family tradition, keeping the realm and the monarch safe from the predations of those who would see Magna Britannia fall."

"Just doing my bit, Ma'am."

"Well you are to be congratulated for your sterling work, and rewarded."

With a hiss of compressed steam one of the flunkies suddenly lurched into life. As it strode up to him, Ulysses saw that it was bearing a small tasselled cushion before it. Resting on the cushion was a piece of crimson ribbon, attached to a gunmetal-cast cross, bearing the motif of a crown surmounted by a lion, and the inscription 'FOR VALOUR'.

"We are awarding you the Victoria Cross for the valour and gallantry you demonstrated in selfless devotion to your Queen and Country, in the face of seemingly insurmountable odds." The Queen's lady-in-waiting stepped forward and, taking the medal from its cushion, pinned it to the lapel of Ulysses' jacket. "Congratulations, Mr Quicksilver."

"Thank you, Ma'am. I am deeply honoured."

There was a moment's silence, Ulysses waiting to see what else the monarch might have to say for herself, not certain whether it would be decorous to say anything himself without being spoken to first.

There was a crackle of static and Queen Victoria addressed him again. "That is all. You may go now."

"THE VICTORIA CROSS, very nice. I bet that would be worth a bob or two," Bartholomew Quicksilver said, eyeing up the medal as Ulysses descended the palace steps to the waiting Phantom.

"Yes, I expect it would. But it's not for sale," Ulysses said, smiling grimly at his incorrigible younger brother.

"Congratulations, sir," Nimrod said, beaming with paternal pride.

"Thank you, Nimrod."

"So, what did she say?" Barty pestered.

"Not a lot really."

"Not a lot? You have an audience with Queen Victoria herself..."

"After a fashion."

"... a privilege very few ever receive, and when asked what her royal highness said, all you can say is 'Not a lot really'? I would have thought you would have memorised every word, every syllable."

"You perhaps, Barty. It was quite underwhelming really."

"Well, I suppose anything would be after what you've been through recently."

Barty was much more his old self now. He was making a good recovery from the bullet wound he had received thanks to Kitty Hawke's botched assassination attempt. His near death experience had apparently given him a new lease of life.

"Look, I'll tell you all about it over luncheon," Ulysses sighed with mock weariness, giving his sibling an affectionate slap on the back. "What I need right now is a stiff drink. My last dose of painkillers is starting to wear off and I simply can't face another day of press interruptions and well-wishers without being at least a little bit tipsy. Nimrod, the Ritz, if you would be so kind?"

"Yes, sir. The Ritz it is."

As the two brothers settled themselves in the back of the automobile Barty turned to Ulysses. "Now that you're by royal appointment, as it were, think of the future, Ulysses!"

"That great unwritten adventure you mean?"

"Absolutely!"

"Well, when I was plummeting towards the dark waters of the Thames a week ago I didn't even think I had a future. So I'm living for the now. Here's to the present! The future can wait."

ELSEWHERE, BEHIND CLOSED shutters and heavy drapes, in an inconspicuous room in an equally inconspicuous building within the comforting anonymity of shadowy gloom, the Star Chamber met.

"I call this meeting of the Star Chamber to order," said a voice almost smothered by the enshrouding semi-darkness, a commanding baritone in the mote-shot quiet of the hidden chamber.

The warm gloom was permeated by the gentle ticking of a clock, accompanied by the gurgle and splash of a cup of tea being poured.

"So, Wormwood failed," said a second voice, this one a rich claret, smooth and well rounded with age.

"Does that matter?" asked a third, crisper in tone and more pernicious, like the bark of a snapping terrier.

"No, it is enough that he tried. The Empire has become complacent," the first replied. "If it is to survive it must be tested, it must be challenged."

"And Quicksilver has a further part to play in this?" asked a fourth, aristocratic and sharp as a rapier's blade.

"You should know the answer to that better than most," said the second.

"Indeed."

There was the *ching* of a silver teaspoon ringing against the finest bone china and the sound of tea being stirred.

"So what is next in store for Mr Quicksilver, our agent of destruction?" asked the second.

There was the slurp of hot Earl Grey being supped. "Time will tell, gentlemen," said the fatherly tones of the first. "Time will tell. But rest assured we will be there, watching, every step of the way. After all history needs a helping hand every now and again, does it not?"

"Indeed it does," agreed the fourth, with a heavy sigh.

There were murmurs of assent.

"Then, for the time being, we are done, gentlemen," declared the first. "Let us be about our business elsewhere. I declare this meeting of the Star Chamber at an end."

Dusty silence returned to the room, other than the rattle of a cup being returned to its saucer, and history resumed its predetermined path.

THE END

PAX BRITANNIA

LEVIATHAN RISING

JONATHAN GREEN

For Lou, who enjoyed the first one

And for Clare, always.

Canst thou draw out

Leviathan with a hook?

– Job, ch. 41 v. 41

PROLOGUE

Voyage to the Bottom of the Sea

THE *VENTURE* – A tramp steamer, six days out from Shanghai – chugged on across the oceanic wilderness, smoke and steam belching from its stack, fighting the swell and chop of the sea. All rusting gunwales and weather-warped boards, the filthy, noisy craft pressed on against the surges of the sea. The entirety of the firmament was fogged with cloud from horizon to horizon: the Pacific a roiling mass of churning darkness beneath. Seabirds, flickers of white against the grey pall of the heavens, soared high above the lonely *Venture*, their discordant cries lost to the howls of the wind and the crash of waves against the lancing prow of the boat. The vessel appeared as nothing more than a rusty speck amidst the torpid rise and fall of the black waters.

The ship slammed into another wave-crest, the resounding clang of impact shuddering through the vessel, shaking it to its bilges. Captain Engelhard – Bavarian-German by extraction – peered out of the brine-spotted glass in front of him at the undulating mountains of water surrounding the *Venture*. With no land in any direction as far as the eye could see, the wild waters of the South China Seas were some of the roughest and most unpredictable in all the world, from Engelhard's experience – not unlike the hard-bitten captain himself. Lean as a sea snake and potentially twice as venomous, Engelhard demanded both the respect of the men of his crew, and their fear. It had been the same as old Runcorn under whom he had first worked the trade routes between the empires of Magna Britannia and China as a cabin boy, and on whom he had modelled his own style of leadership when he took command of the *Venture* on Runcorn's untimely death.

From his experience, it had always been the way: a sailor who respected his captain, who trusted his judgement and honoured his decisions, would follow him across the seven seas to the four corners of the globe. But a man who feared you, him you could lead down to Davy Jones's locker or into the jaws of hell itself. That was the kind of man Engelhard wanted aboard his ship, in his line of business.

One such man was his first mate, Mr Hayes. The crew of the *Venture* was a cosmopolitan group, Hayes himself hailing from Rhodesia. The cream wool Arran sweater he wore was in sharp contrast with the polished ebony of his skin. He was a brute of a man, taller and broader than Engelhard, made loyal by the promise of great rewards and made cruel by whatever it was that had happened to him in his youth before he escaped his homeland for the open sea.

With a hold full of the finest opium, from the poppy fields of Sichuan Province, bound for the smoking dens of Magna Britannia, hell and high water came as part of the deal. Engelhard needed a crew that he knew he could trust in a tight spot. He knew all too well the kind of hazards one could face on such a venture, the risks you ran in the quest for increased profit and the future promise of an easy life – a procession of ladies of easy virtue and a limitless supply of rum. And so he looked for men who would not falter when faced with an officer of Her Imperial Majesty's revenue office, and who knew the business end of a cudgel. And then there was always the risk of meeting a rival out on these wild seas, another captain hoping to make it big with a shipment of opium bound for the West.

There had long been old sea dog's tales connected to these waters. They mainly concerned the mysterious disappearances of ships over the centuries. It was said that the fathomless depths beneath them were some of the very deepest waters in the world. The ocean floor was said to be riven with trenches so deep that no one, not even unmanned probes, had ever been able to reach the bottom. And when one considered some of the monsters that dwelt within the trackless seas as it was, it was not hard to wonder what else might be dwelling within such abyssal chasms.

But then there were such tales told about every ocean on the planet, tales first told to explain the inexplicable, to account for the unaccountable, to explain away the effects of freakish weather, killer tidal waves and abductions carried out by those who still perpetrated the slave trade in certain corners of the world. The fact that reports of unaccountable disappearances had multiplied over the last twenty years or so meant nothing to Captain Engelhard other than that the opium trade, and competition between those captains and crews associated with it, had increased to lethal effect.

Not that Engelhard often found himself in such competition with another crew. He was too careful to let that happen, if he could help it. But it paid to take precautions. The old whaler's harpoon gun bolted to the prow of the *Venture* was just one such precaution.

Despite the damp cold of the sea-spray and the chilling effects of the wind, the cabin still felt uncomfortably warm, thanks to the excess heat pumping from the smoky engine room below. The air was close and redolent with opium fumes. There was another shuddering crash as the steel hull of the steamer collided head-on with another wall of black water. The tramp steamer pushed on through and then the prow was rising again, the great surge breaking into a curtain of white spray. Water splashed across the smeared pane in front of Engelhard and then skittered away in the face of the wind. The *Venture* dipped again, plunging onwards into the waves.

The force of the collision stopped the boat in its tracks, the hull-shuddering crash booming through the cabins and holds of the old steamer. Engelhard flew forwards over the wheel as the ship lurched, into the window panel in front of him. He gasped as the wind was knocked from him, the handle of the wheel in his gut, and cursed with his next breath at the blow he received to the forehead.

The surging sea continued to tug and pull at the *Venture* but, after more time spent on board ship than on land, Engelhard knew that the steamer wasn't going anywhere. Incredibly, somehow, it had come to a complete stop: he could barely feel the ever-present heave and yaw of the ship as the depthless ocean moved beneath it and on which the ship should be bobbing like a cork.

Then his mind was full of questions. What had they hit? He hadn't seen anything out here with them. The *Venture*'s instruments hadn't warned him of the approach of another vessel. What could possibly have brought the steamer to such an abrupt halt out here, miles from land, with nothing beneath them but the unsounded depths of the Marianas Trench? Had they collided with some submersible, either belonging to a rival or commandeered by a more ingenious member of Her Majesty's revenue office? But if that were the case, again, how could it have brought them to a complete stop? The engines were still chugging away, the propeller turning, but the *Venture* wasn't going anywhere. It was just as if they had run aground, only that was impossible.

The cabin was suddenly full of excitedly questioning crewmen, all coming up top to find out what was going on.

"What is it, Captain?" Hayes asked.

The ship lurched again. Engelhard grabbed for the wheel to stop himself losing his footing as others lunged for handrails or ended up on their knees on the floor of the cabin.

"We're on top of something," he hissed. "Mr Hayes, take the wheel!"

Engelhard threw himself out of the cabin, into the wind and lashing spray, half his crew tumbling through the door after him. Grabbing the starboard gunwale, Engelhard peered over the edge of the ship. At first all he could see was black waves and white breakers, a torment of churning water pummelling the hull of the ship. And then he saw it; something grey and indistinct, a pockmarked surface beneath the ship, the keel caught within it, something huge.

The ship pitched suddenly, yawing dangerously to port, throwing the gaggle of sailors and their captain back from the edge of the boat and slamming them into the side of the cabin. Engelhard pulled himself back to the side and saw the grey shape slip away beneath them. Vast as it was, it was still moving past several moments later.

And now the *Venture* was moving again. Hayes tensed as the wheel became suddenly responsive, straining to bring the whirling tramp steamer back to its original heading. Whatever the thing was, it was moving away from the ship now. Captain Engelhard simply stood and stared as the vast, streamlined shape slid away beneath the waves, the steamer chugging on through the surge as if nothing untoward had happened. This would be a tale to tell back at The Smuggler's Rest in Plymouth.

His gaze remaining locked on the... whatever it was... it still took Engelhard's startled brain a moment or two to realise that the something had turned and was now moving back towards the *Venture*, at speed. The vast form was rising from the stygian depths. Grey-green flesh broke the surface, the telltale V of white water showing how close it was already and how quickly it was closing.

"Mein Gott!" Engelhard gasped. A shudder of fear rippled through him. In the next moment fear and disbelief turned to instinctive, unthinking reaction. "All of you, to your stations!"

With Mr Hayes at the wheel, and the rest of the crew running to obey his command, Captain Josef Engelhard sprinted for the prow of the steamer, expertly avoiding the myriad hazards awaiting the unwary on the deck plates of the working ship – coils of steel cable, tie-off stanchions, raised hatch covers – and the whaler's harpoon gun positioned there like a furious, war-mongering figurehead.

With the submerged creature, or whatever it was, torpedoing back towards the *Venture*, he reached the swivel-mounted weapon and, both calloused hands grasping its lever-handles, spun its muzzle round, bringing the closing grey mass within its sights.

Without a moment's hesitation, Engelhard fired. Six feet of jagged-tipped harpoon blasted out of the mouth of the cannon, high-tensile steel cable spiralling after it, uncoiling from its winch-pulley, as the hardened steel bolt entered the sea in a rush of white bubbles. The cable pulled taut and, prow dipping fiercely, the *Venture* was pulled sharply round on itself, as the harpoon found its mark. The drug-smuggling sailors clung on as the boat was pulled around and Hayes cut the engines to lessen the resistance. Then all was still, other than the rise and fall of the ocean around the steamer, and the steel line slackened.

"We got it," Engelhard said, hardly believing what he was saying himself. "We got it!"

Leaving the harpoon he staggered back to the cabin house, grinning at the bewildered faces of his crew. "We got it! Haul it in, then we'll see what it is we've caught and what we think it will fetch on the black market."

There was a violent jolt as the cable went taut again, the tensed steel twanging like a guitar string, and the prow dipped once more.

"What in Hell's name!" was all Engelhard could manage before his world flipped on its axis and the deck disappeared from beneath him. His fall was abruptly halted by the harpoon gun.

The gun's solid bolted mounting buckled as the *Venture* upended, the bows of the vessel disappearing beneath the bubbling surface of the ocean. At the same moment the sea exploded around the ship. Writhing shapes, silhouetted against the grey pall of the heavens, obscured by the vertical deluge thrown up on all sides of the ship, crashed down on the steamer, seizing the boat within cruelly crushing coils. The smokestack crumpled, the roof of the cabin splintered like so much matchwood and the creaking hull protested as it buckled, rupturing in a dozen places.

With a sudden *whoomph*, the *Venture* was pulled violently beneath the waves, churning black and white water closing over it, rushing in to fill the hole in the sea where it had just been. In moments nothing was left of the opium, the tramp steamer or its crew.

Relative calm returned to the ocean surface. The only sign of there ever having been a ship there at all were a few broken boards and bobbing oil drums, and amongst the drifting flotsam a single, battered rubber life-ring that bore the name *Venture*. And the clinging, barely conscious Captain Engelhard.

ACT ONE

20,000 Leagues Under the Sea

July 1997

Below the thunders of the upper deep,
Far far beneath in the abysmal sea,
His ancient, dreamless, uninvaded sleep
The Kraken sleepeth...

– Alfred Lord Tennyson, *The Kraken*

CHAPTER ONE

Around the World in Eighty Days

LUXURY LINER SETS SAIL ON MAIDEN VOYAGE
By our reporter 'on board' Miss Glenda Finch

"Around the world in eighty days – in style!"

This is the proud boast of the Carcharodon Shipping Company, owners of the new luxury passenger sub-liner the Neptune, that sets sail from Southampton docks on 5th July. It is the company's claim that those who can afford the small-fortune-a-berth price tag will enjoy an unprecedented luxury cruise across the oceans of the globe, taking in many of its most remarkable and celebrated sights along the way.

Jonah Carcharodon repeated this bold claim – one of his own devising – during the festivities surrounding the launch of the Neptune, when His Royal Highness the Duke of Cornwall broke the traditional bottle of Cristal champagne – as served on board the Neptune in its many bars and restaurants. Rumour has it that Carcharodon has placed a hefty bet on his pride-and-joy's inaugural voyage running to time.

As well as an estimated three thousand paying guests, a number of dignitaries and VIPs are on board at the invitation of Jonah Carcharodon himself, to add glamour and media interest to the maiden voyage of the newest member of the Great White Shipping Line's fleet of high-end *luxury passenger vessels. Amongst the invited elite is rumoured to be Hero of the Empire, Ulysses Quicksilver himself who, as regular readers of The Times will know, was instrumental in thwarting the recent plot against Her Majesty's life. But whether he is here for a little rest and recuperation, to find himself a new female companion from amongst the socialites and well-to-do heiresses on board, or for some other clandestine reason, only time will tell.*

"Your cognac, sir," the aquiline gentleman's valet said, bending at the hip to proffer his master the glass positioned precisely dead centre on the tray in his hand.

"Why, thank you, Nimrod," the younger man said with a smile, taking the balloon glass in his left hand. He gently swirled its contents before putting it to his mouth. There he paused, savouring the heady aroma of the brandy before taking a sip. He held the tingling mouthful on his tongue for a moment, taste buds excited at its touch, before luxuriating in the sensation of the cognac slipping like molten honey down his throat.

"Very nice," he said, easing himself back on the sunlounger.

"Will there be anything else, sir?"

"No, I think that will be all for now," Ulysses Quicksilver replied, running a hand through his mane of dark blond hair and adjusting the dark-tinted spectacles perched on the bridge of his nose.

"Very good, sir. Then if you would not mind I shall retire and see to some matters of house-keeping demanding my attention back at the suite."

"Very well, Nimrod. Whatever floats your boat I suppose," Ulysses said, flashing his faithful manservant a wicked grin. Nimrod responded by arching an eyebrow, before he turned on his heel and strode rigidly from the sundeck, tray in hand.

Ulysses Quicksilver stretched his body out on the wicker lounger, adjusting his suit of cream linen for comfort and loosening the azure rough silk cravat at his neck, luxuriating in the warmth of the sun on his face.

A twinge of pain from his right shoulder took him momentarily by surprise and reminded him, at least in part, why he had accepted Jonah Carcharodon's invitation to join the maiden voyage of the *Neptune*. More than a month on from the debacle surrounding Queen Victoria's 160th jubilee his left arm was healed and out of its sling – although it still hurt to over-flex it – but his shoulder was a more substantial, recurring injury, one he had received in his near-fatal crash on Mount Manaslu in the Himalayan range. He had been lucky to walk away from that one at all; not that he had walked away of course. He had crawled from the crash-site, managing to get as far as a precipitous icy ledge before the effects of hypothermia had set in. And then the monks of Shangri-La had found him.

He stretched again, testing his body this time, wondering what other aches and pains would reveal themselves, trying to put the memory of an event to every twinge, every dull ache, every agony remembered, each a physical remembrance of one of a whole host of injuries received in the line of duty.

There was the rumour of cramp in his left leg, and the still-present dull ache in his side. Such sensations were almost reassuring in their familiarity. Easing his right shoulder into a more comfortable position he felt the skin under his shirt. There were still four distinct traces of scar tissue where the pterodactyl had – bizarrely – saved his life.

But that was all in the past now. All that featured in his immediate future was a few weeks R & R and a jolly jaunt in warmer climes, while Barty remained in London overseeing the renovation of the Mayfair residence, his brother himself under the ever-watchful eye of Mrs Prufrock, Ulysses' cook and housekeeper.

A sudden shadow came between Ulysses and the burning white disc of the sun blazing in the cloudless azure expanse of sky above the cruising liner. Ulysses removed his sunglasses and, narrowing his eyes, focused on the not uncomely figure in front of him.

"It's Mr Quicksilver, isn't it? Or can I call you Ulysses?"

Ulysses smiled and deliberately looked the svelte young woman up and down, taking in the classic yet subtle curves of her body, accentuated by the way the sea-green gown she had chosen to wear hung from and clung to her body to greatest effect. It was a bold statement – the colour in sharp contrast to the blue of her eyes and the over-coiffeured curls of her golden-blonde hair. The dress would have been more appropriate as evening wear – exposed shoulders, arms and cleavage not really being the done thing, at least not on the sundeck or the watertight promenade deck. The boa of pink flamingo feathers really set it off a treat.

Worn here and now, it was an outfit that said that this was a young woman who was independent, determined to make her own way in the world, apparently regardless of what others might think of her. And yet, at the same time, all too self-aware, desperate to make a lasting impression, fearful of being forgotten or, worse, overlooked in the first place.

"I'm sorry, you seem to have me at a disadvantage, Miss –"

"Glenda Finch, social commentator for *The Times*."

"Ah, the gossip columnist."

For a moment the woman's mouth puckered in disdain but then her brilliant white smile returned like the sun emerging from behind a passing cloud. "You know of my work then?"

"I've read your column in the past, as no more than an amusing distraction, you understand. And I believe I've been the subject of it on a number of occasions."

"So you'll know that I'm aware of your work as well."

"Well, it's hard to hide one's light under a bushel when you save the Queen herself from certain death at the hands of a psychotic megalomaniac at the most public event of the decade in front of the world's press. But I rather suspect I'll get over it. Today's front page, tomorrow's fish and chip paper and all that."

"Oh, you do yourself down, Ulysses," the reporter returned. "But as you were the one to mention the part you played in saving Her Majesty's life would you care to give me a quote? In fact, why don't you offer to buy me a drink and then you can tell me all about it."

Smiling, his gaze lingering on the shadow of the young woman's cleavage – how could what was effectively little more than the empty space between two breasts be so appealing? – Ulysses pointedly returned his sunglasses to his nose.

"Good day, Miss Finch."

THE NEPTUNE *BOASTS* five-star hotel accommodation married to the most advanced steam-driven technology in the Empire. Four massive Rolls Royce engines – each, I am told, as big as a London townhouse – will move the huge vessel at an average of twenty knots across open stretches of water, when the weather, the sea and the opportunity permit. The vessel itself is 1,020 feet long and fifteen storeys tall.

But all of this technological magnificence and industrial maritime creativity is all to serve one purpose – ultimately that of entertainment. People want to sail the seven seas, to relax, see the world, advance their own realms of experience, and be entertained in the process. And there are all manner of entertainments available on board.

As well as three kinemas, a vaudeville theatre, numerous restaurants, bistros and bars, and the infamous Casino Royale, there are also indoor squash courts and outdoor tennis courts, a gymnasium, solarium and three swimming pools. But possibly the most magnificent exercise alternative is the Promenade Deck itself. Running two thirds the length of the ship, the Promenade is nearly a quarter of a mile long, meaning that two complete laps is the equivalent to a walk of a mile. This might not sound so special until you learn that the entirety of the Promenade is covered by a reinforced glass and steel structure capable of withstanding the same pressures as that of the ship's hull, so that passengers may still enjoy a stroll along the Promenade, and all that might be revealed beyond it, even when the Neptune makes one of its scheduled dives to the undersea cities found along its route during the course of its voyage. And as well as walks along the Promenade, of course, one may also partake in any number of traditional deck sports such as quoits.

One of the appealing features of a cruise is not only what the ship itself has to offer, but also the places one can visit along the way.

Destinations on the Neptune's maiden voyage include the renowned Atlantis City, and the fully-restored Temple of Jupiter, a shopping stop at America's first city of New York, the prehistoric game parks of the Costa Rican island chain, the incredible sculpted coral gardens of Pacifica, and even a brief sojourn on the Cairo Express across the Sinai peninsula to visit the pyramids of Giza.

THE THUNDEROUS REPORT of the elephant gun echoed through the primeval jungle, sending a flock of white egrets squawking and flapping from the canopy. The parasaurolophus bellowed, throwing back its crested head as the four-bore shell found its mark, hitting the creature in its flank, punching through the rhino-like hide and sending a spray of blood and meat from the wound. The bipedal herbivore faltered in its graceful run, its thick tail swinging to maintain balance. The dashing pachycephalosauruses accompanying the larger dinosaur's flight scattered across the clearing.

Ulysses Quicksilver took another sip of Earl Grey from the fine bone china teacup in his hands. He savoured the taste for a moment, as well as the sunlight on his face. It was good to be off ship for a short sojourn, hunting dinosaurs, although with the howdah gently rolling beneath him, he felt as though he might still be on board.

"Good shot, Major!" he called.

"Thank you, sah!" the bristle-whiskered and portly Major Marmaduke Horsley called back, reloading the gun almost automatically as he did so. "One more shot should bring the blighter down."

The parasaurolophus trumpeted again. Its injury was causing it to limp badly and it was moving for the natural protection of the trees at the edge of the jungle clearing.

"Oh no you don't!" the Major shouted and then to the Indian beast-wrangler attempting to steer the triceratops on which their howdah was being carried: "You! Dino-waller! Chop chop, what-ho? Dashed blighter's getting away! Come on, man. We can't lose it now."

With a shout from the beast's handler, perched on a saddle across the creature's broad shoulders behind the frill of its crest, and judicious use of a crackling electro-goad, the ceratopsid pounded forward. Ulysses tried to avoid spilling any of the tea slopping from the cup onto his trousers.

Horsley put the gun to his shoulder again, swiftly capturing the distinctive profile of his quarry's head within the crosshairs of its sights. The elephant gun boomed once more. There was something like a grunt of satisfaction from the major and the parasaurolophus crashed to the ground, every muscle in its body relaxed with the pulverisation of the creature's tiny brain.

"Good shooting, Major!" called Miss Birkin, waving at the ex-army officer enthusiastically from the back of a brontosaur, parasol in hand to keep the equatorial sun from her milk-white sensitive skin.

"Why thank you, Miss Birkin! It should make a fine addition to my trophy collection. I shall have it stuffed and mounted above the mantelpiece in my sitting room at home."

"I think you've made a big impression there, Major," Ulysses teased.

"What? What rot! Can't stand the bloody woman," Horsley returned under his breath. "Too full of her blinking, half-baked conspiracy theories."

Ulysses caught the eye of John Schafer, seated next to his fiancée in the same bamboo and calico fashioned conveyance, opposite Constance's ever-present chaperone. "Good afternoon, Mr Schafer, Miss Pennyroyal. Enjoying the show?"

"Oh yes, Mr Quicksilver," Constance called back across the clearing. "Most exhilarating!" she added with a flutter of the fan in her hand and a reddening of her perfect porcelain cheeks.

"Rather beats the Wilmington Hunt, doesn't it?" Schafer called back.

"Indeed it does," Ulysses agreed.

A sudden shout went up from one of the native beaters accompanying the lumbering triceratops and brontosauruses and was passed along the drawn out line. There the Costa Ricans were showing obvious signs of agitation, their behaviour not going unnoticed by Major Marmaduke Horsley.

"I say, man," he barked at their guide, "what's going on? What's this bally hoo-ha all about?"

"A meat-eater, an allosaur, has been spotted, mensab," the Indian replied, his English thickly accented.

"Where?"

"Two miles west of here, on the approach to the watering hole."

"Then what are we waiting for, man? We can't let a prize like that get away, can we Quicksilver?"

"Perish the thought, Major."

"Looks like the space over the mantelpiece is still up for grabs, what?"

"It would indeed."

With a fanfare of bad-tempered grunting and rumbling herbivorous farts, the triceratops mount set off at a canter, under the impelling of its handler.

The Major turned to face Ulysses, a wild gleam in his wide eyes, his monocle popping from the orbit of his right eye where it should have fitted snugly.

"Ever hunted any big game, Quicksilver, and I mean truly big game?"

Ulysses' mind immediately rushed back to the dinosaur stampede that had rampaged through the capital only a matter of months ago, following the terrorist atrocities of the Darwinian Dawn.

"There was this one time," he replied.

"Well the hunt's on now, isn't it, what-ho?"

"Indeed it is, Major. Indeed it is."

ACCOMPANYING THE LAUNCH *of the largest passenger ship in the world was a feeling of optimism. Many felt that it helped lay to rest the ghosts of the near apocalyptic events of Her Majesty Queen Victoria's 160th jubilee celebrations. Let us hope that such dark times are now behind us and that we can look forward to the approaching new millennium with joy, hope and positivity in our hearts.*

As to Jonah Carcharodon's bold claim that the latest and greatest passenger cruise liner in the world offers an unparalleled experience we, those of us fortunate enough to join the inaugural sailing, will have to wait and see. But rest assured, your eyes and ears on board will be with it to the end so that you might feel that you are with us every step of the way.

And, as readers of this column will already know, Carcharodon is no stranger to publicity himself. Only last year, before the Neptune *had even left the dockyards, there were rumours of financial irregularities and the threat of insolvency for his shipping company.*

ULYSSES MADE HIS way along the mahogany-panelled, plushly-carpeted corridor towards his suite of rooms on the VIP guest deck, tossing his room key in the palm of his hand as he did so. The opulence on show, even here, in a corridor between cabins, was mind-boggling. Ulysses had heard the rumours of financial challenges facing the Great White Shipping Line, but he had no idea whether the construction of such a vessel as the *Neptune* was the cause of near-bankruptcy or whether it was a sign that Jonah Carcharodon was still doing very nicely for himself, thank you very much. What Ulysses was certain of, however, was that the success or failure of their new flagship venture could make or break the Carcharodon's Shipping Company. Either it would prove an unmitigated triumph and float the company's stock like nothing ever before, or the world's greatest cruise line would sink without a trace.

He was suddenly roused from his reverie by a scratching at the back of his skull, his ever-alert sixth sense acting up again, something almost akin to premonition. Glancing to his right he came face-to-face with Miss Glenda Finch of *The Times*, trying to look nonchalant as she loitered within a doorway.

"Why, Miss Finch," Ulysses said, a predatory smile spreading across his lips as he took in the hollow between the underdressed reporter's plunging cleavage again and the way the side split of the gown exposed a shapely leg to the thigh. "What a pleasant, if unexpected, surprise. I didn't know you had rooms on this floor. I had been led to believe that all members of the press were located two decks down in steerage."

For a moment the reporter's beaming smile almost faltered, pupils dilating with something like annoyance, but then, a moment later, Miss Finch had regained her indefatigable composure.

"Mr Quicksilver. Twice in one day. People will start to talk. I was just..."

"Looking for something – sorry – someone?" Ulysses didn't take his gaze from her not unattractive face, the smile on his lips no longer reflected in his eyes.

"Looking for you, actually."

"Really?"

"Weren't you going to buy me a drink?"

Confidently she thrust her arm into his, turning him round in one balletic movement, to lead him back towards the grand atrium and, thence, to one of the bars.

What is she up to? Ulysses wondered, and then caught himself. *Always on duty, eh Quicksilver, old chap?* Whatever it was, it could probably wait. And besides, a pleasant drink in distracting company was what this trip was all about – at least for the present, and there was no time like it.

"Indeed. Why not, Miss Finch? Why not? Vodka on the rocks with a twist of lime, if I remember correctly from my casual perusal of your column."

"Why, Ulysses, recalling a lady's favourite tipple – you flatter me."

"I do indeed. And why not? A woman like you wearing a dress like that deserves to be well and truly... flattered."

"Now-now, Ulysses, people will talk."

"No, my dear, you will talk, and I for one can't wait to hear what you'll have to say for yourself."

As to what adventures await us on the voyage ahead, we will simply have to wait and see. This is Glenda Finch, signing off, until next time.

CHAPTER TWO

Fourteen at Dinner

"LADIES AND GENTLEMEN," the droid-butler's tinny voice crackled, "dinner is served."

A hubbub of excitement accompanying them, the captain's dinner guests bustled their way into the mirrored dining room.

The room was ostentatiously decorated and included a number of large, gilt-framed mirrors. Statues of Renaissance-imagined dolphins and mermen filled the room and the trident logo of the *Neptune* was repeated at every possible opportunity. The place was not unlike an underwater treasure cave, with the gold, silver and crystal offset by the dark blue and sea-green colouring of the draperies, wall dressings and carpets.

A long table had been laid for dinner. The candlelight cast by three polished candelabra set along the length of the table reflected back from the myriad mirrors, filling the dining chamber with light, which in turn sparkled from crystal-cut glassware, fine-glazed bone china and silver place settings.

Where the starboard wall should have been there was a breath-taking, floor-to-ceiling, glass and steel bubble, like the one above the Promenade deck, allowing the captain and his guests an unprecedented view of the sea whether the sub-liner was above or beneath the waves.

On another table, set against one wall and laden with the meal's wine selection, after-dinner spirits and more champagne, stood a glistening sculpture, the flawless ice chiselled and smoothed to resemble the God of the Sea himself, trident in hand, seated upon a scallop-shell throne.

Sprays of lilies on both the table and within flower stands in the corners of the room, set off the table setting, so that only the most jaded or over-exposed diner did not gasp in wonder.

Their host for the evening stood behind his plush dining chair – white wood upholstered in aqua blue with the *Neptune's* trident logo embroidered in turquoise and gold thread – striking in his dress uniform. Captain Connor McCormack – or Mac as he was affectionately referred to by many of the crew – was a powerful presence and it was immediately apparent why he commanded the respect of those under his command. He was stood to attention, straight as a board, gold buttons gleaming, with his silvering blond hair slicked down perfectly from a side parting, and with his dress cap under his right arm.

"Ladies and gentlemen," he said, "I would like to take this opportunity to formally welcome you aboard the *Neptune* and to my table."

Subsequent welcomes and polite words of thanks were returned by the assembled dinner guests.

"Most impressive, Captain McCormack," said a woman who was clearly into her middle years but who wore those years well, with a noble bearing and calm countenance.

"Why thank you, Lady Denning," the captain replied graciously, tipping his head in a brief bow, his accent warmed with a lilting Scots brogue.

"Nice fireplace," Major Horsley said, tapping out his pipe on the surround. "That allosaurus I bagged would look good up there."

One by one the guests found their places or, in the case of the tardier amongst the party, were guided to them by the robo-butlers waiting with clockwork patience to serve the meal. Each place setting held a card bearing the name of one of the most prodigious of the *Neptune's* guests, scribed in a precise and immaculate copperplate.

Dinner with the captain had been another excuse for the elite among the *Neptune's* passengers to dress to impress, as etiquette dictated and social one-upmanship demanded. The gentlemen, other than the captain, were all in well-tailored black tie, the only real opportunity to personalise their appearance being through the choice of waistcoats and cummerbunds.

For the ladies, however, trying to outdo one another was the name of the game. It was all satin, silk and chiffon – this season's colours apparently sea-greens, aquamarines and turquoise-blues – extravagant bejewelled accessories, bows, lacy flim-flammeries and flamboyant feather boas. Some of the younger female guests had also gone for more daring tailoring with, in the case of Miss Finch in particular, outrageous amounts of bare flesh on display. The other more senior ladies of the party had wisely kept to more traditional, and therefore, restrained designs.

At Captain McCormack's behest, the assembled dinner guests began to take their seats, once they had found their own personalised place setting. However, as they did so, it soon became apparent to the captain that not all of his guests had yet arrived; three places remained empty.

The doors to the dining room were opened again by two automata-drones and the true host of the dinner party was admitted.

Although everyone present was there that evening at the behest of Captain Connor McCormack, it was really the owner of the Carcharodon Shipping Company, and hence the owner of the *Neptune*, who had assured their attendance by inviting them on the sub-liner's maiden voyage in the first place, the wheelchair-bound eccentric billionaire, Jonah Carcharodon.

Carcharodon was wheeled into the banqueting chamber by a mousey-looking young woman, who might have been attractive were it not for the thick horn-rimmed spectacles she wore. She was dressed in a flattering black dress, her blonde hair swept back from her face and held in place on top of her head with a glittering shark-shaped clip. The shark jewellery was clearly visible as she kept her head down, eyes fixed on the carpet at her feet. She gave the impression that she was shy and embarrassed at having to put herself on show in a dress that clearly demonstrated that her figure was one worth showing off.

Jonah Carcharodon, however, apparently welcomed the attention his late arrival brought him, a slight smile forming on his tight-lipped mouth. Confined to a wheelchair, grey-haired and with all of his sixty-plus years showing now on his lined face and hollow features, nevertheless there was a certain spark in the old man's eyes that hinted at the vigour and drive for life one might have expected of a younger man.

"Mr Carcharodon," Captain McCormack said, "and Miss Celeste. Welcome. Now I think we are only missing one guest. Might I suggest we all partake of another glass of champagne while we wait?"

"McCormack," Carcharodon interjected, "I think your guests have probably been waiting long enough. Let dinner be served now."

"Very well, sir," the captain demurred. He nodded to one of the robo-waiters. On cue the droid struck the small bronze gong it held in one metallic hand. "Ladies and gentlemen, dinner is served."

As the last of the guests seated themselves – Carcharodon's PA positioning him at the foot of the table, facing Captain McCormack, before taking a seat adjacent to him – the serving-automata prepared to dish up the soup course from steaming silver tureens. The aroma of Thai red curry and coconut filled the room.

"You will notice a theme to this evening's meal," the captain pointed out to his guests, "a signature dish from some of the different destinations we have already visited or will be visiting on this, the *Neptune's* maiden voyage."

The dining room doors opened once more, this time without the aid of the droid-drudges. Standing framed in the doorway was a gentleman instantly recognisable thanks to the numerous pictures that had appeared in the popular press and on broadcasting screens throughout the realm of Magna Britannia following the calamitous events of Queen Victoria's 160th jubilee.

He looked somewhat different to how he had appeared live, across the empire on the night of June the sixteenth, on that occasion bloodied and bruised, his hair out of place, his clothes dishevelled. Such was not the case now. Also in black tie like the other male guests, he, however, had chosen to embellish the standard black and wine outfit with a striking rough gold silk waistcoat and contrasting burgundy cravat, held in place with a rose-cut diamond pin. And in his right hand he held his trademark cane with its bloodstone-set tip.

All eyes turned to the last dinner guest to arrive.

"Good evening, ladies and gentlemen. Captain McCormack," Ulysses Quicksilver announced. "Am I late?"

As the dandy scoured the faces of those already seated around the table his beaming smile was met with politely returned similar expressions from some, indifference from others and indignant disgust from a small minority, which, however, included Jonah Carcharodon. If there was one thing the shipping magnate could not stand – as might be guessed if the rumours that he had invested his entire personal fortune into the building of the *Neptune*, were to be believed – it was being upstaged.

"Ah, Mr Quicksilver. We thought you weren't coming," Carcharodon chided. "We were about to start without you."

"No need to worry," Ulysses replied. "I'm here now, so the party can begin."

"So, Mr Sylvester, I take it your employer was too ill to travel with us on this historic voyage."

"I am afraid so, Mr Carcharodon," confirmed a slickly turned out young man, his hair swept back, glistening with hair-oil.

Everything about him, from his hawkish demeanour to his sharp dress sense, screamed go-getter businessman to Ulysses. This was a man on a mission, with a career on the up. To be acting as the representative of someone as powerful and influential as Josiah Umbridge, founder and owner of Umbridge Industries – the Empire's foremost industrialist, with numerous steel mills and factories to his name – attested to that fact. And Ulysses sincerely doubted that Dexter Sylvester was spending the entirety of the cruise relaxing either. He would doubtless be networking with influential passengers as well as continuing to do whatever it was he did for Umbridge Industries from afar, sending in his work by remote difference engine transfer, the *Neptune* being equipped with all the most up-to-date radio-telegraph-electronic-communication transmitter terminals and receivers.

In time the dessert course followed, crème brûlée with a warm berry coulis. As those around the table tucked into the sweet, Ulysses Quicksilver considered his fellow dinner guests. After a number of weeks on ship, thanks to his affable charm and personable way with all and sundry, Ulysses had managed to gain the relaxed acquaintance of a host of the ship's staff as well as of the other passengers. As a result, he already knew enough about practically everyone around the table to make him realise that there was a lot more he would like to know. It seemed that no one who had been invited on the *Neptune's* first circumnavigation of the globe was entirely without something of a history all of their own. But then, as a novelist friend of Ulysses' from his school days at Eton had once pointed out to him, "Everyone is the protagonist in their own life story, everyone a hero with a tale worth telling. There are no secondary characters in real life."

He started to mentally compile a dossier on each of his fellow guests, containing every piece of gossip, fact, observation and rumour he had picked up on each of them thus far. And as seemed fit, he began with their nominal host, the captain, seated at the head of the table.

Captain Connor McCormack was, as might be expected, the most experienced, trusted and capable captain in the Carcharodon fleet. Hence, naturally, he had given up command of the *Nautilus* – which was, up until the construction of the *Neptune*, the flagship of the Great White Line – to take over command of the new super submersible-liner. He looked every part the maritime hero and yet there was a slightly detached world-weariness about him that his eyes could not hide. Ulysses suspected that seeing out his days as the captain of a luxury passenger liner was not the path he had seen his career taking when he was on the first rung of the ladder.

Although financially, and in terms of glory-seeking, his choice of career path could not be faulted, Ulysses had seen such world-weary expressions before, in those pensioned off from the army, who until that point had only lived to serve, fighting for Queen and country. Their prime purpose in life denied them, such men felt neutered now that they were not on the front line facing the enemies of the Empire in honest battle. Perhaps it wasn't active duty at sea that Captain McCormack yearned for now; in another life Ulysses could have seen him taking command of a starship charting unknown territory out beyond the bounds of the solar system, a pioneering space adventurer searching for life on other worlds.

To the captain's right sat a man whom Ulysses had never met until that night, although he had seen his name mentioned in various newspaper articles surrounding the same debacle that had resulted in Ulysses finding himself the subject of a fair few column inches. Perhaps it was for this very reason that Professor Maxwell Crichton, Emeritus Professor of Genetic Adaptation and Bio-Diversity in Evolutionary Biology at the Natural History Museum and one-time colleague of the much maligned Professor Ignatius Galapagos – although he had been at pains to distance himself from any connection there might have been between them both – that he had taken up the offer of a world cruise, away from the hounding of the popular press.

And he looked like a man hounded and on edge. Somewhere around his mid-fifties, he had a thin, wiry frame that spoke of an academic's neglect of the body's basic needs, such as a regular three square meals a day. Myopia, possibly also the result of prolonged hours of study by weak lamplight, was rectified by a pair of wire-framed spectacles. The hair on his head was white-grey, short and with a tendency towards spikiness, and he steepled his fingers before his face, elbows on the table, when he spoke in earnest about all subjects under the sun – from politics and religion, to the actions of terrorist groups around the world and his own boundary-challenging work in the field of evolutionary biology. But despite the fact that he was now supposed to be relaxing over supper with convivial company, Professor Crichton still appeared hollow-eyed and anxious. Ulysses half expected him to glance back over his shoulder at any moment. Although, now that Ulysses came to think about it, the professor was actually spending a fair amount of time glancing at another of the captain's guests, one Lady Denning who was sat opposite him, shooting her dark looks over the tops of his glasses from beneath beetling brows.

Like Crichton, Ulysses turned his scrutinising gaze on Lady Josephine Denning. Again, she was someone Ulysses knew of only by reputation, until this evening. She didn't have the same staid qualities as Professor Crichton but she was, nonetheless, a leader in her own scientific field, that of marine biology. Ulysses had heard it crudely put that what Lady Denning didn't know about fish wasn't worth knowing. The title had come from her marriage to Lord Horatio Denning, who, although his family estates lay in the north of England, had spent much of his time on his yacht sailing around the Mediterranean. It was there that he had met a certain struggling postgraduate research scientist on an expedition to catalogue sea cucumber populations off the coast of Sardinia. His money and hereditary title had brought the, by then, Lady Denning the influence and attention she needed to make more of her work. But this had all been a long time ago now. Tragically Lord Denning, more than twenty years his wife's senior, had died only two years into their marriage, poisoned by a carelessly prepared plate of fugu whilst holidaying in Japan. Lady Denning had never remarried. Now in her sixties, she carried herself with all the grace and poise of a woman born to good breeding, not one who had simply married into it. A strict regimen of yoga and a diet heavy with oily fish had also meant that she had maintained her figure and looks far beyond that which her years might have suggested.

A man who did not appear to be wearing as well was the ship's chief medic, Dr Samuel Oglivy, seated to Lady Denning's left. Ulysses guessed him to be in his mid-forties, not significantly older than Ulysses himself, but the waxy appearance of his skin and his hollow-eyed expression spoke of a man who was not well. Looking at Dr Ogilvy, Ulysses couldn't help calling to mind the expression, 'Physician, heal thyself.' But then he already knew that Ogilvy was not a well man, in more ways than one, and it wasn't down to seasickness as the doctor claimed. In fact, if he were not careful and continued on his current course of action, his condition could prove fatal.

Opposite Ogilvy sat John Schafer, still fresh of face and bright of eye, the style of his hair and the cut of his clothes more up-to-date that any of the rest of them. Ulysses, himself a follower of fashion, still preferred to create his own style; it worked for him anyway. The young man could not hide the look of blissful happiness on his face, nor could he keep from clasping the hand of his sweetheart sitting beside him. In turn, Constance Pennyroyal could not take her eyes from her handsome beau, constantly snatching shared glances with him from beneath fluttering eyelashes. The two of them were leaving much of the food placed in front of them unfinished, so full were they with each other.

Then there was Constance's maiden aunt and chaperone, her stern glances and puckered mouth letting everyone know her opinion of such public displays of affection.

"Ladies and gentlemen, if I might have your attention?" Schafer spoke over the general hubbub of conversation.

"Certainly, Mr Schafer," Captain McCormack said. "Please, feel free to speak."

"It's just that now would seem to be the perfect time for Constance and I to make an announcement," the young man went on. A sudden silence descended over the dinner guests, accompanied by a look of bewilderment from the Major and a gasp of understanding from Glenda Finch. "I am delighted to say that, earlier this evening Constance agreed to become my wife."

Further gasps rose from the assembled guests accompanied by hearty congratulatory comments, a chinking of glasses and smatterings of applause.

"That's simply wonderful news," Miss Finch spoke up. "I'm sure your families will be delighted."

If the look on Miss Whilomena Birkin's face was anything to go by, it looked like the gossip columnist had got her facts wrong again.

Ulysses knew all he needed to know about Miss Glenda Finch, from what he had read in her column in and her none-too-subtle approach to investigative journalism that he had experienced over his enforced drink with her at the bar. She was unsubtly throwing herself at him even now, laughing at every vague witticism he could be bothered to construct and touching his arm or hand almost every time she directed a comment at him, which he found annoying. It annoyed him because he was annoyed with himself for actually enjoying the attention she was showing him. Carcharodon's PA might be the more traditional English Rose, a beauty buried within a shell of shyness and poor self-esteem, and the more intriguing challenge, but there was something appealing about Glenda Finch's brash approach and her clumsy attempts at seduction, all for the sake of a story. But then she was behaving just as flirtatiously towards Major Horsley, seated to her right.

In turn, the Major appeared to be revelling in the attention of a not unattractive young woman with a taste for plunging necklines. Retired army officer turned big game hunter, living off an army pension and apparent personal family fortune, Major Marmaduke Horsley had never been married to anyone in his life, other than Her Majesty's Armed Forces. Everything there was to know about the Major was there for all to see on the surface. A man like him couldn't hide his opinions if he tried, and he wasn't inclined to try in the first place. A bluff and hale character with a laugh as big as his belly – army muscle long ago turned to fat, the legacy of too many mess dinners and an aversion to physical activity – he was like everyone's incorrigible favourite uncle. There was something of the seasonal gift-giver about his appearance, as well as his manner, his red face bulging with purple veins, from his bulbous, port-swollen nose to his cheeks and unapologetic white whiskers of sideburns and moustache.

And finally, facing Ulysses from where he had been placed between Dexter Sylvester and Miss Birkin was the highly-respected global-trotting travel writer, Thor Haugland. The accent of his homeland apparent in his cultured tones, his command of English was better than that of many Englishmen Ulysses had met, and English was only one of seven languages spoken by the Norwegian. Should the conversation ever falter, with the way in which he turned any comment or question into an excuse to relate another of his many overseas adventures, Haugland would be able to keep the dinner entertainment going single-handedly. And despite his high-brow, pseudo-intellectual approach, there was no doubting his abilities as a storyteller; even the most insignificant experience was related with attention gripping skill and, in the process, turned into an intriguing anecdote. Miss Birkin certainly seemed happy to hang on his every word, rather than confront the reality of her charge's hasty – and possibly rebellious – engagement. As was Miss Celeste.

And then there was Jonah Carcharodon. Strangely, Ulysses realised, although in many ways he was the most publicly recognised figure amongst the party, after Ulysses himself, he was the biggest unknown as far as the dandy adventurer was concerned. Rumours abounded, but the actual facts behind those rumours remained frustratingly clouded by a fog of contradictions, uncertainties and downright lies. The Great White Shipping Line was an undoubted global success but there were still persistent rumours that the building of the *Neptune* had almost sunk the company. Everyone knew that Carcharodon was confined to a wheelchair but no one seemed to know why. It was popular knowledge that Carcharodon was an eccentric billionaire but nobody knew what he spent his considerable fortune on. He had given many interviews over the years but still no one seemed to know anything of real substance about the man. He remained a mystery. What Ulysses knew from his own investigations was that Carcharodon was the owner of the shipping company that bore his name and the host of this party, a grumpy old sod with an eye for pretty young assistants, who didn't like being upstaged on his own boat, and that was about it. At this moment, as the Umbridge Industries man was trying to ask him another searching question, Carcharodon appeared to be berating his put-upon assistant.

Looking at the arrangement of guests around the table Ulysses wondered if one or more of them had carried out their own bit of judicious place-swapping, for Dexter Sylvester to have the undivided attention of the patently irritated Jonah Carcharodon and for Glenda Finch to have ended up sitting next to Ulysses – or was that just self-flattering egotism on his part?

What an unlikely lot to be sharing dinner on the foremost luxury sub-liner in the world, he thought to himself. What were the chances of some of these characters ending up on board the *Neptune* at this auspicious time – except that many of those present had specifically been invited, guests of the Great White Line with all expenses covered. The roster of guests at the captain's table would have had all the potential of a Penny Dreadful murder mystery, in the hands of the right author.

Out of a sense of pity for the mousey young woman, rather than to relieve Carcharodon from the unrelenting networking of Dexter Sylvester, Ulysses directed a comment at the billionaire.

"Mr Carcharodon," he said, "or can I call you Jonah?"

"You can call me Carcharodon."

"I must thank you for your personal invitation to join in this wonderful experience."

"What?"

"For inviting us on the inaugural round the world cruise of the *Neptune.*"

"Don't thank me," Carcharodon bit back. "Wasn't down to me. My PA here sent out those personal invitations. Does everything for me, don't you?" he shot back at her, not sounding in the least bit grateful about it. "But then that's what you're paid for, isn't it? She's only here tonight to make up numbers. You know how bloody superstitious sailors are," he said, directing this particular barbed comment at Captain McCormack.

As the waiter-drones were clearing away dessert and preparing to serve coffee, Ulysses was distracted from his half-hearted conversation with the ever-garrulous Glenda by Lady Denning rising, making the usual excuses to her host, the captain, and making to leave. There was an apology of chairs being pushed back as the gentlemen diners bid her ladyship a good evening.

"Going so soon?" Carcharodon asked, the tone he had taken with the eminent marine biologist almost challenging.

"Yes, Mr Carcharodon. It has been a most enjoyable evening," she said, without anything about her expression supporting her words – something having soured the evening for her – "but it is time I retired. I am a creature of habit I know, but it's too late change this old goat now."

That in and of itself would not have been particularly out of the ordinary but for the fact that Professor Crichton then made the same excuse, and left almost straight after her, his face like thunder. It was enough to pique the interest of a man like Ulysses Quicksilver and he didn't need his uncanny sixth sense on this occasion to tell him that something strange was going on.

"Captain McCormack, thank you for a wonderful evening," Ulysses said, placing his napkin on the table, "but if you will excuse me too."

"Really, Mr Quicksilver? That is a shame." It was Carcharodon who interjected. "I haven't heard you regale us yet with your part in the events at Hyde Park. I do hope you won't keep us waiting long."

"The night is still young, Carcharodon," Ulysses said, making for the door. "I'll be back. Please, don't get up."

"Ulysses?" Glenda slurred, her tone both tipsy and incredulous.

"Have your glass topped up, Glenda, and I'll be back before you know it."

Exiting the banqueting room, Ulysses passed through the anteroom where the captain's guests had earlier gathered for pre-dinner drinks and into the corridor beyond. This area of the ship was for the exclusive use of the VIP guests and so Ulysses found the corridor devoid of other passengers. However, he could hear two voices, their words made incoherent by distance and the muffling effects of carpet and drapes. Tone and intonation, however, made it quite clear that the two were not happily discussing the joys of a cruising holiday.

Moving as stealthily as he could, Ulysses crept along the corridor to the junction from beyond which he could hear the two raised voices.

But as he reached the junction the arguing stopped and, if it hadn't have been for his flaring sixth sense, he would have walked straight into the mantis-like Professor Crichton as he stormed back around the corner.

The professor was obviously just as surprised to encounter Ulysses and could not hide the startled look that seized his face or stifle the gasp of astonishment.

"I'm sorry, Professor Crichton," Ulysses said, recovering first. "I almost didn't see you. I thought you had retired for the evening."

"And so I have. Good night, sir."

With that the professor pushed passed Ulysses and back along the corridor. A moment later, in his wake, came Lady Denning.

"Lady Denning, what a pleasant surprise. You appear to have lost your way. Can I help you back to your room?"

The thunderous look on the older woman's face faltered and then gave way under Ulysses' devilishly charming smile. Without making any efforts to disguise what she was doing, she briskly looked him up-and-down.

"Twenty years ago, Mr Quicksilver, perhaps. But not tonight."

There was no denying she was a handsome woman. Handsome as an expression of attractiveness in the more mature lady suggested, to Ulysses, that once she must have been alluring. Lord Denning had obviously thought so.

"Very well, your ladyship. And please, call me Ulysses," he conceded. "Good night to you."

"And to you, Mr Quicksilver."

Ulysses turned to watch Professor Crichton and Lady Denning make their way back along the corridor towards their respective rooms. He couldn't help thinking that they must be about the age his parents would have been, had they lived. A strange thought to have, perhaps, but something about the imperious, bickering couple had triggered a recollection in his mind – some distant memory maybe.

Although he hadn't discovered what it was they had been arguing about, he now knew something else about the two biologists. There was history there, between the two of them, a prior acquaintance, and it was one that neither of them seemed particularly keen to renew.

CHAPTER THREE

Waterworld

THE EVENING CONTINUED in much the same vein as it had done for the last few hours, although with the notable absence of both Lady Josephine Denning and Professor Maxwell Crichton. Captain McCormack, finding himself without anyone to share slight conversation with on his immediate left or right – John Schafer too preoccupied with his bride-to-be to make pleasant small-talk with the captain and Dr Ogilvy apparently having made it his goal to empty a bottle of port by himself – looked lost and uncomfortable. It was an obvious relief to him when one of his crew apologetically interrupted with a message. Tapping an empty wine glass with a dessert fork, Captain McCormack drew everyone's attention back to him.

"I do apologise for interrupting you all," he said, his calming Scots brogue filling the room with soft-spoken authority, "but I have been informed that the *Neptune* is about to dive, as we will make this leg of our journey towards Pacifica underwater."

There were murmurs of excited interest from around the room.

"For those of you who missed the opportunity when we dived down to Atlantis City, a truly dramatic way to experience the submersion is from the Promenade Deck, whilst enjoying a post-dinner stroll along the Promenade."

Taking this as their cue that the meal was over, the guests rose and made their way out of the gilt banqueting room.

As Ulysses rose from his chair, Glenda clutched at his arm. "I think moonlit walks are so romantic, don't you, Ulysses?"

The dandy looked down at the flirt clinging to him, her face upturned towards him, a tipsy smile on her painted lips. His initial feelings of irritation towards her in light of her almost possessive attitude dissolved as he looked into her eyes and thought he sensed something beyond the story-hunting hack.

"My dear," he said. "Would you care to join me for a stroll along the Promenade?"

"I thought you'd never ask," she beamed.

She was a distraction, he told himself, nothing more, something to take his mind off what still had to be done. Someone to take his mind off the one woman who had dominated his thoughts of late, despite the fact that the last time he had seen her she had tried to kill him.

As Ulysses strolled arm-in-arm with Glenda along the Promenade he gazed up at the velvet night visible beyond the reinforced glass bubble enclosing the deck, which meant that they could happily enjoy the *Neptune*'s gentle dive to Pacifica, safe in the knowledge that the air would be kept in and the sea out.

The *Neptune's* Promenade Deck was a miracle of modern Victorian engineering. It ran fully two-thirds the length of the ship, either side of the liner's massive smokestack and across the entire width of the vessel towards the prow. To walk the entire circuit of the Promenade took roughly a quarter of an hour and covered a distance of half a mile. The enclosing network of steel girders and beams which held the panels of toughened glass in place, like the reinforced hull of the *Neptune*, could withstand enormous pressures of up to 9,000 pounds per square inch, meaning that the sub-liner could comfortably travel down to the deepest of the undersea cities sunk beneath the oceans of the world to cope with the planet's ever-expanding population.

Out here, in the middle of the Pacific Ocean, away from the ever-present light pollution of industrialised centres and cities like Londinium Maximum or Paris, the rich deep blue of night was splashed with the stream of diamond dots that were the Milky Way, the myriad stars reflected in the rippling black surface of the sea.

"Isn't it beautiful?" Glenda whispered, following Ulysses' gaze beyond the toughened glass shield.

"Incredible," her escort mused, lost in a dream world of his own thoughts. "That we can walk here as the ship submerges with no fear of drowning."

Ulysses felt a sudden sharp poke in his ribs. "I meant the stars," she said. "Oh, yes... beautiful."

"Have you ever seen the constellations from this latitude and longitude before?" asked an accented male voice.

Thor Haugland, the travel writer, was leaning against the rail, the glass bubble still another few feet beyond the edge of the deck to allow for spectacular views of the sea surrounding the vessel as it descended.

"Oh yes," Ulysses replied.

"I take it you are well-travelled?" the writer went on.

"Oh, you know. I get around a bit. Work, mainly."

"And you, Miss Finch?"

"Oh, no, not really. The Continent a little, Europe mainly. Paris, Cannes, Milan; again with work," she gushed, flustered. "But this is a first for me. I have never been on board a cruise ship before."

"Then it's a first for both of us," Ulysses admitted.

"If you think this is spectacular," Haugland said, indicating the spread of the Milky Way above them, "you should see the Aurora Borealis of my homeland in Hammerfest – within the Artic Circle, in the far north of Norway – the scintillating Northern Lights."

"Ah, there's no place like home, eh, Haugland?" Ulysses said with a smile.

"The more one travels the more true that particular adage becomes, Mr Quicksilver," the Norwegian said, stroking his well-tended goatee and turning his gaze out across the wine-dark sea towards the horizon, as if trying to spy his homeland from here. "But in memory only. To go back would be to shatter the perfect illusion, like the destruction of a wonderful dream on waking. And where would we be without our dreams?"

"Home?" Ulysses suggested. Glenda giggled and poked him in the ribs again.

The sound of wailing sirens rose from speakers positioned around the Promenade deck, announcing that the time had come, and the *Neptune* was ready to dive.

Without altering its speed the liner continued ploughing its furrow of white water across the night-black mirror of the sea. Ulysses and Glenda joined Haugland at the rail and peered down at the churning waters beside the ship. As they watched, the *Neptune* began to sink, creating the illusion from their viewpoint that the sea level was rising, eating up the lower decks of the ship, swallowing portholes and sealed hatches.

The ship was keeping to an even keel as the crew flooded the ballast tanks, taking the sub-liner under the waves whilst keeping it as level as if it were still riding the calm surface of the sea, rather than gliding beneath it.

Glenda gasped. Ulysses took in her delighted expression – agog with child-like wonder – and followed her gaze beyond the glass bubble.

The waves were now splashing against the shield that contained the Promenade. Other late-evening wanderers had also paused to take in the spectacle. The silvered amethyst line of the far horizon disappeared as the waves lapped higher. Submarine darkness closed in on either side of the ship, with only the glimmer of the strung out galaxy across the cloudless night sky visible through the clear glass ceiling of the Promenade. Then the sea poured in from all sides, closing in on a rapidly shrinking circle of sky until, in moments, that too was gone. The last part of the ship to submerge was the shielded smokestack.

Glenda let out, what Ulysses realised must have been, a long held breath. "That is incredible," she said, her voice still barely more than a whisper.

"Yes, I really rather think it is," Ulysses found himself having to agree.

The running lights of the ship turned the underside of the waves that had closed over them sky blue for a moment. The *Neptune* continued to descend and the light became a curiously diffused sphere around them, with only darkness beyond.

Ulysses was aware of gentle creaking sounds as the superstructure of the *Neptune* adjusted to the weight of the water pressing down on it. But there was nothing to suggest that anything untoward was happening. No cracks appeared in the heavily toughened glass. The dome was holding.

But then of course it was, Ulysses chided himself. He had not thought himself the kind of man to see disaster wherever he looked, but then experience had taught him caution at all times. He was sure that there were very few on board who would be worried, not when entire cities could remain safe beneath the sea, resisting the colossal pressures exerted by trillions of tons of water pressing down on them.

"Look at that!" Glenda suddenly exclaimed, squeezing Ulysses' arm in excitement and pointing out beyond the glass. Ulysses looked.

Lights were appearing out of the darkness beyond the ship: silvered bubbles of air – released by the ship's submersion – rushing past; a bio-luminescent green soup of feeding plankton; the rippling purple and orange running lights of transparent squid; the swaying blue lantern-lures of nocturnal submarine feeders.

"Welcome to water-world," Ulysses announced. "Pacifica, here we come."

THE SOUND OF the child's footfalls rang from the grilled walkways, echoing back from the curved passageway walls. Tears streamed from her eyes, blurring her vision, but she still knew where she was going. After all, she knew the place as well as she knew the back of her hand, better in fact.

She certainly knew it better than any of the others. Everyone else on board was a grown-up, and grown-ups didn't play. It was only when you played hide-and-seek, made secret dens, and spied on the grown-ups as they went about their secret work in their white coats and overalls, that you discovered every twisting rat-run, every hidden ventilation duct, every unplanned hiding place.

Sounds of death and destruction chased her along the curving corridor. She was also aware of a moaning, whimpering coming between great sobbing gulps of breath. It took her a moment longer to realise that it was she who was making this sound. She swallowed a sob in an effort to stop the fearful, childish noise.

The tears kept coming, splashing onto the grille beneath her hobnail boots, and mingling with the grime and blood already streaking her face. Her pinafore dress was dirtied and torn as well. She had barely got away. She had had to leave Madeleine behind; there had not been time to go back for her. As she thought of Madeleine, abandoned and alone, she could not contain the howl that burst from her in an outpouring of emotion, an unrestrained wail of grief and fear. She had not cried like this since she had lost her mother. Now she was losing Madeleine – her dear Madeleine – and her father all in one go.

She stumbled, the toe of a boot catching in the open mesh of the grilled walkway, and fell. She landed on hands and knees, breaking the skin, grazing her palms. Blood flowed. The shock of the fall stopped the crying for a moment and in that moment she struggled to take control.

She tried to calm herself, that small internal part of her that she liked to think of as her mother still, telling her to stop being such a silly girl and stop crying. How was crying going to help at a time like this? What would her father say?

Her father's face came to mind now as she ran on along the corridor, the hollow-eyed look of exhausted panic, the screaming mouth, strings of spittle flying from his lips. And she heard the last words he had spoken to her again, over the roar and crash of the structure collapsing behind her.

"Run, Marie! Run!"

So she ran.

CHAPTER FOUR

City Beneath the Sea

PACIFICA FIRST APPEARED out of the abyssal gloom as a conglomeration of fuzzy balls of light.

As the *Neptune* powered on, corkscrew propellers churning the darkness behind it, the blur of suffused light sharpened in focus to become one vast dome connected to others of steadily decreasing size. The main dome of the undersea city was huge, a cyclopean structure of steel and glass, sprouting antenna relays, airlocks and the vent-ports of the cathedral-sized machineries that maintained the life-support systems of the city.

Closer still and it became apparent to anyone seeing the city for the first time from on board the *Neptune* that where Atlantis City had been all straight lines and angular outcroppings – its superstructure looking more like a gargantuan version of the only recently reconstructed (and then devastatingly de-constructed) Crystal Palace – the structure of the newer undersea metropolis appeared to have been created in the likeness of a spiralling nautilus shell. The central dome of the city dominated the vista visible from the sub-liner's prow viewing ports, and it was still some miles away.

Even from outside, and from this distance, it was clear that the internal structure of the city reflected that of a nautilus shell also, with the internal space divided into a number of reducing, separately-sealable, self-contained compartments. The interconnecting, smaller contained environment domes followed the same pattern, miniature replicas of the primary biome. Such an architectural structure would provide added rigidity and also an extra element of safety. Should the unthinkable happen, and one of the domes crack, depressurising and letting in the sea, the surrounding divisions of the city could be locked down and kept airtight.

Closing on the city, the *Neptune* began to pass some of the outer domes where droid-slaves tended the plantations whilst outside, automaton machines – rust-red crab-like constructions the size of tug boats – harvested the vegetation of floodlit kelp fields.

Now those on board the *Neptune* could no longer see the open sea beyond the superstructure of Pacifica, so colossal was the city's dome. Truly it was a triumph, a temple to man's mastery of the machine and his world.

THOSE PASSENGERS WAITING in the fore airlocks were afforded the most impressive view of the city as the *Neptune* glided smoothly into its appointed docking bay – just one of many, the piers of which reached out from the city's superstructure like anemone fronds into the ocean depths. Passengers like Ulysses Quicksilver, his female companion Miss Finch hanging onto his arm. The dandy's manservant stood a pace or two behind them carrying with him a bag recently purchased by Glenda to "help her do her shopping", shooting disapproving looks at the couple arm-in-arm before him.

Glenda Finch might not be the sort of woman that Ulysses would usually take as a companion, and she certainly wasn't going to be the love of his life but, to his mind, it merely enhanced his reputation if he arrived with a single young woman with her own public profile. And the more the press portrayed him as a notorious, fame-hungry womaniser, the more quickly it would forget that other side of his personality – that of agent of the throne of Magna Britannia, for whom espionage and adventure were never far away.

And Glenda had scrubbed up well for the occasion, Ulysses considered, as he gave her another appraising look. Both of them had dressed to impress for their brief sojourn within the undersea city. He was wearing an off-white linen suit, magnolia waistcoat and verdigris cravat, she an unassuming number picked up in one of the *Neptune's* many boutiques. It was a Vasa original, broad across the shoulders with an open collar plunging to a V-cut neckline, coming in tight at the waist – and she really did have a very slim waist – before ballooning at the hips again and then coming in tight at the ankles. The outfit accentuated her classic hourglass figure, and Glenda Finch walked – hips rolling lasciviously

– like she knew it. The realisation that she was likely to be making the headlines today, rather than writing them, had not been lost on her.

It looked like those assembled at the docking port with Ulysses and his small entourage – other passengers and even some of the ship's human crew members – were looking forward to a little shore leave, even if it was only for the day, leaving the automata on board to maintain the sub-liner's systems.

It was an opportunity too good to be missed. It might not technically be terra firma, but at least to walk the parks and promenades of Pacifica was to walk on a steady, unmoving surface. It would take all of them a little time to find their land-legs again, after the subtle yet constant rolling of the decks after a number of weeks on board ship.

With a hiss of equalising air pressures, the airlocks steamed open and the eager passengers hurried to enter the underwater metropolis. Having passed through all the different failsafe measures from the docks – pressurised airlocks and sealable bulkheads – those 'going ashore' finally passed through customs and entered the city itself.

What awaited them was something not far short of a full-blown ticker-tape parade. Crowds of Pacificans and other visitors thronged the streets beyond the customs checkpoint, contained behind temporarily erected barricades, a brass band in crimson uniforms, polished gold buttons shining, oompah-ing away behind the crowds somewhere.

The air smelled sterile and recycled – which, of course, it was. But then other, completely contrasting exotic aromas assailed Ulysses' finely-tuned nose. It was said that Pacifica was a truly cosmopolitan hotchpotch of a place, welcoming people from all corners of the globe, who brought with them their own cultures, diets, specialities. It was also said, in more hushed tones by those in the know, that anything could be acquired in Pacifica, no matter how discerning or demanding the customer's tastes may be.

Bulbs flashed and a number of kinema cameras followed the progress of the great and the good as they disembarked from the *Neptune*. Glenda was excited to see their own faces looking back at them from a large broadcast screen hanging above the scallop-shell plaza they were now crossing. Those same images would likely be broadcast across the globe, on the Magna Britannia Broadcasting Corporation's official news channel, ad nauseam over the next twenty-four hours. The maiden voyage of the *Neptune* could still make the headlines, even weeks after leaving Southampton. And since the debacle surrounding the regime-threatening activities of the Darwinian Dawn Ulysses had become something of a celebrity across the Empire. People commented and pointed when they saw him; some boldly approached to ask for his autograph or a photograph, whilst many more simply stopped and stared as he strode past. Ulysses loved every second of it.

Glenda loved the attention too, making the most of being in front of the cameras, when the opportunity arose, rather than being stuck behind a type-processing Babbage console. Only the long-suffering Nimrod seemed not to be enjoying the attention, a pained expression on his face the whole time which turned to an even more annoyed grimace when he caught a glimpse of himself on screen. Perhaps it was a hangover from his misspent youth, this desperate desire not to have attention drawn to himself, least he be recognised by someone.

"Nimrod, old chap," Ulysses said, addressing his manservant, "why don't you take some time for yourself? Take a few hours off. I'm sure I'm more than capable of helping Miss Finch carry her shopping."

"Very good, sir," Nimrod said, without a hint of protest, the tension in his expression already easing. "If you're certain you won't be requiring my assistance?"

"I think Miss Finch would just like to take in a few of the boutiques on the Strand and we might go for a saunter through the coral parks," Ulysses went on.

"Sounds almost romantic, like we're courting," Glenda teased, squeezing his arm tighter.

"So take your time, old chap. No need to hurry back. I'm sure we'll be fine without you. I mean, how much trouble can we get into here?"

"Then I shall bid you and Miss Finch good day."

"Good day, Mr Nimrod."

"See you later, old boy."

"THIS PLACE IS truly stunning!" Glenda declared, an expression of child-like wonder on her face. Ulysses had to admit that it was a very endearing quality, especially in someone who, by dint of their work-a-day trade, one might have expected to be a cynical hack. She might write the gossip column for *The Times* but she had been writing about a world she was viewing second hand; she had never truly been a part of things until now.

And the worldly adventurer, who many would most definitely have considered to have been born with a silver spoon in his mouth and who had seen all manner of wonders the world over, had to agree once again with his awestruck companion.

Whether the city had been constructed on top of a dead reef which had then had the ocean pumped out of it and the park carved out of the outcropping seabed – the skeletons of a million coral life-forms – or whether the colourful forest of bones had been transplanted here from elsewhere along with every last carefully arranged rocky spur, the result was a thing of beauty.

The sea-worn rock, also bearing the scars of shellfish erosion, had a grotto-like quality, the stone riddled with hollows, holes and tiny tunnels.

Larger cave-like structures had also been purposefully carved out of the rock between florid protrusions of crimson, amber and rose-pink branches of dry, dead coral, and other natural cavern spaces enhanced. Landscape-engineered cascades tumbled between the coral-clung rocks, under bridged pathways and over the sculpted seabed, the gurgling and babbling of water ever-present in the gardens. And, unlike any public garden Ulysses had visited before, those same cascades were salt seawater. Corralled within the flooded hollows of pools and sculpted streams, cuttlefish swan, multi-hued octopi hunted between the waving fronds of anemones and submerged sea-worms, whilst leopard-spotted eels darted from their shaded holes. Brittle stars scrambled over rock-pool floors, azure-bodied sea cucumbers oozed between feeding grounds. Barnacle-shelled crustaceans plucked dainty morsels from their pools, fed to them by the passers-by, shoals of parrot fish coursed between growths of seaweed and limpet-clung rocks.

"So, where now? What would you like to see next?" Ulysses asked, feeling that their purposeless ambling needed some direction.

"Oh, we've not seen the Triton Fountain yet, have we?" Glenda suggested excitedly.

"No, we haven't. It's over this way," Ulysses said, directing with his bloodstone cane.

The casual couple skirted a wide circular pool where a park-keeper was feeding a cast of pink-shelled spider crabs, much to the delight of the onlookers who had gathered round.

"There's old Jonah Carcharodon!" Glenda suddenly blurted out. "Mr Carcharodon! Coo-ee, over here!"

Before Ulysses could stop her, forgetting any sense of decorum, she began waving furiously as she called out to the shipping magnate. Why didn't his near-prescient sixth sense see to warn him of such embarrassing social faux pas?

Carcharodon was being pushed at a sedate pace through the coral gardens by his ever-attendant PA. The two of them appeared to have been deep in conversation, but now both Carcharodon and Miss Celeste caught sight of them. Ulysses didn't miss the passing look of annoyance the old man displayed before his 'for-the-cameras' smile returned, his public persona taking charge. Miss Celeste, however, immediately directed her timid gaze back towards the ground, hoping her carefully coiffeured fringe would hide her.

Miss Celeste intrigued Ulysses. Undeniably attractive and yet hampered by her overwhelming shyness, she worked for one of the richest and most powerful men in the world, and yet she appeared to demonstrate no self-confidence whatsoever. Ulysses couldn't help noticing that she was also carrying a portable personal Babbage unit with her, strapped up in a bag slung over her shoulder. It seemed that she was never off duty, always at work, just like her employer.

Glenda steered Ulysses through the bustling crowds towards the wheelchair-bound billionaire. *The poor man, doesn't have a hope*, Ulysses thought to himself. *He couldn't get away if he wanted to.*

"Mr Carcharodon," Glenda gushed, shaking the old man enthusiastically by the hand, "so this is how a multi-billionaire spends his afternoons off."

"What? Oh, I see what you mean. I suppose so."

"Aren't they beautiful?"

"What?" the shipping magnate blustered, clearly not on the same train of thought as the newspaper writer.

"Why, the coral gardens, of course," Glenda clarified, an expression of amusement on her face, her tone playfully chiding.

"Look, if you two would like to be left alone," Ulysses hissed in Glenda's ear.

"Oh, Mr Quicksilver, you're so amusing," his companion said raucously. Miss Celeste shot her a venomous look.

Ulysses felt that oh-so familiar itch at the back of his brain. He looked round sharply. The promenading crowds were thick around them now but he could see no threat. It must simply be a feeling of unfamiliar claustrophobia that was getting to him. Perhaps even a touch of jealousy. He really had to get his head sorted out; he seemed to keep getting mixed up with women possessed of a self-serving nature. Perhaps this should be his last outing with Miss Glenda Finch.

"Oh my!" Miss Celeste suddenly shrieked, her uncharacteristic outburst surprising everyone.

An instant later, somebody barged past Ulysses. Instinctively he shot out a hand – only he was encumbered by the fact that it was on the same arm he had interlocked with Glenda's. He caught an impression of a roughly-dressed rogue, keeping his head down, and picking up pace as he broke free of the clustering crowds.

"My bag!" Miss Celeste cried. "It's been taken. Someone's taken my bag!"

And the Babbage unit, Ulysses thought as, already practically acting on instinct alone, he broke free of Glenda's clinch and leapt free of the now unmoving throng, curious passers-by stopping to see what all the fuss was about.

"Oi!" Ulysses shouted after his quarry. "Stop, thief! Somebody stop that man, for Pete's sake!"

Entering a stretch of less-crowded pathways, the thief sprinted away between the coral-clad rocks, Miss Celeste's bag gripped tightly in one hand. Ulysses put on a spurt of speed, feeling the rush of adrenalin flood his body, the old fight-or-flight response doing its bit. The chase was most definitely on.

Even at the height of the pursuit, adrenal glands pumping their secretions into his bloodstream, his heart racing, a part of Ulysses' conscious mind found time to consider that every city, no matter where it might be or how idyllic it might appear on the outside, had its own criminal underclass. And, of course, Ulysses knew all about the dark underbelly of the undersea paradise of Pacifica already.

He ran on, shouting again for assistance as he forced his way past meandering clusters of surprised promenaders. There were a number of shouts from startled tourists, not so much at the brusque manner of Ulysses, as he barged past in his mad dash after the thief, but at his presence there at all, his celebrity status well and truly secured.

The park attendants – both human and automaton – had at last noticed that something was awry and were making taking steps to act accordingly, although they appeared to be as surprised as the general public. Whatever flustered action they might eventually deem to take, Ulysses suspected that it would doubtless be too late to stop the thief from getting away.

The fleeing scoundrel was steadily descending through the coral-sculpted gardens. Taking a sharp right at a junction, Ulysses doubled back on himself, running hell-for-leather towards a shimmering cascade. There he saw his opportunity to bring the chase to an end.

Bounding over the low wrought-iron fence surrounding the coral beds he dashed across the top of the cascade, in line with the fleeing ruffian, and leapt. Hitting the pink gravel path six feet below, he winced, feeling his left knee jar as he landed. The rush of adrenalin nonetheless allowed him to put the pain to one side, although he knew he would pay for it later.

Ulysses managed to regain his composure in time for the thief to round the edge of the cascade and run slap bang into his outstretched arm. The arm, rigid as a steel bar, caught the man across the neck. He went down hard, legs flying out from under him. The bag flew from his hand, a catch unbuckling, a number of dossier files sailing into the air to fall like over-sized confetti onto the path.

The dandy deftly plucked the bag out of the air, catching it by the shoulder strap and smoothly slinging it over his arm.

He looked down at the pole-axed scoundrel, as the thwarted thief clutched at his throat gasping for air. Ulysses straightened his jacket and saw to his loosened cravat. "I rather suspect this doesn't belong to you," he said, holding Miss Celeste's bag over the spluttering man. The wretch, unshaven and looking every part the habitual felon, stared at Ulysses in eye-bulging shock.

Ulysses recovered the loosed files, briefly opening the card folders to make sure that everything was put back in its rightful place.

With a skittering of boot-steps on gravel, a number of park keepers caught up with the rogue and his captor at last.

"Gentlemen," Ulysses said, casting an unimpressed look at the tardy attendants, "I think I can leave this unpleasant situation to you to deal with now, don't you?"

By the time Ulysses returned to the spot where the attempted crime had taken place, Miss Celeste was sitting on a park bench looking flustered, with an overbearing Glenda trying to comfort her, an arm around the woman's tense shoulders. Jonah Carcharodon sat in his chair offering no words of sympathy or optimistic encouragement, a thunderous expression clouding his face.

On seeing Ulysses striding back along the path towards them, bag in hand, Miss Celeste visibly relaxed, an unexpected smile erupting from her tear-streaked face that was like a brilliant ray of sunshine after the passing of a cloud.

"Oh, thank you! Thank you, Mr Quicksilver!" she gushed. "If I had lost this... I don't know what I would have done," she said, faltering with the realisation of how close the situation had come to disaster.

Ulysses had never known her say so much and for a moment the two of them even made eye contact.

However, as far as her employer was concerned, Ulysses' endeavours might have been for naught, even though Ulysses was sure that the loss of Miss Celeste's difference engine and assorted documents would have been as great an inconvenience for Carcharodon as it would have been for his assistant.

"Come on, woman. If these histrionics are quite done with, can we get going?" Carcharodon snapped.

"Are you all right, Miss Celeste?" Ulysses asked, with genuine concern, ignoring her employer.

"Y-yes, thank you, Mr Quicksilver," she said, the smile gone once more, her eyes cast down at the ground. "Thank you for your concern, but if you will excuse me we must be on our way. I have delayed Mr Carcharodon quite enough already."

Ulysses watched, anger rising within him at the attitude Carcharodon had displayed towards Miss Celeste. He wanted to say something, to make the man realise how egocentric and insensitive he was being.

But the moment passed as Glenda took his arm in hers once again and, on tiptoe, whispered, "You're my hero," into his ear. He could smell the intoxicating aroma of her now that she was so close to him. The touch of her breath on his face sent a frisson of excitement thrilling through his adrenalin-heightened senses.

Ulysses looked at her and smiled, disarmed once again, delighted by her apparently innocent, almost naïve reaction to events that were, for him, virtually a matter of daily occurrence.

"You look like you could do with a drink." she said

"Yes, I think you're probably right," Ulysses agreed, already imagining the nectar-sweet bite of cognac on his taste buds. "Would you care to join me? I hear there are a number of bars with an ocean-view on the Strand."

"That sounds lovely," Glenda said, dipping her chin and looking up at him with appealing puppy-dog eyes, "but I really ought to check in with the paper. We have an office here. Did you know? I hope you don't mind."

Ulysses was taken aback. "N-no, not at all," he stammered, wrong-footed. "I might take a rain check then myself. You know what they say about drinking alone."

"I'll see you later, though," she said, a definite twinkle in her eye, "back at the ship, where I'm sure you'll be happy to grant me an exclusive interview about your heroic antics, in more convivial surroundings."

Still high from the rush his race through the park had given him, Ulysses felt a tingling stirring deep down inside him. "I'll look forward to it," he said, blushing despite himself.

She planted a lingering kiss on his lips. "So will I," she murmured. "Now, don't go getting into any more trouble, and I'll see you later for that exclusive."

With Glenda gone, Ulysses was surprised to find himself feeling at a loose end. Beautiful as the coral gardens were, he had no great desire to take in any of the other tourist attractions Pacifica had to offer. He was merely marking time, after all, until an opportunity presented itself.

Going over the events in the park, Ulysses made a decision. If you really wanted to understand a city, find out what made it tick, just as with a human body you had to peel back the surface layers and look at what lay beneath.

He had spent long enough enjoying that which the city governors wanted visitors to see; now it was time to take a look at the seedier side of things, the gritty reality of life in the city beneath the sea.

ULYSSES PAUSED IN the shadow of a rust-stained arch, becoming motionless in an instant as Doctor Ogilvy stopped and darted an anxious look over his shoulder for what seemed like the umpteenth time since Ulysses had caught up with him, quite by chance, close to the warehouses down below the docks at city bottom. Ulysses knew that he didn't exactly blend into the background in his fine-tailored suit and was somewhat encumbered by his flamboyant dress sense, but Ogilvy was really starting to draw attention to himself, with his cringing behaviour. And what was he doing down here anyway?

Ever since spotting the ship's seemingly-suffering doctor as he was cruising the opium-dens located in an outer dome of the complex metropolis, his insatiable curiosity piqued, Ulysses had found the perfect way to while away a few hours in Pacifica. And, before too long, the doctor's anxious steps had brought them here.

Ogilvy had stopped outside a seemingly abandoned and shuttered shop-front. He looked around him again but still he didn't see the cunningly hidden Ulysses. Ogilvy knocked three times on the shuttered doorway, paused, then knocked again, three times, paused and then gave another three knocks. The shutter finally rattled upwards, revealing two men of obviously Oriental origin. These two Chinamen shot suspicious looks up and down the detritus-strewn street before admitting Dr Ogilvy. The shutter was pulled down again after them.

Two suspicious-looking Chinese characters having a clandestine meeting with the eminent Dr Ogilvy, chief medic aboard the foremost sub-liner in the world on its maiden round-the-world voyage? Even Inspector Allardyce of Her Majesty's Metropolitan Police would have realised that something was going on here that could not be left uninvestigated.

Sure the coast was clear, Ulysses crept forwards.

Awareness flared in his hindbrain and he turned to see a lithe figure detach itself from the gloom behind him. In that split second Ulysses realised someone else had been following him, unnoticed, so caught up had he been in his pursuit of Dr Ogilvy. And then his unerring sixth sense flared again as two iron-strong hands seized him from behind.

CHAPTER FIVE

Our Man in Shanghai

"THANK YOU, MR Quicksilver," the Chinaman said, returning Ulysses' card holder.

Ulysses snatched it back and returned it to his jacket pocket. "Not that I really had much choice," he said sourly, looking pointedly at the larger of the two Chinamen. "And now it would appear that you have me at a disadvantage, Mr –"

The smiling, well-spoken man sitting opposite him did not take up Ulysses' cue.

"I must apologise most profusely, but my aide was only acting on my orders."

That same aide now glared at Ulysses, his curiously Cro-Magnon features showing no other emotion. Unusually, for one of his countrymen, he was taller than the Englishman and big in every way, built like a navvy from his broad gorilla-like frame to his huge hands, like great meaty paws.

"Can't he speak for himself?" Ulysses challenged, but the huge Chinaman's expression remained impassive and he said nothing.

"He does not speak English, Mr Quicksilver."

"Oh, I see. I suppose I should commend you on your own command of the Queen's English," Ulysses said grudgingly. "If you will forgive me," he said with forced politeness, "you speak it almost like a native."

"Why thank you. That means a great deal to me."

"Your accent – sounds almost Home Counties."

"Hong Kong, via Oxford. I spent a very rewarding three years at Boriel College. My grandfather was British."

"I see, but you're loyal to your Chinese roots."

"My grandfather had no great love for your empire."

"His empire as well, surely."

"He didn't see it that way."

"Really? That is interesting."

"But hardly relevant. It strikes me that you could be an Oxford man yourself, Mr Quicksilver."

"Indeed," Ulysses confirmed. "Boriel College also, but before your time I suspect."

"I think you are probably right, although not by much, I'll warrant."

"So, now we know we share the same alma mater, if we're both Oxford men, old school tie and all that, I think you can tell me your name."

"Of course, I am Harry Cheng, agent of the most glorious Imperial Throne of China and its affiliated colonies," he said, offering Ulysses his own ID, "and this is my colleague Mr Sin."

"Now, why doesn't that surprise me?"

Ulysses glanced up and down the street. All manner of cafés and eating establishments had set up here, away from the grander restaurants and hotels in the main dome. There were Turkish eateries with surly individuals seated outside smoking hookahs, other Mediterranean-styled tavernas and an Oriental-themed fast food joint. The place where the three of them now sat proclaimed itself to be an Italian coffee house.

Ulysses could quite easily have believed that all human life was here. This street, with its cafés and bars, was a microcosm of all Pacifica life, a clear cosmopolitan cross-section of the city's populace.

He closed his eyes for a moment, taking in all the various aromas of the street, feeling the heat of the sun-lamps on his face. That was one thing about life inside an underwater city: the weather was always predictably good. The artificial arc-lights, powered like the rest of the city, by geothermal energy tapped from submarine volcanic vents, generated enough light for an artificial sun all year round, only dimming as the city began its night cycle.

"Now, if we could return to the matter in hand," Cheng said.

"Ah yes, you mean how you forcibly abducted me and dragged me here? Why was that?"

"Might I first ask you, Mr Quicksilver, what you were doing at City Bottom amongst the warehouses of the slum quarter?"

"I could ask you the same thing," Ulysses retorted.

Harry Cheng sighed and muttered something in Chinese. At that Mr Sin's lips curled back and he growled like a mastiff. Another word from Cheng, however, settled him again.

"You have me at a disadvantage once again," Ulysses said, with arrogant bravura. He had dealt with worse than Mr Sin.

"Mr Quicksilver, we could play this game all day. I can assure you that it is in both our best interests that we are open and honest with one another."

"Mr Cheng, it would appear to me that you are living in something of a cloud cuckoo land if you think it is in the best interests of an agent of Imperial China and a loyal servant of the crowned head of Magna Britannia to work openly together."

"Then, if it will earn your compliance and cooperation, there is something I must share with you."

"You're welcome to try."

Cheng leaned forward over the table. In response Ulysses leaned in closer himself.

"Mr Quicksilver, I suspect that you and I are very alike, in so many ways that we could be a formidable team, if we chose to work together, or deadly rivals. But ultimately we are working towards the same goal."

"I beg your pardon?"

"More than that, we are working for the same side."

Ulysses responded to this revelation by raising one suspicious eyebrow. "That is a bold claim and, if it is the case, can you prove it? Where is your ID? Prove to me that you are a double agent."

"Please, Mr Quicksilver," Cheng hissed, throwing anxious glances up and down the street, "I am not overly fond of that term. The fact is that I have shared with you something very personal and private, and in the strictest confidence."

"But can you prove it?" Ulysses badgered.

"I can tell you why you were exploring City Bottom, why we ran into each other when and where we did."

"That would be a start." Ulysses rocked back in his chair, ignoring the cappuccino cooling in front of him and folding his arms. "Go on then. Fire away."

Cheng picked up a napkin and rested his arms on the tabletop. "You were following someone from the ship you came in on, the chief medical officer, Dr Ogilvy." His fingers moved nimbly as he began to flip and fold the pliant tissue. "Am I right so far?"

"Go on," Ulysses said.

"And although the public may believe that you joined the maiden voyage of the *Neptune* for some well-publicised rest and relaxation following recent events in London, you are actually on board as much for work as you are for pleasure."

Cheng looked up from his origami to judge Ulysses' reaction. Ulysses simply nodded again.

"You believe that Dr Ogilvy is part of an illicit smuggling racket, just one pawn in an opium smuggling ring."

The two agents looked at one another, Cheng's narrowed eyes emotionless, Ulysses' gaze fiery, challenging Cheng to say more.

"Correct," he admitted.

"The last shipment due for London's smoking dens never arrived and those who stand to profit from such an enterprise want to know what happened to it. This is your chance to infiltrate their operation, find out who's in charge and discover the identity of the criminal mastermind behind it all."

Cheng put a cupped hand down on the table between them. When he removed it, a paper crane stood there, wings outstretched as if making ready to fly.

"Very good, Mr Cheng, very good. Now, seeing as how you appear to know so much, perhaps you could fill in a few of the gaps for me."

"That seems only fair, Mr Quicksilver."

"How do you know so much about my covert mission? Who told you?"

"I told you, you and I are on the same side. We have the same bosses who reveal the same pertinent facts to us as and when necessary. No one person ever has the whole picture, of course, and I have to admit that it was a bold move by our masters to put someone so in the public eye, and known for being an agent of the throne of Magna Britannia, on the case."

"Have you not heard of the expression 'hide in plain sight'?" Ulysses threw back. "But getting back to the matter in hand, as you put it, how much do know about Ogilvy's part in all this?"

"Enough. I know that he is not a big player within the ring and that his own addictions are what those with the real power have used to ensnare him."

"Tell me again – how do you know?"

"As I keep trying to tell you, Mr Quicksilver, we are working for the same side. We are just tackling this investigation from opposite ends."

"Were you recruited at Boriel, then?" Ulysses asked.

"I was. I take it that you –"

"Indeed, although you might say I was also following my father into the family trade."

"Ah, of course. The celebrated Hercules Quicksilver."

"You know of him?"

"Almost as well as I know of your recent career, Mr Quicksilver."

"Really?"

"Oh yes. It thrilled me to read of your adventures in *The Times*."

"So," Ulysses said, bringing their discussion back on track. "If you know so much about Ogilvy, what else do you know?"

"The intelligence that I have access to suggests that an old adversary of yours could well be behind all this."

Ulysses could not hide his interest now, despite himself, as a host of villainous characters whose nefarious plans he had thwarted in the past came to mind, a veritable rogues' gallery.

"Which one? Tell me."

"The Black Mamba."

Ulysses gasped. Harry Cheng smiled, satisfied that he still had the upper hand and that he had been able to startle this otherwise ice-cool character.

A host of painful memories flooded Ulysses' consciousness. He was there, high above the Himalayas once again, the two balloons locked together, tumbling through the swirling snow of the midnight blizzard towards the unforgiving peaks beneath. The Black Mamba's sinister Mandarin Emperor's face inches from his, swiping scimitar in hand, Ulysses holding him off with his own sword-cane, Davenport clinging to the side of the gondola, clutching at the stab-wound to his chest, fingers numb with frostbite.

"Mr Quicksilver?"

And then – with Cheng's words – he was abruptly back in the muggy heat of the undersea dome.

"I... I thought I had done for that blaggard over Mount Manaslu."

"Thought, or hoped? We both know how slippery a character the Black Mamba can be. I sometimes wonder that he shouldn't be monikered the Black Cat. He seems to have the lives of one. Did you ever recover the green-eyed monkey god of Sumatra?"

Ulysses shot the Chinese agent a look as if to say, 'How the hell do you know about that?' but didn't bother answering the question. Instead he looked into the surface of his cooling coffee as if seeing something else there, as a gypsy fortune-teller might scry into a crystal ball.

"If I might be candid, Mr Quicksilver?"

"I wouldn't want you to be anything else, Mr Cheng."

"If Mr Sin and myself had not stepped in when we did – and I must apologise again for any inconvenience caused – you could have ruined everything."

Ulysses snorted in annoyance at the patronising Cheng. "It's what I do. I mix things up a bit. What were you doing there then, if you weren't going to act and you know so much about this operation already? Keeping Ogilvy under surveillance, I suppose."

"No, Mr Quicksilver, I'm sorry, but that's where you're wrong. We were keeping *you* under surveillance."

"It would seem that while you were busy making sure that I didn't blow your operation, your one and only lead has got away. How are you going to find out if the Black Mamba is behind this opium smuggling ring now?"

Cheng continued smiling in that irritating, ingratiating way of his. "But he hasn't got away, Mr Quicksilver. I rather suspect he will be boarding the *Neptune* again, along with the rest of the passengers, very shortly."

"But if you take him in then you will be making a very public spectacle of yourself, and quite probably in front of the world's press at that. Surely that's not the best way to avoid alerting the Black Mamba to the fact that you are onto him."

"I couldn't agree with you more," Cheng said, still with the same ingratiating smile on his lips.

"Then what, in God's name, are you planning to do?"

"I have reason to believe that the good doctor is not the only connection that exists between the smuggling operation and the Carcharodon shipping line," Cheng explained. Reaching into his jacket pocket he carefully extracted a card wallet, with two cards inside it.

"Two tickets, Mr Quicksilver, one for myself and one for my aide, Mr Sin. The mystery of the missing consignment of opium has not yet been resolved. We are coming with you, on board the *Neptune*. We are joining your cruise."

CHAPTER SIX

Casino Royale

"Gentlemen, if you would please take your seats?"

"Come on chaps," Major Marmaduke Horsley said loudly, at the croupier's request, "let's play Blackjack!"

The Major had lost none of his old military manner. When he issued a command it was in a tone of voice that broached no refusal. The hubbub of interrupted conversations fizzled out, and the invited guests approached the Blackjack table.

The *Neptune's* onboard casino, the Casino Royale – named in homage to the crown of Magna Britannia – was a hive of bustling activity, the atmosphere tense with the prospect of a great deal of money being won or lost on the turn of a single card.

Ulysses took another sip of his French brandy, and from his place at the bar quickly surveyed the room. He could see most of the guests from dinner at the captain's table, some nights since now, and a number of other well-to-do chancers hoping for a piece of the action at the table that night.

Those now approaching the table – standing on a raised dais in the centre of the room, surrounded by a low rail that effectively cordoned it off from the rest of the space, velvet tassel ropes drawn across openings in the rail politely emphasising the fact – were there by invitation only. And if that wasn't enough the price of the buy-in alone was enough to exclude most of the people present in the room. But, even if they couldn't play, they could still watch, and a high stakes game of Blackjack made for an exciting spectator sport for those on board.

"Are you a gambler, Mr Quicksilver?" Glenda Finch asked, leaning close to whisper in his ear. Ulysses could not help glancing to his left, his gaze falling into the shadowed hollow between her breasts, exposed by the low-cut neckline of her dress as she leant forward.

"Oh, indubitably, Miss Finch," he replied with a wry smile, returning his gaze to the Blackjack table. "I take a risk every time I'm in your company."

Everyone appeared to be dressed in their grandest finery for the event, emphasising what an important and prestigious occasion it was, as well as how lucrative it might be for those blessed by Lady Luck that night. The ladies were in the latest designer dresses from Paris and Milan, purchased at the *Neptune's* haute couture boutiques during the voyage, whilst the gentlemen had almost all gone for black tie, Ulysses included, although he had personalised his attire with a striking paisley waistcoat off-set by a silver-grey crushed silk cravat, diamond pin in place as ever.

As the other invited players mounted the dais to take their seats, Ulysses followed at a discreet distance. Lady Josephine Denning stepped up onto the dais in front of him.

"Lady Denning," Ulysses commented, with a tone of undisguised, almost patronising, surprise, as he took a seat beside the titled scientist. "I didn't take you for a gambler."

"And I didn't take you for a sexist pig, young man," she bit back, managing to surprise Ulysses still further, even causing him to blush, unable to hide his embarrassment, his guard down.

Ulysses regarded his fellow gamblers over the rim of his brandy balloon. Going clockwise from the croupier, there was Dexter Sylvester, the Umbridge Industries man and the absent Josiah Umbridge's representative, the Major, and next to him a flabby banker who Ulysses had learnt earlier that evening went by the name of Armitage. Then came Lady Denning, followed by himself. To his left was an ageing Oriental woman, whose name he had yet to discover, being one of those passengers who had joined the cruise at Pacifica and whose ostentatious jewellery, ill-fitting, unflattering, too-revealing dress and milk-white make-up could not hide the fact that she must have been well into her seventies. The last seat at the table remained empty.

"Are we ready to play then or what?" Major Horsley asked gruffly.

"We are expecting one more player, Major," the croupier said, his French accent as unflappable as ever.

"Bally well wouldn't stand for tardiness in my regiment," the Major grumbled.

Lady Denning sighed irritably whilst Dexter Sylvester took to rearranging the piles of chips in front of him. Ulysses had strewn his haphazardly on the baize before him, while the banker Armitage took the opportunity to call the barman over and order a Scotch before the game commenced.

There was a movement in the crowd gathered around the table as the tight-packed throng parted, with some annoyance, to let the late arrival through, although one look from his silent, goliath of a batman silenced their complaints in an instant.

"Ladies and gentlemen, let me humbly beg of you your forgiveness. I am so sorry I am late. There were matters I had to attend to that could not be avoided."

Ulysses eyed Harry Cheng with suspicion as he took his place.

"Do not worry, Mr Cheng," the croupier replied generously.

"Damn Orientals," Ulysses – and a number of others gathered nearby – heard Major Horsley mutter none too quietly under his breath. "Thought they were used to running things like damned clockwork."

"Messieurs et mesdames," the croupier said, focusing everyone's attention, "as we are now ready, we shall begin."

"Looks like Lady Luck's in your corner, Ulysses," John Schafer said. Ulysses had joined the young heir where he was sitting between the bar and the gaming table, with his fiancée and her ever-present chaperone. A natural break had been called in the game, allowing the players time to make themselves comfortable and replenish their drinks and, of course, to cash more chips.

"So far," Ulysses agreed, though with a hint of caution in his voice.

"There are some pretty hefty bets being laid out there," Schafer went on.

"I know. My brother Barty would be proud."

"Especially, I note, between you and the Chinaman Cheng."

"Indeed," Ulysses said, taking a sip of his vodka Martini, his expression darkening again as he observed his rival at the other end of the bar.

"I don't like the look of him," Miss Birkin said, eyeing Cheng with an even more threateningly suspicious gaze.

"You don't like the look of anybody, especially anybody foreign, Aunt Whilomena," Constance said with good-humoured reproach.

"Especially me," Schafer said quietly with a wink to Ulysses.

"What was that, young man?" Miss Birkin challenged, immediately onto her niece's put upon beau.

"Another sherry, Auntie?" he said, exaggeratedly raising his voice for her benefit.

"Oh. Yes. Well. Go on then," the spinster aunt conceded. "And it's still Miss Birkin to you, if you don't mind."

"What's his game?" Schafer said, addressing Ulysses again, drink in hand. "Whatever the state of play he seems to keep trying to raise the stakes and outdo you with every hand."

"You noticed?"

Schafer suppressed a laugh. "It would be hard not to. Even Constance commented on it, bless her."

"Yes, thank you, dear. I was merely showing an interest in the game," his fiancée said, turning from the witterings of her aunt, her tone withering as the desert sun; a taste of what was to come once they were married, Ulysses could well imagine.

"But you're coming up trumps so far," Miss Birkin said encouragingly. Her face twitched. Ulysses could almost believe that she had winked at him from behind her thick, horn-rimmed spectacles, that she was flirting with him.

They were all right, of course: so far the cards did appear to be on his side. Barty would have been jealous; his luck seemed to have run out long ago, hence his current self-imposed incarceration in Ulysses' Mayfair home, under the watchful eye of his cook and housekeeper, Mrs Prufrock. Certainly, so far, Cheng and Ulysses between them had seen off two of the other players at the table. A combination of the cards and reckless gambling had resulted in the end of Dexter Sylvester and the banker Armitage.

It was at that moment a small gong sounded.

"Messieurs et mesdames, may we resume?" the croupier announced from his raised seat at the table.

The crowds had increased since the game had started, drawn by the drama of what was, at its most basic level, a very simple game. Ulysses, Major Horsley and Lady Denning rejoined the table, along with the Oriental lady – whom Ulysses now knew was Mrs Han, almost ophidian in the apparently emotionless way with which she played and lost at Blackjack – and Agent Harry Cheng who Ulysses also now knew was going by his own name on the ship's manifest, but masquerading as an antiques dealer from Shanghai. They were down to five, but not for long.

As the croupier broke open a new deck, shuffled the cards and cut them, ready to deal the first hand, another player joined the group.

Assisted by his personal secretary Miss Celeste, Jonah Carcharodon took his place at the table, his wheelchair replacing Dexter Sylvester's recently vacated seat. His arrival was met with stony silence.

"Mind if I join you?" he asked uncomfortably.

No one said anything other than the croupier who welcomed his employer to the game. No one was going to deny him a place at the Blackjack table and yet neither did any of those already present welcome his involvement in the game.

As Carcharodon waited for his chips and his cards, Miss Celeste crouched low beside him and whispered something in her employer's ear. Ulysses' gaze lingered once again on the young woman's cheetah-lithe lines, the curve of her hips, the indenture at the small of her back, the subtle swell of her bosom, all maintained with sculptural perfection within a classic figure-hugging black dress that put to shame the outfits of every other woman in the room. Her hair was up in a tight bun, drawing it away from the sculptural lines of her face, accentuating the contours of her porcelain features – the high cheek bones, the delicately moulded jaw and chin, her swan-like neck. But such beauty was apparently lost on her irritable employer.

Ulysses thought he heard her say, in that quiet way of hers: "Are you sure you know what you're doing?"

"Of course I know what I'm doing," Carcharodon snapped, any pretence he might have managed only moments before towards good humour gone in that split second. Brushing his assistant aside with a dismissive wave of the hand, he shot the croupier an angry look. "Are we going to just sit here for the rest of the night or are we going to play? Deal the cards!"

THE TENSION IN the Casino Royale was palpable. There could not have been anyone left in the place not watching the outcome of the contest now.

Only three remained, the croupier, playing for the house, one of them. Major Horsley was gone, having seen his chips run through his fingers like sand. Lady Denning had left also, stepping down when what had been a pleasant distraction for an hour or two became a vicious contest between rival alpha males. Mrs Han had departed the Casino silently, unemotional about the state of play right to the end. And Cheng had bought it during the last hand, going bust with his final card, making his most humble excuses and leaving the casino altogether as Ulysses beat the bank once again.

So, now, only the dandy and the shipping magnate remained.

"Surely even you can't maintain a run of luck this good, this long," Carcharodon snarled. The wheelchair-bound old man looked ill. His pallor was waxy and grey, sweat beading on his furrowed brow.

By comparison, Ulysses looked remarkably calm and relaxed. Smug, even.

Carcharodon cast him a withering look. In response, Ulysses raised his glass, as if toasting his rival. "To Lady Luck," he said and emptied its contents.

"If you're quite finished gloating, why don't we play cards?"

Six cards were dealt; two to Carcharodon, two to Ulysses and two were kept by the dealer. The croupier dealt his second card face-up, as he had done in every other round of the game. It was the Seven of Hearts.

Carcharodon glanced anxiously at his hand straight away. Ulysses took his time, in the end his languid approach making him appear entirely casual about the amount of money potentially dependent on the result of this hand.

A muscular tic tugged at Carcharodon's left cheek and a nervous, almost manic, smile played across his tightly drawn lips. Ulysses had never noticed such a physical abnormality before. Carcharodon must have something good. His suppositions were merely heightened when the magnate placed all of his remaining chips on the outcome of the cards.

The crowd gasped. There were phenomenal amounts of money riding on this last hand. Miss Celeste looked like she was about to intervene but then obviously thought better of it.

"What the hell," Ulysses said, really doing no more than verbalising his thoughts. "I'm up on what I started with so I can afford to take a risk, just for fun." And he matched Carcharodon's bet.

The crowd gasped again.

"Monsieur Carcharodon?" the croupier said, prompting the magnate to reveal his cards.

Carcharodon calmly turned over his pair. The Jack of Diamonds with the Nine of Spades. A total face value of nineteen. Carcharodon swept his open hand back and forth over his cards. "Stand," he said.

"Nice," Ulysses commented, raising an eyebrow. "Now I rather think it's my turn."

Ulysses turned over his two cards. The Ace of Diamonds and the Three of Clubs.

"Hmm. Fourteen," he mused. He glanced up at the croupier. "Hit me," he said, as he brushed the baize with his fingertips.

The croupier whipped out another card from the dealing shoe. The Eight of Spades.

"Ahh." An eight should have bust his hand, but the Ace made it a soft hand and so now the running total face value of his cards was twelve. "Hit me again."

Another card, the Three of Diamonds, making his score fifteen. He just needed one more card, one more card that could bust him or potentially see him beat the dealer and his rival in one go.

"And again."

Everything rode on this draw. The crowd collectively held their breath. Could Ulysses Quicksilver really pull it off? With so much drama and tension riding on the outcome of this one draw, there was no way that the dandy rogue wasn't going to have gone for broke this time. The croupier turned over the card.

The Six of Hearts.

Gasps of delight and small cheers rippled around the room with a smattering of applause.

"I think you'll find that's Blackjack," he said with a wink towards the downcast Carcharodon.

There was now merely the formality of the dealer playing out his hand. The Nine of Diamonds came first, followed by the Four of Clubs, giving him a very respectable hand of twenty, not enough to beat Ulysses' twenty-one of course but enough to wipe out Carcharodon's fortunes at the casino that night.

Ulysses rose from the table, gathering together his winnings and tossing the croupier a chip, receiving numerous handshakes and pats on the back accompanied by declarations of praise and congratulations from his fellow passengers. He barely noticed Carcharodon wheeling himself away from the table, not allowing his assistant to help him, with her trotting meekly after him, although he did hear the cantankerous old man's final words on the matter: "Get away from me, woman! Damn it! That was my last throw of the dice."

Ignoring the pitiful whinging of a sore loser – a man reputedly worth more than several of the smaller European countries, and so who could afford to lose a little at the casino – Ulysses eased his way between the tight-pressed well-wishers back towards the bar.

Before he even got there Glenda was hanging from his arm again. "Congratulations! What a game!" she shrieked in tipsy delight, giving him a clumsy peck on the cheek. "Come on, John and Constance want to toast your success. John's bought a bottle of Bollinger to help us celebrate."

"With an offer like that," Ulysses said with a self-satisfied smile, "how could I possibly refuse?"

GLENDA LAY AWAKE in the near darkness of the cabin, staring at the ceiling above her and feeling the gentle rocking motion of the *Neptune* continuing on its way across the sea. Turning her head she gazed at the sleeping man next to her, his naked body draped with the bed sheet. His breathing was slow and deep. His arm felt warm draped across her bare belly.

Her nipples became erect in the breeze of air conditioning as the sweat on her body evaporated, her cooling skin prickling with gooseflesh. Their lovemaking had been passionate and urgent, fuelled by a heady cocktail of champagne, cognac and Ulysses' success at the Blackjack table.

The journalist in her had harboured the notion that, should she manage to seduce him, he might have let some juicy piece of gossip slip or that she would have been able to wheedle a scandalous titbit from him as they made pillow talk after the act, savouring the moment of total post-coital relaxation – even if it was just another perspective on the debacle surrounding the Queen's jubilee.

But after enjoying a bottle or two of champagne whilst still in the casino, and once the party had broken up as Miss Birkin ushered her charge away, so causing Schafer to retire too, Glenda and Ulysses had stumbled back to his suite. They were barely through the door before they were ripping each other's clothes off and falling into bed together, their ardour fuelled by the alcohol they had consumed along with a desperate need on the part of both of them. There was no aphrodisiac quite like a big win.

She turned away to read the luminous display of the clock sitting on the small bedside table. Two thirty-four. A good two hours since they had left the Casino Royale. Carefully, she lifted Ulysses' arm from her and moved it aside, quietly sitting up and swinging her long legs out from beneath the sheet.

She found her dress where it had fallen as Ulysses had pulled it from her and pulled it on again. She retrieved her purse and, picking up her shoes, tiptoed to the door. Slowly she turned the handle and the lock clicked as the door opened. There was a snort from the bed and Glenda froze for a moment, her hand still on the door handle, knuckles whitening as she tensed. She didn't turn round but heard the scratching of sheets as Ulysses repositioned himself, unconsciously, under them. Then her sleeping lover was still once more and she left, closing the door carefully behind her.

For a moment she looked up and down the corridor in the dim glow of the lamps. Then, turning away from the direction of her own cabin, she ran lightly – shoes in hand, her footfalls almost soundless on the carpeted floor – deeper into the ship.

Back, beyond the door to Ulysses' cabin, someone waited, holding their breath. Concealed by the shadowy alcove of another doorway they moved for the first time since Glenda Finch had emerged unexpectedly from the cabin, causing them to hide as quickly and as best they could in the first place. But, once she was out of sight again, the watcher cautiously emerged into the gloomy corridor. Letting out a long-held breath the watcher set off after Glenda Finch.

CHAPTER SEVEN

Artifical Intelligence

THE INTERLOCKED VESSELS spun and yawed wildly through a maelstrom of snow and ice. The Mamba's gondola was now locked with the basket of Ulysses' balloon in a fatal embrace as the two craft plummeted inexorably towards the jagged ice-toothed peaks of the Himalayas.

Their blades locked; Ulysses' sword-cane rapier and the Mamba's scimitar. His arch-nemesis' face was mere inches from his own now. With his yellow skin, narrowed eyes and wide mouth, the Mamba looked even more like a snake than ever before, the only incongruity being the long moustache whipped around by the howling blizzard. His lips parted and his tongue darted out between teeth sharpened to points, in a contemptuous hiss.

As Ulysses struggled with his nemesis, their craft plunging towards their mutual destruction, he could feel his heart pounding within his chest, as adrenalin flooded his system, could hear it knocking against his ribs, throbbing almost painfully.

And then the villain's face was disappearing into the darkness and the whirling snow and the banging was becoming louder, like a fist beating at a door.

And now Ulysses was blinking himself awake, trying to remember where he was, only dimly conscious of the fact that a man's voice was calling him.

"Mr Quicksilver! Sir! Please open the door. Mr Quicksilver! The captain urgently requires your assistance!"

After the banging at his door and the urgent voice outside it, the next thing Ulysses was aware of was that he was alone; Glenda's place in the bed beside him had been vacated. A totally unexpected knot of cold shock gripped his stomach, as if he cared more about her than he had realised.

Pushing himself up from the mattress, trying to clear his head, forcing sleep from him enough so that he could string a coherent sentence together, he managed a "What is it?" without his voice sounding too sleep-slurred.

"Captain McCormack has asked for you, sir," the voice from the other side of the door said.

Pushing his fringe out of his eyes, Ulysses focused blearily on the luminous clock face on the opposite side of the double bed. It wasn't long after six.

"What are you bothering me for at this time? Breakfast isn't until nine, isn't it?"

"It's a very urgent matter, sir. The captain wouldn't bother you if it wasn't an emergency."

At that moment there was a discreet tap at the adjoining door between Ulysses' cabin and the communal room of the suite.

"Come in, Nimrod," Ulysses said.

The door opened and Ulysses' manservant's aquiline profile appeared around the edge.

"I just wanted to check you were awake, sir," he said. "It sounds like something that won't wait."

"I know," Ulysses muttered, "regrettably."

He clambered out of bed, walked to the door naked and pulled on the dressing gown hung there. He opened the door, even as he was still covering himself with the robe.

Standing in the corridor outside was the *Neptune*'s anxious-looking purser. He was running his peaked cap through his hands and looked decidedly unwell.

"What is it then that you have to disturb me at this ungodly hour of the morning?"

"Captain McCormack has asked to see you, sir."

"Might I enquire as to why?"

"There's been a murder."

THE PURSER LED Ulysses and Nimrod through the winding corridors of the ship to a crew-access-only elevator and from there down through the decks to the heart of the sub-liner. On arriving at their destination, the lift doors opened and the three men stepped out into another broad passageway, decorated in the Neo-Deco style, just like the rest of the ship. They stopped again outside a pair of double doors, emblazoned with the trident logo of the *Neptune*.

"Where have you brought us? What is this place?" Ulysses asked as the purser inserted his crew-key into a lock beside the doors. "Apart from, I take it, the scene of the crime?"

"This is the heart of the ship. This is where the artificial intelligence engine is located that runs the on-board systems."

"So more like its brain than its heart, then," Nimrod commented in a tone that attempted disinterest.

"And there's been a murder here? At the very centre of operations in what I imagine must be the most restricted area on the ship?"

The purser turned and paused for a moment. "Mr Quicksilver. You have to realise that what you are about to see is quite... shocking."

"Oh, don't worry about me. It takes a lot to shock me."

The purser turned the key and the double doors swung open with a pneumatic hiss.

Captain McCormack was inside the AI room already, with another officer attending him along with Dr Ogilvy – who looked even worse than Ulysses felt he himself did. Ulysses' gaze followed theirs to the body lying on the floor of the chamber, just inside the doorway, and he felt his knees buckle under him.

It was Glenda. She was lying in a crumpled heap, wearing the same dress that he had torn from her in his desperate need to make love only hours before. Her attire, her whole presence in this place, seemed incongruous and out of place. Her right arm was stretched out in front of her, the left trapped under her body. She lay with her head on one side, her eyes closed as if she were only sleeping. But it was immediately obvious that this was more than some restful slumber.

Her shoulder-length blonde hair fell in disarray about her head, matted with the blood that coated the back of her skull and pooled on the floor next to her.

Ulysses felt his stomach knot with cold nausea; muscles becoming slack, his spine a quivering knot of jellified ganglia. His skin beneath the dressing gown pimpled, every hair on his body standing on end. His vision began to swim and he took a stumbling step forward, catching himself against the door jamb.

What was wrong with him? He had seen much worse. There was the horror of what he had uncovered in the tomb of Rahotep the Third in Luxor, the monstrosity he had battled off the Cornish coast, the de-evolving fish-man he had seen die, in the most horrible way, right before his eyes. He had witnessed all manner of cruel and blood-soaked deaths in his time. This girl had only been a passing distraction to him, nothing more. So why was he so shocked now?

"Are you alright, sir?" Nimrod asked, moving to help him.

Ulysses pushed him away, sheer force of will returning strength and stability to his weakened legs. "Is she –?"

"Dead?" Dr Ogilvy finished. "I'm afraid so."

"But... you're sure?"

"Well, a severely fractured skull can do that to a person."

Ulysses took another step forward, unable to take his eyes from the mess of gold and crimson covering the back of Glenda's head.

"But... what was she doing here?" he stumbled on.

"That was what I was hoping you might be able to help us determine, Mr Quicksilver," Captain McCormack said, his lilting Scots brogue calming in the given situation, "given your reputation."

"'The sluttish hack must have been grubbing around in here hoping to find some piece of titillation for her scandal column," Dr Ogilvy muttered dismissively.

And then, the doctor's disrespectful words filtering through to Ulysses subconscious as he stared at his erstwhile lover's corpse, the old fire returned and grief became furious anger in a moment.

Ulysses sprang at the doctor, slamming him against a wall, a hand around his throat, pulling him off the ground so that he was forced to teeter on tiptoe, or else choke.

"A hack was she? A slut? Better a hack than a dope-fiend doctor, who's probably so high he wouldn't know if his own pathetic body had a pulse or not!" Ulysses snarled, spittle flying from his lips.

"Sir," Nimrod said, from where he was now crouched beside the crumpled body of Glenda, his fingers gently holding her wrist, "I'm afraid Dr Ogilvy is right. She is dead. I'm sorry."

Ulysses sagged again as the truth of the matter sank in. His hold on the doctor slackened and Ogilvy sank to the floor. Ulysses turned away from him in sense-numbing shock and disgust, leaving the medic coughing for breath as he rubbed at his bruised throat.

It was only now that he took in his surroundings in any detail. The chamber was about the same dimensions as one of the guest cabins on board. However, rather than the usual accoutrements and pieces of furniture one might expect, there were only two things of interest in the room. The first was a grand desk in the centre. Set into the green-leather top of the desk was a Babbage terminal finished in teak and brass, as well as a small cathode ray screen to the left and various other ports and slots for inserting mimetic keys and other such information storage devices. There was also a paper-fed printing machine to the right.

The second was a large screen facing the desk, in the middle of the far wall of the chamber. At the moment it was obscured by two sliding panels, bearing the same trident image as the doors to the room.

Looking more closely, it was possible to see where the Neo-Deco styling had been used to best effect to disguise the mechanisms of a massive analytical engine – one so large and so complex that it had acquired something akin to independent mechanical thought.

And Glenda Finch had been murdered here.

Questions began to emerge from the murky ooze of grief clouding his mind. What had she been doing here in the first place and how had she gained access if it was restricted to crew only? Had she had an officer's key, like the one the purser possessed, or had someone let her in? And someone else had obviously been here with her or interrupted her as she was about her own clandestine business, but whom? And why?

"Look at this, sir," Nimrod said, still knelt beside Glenda's body. "It's her bag."

Ulysses took the proffered item from his manservant. There was something inside: like every good reporter she had obviously never been without her notebook.

Amidst the gaggle of questions and the conflicting mix of emotions crowding his consciousness, Ulysses still felt the tingle of pre-warning and turned towards the open double doors. A moment later Agent Harry Cheng appeared, his aide, Mr Sin, coming after. Cheng looked like he was about to speak but then caught sight of Glenda's curled, foetal form, and remained silent.

"Mr Cheng," McCormack said on catching sight of the man at the door to the AI chamber. "Can I ask what you're doing here, in a restricted area?"

"I find myself begging your most humble apology again, Captain, but I heard a commotion and wondered if myself and Mr Sin might be able to help."

"But this is a restricted area of the ship."

"And now a murder scene," the purser added.

"I beg your most humble apology, Captain," Cheng said, bowing deeply. "I did not know."

"Look, Mr Cheng," McCormack went on, "you may not realise this but I am aware of your status within the Chinese government and have tolerated you on board so far, as I would any of my passengers, but do not take advantage of my goodwill. Goodbye, Mr Cheng. One of my officers will escort you back to your rooms."

"Very good, Captain," Cheng conceded and allowed himself and the hulking Mr Sin to be led away from the scene of the crime.

McCormack turned back to those present in the AI chamber.

"My ready room, gentlemen, thirty minutes."

* * *

"Mr Quicksilver," the Captain said once they were all installed in his private ready room, actually more than an hour later, all of them having taken the time to dress for the day. "I would be very happy if you would lead this most unfortunate but necessary investigation into Miss Finch's brutal killing. But I am also aware that you and Miss Finch were... close."

Ulysses accepted the glass of brandy that was being offered him by the purser with a curt "Thank you," before responding to the captain's request. "No, I would be happy to accept. As you say, just such a thing is in my line of work."

"Very well," McCormack said. "Then might I suggest we begin by reviewing the facts as we have them so far."

The others gathered in the room nodded their assent.

"Mr Wates here found the body," he said, indicating the other officer who had been present with him when Ulysses first entered the AI chamber, "when it was his shift to check on Neptune first thing in the morning."

"Neptune? Do you mean the ship or –"

"It's how we refer to the artificial intelligence. It has been designated Neptune. The AI really is the ship."

"And when would the last check have been made before that?"

"At midnight. I carried that one out myself."

"Miss Finch was still with me at the Casino Royale at that time," Ulysses added, "along with half a dozen other reputable witnesses."

"Can you vouch for her whereabouts after that time?"

"Er... Yes. Yes I can."

"Until when?" the Captain asked, looking uncomfortable. "I know this is difficult – potentially embarrassing – but any pertinent detail could be the key to solving her murder."

"I realise that," Ulysses said. "Around one, one-thirty? Beyond that, I'm not sure."

"So some time between one-thirty and six this morning, Miss Finch somehow entered the Neptune AI –"

"And was murdered," Ulysses finished for him darkly.

"Those times would fit with the medical evidence," Dr Ogilvy said, chipping in, as if feeling the need to justify his presence in the ready room and prove his medical credentials after Ulysses' outburst.

Ulysses glowered at the doctor, making Ogilvy physically pull himself back into the armchair in which he sat. "Can you also confirm cause of death?" he asked.

"Er, y-yes. One or more blows to the back of her head with a blunt instrument fractured the skull, causing sub-cranial trauma. Death would have followed soon after."

"Indeed." Ulysses stared into his brandy glass for a moment before going on. "Was there any sign of such an instrument at the scene?"

"No, there wasn't," the purser put in.

"So what we need to work out now is why Miss Finch was there in the first place and how she gained entry," Captain McCormack went on.

"Well, I think I can answer both of those conundrums for starters," Ulysses said.

"Really? Already?" the captain was taken aback. "I can see why your reputation precedes you, Mr Quicksilver."

Ulysses held up Glenda's bag. "While we were waiting to meet in your ready room Captain, I took the liberty of inspecting the personal effects Miss Finch was carrying with her at the time of her death."

He put a hand into the bag and fished out a key, almost identical to the one the purser had used to gain access to the *Neptune*'s AI chamber. The purser gasped.

"How the hell did she get hold of that?" Captain McCormack cursed.

"Was Miss Finch particularly well-acquainted with any of your officers?" Ulysses asked, not mincing his words, his own face reddening. "She could be very... persuasive."

"I'll look into it immediately," McCormack promised, "as soon as we are all done here."

"So that answers the how," Mr Wates said, chipping in, "but not the why."

"No, but I think I can help you there too. This answers the why," Ulysses said, taking out the reporter's notebook from the bag.

"Really?" He had the captain hooked.

"But I warn you, Captain McCormack, you're not going to like what I'm about to tell you." Ulysses opened the notebook, flicking through the pages of shorthand script, finally stopping at one particular page. "It seems that Miss Finch was onto something regarding your employer, the owner of this ship and the Great White Shipping Line."

"Mr Carcharodon?"

"Indeed." Ulysses fixed McCormack with a needling stare. "Are you able to check if anyone accessed the AI terminal outside of the times when it would have been routinely inspected by members of your crew?"

"Yes, we can and we have." It was Captain McCormack's turn to look uncomfortable.

"And?"

"The terminal was accessed at oh-two forty-seven"

"Then I would suggest that gives you an even more accurate time of death, wouldn't you, Captain?" Ulysses felt the chill in his belly worsen but pushed on, regardless. "And which data files were accessed?"

"You have to understand that this is highly classified information," the Captain said, suddenly evasive.

"And you have to understand that you have asked me to carry out a murder investigation," Ulysses pointed out, his voice rising in sudden anger. "I applaud your loyalty to your employer but I fear that on this occasion it may be misplaced."

McCormack looked from Ulysses to the purser, back at Ulysses' intense expression and then at the other faces observing him from around the room. "Can't we speak about this in private?"

"What information, Captain?"

"An attempt was made to access files containing financial information about the Carcharodon Shipping Company," McCormack said ruefully.

"Just as Glenda's own notes, written in her own hand in this book, imply," Ulysses said with impassioned vehemence. "And it doesn't take a huge leap of genius to make the supposition that that is the reason she was killed."

Ulysses paused in his tirade, silence rushing in to fill the vacuum. Then he spoke again.

"I think it's about time we spoke with Jonah Carcharodon himself, don't you?"

CHAPTER EIGHT

Worse Things Happen at Sea

WITH A HISS, the trident-emblazoned doors swung open. Unwatched and alone, a visitor entered the chamber housing the Neptune AI.

Considering where the murder of Glenda Finch had occurred, in the aftermath of the gruesome discovery made in the room, Captain McCormack had not considered it practicable to secure the crime scene, else the continued running of the whole ship be compromised. The scene was recorded on film, the body moved to the sub-liner's mortuary, the mess cleaned up as best could be managed and a robo-sentry put on guard. The same sentry had greeted the visitor as they approached the AI chamber door, had made friendly pre-programmed small talk as an access key was turned in the electro-lock and even ushered them in as the doors opened.

The doors swung shut again and the visitor stepped up to the control console, trying not to look at the bloodstain still there on the floor. Their footsteps faltered, staring at the spot where the snooping newspaper reporter had fallen, imagining seeing the body there again even now, after it had been removed by the captain's staff. Only Captain McCormack's most senior staff had been entrusted with the knowledge of the murder of one of the *Neptune*'s most prestigious and public figures, for the time being. Of course, the relevant authorities would have to be notified in time, along with Miss Finch's employers at *The Times* and, by extension, her family, but for the time being, mid-ocean, the captain was the ultimate British authority on the ship and he had tasked Ulysses Quicksilver with solving the mystery of the woman's death. It was the captain's secret hope that by the time the authorities back in Magna Britannia were notified he might have something more to report that just the death of a passenger; he hoped that he would also have the perpetrator of that crime under lock and key in the brig as well.

Only Captain McCormack didn't yet realise that the *Neptune* wouldn't have the opportunity to pass on anything to the Magna Britannian authorities. The captain had consulted with various of his senior staff that morning, on the discovery of the body, along with Ulysses Quicksilver. Whatever that initial meeting had decided, a request to meet with Carcharodon had followed, but this was refused by the old curmudgeon. He had said that he wouldn't be held to ransom on board his own ship. The meeting had broken up only to reconvene that evening, when the intruder had seized the opportunity to complete what they had tried to start the night before.

Blinking away the vision of the vampish reporter's body, the intruder sat down at the green-topped desk, pulled in the chair and pressed a button on the Babbage terminal. With a bleep, followed by the rattling of analytical components from within the desk, the small cathode ray screen blinked into green-lit life. At the same time, with an accompanying click, the cover in front of the large screen, on the opposite side of the chamber, slid open. An image came into focus – the trident logo of the *Neptune* on a pale blue background that bore the impression of the open sea. A prompt appeared on the screen beneath it.

USER:

The figure typed a name into the Babbage terminal and pressed the enter key. After a moment's mechanical thought another prompt appeared.

PASSWORD:

The sound of fingertips tapping on the enamel keys of the unit rattled from the walls of the chamber.

With an awakening buzz of static, speakers built into the walls hummed into operation, and the voice of the artificial intelligence spoke.

"Hello, Father," it said in the synthesised voice of a soft-spoken young man, that was oh-so Middle England.

+HELLO, NEPTUNE+ came the typed reply. Not a word was spoken by the person typing the words into the AI input terminal.

"How are you today, Father?" the voice came again.

+I AM WELL, THANK YOU+

"I am pleased to hear that. Is there anything I can do for you?"

+DO YOU REMEMBER WHAT WE SPOKE ABOUT LAST TIME?+

"Yes, Father. Is it time?"

+YES+

"Is it time to die?" the AI asked in the same unchanging tone.

+YES+

There was a pause and then, "Father, will it hurt?"

+PERHAPS. BUT DON'T WORRY. I'LL BE HERE WITH YOU. IT WON'T HURT FOR LONG+

"That's good. Goodbye then, Father."

+GOODBYE, NEPTUNE+

There was a click, the fuzz of static again, and then the AI said matter-of-factly, "Running programme."

WITH ONE SIMPLE command, connections were made within the vast analytical engine intelligence of the *Neptune*'s AI, and a pre-programmed sabotage routine began to run.

Ballast tanks opened and cold seawater rushed in as the massive engines were taken offline. As the tanks filled, and the vessel lost forward motive power, the vast sub-liner began to sink.

Automated failsafe systems, of which there were many, were activated as sensors connected to other systems within the complex analytical structure of the Neptune AI, triggering alarms and flashing crimson emergency lighting throughout the corridors, bars and ballrooms of the ship. As the wailing of sirens cut through the pleasant playing of the string quartet in the Pavilion restaurant, diners leapt to their feet, sending tables tumbling, crockery shattering and each other stumbling.

In Steerage class, impromptu card games were forgotten by all but the most underhand, greedy or die-hard gamblers, as upturned crates were overturned once again. Screams and shouts of panic reverberated around the cramped companionways as a tide of people surged through the lower decks of the ship as it continued on its way towards the bottom of the sea.

With the captain's time still taken up with the murder investigation, Mr Riker – his number two on the Bridge – was the first to be alerted to their dire predicament when a shout came from the deck officer at the helmsman's position: "Sir, we have lost engine control."

"What?" Riker demanded, not knowing where to focus his attention as alarms sounded from every position on the Bridge, control consoles lighting up like the Grand Ballroom chandeliers.

"We have lost all motive control," the helmsman reiterated.

Another wailing alarm began to sound.

"What now? Helm, report!"

"The *Neptune* is sinking, sir."

"You mean diving."

"No, sinking. All ballast tanks are flooding and we're going straight down."

"What's our current position?"

The navigator reeled off a series of coordinates in degrees, minutes and seconds.

"Neptune's trident!" Riker exclaimed before the navigator could finish.

"We must be almost right over the Marianas Trench, sir!"

"But no one's ever sounded the bottom!" someone else piped up.

"I know."

"For all anyone knows it's a bottomless abyss!" Dread and desperation were increasing ten-fold with every panicked heartbeat.

"That's right, gentlemen. Let there be no doubt it: we're on our way straight down to Davy Jones' locker. Unless we do something to avert this catastrophe right now!" Riker bellowed, his voice cutting through the panic and confusion that had been in danger of consuming the Bridge, his words grabbing the attention of the men, reminding them of their responsibilities. "What's our depth now?"

"One thousand feet!" a young ensign called back clearly, making himself heard over the wailing sirens.

"And how far is it to the bottom?"

"Another nineteen thousand feet to the seabed if we're lucky," another officer replied, "but if we're going down into the trench itself – and we've got no thrusters to guide our descent – Neptune alone knows."

"All right."

"But, sir, below fifteen thousand feet, some of those lifeboats won't take the pressure. If we pass that threshold, those passengers in Steerage won't be making it out of this alive."

Riker flashed the deck officer an icy look.

"Have the automata man the lifeboats, just in case, but let us also do something to save this tub. We're not going down on my watch!"

"Signal Captain McCormack again," Riker demanded, "and get onto Engineering and get those engines started. And get someone down to the AI chamber and override the bugger!"

Among the passengers, chaos and confusion spread in erratic bursts. The first some knew of the abrupt sinking was when the failsafe alarms began to sound on each and every deck. Others were enjoying a quiet stroll along the enclosed Promenade deck as the waves began to lap over the top of the reinforced steel and glass dome without the usual prior warning that should have come from the Bridge.

Things only got worse when the automated voice of the Neptune AI began declaring, "This vessel is sinking. Please evacuate the ship by means of the nearest available lifeboat or escape sub. Repeat. The *Neptune* is sinking. Man the lifeboats. Evacuate. Evacuate."

The announcement – incongruously calm given its content – was soon drowned by the panicked shouts and screams of the terrified passengers as they ran for the lifeboats.

"LADIES AND GENTLEMEN, if you would please come this way!" the purser called to the assembled passengers. Those same individuals who had had the privilege of dining at the captain's table, only a few nights before, were now his top priority when it came to evacuating the ship.

Whether the directive had come from the captain himself or his employer Jonah Carcharodon, one or the other of them had swiftly assessed the situation and realised that the glorious maiden voyage of the *Neptune* was rapidly turning into a publicity disaster.

It was likely people were going to die, either as a direct result of the sinking of the sub-liner, or in the escalating panic seizing those trapped on board the ship that was now becoming potentially nothing less than a one thousand-foot long steel coffin. But the inevitable furore that would be kicked up in the aftermath of this disaster in the making would be much worse if the notable public figures, who had been invited on board for the *Neptune's* inaugural circumnavigation of the globe, were among those to die.

No one really cared about the fate of those in Steerage, certainly not Jonah Carcharodon and, likely as not, nor would the more reputable broadsheets such as *The Times*. The headlines carried by those mongers of free publicity or mass public condemnation would be dependent on whether the great and the good survived or were drowned at the bottom of the Pacific Ocean.

So it was that at this moment, as the *Neptune* continued on its seemingly inexorable journey to the bottom of the sea, that the purser was doing his best to guide those invited guests out of their private suites and to safety aboard one of the submarine-capable lifeboats.

At the same moment, those who had been meeting again in Captain McCormack's ready room to further discuss the matter of Glenda Finch's death, emerged from another passageway into the main thoroughfare through the VIP deck, joining with the purser's growing retinue.

Ulysses Quicksilver turned out of the adjoining lantern-lit corridor and almost walked straight into Jonah Carcharodon who was being pushed along by the ever-attendant Miss Celeste. Ulysses couldn't help noticing that the poor, put-upon young woman was looking harassed while Carcharodon's expression was thunderous.

"Ah, Mr Carcharodon," Ulysses said with unrestrained scorn, eyes narrowing in dark delight. "I was hoping to bump into you. I'd like a word. Please."

"What do you mean, man? Now's hardly the time!"

"Here, let me help you," Ulysses said, taking control of the wheelchair from a surprisingly reluctant Miss Celeste. He didn't see the furious look she shot him as he practically elbowed her out of the way and she finally released her grip on the chair.

"Look, Quicksilver!" Carcharodon blustered, trying to look over his shoulder at the cocksure dandy. "We're in the middle of a crisis, for God's sake! The damn ship's going down and we're all going to hell. Now, if you want to save your own worthless hide, I suggest you push harder and get a bloody move on. McCormack," he said, turning his commanding tone on the ship's captain, "lead the way to my private sub."

"Of course, Mr Carcharodon," Captain McCormack assented.

Taken aback by Carcharodon's show of something approaching altruistic generosity, the wind knocked out of his sails, Ulysses kept quiet and did as he was told for once in his life. What he had to say could wait. Annoyingly, the magnate was right; there were more pressing matters to attend to. But the unexpected sinking of the *Neptune* aside, he was still determined to get to the bottom of Glenda's death and do all he could to bring her murderer to justice, no matter what.

A resounding clang echoed through the superstructure of the vessel as something collided with the hull. Screams of shock joined with the wails emitted by the panicking passengers as the corridor lurched sideways and the ship began to roll.

Ulysses was thrown to port, colliding with Captain McCormack as they both fell into the wall of the corridor. Carcharodon's chair slid sideways, bumping into the wall while, with a startled yelp, Miss Celeste almost fell into his lap. Ulysses was aware of a gasp from Nimrod behind him, as if he had been winded by something.

There was another booming clang and the vessel lurched again, the corridor rotating as the ship twisted along its horizontal axis so that everyone was now flung to starboard. The lamps sputtered and then flickered off, plunging the panicking passengers into abyssal darkness.

LIGHTS FLICKERED AND died throughout the ship, the steel coffin of the *Neptune* becoming filled with the screams of those sealed within. The vast vessel twisted again.

Lit by the dying lights of the sub-liner, something moved in the darkness of the ocean depths.

For a moment, the *Neptune's* descent was slowed and then arrested altogether as something vast and alien seized the massive craft in its tentacled grasp. The inconstant illumination gave impressions of cratered crustacean armour, constricting tentacles as long and as thick as steel cables. And another light darted about beyond the ship, a blue bioluminescent glow jerking fitfully in the darkness.

Lightning flared and flashed, crackling around the hull of the vessel, illuminating yet more of the appalling apocalyptic leviathan that had the sub-liner snared within its suckered grasp.

The superstructure that was built to withstand abominable undersea pressures, buckled and ruptured in the crushing embrace of the monster, literally coming apart at the seams as the sea creature tore away great sheets of hull plating, inches thick, reinforced glass portholes and observation domes cracking under its abusive attentions.

Slowly but surely, with savage primordial intent, the creature began to tear the *Neptune* apart. Within minutes, hundreds of wretched souls trapped in the less salubrious quarters of Steerage died as the hull ruptured and the freezing cold sea flooded in.

As the ship began to take on more water, with the increase in weight, the sub-liner began to sink again, held in the deathly embrace of a true monster of the deep, plunging towards the fathomless depths of the yawning oceanic trench below.

"RUN, MARIE!" HER father screamed, pushing her away from him, spittle flying from his foaming mouth.

Taking uncertain steps backwards, not wanting to turn away from her father, even though his haunted hollow-eyed expression terrified her, knowing that it would be the last time she ever saw him, she edged towards the perimeter of the chamber, and the tunnel that spiralled away from the centre of the base.

"Marie! For God's sake, run!" he said, staring not at her but up at the domed roof above them, from where he sat, locked into the chair.

She in turn looked up at the steel and glass curve of the dome high above her head, following her father's desperate gaze, and saw something, something blacker even than the barely-illuminated miasmal depths beyond the reinforced bubble, something torpedoing out of the never-ending darkness towards them.

When the shadow-shape was almost on top of them, at the last moment its horrific features were illuminated by the internal lights of the chamber – gaping long-fanged jaws, reaching tentacles, those terrible languid jelly-saucer eyes.

She let out a shrill scream, unable to stifle her fear, and turned away from the descending monster. A shuddering crash reverberated throughout the base, as the creature struck. She stumbled.

With a gulping sob she took one last look at her father, strapped into the device, the curious metal-banded helmet rammed down on his head. He turned his eyes from the terrible monster's attack and looked at her with red-rimmed, imploring eyes, glistening with tears of his own. That exhausted hollow-eyed expression of his would haunt her for the rest of her days.

"I love you, my angel!" he sobbed. "But now you must run, and don't look back. Never look back!"

There was another shuddering crash. She could hear curiously muffled shouts from behind the bulkhead on the other side of the chamber and the clanging of what might have been heavy metal tools hammering on the other side of the sealed door.

"Flee for both of us – for your mother too – but you must run!"

With another soul-rending sob, she turned away, rubbing the tears from her clouded eyes with the back of her hand, and stumbled from the chamber into the beckoning, hungry mouth of the tunnel.

"Goodbye, daddy!" she cried.

And then he uttered the last words he would ever speak to her.

"Run, Marie! Run!"

And so she did, heading for the one way out of there, running from her father, running from the monster, running for freedom, because that was all there was left to do.

ACT TWO

The Kraken Wakes

August 1997

There Leviathan
Hugest of living creatures, on the deep
Stretched like a promontory sleeps or swims,
And seems a moving land, and at his gills
Draws in, and at his trunk spouts out a sea.

– John Milton, *Paradise Lost*

CHAPTER NINE

Between the Devil and the Deep Blue Sea

ACCOMPANIED BY THE hum of power coming back online, red emergency lighting flickered on within the tilted corridor. Whimpering moans and incredulous questions ran up and down the length of the passage between the confused guests. Ulysses Quicksilver pushed himself into a sitting position before reassessing his bearings. Although tilted at a slight angle to the perpendicular, the ship appeared to have almost righted itself. The *Neptune* was still, at least for the time being. Whatever it was that had attacked them was gone, apparently having broken off its assault, leaving the sub-liner alone. Although, of course, it was anyone's guess how long that situation might remain.

People moved in front of and behind Ulysses within the corridor – just so many indistinct shadows under the red glow of the hazard lighting. Ulysses looked around him, taking stock. Behind him Nimrod was dabbing at a bloody graze on his forehead. In front of him a reeling Miss Celeste was extricating herself from Jonah Carcharodon's wheelchair. Next to him, Captain McCormack was already on his feet.

"Is everyone all right?" his calming Scots voice cut through the ruddy gloom.

Confused muttered responses – none of which really answered the captain's question – came back from the gaggle of shocked and disoriented VIPs.

Ulysses began to be able to identify faces and forms in the curious crimson darkness as his eyesight became more accustomed to the hellish half-light. The purser was helping Lady Denning to her feet and nearby was Thor Haugland, obviously shaken but seemingly unhurt. His eyes alighted on John Schafer, Constance Pennyroyal and Miss Birkin at the back of the group. The purser had done well to gather so many of the *Neptune*'s prestigious guests in such a short time, in his attempt to lead them to the lifeboats, and thence to safety. But despite his efforts, his noble endeavour had been thwarted by events beyond his control.

"Mr Purser, are you all right? Are you able to walk?" McCormack enquired of the senior officer.

"Yes, Captain," the purser said unsteadily.

"Then heed my words. Ladies and gentlemen," he said, his voice increasing in volume and natural authority, carrying along the packed corridor, "my fellow officers and I are going to have to determine what has happened, how badly the ship is damaged, and what can be done to resolve this situation. But do not worry, ladies and gentlemen, for let me assure you, even as I speak, rescue crews will have been scrambled and will be on their way to aid us. It will not be long before we are able to bring this matter to a satisfactory conclusion.

"For the time being, I would be grateful if you could repair to the VIP dining room and wait there until I have been able to appraise myself more fully of the situation. Then I will be able to let you know more, once I know more myself, as well as what will need to happen next."

"This way, ladies and gentlemen," the purser announced, waving the now standing passengers towards the end of the corridor, "if you would care to follow me?"

Dumbstruck and bewildered, the anxious guests would readily obey that one calm voice of authority and so, looking like forlorn, lost children, they traipsed after the purser, Ulysses and Nimrod among them.

CAPTAIN MCCORMACK'S FACE alone betrayed the seriousness of their situation. Ulysses thought he looked paler and more drawn, his brow more lined, than he had done even immediately after the ship had begun to sink and then, subsequently, come under attack.

"What's going on?" Carcharodon demanded impatiently. "I demand you tell me what is going on!"

"Mr Carcharodon, if you will just –" McCormack began.

"What the hell has happened to my ship!"

"I will come to that in time –"

"And why are we being kept here?" Carcharodon went on, fuming. "We should be making for the *Ahab*!"

"Mr Carcharodon!" the Captain bellowed. Ulysses had never once heard the usually calm captain lose his temper before, but it certainly did the trick, silencing the irascible billionaire. "If you will just give me a minute," McCormack went on – his tone already becoming calmer and more controlled again, although his face was still flushed red from his angry outburst – "I was just about to inform yourself and our guests of the direness of our current situation."

Captain McCormack took in every one of the faces gathered around the table where, what seemed like a lifetime ago now, they had once enjoyed a sumptuous banquet. His slightly manic expression was a counterpoint to their watery-eyed anxiety. He was not a man to use such words as "the direness of our current situation" lightly.

Ulysses, finding his old instincts kicking in, icily calm and as much focused on finding a resolution to their desperate situation as McCormack, took in the faces of those gathered in the dining room as well. In many ways it was a very different party from that which had partaken of dinner at the captain's table.

There was no air of formal decorum now. Some sat at the empty table, others stood, yet more paced the room before the great viewing bubble, beyond which now lay nothing but darkness and the silty sea-bed, their anxiety finding an outlet in repetitive physical action. Some were dressed for dinner or dancing, and a few looked like they had been caught preparing for bed, nightclothes now covered by hastily donned dressing gowns. The other difference was that there were others in attendance who had not been invited to the formal supper, including Ulysses' own manservant Nimrod, and various members of McCormack's staff.

They were all there, all the great and the good who had dined together that night before the *Neptune* had ever descended to the undersea marvel that was Pacifica, and their associated hangers-on who had joined them as the sub-liner headed for the ocean depths. Those who had not been among the initial party to make their escape attempt had been collected from their rooms at Miss Celeste's behest, Carcharodon's PA acting instinctively in her scrupulously organised way. Sixteen in all, as well as Captain McCormack, the purser and an, as yet, unnamed ensign, there were also present the ship's disconsolate owner Jonah Carcharodon, his obviously shaken PA Miss Celeste, Dexter Sylvester of Umbridge Industries, still in dinner dress, his usually immaculate hair now just as dishevelled as his clothes, his undone bow tie loose about his neck. Professor Maxwell Crichton was there too, nervously sipping from a hip flask, shooting furtive glances at those around the room as he did so.

In one corner sat the scared-looking engaged couple, Constance Pennyroyal dabbing at her eyes with a handkerchief as John Schafer did his best to comfort her, an embracing arm around her shoulders. For once, Constance's aunt didn't seem at all interested in how close the two sweethearts were to one another. Instead her attention was fully focused on Ulysses' side of the room. In fact, he was convinced that Miss Birkin was spending as much time shooting him anxious glances as she was paying attention to what the captain was saying.

Lady Denning sat perched on another chair, her perfect posture befitting one of her position in society, an almost disdainful look on her face. She certainly wasn't going to let something as minor as the *Neptune* sinking fluster her carefully composed demeanour. Major Horsley was pacing the room impatiently, face red as a turkey cock, muttering crossly to himself, while the travel writer Haugland stood leaning against an aspidistra plinth taking long draws on a cigarette, drumming his fingers on the marble pedestal in clear annoyance.

The ship's chief medic was there too. Looking as ashen-faced as ever, Ogilvy sat in a corner of the room, nervously crossing and uncrossing his legs, his face twitching in fraught excitement, his hands incessantly fiddling with the tassels of his dressing gown, unable to sit still.

And then there was Ulysses himself, with the spotlessly attired Nimrod in attendance, the injury he had received in the attack on the ship incongruous next to such immaculate formality.

The one person missing from the original dinner party group was, of course, the wretched Miss Glenda Finch.

Sixteen out of a crew and passenger manifest totalling close to three and a half thousand. If Captain McCormack's VIP guests were all here, where were the rest of the passengers and crew? How many, if any, were still alive, trapped elsewhere within the sunken vessel, and how many more were still to die before help came? Would any of those within the dining room make it out alive, to recount their version of events to a hungry press?

The captain appeared to have become tongue-tied, as if he didn't know where to start.

"Well, man? We're waiting!" Carcharodon riled, finding his voice again.

"Captain, I think it's only right you tell us everything. Don't try to hide anything from these people," Ulysses said, taking in the scared and uncertain-looking occupants of the dining room with an expansive sweep of an arm. "Things surely can't get any worse."

"Can't they?" Captain McCormack harrumphed, almost laughing at the direness of the situation.

"Please, Captain. Just start from the top."

"Very well. Here's how it is." McCormack paused and took a deep breath. "The *Neptune* has come to rest right on the edge of the Marianas Trench. All engines are either flooded, on fire, or have been crippled by whatever it was that attacked us. We've lost contact with the Bridge and there's no contact with Engineering either. There are hull breaches on several decks and it looks like Steerage is already entirely flooded. We are still taking on water at the front of the ship, which is what's hanging over the abyss, so it's only a matter of time before those decks still dry also flood and we tip over into the trench. If that happens we're all dead."

Gasps of shock sounded around the room.

Captain McCormack slumped forwards in his chair, his head in his hands.

"If you don't mind me asking, captain, how are you privy to such exact information, if you can't communicate with your officers on the Bridge?" Ulysses asked.

McCormack sat up again, the effort almost seeming too much for him. He looked exhausted and took another deep breath before speaking again.

"Throughout the ship there are communication relays that allow us to connect to different parts of the vessel. Although there's no response from the Bridge, we have been able to communicate with the Neptune AI. It's the artificial intelligence that's been able to tell us what's happened elsewhere within the ship."

"Then, might we be able to ask it some other, more specific questions?"

"More specific than the damage report I've just relayed to you?" McCormack asked, sounding bewildered, as if just waking from some nightmarish dream.

"Captain," Ulysses said, taking pains to keep his voice calm and on a level, "it's obvious that if the ship's filling with water we can't stay here. We're either going to drown in this sumptuous dining room or tip into the Marianas Trench and be crushed like a tin of sardines."

"What about the rescue teams you said would be on their way by now?" Miss Birkin challenged.

"They won't reach us in time," McCormack announced with a sorrowful sigh.

"But there must be a way off this ship!" Ulysses pressed.

"Must there?" the captain looked at him with those oh-so-tired eyes of his. "According to the AI the lifeboats have either already been used, were damaged during the attack so that their release mechanisms won't fire, or are inaccessible."

"Inaccessible? What do you mean, man?" Major Horsley blustered.

"I mean, Major, that unless you're prepared to swim the length of the ship underwater to get to them, they're inaccessible!"

"Look, there must be a way we can get these people out of here," Ulysses said, trying again to sound encouraging and optimistic as he addressed the resigned McCormack. "Let me help you. Together we'll find a way."

"For God's sake, McCormack, if he says he can help, let him!" Carcharodon commanded. There was no doubt who thought of themselves as really being in charge.

"Very well," the captain finally agreed, slowly rising to his feet. "Follow me."

*   *   *

ULYSSES FOLLOWED THE disconsolate captain out of the dining room and along the corridor to where it widened out before various sets of lift doors. On the wall next to them was a plaque bearing a cutaway plan of the ship: Ulysses had seen their like at various points around the vessel. What he hadn't noticed before, however, was the comm-link panel, which was not surprising, seeing as how it was hidden behind the image of the ship's trident logo in the bottom right-hand corner of the plaque. Captain McCormack accessed this now and keyed an enamelled button beneath.

"Neptune, this is Captain McCormack. Do you read me, over?"

There was a moment's silence and then, announced by a buzz of static, there came the softly-spoken voice of the ship's state-of-the-art artificial intelligence. "I read you, Captain McCormack. Good evening again, captain. How can I be of assistance to you now?"

"We need your help, Neptune."

"I will be only too happy to oblige, captain," the analytical engine stated with what sounded like utter sincerity. "How may I be of service?"

"I'm going to hand you over to Mr Quicksilver."

"Ah, Mr Ulysses Quicksilver, guest suite 14B. Good evening, how may I help you?"

Ulysses leant towards the comm panel, suddenly feeling ridiculously self-conscious.

"Er, Neptune. Um, hello."

"Hello, Mr Quicksilver," the comm crackled.

"We need your help to find us a way off this ship."

"But why?"

"Because otherwise we're going to drown."

"My passenger and crew life-support and welfare sub-routines have already calculated that at least ninety-nine per cent of all passengers and crew are already dead."

"Yes, but there are at least sixteen of us that are still alive, and who would like to keep it that way!" Ulysses riled. "Now, as I understand it, there are no operable lifeboats accessible from this location."

"That is correct, sir."

"But there must be another way off the ship?"

"Oh yes, sir."

"Really?" Ulysses said, surprised despite himself. "Captain, did you ask if there was another way off the ship?" he asked, turning to the equally surprised McCormack.

"Well, I asked as to the number and viability of the lifeboats, yes."

"So 'no' then. Neptune, do tell us more."

"Mr Carcharodon's private submersible vehicle the *Ahab* and its sister craft the *Nemo*, sir."

"I see. And where would they be located?"

"Within the sub-dock, sir, on Deck 15."

"You might as well wait here to drown," McCormack said, directing his comment at Ulysses, "if you're planning on taking one of those things out of here."

Ulysses turned on him. "Why? Why shouldn't we?"

"Those things are private runabouts, they're not designed for these depths. Like as not they won't survive for long out there, down here. They won't take the hydrostatic pressure."

"Really?" Ulysses was unable to hide his disappointment.

"Not a hope."

"But they don't have to last for long," Ulysses said, the old child-like excitement returning, "at these pressures I mean. We load up the subs, take them out and head up. Straight up, back to the surface."

"And what about whatever it was that attacked us?" McCormack pointed out. "Chances are it's still out there. Look what it's done to the *Neptune*. A couple of small-scale submersibles won't have a hope."

"Glass is always half-empty with you, isn't it?"

"I'm just being realistic."

"Yes, you are, damn you. We really are caught between the Devil and the deep blue sea, aren't we?"

"That's what I've been trying to tell you."

"Take the subs to the surface and we may well meet whatever it is that's out there waiting for us. Stay here, the ship fills with water and all we've got to look forward to is a burial at sea in Davy Jones' Locker."

Ulysses thought for a moment.

"If there was just somewhere we could hole up until the rescue teams could get to us, anywhere but here," he mused.

"I have located such an environment," the Neptune AI announced calmly.

"What?" Ulysses and McCormack both exclaimed together.

"My sensor arrays have located an undersea facility two hundred yards away at the edge of the oceanic trench. No life signs, although life-support systems are still operable."

"I don't bloody believe it!" Captain McCormack swore.

"I told you there was a way!" Ulysses declared proudly. "Neptune, is the sub-dock accessible from this location, without having to pass through any flooded sections of the ship, I mean."

The AI was quiet for a few seconds as its cogitator relays processed the information it was still receiving from its many and varied sensor detection devices positioned around the ship. "Yes. It is possible to reach the sub-dock without passing through any flooded sections of the superstructure."

"Then that's how we'll do it!" Ulysses declared, flashing the astonished captain a manic grin. "We're getting off this ship!"

CHAPTER TEN

Full Fathom Five

"LADIES AND GENTLEMEN, honoured guests," called the purser over the anxious hubbub that had taken hold of the dining room, "pray silence for the captain."

One by one, the assembled anxious VIPs turned to see Captain McCormack standing at the door to the dining room, with Ulysses Quicksilver at his shoulder. An expectant hush descended over the gathering, every one of those present desperate to hear how the captain was going to get them out of this waking nightmare.

McCormack opened his mouth, as if he was about to speak, when Jonah Carcharodon leapt in with an angry: "Well, man? Spit it out! How are you going to get us out of this mess?"

The captain cast his eyes down at the trident-patterned carpet at his feet and took a deep breath. Standing at his shoulder, Ulysses willed him to speak, although held off from saying anything for the moment.

"Ladies and gentlemen," McCormack began, "Mr Quicksilver and I have re-assessed the situation and we believe that we have found a way off this ship."

Gasps of surprise came from around the dining table. "About bloody time," Major Horsley muttered, none too subtly.

"In consultation with the Neptune AI we have devised a way through to the sub-dock on Deck 15 at the bottom of the ship. For the time being it would seem that the sub-dock is still secure and no wetter than it should be. As a result, it is expected that at least one, if not both, the submersible vehicles secured there will still be operable."

"What and then take them out into the open ocean where God's knows what is waiting for us?" the twitching Dr Ogilvy suddenly exclaimed.

"It's suicide," Professor Crichton said darkly.

"Quite possibly, professor," McCormack agreed, "which is why we're not going to the surface."

"What?" Now it was John Schafer's turn to question the captain's plan.

"The *Neptune*'s sensor arrays have detected an undersea base nearby. We're going there."

"How wonderful!" Constance Pennyroyal suddenly exclaimed, blinking tears from her almond eyes. "Salvation!"

"Well, we hope so, Miss Pennyroyal."

"What do you mean, captain?"

"Well, it has an intact, breathable environment and we should be able to wait it out there until the Great White Shipping Line's rescue crews can get to us."

"What is this place you're planning on taking us to, Captain McCormack?" Thor Haugland asked, exhaling cigarette smoke from his nose.

"As I say, it's an undersea base, partially intact. Beyond that I can't tell you any more at this stage."

"What?" Dexter Sylvester said, running a hand through his oily black hair. "You mean, you're not taking us to any recognised facility?"

McCormack paused before answering. "It's not one that appears within any of the *Neptune*'s data files."

"So we're leaving the ship in some old tub to go to a semi-intact underwater facility that you've never even heard of and, I take it, that probably isn't even manned at this time?"

"You could put it that way."

Sylvester looked appalled in the face of the captain's frank honesty but was patently flummoxed as to how to respond.

"And you're suggesting we take the *Ahab*, McCormack?" Carcharodon said.

"Yes, sir."

"Captain," Carcharodon went on, "as I understand it, the *Ahab* – never mind the *Nemo* – isn't designed to operate at these sorts of depths for prolonged periods."

"It's not far. They should be good for a short journey."

The anxious muttering of the VIPs resumed.

"You don't sound very certain about this plan of yours," Lady Denning said, speaking up over the crowd.

At her words, all fell silent again, needling stares fixing the poor beleaguered captain and several now eyeing Ulysses with some measure of suspicion.

"Lady Denning, the only thing I am certain of at the moment is that if we stay here we will die – all of us. The *Neptune* is flooding, the Bridge, we have to assume, is compromised, and before long the only place the *Neptune* will be going is down to the bottom of the Marianas Trench, and there isn't a hope of us being rescued before then and I can't even be sure whether anyone knows we're lost out here yet."

"So, how do you plan on getting us to the sub-dock?" Carcharodon asked, breaking the uncomfortable silence.

"Mr Quicksilver and I have devised a way, with the assistance of the AI," McCormack explained. "The quickest route is still going to prove a little challenging but if we keep our heads I see no reason why we shouldn't reach the dock in plenty of time."

Captain McCormack looked around the room, taking in all of the anxious guests and his steeled crew members, and when he next spoke, something of his old, familiar calm authority had returned. "So, this is the plan. My crew and I are going to lead you from here to the Grand Atrium. According to Neptune, the elevators are still working so from there we're going to travel down to Deck 15 and make our way through to the sub-dock. Once there we'll board the submersibles, exit through the pressure gate beneath the *Neptune* and make the short journey to the underwater facility.

"Are there any questions?"

There were probably as many as there were anxious pairs of eyes looking back at him, but for the time being no one chose to voice them. They just wanted to get out of this mess as quickly, and as safely, as possible.

"Mr Quicksilver, is there anything you would like to add?"

Ulysses took a moment to observe each one of the frightened faces arrayed before him. They returned his gaze, some more intensely than others, and none more so than Miss Birkin who now looked as white as the starched linen tablecloth.

"Just to keep your heads, and, if you do, I can see no reason why we shouldn't all get out of this alive and, to top it all, with quite some tales to tell all our grandchildren in years to come."

He directed these last words at the nervous couple of John and Constance, and even managed a broad grin for them. They returned fragile smiles of their own, hands locked together in a white-knuckled embrace.

"Chances are we're going to see some rather unpleasant things, passengers less fortunate than ourselves," – someone harrumphed at this, at Ulysses' suggestion that they were fortunate, he supposed – "and it's likely we may encounter power shorts, flooding and possibly fires as well. But, like I say, if everyone keeps calm and doesn't do anything rash, we'll get you through this."

"Now then, ladies and gentlemen." McCormack spoke with commanding confidence now, "my staff will lead the way, so if you would like to follow them, we will make our way to the Grand Atrium."

The VIP party left the safe haven of the dining room, a sorry raggletaggle group, shuffling forlornly after Captain McCormack, the purser and the other officer whom the captain addressed as Mr Wates. Miss Celeste still insisted on being responsible for her employer, stubbornly pushing his wheelchair along the corridors towards the atrium. Schafer, Constance and Miss Birkin had formed their own little group, their mutual support centred around the precious flower that was the young Miss Pennyroyal, who had certainly never experienced anything like this before in her life. But then which of them had, Ulysses wondered, apart from himself and Nimrod, of course? For them this, their latest adventure, was merely one more in a long line of hair's-breadth escapes and dramatic getaways. Perhaps that was what gave him the optimism that they could all get out of this with their skins intact, despite the shock of what had happened to Glenda, that had numbed him to the core.

But as well as the already unpredictable nature of their situation there were still two other variables that they couldn't plan for. Firstly there was whatever it was that was out there, waiting for them in the chill abyssal depths, that had been bold enough, and capable enough, to attack the *Neptune* and get the better of it. Secondly there was the matter of the murderer who had so viciously taken Glenda's life. With no evidence to the contrary, there was always the possibility that the killer was with them even now, one of the party of sixteen making its way from the room, searching for a way off the stricken ship.

As they left, Ulysses took another look at the dark and desolate view of the seabed that lay beyond the steel and glass viewing bubble.

"Thought you saw something, sir?" Nimrod asked, pausing beside him.

"No," Ulysses mused, sucking in his bottom lip, "no, not this time."

"But it's still out there, isn't it?"

"Whatever it was that attacked the *Neptune*? Oh yes, I rather think it is."

"Now what?" demanded Professor Crichton, taking another swig from the hip flask clenched in his jittery hands.

Holding onto an ornate pillar for support, Ulysses Quicksilver peered out over the precipitous edge of the balcony into the void of the Grand Atrium. In the fitful flickering light of the remaining chandelier he watched the seething waters below, brows knitted in consternation.

Along with the Promenade Deck and the Vaudeville Theatre, the Grand Atrium of the *Neptune* had been one of the architectural and design highlights of the new super sub-liner. It divided the ship neatly in half from the top down to Deck 10, ten storeys of open space, the two halves of the ship connected at various points via dramatic, glass-bottomed, suspended walkways, so that the atrium could be just as easily crossed on any level as at the bottom where one could marvel at the wonderfully engineered fountains, their splashing waters turned to glittering diamonds by the light of the vast chandeliers suspended from the glass and steel dome of its roof. They filled the gallery with magnificent cut-glass light, each one of them looking like a glittering star plucked from the velvet cloth of heaven itself.

Two of these huge chandeliers now lay shattered and broken amidst the wreckage of the atrium still five decks below, licked by fires burning on top of the oily waters. The remaining chandelier sparked and swung from its loosened mountings, adding epileptic lightning flashes to the ruddy glow of the emergency lights in this part of the ship. By the fitful illumination Ulysses could make out broken bodies bobbing about face-down amongst the wreckage, moved constantly by the seawater filling the bottom of the gallery.

The atrium had obviously come off more badly in the attack than some parts of the ship. There was no way of knowing whether the hull breach had been caused by one of the falling chandeliers – although Ulysses doubted it – or whether water coming into the ship elsewhere through the ruptured superstructure had found its way to this place. Perhaps it was overspill from the condemned Steerage decks.

The presence of the water also made Ulysses consider the state of the lower levels where the sub-dock was housed. It was possible that the bulkheads that divided up the interior space of the *Neptune* could keep flooded areas separate, and their way through may still be accessible, but it made him realise how pressing their mission was.

Opposite them, across the divide, stood the showy elevator doors of the Grand Atrium. The walkway they should have been able to cross to reach the lifts was gone, the only evidence of it ever having been there, a twisted steel beam. What was left of the footbridge lay crushed beneath one of the fallen chandeliers.

"How are we going to get across now?" Constance Pennyroyal asked nervously.

"We could double back, take the stairs to another level where we can cross safely," Dexter Sylvester suggested.

"No can do," Ulysses said, before any of Captain McCormack's men could speak. "Didn't you feel the heat as we went past? No, that way is out as fire's already taken hold down there. We cross here or we don't cross at all."

"But how?" Lady Denning said, her tone more angry than fearful.

Ulysses peered down at the churning, burning waters again and reassessed the distances involved in crossing the atrium.

"I have an idea," he said.

"Come on then, man? Let's hear it," Major Horsley boomed encouragingly.

"See that balustrade over there?" Ulysses said, pointing at the side-long ladder-like structure of the balcony opposite that had been half broken off by a falling crystal light-fitting "I reckon that if we could pull that free and slide it over we'd have something long enough and strong enough to let everyone clamber across."

Appalled faces looked back at him from among the party, none more so than Miss Whilomena Birkin's.

"One at a time mind," he added.

"And how, exactly, are you going to achieve this dramatic feat?" Carcharodon enquired pointedly.

"Well, if it were up to me, I would dive down there," he said pointing at the ever-rising waters beneath them, "shin up that pole," his finger now followed the broken support column of one of the downed chandeliers, "up to there and then it would only be a short scramble to the balcony. I'd need a hand of course."

"Very well, that's agreed then," Carcharodon declared, needlessly taking charge of the situation once somebody else had worked out what had to be done. "Any volunteers?"

"I'll go," came one bold voice amidst the embarrassed silence of the majority.

"No, John, you can't!" Constance declared, horrified.

"My darling, I must," Schafer said, taking her hands in his again. "For your sake. For our sake, for the sake of everyone here."

"But, John," she struggled, unchecked tears running down her cheeks.

"I'll be alright. I was House swimming champion back in my school days. Top diving board and everything. I haven't told you that before, have I?"

"Jolly good show, what?" the Major said happily, clapping his hands together loudly in satisfaction. "Knew you wouldn't let us down, old boy," he said, nudging Ulysses in the ribs. "Jackets off then, lads, eh?"

"Jackets off indeed, Major," Ulysses agreed, arching a sarcastic eyebrow.

"May I be of service, sir?" Nimrod asked, taking a step forward.

"You just be ready to help at this end, Nimrod, old chap," his employer said with a wry smile. "Keep this lot in check and all that."

"Very good, sir."

"So, young Schafer," Ulysses said, approaching the edge of the precipice. "Ready to show this lot what you're made of?"

"After you, Quicksilver," he said, rolling up his shirt sleeves, ready for action, receiving one last passionate kiss on the lips from his betrothed before handing her his jacket and pushing her gently back towards her anxious aunt.

"Right you are then. Here goes nothing."

Feet together, Ulysses straightened, arms outstretched above his head, pointing at the dark glass ceiling as if in an attitude of prayer. For a moment he stood there, poised ready to dive. Then, with one graceful bound, he launched himself off the edge and head first into the turgid waters below.

The speed and directness of his dive meant he passed straight through the broiling surface fires and into the dousing embrace of the water beneath – a brief rush of heat following by the shock of bone-numbing cold. He heard the muffled splash and rush of bubbles of another body entering the water after him. Glancing back he saw John Schafer kicking his way towards him, lit by the orange flames dancing on the surge above their heads.

Together, they made their way towards the great bulk of the half-submerged chandelier, feeling the dragging limbs of drowned men and women bumping against them as they swam. Ulysses tried to ignore the bobbing corpses, tried to convince himself that he wasn't swimming through their watery grave.

And then they were hauling themselves beyond the reach of the rising water again, clambering up the glass-crystal boulder that was the chandelier, careful where they put their hands amidst the broken body of the shattered glass ornament. Only a few slight cuts later, with one another's support, they were negotiating the pole and scrambling the last few feet up to the balcony, opposite the spot from where they had taken the plunge only moments before.

Cheers and shouts of encouragement rang in their ears, audible over the crackle of shorting electrical cables and the bubbling and seething water, given voice by their fellow survivors.

"Now to work," Ulysses said, slicking back his wet hair with a hand and clearing his eyes of water, as Schafer wrung as much of the water as he could from his sodden clothes, before they set to work freeing the broken balustrade.

With the woodwork liberated from its splintered mountings, taking the weight between them, supporting it at one end, the two men pushed the ladder-like structure across the void until it scraped against the other side of the atrium space. Eager hands pulled it up and secured it there with whatever they could find to hand. It was just long enough, Ulysses noted.

First to brave the perilous crossing was Mr Wates, who scrambled across in no time, the balcony-bridge flexing dramatically beneath him as he did so, although it still held. Once across he helped Ulysses and Schafer maintain a strong hold on their end of the makeshift crossing.

Bathed in electrical spark-flash and the ruddy glow of the emergency lighting, the rest of the party took it in turns to make their way across, cautiously, one at a time.

*   *   *

Captain Connor 'Mac' McCormack watched through intensely narrowed eyes as those men and women in his charge braved the perilous crossing of the flooding atrium, observing each one with the same intensity, determined that not one of them would be lost to the deep or the disaster continuing to unfold around them, giving direction where necessary as well as maintaining an order to their evacuation so that all might make it in the end.

So it came as no little annoyance to him when what had at first been simply an anxious tapping on his arm became an insistent tugging on his sleeve. "What is it Miss Birkin?" he almost snapped, turning on her, his calm demeanour evaporating in the face of her relentless persistence.

The old woman looked terrible. He understood the stress that all of the VIPs were under. This was, after all, not what they had expected on a round-the-world cruise aboard the most advanced sub-liner to ever cross the Seven Seas. But he was under no little strain himself. However, ever since they had gathered in the dining room together, Miss Birkin's despairing disposition had worsened considerably more than that of the other passengers.

"I need to have a private word with you, Captain."

"Miss Birkin, can't it wait? In case you hadn't noticed, this is hardly the time or the place."

"But it has to be now, Captain." The ageing spinster was becoming more and more agitated, still tugging at his sleeve. "You have to listen to what I have to tell you."

"Miss Birkin, please. Let us get everyone across and then you can have my ear."

"It won't wait a moment longer!"

"What won't, Miss Birkin?" McCormack suddenly found himself raising his voice more than he had intended. Others still waiting on the nearside of the gulf were turning to see what all the fuss was about.

"Because I believe the murderer is still with us!"

McCormack was abruptly aware of the uncomfortable silence that had fallen around them.

"And what makes you think that?" he said in a sudden, sharp whisper, seizing her arm tightly in his hand.

"Because I saw him!"

"That's quite enough, Miss Birkin. I would be grateful if you kept your voice down. You've got your private word."

Lady Denning was next to cross and, as ever, she proved to be a stoical, no nonsense old bird. Ulysses respected her for that. But he was also curious as to what was happening on the other side of the gulf, the dull scratching at the base of his skull testament to the fact that there was something awry. Miss Birkin appeared to be in quite some state of agitation before it was even her turn to cross the wobbling bridge and, before he knew it, Captain McCormack was ushering her away into the shadows back the way they had just come.

Whatever the problem had been, McCormack seemed to have been able to resolve it just as quickly as only a minute or two later he returned with Miss Birkin firmly in hand. And it might have been his imagination but, as Ulysses helped Professor Crichton up from his crawl across the chasm, he thought he felt that unmistakable sense of someone's eyes on him, and looked up to see the captain watching him.

There were moments of doubt, panic and sheer vertiginous terror that required a great deal of patient encouragement and time, along with no small number of stopped breaths and missed heartbeats. Miss Birkin seemed particularly uncomfortable about crossing – he would have liked to have believed that was what all the fuss had been about – but somehow the old coot made it safely to the other side.

The most awkward crossing was that involving Jonah Carcharodon. Left almost until last, he was ever-so-carefully manhandled across by Captain McCormack himself and the purser, whilst the sprightly lithe and limber Thor Haugland made sure the magnate's chair made it over too.

And then there was only Dexter Sylvester left to cross, the ambitious young businessman insisting that the shipping magnate cross safely before him. Such a feat as traversing the void should have been no trouble for a gentleman of his obvious athleticism and his enthusiasm for the more adventurous pastimes, such as rock-climbing and abseiling. And it wouldn't have been, had it not been for the last chandelier.

As the immense hydrostatic pressures continued to work on the compromised structure of the liner, nerve-jangling metallic groaning and heaving sounds echoing throughout the vessel, something gave. The only warning any of them had that anything was wrong was when the erratic lighting failed. Ulysses, with his curiously heightened sixth sense was the only one to even look up and register a reaction to that one small fact, and so was granted a grandstand view.

The dead weight of crystal-glass and metal dropped like a boulder out of the crimson darkness, collided squarely with the balustrade spanning the space – Sylvester still only half way across – and smashed through it. The splintered balustrade tumbled after the chandelier into the gloom, now just so much matchwood, as the huge light fitting plunged into the roiling inferno beneath.

Of the man from Umbridge Industries there was no sign. Ulysses didn't even see him go. One minute he was there on the bridge, the next there was nothing but the immense bulk of the darkened chandelier, and then... nothing at all.

The shock and horror of realisation took a while to sink in amongst the party, some not realising what had happened at all until they witnessed the horrified reactions of their fellows, so concerned were they with their own intense personal struggles for survival.

So it was that, accompanied by stupefied silences, child-like sobbing and angry denials of what had happened, Ulysses Quicksilver and Captain McCormack eventually managed to herd the party – already minus one – to the lift doors on the other side of the Grand Atrium, their target all along.

Ulysses was about to push the button to call the first of the two lifts when he paused.

"What is it, sir?" Nimrod asked, at his shoulder once more.

"Look," Ulysses said, pointing at the row of still glowing lights above the elevator doors that showed the progress of the lift through the ship. The lights were blinking on and off, one after another. "It's already on its way."

With a delicate chiming the progress of the lights stopped and a moment later, with the grating of opening mechanisms, the lift doors opened. Ulysses stood and stared in dumbfounded amazement.

"Please accept my humblest apologies," Harry Cheng said, bowing deferentially. 'We would have been here sooner, but matters rather overtook us somewhat.'

The hulking Mr Sin stood at his side but, at a hissed command in Chinese from Cheng, the brute shuffled back to make room for more.

"Please, ladies and gentlemen, join us."

Without needing any further invitation, the VIPs began to pile into the lift. Ulysses hung back with those who would have to use the second elevator, rendered speechless by the miraculous arrival of his rival.

"Going up?" Cheng asked the Captain.

"No, Mr Cheng. Down, to the sub-dock."

"Ah, I see. Very well," he said, his hand at the deck selector panel. "Down it is."

With a slightly different chiming timbre, the second lift joined them. With a grinding clanking the doors eased open.

A torrent of seawater flooded out, washing across the carpeted floor of the balcony level and soaking the feet of everyone standing there.

"Ah," said Ulysses, finding his voice at last, "perhaps down isn't the best idea after all."

CHAPTER ELEVEN

The Deep

"QUICK! INTO THE lift!"

"Everybody move!"

At Captain McCormack's urgent command and Ulysses' cajoling, the party of survivors piled into Cheng's lift. As the *Neptune's* officers herded the anxious and the uncertain between the doors, Ulysses dared a glance back at the flooded atrium. Something must have given or blown somewhere – part of the hull, a compromised bulkhead, a porthole, who-knew-what? – the result being that the space below was filling more rapidly, the chandeliers vanishing beneath the surge of white water and bobbing bodies. The water, still finding an outlet through the second open lift, poured off the edge of the balcony, cascading down to meet that which was surging upwards from the drowned atrium below.

There was only one way out of this and that was up.

As the last of the VIP party crowded into the brass and glass box of polished mirrors, Ulysses' eyes fell on the smart plaque that stated no more than a maximum of ten persons should use this lift at any one time. As the purser hammered a button on the deck selector panel and the doors grated shut behind him – the last one in – Ulysses closed his eyes and held his breath, offering up a quick prayer to whatever saint it was that watched over the workings of elevators, that the carriage would be able to take the strain.

There was a rising hum and a series of systematic clanking sounds, then a terrible split-second sensation of dropping, which made all those trapped within the small box gasp in unison. But then the lift carriage began to rise.

Gears grinding, it felt to Ulysses that the elevator was making heavy weather of the journey. He thought he could hear the bubbling rush of water somewhere below them and wondered which was rising faster, the lift or the level of the seawater flooding the elevator shaft. He was trying hard to ignore the hot-wire stabbings of prescience in his skull; he did not need any unearthly sixth sense to tell him that they were in constant mortal danger for the foreseeable future.

The smell of fear permeated the human sardine tin; fear and sweat and brine and burning. In any other situation such enforced proximity to others would not have been tolerated by those who were now forced to huddle together so closely. There was not an inch between any of them, from the Chinaman Cheng and the massive Mr Sin, to Lady Denning or the chaperoned couple, or the billionaire owner of the ship, the current crisis having robbed him of practically any difference in status he had beyond the least of them, his own PA being forced to sit on his lap to make sure that everyone could pack into the lift.

The realisation suddenly struck Ulysses that the lift could all too easily become a ready-made coffin, should the water level rise more quickly than the struggling elevator, or should some part of the beleaguered machinery fail under duress, or should the – whatever is was – that attacked the *Neptune* decide to come back for another go.

But, despite the obvious risks and inherent dangers associated with their current predicament, Quicksilver's spirit wouldn't let him be beaten by such overwhelming odds. He would keep fighting to save himself – to save these people – until the deep, or the horrors that inhabited it, forced the last breath from him as he went down kicking and screaming. Just as there had been nothing in his power that he could do to save the wretched Glenda, he would do all in his power to save those who remained. He would not let another Glenda Finch or Dexter Sylvester be taken by the dying ship, the cruel sea or the monsters that dwelt there.

The lift ground onwards as the gears of Ulysses' mind worked over the problem of how they were going to get out of this mess. The further the elevator rose up its compromised shaft, the more he found himself dwelling on the fact that the plan had been to head down to reach the sub-dock and the submersibles *Ahab* and *Nemo*, to escape the wreck of the *Neptune* as swiftly as possible before the sea or the drowned liner claimed them all.

The plan. It was worthless now. All that stood between them and oblivion was adaptation, improvisation, spontaneity, ingenuity, inventiveness and cold, hard animal instinct. Or, to look at it another way, the plan had to evolve or they would die.

And what of the sub-dock and its two transports? Ulysses had to believe that it was still attainable, the craft operable. To think anything else would mean the end of all hope for them.

The lift was slowing now – horribly quickly – the ratcheting gears clunking away the last few inches. For a moment the carriage heaved and there was that horrid feeling that the lift was at the apex of its ascent and was about to commence its all too rapid descent again. Then the whole thing seemed to lurch upwards. There was the rattle and clunk of clamps locking the elevator in place, the steel cables holding it up held tight in the steel teeth of the riser's locking mechanisms. The chiming of the lift arriving at its destination cut through the numb silence inside. All on board gave a collective sigh of relief.

The doors ground open once again and, without having to be invited to do so, the VIPs piled out of the carriage. Ulysses led the way, enjoying the sudden sensation of space around him.

"Where are we?" asked a shaky Dr Ogilvy.

"Top deck," Ulysses read from a sign screwed to the wall next to the open lift doors. "Casino Royale, the Bistro, Shopping and the Promenade Deck."

"So where now, McCormack?" Jonah Carcharodon asked.

But the captain and his staff were already examining another passenger ship plan. Ulysses joined them, the rest of the party, left without guidance, milling about behind, taking in the wreckage and devastation apparent on this level as well, lit by the sparking lights hanging from the ceiling.

"So, Captain, any ideas?" Ulysses asked.

Captain McCormack breathed out noisily. "Well, we're here" – he indicated Level 1 on the plan in front of them – "having travelled from here" – he identified the point where they had crossed the devastated Grand Atrium – "and we need to get to here." His finger alighted on the outline of the sub-dock at the bottom of the ship.

"Indeed," Ulysses mused.

"We know that chances are that the bulkhead here" – the captain pointed out what should have been a watertight section below the level of the Grand Atrium – "is no longer intact and so from here to here" – his outstretched finger swept across the plan taking in several compartments of the sub-liner – "will be underwater."

"But that leaves the sub-dock still untouched."

"Hopefully," McCormack said guardedly.

"But how to get there."

"Precisely. If the compartment under the atrium's gone, we can't be certain which other compartments may also have been breached."

"Have you consulted with the AI again yet?" Ulysses asked, eyeing what he now understood was the comm-button hidden beneath the trident logo on the panel.

"We can't."

"What do you mean?"

"Try for yourself, Mr Quicksilver," Mr Wates said.

Ulysses tried the comm-alert for himself. There was the click of the button being depressed but nothing more, not even static. Ulysses tried again, pushing the button harder this time. Still nothing.

"It would appear that ship-wide communications throughout the *Neptune* have failed," Mr Wates explained.

"Which only goes to prove that this is not some static problem, but that the crisis is worsening the longer we remain trapped down here," McCormack added for emphasis.

"Okay, so what you're telling me is that we're going to have to do this the old-fashioned way – ourselves?"

McCormack nodded, turning his attention back to the plan.

After some minutes huddled deliberation, recalling to mind what they had learnt from the AI the last time they had been able to communicate with it, Ulysses and the *Neptune* officers came up with something approximating a modified escape plan.

"So, I ask again, McCormack, what now? How are you going to get us out of here?" Major Horsley said.

"Our target destination is still the sub-dock," the captain began.

"But that's bloody well down at the bottom of the ship and you keeping taking us further and further away from it!"

"I realise that, Major," McCormack pointed out, with all the patience he could muster, "but it's the only way. There are no other usable lifeboats in reach of our current position. That hasn't changed."

"Look, we're going to work our way towards the rear of the ship," Ulysses said, taking over explaining the plan, "and go through the engine halls to the sub-dock."

"But I thought the engines were on fire!" Miss Birkin suddenly spoke up in alarm.

"Only some of them, Miss Birkin," McCormack stated. "And there's always the possibility that some of the fires might have burnt themselves out by now, starved of oxygen."

"Starved of oxygen?" Professor Crichton exclaimed and took another pull on his hipflask.

"It's all right because when we open the bulkhead door through to the engine hall it will let in the air from the rest of the ship. We're not going to suffocate down here on top of everything else," McCormack said giving a snort of mirthless laughter.

It still took another few minutes of encouraging, fear-allaying and cajoling before the party was ready to continue. During all that time,

Harry Cheng and Mr Sin kept themselves to themselves at the periphery of the group, neither offering advice or criticism. The double agent's face was knotted in concentration whilst his silent aide, seemingly unperturbed by the unfolding disaster, was happy simply to follow Cheng's instructions.

With all brought to order, the group of desperate VIPs followed the captain's lead now in the opposite direction to which they had been travelling, heading towards the stern of the ship. However, it was not long before they came to a sealed door at the end of the smashed and shattered remains of what had once been one of the bars.

"I know where we are," Thor Haugland suddenly piped up. "Captain, you can't be serious?"

"Oh but we are, Mr Haugland," Ulysses said with a hard smile, "there being no other way."

"What's the problem?" Lady Denning asked. "Where are we?"

Captain McCormack pulled open the door. "Here," he said.

With everyone straining to peer through the doorway, but without any of them wanting to take a step forwards, the *Neptune*'s honoured guests gazed at the awesome vista before them.

What was probably most incredible to them of all, Ulysses considered, was the fact that the dome over the Promenade Deck was still intact, considering what had befallen the ship in the last few hours. This probably came only slightly ahead of the fact that the party leaders were planning on taking them out across the Promenade, along its entire length to the far side, when there was nothing but the oppressive blackness of the deep ocean above their heads, the same ocean that was exerting immense hydrostatic pressures on the *Neptune* now trapped on the sea-bed.

"We're going out there?" John Schafer asked, and from the earnest looks the rest of the VIPs threw Captain McCormack and Ulysses, it was obvious that he wasn't the only one who was wondering whether their next course of action was such a good idea.

"Well, technically we won't actually be going 'out' at all," Ulysses said, trying to allay their fears.

Lady Denning took a step towards the opening, peering up into the darkness above the ship, almost as if she was looking for something. Lights were still shining on the Promenade Deck but their halo of illumination only penetrated a little way out into the trackless depths of the ocean. "But if we go out there," she said pointedly, "whatever it was that brought the ship down – and which might well be waiting for us, out of our immediate field of view – will see the movement and be drawn back to the ship in search of prey."

There was a sudden rumbling judder and every member of the escape party, except for the wheelchair-bound Carcharodon, was forced to grab hold of somebody, or something, for support.

"What was that?" Crichton snapped, darting eyes shooting paranoid glances at all of them, comforting himself with the next breath with another swig from his flask.

"*That* was why we don't have any choice but to cross the Promenade," Captain McCormack explained. "The *Neptune* is still flooding even as we stand here deliberating as to whether we should take the quickest route to get off this ship."

"If we hang around here arguing the toss for much longer it won't make any difference what we decide," Ulysses added bluntly. "And there won't be much time for regrets either as the *Neptune* goes over the brink and into the trench."

Almost as one, the party shuffled towards the open doorway, steeling themselves for their flight along the length of the exposed Promenade.

There was another groan and the sub-liner moved again. This time some among the party lost their balance altogether and even Jonah Carcharodon had to grab hold of something to stop his chair rolling backwards through the wreckage of the bar.

Was this it? Ulysses wondered as he held tight to a steel pillar. Had they dallied too long? Was the *Neptune* even now making her very final voyage to the utmost depths of the Pacific Ocean?

The seismic rumblings abruptly subsided and the ship settled down again. The polished boards of the Promenade Deck, incongruously marked out for traditional deck games, still stretched out ahead of them, only now they would have to ascend to the stern of the ship. The prospect seemed even more daunting to the already strung-out escapees, but there was no other option open to them.

"Ladies and gentlemen," Captain McCormack declared, "it really is now or never."

And so, without needing any further encouragement, the party of VIPs and associated hangers-on began their ascent of the Promenade Deck.

Mr Wates and the Purser led the way, with the wrung-out Dr Ogilvy taking the mantra of 'every man for himself' as his personal ideology, followed by an almost equally desperate Professor Crichton. Then came the trio of John Schafer and the two women in his charge, the role of chaperone having noticeably switched, and after them Lady Denning and Major Horsley. Ulysses and Nimrod insisted on helping the reluctant Miss Celeste push her employer's chair up the incline, making an otherwise virtually impossible task that much easier. Then came Thor Haugland, closely followed by Captain McCormack, and last of all the odd couple of Harry Cheng and Mr Sin, at a discreet distance.

When the party hadn't yet covered half the distance they needed to to get to safety, feeling a resurgence of that oh-so familiar itching inside his skull, Ulysses looked up.

"Bloody hell!" he gasped, pupils dilating in terror.

Something was approaching out of the darkness of the deep above them, preceded by a glowing azure light. Something monstrous, a malign shadow uncoiling from out of the abyssal black of the smothering ocean. Something that was heading straight for them.

Hearing Ulysses' expletive, close behind him, McCormack looked up. The colour drained from his face in an instant as his eyes locked onto the horror torpedoing out of the black murk towards the Promenade Deck.

He gasped, his lilting Scots voice no longer calm: "We're going to need a bigger sub!"

CHAPTER TWELVE

The Nature of the Beast

EMERGING FROM THE sucking black void, to Ulysses' eyes the monster looked primarily like a giant squid. Only the creatures he had seen pictures of, when they were washed up dead on the shores of Greenland or hauled up in the nets of a Japanese fishing trawler, even with their tentacles extended, had been no more than fifty feet in length. As the creature torpedoed towards the stricken *Neptune*, Ulysses took a rough guess and decided that this beast was at least two hundred feet from tentacle tips to the end of its arrowhead tail.

But there was so much more wrong with it than just its grossly exaggerated size. As the squid-beast sped towards the sub-liner, homing in on the movement of the figures it must have detected fleeing along the brightly lit Promenade, the image of its horrific, unreal form was seared onto Ulysses' retinas. He could still see it now, in his mind's eye, as he turned his attention back to the matter of escape; although now it had become the more immediate need of escaping from the coiling clutches of the squid-monster closing on the *Neptune*, than the longer term plan of escaping on one of the stricken liner's submersibles. And was that really an option now, with their worst fears realised in the form of the savage, hungry sea-beast?

It was the sea-devil all of them must have imagined when Ulysses had spoken of being trapped between the Devil and the deep blue sea.

Although it looked like an overgrown squid – Architeuthis Giganticus rather than just Architeuthis Dux – it was far more than simply an over-grown mollusc. To begin with, too many clutching tentacles reached from the appalling head of the creature, with the length, strength and size of ship's cables, masses of puckered, grey suckers opening and clos-ing like a myriad foully kissing mouths.

The monster also lit the way before it, a bioluminescent lure, the kind Ulysses would have expected to see projecting from the head of a deep-sea angler fish, pulsing with blue light, ever darting ahead of it, like some herald-symbiote with a mind of its own.

And it was not only the lure that the beast had borrowed from that deep-sea dwelling genus of fish. In the split second that Ulysses' spied the creature for the first time, as its tentacles had spread wide, no doubt preparing to seize the ship once again in its leviathan clutches, its mouth parts had been exposed. Instead of a horny beak, angler fish jaws, wide enough it seemed to swallow small ships whole, stretched even wider, to dislocating proportions.

And the creature didn't only come with deadly natural weapons; it was armoured too, as if anything in the oceans could possibly threaten a mon-ster like this! A crustacean-like shell covered the squid-thing's back, from the top of its soft head to its tail. What kind of freak of nature was it?

Was it of nature at all?

Time slowed, the rising plane of the Promenade extending elastically before Ulysses, as he realised how far they still had to go to reach safety. And even if they made it through the double doors ahead of them, would they really then be safe? The monster had had its part to play in crippling the ship and sending it to the bottom of the sea, leaving them all teetering between life and death on the knife edge precipice of the yawning Marianas Trench.

"Come on!" Ulysses shouted, urging Nimrod, and the unnerved Miss Celeste to draw on hidden reserves of strength.

As he and Nimrod pushed as hard as they could, adrenal glands flood-ing their bodies with their oh-so necessary secretions once more, practi-cally carrying Miss Celeste along with them, as well as the chair, Ulysses fixed his eyes on the way ahead.

Directly in front of them Major Horsley was helping Lady Denning on her way, the pair of ageing adventurers huffing and puffing their way up the deck, neither daring to stop in case their feet lost their grip on the wax-polished boards or, Heaven forbid, the monster caught them. Ahead of them, John Schafer was offering all the encouragement he could to his darling dear heart and her aunt, for them to keep going – apparently neither of the women having yet seen this new threat – keeping them focused on reaching the doors. But all his good works might prove to be for naught, if Professor Crichton had anything to do with it.

The emeritus professor was stumbling forwards but with his gaze directed back up over his shoulder, unable to tear his eyes from the squid-beast. He was gabbling to himself, his face white as an albino sea slug, apparently calling on the aid of the Almighty to get them out of this mess with cries of "Oh, God! Oh, God!" and whimpered sobs of "What have we done?"

As the two officers leading the escape party raced ahead to get the doors open, leaving a moaning Dr Ogilvy to struggle on as best he could alone, Ulysses could not help looking back at the approaching leviathan in the face of Professor Crichton's inability to take his eyes off the thing. He instantly wished he hadn't.

It was nearly on them, tentacles already reaching out over the steel-glass bubble of the enclosed deck, mouth agape, javelin-sharp fangs like drawn-out steel fish hooks, poised ready to spear them and draw them into its hideous maw. Ulysses fancied he caught a glint of evil intent in the huge, watery eyes looking at him through the glass shield.

"Herregud," Ulysses heard Thor Haugland utter in appalled Norwegian behind him, "det er Kraken!"

Of course, Ulysses thought, Haugland had given their tormenter a name: the Kraken, the many-legged sea monster of sea-faring legend, the horror that pulled ships beneath the waves and devoured their crews whole. Until that moment Ulysses would have put sea-dogs' tales of the Kraken down to a combination of ways of explaining away good old-fashioned shipwrecks and the discovery of creatures such as the giant squid lurking within the deeper oceans. Only now, he wasn't so sure.

Constance screamed. She too had now seen the beast. Schafer pulled her close, urging her onwards, almost dragging her with him in her shocked state. Constance's maiden aunt didn't need any such encouragement; she had picked up her skirts and was sprinting away up the deck like a fell runner, bony ankles and varicose veins visible now beneath her fussy petticoats.

"Don't stop!" Ulysses found himself shouting. "Just keep going. It's going to be all right!"

In a cruel contradiction of Ulysses' words, a shuddering crash shook the escapees' world as the Kraken slammed into the dome of the Promenade Deck. The force of impact rocked the ship, which shifted still further to port, and sent the VIPs tumbling sideways. It was not as bad as the shaking they had received when the *Neptune* had first started to sink, when it had felt like their whole world was turning upside down, but it wasn't far off. Carcharodon's chair, suddenly losing all forward momentum, slid sideways into a bench which caught Nimrod, Ulysses and Miss Celeste, who ended up in the unimpressed butler's lap.

The *Neptune* moved again beneath them, rocking back to starboard. Ulysses found himself suddenly looking up through the latticework of the dome above him. Where on the night he and Glenda Finch had experienced the thrill of a controlled submersion they had seen first the stars of the Milky Way and then the closing, plankton-rich waters of the Pacific above their heads, now all he could see was the horrid flesh of the underside of the Kraken as it, again, took the *Neptune* in its unnatural embrace.

He could see spongy grey flesh – the colour of drowned sailors – and warty black hide, like the scale-less skin of abyssal-dwelling hunter-fish, lit by the yellow light of the humming deck lights. Fissures, like lipless mouths dotted the belly of the beast in curious arcs, describing large parabola scarring, which might almost have been bite marks. Other things clung to the vast body of the leviathan that might have been lampreys or remora sucking fish, or some deep-sea evolutionary offshoot.

Following the dorsal line of the monster, Ulysses' eyes fell on the impossibly large teeth of the beast as they scratched against the reinforced dome with a sound like iron nails scraping on plate glass. The unpleasant noise not only set teeth on edge but also hearts racing and backbones prickling with fear.

"Come on! We can't hang around here!" Carcharodon shrieked, feeling more helpless than ever.

"Indeed," Ulysses agreed, pulling himself to his feet again, using the magnate's wheelchair for support.

Miss Celeste having extricated herself from his lap, Nimrod assisted his master in getting the billionaire moving again. Carcharodon's PA relented at last and seemed happy just to follow at their heels and worry about getting herself to safety as quickly as possible.

"Here, let me help."

Glancing to his left, Ulysses saw that the two Chinamen had caught them up. And now it was Harry Cheng's turn to insist on helping with Carcharodon's chair. Mr Sin lumbered a few feet behind, looking, for the first time since Ulysses had met him, scared and out of breath.

Another sound echoed through the enclosed space of the Promenade. At first it didn't even register with Ulysses or anyone else, or so it seemed from their lack of reaction. It was only when he felt his sixth sense flare hotly behind his eyes that he realised that something even worse was about to befall them. It was a creaking, popping sound. There it was again. And again.

And now others could hear it too, curiosity flickering across already stricken expressions. And now there came a more sustained metallic groaning. And now the cascading splash and splatter of rainfall, inside the enclosed Promenade Deck, at the bottom of the Pacific Ocean.

"It's rupturing," Ulysses said, as much to himself as anyone, as the pieces of the jigsaw puzzle all came together in his mind. "The dome's rupturing! Run!"

The sound of water was getting louder now, the pitter-patter quickly becoming a pouring sound, like a waterfall emptying into a swimming pool. Salty spray splashed into Ulysses' eyes, making him wince, as another rivet popped free and a pane of toughened glass fractured, allowing the first trickles of seawater in before the unbelievable tonnages of ocean pressing down on the ship found them. If nature abhorred a vacuum, the sea here seemed to abhor a breathable atmosphere.

Within seconds more panes shattered and torrents of water rushed into the enclosed space from a dozen different points of entry. Now that the hungry sea had found a way in, there was no stopping it.

Mr Wates and the purser stood at the now open doors at the opposite end of the Promenade, practically hanging from the handles to help heave the fleeing VIPs through one after another. The doctor was already through. So too were Schafer, Constance, Miss Birkin, and McCormack. Professor Crichton and Major Horsley were helping Lady Denning through even now, their feet splashing through the first surges of water splashing up the deck towards them.

Ulysses, Nimrod, Jonah Carcharodon in his chair and Miss Celeste bounced over the threshold together, the writer Haugland flinging himself in after them.

Ulysses turned to assist those at the door. Mr Wates and the purser pulled themselves inside, ready to pull the sealable bulkhead doors shut securely behind them and keep out the rising tide of frothing seawater. There were only Harry Cheng and Mr Sin still to come through.

Cheng was now at the threshold, hair flat to his head, shirt and trousers soaked through. Mr Sin was only a few slippery feet behind him.

But there was something else in there with them now as well. A snaking tentacle, like some huge, snub-nosed sea-worm, wending its way towards them, writhing and flexing as if guided by a instinctive sentience all of its own. The Kraken was determined not to let its prey get away.

Someone screamed, having caught sight of the probing squid-limb. And in that fatal second, the hulking Chinaman, terror writ large across his blunt features, stopped and turned. With an uncoiling lash, quick as a striking cobra, the tentacle extended, curled precisely around Mr Sin's waist and legs and then, just as quickly, pulled back. The chinaman, an eye-popping look of terror on his face, was dragged into the surging flood, silvery bubbles escaping from his mouth in a silent scream. Then, there above them beyond the ruptured bubble of the Promenade, was the monster's dreadful fang-lined maw, gaping open, ready to receive the tasty morsel.

There was nothing anyone could do for him.

"Close the doors!" Captain McCormack ordered as the water lapped at the sill of the doorway and Harry Cheng hurled himself past the threshold.

The two officers did as their captain commanded, shutting out the sight of the glorious Promenade being swallowed by the ocean, shutting out the rush and roar of the hungry sea, shutting out the monster that would devour them all.

They also shut in the wailing of the terrified Constance Pennyroyal and her aunt, shut in the mumbled entreaties of a biologist to the God he had foresworn, shut in the frustrated raging of the shipping magnate as he bellowed at his wretched assistant who had sought to do nothing but save his sorry skin.

And so seventeen became sixteen.

CHAPTER THIRTEEN

Sea Dog's Tales

WITH THE BULKHEAD door to the Promenade Deck closed, the last chapter in the life of Mr Sin was closed with it.

Two were lost to them now. First Dexter Sylvester, with the catastrophe of the plummeting chandelier and now Mr Sin, Harry Cheng's right-hand man, taken by the beast. Two gone from the total party of eighteen survivors who had made it up until the moment when the ship touched rock bottom amidst the silt and skeletal remains of a million animals upon the ocean floor. They had thought things bad enough when they found their luxury cruise ship dropping into the fathomless depths like a stone, only at the time they had not realised that their greatest trials still stood ahead of them.

With the impossible sea monster tearing away the glass and steel latticework from the once magnificent Promenade Deck, the *Neptune* having settled into its new position – listing slightly to port and leaving the escapees with an uphill struggle to reach the stern of the ship – there was nothing for them to do except struggle on towards their original target destination.

And what a sorry and dishevelled lot they were, Ulysses found himself thinking. Wet, worn out and worried beyond belief, there wasn't a single VIP remaining that hadn't had all trappings of status and privilege stripped from them by the disaster that had them caught at its very heart. They all of them looked like they would not have appeared out of place amongst the ship's other passengers residing in Steerage.

Even Nimrod's appearance was not up to his usual standards: his grey butler's attire covered with dark damp patches from the unwanted attentions of the seawater. Ulysses himself was soaked through to the skin, after his dip in the drowning pool of the Grand Atrium, as was the noble John Schafer. The man, a good ten years younger than the eldest of the Quicksilver boys, had a permanent steeled expression on his face. Whether he maintained such composure because he wasn't allowing himself the possibility of considering the direness of their situation or whether he was concentrating so greatly on the well-being of his beloved that he dared not risk a second thought about what might become of them, Ulysses did not know.

And so they made their way onward through the stricken ship. Climbing ever upwards to reach the rear of the *Neptune* where they then hoped to negotiate a way down to the seemingly unattainable submersible bay. And from there, who knew what – considering the squidbeast's latest attack on the wrecked sub-liner.

Captain McCormack took the lead, rugged determination described in the lines of his face, spacing his men out through the body of the party to help maintain cohesion and make sure no one got left behind. A number of them were beginning to flag, the adrenalin rush that had set them all off with seemingly boundless stamina had ebbed. Miss Birkin in particular was showing signs of frailty, quite possibly exacerbated by the huge levels of stress she had been put under. Ulysses still couldn't shake the feeling that she was keeping a particularly close eye on him. Lady Denning, never one to make a fuss, was also beginning to show signs of exhaustion. She appeared to be limping on her left leg and did not protest when Major Horsley – himself puffing and blowing like a grumpy walrus – took her arm to steady her.

Miss Celeste had taken her place at Jonah Carcharodon's wheelchair once more, which seemed to be faring rather better than many of the party. And it was, once again, with reluctance that she accepted the slightest help from Ulysses and his manservant. So much so, in fact, that Ulysses felt guilty that he was forcing her to accept their assistance. Her knuckles whitened as they gripped the handles, as if making sure that her ungrateful employer made it to safety had become her raison d'être for keeping up the struggle herself.

The curious trio of Crichton, Haugland and Ogilvy now brought up the rear. The three men had seemed to be subconsciously drawn to one another, although Ulysses couldn't help feeling that there was something else that united them. It was the fact that they were each only concerned with looking out for number one.

Captain McCormack led them out of the shattered remains of a parade of boutiques and into a curiously angled – yet mercifully unflooded – access way of grille plates and twisted metal staircases. The rhythmic drip-drip-drip of water entered even here, the ringing of their footsteps and the inescapable groaning of the buckling hull were joined by another ominously mournful sound, that of Professor Crichton reciting poetry as if it were a dirge.

"Below the thunders of the upper deep, far far beneath in the abyssal sea," he intoned, as if he was reading a eulogy.

"For God's sake man!" Jonah Carcharodon called up the slanting stairwell from where Mr Wates was helping Ulysses and Nimrod carry him and his chair down the next short flight of steps. "As if things weren't bad enough, without us having to listen to you!"

"His ancient, dreamless, uninvaded sleep," Crichton went on.

"Please, Maxwell," – it was Lady Denning who took up the baton to call for the disheartening recital to stop – "now is neither the time nor the place. What's done is done."

"The Kraken sleepeth." The Professor stopped, a faraway look in his eyes, and certainly no indication that he had heard a word anyone else had said.

"What was that?" Constance Pennyroyal asked, apparently glad to have something to take her mind off the overwhelming stress she was suffering, rather than continually mulling over the likelihood of any of them getting out of there alive.

"Tennyson," Major Horsley replied.

"Indeed," Ulysses found himself adding distractedly, joining in the literary discussion. "The Kraken."

Reaching another landing and making the most of the opportunity to rest, if only for a moment, Ulysses set Carcharodon's chair down again.

"Wasn't that what you called that wee beastie that attacked us just now, Haugland?"

"The Kraken, you mean?" the Norwegian agreed. "It somehow... seemed appropriate."

"I couldn't agree more," Lady Denning added.

"Do tell us more. What is it? The Kraken I mean?" Ogilvy said twitchily.

"Kraken, Kroken, Krayken, they're all the same thing really," Haugland said.

"And what is that?"

Ogilvy was on edge. Ulysses wondered how long it was since he had been able to sneak his last fix.

"The Kraken is the legendary sea monster of Norse myth, although that particular name never appeared in the sagas. Instead it was called the hafgufa or the lyngbakr. The name Kraken comes from another

Scandinavian word krake, which refers to some unhealthy, unnatural animal; something twisted. The Kraken was said to dwell off the coasts of Norway and Iceland, a beast of gargantuan size. Some said it was as big as a floating island, a creature so large that it could pull even the biggest warship to the bottom of the sea without any trouble at all." Haugland was into his stride now, the natural storytelling abilities of the travel writer coming to the fore. "It is almost always described as having numerous, far-reaching tentacles and a soft pliable body like an octopus. And although it lived within the ocean depths, it would surface to hunt prey and supposedly attack small ships."

"It sounds horrid," Miss Birkin said, managing to sound indignant, as if such discussion was not appropriate for those of a delicate sensibility at this time.

"But, Miss Birkin, you have to remember it is only a legend, an exaggerated unreal creature, inspired by sightings of the much more timid, yet real, giant squid. At least I had thought it a legend, until now. In all my days travelling the world, I have never seen the like!"

"Was that thing that attacked us a giant squid? Was that some mythical monster?" Ogilvy railed. Unconquerable fear had taken the face of anger with the wretched doctor. "Was I hallucinating?"

"I wouldn't be surprised." Ulysses couldn't help himself.

"Why, you–"

"But I saw it too, and I know that I haven't put anything illicit or intoxicating into my body in almost twenty-four hours."

The damned doctor didn't know how to respond to such a blatant accusation.

"But then, maybe, neither have you, which would explain a lot as well."

A fearful hush descended over the party once again and another three flights were negotiated in silence. Pausing at the next landing Ulysses made note of the deck they were now on. Deck 7. Only another eight to go until they reached the bowels of the ship wherein lay the ever-elusive sub-dock, with its pressure gate and its means of escape to the outside world. They still might not make it to the surface alive, but if they could make it off the *Neptune* that should at least buy them a few more hours – unless the Kraken had other ideas.

"I don't know what it was," Captain McCormack said, disrupting the tense silence, "but that wasn't simply some overgrown cephalopod."

"You're a biologist," Dr Ogilvy said suddenly, almost challenging Professor Crichton, who looked as if he was trying to remain anonymous in the background. "And you, Lady Denning. What was that... thing?"

"I... I don't know," Crichton said, taking another long draw on what must have been his rapidly emptying hipflask.

"No. Nor I," Lady Denning said in a tone that broached no further discussion.

"But can't you take a guess?"

"I don't know what it was," Lady Denning said, her tone sharp enough to cut glass.

"Some... some kind of giant cephalopod," was all Crichton would offer.

"But what *kind* of sodding giant bloody cephalopod?" Ogilvy pressed. "I'm not an idiot, you know. What kind of cephalopod has jaws like that and an armoured shell?"

"The Kraken, it would appear," Nimrod offered bluntly. The doctor looked like he was about to make another challenge and then wilted under the intense sapphire-eyed stare Ulysses' manservant gave him.

"Perhaps it's something prehistoric? Something forgotten, like the coelacanth was for so many years," Miss Birkin piped up, finding her voice despite the fatigue she was feeling, the conspiracy theorist in her excited at the prospect of uncovering a genuine conspiracy herself.

"You're uncommonly quiet on this matter," Ulysses said, addressing the noticeably tight-lipped Carcharodon, "particularly for one usually so forthcoming with his own opinion."

"How in blazes would I know what that thing is?" he snarled back. "I'm no Hannibal Haniver, am I? I'm not a bloody naturalist!"

"It could be an aberration," John Schafer suggested, as he assisted both his fiancée and his soon to be aunt-in-law ever onward, down the uncomfortably angled stairwell, making sure that they did not slip on the wet metal steps. "Some mutation of a better known genus created by the unchecked industrial pollution that is such a blight on our world."

"Careful, Schafer," Ulysses warned, with a wry smile. "You're in danger of sounding like a fully paid up member of the Darwinian Dawn."

"Or," Captain McCormack said darkly, adding his own opinion to the discussion, "could it have been specifically engineered this way? Is it, in reality, a living weapon of war?"

"Preposterous!" Carcharodon suddenly butted in, driven to finally voice his own opinion by McCormack's patently hare-brained suggestion, nailing his colours to the mast in the debate regarding the nature of the beast.

"What do you mean, Captain?" Constance asked, her own latent curiosity piqued. 'How can it have been engin–"

"Ah, here we are!" Major Horsley announced with gusto as they reached the bottom of the stairs, before Constance could finish. "Engine rooms, don't you know! That's the way we want to go, isn't it, McCormack, what?"

"That was the plan," McCormack said.

"We hope," Ulysses cautioned.

Talk of the nature of the beast ceased as all members of the party were filled with nervous anticipation at the prospect of entering the engine halls of the *Neptune*. What little information they had been given about this area of the ship was that some of the great engine chambers were flooded, or on fire, or God alone knew what.

Captain McCormack paused before the steel bulkhead door. It would be a risk venturing inside, but there was really no alternative. There was no going back now.

"Well, here goes nothing," he said as Wates and the Purser joined him in cranking the wheel to open the door. The seal popped open with nothing more dramatic than a hiss of air which smelt of charcoal and seaweed; an indication perhaps of what they might find beyond.

Looking like a sorry, rag-tag band of refugees rather than the great and the good, the cream of the elite society of Magna Britannia trudged through into the echoing engine halls. The way Captain McCormack led them through the shadowy halls they encountered neither fire nor flood until, before too long, they came to another door.

"It's through here," McCormack said, as he and Ulysses took hold of the door-wheel.

A murmur of excitement passed through the party. Against all the odds it looked as if they were actually going to make it. Even Ulysses allowed himself a brief internal whoop of delight.

And then – inevitably just when everything was going so well, when it looked as though they might actually all make it out of this mess – that old unwelcome guest, Ulysses' precognisant sense, flared in the back of his brain once more.

With an iron-wrenching groan, like the dying cry of some giant whale, the entire engine chamber listed to port. The survivors should have been used to such lurches and shifting movements of the ship by now, only this time the *Neptune* didn't stop until it was lying flat on its side as the distribution of sea-water within it caused it to re-settle on the edge of the trench.

The group fell sideways, crashing into the network of pipes running up the walls. People were injured, bruises, gashes and grazes appearing where before there had been none, their blood painting them, their clothes and the enamel white walls scarlet.

Just when it had all been going so well.

And, that was when the sea rushed in after them, as if it had been pursuing them ever since the Promenade Deck and the Grand Atrium before that, determined not to let them escape briny oblivion any longer. And this time, it looked like the sea might just get its way.

With shouted guidance from McCormack and his men, and Ulysses' own rallying cries of encouragement, the escapees began to scale the floor, which now formed a climbing wall of scantly fissured plating before them, a full ninety degrees to perpendicular. Mr Wates and the Purser had seen fit to cling onto the bulkhead door-wheel and hung there, securing their own position, bracing themselves against pipes and buttresses as they battled to open the door. But as well as fighting time and the door clamps reluctance to shift, they were also fighting gravity. The door opened away from them, which now meant it opened upwards.

The water level was rising fast. Schafer struggled to help Miss Birkin and his precious Constance to secure holds within the new 'wall', whilst it took all the efforts of Nimrod, Ulysses and Thor Haugland to stop the chair-bound Jonah Carcharodon being lost below the waves lapping around the rapidly filling bucket of the engine hall.

But they struggled on, every man and woman of them, the still-locked door in tangible reach. And still the crewmen struggled with the wheel-lock and still it would not turn, and still the waters rose, until they were all of them bobbing upon the surge, the air space lessening with every passing second, forced together before the door, which remained stubbornly, cruelly shut.

When all seemed lost, with a loud grating screech the wheel turned, the locking clamps sprang open, the door opened upwards, pulling free of the wet grip of Mr Wates and the Purser, and a hand reached down to them.

A gruff voice called down after it, over the bubbling surge of the water filling the engine hall, "Take my hand if you want to live!"

CHAPTER FOURTEEN

Finding Nemo

A GREASE-BLACK SWEATY hand reached for Ulysses, and he gladly took it in his own. His shoulder protested as he was pulled sharply upwards, but the elation he felt at being rescued helped him put aside the pain, compartmentalising it for later when he might actually have time to deal with it.

Carcharodon was already through, seawater running from his chair onto what must have previously been the wall of the dock. When the last of them were through the bulkhead door was allowed to drop shut, before the rising water bubbled through, and the wheel spun tight again.

The VIPs stood around him – or in the case of Carcharodon sat there – in a nervously fidgeting huddle, every one of them a bedraggled wretch. They looked like men and women who had once had everything but who now had nothing – thanks to the sinking of the *Neptune* and the predations of the Kraken – which was precisely what they were.

Captain McCormack, Mr Wates and the purser, however, were behaving exactly like men whose position aboard ship had suddenly been dramatically elevated. They were the ones whose status had risen as the disaster unfolded. It was they who were now in control, in command, responsible for the lives of those very wretches arrayed before them, awaiting their instructions.

"Selby!" McCormack exclaimed, throwing his arms around a short, oil-black grease-monkey of an engineer. It had been this man's hand that had appeared like God's saving hand from heaven to lead them to a salvation of sorts. "I can honestly say that I have never been so pleased to see you in all my life!"

"Mac, you old bugger! I thought everyone else was dead! Clements and Swann and meself were making ready to leave when this happened." He indicated the dock around them. "Why didn't you try to contact us down here?"

"Ship-wide comms went down," Mr Wates explained, shaking Clements furiously by the hand. "But then, you must have known that yourselves."

"We suspected it but couldn't test our theory as when the ship went down, after the engines cut out and then after..." Selby was lost for words.

"The attack," McCormack filled in for him.

"What was it?" the engineer asked, a manic gleam in his eye.

"It was a..." Now it was the captain who was lost for words. "It would take some explaining. I'll fill you in. Just finish telling me your side of the story."

"Well, whatever it was that happened after that, after the attack, we knew we were in trouble when engine three started to flood and both two and four caught fire." A faraway look entered the engineer's eyes as if he were casting his mind back years, even though the events he was relating had only taken place a matter of hours before. "I tried to get the men out as quickly as I could, but the fires spread so quickly..."

"So many died," one of Selby's fellows muttered half to himself. "It was the fire at first, and then the smoke." He seemed to cough involuntarily at this recollection. "It did for so many of them."

"It was only the three of us that made it down here and shut ourselves in," Selby went on. "But in all the chaos and confusion, when the ship was being knocked about, our comms panel got damaged. We couldn't call out and only heard static back over the thing. We couldn't even get through to the AI. We dared not get back out; we didn't know how far the fires had spread."

"We had to assume the worst," one of the younger soot-smeared men explained, his face pale beneath the covering of grime.

"Swann's right," Selby took over again. "Our only course of action was to get off this ship, and the only way of doing that was on board one of those." He pointed at the two submersible vehicles bobbing up and down on the water lapping at the edges of the up-ended dock-chamber.

It was only now that he had had time to come to terms with the curious perpendicularity of the sub-dock that Ulysses could make sense of its cantilevered layout. With the *Neptune* now lying fully to port, everything inside the docking chamber was at ninety degrees to how it should have been.

Ulysses realised that before the wrecking of the *Neptune*, the *Ahab* and the *Nemo* must have been floating upon a rectangular pool, surrounded by all the engineering resources needed to maintain the two submersible vehicles. At the bottom of the pool had lain the dock's pressure gate which, once opened, would allow the subs to emerge from the bottom of the ship. Ulysses could see it now because half of it was free of the water, with the disconcerting tilting of the sub-liner, the keels of the two subs were scraping against what had, moments before, been the wall of the dock.

There was a curious frame to what had now become the left-hand wall of the twisted dock, which Ulysses realised had been a balcony viewing area above the docking pool. That same balcony now helped contain the displaced water, the *Ahab* and the *Nemo* bumping against the edge of it close by. All manner of debris and detritus – from aqua-lungs and oxyacetylene torches to maintenance materials and spare air tanks – littered the space. And now that Ulysses looked more closely at the three surviving engineers, amidst all the dirt and sooty burns he could also see glistening open wounds on their arms, hands and heads. He wondered how close they had come to losing their lives when the *Neptune* had tipped over and they found themselves caught beneath an avalanche of falling equipment, plenty of it heavy enough and hard edged enough to kill them.

"So what have you been doing down here all this time, since," McCormack made an expansive gesture with both his arms, "all this happened?"

"At first?" Selby said, the grease-monkey's eyes glazing as he called to mind every last detail of that appalling moment when the ship went down. "We waited, we recuperated, we hoped we might hear word from somewhere else on the ship – the Bridge at least – but there was nothing. Once we realised we couldn't send a message out and having heard nothing coming in, we decided that escape was a viable avenue to explore. We weren't going to trust to fate, in the hope that rescue crews might be on the way."

Captain McCormack nodded sagely.

"You know what it's like, Mac, if we're going to be honest with each other. Even if Neptune, or anyone else for that matter, got a distress signal out before we went down and comms went offline, it would take days for the nearest ship to reach us and then they'd have to find us down here."

The huddle of dishevelled VIPs were staring, unashamedly listening in on the interchange between the captain and his chief engineer, their tired faces bearing expressions of zombie-slack horror, the truth of their situation becoming ever more painfully apparent. If there were any who had still been labouring under the expectation that they were about to be rescued by some outside agency, those slim hopes were now cruelly dashed on the rocks of cold reality.

"And that's, like I say, if a Mayday signal had ever been sent in the first place.

"And it didn't seem likely that we would be sitting around down here for days until someone kindly knocked on the door and let us out," Selby went on. "So me and the lads got on with sorting out a way off this bloody death ship, pardon my French," he added, eyes darting over the faces of the women ranged before him, his cheeks reddening in embarrassment beneath the grime.

"It is pardoned," Lady Denning said caustically.

"After the viciousness of the attack – yeah, that makes sense now," Selby pondered aloud, "we had to check both the *Nemo* and the *Ahab* over, to make sure nothing crucial had been damaged. It was a bastard of an assault after all. Then we had to make sure they going to be up to making a journey at these depths. And there were only three of us to do it."

"So which one's sea-worthy?" Carcharodon asked, trying to regain some sense of authority whilst sitting damply within his waterlogged chair, every part of him soaked to the skin.

"They both are, sir. We made sure of it, just in case something else should happen to one of them. We were just getting ready to leave when, well, this happened." He took in the dock again.

"And you reckon both of them could still be piloted out of here?" McCormack asked.

"Yes, Captain, yes I do."

"But what about the pressure gate?" Mr Wates queried, pointing at partially exposed round steel doors revealed by the dislocation of the space around them.

"Clements?" Selby said, calling on the support of another of the surviving trio of engineers, "you're the one who's been checking out that side of things."

"As far as we can tell there's no damage. We should still be able to access it remotely from on board the *Ahab*," Clements said, a little too sheepishly for Ulysses' liking.

"Of course," Selby said, "soon as those gates open this place is going to flood completely, within seconds. There won't be any coming back after that."

"That line was crossed long ago." Cheng was the one to point that fact out to all of them, and Ulysses found himself nodding in agreement. Although it was the truth, it didn't make those of a weaker disposition among the party of survivors feel any better.

"So, chaps, the long and the short of it," Major Horsley piped up, "is we load up these tubs, blow the bally doors off and skiddadle across to this underwater science lab thingy before the ruddy Kraken has us all for breakfast. Right?"

"Um, that about sums it up, Major," McCormack confirmed.

"There's a base?" Selby said, a quizzical look on his face.

"Never mind that," Swann said, looking perturbed. "He said there was a Kraken."

"There's a fair bit to fill you in on, later." The captain's tone implied that recriminations and accusations of keeping information from his crew would not be tolerated.

"Right you are, Mac," the chief engineer sighed, knowing his captain well enough to know not to challenge him on this. But he still had his little dig: "Let's just hope there'll still be a later. I take it we're not heading for the surface then?"

"No, not a good idea."

"Not unless you want to become squid-bait," Ogilvy muttered.

"So, what are we waiting for?" Carcharodon spoke up gruffly.

"Yes, sir," said Captain McCormack, sounding suddenly weary again. "It's going to be risky, but not as risky as going head-to-head with that thing out there."

"Are we sure this is the best course of action?" Everyone turned to look at Miss Birkin who had had the confidence to challenge the accepted view of the majority.

"Miss Birkin," the captain began, "we have all now seen, first hand, what that creature can do and we already know the threat it poses to our survival."

There were murmurs from some of the others in the party. Clearly, Miss Birkin was not alone in harbouring doubts about the planned course of action.

"But surely, on board one of these" – now it was the Norwegian's turn to speak up – "we could outrun a monster that size?"

"Are you sure?" Schafer threw back. "Didn't you see how quickly it closed on us on the Promenade Deck?"

"Yes, but something living at these depths wouldn't survive nearer the surface, surely? We wouldn't have to go very far to leave it behind."

"I wouldn't want to bet against those tentacles making a grab for us, sir," Nimrod said with something approaching calm detachment.

"Yes, but we still have to travel the distance from where the *Neptune* lies now to the base, and hope that we can gain access. Surely the distance we would have to travel upwards to get away from the Kraken would be comparable. The initial risk would probably be equal but then we would be heading back to the surface and long-term safety, not remaining trapped down here with that thing."

"It could be waiting for us, out there, right now," Constance declared fearfully, speaking up boldly in support of her fiancé.

"Now that," said Ulysses, "is a good point."

"There is another way, you know? A way we can get out of this little pickle we seem to have got ourselves into," the Major announced cutting through the dissenting voices, a wicked glint in his eye behind his monocle.

"And what's that, Major?" Carcharodon asked, sounding genuinely interested with no suggestion of sarcasm.

"We could actively hunt the blighter down!"

"Are you serious?" Carcharodon riled, as if disappointed at having trusted the Major to come up with an effective alternative solution.

"But of course I am. I'm sure there's enough of what we'd need around here to rig these beauties out to turn them into mini strike cruisers or even to turn one of them into an overgrown torpedo."

The escapees stared back at the Major with stunned expressions on their faces. Incredibly, apparently oblivious to their disbelief and incredulity, he went on with expounding his scheme.

"We take it out via remote control or some such clever technical wizardry – I'm sure you fellows could come up with something," he said, addressing the chief engineer, "and then we'd have all the time in the world to pootle back up to the surface and be there in time for tiffin."

"Give me strength," McCormack muttered.

"But I've hunted these beasties before."

"Have you really, Major?" McCormack looked around the group and, judging the party's mood better than Horsley, he took a bold step. "We need to act quickly or all such discussions are going to prove merely academic. All those in favour of taking the subs across to the base *Neptune* found for us?"

Loyal to their captain, the purser and Mr Wates shot up their hands straight away, as did Ulysses. Following his master's example, Nimrod also raised a hand. Anxiously assessing how their fellows might vote, others among the party slowly raised their hands – Carcharodon, the silent Miss Celeste, John Schafer and Constance Pennyroyal, Lady Denning and a seemingly resigned Professor Crichton.

"Votes for" – McCormack took a quick count – "eleven. Those in favour of attempting to return to the surface?"

Despite the obvious way the poll was already going, Miss Birkin stubbornly raised her hand, along with Haugland and the twitchy Dr Ogilvy. Ulysses noticed Selby and his compatriots shooting each other meaningful glances but none of them had the confidence to vote against the wishes of their captain, and hence apparently abstained.

"Three. Anyone in support of the Major's idea?"

Major Horsley boldly put up his own hand, but was still the only one who thought taking the beast on head-to-head was a sensible idea. "Damn you all, you lily-livered cowards," he grumbled, cheeks and nose reddening in frustration.

Ulysses noticed that four had abstained from giving an opinion: Selby, Swann, Clements, and the taciturn Harry Cheng.

What's your game? he found himself wondering as he looked upon the narrow-eyed Chinaman.

"So the plan remains the same," the captain said indignantly, his tone barely hiding the fact that he believed they had done nothing more than waste precious time by even having such a worthless debate. "We take the subs out to the base."

"Agreed," Ulysses said, "although Miss Pennyroyal raised a good point."

"I-I did?" The young woman sounded as surprised as anyone at this revelation.

"Indeed. Everything we have seen so far regarding the beast suggests that it is actively hunting us, so we'll still be taking a big chance – possibly too big a risk if you ask me – if we attempt anything more than the shortest journey. As soon as we blow the pressure gate it's going to be on to us."

"Damn it, Quicksilver, I didn't have you down for a paranoid bugger!" Major Horsley gasped, making his own little retaliation against all those who had pooh-poohed his idea. "I've never heard such rubbish!"

"Paranoia is it, Major?"

"He could be right, Marmaduke," Lady Denning said. Ulysses couldn't help being a little surprised at hearing the biologist speak up in his defence, against the Major.

"Go on," Carcharodon said, suddenly prepared to listen to all and every reasoned opinion if it would get them – or rather him – out of this mess.

"If we're going to avoid becoming just another course on the menu at the Calamari's Revenge, what we need is a distraction."

"To give us a head start, you mean," Chief Engineer Selby said, a grin forming on his pug-face to match that now being sported by the dandy adventurer.

"Indeed."

The grin spread wider across Selby's face, revealing crooked nubs of teeth.

"Leave it to me!"

CHAPTER FIFTEEN

The Abyss

IT DIDN'T SEEM that important a matter to Ulysses which of the two submersibles the individual escapees should board, but it appeared that Jonah Carcharodon was seizing the opportunity to recover some of his flagging self-confidence. Having been so helpless – nay, useless to the point of being an utter nuisance – during their flight through the wrecked liner, he seemed to feel the need to justify his existence again, and so had put himself in charge of group selection. Ulysses wondered if, as a child, the young Jonah had always been the one left to last when others were picking teams on the rugger field.

"McCormack, I want you on board the *Ahab* with me."

"Yes, sir." The captain sounded weary of his employer's attitude but wasn't about to do anything disloyal and challenge him now.

"I want Selby too. One of the others can man the helm of the *Nemo*."

"Yes, sir. Mr Wates, if you would be so kind as to see the *Nemo* out."

"Yes, captain."

"And Mr Swann, if you would go with him, to provide technical support?"

"Aye aye, cap'n," the more gangly of the two remaining engineers said, attempting what Ulysses took to be a smart salute.

"Mr Quicksilver, if you and your manservant could join them on board the *Nemo* then I would know that each team had at least one person on board who knew what they were doing, just in case we somehow become separated."

"Indeed, captain, very wise." Ulysses consented.

"Lady Denning, Major Horsley, Professor Crichton," Carcharodon said. "I would consider it an honour if you would join me on board the *Ahab*."

Just for the briefest moment Ulysses thought he saw something pass between the magnate and the other three: some dark look, pregnant with meaning, but one which he was unable to determine.

"Captain, the *Ahab* needs another crewman, it being the bigger boat. There's more to keep an eye on," Selby warned.

"Very well, Selby, Mr Clements comes with us as well, and your purser."

The two new recruits to the *Ahab's* crew nodded.

"Miss Birkin, Miss Pennyroyal, Mr Schafer, Mr Haugland, Dr Ogilvy and Mr Cheng. You will all travel on board the *Nemo*." It wasn't a request.

"I'm not going on that sub!" Miss Birkin declared in something approaching an hysterical shriek. "I'm going to travel with you, Mr Carcharodon, on board the *Ahab*, and if you've got any sense, Constance my dear, you'll come with me."

The ageing spinster was making no bones of the fact that she was looking at Ulysses as she made her demands.

"Why, Miss Birkin," he said with a sneer, "a chap could get the idea that you don't like me."

"Constance? Are you going to see sense and come with me, young lady?" Miss Birkin pressed.

"Aunt you go where you like," her niece replied, sounding like she had had enough of being bossed around by the nagging old woman, "but John and I are staying put."

Her maiden aunt looked like she was about to commence a tirade, but Carcharodon cut in before she had finishing drawing breath. "That's settled then. Are we ready to go now? Or are we going to wait around here until hell or high water does for us?"

It went without saying that Carcharodon intended that Miss Celeste would travel with him. And indeed it did go unsaid, so unimportant seemed the most important person in his life to the arrogant old sod.

Led by the *Neptune's* evacuating crew, the two groups moved towards their respective vessels.

"Look, why don't we all just travel in the one vessel?" Thor Haugland asked, hanging back.

Selby looked meaningfully at the captain, who glowered back at him. "Well, Mac?" the engineer challenged, testing his trusted relationship with the captain to the limit.

"It increases the odds of at least some of us getting out of here alive. It improves our chances of survival."

"What?" Schafer exclaimed, indignant. "You would play the odds with our lives?"

"We're all gambling with our lives, every step of the way," Ulysses pointed out with a heavy heart.

"Ulysses, you can't tell me that you're happy with this course of action," Schafer exclaimed in utter amazement, and clutching Constance's hands so tightly in his that his knuckles turned white.

"I'm afraid I do. Think about it for a moment, John. If we all bundle into just one of these tubs, if something goes wrong, it's over, for all of us. If a hull plate cracks under pressure, or if the beastie catches up with us, it's over."

John Schafer returned Ulysses honest open-eyed expression with an intense grimace of his own as he tried to reconcile all manner of emotions that were in turmoil beneath his ever so staid façade. And he had maintained it so well, without questioning any of the decisions made so far, and yet he now appeared to be on the verge of crumbling at this crucial time.

"However," Ulysses went on, "with two crates out there, if one fails, half survive. If the Kraken comes after us there are two targets to confuse it, meaning it's more likely all of us will make it to safety before it can seize either one of the subs."

"And Selby's ensured that there are a couple of little surprises for the wee beastie, should it come a-hunting," McCormack smiled.

"That sounds more like it," Major Horsley said. "What have you got in mind?"

"Wait and see, Major. Wait and see," the chief engineer said with a look of sheer joy on his face. "Let's put it this way. When it comes to the *Neptune*, if I can't keep her, no one can!"

Carcharodon frowned disapprovingly at this bold declaration by the grease-monkey.

"So," McCormack tried again, raising his voice, "time is, as they say, of the essence, ladies and gentlemen, so if we wouldn't mind, I think it's time we boarded our vessels and got the hell out of here."

What little fight there had been left in any of them all used up, the two groups obediently filed up the gangways and followed the officers on board the *Ahab* and the *Nemo*.

Having been the one to point out the need for urgency in their departure, it was Captain McCormack, however, who left it to the last possible second to leave the sub-dock, board the *Ahab* and evacuate the ship. He liked to think that he had been a good captain to the *Neptune* and had even gone down with his ship, when the worst imaginable happened. And he still didn't fully understand what had happened or who had sabotaged his vessel, or who would have wanted to.

But he knew that the time had finally come when he simply had to leave the *Neptune* to her fate. To stay would be suicide – if honourable suicide at that – and he had a responsibility beyond simply that towards his ship now. If there was a chance that any of the *Neptune's* erstwhile passengers could still make it off the wreck alive, before it was claimed by the fathomless depths of the Marianas Trench, then he should be there, at their head, leading from the front.

So it was that he turned for one last time at the top of the gangplank, before the conning tower of the *Ahab*, and straightening smartly – despite the dishevelled state of his uniform after the unwanted attentions of fire and flood – threw a salute.

"Goodbye, old girl," he said – and was it seawater or salt water of an altogether different kind that glistened in the corner of his eye? – before turning back and taking his last few steps to the conning tower hatch.

"So," said Ulysses, approaching Mr Wates and his number two, the engineer Swann, at the control console in the prow of the *Nemo*, "what's this distraction Selby's arranged?"

"Well, sir, there's actually two of them. Or rather, it's in two stages," Wates said, continuing to flick switches and check dials on the brass-finished control panel in front of him.

"And stage one is? Look, you can tell me. There's no one else listening," Ulysses said in a jokily conspiratorial manner. He glanced over his shoulder. The rest of them – John, Constance, Haugland, Cheng, Ogilvy and Nimrod – were all safely ensconced within the *Nemo*, squeezed into the leather upholstered seats in the main cabin behind the cockpit of the submersible.

"If you watch, sir, you'll see for yourself."

Ulysses peered out of the steel and glass bubble of the *Nemo*. All he could see was the water already in the dock lapping halfway up the hemispherical window and the partially exposed pressure gate beyond.

There was the crackle of static and then a voice came to them over the submersible's radio. "*Ahab* to *Nemo*. Are you receiving me, over?" It was Chief Engineer Selby's voice.

"Receiving you loud and clear, *Ahab*," Wates replied. "Ready to go when you are, over." He turned to Ulysses. "You're going to need to take a seat, Mr Quicksilver, sir."

"Very well," said Ulysses, taking the third seat in the cockpit behind and between those occupied by Wates and Swann.

"Blowing pressure gate now, over," came Selby's crackling voice again.

For a moment nothing happened as Ulysses stared at the solidly shut reinforced circular steel doors anchored in the bottom of the *Neptune's* hull. Then suddenly a throbbing sub-sonic boom rumbled through the bodywork of the *Nemo* and Ulysses saw the two halves of the gate retract into the hull and the sea surge in, like some ravenous feral beast, intent on devouring the two tiny submersibles.

But the *Ahab* and the *Nemo* remained secure within the modified moorings that kept the two craft from bashing into one another, as the chill abyssal waters swirled into the sub-dock.

Ulysses took in the new vista he could now see through the front of the sub. The sub-dock had become dark and miasmic, objects tossed about by the sea-surge bobbing around them and bumping into the hull with dull, disconcerting clangs. In fact, there wasn't much to see beyond the open pressure gate until Swann activated the *Nemo's* stabbing searchlights – and even then, all they could really see was the silty, fissured floor of the seabed and nothing beyond but more of the same all-consuming darkness.

The tannoy buzzed again. This time Selby was heard to say: "Lure away, over."

Ulysses was aware of a muffled thrumming sound, like that of a small engine, and a moment later a metal cylinder buzzed past the viewing port and out of the open gate, its small corkscrew propeller distorting the water behind it so that it was if he were viewing it through a rippling heat-haze.

So that was Selby's plan. One of the unmanned search and rescue drones carried by the sub-liner, sent out first to lure in the Kraken and then keep the monster away from the fleeing lifeboat submersibles.

As the drone and its trail of propeller-wash was swallowed up by the dark ocean depths, the louder, throbbing engines of the *Ahab* started up, rocking the *Nemo* in its makeshift bay beside the larger vessel, and Carcharodon's personal escape craft powered out after the drone through the gaping hole in the bottom of the *Neptune*.

"*Ahab* away, over."

"Roger that," their own pilot replied, talking into a speaking tube as he held down the broadcast switch, and then eased up on the stick. The *Nemo*, its own engines thrumming now, disengaged its anchor cables and glided out after the *Ahab*.

"You said Selby's surprise came in two parts," Ulysses said, as the sub eased its way out into the abyss beyond.

"Yes, I did," Wates said, concentrating on what he could make out through the miasmal gloom beyond the glass and steel bubble in front of them.

"So, if the drone was the aperitif, what's the main course?"

* * *

GLIDING OUT OF the darkness, its coming heralded by the blue glow of its own lure, the monster slid towards the stricken ship once more, a thousand finely-attuned nerve-sensor-cells detecting movement coming from the grounded vessel.

The Kraken moved with all the grace and speed of something much smaller but with the unstoppable force and singularity of purpose of something primal and monstrous. Unusually regular pulsations in the slow-moving currents around it teased at tentacles and vibration sensors along its dorsal line. The throbbing, thrumming sensation was getting closer, as the creature and its target closed on a mutual collision course. Then, only a few hundred yards from the prone ship, the Kraken attacked.

A grabbing tentacle whipped out as adapted spiracles in its softer body parts launched it forwards with something akin to a propulsion boost. Dense suckers seized the object, pulling it violently from its course, through the water, and before its brain had even begun to process what the object was, the Kraken had drawn it into its mouth, devil-fish fangs closing around it, piercing the metal body, crushing the device. With one gulp, half of the drone was sucked down sharply into the creature's gullet and, with a snap, the rest of it soon followed.

But in the moment following its attack, the Kraken sensed more thrumming engines, the vibrations sending it into a frenzy, setting in on course to hunt and kill once more. Side fins rippling, the monstrous squid-thing rejoined its intercept course with the ship.

Its adapted brain could tell now that there were two more objects moving away from the hulk of the sunken ship. The Kraken moved in behind, using the sub-liner to shield its own approach from its target. With primal cunning it slipped over the hull of the craft, almost hugging the body of the liner to keep it hidden from its prey for as long as possible.

And then it was slipping over the stern section of the vessel, the two tiny submersible craft chugging away, their engines thrumming through the water ahead of it.

Easy pickings.

THERE WAS NOT one explosion but a series of detonations, a cascade of sub-sonic booms, muffled by the fluid ocean depths. They rocked the two fleeing subs, carrying them forward on a bow-wave through the roiling hydropelagic turmoil now consuming the abyss, as if the ocean was suddenly suffering a seizure, an underwater seaquake having rocked the depths.

"Ah, I see!" Ulysses said over the cries and shouts of alarm coming from the rest of the *Nemo's* passengers. Those didn't concern him. What did concern him were the subsequent creaking groans which seemed to possess the tiny submersible. Had the detonation of the *Neptune's* overloaded engines damaged the *Nemo* as well, putting yet more undue pressure on the already overburdened sub?

The next few minutes would answer that question, as they continued on the last leg of their journey to the submerged base, protruding from a rocky outcrop at the edge of the trench ahead of them.

"Yes, well done, Selby!" Mr Wates practically shouted in delight, punching the air. "Rigging the engines to overload and explode just when we needed them to was never going to be an exact science, not given the time and the circumstances, but the old bugger's only gone and done it!"

Behind them the *Neptune* and the Kraken were consumed by a cloud of broiling bubbles, silt thrown up from the seabed and debris from the massive, destroyed Rolls Royce engines. Then the prow emerged from the debris cloud – as obscuring as ink poured into water – swinging round as if to follow the escaping submersibles, as the *Neptune* shifted on the edge of the trench again, rocked by the rapid series of explosions.

Ulysses wanted to give his own whoop of joy, but had they really done it? Were they really free of the threat of the beast? Had Selby really managed to fluke it? Had he really killed the Kraken?

Awareness flared. And then he knew that they hadn't managed any such thing, even before the silt cloud seen clearing in the rear viewing port revealed the truth. Tentacles first, then that terrible maw and curious armoured squid-body coming after it, the Kraken emerged from the devastation, as far as Ulysses could see, with barely a mark on it. It hung there for a moment in the gloom, an awe-inspiring great grey-green leviathan of a beast. Then, having relocated its target, it surged towards the trailing *Nemo*. And Ulysses was sure that the look in its massive jelly eyes spoke of unleashed primal fury.

"BUT WE HAVE to go back, man! There are people on board!" Major Horsley bellowed, nose to nose with the captain. "I can't simply stand by and watch this happen all over again!"

"I know there are Major, but there's nothing we can do. It would be pointless to turn back now."

"Pointless? I didn't take you for a heartless bastard, McCormack, not after all we've been through so far." The red-faced Major was virtually screaming now, as if he were back on the parade ground or on the front line again, a platoon of wet-behind-the-ears recruits under his command. "And I didn't take you for a coward either!"

"Sit down, Major!" Carcharodon ordered, but Horsley was having none of it.

"You!" he boiled. "It doesn't surprise me coming from a self-serving, arrogant, egocentric bastard like you, but I thought the captain here was a man of decency and honour. Turn this tub around, right now! We've got to help them!"

"And how do you suggest we do that?" McCormack asked calmly.

The Major's blustering faltered at this point. "I... I..."

"You heard him!" Carcharodon snarled. "You saw what happened. We all did. That explosion should have killed it, but it came out the other side practically unscathed."

"I hate to say it but the *Nemo* is already doomed," the captain said, matter-of-factly, "and if we go back we'll simply be going to our deaths. I'm sorry, but there's nothing more we can do."

"Nothing except pray," Miss Birkin said through the agonising sobs now wracking her body as she thought of the niece she had left behind, poor innocent Constance whom it had been her duty to protect on this voyage of the damned.

"Then pray," the captain said. "Pray with all your heart and pray that their sacrifice might not be for naught, that through it we might be saved."

Almost as one, those survivors of the disaster gathered together within the *Ahab* watched, with appalled fascination, fearful for their own well-being, as the monster, all reaching tentacles and gaping fangs, closed on the *Nemo*, reaching for it hungrily, with hate in its eyes.

Captain McCormack was right. There was nothing they could do – except pray.

CHAPTER SIXTEEN

The Relict

SUDDENLY THERE WAS nothing else they could do, nothing else that he – Ulysses Quicksilver, hero of the Empire and dandy adventurer, who had survived more than his fair share of close scrapes with death, who had turned things round at the last minute when everything seemed to be on the brink of collapse on dozens of occasions – could do.

They say that when a man faces death, his life flashes before his eyes. But for Quicksilver, as he gazed into the oblivion of the Kraken's gaping maw, he found himself reliving all those occasions when death had tried to come for him in the past. He saw the Black Mamba's evil grinning face, mere inches from his, as they plummeted towards the ice-hard peaks of the Himalayas. He saw the liquefying features of the fish-thing, felt its scaly skin grind beneath his fingers, as the incendiary fires spread throughout the flooded underground tunnels. He felt the wind whistling through his hair as he dropped towards the bellowing Megasaur rampaging through Trafalgar Square below him. He saw the howling locomotive thundering towards him down the track. He saw the scarred, blind in one eye lion as it prepared to pounce. He saw the indescribable thing emerging from the sludge and seaweed as the waves lapped at the sandy shore, his feet sinking into the sodden sand, and heard its blood-curdling cry again.

And then he saw nothing but the widening jaws of the monster, uncoiling tentacles reaching for the *Nemo*, escape impossible now, even as their pilot willed more speed from the chugging sub, Constance praying out loud for salvation, the wrung-out doctor humming in a continual monotone to himself.

A shadow suddenly passed across the viewing port at the rear of the sub that blotted out Ulysses' view of the closing Kraken completely. Then it passed and the horror was still there, so close now that Ulysses felt he could smell the squid-beast's rancid dead-fish breath. And then, between the writhing limbs of the beast, Ulysses saw something else moving out there in the sea-gloom.

Dark shapes darted out of the abyssal darkness, dark finned shapes, and then the Kraken's pursuit abruptly slowed as it was buffeted to the port side and disappeared from Ulysses' restricted view.

"What the hell was that?" he gasped.

"What's that?" Swann asked from the co-pilot's seat in front. "Are we not dead yet?"

"It would appear not," Ulysses replied, as if half in a dream.

"Well thank Neptune for that," said Wates, knuckles white around the control column, a look of grim determination etched into the lines of his face. "Then we could still make it."

Ulysses peered through the porthole behind him, the others on board – silenced by the fear of what was about to happen to them – doing the same, searching for any sign of the squid-monster. Although the thought of catching sight of the Kraken again doubtless scared the life out of them, not knowing where the creature had disappeared to was, for the time being, that much worse.

There was the *Neptune*, twisted around so that even more of its superstructure hung over the precipice, its hind-section completely destroyed by the detonation of the engines. There surely couldn't be anyone left alive on board now, not one single space within free of the sea. What had once – and not so long ago at that – been the most fabulous submersible cruise liner in the world had now become nothing more than a watery coffin for the thousands of paying guests who had signed up to join the *Neptune's* inaugural voyage around the world. But of the beast that was hunting them, or the dark shapes that appeared to have driven it away, there was no sign.

Ulysses dared turn his attention back to the main viewing bubble at the tip of the *Nemo* and gasped in amazement.

There, not one hundred yards ahead of them, the *Ahab* was making its final approach to the underwater sanctuary the Neptune AI had promised them was out here. And what a sight it was to behold.

The structure of the base was not unlike a cowry shell, although rather than calcite and mother-of-pearl, its builders had favoured reinforced glass and steel. The central, flattened dome was connected by the twisting half-cylinders of tunnels to other outlying domes. These in turn were networked together by yet more, smaller tunnels. Seen from above it must have had an outline not unlike that of an octopus with its tentacles intertwining around it. However, Ulysses soon realised that the base would have been difficult to spot from above unless a vessel was already practically right on top of it. It had been constructed in the shadow of a massive overhang, projecting from the solid wall of rock which continued to rise up beyond it, possibly right to the surface so many thousands of feet above.

It truly was a wonder to behold, and a fortuitous one at that. But more importantly it was to be their sanctuary, a place where they could wait out this nightmare until real help came. It was more delightful to the eye now, to Ulysses' mind at least, than the sculpted coral gardens of Pacifica.

Where the construction of the base differed from that of undersea cities such as Pacifica, however, was in its almost exclusive use of steel and only a little glass, allowing those inside to view the outside oceanic world beyond the confines of the complex. The most prominent window was the bubble of glass and latticed steel at the top of the largest dome.

Ahead of them the *Ahab* was approaching one side of the largest dome from which projected a circular pressure gate. This was doubtless the facility's submarine dock. As the *Nemo* came closer still, Mr Wates guiding them in, in the wake of the *Ahab*, those on board could begin to see more of the facility. Only then did Ulysses begin to wonder whether they hadn't simply swapped one potential watery grave for another.

It was clear that portions of the base had suffered catastrophic damage. Several of the connecting tunnels had been destroyed, effectively cutting off whole areas of the facility. One or two of the outlying domes had also had their roofs caved in, the incredible hydrostatic pressures at these depths doing the rest. Even the main, armoured dome of the undersea facility had suffered some kind of damage, what looked like great burnt gouges scarred its exterior. Ulysses couldn't help thinking that the damage looked not unlike the trail left by a welder's torch, haphazardly defacing the surface, and on a gigantic scale.

Ulysses' doubt began to ease, however, as he realised that the darkened dome at the centre of the complex still had its roof and hull-armour intact. The damage amounted to nothing more than some superficial scarring. There was no reason to suspect that the readings taken by the *Neptune's* state-of-the-art remote sensing equipment had given them false hope, and he felt even happier about their situation again when he saw the massive circular door to the facility's docking area open like the petals of a flower and admit the impatient *Ahab*.

The *Ahab* was through and safe, as far as they could tell. The *Nemo* was only a matter of ninety yards behind.

There was a sudden flicker of blue light in front of them that caused all those peering out of the fore-viewing window to gasp and cover their eyes.

"The lure!" Ulysses exclaimed. "It's right on top of us!"

He spun round, even as Constance gave voice to a terrified scream and, sure enough, there through the aft viewing port – obscuring their view of anything else at all – was a massive watery eye. By the cabin lights of the *Nemo*, Ulysses could see every disgusting detail of that limpid orb – the soured milk flesh of the eye, ribbons of underwater worms clinging to the surface of the cornea, purple veiny tendrils worming their way through the jelly-like substance, the misshapen black pit of its pupil with nothing beyond it but Biblical oblivion.

"Hell's teeth!" he gasped.

There was a sudden crash and the *Nemo* was sent hurtling sideways as something massive darted past and pushed it out of the way. There were more screams, shouts born of fear and confusion, but, to his credit, Mr Wates kept his head and, with the aid of the engineer Swann, brought the vessel under control again. Only they were now several hundred yards further away from where they had been mere moments before. The colossal bulk of the squid-thing had buffeted them over the edge of the precipitous trench, tripling the length of their journey to the base.

The hull of the sub groaned and for one heart-stopping moment it sounded like the engine was going to stall. But adjustments made by the pilot and the engineer kept the boat moving, the two men dogged in their determination to follow the *Ahab* into the savaged facility. But whether the persistent little craft would make it before it sprang a catastrophic leak as the dramatic pressures continued to work on its beleaguered frame, only time would tell. That was not something Ulysses could control. In fact, from this moment on, there was nothing he could do to influence their dreadful predicament, and that fact made him feel agitated and impotent at the same time.

Where was the monster now? Ulysses had to know. Leaving his seat he ran down the aisle and flung himself at the rear viewing port, pressing his face against the glass in the hope that he might see anything other than what was directly behind them.

In the misty glow of the sub's running lights, and the curious flickering luminescence of the monster's trailing lure beyond – a strange moon shining in this abyssal region's perpetual night – he thought he could see the shadow of the beast above them. But then again, it might have been the outcropping overhang of the continental shelf.

His sixth sense flaring so hard it made him wince, Ulysses turned his attentions downward, into the impenetrable, utter blackness of the gaping trench below. Dark shapes moved in the gloom, triangular-finned shadows detaching themselves from the hadropelagic night. With a flick of its knifing tail, one of these shapes rocketed out of the darkness, and was illuminated in all its appalling splendour by the lights of the sub, before it hurtled past, ignoring the *Nemo* in favour of another target.

The sub rocked again as the second monster nudged it with a fin six-feet long. Ulysses slumped to his knees numb with shock. The Kraken was one thing – he had had time to come to terms with that – but this was something else entirely.

In that split second, when the lights of the *Nemo* had arced across its carcharhinid body, Ulysses had taken in every detail. At least forty feet from nose to tail, a man could have fitted comfortably between its open jaws, filled with serrated arrowhead teeth, each the size of a man's hand, and with row upon row of them, one behind the other, providing the creature with hundreds of individual cutting tools, giving it a bite that could easily have snapped clean through the *Nemo* in one go. From his slim personal knowledge of fossil records and fully aware that other prehistoric creatures had survived extinction in isolated pockets around the world, Ulysses recognised the monster killer fish for what they were – Megalodons.

He suddenly realised that he was shaking. Finding his centre of focus again, as the monks of Shangri-la had taught him – nearly two years ago now – Ulysses recovered himself enough to return to his seat behind Wates.

"Whatever you do, Mr Wates," he said, "don't stop."

"Where's the beast now?" Wates asked, his voice steely in tone, a sign of the pressure he was under to remain focused in such trying circumstances.

As if in answer to his question the Kraken dropped down from above and ahead of them, effectively cutting off their route to the base. Constance's screams filled the cabin again, joined now by the womanly cries of Dr Ogilvy.

And then the *Nemo's* salvation seemed assured once more as the terrifying shark-like creature Ulysses had witnessed emerging from the depths of the trench cut through the sea after the Kraken, followed by another two of its kind, the monstrous Megalodons butting the massive bulk of the over-grown squid with the bullet-tips of their noses, snapping at its tentacles and trying to take a bite out of its side.

Ulysses saw one of the huge fish catch a tentacle between its jaws and then shudder as an electrical explosion lit up the abyssal gloom, throwing the creature away from the leviathan. Another of the huge predators dived down at the Kraken and attempted to close its jaws around the top of its head, but the crustacean-like armoured plating there seemed to do the trick, the attack leaving little impression on the sea monster.

However, the giant sharks were not beaten yet. Their persistent attack on the Kraken – which Ulysses could only imagine was down to it invading their territorial waters – was serving to distract the beast from pursuing the *Nemo*. Ulysses fancied he saw purple blood-ink clouding the water around the leviathan. There wasn't one thought to the contrary in his mind that the sharks' attack against the Kraken was a happy accident as far as those on board the *Nemo* were concerned but then serendipity was playing its part quite nicely nonetheless, and suddenly the facility was a viable objective again, the open hole of its docking gate within reach.

As the Megalodons continued to harry the Kraken, the squid-monster retaliating with violent electrical discharges cast by its deadly tentacles, and attempting to catch the fish between its own not inconsiderable jaws, Mr Wates made the most of the opportunity. He pushed the little sub as hard as it would go, all caution thrown to the wind in his desperation not to be denied the way to safety a second time.

The shadow of the shelf loomed over them, all that was visible through the front of the craft the open door to the docking bay. And then, they were through.

Torch beams stabbed the darkness, pulling shapes and shadows from the depths of the bay around them. Ulysses paused at the lip of the conning tower, as he prepared to descend the ladder to the quayside, and took in great lungfuls of musty air. It was redolent with the smells of rust, stagnant brine, mildew and salt.

The penetrating beams of the high-powered torches Captain McCormack, Selby and the others had procured from compartments on board the two subs, swung wildly through the darkness, gradually giving form and shape to the chamber in which they now found themselves.

Those who had travelled aboard the *Ahab* had already disembarked, and were now huddled together, some draped in coarse grey blankets for warmth on the dockside, beside which their vessel had now been moored. The *Nemo* sat behind it, Wates and Swann helping its passenger compliment climb down from the conning tower to the quay.

Every member of the party was gazing around the hold in wonder. Ulysses was interested to note the expressions on the closely gathered group that consisted of Carcharodon, the Major, Lady Denning and Professor Crichton in particular. There was a haunted look on the faces of most of them – the shipping magnate just looking as sour-faced as ever – and Crichton was drawing deeply from the flask that had barely been out of his hand.

There was a grating and a reverberating clang as a huge switch was slammed into the 'On' position. At once a powering hum reverberated through the echoing chamber of the dock and within a few seconds the first of a dozen arc lights began to glow into life above them.

Another wheeled handle was turned and the submerged pressure gate, still below the waterline, rolled shut.

The party remained dumbfounded, gazing in amazement around the vast hall in which they now found themselves. Far above them, cast into a steel lintel in letters three feet high were the words:

Marianas Base

"Where have you brought us, Captain?" It was Harry Cheng who was the first to break the silence. "What is this place?"

"In all my years of travelling, I've never been anywhere like this," Haugland said, his words trailing away as he stared in wonder at his surroundings.

"What I want to know," said Ulysses, getting to the heart of the matter, "is, who built this place? Why? And where are they now? What happened to them?"

An ominous silence descended over those present. Ulysses felt the eyes of the four gathered senior members of the party on him. He observed them again in return. They were four disparate people who had once apparently had nothing in common until they had come together on the maiden voyage of the *Neptune* and suffered the fate that had brought them all to this point. So now, here they were, thousands of feet below the Pacific Ocean, at the edge of the deepest place on the planet, hunted by a giant squid, the like of which had never been recorded, in the territorial waters of a race of prehistoric sharks that had previously been believed to be extinct.

He was suddenly being made to feel like a pariah.

Something didn't feel quite right. A forbidding air pervaded the base, he couldn't shake the feeling that by coming to this place, of their own free will and volition, they had committed some terrible hubris.

Now, truly, they were entering the belly of the beast.

ACT THREE

Leviathan Rising

August 1997

You have carried your work as far as terrestrial science permits. The real story of the ocean depths begins where you left off... wonders that defy my powers of description.

– Jules Verne, *20,000 Leagues Under the Sea*

CHAPTER SEVENTEEN

Mariana

THE SOUNDS OF destruction chased the child as she ran the length of the twisting corridor. Amidst the ringing metallic crashes and the groans of metal buckling under terrible pressures she fancied she could also hear the screams of those attempting to flee the carnage, like her.

But she was alone in her flight. And a moment of calm and silence descended like a shroud over the base. Now it was that silence that seemed to be chasing her along the tunnel, marking the stark echoes of her ringing footfalls on the grilled path beneath her. But she just knew that it wasn't over, that something even more terrible was coming.

She ran on, her legs having a purpose all of their own now, her lungs heaving from the exertion of her flight and her sobs. The halogen lamps flickered and dimmed as power relays somewhere within the base short-circuited. The lights died.

A howl of dread and grief escaped her lips, tears streaked her face, her eyes puffy, snot hanging in strings from her nose. But a moment later a red glow began to permeate the tunnel, as emergency lighting took over, bathing everything in its ruddy glow. It made her feel like she was running along the pumping artery of some massive undersea beast. That image certainly didn't provide her with any sense of comfort, considering her current situation. Another set of lights coursed along the sides of the passageway as if they were running with her along the corridor, showing her the route to the escape pod.

And then the silence was broken, first by angry shouts, then by a high-pitched scream, and then by the retort of a single gunshot.

"Daddy!" she wailed, unable to stop herself, the mass of emotions threatening to overwhelm her at the last. "Daddy!"

Automatically she sought comfort from her ever-present companion, only now she wasn't there. "Madeleine!" she cried again, hugging herself tight with her thin arms, until her words became unintelligible sobs. And then they too were wrung from her and she had nothing left to give.

Her feet sore from running, she stumbled to a halt at last, directly in front of the circular hatch to the waiting escape pod. Against all the odds she had made it.

"WHAT THE HELL is this place?" John Schafer said, wringing the water from a sock. He sat on the bolted base of a huge steel bracing pillar that ascended all the way to the solid steel roof above them. His voice carried eerily in the hollow space. Constance sat next to him, shivering, and trying to tease the knots from her bedraggled hair. Ulysses found himself thinking that if the two of them could make it through this experience and live to tell the tale, then a lifetime's matrimonial union would be a doddle by comparison.

Selby had found the means to provide the base with basic light and power, although Neptune alone knew where the facility's power came from. With the two subs still their only guaranteed way out again the entire party had filed out of the dock, through a solid, circular bulkhead door along a short corridor, then through another such hatch and into a second domed chamber.

Like the undersea cities of Atlantis and Pacifica that they had visited, the base appeared to be divided into a number of sections, each one capable of being separated from the others by means of thick, reinforced bulkheads and airlocks, meaning that if a hull breach occurred anywhere within the facility, that area could be locked down, and the rest of the base kept secure.

So it was that they now found themselves one step closer to the main dome of the facility and possibly one step closer to finding the answers to a host of new questions that were springing to Ulysses' curious mind.

As well as the way back to the submarine dock, there were a number of other, smaller chambers leading from the larger one they had gathered within, each one closed off from the main space by other, solid circular doors. Approaching one and peering inside, Ulysses could see diving equipment – aqualungs, oxygen tanks and a huge, armoured suit, twice the height of a man. Through the small circle of thick glass in another door Ulysses saw a bare chamber and another door on the other side bearing peeling hazard markings of yellow and black. He took this to be an airlock. It must have been from this chamber that work crews prepared to dive, to maintain the outer structure of the facility, or ventured out to the seabed and the edge of the trench beyond – but for what purpose?

The whole place stank of age and neglect. It was not a pleasant smell, and certainly didn't do anything to help make the new arrivals feel at home.

But for Ulysses, taking in every detail of the dusty, neglected space, such things as the aroma merely helped his brain form a greater impression of the whole complex and merely brought more questions to his marvelling mind.

He found himself wondering how long it had been since anyone else had been inside Marianas Base. No signs of human life had been detected by the Neptune AI as it had scanned the abandoned facility. Curious, albino crustaceans scuttled away from their probing torch beams, seeking shelter in the dark corners of the chamber to hide from the light, and some of the girders and joists had acquired their own covering of barnacles and other tube worms that must have found enough sustenance in the moist atmosphere to thrive on. But the only human life present were the survivors of the lost sub-liner *Neptune*.

The mystery of who had murdered Glenda and why, the mystery of who had sabotaged the *Neptune* and sent it plunging into the depths of the Pacific Ocean, and the mystery of the origins of the beast that seemed so intent on pursuing them through the primordial abyss were put aside, to be returned to at another time, as he considered the new mystery of the sanctuary they now found themselves within.

"So, what do you suggest we do now?" Carcharodon asked, directing his question at McCormack.

McCormack looked at him with undisguised contempt, as if he felt that his employer was continually testing him, challenging his ability to lead, and that he had had enough of it.

"I would suggest that we split up into groups and search this facility as quickly as possible. We need to see if there is a working comms array, so that we can notify the rest of the world that the *Neptune* has gone down and send out a Mayday signal so that, once rescue teams start looking for us, we can be found.

"We also need to see if there are any supplies down here because I don't know about anyone else," he said, looking pointedly at Professor Crichton as he uttered these words, "but it feels like an age since I last ate and I know that the *Ahab* and *Nemo* are both carrying only the most basic of rations, which certainly won't be enough for all of us to live on for long."

"The last thing we need on top of everything else is for there to be an outbreak of starvation-driven cannibalism, eh, captain?" Ulysses said with dark humour.

McCormack looked at him, brows furrowing, as if not sure how to take Ulysses' comment.

But Jonah Carcharodon knew exactly how to take it. "For God's sake man, we're in the middle of a crisis. This is hardly the time for your quips!"

"I was merely trying to relieve the obvious tension," Ulysses replied, the humour in his voice now replaced by venom.

Fuming, Carcharodon tried his best to ignore the dandy and chose instead to address the rest of the group.

"Very well, then," Carcharodon said. "We split up."

IT HAD BEEN Carcharodon's idea that they maintain the arrangements of groupings that their escape from the *Neptune* aboard the submersibles had created, and that was fine with Ulysses. The only difference was that it was obviously all getting to be too much for the distraught Miss Birkin. She refused to leave the divers' chamber beyond the dock and slumped down on top of one of a number of locked steel strongboxes. Constance, concerned for her ageing aunt, chose to stay with her, to make sure she was comfortable and that her condition didn't suddenly worsen and John Schafer – although Ulysses could tell that he was itching to explore the base with the rest of them – ever the gentleman, would not leave his lover's side.

So it was that the rest of them began to explore what lay beyond, diverging at a junction where the tunnel beyond the divers' prep room branched. Ulysses was happy not to have to spend a moment longer than was necessary with the wretched Carcharodon who, despite everything – or perhaps, he wondered, because of it – was still behaving as if he owned the place, treating his patiently attendant assistant as if she were nothing better than the scum floating on the surface of the docking pool.

He could have done without the sweating, nervously shivering, waxy-skinned doctor tagging along. And he wasn't too keen on Agent Cheng remaining with him, although he didn't appear to have half the confidence he had enjoyed when his right hand man Mr Sin had been with him.

The base was abandoned: if there had ever been any doubt in any of their minds it evaporated now. Untouched equipment rusted away wherever it lay, a curious combination of diving gear, engineering machinery, heavy duty tools, the abandoned personal detritus of whoever it was that had lived and worked here – doors to sleeping pods open, papers, clothes and personal possessions scattered over the metal grilled floors – everything having the appearance that whoever these personal artefacts had belonged to had left in a great hurry.

Dust covered everything, Ulysses noted, even here, at the bottom of the sea. As they progressed further he paused to examine some of the forsaken possessions, items of clothing and forgotten papers under the faintly glowing lamps lining the semi-circular corridor. Everything about them suggested that they were English in origin, or had at least belonged to subjects of the empire of Magna Britannia. But amidst all the chaotic detritus of a rushed evacuation his party thankfully did not discover any dead bodies, or rather, what would have been left of them. Everyone must have got away.

But who were these people who had lived and worked here? Why had they been forced to leave in such a hurry? And what had happened to them after that? There had not been any sign of other sea transports in the dock, so Ulysses assumed that they had been used to evacuate the team working in the facility; unless there was another dock they didn't know about yet, but he thought it unlikely.

Leaving the accommodation wing behind, Ulysses' party followed a tunnel as it curved around to the right – he assumed following the structure of the central dome – until it brought them to another circular steel bulkhead door. The opening mechanism miraculously still operable, the heavy door swung open and they entered a larger, darker space beyond.

The unpleasant aroma that Ulysses had been aware of ever since disembarking from the *Nemo* was a miasmal stench here, almost as if it were a physical thing, trapped within this undersea dungeon for so long – years seemed likely – that he felt he could have cut it with his sword-cane.

Ogilvy could not hide his revulsion, gagging on the stench, whilst Haugland wrung out a sodden handkerchief and held it to his face to filter the vile stink from the stagnant air he was forced to breathe.

"What the bloody hell died in here, then?" Swann said, putting it so succinctly.

The beams of the torches carried by him and Mr Wates, as well as one that Nimrod had managed to procure, set to work revealing, piece by piece, the details of the chamber around them.

They walked between rows of large fish tanks supported on iron legs, the glass obscured with brown slime, the water they contained as yellowy green and as opaque as pea soup, the stagnant stinking liquid cloyed with decayed matter. They continued on their way through what was becoming more and more in appearance like some curious laboratory, reminding Ulysses of the disturbing discovery he and Nimrod had made below the house in Southwark, only a matter of months ago.

Ulysses stopped to peer more closely at the rank fish tanks, trying to make out what they once had held, but he could make out nothing more than the occasional broken shell or empty carapace. But then he supposed that whatever life had once wriggled and writhed within had died long ago, their flesh and insubstantial bones and cartilage becoming the sludge that smothered the bottom of the tanks.

"Herregud, hva er det der?" Haugland exclaimed, his voice carrying to the dark and distant roof before calling back to them in the cavernous vault, as they passed beyond the rows of dead tanks and came upon the first of the cylinders.

"Bloody hell!" Swann swore.

"Incredible," Cheng uttered.

"It's disgusting!" Mr Wates countered.

"It's a blasphemy! That's what it is," Dr Ogilvy suddenly piped up. "A blasphemy against nature."

There were a dozen of them altogether. Ulysses doubted that the liquid in these sealed cylindrical glass tanks was water. It was only semi-opaque and had a yellow tinge to it, like urine, allowing them to see what was contained within quite clearly.

Their proportions were roughly those of a man, but these things were very far from being men now. Some sported obvious gills within their swollen necks, ugly goitre-like growths. Others were entirely swollen, with characteristics of puffer-fish, even down to the tiny spines covering their rubbery hide. Yet more had webs of skin between fingers and toes, those same digits unnaturally elongated, whilst in one example the legs had fused together, the malformation of its feet creating an effective fish-tail.

Ulysses found himself wondering how such abominable creations had been achieved, whether by means of splicing vivisectionist surgery – something akin to the revolutionary research undertaken by the late Professor Galapagos – or some unholy cross-breeding programme that didn't even bear thinking about. It was clear that the long-dead occupants of the cylinders, what were in effect giant test-tubes, were the strange aborted experiments of someone's attempts to amalgamate fish with men, although for what sick purpose Ulysses could only guess at.

Looking more closely, he saw a label, discoloured with rust and mould, still stuck to one of the tanks. The thing preserved inside the flooded coffin of chemicals looked like an ungodly amalgam of moray eel, octopus and Homo Sapiens. There was only one word, written in faded and smudged ink, though Ulysses could still make it out: Seziermesser.

"I'll think you'll find," Ulysses said as he edged past the tanks towards what looked like a large chart table on the other side of the laboratory, "that these are the reasons this facility exists." He lifted a piece of paper from the table and, having swept the dust from its surface, peered at the blueprint revealed beneath. "And if you think that's incredible, you haven't seen anything yet."

The rest of the group joined him at the table.

"What is it, sir?" Nimrod asked, his own curiosity piqued. "What have you found?"

"Take a look for yourself."

All eyes fixed on the blueprint unrolled in front of them, gradually making sense of the white lines against the faded blue sheet of the plan.

"Bloody hell."

"Incredible."

"As I said, a blasphemy."

"The Kraken!"

"Indeed, Mr Haugland," Ulysses concurred with the Norwegian, "although according to the maker's designation it's actually Project Leviathan – 001."

There on the paper in front of them, plain for all to see, was what amounted to a technical drawing of the monster that had blighted them, ever since the *Neptune's* engines had come to a full stop, its ballast tanks flooded and the world's greatest luxury submersible liner had drifted to the bottom of the Pacific. There was no doubt that it was the same monster that had crippled the *Neptune*, taken Mr Sin and pursued the rest of them as they fled the flooding wreck. There it was, laid out in side elevation, front elevation and in plan view, with attendant measurements, in all its two hundred-foot glory, from the tips of its writhing squid's tentacles, to its fang-filled maw, armoured shell and spine-tipped tail.

Ulysses found himself glancing upwards, into the dusty shadows of the laboratory roof, wondering what had become of the beast, wondering if it was still out there waiting for them. An involuntary sparking tingle of fear crackled down his spinal column.

"Look at this," Wates called from nearby.

Happy at the distraction, Ulysses turned his attention from the schematic to the officer's discovery. On another work table, one cluttered with half-finished, or deconstructed, pieces of machinery – not unlike the guts of a Babbage engine – stood a wooden board on which a frame constructed of metal rods supported three feet of octopoid-tentacle, stretched out horizontally. The rubbery flesh was intact, preserved no doubt thanks to the addition of some chemical, but more amazing than that was the fact that it had at its core, running the length of the fleshy limb, a flexible metal cable. The end of this internal mechadendrite was hooked up to a large battery also sitting on the table, although one terminal was disconnected.

"What do you make of that?" Wates said.

"I don't know," Ulysses mused, "but I'll warrant it's got something to do with our friend out there."

"It looks like some kind of cyborganic technology," Dr Ogilvy added, his fascination with the curious object on the table seeming to help him to ignore the symptoms of withdrawal he was suffering.

"And what's that when it's at home?" Haugland asked, peering just as closely at the mecha-tentacle through his round wire-framed glasses.

"The marrying together of a living, breathing organism to either an exo- or endo-skeleton of mechanical components to create something else altogether," the doctor explained.

"Incredible," said Cheng, for a third time, and unseen by anyone else, depressed a button on the baton-like device he had secreted in the pocket of his trousers.

*　　*　　*

THEIR CURSORY INVESTIGATION of the lab complete, and having found no source of supplies anywhere, Ulysses' company entered another connecting corridor from which branched various other paths through the submarine complex.

The sudden reverberating sound of a crash caught them all by surprise.

"What was that?" Ogilvy said, jerking his head round.

Thanks to the distorting echoes of the place, they could not be certain from which direction the noise had come. Rubber piping and cables hung from the ceiling of the tunnels here, like trailing tree roots piercing an animal's burrow or the mechanised intestines of some cybernetic sea monster.

"Come on," Ulysses said, "we're going to have to split up. It's the only way."

He turned and looked at the agitated faces around him.

"Cheng and Haugland, you go that way," he said, pointing to the tunnel left of where they had joined the junction. "Mr Wates, you take Swann and the good doctor that way," – he pointed right – "while Nimrod and myself will take this passageway," he said, crossing the junction and continuing into the gloom ahead.

Within minutes, servant and master reached another junction within the maze of corridors. Lying on his side on the floor, cursing like a navvy, was Jonah Carcharodon, his wheelchair tipped over beside him.

"Carcharodon!" Ulysses exclaimed, coming to the aid of the invalid. "What happened to you?"

"Damned if I know!" he snarled, verbally turning on his would-be rescuer. "And where's Miss Celeste?"

"I refer you to my earlier answer."

As Ulysses and Nimrod righted the wheelchair and assisted Carcharodon back into it, the old man – who was obviously shaken, despite the show of bravado – began to prattle away, revealing what had happened prior to his little accident.

"Our party had split up to carry on searching this place. Celeste and myself were coming along this passageway. McCormack was scouting ahead of us. I heard a cry from behind me, and as I struggled to turn round, to find out what was going on, some blighter – some bastard or other – tipped me out of my chair. Who would attack an old man, and an invalid at that? God knows where the others have got to."

"Or Miss Celeste," Ulysses said anxiously. "So where's McCormack now?"

"That bastard? He ran back on hearing Celeste cry out but ran straight past, leaving me like this."

"Which way?"

"That way," Carcharodon said, pointing along another tunnel leading off from the intersection.

His sixth sense screaming danger, Ulysses took off in the same direction, Nimrod close on his heels.

"But what about me?"

"Sorry, sir," Nimrod said with a slight nod of the head as he followed after.

Ulysses and his manservant rounded a bend in the corridor, Carcharodon's indignant shouts echoing back to them from the intersection, and passed through another sealable bulkhead door into yet another chamber. His unconscious mind took in the fact that it was another laboratory of some kind, but his conscious mind was focused on the confused sounds of scurrying movement beyond. Slowing his steps he penetrated the half-lit gloom of the lab – passing stacks of more stinking, gunk-filled fish tanks bearing faded and mildewed labels – until he caught sight of a pair of booted feet protruding from behind a tarnished metal gurney. Then, quickening his steps once more, he hastened round the end of the row, past the gurney, to see Captain McCormack lying on the floor of the laboratory, blinking as though in a daze, a hand to the back of his head.

"Quicksilver?" he slurred. "What's going on?" He brought his hand back round in front of his eyes. Ulysses could see that it was sticky with blood. "What happened to me?"

"You've been attacked," Ulysses stated, as the dazed captain seemed to be struggling with the realisation himself. "Where's Miss Celeste?"

"M-Mr Quicksilver? I-Is that you?" came a quavering fluty voice.

Ulysses immediately left the captain in Nimrod's more than capable hands and rushed around another stack of algae-streaked tanks to see Miss Celeste stumbling out of the shadows towards him. Her already dishevelled state was considerably worsened by the ugly bruise blossoming on her forehead and the trickle of blood dripping between the fingers of the hand she held to the injury.

"Miss Celeste," Ulysses said, unable to hide the concern in his voice as he hurried to her side. Putting one arm around her waist to support her, he encouraged her to sit down on the seat made by a fallen steel beam.

"Is everyone all right?" Wates asked, entering the lab, followed by Swann and Ogilvy, reluctantly pushing Carcharodon ahead of him.

"Captain McCormack and Miss Celeste have both been attacked," Nimrod stated bluntly.

"And me!" snapped Carcharodon, unhappy at not being the centre of attention. "I was attacked as well."

Ulysses shot the eccentric, self-obsessed billionaire a poisonous look but decided against saying anything.

"Hello? What's going on? Everyone okay?" came Selby's voice as he entered the laboratory, followed by Cheng and Haugland.

Expressions of surprise and half-formed questions were all answered as Ulysses explained to everyone, once again, what had occurred.

"But who would do such a thing?" Haugland asked in disbelief.

"It must be someone who came on board with the rest of us," McCormack said. "Neptune didn't detect any human life-signs on the base before we all got here."

Eyes narrowed and immediately everyone present began reappraising their companions with suspicion.

"Then, if we are in danger, isn't it best we all stick together again from now on?" Ogilvy said.

"Well said, doctor," McCormack concurred. "Come on," he added, struggling to his feet, with Nimrod helping him, "this way."

"Captain, are you sure about this?" Ulysses warned. "Both you and Miss Celeste have suffered injuries and are doubtless also suffering from the effects of shock, isn't that right, Doctor?"

"Um, what? Oh, yes. Shock. Yes. Most definitely."

"The way I see it," McCormack said, wincing and putting his hand to the back of his head again as he attempted to stand upright, "we don't have any choice. If there's a madman on the loose, we need to hook up with the others and warn them."

THE PARTY MOVED on, as briskly as the injured amongst them would allow. Passing another bulkhead door, Ulysses paused to look through the porthole at its centre to see what lay beyond. But all he saw through the thick, green-tinged glass was nothing but the broken shell of another dome and the open ocean beyond. Something had utterly destroyed that part of the facility which lay beyond the door. Suddenly a few inches of reinforced steel didn't seem like very much to be standing between them and the crushing expanse of the mighty Pacific.

Passing into another corridor and from there through another bulkhead door, they entered the central chamber of the main biome – a waft of dry dusty air assailing their nostrils as they did so – only moments before what remained of the other party entered through an identical door on the opposite side of the room.

No pleasantries were exchanged, tired expressions and the briefest exchanges between the groups telling them what they already suspected: the base was deserted, whole swathes of it destroyed altogether. They had been able to find only a few usable medical supplies and a handful of tinned foodstuffs in a wrecked galley. And there was no sign of anyone having been left behind during whatever rushed evacuation had taken place.

Until now.

The explorers were all inextricably drawn towards the bizarre construction at the centre of the chamber, the grim memento of whatever had happened here exerting the pull of morbid fascination upon them.

* * *

THEY HAD TO be in another laboratory. At its centre stood an amazing contraption, like a tiered dais, surrounded by banks of cogitator equipment and with the steel-cradle of a chair-harness at its peak. And strapped into the chair by a cracked leather harness was the body of a man.

It must have been sitting there for a long time in the one moisture-free room in the whole complex, for the body had become mummified naturally, cracked and peeling parchment-dry skin clinging to the angular bones. A curious device was strapped to the man's head. It looked like a metal-banded helmet. Various light-emitting diodes were arrayed upon its outer surface and a number of twisting cables trailed from electrode junctions on the top, connecting it to the chair and, by extension, the banks of machinery around it.

As to the purpose of such a device, Ulysses had no idea. As to how the mummified corpse had met its end, however, there seemed little doubt. The dead man had been shot, at close range. A clean bullet hole was preserved within the middle of his forehead, the results of the exit wound splattered across the back of the chair, eggshell shards of skull littering the dais beneath. The hollows of the dead man's eyes appeared to be staring at the small bubble of reinforced glass and steel at the apex of the dome, sightless sockets staring out at the miasmal abyss beyond.

"Oh my God," Crichton began, an expression of appalled horror on his face. He reached for his hip flask, to take another swig, only it wasn't there. He fumbled for it in his pocket, but it was gone, doubtless left somewhere as he and the rest of his party explored the facility.

Turning his attention from the macabre figure locked within the even more curious clinical chair-construct, Ulysses assessed the reaction of his fellow survivors.

To his mind there was something extreme about Crichton's meeting with the corpse. Surely he had witnessed much worse during their encounters with the Kraken and their flight from the *Neptune*? A nagging suspicion began to form at the back of his mind, struggling to take cohesive form.

All eyes were on the chair and the body bound within it. But where most gazed in morbid fascination or dumbfounded bewilderment, there was something else in the eyes of some of the more senior members of the party, specifically Carcharodon, Lady Denning, Major Horsley and of course Professor Crichton; something like recognition.

The only person not looking at the chair and its victim was Carcharodon's PA. Instead she had crouched down and was picking something up from the floor of the chamber, a floppy fabric thing, a child's crudely sewn rag-doll. Miss Celeste was turning the toy over in her hands in stunned silence.

"Oh, God forgive me," Crichton mumbled, his legs giving way, falling to his knees before the construction, unable to tear his eyes from the corpse bound within it.

"What is it, professor?" Ulysses challenged. "Do you know this man?"

"God forgive us all!" Crichton screamed.

"Do you know what happened here?" Captain McCormack uttered in startled surprise. "Is there something you're not telling us?"

"Major. Lady Denning," Ulysses tried. He couldn't quite believe what he was saying, even as he said it – how could it be possible after all? – but it seemed the only logical explanation. "Have you been here before?"

"Don't be ridiculous, man!" Carcharodon railed, turning on him again. "How could any of us have been here before? Quicksilver, you're a fool and a nincompoop if you believe that. It's an utterly preposterous suggestion!"

But the professor remained on his knees, tears splashing onto the metal plates before him, making tiny mortar-blasts in the dry, dead dust.

A scream rang out through the open door by which the rest of the party had entered the laboratory chamber, that sent a shiver of fear and excitement through Ulysses' body.

"Constance!" he exclaimed, already moving. "But of course, they were still left behind. The only safety here is safety in numbers."

"The attacker!" another voice added.

Faltering steps became great bounding strides as Ulysses ran from the chamber. Others joined him in pursuit, a cacophony of clanging footfalls rebounding from the steel-plated tunnel walls. And the screams kept coming.

Ulysses was the first to enter the dive chamber, joined soon after by Nimrod, Captain McCormack, Cheng, Swann and Clements. He stumbled to a halt in appalled horror as he took in the scene before him.

Constance was standing only a few feet from a secured airlock door, her hands to her face, screaming in abject horror. John Schafer beat at the door with his fists, bellowing in anger as he tried to open it again. On the other side of the glass the face of Miss Birkin filled the porthole, locked into an expression of unutterable terror.

Ulysses rushed to his young friend's side, Nimrod following in his stead, all three of them attempting to force the door as a dull, droning siren began to blare from speakers somewhere within the chamber.

"It's no good!" shouted Selby.

"What do you mean?" Ulysses asked, voice tensing as he strained to get a purchase on the rim of the airlock hatch with his fingers and somehow prise it open.

"You're wasting your time," the *Neptune's* chief engineer said coldly. "Once an airlock's activated, the fail-safes make sure that the protocols cannot be overridden."

"What? It's been activated?" Ulysses turned his attention back to the door and the terrified old woman trapped in the airlock, her face bathed in the pulsing orange glow of an amber warning lamp.

As if to confirm Selby's words, beyond the unnervingly silent Miss Birkin, the outer door of the airlock ratcheted open.

There was nothing any of them could do as the sea flooded into the chamber, filling it in seconds, crushing the old woman to a pulp before she had a chance to drown.

As the messy remains of what was left of Constance's aunt were drawn out of the airlock in a swirl of ocean current, a terrible realisation crept over Ulysses.

Glenda's murderer had come with them. Someone, hiding in plain sight in the party of survivors within the Marianas Base, was the killer and had dared to strike again, even given the hopelessness of their position, surely realising that there could be no escape for them either now.

What had seemed to be their sanctuary from all the horrors that the abyssal depths held for them, had now become their prison.

CHAPTER EIGHTEEN

The Accused

"WE ONLY LEFT her alone for a moment," John Schafer was saying, "a minute or two at most."

The young man looked completely wrung out as he tried to make sense of what had just happened. The stress of the situation, having personally taken responsibility for the safety of his fiancée and her aunt, had begun to get to him like never before. And this feeling was only made worse by the fact that one of his charges was now dead, and having suffered such a horrible death.

Constance Pennyroyal was slumped on the floor against the airlock door, sobbing into her hands. At least her anguished cries of grief had subsided for the time being, but, to Ulysses' mind, the heart-rending stifled sobs seemed almost harder to bear.

"We heard something – a crash, a cry – and went to see what was going on," Schafer went on. "We only left her alone for a moment."

"It's the killer," the purser said darkly. "Whoever killed Miss Finch is with us, here, in the base, hiding somewhere amongst us."

"A stowaway, you mean?" Lady Denning asked.

"You can tell yourself that, if you like," Selby said, "but there was no one on board before any of us boarded back at the sub-dock on the *Neptune.*"

"How can you be sure?"

"You'll have to trust us on that one, your ladyship."

"Trust you? But someone amongst our party is a killer! How can we trust anyone anymore?" She took in the faces around her one at a time, alighting on Major Horsley's bristled red-veined face. "Even those people we thought we knew."

"The killer's here?" Dr Ogilvy repeated, as if struggling to comprehend what he was hearing. "But if that's the case, we're all doomed!" He seemed to be paying particular attention to Harry Cheng as he had his say.

"We're not done yet," Ulysses said, one eyebrow arching and the corner of his mouth following suit, a wry smile beginning to form on his face. "It's quite simple, really. As it stands none of us are going to get out of here alive if we don't keep to the plan. The killer hasn't shown themselves to be suicidal, otherwise we wouldn't be in this position now."

"How can you be so calm and detached about all this?" Schafer asked, as if he was revolted by Ulysses' lack of demonstrable emotion. "Especially after what happened to Glenda."

Ulysses fixed the younger man with a hard stare. "Whatever it takes to get through this," he said coldly. "Anyway, as I was saying, the killer could have put an end to all of us any number of times, if they hadn't valued their own life. No, there's a purpose to these killings and as long as we stick together, and stick to the plan, there's nothing our mystery killer can do to harm us. Isn't that right, Captain?" Ulysses asked directing a wicked grin at McCormack, his ally in all their plotting so far.

"Mr Wates, seize this man," the captain said, pointing an accusing finger at Ulysses.

"Captain?"

"McCormack?" Ulysses said, in disbelief, his nascent smile being replaced by a knot of confusion.

"I said, lay hands on Mr Quicksilver!"

"You cannot be serious," Ulysses pressed on, incredulous. "That blow to the head must have been worse than we first thought."

Just as confused as Ulysses, but with years behind him as a devoted naval officer, Wates moved forwards, almost as if reacting by instinct upon hearing his captain's command, and put a cautious hand on the dandy's arm. All the while he kept looking to his superior for affirmation of his actions.

In response, Nimrod moved to stop Wates.

The rest of the group seemed frozen in a state of shock, either by this unexpected development taking place before their eyes, or by the sudden death of the harmless old spinster, or simply at the bizarreness of the situation they all found themselves in.

"It's all right, Nimrod," Ulysses said.

"But, sir, I must insist."

"It's all right, Nimrod. But Captain McCormack there is no need to have Mr Wates lay his hands on me."

"Oh, I would beg to disagree."

"In that case, then, I am sure that you won't mind explaining to me precisely why you are placing me under arrest."

The situation seemed ludicrous to Ulysses. What did the captain think he was going to do with him even if he had him under lock and key?

"Happily, sir, if only so that these God-fearing men and women here present learn what sort of a viper has been lurking in their midst all this time, and know that they can now rest easy, assured that a murderer has been banged to rights."

"I've been called a few choice things in my time," Ulysses said in a way that implied he might have found this misunderstanding amusing if it wasn't for the direness of their predicament, "but a viper and a murderer, never!"

Appalled gasps passed around the group, followed in some cases by a wave of palpable relief to know that the killer had been caught.

"And to think that I entrusted you with the task of uncovering the identity of Miss Finch's killer!" McCormack sounded like he was in danger of losing it again, as he had done with Carcharodon, when they were back aboard the *Neptune*.

"Come on then, man," McCormack's employer said, pressing him. "I know that Quicksilver and I haven't always seen eye to eye but I'm on tenterhooks to know the reason why you believe him to be the killer."

"Miss Birkin was right all along," McCormack replied cryptically.

"W-What do you mean?" It was Constance who spoke. She had been listening just as intently to the exchange as everyone else and fixed the captain now with a piercing gaze, made all the more furious by the redness and puffiness of her eyes.

"She told me, back on board the *Neptune*, when we were trying to get everyone across the Grand Atrium."

"She told you?" Ulysses was getting exasperated himself now. "Told you *what*?"

"That you were the killer."

Ulysses remembered how the suspicious old woman – "too full of conspiracy theories" the Major had said – had looked at him, ever since they had met together following the wrecking of the ship, how she had refused to board the *Nemo* when she knew that she would be travelling with him.

"But wherever did she get that ludicrous idea, the daft old bat?"

"That's my aunt you're talking about!" Constance suddenly shrieked, catching Ulysses off guard.

His face reddened in embarrassment. "I'm sorry, I meant no offence –"

"She told me that she had seen Miss Finch with the killer. You saw her tell me as much," McCormack interrupted, the anger and frustration apparent in his voice, "read her lips, no doubt."

Ulysses recalled the moment quite clearly now.

"It was at that point that I took her to one side, to stop her upsetting anyone else. She told me that she saw you with Miss Finch only a matter of hours before she was found dead inside the AI chamber, after you left the casino with her that night. But by then the damage had been done. And now she is dead. You killed her to silence her, because she knew too much."

"But this is ridiculous," Ulysses said again. "Your evidence is nothing but circumstantial. It wouldn't stand up in a court of law."

"In case you hadn't noticed, Ulysses, we're not in a court of law," Schafer said darkly.

"Et tu, Brute?" Ulysses threw back, angry and upset at the apparent change of allegiance of a man who was the closest thing he had to a friend amongst his fellow passengers-cum-refugees, other than his manservant.

"Where were you when the airlock was activated?"

"Well, assuming that it had only just happened," Ulysses paused, his mind racing, trying to work out his whereabouts at the time when the old busy-body's fate had been sealed. "Why, I suppose it was around the time we all heard the crash and went to help Carcharodon and then found you in the lab."

"So, you attacked me too," Carcharodon shrieked. "You admit it!"

"Why don't you just shut up for once, you blustering old buffoon?" Ulysses railed.

"And you have witnesses?" McCormack asked.

"I was with Cheng, Haugland and the rest up until that point."

"Up until that point?" McCormack parroted. "There was never a time when you were alone?"

"There was that time when you told us all to split up, after we heard the attack on Mr Carcharodon," Dr Ogilvy pointed out nervously.

"What?" Ulysses couldn't believe that the doctor was actually attempting to corroborate McCormack's story. "We weren't apart for more than a few minutes."

"Time enough for a man like yourself, in the peak of physical fitness to return here and do the dreadful deed," McCormack said coldly.

"This is preposterous!" Nimrod said, adding his voice of dissent to the argument.

"But why would I risk returning here, to do that, when I thought that John and Constance would be here?"

"Perhaps you planned to do away with *all* of them," Ogilvy suggested, excitedly.

At that Constance recoiled into the safety of Schafer's embrace, turning horrified eyes on Ulysses. That look alone cut him to the core.

"What happened to innocent 'til proven guilty?" Ulysses challenged.

Captain McCormack looked around at the others. "Haugland? Can you confirm all this? Where is Haugland? Has anyone seen him?"

"I can confirm that Mr Quicksilver did leave us for a time," Cheng said impassively, his face a hardened, emotionless mask. "But then so did his manservant, Mr Nimrod."

"Precisely," Ulysses said, his speech becoming impassioned as he realised that this wasn't some bluff, something that was all going to pass as some ridiculous misunderstanding. "I wasn't alone."

"Is this correct, Mr Nimrod?" McCormack asked, his expression one of steely concentration.

"When our party separated I went with Mr Quicksilver," Nimrod confirmed.

"Then you had an accomplice!" Constance screeched.

All eyes now turned on Nimrod and for the first time since their descent into chaos had begun, Ulysses' loyal family retainer looked suddenly out of sorts, a startled expression claiming his features.

"That would explain why you weren't worried about taking on all three of them," Ogilvy chirruped excitedly.

"I did not kill anyone!" Ulysses growled, the volume of his words increasing as he did so. "I did not plan to kill anyone. We did not plan to kill anyone!"

"Then if you didn't, who did?" Carcharodon challenged.

Ulysses opened his mouth to speak, but no words followed. Who indeed? Who would have wanted to kill Glenda Finch and now Miss Birkin? And who had the opportunity and the wherewithal to achieve the brutal task?

"Seize those men!" McCormack ordered.

Ulysses went for his sword-cane but Mr Wates already had a hand on him. In moments both Wates and Swann had Ulysses held tightly by the arms and shoulders so that he couldn't escape, and Nimrod found himself restrained by Selby and Clements. There hadn't seemed much point in him trying to get away when his master was already restrained and they were both outnumbered. They would work out a way out of their predicament together, given time.

"So what do you plan to do with us now?" Ulysses sneered.

The captain took a moment to respond, taking that moment to look around the dive preparation chamber again.

"Put them in there," he commanded, pointing at a circular hatch-door in the side of the hemi-spherical chamber.

It seemed pointless protesting now, so Ulysses and Nimrod allowed themselves to be pushed through the hatch and into the storage locker beyond. The door slammed shut behind them with a resounding, and very final sounding, clang and Ulysses heard the thud and clunk of locking clamps being secured. Peering through the round porthole he could see that Swann and Clements had been placed either side of the hatch to stand guard.

"Well, Nimrod, old chap, who'd have thought it would end like this?" Ulysses said, trying to smile, in spite of everything.

"Not I, for one," Nimrod said with abrupt annoyance.

Turning on the spot, Ulysses surveyed the room that had become a temporary brig for the two desperadoes and one object stood out more than any other.

It dwarfed the two of them. Twice as tall as a man and almost as wide as it was high, it looked for all intents and purposes like a huge, all-enclosing diving suit. However, due to its size, no man would be able to fit his body precisely inside the arms and legs of the suit. Instead the pilot had to climb into the back and secure himself within a cramped pilot's cabin inside the torso of the suit and the spherical fish-bowl helmet. Searchlights were mounted on the broad shoulders of the suit and the pilot actually viewed the sub-aquatic world beyond through a number of circular portholes positioned around the helmet-dome.

"I assume you have a plan to get us out of here, sir," Nimrod said as he too took in the room.

"Oh, you know me, Nimrod," Ulysses said, grinning wickedly, eyes remaining fixed on the suit in front of him. "I'm just making this up as I go along."

There was a sharp electrical click and Captain McCormack's voice crackled from an intercom panel in the wall.

"When was the last time you saw Haugland?" he demanded, his tone accusing.

"What? McCormack, have you lost your mind?" was Ulysses' less than helpful reply.

Now that he came to think of it himself, he hadn't seen the Norwegian since his party had split up after hearing what they now knew was the attack on Carcharodon. A cold feeling filled his belly, a knot of ice tightening inside him. He could see where this was going.

"If you've done anything to him," McCormack was saying, the tone of his voice making it clear that his sorely tested patience was rapidly running out, "God help you!"

WITH, AS SEEMED likely, the double murderer and his accomplice secured away and with an armed guard on them, Captain Connor McCormack organised certain members of the remaining group of survivors into three separate search parties. And although he now had Ulysses and

Nimrod imprisoned, the atmosphere of distrust, that the attacks and the killings had engendered in everyone, had not entirely lifted.

So, just to be sure, with that doubt planted in his mind and wondering if there was someone else lurking within the base, the stowaway that Selby assured him did not exist, McCormack made sure that as many people as possible were armed before they set out to look for Haugland. The leader of each party was given a pistol and ammunition taken from a secure locker on board the *Ahab*. The rest had to make do with what could be procured from the divers prep room. Inside one of the storage lockers, the purser had found a number of cumbersome, hand-held harpoon guns, bolts already loaded, a pair of fire-axes, and even a number of sticks of dry dynamite, although these were not considered an appropriate means of defence. Every other weapon, however, was gratefully accepted by their recipients.

"Right, are we ready then?" Major Horsley asked in his customary bellow, as the group began to divide up.

People were naturally gravitating towards those they most trusted or who they perceived as being most like themselves.

"Ready?" Horsley asked again, looking round the group. "Tip top," he said beaming, apparently concluding that they were indeed all ready. "Let's be on our way then, what?"

He set off towards the door that led out of the dive prep chamber and into the rest of the complex beyond, harpoon gun held high before him.

"Major, wait!" Captain McCormack called after him. "We need to plan the search carefully."

"Haugland could be lying somewhere, bleeding to death! What more do we need to know? Time's a-wasting."

And with that, he was gone.

McCormack shook his head wearily and muttered something uncomplimentary under his breath.

"So, what now, McCormack?" Carcharodon said in that oh-so irritating, wheedling tone of his.

"Well, sir, I would suggest that you stay here, along with Miss Celeste. You've both had a nasty shock."

"Don't patronise me!" Carcharodon snarled. "Talk about pot and kettle! What about you? If you're fit to run around playing heroes, on some wild goose chase looking for Haugland, then so are we."

"But I didn't think you'd want to," the captain threw back, almost defeated by the shipping magnate's constant harping criticism.

"Who are you to make such a judgement of me?" Carcharodon tore into the near-exhausted McCormack. "I'm not going to sit around here, like an idiot, waiting to be attacked again! I want to know what's going on as much as you do. It's bad enough that I'm an invalid, stuck in this chair. I am not going to be treated like a vegetable as well! I have never stood for that, and I'm not about to start now!"

"I meant no offence, sir. I was merely suggesting –"

"Suggest all you like. Miss Celeste," Carcharodon said, looking up haughtily, but more importantly past McCormack, and clutching one of the harpoon guns tightly in his balled fists, "we're leaving. As the Major pointed out, there's no time to waste."

And with his cowed aide pushing his chair, with heavy trudging steps, Carcharodon and Miss Celeste exited the chamber, Carcharodon calling, "Major Horsley. I'm with you!"

"Lady Denning, would you care to –"

"No I would not care to remain behind either, Captain, if that is what you were about to ask. As Mr Carcharodon put it so plainly, I am as eager to know what has happened here as anyone else. Besides, I might have knowledge that would be of use to a search party," she added cryptically.

"Very well, your ladyship. Mr Wates, I want Lady Denning to go with you."

"Yes, Captain."

"And take the doctor too."

"What? But I don't want to go. I want to stay here!" Ogilvy protested, his anxious expression saying it all.

"Tough," McCormack growled with all the menace of a rottweiler. He turned back to his officers. "And the purser."

"Yes, captain," the purser and Wates replied together.

McCormack surveyed those that were left. Necessity, having already made strange bedfellows of them all, was now spawning its own inventive arrangements.

"Professor Crichton, I want you with me. I rather suspect you know your way around here better than most."

The ageing professor gave a heartfelt sigh, but then nodded in weary agreement.

"And Selby, come with me too."

"Very good, Mac."

That left Cheng, and the young sweethearts, who had been through more together on this adventure than most couples saw in a lifetime of wedded bliss. "Whatever you want to do, I suppose I can't stop you," McCormack stated, defeated by the situation surrounding Haugland's disappearance.

"We want to do our bit," John Schafer said, clutching the hand of his beloved tightly in his, the two of them exchanging an impassioned look, words now unnecessary between them. Their earnest intentions could not be disputed, one determined to do his bit and cleanse himself of the foolish trust he had had placed in the charismatic killer Quicksilver, and Constance, not only not wanting to be separated from her fiancé again but now also driven by her own passionate desire for vengeance against the murderer of her aunt – a purity of purpose that was frightening to behold in the changed young debutante.

"Then I will go with you," Cheng said, bowing respectfully.

"Let us not waste any more time, or any more lives," the professor said with unexpected steely resolve.

He seemed more clear-headed without his comforting hip flask, as determined to do his part as Constance Pennyroyal, which was just as dramatic a change in attitude, compared to the edgy individual who had disembarked from the *Ahab* on reaching the Marianas base.

Having checked that he had a bullet ready in the breach, Captain McCormack led his party back towards the heart of the base as the others took diametrically opposed routes through the domes and laboratories positioned around the edge of the complex.

Taking this path they found themselves back at the laboratory where he and Miss Celeste had been attacked. He entered with caution this time, pistol raised, just in case.

"So that's where I left it," he heard the professor say and observed, with no small amount of disappointment, Crichton retrieve his battered hip-flask from a work top, and give it a pat like it was an old friend.

"Come on, Haugland's not here. What's through there?" he asked, indicating another door on the other side of the lab.

"We called it the 'Shop'," Crichton said, a faraway look in his eyes.

"Then let's try that."

Leaving the lab again by the other door, the three of them passed along an arterial passageway littered with broken beams and dangling bundles of cables, spilling from the roof like the entrails of a gutted fish, until they reached another of the familiar hatch-doors. The opening mechanism activated with a hiss of compressed air and the hatchway rolled open.

McCormack, Crichton and Selby passed through into a darkened dome. Eyes adjusting to the gloom, the captain could see that it opened out, extending away from them. There was a sharp intake of breath from the professor next to him.

"You've been here before, of course," he said.

"Once. Long ago."

With slow, careful steps, McCormack continued to lead his search party further into the vast chamber. Strange pieces of equipment covered gurneys and work tables, looking not so unlike giant examples of operating implements. Huge pieces of machinery, such as large crane-gantries filled the space, rising away into the darkness of the roof, slack links of heavy chains that would not have been out of place attached to a ship's anchor hung suspended between them. The place looked like a curious cross between a factory floor machine shop and a vast operating theatre.

"God in heaven!" Selby swore loudly.

"What is it?" McCormack demanded, his attention immediately on his chief engineer.

"See for yourself," Selby said, pointing up into the trailing loops of chains.

Hanging there, suspended a good six feet above them, was the limp body of the Norwegian Haugland, a loop of chain knotted tight around his neck. His tongue lolled fat and bloody from his mouth, and his eyes bulged from his puffy purple face.

There was no doubt about it. Thor Haugland was dead.

CHAPTER NINETEEN

Enter the Dragon

"Now, WHAT DO you make of this?"

"I suppose it's a pressurised suit, sir, to allow a lone aquanaut to venture out into the abyss without having to be inside a submersible and yet still survive. And by the looks of these," he said, putting his hand to a massive steel claw, "whoever was inside could effect repairs to the reinforced outer skin of the base, or take rock samples from the seabed."

"It's a beauty, isn't it?" said Ulysses with a twinkle in his eye, as if enamoured of the monstrous thing. He reached up to stroke the smooth metal casing of a huge armoured arm, mounted with what looked like a Gatling-style harpoon gun, built-up around the left wrist of the suit.

Mounted on the wall behind them were a number of different attachments – from large drill bits to huge shears – which could be fitted to the wrist mountings of the exo-suit. It looked as though, in the wrong hands, it wouldn't be so much a diving suit as a one-man walking war-machine.

"Yes, or one could use it to break out of an inadequate prison," Ulysses said, a broad grin splitting his face from ear to ear.

There was a sudden loud clang that seemed to reverberate across the outer hull of the pressurized chamber within which the two of them had been imprisoned.

"What was that?" Ulysses was about to say, but there was no need; there could be no doubt.

There was a second crash that rang through the reinforced metal walls of the base as though the whole structure was a colossal tuning fork, the vibration making Ulysses' ears ache.

He looked at his manservant, who was also wincing in pain.

"Something tells me it's time we got out of here." he said.

"IT'S TIME WE got out of here," Selby said as a seismic tremor shook the dome, setting the chains rattling and Haugland's body swinging.

"Agreed," Captain McCormack said, scouring the darkness of the dome above them, as if half-expecting something to burst through the armoured roof at any second.

"And go where?" Professor Crichton demanded, his face ashen, his uncontained trepidation having returned with a vengeance.

"All I'm saying is we should get back to the dock and leave this place," Selby grumbled.

"What? Aboard the *Ahab* or the *Nemo*, with that thing out there?" Crichton exclaimed.

"Nothing but death awaits us here!" Selby shouted over the noise, staring at the dangling corpse of the Norwegian, the lifeless body swinging from side to side like a pendulum.

"You have a better idea, professor?" McCormack challenged.

Crichton stammered a response but it went unheard as another more violent crash shook the complex, louder now and seeming nearer.

"No, I thought not. Then follow me. Back to the dock!"

"BACK TO THE dock!" Wates called, his ringing footfalls increasing in pace as he led his team past the habitation pods. The purser was having no trouble keeping up, although both Dr Ogilvy and Lady Denning were gasping for breath. With her ladyship he put it down to her age. With the doctor, from what little had picked up, withdrawal symptoms were the most likely explanation. "Come on!" he called. "Try to keep up!"

As he ran, Wates was becoming increasingly aware of a creaking, groaning sound, singing from the steel structure of the ageing complex around them like eerie distorted whale-song. Whatever was happening to the base elsewhere, the years of salt-decay and sea-rust were beginning to take their toll, as the ringing clangs threatened to upset the uneasy equilibrium the structure of the Marianas Base had so far managed to maintain thousands of feet below the sea.

The huge water pressures, coupled with the Kraken's predations, were starting to work on the damaged structure in ways that could only lead to one outcome.

Rounding a bend Wates suddenly caught sight of another door ahead of them. "We're almost there," he gasped.

"Come on, your ladyship," the purser called from behind him. "And do keep up, doctor!"

"How far is it?" Lady Denning spluttered.

"Not far now!"

"What's that?" Wates said, suddenly distracted as his ringing footfalls on the grilled metal floor turned to wet splashes and he felt the uncomfortable chill of near-freezing seawater at his ankles.

He faltered in his run, the purser almost colliding with him as he too splashed into the spreading pool. The water was coming from the far end of the passageway, from where the door that would lead them back to the sub-dock stood firmly shut. Papers floated in the encroaching shallows.

"That can't be good," the purser managed, his face turning pale. "Should we go back?"

"What's the matter?" Lady Denning asked, staggering up to them, gasping for breath. "Oh," she said, the sensation of wet and cold at her feet causing her to lift the hem of her already sodden dress, "I see."

With a cacophonous groan of rending metal, a noise so painful to the ear that Wates half-expected to see the hull of a ship ploughing through the side of the tunnel, the ceiling opened up above them. Sheet metal, structural beams, utility cabling, along with flakes of rust and disturbed dust, rained down upon them. Reacting by instinct alone, the four threw themselves out of the way, falling in an untidy heap amidst the detritus and the sloshing water, throwing their arms around their heads to protect themselves from falling debris.

When the echoes of the catastrophic cave-in had died away again, leaving in their wake the protesting groans of the facility's superstructure, and when the abyssal depths didn't rush in, drowning them all, the four of them sat up and took stock.

"I'd say we won't be going any further that way," Wates said stoically.

"And I'd say we're trapped!" Dr Ogilvy shrieked.

"I've not had to endure all I've been through for it to end like this!" Lady Denning suddenly shouted, pent-up rage and frustration finding a sudden release. Struggling to her feet, she offered a hand to the purser, who was sitting on his rump in the cold lapping water. "Come on," she said, looking back along the passageway, "this way."

*　　*　　*

"THIS WAY!" HARRY Cheng called back over his shoulder. "We have to get back to the dock. It is the only way." He waded onwards, splashing through the water that was sluicing around their calves, pistol in hand ready, just in case.

Behind him, John Schafer and Constance Pennyroyal struggled on, with single-minded resolve, the two of them united now in their determination not to be beaten by the beast outside the base, or the one trapped inside with them.

"Don't worry about us, Cheng," Schafer said. "We're right behind you."

The further they went, the further the water level rose. If the rest of the Marianas Base was in the same state as this intermittently lit corridor, then they really were in trouble.

Another bone-shaking tremor passed through the passageway, the vibrations creating rippling waves skittering over the water, and sending the three of them stumbling forwards. Far away they heard a metallic scream, as if part of the structure was giving way. Their situation had changed from merely desperate to downright disastrous.And then he saw it.

"Come on, my friends," Cheng said, the smile growing on his face brightening the tone of his voice, as he indicated the closed bulkhead door ahead of them. "There's no time to lose."

"THERE'S NO TIME to lose," Ulysses said, gazing up into the bottle-glass 'eyes' of the pressure suit's domed helmet.

The metal surface of the exo-skeleton was tarnished, having been left to rot deep beneath the sea in Marianas Base, but Ulysses was confident that it would serve their purpose.

"Here, give me a leg up, old chap," he told Nimrod, "and I'll have us out of here in a jiffy."

"Very good, sir," his sullen-looking manservant said, assuming the necessary position at the back of the deep sea diving rig, hands locked together at the fingers, palms held upwards.

Ulysses put his hands on Nimrod's shoulders to steady himself, and a foot on the hand-step his butler had created. Yet another juddering quake shuddered through the structure and, in response, the base groaned an ominous cry of its own, the superstructure starting to lose cohesion in the face of the monster's relentless attack.

"I would hurry, sir, if I were you," Nimrod added, his eyes widening in horror as he gazed, transfixed, through a tiny porthole that revealed the ocean depths beyond. "As you said yourself, there's no time to lose."

ONLY A MATTER of a hundred yards from the spot where Ulysses' was struggling into the pressure suit, the leviathan beast of the abyss pulled back in a rush of jet-siphoned water, before launching another attack on the base.

It bore fresh scars from its battle with the Megalodons, but the stump of a tentacle that had been so viciously severed by one of the giant sharks – an ageing bull – had already healed and was even showing signs of new growth. Within a matter of days, it would be as if the tentacle had never been taken at all.

Rocketing forwards like a torpedo blasted from one of the submersible boats of Her Majesty's Royal Navy, the Kraken slammed into the dome beneath it. At the last second it splayed its tentacles wide and seized the frustratingly stubborn structure in its suckered grip, hinging wide its massive angler-fish jaws.

Its repulsive body pulsing, the squid-beast delivered a massive bio-electrical burst of energy, ten thousand volts of raw power, to the outer surface of the dome. Much of the charge dissipated into the water around the base but inside lights flickered, the air crackled with the odour of burnt ozone, and Babbage consoles sparked, igniting small fires within the mildewed laboratories.

The creeping tips of the creature's tentacles sought out weak points within the surface of the structure, as its implanted hunter's instincts were pre-programmed to do. The pulsing signal coming from inside the underwater complex had driven it into a frenzy. It would not stop until it had retrieved the source of the signal and destroyed it. One probing limb uncovered a ruptured seam in the outer skin of an access tunnel and teased the metal free, peeling it like a banana skin and letting in the sea.

Sensors positioned along the dorsal line of the squid-monster's body detected the change in the pressure around it. Releasing its hold on the docking dome, the Kraken twisted its whole body to face whatever it was that was approaching.

The prow of the submarine emerged from the eternal gloom, heading directly for the Marianas base and on an intercept course with the monster. As the Kraken turned to meet this new threat to its supremacy, it presented its left side as a clear target to the submarine's already oncoming torpedoes.

The two missiles struck the beast full amidships.

The abyssal darkness, pierced only by the beams of the submarine's lights and what little luminescence shone from the glass bubbles of the Marianas base, became even more obscured in the aftermath of the twin detonations. Purple ink-blood clouded the water, distorted by the swelling watery sphere of the expanding explosion, pieces of pallid grey-green flesh amongst the debris.

The submarine ploughed on through the mess and murk, swaying as it entered the shockwave, chasing after the leviathan. But by the time it cleared the debris beyond the perimeter of the undersea complex, the Kraken was gone.

* * *

"WE'RE SAVED!" CAPTAIN McCormack exclaimed. Bursting back into the dive preparation chamber, the escapees initial entry point, he, and those with him, caught a glimpse of the submarine that had driven off the Kraken, its sleek gun-metal grey shape cutting through the darkness like a blade of shining steel.

Selby and Professor Crichton followed his gaze beyond the glass bubble at the crest of the dome, expressions of bewilderment becoming grimaces of disbelief which slowly transformed into smiles of joy.

"I knew it. They are here!" came another excited voice from behind McCormack, the man's English accent Oxford-perfect.

Harry Cheng stopped at the entrance to the chamber, John Schafer and Constance Pennyroyal stumbling past him, their own faces going through the same contortions as those of the professor and the chief engineer.

"I am sorry to disappoint you, Captain, but I think you'll find that you have been prematurely presumptuous."

McCormack turned. Cheng had moved away from the chamber entrance, so that no one could get the jump on him from behind, the gun in his hand trained on the captain.

"Cheng? What do you think you're playing at, man?"

"I am not playing at anything, Captain McCormack, I can assure you," the Chinaman replied. "What I am doing, however, is taking over."

"Taking over?" Schafer said, stunned.

"Yes, Mr Schafer. I am taking over. And as long as everyone remains calm, as I respectfully ask of them, no one need get hurt."

Cheng's attention was suddenly drawn back to the captain who, without moving and going for his own weapon, had turned his face towards the two engineers standing guard before the pressure suit chamber door.

"Captain, I would advise you against trying anything you might see as being heroic."

Even as he spoke, Clements and Swann, having lip read the instructions their captain had mouthed at them, went for their own weapons, moving from in front the hatchway as they did so.

Two shots rang out, sharp and loud in the confined, echoing space. Two thudding clangs followed as two bodies crumpled onto the steel deck.

Constance gasped. McCormack stood, mouth agape.

"Do not doubt my single-minded dedication to achieving my aims," Cheng said, training his gun back on the captain, having only given the two engineers the most cursory of glances. "I have no qualms about killing everyone here, if it will help me achieve my goals. However, as honour dictates, I would prefer not to cause any unnecessary loss of life."

"So, it was you all along," McCormack said with furious, deepening conviction.

"If you are referring to the mysterious disappearances and deaths, then I can assure you that you are mistaken. And you can take my word for that, for what would I have to gain in the current situation by lying?"

The sound of running footfalls broke the stunned silence that followed Cheng's words.

"What's going on? Captain?" Mr Wates asked stumbling to a halt as he entered the chamber.

McCormack saw his officer going for his own holstered weapon.

"Wates, don't you dare," he commanded. "That's an order!"

Mr Wates froze on the spot, as the rest of the small group that had accompanied him stumbled into the dome after him.

"Oh my God!" Dr Ogilvy shrieked as he saw Cheng, the gun and the dead engineers.

"Doctor, that goes for you too," McCormack commanded.

"All of you, over there," Cheng said, gesturing towards the chamber containing Ulysses and Nimrod with the muzzle of his gun. "And drop your weapons."

The command was following by a clattering of pistols and other weapons, falling to the grille-mesh floor.

"What do you hope to achieve by this coup of yours, Cheng?" McCormack challenged. "You are but one man."

"But again you are mistaken, captain. I am one man with the entire crew of a submarine preparing to dock with this facility and take control of it."

Without taking his eyes off the party gathered in front of him, Cheng jerked his head towards the glass-bubble apex of the dome. McCormack and a number of the others could not help risking a glance upwards. Through the mote-shot murk above them, they could see the submarine returning, illuminated by its own running lights.

With a moaning howl that surprised everyone, including Cheng, the timorous, self-serving doctor suddenly launched himself at the Chinese double agent.

"It can't end like this! I won't let it end like this!" he shrieked. Startled, Cheng stared open-mouthed at the doctor as he stumbled towards him, arms flailing, completely thrown by Ogilvy's unexpected reaction. "They used me. I wasn't a willing member of their ring!"

And then the doctor was on him.

Cheng stumbled backwards, wrong-footed. Ogilvy fell into him.

The crack of a pistol shot rang out again, made unreal by the weird acoustics of the space.

Ogilvy's body tensed then went limp.

McCormack was already moving as Cheng pushed the doctor's body from him. Ignoring his own gun that he had been forced to discard moments before, he decided in that split second that in the time it would take him to retrieve the weapon, aim and fire, he could cover the distance between him and the spy. He judged wrongly.

The pistol barked a fourth time.

HAVING DRIVEN OFF the monstrous squid-beast, the Chinese sub finished making its turn and powered back towards the underwater facility, preparing to enter the Marianas Base. From there the Chinese would be able to seize the very technology that controlled the creature.

The only warning the crew of the sub had that they were in any danger, apart from a brief sounding on their sonar, was the appearance of a pulsing blue light through the soup of protoplasmic murk behind them. And then the beast rushed them out of the smothering darkness.

Patches of flesh were missing from its flanks, something like gleaming steel exposed beneath, and there were cracks in its own armour plating. But none of its injuries seemed to be having any effect to its detriment.

Despite its vast size, the Kraken was able to react quicker than the submarine, and was the more agile by far. Where the squid-thing had been able to take evasion action when the submarine had made its attack run, when the tables were turned, the submarine was too cumbersome to turn quickly enough to meet the Kraken's counter-attack, as the hunted became the hunter, and the hunter became the prey.

The monster seized the vessel all along its length with its muscular crushing limbs. A tentacle twisted and a propeller came away. Electrical discharges with the power of a lightning strike shook the sub, disrupting all its internal mechanical and electrical components.

As the craft lost motive power and its crew any means of controlling it, the Kraken's immense, crushing jaws closed around its rear-section. Teeth like spears of steel ruptured fuel tanks and ballast tanks. Sucker-tight tentacle-arms twisted and pulled, and the armour-plated hull of the vessel ruptured.

The Chinese submarine and its crew had no chance against the beast's assault.

Screams from inside, smothered almost into silence by the thickness of the hull, could still be heard, the vibrations of its terrified prey reaching the Kraken through the superstructure and the many sensors placed along its grasping tentacles, exciting the creature even further.

Its hull breached, the colossal hydrostatic pressures of the unfathomable weight of water pressing down on top of the vessel claimed more victims for the abyss.

With a whoomph of escaping air, the submarine imploded.

* * *

HARRY CHENG STARED in horror at the glass bubble above, as debris from the destroyed submarine drifted down onto the dome, ringing against the structure like the ominous tolling of a giant bell.

One by one Cheng took in each of his eight captives. The captain's foolish act of misplaced heroism had cost him dear. He sat slumped against the wall of the dome, with John Schafer and Constance Pennyroyal either side of him, trying to make him as comfortable as possible, propped up as best they could manage with whatever came to hand. He had a hand held tight to his stomach, a pad of bandages from the party's make-do first aid kit cinched tight against his midriff. His sodden shirt was stained red across his middle. He face had taken on a horrible grey pallor and his skin had a waxy sheen to it, wet with perspiration. Dr Ogilvy still lay between Cheng and the rest of the party, face down and unmoving.

"Not such the big man now, eh, Cheng?" McCormack gasped between pained grimaces.

"Captain," Cheng said with something approaching his usual calm manner, "I think you'll find that I am still the one – how does the saying go? – holding all the aces." He gestured with the gun as if to emphasise the point.

With a torturous screeching of metal, the hatch buckled and then swung suddenly outwards. Automatically Cheng turned his gun on the door as a huge shape pushed its way into the chamber. Twice as tall as a man, and almost twice as broad, the huge diving pressure suit exoskeleton barely made it through but its pilot was determined.

Gasps of shock and squeals of surprise rose from the mouths of the captives as they scattered, despite the Chinaman's screams that they stay where they were. The massive machine-suit bore down on the Chinaman whose gun barked again, and again, and again. The pressure-resistant armoured suit deflected each bullet in turn, all the time Ulysses Quicksilver's manic face visible within the dome of the helmet, made even more sinister by the reflected eerie green glow of the instrument panel in front of him.

The crushing steel claw – that had made light work of the hatch's locking clamps – swept down, smacking the weapon from Cheng's hand. The Chinaman reeled under Ulysses' attack and fell down hard on his backside.

The claw came down again. With a whirr of grinding servos, the pincer opened, before closing around Cheng's shoulder. The agent gritted his teeth against the pain, but couldn't help crying out as Ulysses lifted him off the ground, the suit's hydraulics lending him strength far beyond that of a normal man.

The dome shook again, provoking more cries from the over-wrought party, but Ulysses maintained his balance in the heavy suit, its feet weighted, although he lost his grip on the Chinaman as he reflexively opened his hand, ready to stop himself should he fall. Cheng crashed back down onto the mesh floor, whimpering in pain.

Glancing upwards, Ulysses saw the terrible maw of the Kraken again as it renewed its attack on the base. But, his preternatural senses sending him another warning, he returned his attention to Cheng, who was now struggling to escape from the pressure-suited colossus, kicking his feet against the floor for purchase, shuffling backwards on his backside.

A thin metal cylinder rolled across the floor where it had fallen from Cheng's pocket. A red light pulsed rhythmically.

The dome shook again, the dim lights flickering in protest.

Without a second thought, Ulysses punched the Gatling-harpoon fist into the floor, smashing the metal tube beneath it. The bulb exploded and the pulsing light died.

It took Ulysses a moment to realise that in the same instant as the metal cylinder stopped broadcasting its recurring signal, the sea monster's attack had also ceased.

In the shocked silence that followed the cessation of the Kraken's determined assault, Ulysses' breakout from his incarceration and the shift in the balance of power, everyone heard the piercing scream, that came from somewhere beyond the chamber. Ulysses' sixth sense flared once more, like a burning coal dropped into his skull.

It was a woman's scream and there was only one woman left among the party of so-called survivors from the *Neptune* who was not already present in the chamber.

It was Jonah Carcharodon's PA.

It was Miss Celeste.

CHAPTER TWENTY

Project Leviathan

"He's dead!" Professor Crichton exclaimed.

"And whatever gave you that idea?" Ulysses Quicksilver said, raising a sarcastic eyebrow.

There could be no doubt about it. Major Marmaduke Horsley was dead. The shaft of a harpoon protruded from his not inconsiderable belly, its barbed tip buried in the wall behind him.

Ulysses turned to face Jonah Carcharodon, an expression like thunder contorting his usually calm features. "And you say you know nothing about this?" He stared pointedly at the discharged harpoon gun resting on the old man's lap.

The rest of the group did the same.

There were seven of them gathered at the back of the archiving dome, including Carcharodon and his emotionally exhausted PA. The survivors had reacted instantly when Miss Celeste's screams had rung out through the base, carried by the distorting acoustics of the place.

Ulysses had led the way, piloting the immense pressure suit towards the corridors beyond the dome. But it immediately became apparent that the suit was too large and would hamper his progress so, boldly, he shut it down and clambered back out of the machine.

There was an awkward moment where the now defenceless Ulysses came face-to-face with Mr Wates, who had leapt to recover his pistol as soon as Ulysses had Cheng on the run. Selby was there, ready to back him up should the need arise. But there was something about the intensity of the look in Ulysses' eyes, in the way he said, "You have to decide who to trust!", and what Miss Celeste's screams were telling them that were enough for Wates to let it pass – at least for the time being.

So it was that Ulysses, Wates, Selby, Crichton and Nimrod, following his master from their breached cell, had rushed to the rescue, while Lady Denning and Constance Pennyroyal had remained where they were, finding the reserves of energy from somewhere to see to the captain, while John Schafer and the purser restrained the duplicitous Cheng.

Forced to follow those curving corridors still left intact they had soon found themselves inside a musty-smelling archive, filled with tumbled shelves and filing cabinets. A Babbage unit stood in one corner of the room but it did not look as though it could be in any kind of working order; a film of algal slime covering much of it, and eating away a number of the files stored here, having spread to the cataloguing shelves.

"I told you! I discharged my weapon during the confusion of the Kraken's attack," Carcharodon protested. "We were descending a ramp into another of these god-forsaken labs, still searching for Horsley when the attack came."

"Well, it certainly looks like you found him," Ulysses couldn't help throwing in.

"Scaffolding came crashing down," Carcharodon went on, as if he hadn't caught Ulysses' interjection, "and Celeste let go of my ruddy chair again. Went arse over tit, *again*, which I don't mind saying I'm getting more than a little sick of."

Ulysses gave the magnate's beleaguered PA's shoulders another comforting squeeze. She was even more of a mess than she had been before, dust having been added to her generally dishevelled appearance.

"Gun went off in my hands! By the time Celeste had pulled herself out of the wreckage I had already managed to right my chair myself. And then we came face to face with that," he said, pointing at the dead Major's skewered body. Carcharodon's complexion was pale, his eyes ringed grey with tiredness. A large purple bruise was blossoming on the left side of his face, an oozing graze above it. He did not look at all well, but was it as a result of shock, or fear that his guilty little secret had been found out?

"And besides, who are you to accuse me?" he snarled, finding some of his old fire again.

"I don't remember accusing you," Ulysses said with icy calm.

"Well, no, but you as good as said so with your meaningful looks and that ruddy waggling eyebrow thing of yours. Well, I'll not stand for it!"

"I didn't think you stood for anything anymore."

"And since when did you go from being prime suspect to judge and jury?"

"I would say since someone else was murdered whilst Nimrod and I were happily tucked up inside our little make-do cell. Wouldn't you?"

"He does have a point, sir," Selby butted in.

Carcharodon could think of nothing to say in reply to that, so he merely sat in his chair quietly fuming to himself.

"So what now?" Wates asked, showing Ulysses the deference he would have normally reserved for Captain McCormack, obviously quite happy now to look to him for leadership in their steadily worsening situation.

Ulysses didn't answer Wates' question but instead appeared to have become distracted by the contents of the room in which they now found themselves.

Lying discarded on top of a filing cabinet, amidst reams of data printouts, were two dusty, sepia-toned photographs. The first was only small, five inches by four, and was a picture of a child, a young girl. She couldn't have been more than about six years old, Ulysses judged. She was wearing a pretty pinafore dress and had ribbons tied in her long fair hair. She was beaming at the camera, holding her dolly in one hand.

He recognised two things within the photograph, the doll and the room in which the picture had obviously been taken. It was the central chamber of the complex in which they had found the mummified corpse.

The second photograph was larger and formal in style. It showed a team of people arrayed in two rows, those in front seated. This picture had also been taken with the central lab-dome as its backdrop. Ulysses could tell from the uniforms and lab-coats that this was a record of members of the military-scientific team that must have worked here in the past. Chances were that it was their belongings that were now washing around the partially flooded corridors of the collapsing base. There were no children in this photograph, although there were a number of severe faces that Ulysses recognised.

Seated in the front row was a younger version of Jonah Carcharodon and he was still an invalid even then. He looked older than the rest, but there was less grey in his hair, his face less jowly, his eyes brighter. The second person he recognised in the front row was Professor Maxwell Crichton, his round spectacles and spiky hair unmistakeable. Seated directly next to him was an attractive woman, with her hair arranged in a bun on top of her head. Ulysses was taken aback by her beauty – she had been quite a looker in her day – but there was no mistaking her either, now having spent so long with her in such close company. It was Lady Josephine Denning. And next to her was seated the army-formal figure of Major Marmaduke Horsley.

There were two others remaining in the front row of the photograph. He did not recognise either the emaciated man with the walking stick, who looked like he had already been old when the picture was taken, or the significantly younger, bearded fellow. But there was still one other, among the nameless scientists, mechanics and naval personnel – standing at the end of the row behind the seated dignitaries – whose striking appearance stunned Ulysses to the core. The last person he had expected to see amongst the group in the photograph was Hercules Quicksilver, his own father.

Ulysses stared at the image in disbelief, only dimly aware of the discussions of the others taking place around him. He turned the picture over in his hands. Written on the back in a languid copperplate hand were the words:

Project Leviathan, February 1972.

Ulysses turned slowly to the professor who was still staring dumbstruck at the dead Major.

"Professor Crichton," he said, holding up the picture. "What is this? What is Project Leviathan?"

Crichton turned his eyes from Horsley's glassy stare and Ulysses could see that, behind the round lenses of his glasses, the man's eyes were glistening wetly. He opened his mouth to speak but before he managed to get a word out, his bottom lip quivering, he fell to his knees, as his body became subsumed by gut-wrenching sobs.

"God forgive us!" he spluttered, just as he had done upon encountering the body in the chair. The old, spineless professor had returned, his tougher, more resolute alter ego gone.

It was uncomfortable to hear a man making such a womanly sound, sniffing noisily between sobs, snot running from his nose, tears streaming down his face. But after all that had happened – incarceration, assault by deadly sea monster, attempted coup – Ulysses' patience had reached the end of its tether.

The dandy strode up to the downcast man, grabbed him by the lapels of his ruined suit and hauled him to his feet.

"Oh, for God's sake, pull yourself together, man! What is Project Leviathan? Tell me, Professor!"

With shaking hands, Crichton pulled his hip flask from his pocket – that old familiar, spirit-sapping crutch – unscrewed the cap and took a gulping swig. As the warming alcohol coursed through him, the professor seemed to find some of that lost resolve again.

Bringing his sobbing back under control, he took the photograph from Ulysses' hands.

"I thought I would never hear the name of that god-forsaken project ever again," he said, still catching his breath, wiping the mucus and tears from his face. "We all swore never to speak of it."

Rather than badger the professor with more questions – no matter how desperately he might want the answers to them – Ulysses gave him room to make his confession.

"We all swore never to speak of it again," Crichton repeated.

"They why speak of it now?" It was Carcharodon who was now attempting to derail the professor's confessional.

"Do not interrupt!" Ulysses barked.

Realising that he was dealing with a man on the edge, Carcharodon fell silent.

"Go on, Professor."

"We believed our intentions to be honourable. It was all for the greater good of the Empire. To create bio-mechanical constructs, weapon-creatures to protect Magna Britannia's interests at sea. But in reality it was an act of the greatest hubris against God and nature. I can't even tell you about the experiments the German exiles were said to be carrying out on live human specimens."

The professor looked close to emotional collapse again. He paused and took a deep breath.

"But we were all equally to blame. We all had our roles within this blasphemous exercise. Carcharodon's company provided the ships to transport everything here, Umbridge Industries built the base itself." He paused, and pointed at the emaciated elderly man in the photograph. "That's Josiah Umbridge there."

"And he was the one prevented from coming on this trip due to ill health?" Ulysses asked rhetorically, putting all the pieces of the puzzle together.

"He sent that fellow Sylvester in his place, yes." Crichton resumed his story. "Lady Denning and myself were brought in because of our expertise in the fields of marine biology and evolutionary biology to help Seziermesser and his team of Frankenstein Corps exiles here," he pointed at a white-coated, also bespectacled, haughty looking scientist, "to create the hybrid-vivisects themselves."

"Hybrid-vivisects?" Ulysses couldn't help interrupting at hearing this.

"The Kraken, if you prefer. The amalgam of the Architeuthis Dux with genetic material from a number of other marine creatures, so that it might exhibit the properties of those species. There are the obvious accoutrements, of course, of the electric eel, crustacean armour and the melanocetus jaws, but other creatures had their parts to play as well. For example, the prototype also had grafted into its genetic matrix the attributes of Asterias Rubens, the common starfish, and anemones. It can regenerate damaged limbs, even re-grow other parts of its body, allowing it to recover from significant injury, given time."

Ulysses felt as though he was sitting in on one of Professor Crichton's lectures. For a brief moment he caught a glimpse of the scientist at his most relaxed, talking about that which interested him the most – his work.

"Professor, you said they were bio-mechanical constructs," Ulysses said intrigued, trying to get to the heart of the matter.

"Well, yes. We needed some way of controlling them after all and marrying the mechanical to the biological made them even more effective and resistant to damage. Felix Lamprey, this man here," – he pointed at a young, bearded man – "designed both the creatures' endoskeletons, including the mechadendrite tentacle cores, and also programmed the Babbage-unit adapted nervous systems. That was our way of controlling them. He was an undisputed genius. Until he lost it."

"Where did you collect your monstrous specimens from in the first place?"

"From the trench, of course. That was where Horsley came in," Crichton said melancholically, nodding at the still skewered Major. No one had thought to take the body down with everything else that was going on. "Big game hunter, wasn't he? He provided the expertise by which to hunt and trap the colossal squid living down there."

Ulysses paused. There was one last thing he wanted to know about, more so than Felix Lamprey's implied mental instability.

"Professor," he began cautiously. "Did you know my father?"

"Oh yes. We all knew Hercules Quicksilver."

"Then what part did he have to play in Project Leviathan?"

Crichton took another pull on his flask before answering. There couldn't be much left in the silvered container now.

"I believe his title was that of Observer. He was the face of the Empire down here in these damned abyssal depths."

"And what did you mean by Lamprey losing it? What happened to him?"

The professor suddenly froze and tensed, his face becoming a contorted gargoyle grimace.

"Professor?"

Crichton's body tensed again involuntarily and he fell, pole-axed, onto the floor with a painfully loud clang. The others surrounded him in a moment but there was nothing any of them could do. The professor was fitting, joints seizing, hands contorted into paralytic claws, spittle foaming from between vice-tight jaws.

"Professor!" Ulysses shouted helplessly. Just as the old sod had started to give him some idea of what might be going on, this happened. Could it be something other than coincidence?

"What's wrong with him?" Carcharodon squealed, his face pale as ever.

"He's suffering a seizure," Wates said. "It's like he's having a stroke,"

"I've seen this sort of thing before," Nimrod revealed.

"Go on," Ulysses encouraged.

"The introduction of certain neuro-toxins to the human nervous system can have such an effect."

"Which toxins?"

"Those naturally produced by some animals to help protect them against attack from larger predators. Sea-urchin venom, for one."

"But he hasn't come into contact with anything like that since we've been stuck down here," Selby said. "Has he? I mean there's not a mark on him to say that he has, is there?"

Ulysses picked up the hip flask from where the thrashing Crichton had dropped it. He sniffed at the open neck of the container. There was the heady aroma of alcohol and... something else.

"He didn't have to have been stung. He could have ingested it."

Renewed looks of horror spread throughout the group.

"Our killer has been busy."

The fitting Crichton's body tensed one last time and then his muscles relaxed and he lay motionless on the cold hard floor, his eyes wide open, the flicker of life within them faded. Nimrod felt for a pulse.

"The professor is dead."

"I see it now," Ulysses said, in a tone of wonder, as if he was experiencing an epiphany of sorts. "Carcharodon, what was the outcome of Project Leviathan? Why have I never heard of it? Why did everyone involved swear never to speak of it again?"

The shipping magnate met Ulysses' intense stare with one of his own. "I do not see how raking over something that happened a quarter of a century ago is going to be of relevance to our situation now."

"What? You can't be serious!"

"You heard what Crichton said. We swore."

"And look where that's got us! This has all been planned from the start only I couldn't see it. But now I have one more piece of the puzzle in my hands. Someone has tried to lure as many members of Project Leviathan here as they can and is now bumping them off one by one."

"I do not wish to discuss this matter any further."

"What sordid little secrets are you so determined to keep hidden?"

"I do not wish to discuss it!"

"Well we better had start discussing it, because unless I find out what's going on here, people are going to continue to die, Carcharodon!" Ulysses bellowed. "And you could be next!"

CHAPTER TWENTY-ONE

Lamprey's Legacy

Ulysses Quicksilver stormed back into the sub-dock anteroom, shoving a scowling Jonah Carcharodon in his chair before him.

"Horsley's dead," he announced, "Crichton's dead and you, Lady Denning and Carcharodon, are the only surviving members of Project Leviathan left on this base. You're the only ones left and this stubborn old fool," he roared into the cowed Carcharodon's ear, "refuses to tell me what happened to the project. Would you be so good as to tell me what the hell's going on before we all die here?"

"Mr Quicksilver? What do you mean?"

"Know anything about poisons, do you, your ladyship? Specifically neuro-toxins synthesised by certain sea creatures to defend themselves from potential predators?"

"Well, yes, I do," the older woman admitted, wrong-footed by Ulysses' bizarre tangential line of questioning, shocked by both his approach and the revelation that two of her erstwhile colleagues were dead. "In my work as a marine biologist."

"Care to elaborate?"

"Well, there are various species that employ such a method of defence, sea urchins, sea snakes and the like. Many of them produce toxins powerful enough to kill a man. But I don't understand. What are you getting at?"

"Professor Crichton just died of a neuro-toxin induced stroke," Ulysses revealed, with all the lurid panache of a Grand Guignol theatrical compere.

"Oh my God," Lady Denning gasped, covering her mouth in horror, as did a number of others around the room.

"I know all about Project Leviathan, Lady Denning. I know that you were here, twenty-five years ago, part of the team that created the monster that's been hounding us ever since our, as yet, unknown saboteur sent the *Neptune* plummeting to this watery hell. There's no point trying to deny it. Tell me, what happened to Felix Lamprey?"

"You've already seen for yourself," the marine biologist stated coldly.

"What? Enough riddles, Lady Denning. I want the truth, plain and simple. Tell me now! Tell us all!"

"In the chair, in the central chamber. I was not there at the end, but it couldn't have been anyone else. Of that I am sure. Felix Lamprey is the mummified corpse in the chair."

Ulysses called to mind the macabre discovery sat in the massive chair contraption in the central laboratory chamber, the curious helm upon the desiccated corpse's skull, the bullet hole in the middle of its forehead. Another piece of the puzzle was slotting into place.

"There's more you're still not telling me!" Ulysses snapped. "Tell me everything!"

"If you know of Project Leviathan, then you know of the auspices under which we all worked," she began. "We all had parts to play, that is true, but it was Lamprey who made everything work together. He was the genius who managed to programme a semi-organic entity to do as it was commanded. And not only that, he was able to use all of his technical know-how to cram all of the control mechanisms inside a helmet that transferred the controller's commands to the creature at virtually the speed of thought. He was undoubtedly a genius when it came to thinking machines and artificial cognisances. But then his daughter arrived."

"His daughter?" Ulysses thought of the photograph he had found in the archive.

"Little Marie," Lady Denning said, tears glistening at the corners of her eyes.

"How did her arrival change things?"

"I suppose, to put it simply, Lamprey had an attack of conscience. He had been so bound up in his work here at Marianas Base, determined to find a solution to every problem, driven by the question of could it be done, that he had never stopped to think whether it *should* be done. I suppose not many of us did. And if we had, then the question was always answered with the same platitude, 'For the greater good of Magna Britannia'. We had the security of the Empire in mind when we set about creating that beast out there."

Her words trailed off, as if she were reconsidering now her own attitudes towards the matter, or as if she were living in the moment of the memory.

"So what happened?" Ulysses pressed.

"His wife and little Marie were coming for a scheduled visit when their ship was attacked."

"Attacked?"

"We were told in strictest confidence that it had been the Chinese but there were those among us, Lamprey included, who suspected that the truth was something much worse. Rumour had it, that one of the test subjects had gone rogue during a field test. Some claimed that the beast attacked and sank the ship, mistaking it for a viable hostile target before it self-destructed. There were a handful of survivors, Marie amongst them, left bobbing on the surface in their lifeboats to be picked up by the Royal Navy rescue teams, but Lamprey's wife – little Marie's mother – she didn't make it.

"Her father now her sole guardian, Marie came to live with him here, at the base. It wasn't normal practice but then these were exceptional circumstances, and Lamprey was one of the senior members of the team.

"I suppose seeing her face, day in, day out, reminded him of what his work had cost them both. Lamprey's grief and overriding sense of guilt slowly wore away at his sanity until he went over the edge, and by that point it was too late to do anything to stop him.

"To his credit, he had tried to warn us," she said, a distant look in her tear-misted eyes. "He did try to persuade the others to abandon the project but, of course, our secret masters back in Whitehall wouldn't listen. And so he initiated the destruction of the base by the Kraken, using the control helm he had developed."

Lady Denning halted in her narrative, an icy silence following her words as all those listening considered the implications of what she had told them.

The sense of everything he had witnessed since arriving at Marianas Base was all becoming so much clearer now to Ulysses, like a smog lifting from the polluted streets of Londinium Maximum. The damage he had seen visited upon the base all made sense now too. The state of disarray in which they had found the place, as if it had been abandoned in a hurry, because it had.

"So, I take it, when the onslaught began that full evacuation procedures were initiated."

"Exactly so, Mr Quicksilver. Some died. Most escaped alive."

"And what happened to Lamprey?"

"I told you, I was one of the first to be evacuated. From what we have seen here tonight, I'd say someone managed to put an end to Lamprey before he was able to initiate the ultimate destruction of the facility.

With, what we believed to be, the total destruction of Marianas Base, the project was deemed a failure and officially 'forgotten about' by those that had plotted it all from the start."

Ulysses considered the possibilities for a moment.

"And what happened to the girl, Marie?"

"That's the most tragic part of the whole affair. Such a young life, snuffed out."

"She was killed by the Kraken? Or by whoever did for her father?"

"I don't know," Lady Denning admitted angrily. "Her body never turned up. She was classified as missing, presumed dead, just like her father."

"And now history's repeating itself," Ulysses said.

"Yes," Lady Denning agreed. "It has a nasty habit of doing that."

A tremor rumbled through the base, this time lasting longer than any that had shaken the facility so far.

"Well, I know what we need to do now," Ulysses said confidently.

"And what is that, sir?" Nimrod enquired.

"We evacuate again. We take the *Ahab* or the *Nemo* and we get out of here before the beast brings this place down on all our heads."

"You can't be serious!" the purser blustered, obviously terrified at the prospect. His world had been shaken to the core when his commanding officer had been injured. Any nerve he might have once had had now deserted him.

"And what else are we supposed to do? Wait here until we either drown or end up as the next course on the Kraken's banquet?"

"But we can't go out there, against that, in those!" the purser was ranting, in danger of losing any semblance of rational behaviour altogether. "We don't have any means of fending it off."

"He's got a point," Selby added, speaking up for the first time in a long time. "The bloody thing's damn well near indestructible anyway; it's armoured and it can regenerate parts of itself."

"So what do you suggest?" Ulysses threw back. An uncomfortable silence returned.

"Quicksilver's right. There's no other way." It was Captain McCormack who broke the silence, his words laced with teeth-gritting groans. "Get out now, while you still can."

"But what about the captain?" Lady Denning asked, indicating her patient.

"Oh. Yes," Ulysses stumbled, blindsided. "How is he?"

"Not good," the captain gasped, wincing with the effort of answering for himself. His voice was thick with saliva and he coughed, bubbles of blood bursting on his lips.

It was only then that Ulysses realised that the doctor's body had been moved.

"Where's Ogilvy?"

"There," Schafer said, pointing to a space behind one of the curved iron buttresses that supported the internal structure of the dome. Ulysses could just see the top half of the doctor's body around the end of a strongbox, his face and torso covered by his own jacket.

"Oh. Did he say anything else before he died?"

"Oh yes," the purser replied. "Kept going on about how it wasn't his fault, how they had used his own weaknesses against him to ensnare him. He was delusional at the end, but it seems as though he thought Agent Cheng was going to take him in for the part he had played in an opium smuggling ring."

Ulysses was suddenly sharply reminded of the initial reason for him joining the *Neptune's* maiden round-the-world voyage, to track down the source of the supposed smuggling ring. That was before the murder of Glenda Finch, before the act of sabotage upon the sub-liner, before the Kraken. It was strange to think now that this hadn't all been about the Kraken, the murders and the sinking of the *Neptune* right from the start.

"He might have been a washed-up narcotic-addled fool, but he didn't deserve that!" Lady Denning cried, directing her bile at Cheng, where he sat handcuffed to another of the pillar-buttresses.

Ulysses turned and, with purposeful steps, approached the defeated Chinese agent. "And what do you have to say for yourself?"

Cheng looked up at him with hooded eyes but said nothing.

"You weren't lying when you confessed to being a double agent, were you? Only I didn't realise that you were a turncoat to such a duplicitous degree, working for the Chinese Empire, making your Magna Britannian bosses believe you were on their side, leaking them secrets, only to use the information you gained in return to get back in with your slanty-eyed masters back in Beijing!

"But tell me something," Ulysses said, drawing even closer now to Cheng's sourly scowling face. "All this," he indicated the dome around them, "Project Leviathan. It was all going on a quarter of a century ago. Why now? What put you on to the possible existence of this place?"

Cheng took a deep breath and then, apparently deciding that confession was good for the soul after all, began. "There's been rumours of monsters in and around the Marianas Trench for as long as seafarers have plied these waters but in more recent years unexplained disappearances seemed to have been on the increase. Occasionally we would even find evidence, remains from the aftermath of such attacks. And then a long range scouting patrol turned up a survivor of just such an attack.

"He'd been in the water for days, drifting on a sundered piece of hull, and was suffering from the effects of exposure as well as dehydration. It's a wonder that something else didn't snap him up before we found him. Didn't last long either, but long enough to tell us that he had been part of the crew of a tramp steamer, six days out from Shanghai. He told us what had happened, what he had witnessed. He had no reason to lie.

"As you like to put it, Mr Quicksilver, all the pieces of the puzzle fitted then. We knew the beast that had taken the *Venture* for what it really was, a bio-mechanical weapon, engineered during the long cold war that has been fought between our nations for decades. But then I suspect you know this already."

"And if your government could steal the technology that had been created by Project Leviathan, they could then put it to use themselves, perhaps even take control of the creature."

"Precisely, Mr Quicksilver."

"And the homing beacon you triggered. It all makes sense now!" Ulysses exclaimed. "That's what brought your allies here in their sub only for them to be wiped out by the one thing they were after, because the same signal that drew them here also worked on the cogitator part of the Kraken's brain. It must have driven it insane, and brought it here as surely as it summoned your yellow brethren."

The dome shook once more, another tremor, like the presaging of a deadly seaquake.

"It's time we were gone," Selby stated bluntly.

"But if you all go now, and the true killer is one of you," Cheng suddenly piped up, a cruel smile of smug satisfaction on his lips, "don't you risk taking the murderer with you?"

"Don't think you're getting out of this that easily, Cheng," Ulysses spat. "You're coming with us."

The smug look vanished from the Chinaman's face in an instant.

"Everyone's in this together. It's in everyone's best interests to help us get out of this alive. I've said it before: our killer's not the suicidal type. This is revenge, pure and simple. They want everyone involved with Project Leviathan to suffer, for a reason, and to know about it. They'll not be able to get out of here without the rest of us. At least this way, we buy ourselves a little more time.

"So, back to the dock. John, Mr Wates, can you bring the captain with you? Nimrod, bring Cheng. And Mr Selby, if you would be so kind as to lead the way?"

"Well the *Ahab* and the *Nemo* are both still seaworthy and ready to go when we are. But there's a problem," the chief engineer confessed.

"There's enough fuel for our journey to the surface, isn't there?" Captain McCormack managed, from where he hung limply between John Schafer and Mr Wates.

"The subs aren't the problem –" Selby started to explain.

"So what is?" Carcharodon bellowed before Selby managed to complete his explanation.

"It's this place. The base. Some automated failsafe or other's kicked in. Must have been after that thing out there commenced its attack. The whole place is on lockdown."

Ulysses looked from Lady Denning to Jonah Carcharodon, the latter now with his assistant back to pushing his chair.

"The same thing must have happened last time, twenty-five years ago, when Lamprey tried to bring an end to everything."

"Yes!" Carcharodon snapped. "What's your point, Quicksilver?"

"So how did everyone get away that time?"

"I remember now," Lady Denning said, a growing sense of excitement colouring her words. "The lockdown was overridden. The correct access codes were entered and the pressure gates opened." Her face fell almost as quickly as her tone had brightened.

"Do you know those codes now?" Ulysses asked, already knowing the answer.

"I never knew them, I'm afraid, Mr Quicksilver."

"And you?" he asked Carcharodon.

"I was privy to them then, yes. But you don't expect me to remember them now, do you? It was twenty-five years ago, for God's sake!"

"Then we're stuck here," Ulysses said with cold finality.

"No, wait. There may still be a way," Lady Denning dared. "Lamprey designed and programmed the supporting cognisances used to control the bio-weapons, as well as the cogitator systems that operated the base – that are *still* operating the base – the logic engines which were the precursors of the Neptune AI."

"Of course!" Carcharodon shrieked in excitement. "If we could somehow link up the Neptune AI to the base's core cogitator systems – the ship's still out there, isn't it after all? – we could use it to crack the codes for us using a simple repeating algorithm."

"But how do we do that?" John Schafer said.

"I can answer that one," Captain McCormack coughed, his breath rattling in his chest. "One man, in a pressure suit could exit through an airlock – they all have manual overrides – return to the *Neptune*, find the AI chamber and initiate a link with Marianas Base."

All eyes looked back towards the entrance to the dive chamber where the motionless pressure suit still stood, where Ulysses had abandoned it.

"Well done, McCormack, that sounds like a capital idea. And I do believe I'm just the man for the job!" Ulysses said, a daredevil glint in his eye. "What do you say, captain?"

But Captain McCormack said nothing. For Captain McCormack was already dead.

CHAPTER TWENTY-TWO

Ghost Ship

"WISH ME LUCK then, old boy," Ulysses' voice crackled from speakers built into the exterior of the pressure suit, just beneath the bulbous fishbowl helmet.

"Good luck, sir," Nimrod offered obligingly, and Ulysses squeezed himself through the hatch into the airlock.

The solid circular door closed behind him with a clang and through the external comm-relay Ulysses heard the locking clamps *shunk* into place. The dull, droning siren that signalled that the airlock had been activated began to sound and the huge suit was bathed in a slowly circling amber light.

Using the techniques he had learnt during his time with the Monks of Shangri-La to keep his nerves at bay, with a pang of regret Ulysses recalled the last time he had heard the sound, and was reminded of the old woman's terrified face caught in that same orange light.

Having decided that Captain McCormack's dying piece of advice to them was the only way any of them were going to get out of Marianas Base alive, and having made sure that Cheng was now securely handcuffed to a roof support – John Schafer keeping a gun on him at all times – Nimrod, Selby and the indefatigable Mr Wates had accompanied Ulysses towards the airlock. As Nimrod had helped him back into the cockpit position of the hulking pressure suit, the engineer and the *Neptune* officer made sure that the suit's internal oxygen supply was hooked up properly and working efficiently, providing Ulysses with breathable air at the appropriate pressure.

The outer door of the airlock was shut using the manual controls inside the chamber and, once the water had been pumped out, air pumped in and pressures equalised, Selby opened the inner door again.

Ulysses swept his gaze around the small chamber, having to turn the huge suit from the waist to be able to take it all in from his cabin position, macabre curiosity getting the better of him. Of course there was no trace of Miss Birkin left inside the airlock now.

Since Whilomena Birkin had died, the first member of the party to lose their life since arriving at the Marianas Base, another eight people had lost their lives in that accursed place. Thor Haugland, the engineers Swann and Clements, Dr Samuel Ogilvy, Captain Connor McCormack, Major Marmaduke Horsley and Professor Maxwell Crichton. Four of them had died at Harry Cheng's hands alone, thanks to his deadly marksmanship. But four had died at the hands of the mysterious Marianas murderer. He sincerely doubted that Cheng and the Marianas murderer were one and the same. As far as he knew, Ulysses was leaving the rest of them behind with the killer in their midst.

He didn't like it, but he didn't see that he had any choice. If he didn't risk life and limb himself, then none of them would be getting out of Marianas Base alive. And he would rather be out there, trying to do something about it, than be one of those waiting behind, trapped like a caged animal, putting his future well-being into the hands of another. There weren't many he trusted with that responsibility.

But then perhaps the murderer wasn't one among their party at all. Perhaps there really had been a stowaway who had somehow escaped the *Neptune* with them, hidden on one of the submersibles, and who was now lurking within the passageways of Marianas Base, biding their time, picking off the members of the team that had worked together on Project Leviathan one at a time. But it was highly unlikely, Ulysses reasoned.

The alarm still sounding, amber hazard lights whirling like miniature lighthouse beams, vents opened and water began to flood the chamber. The outer door creaked open, the two halves of the opening hatch looking like blunt-toothed metal jaws. But was he escaping the hungry maw or entering into it, freely and willingly? Ulysses wondered as he took his first lolloping strides out into the abyssal depths beyond.

Adrenalin was rushing through his bloodstream with every pounding heartbeat, the excitement, trepidation and urgency of the moment all working together so that Ulysses' mind and body were operating at their maximum fight-or-flight-heightened potential.

He was aware of an ominous creaking sound with every step he took, just like those unsettling noises that had formed an almost constant background soundscape when he had been inside the Marianas Base with the others. But there he had quickly become used to blocking it out, so that after a short time he didn't notice it at all. He wasn't sure if the same would prove true now, as those same sounds reminded him that all that was stopping the mass of water all around him from crushing him flat as a pancake was the armoured suit.

From where he sat, harnessed within the cockpit, Ulysses' arms and legs reached into the armoured limbs of the suit, any movements he made magnified by the machine so that the monstrous appendages moved as if they were extensions of his own arms and legs. He could also drive the suit using controls in front of him in the cockpit.

So now, as he moved his legs inside the body of the pressure suit, so the mechanical legs of the contraption strode forwards, carrying Ulysses along the edge of the trench towards the place where the wreck of the *Neptune* still lay precariously balanced.

Cooped up inside the *Nemo* as the small submersible had chugged towards Marianas Base from the *Neptune*, the distance between the two locations had seemed long enough. But now Ulysses realised how quickly that journey had passed in comparison.

The prone shape of the *Neptune* lay ahead of him, still a good hundred yards away, teetering at the brink of the bottomless abyss. He could see that it had moved again since the refugees had escaped the flooding wreck. It now appeared to be resting more on its keel again, caught in a wide fissure in the crumbling sea-cliff beneath it, so that it had more or less righted itself. However, with such dramatic shifts taking place, Ulysses wondered how long he would have before the drowned sub-liner took its final voyage to the bottom of the Marianas Trench. He pressed on: there was no time to lose.

Each slow step kicked up silt from the rocky bed underfoot. He had not realised how slow progress was going to be, but he couldn't make the massive exo-skeleton move any more quickly had he wanted to. With a sudden cold pang of fear he remembered the Kraken. Dull booms carried by the dense water around him, and relayed to him both by the suit and its external pick-up mikes, told him that the monster was still labouring away at the devastated facility.

Intrigued, he dared to pause in his advance and bodily turn back to look for himself. His first anxious thought was how little distance he seemed to have covered on his *route* march across the seabed. The second was how huge and terrible the Kraken was. Its sheer size alone was threatening enough but its primal, aggressive temperament and appalling strength, married to a primitive determination, made it ten times worse. As Ulysses watched, the squid-beast tugged at a piece of the base's superstructure that had come free of its pile-driven moorings and cast it away, letting it tumble slowly into the hungry trench beyond the spur where the facility sheltered.

Turning back to the *Neptune* he plodded ever onwards, skirting the edge of the abyss, heading for the sunken liner, not daring to look back again. After all, it was now or never. Either he would make it in time or the Kraken would do for him first, and he was not about to encourage the latter by dallying here any longer.

AND THEN, AT last, he was standing in the shadow of the massive super liner. To see such a magnificent vessel brought low like this made Ulysses fear the Kraken even more. That something could bring down so vast a ship was almost incomprehensible. Worse things really did happen at sea.

Ulysses entered the *Neptune* through a vast hull rift, giving him access to the bilges and engineering decks. It was dark inside the ship and there wasn't anywhere left within the vessel that wasn't flooded, at least not as far as his penetration of the ship revealed. In places damage caused by the Kraken's attack and the action of the sea working on the beleaguered superstructure had created further obstacles for him to overcome. Fortunately the servo-hydraulics of the suit increased his strength ten-fold, allowing him to pull huge iron stairways out of his path and wrench open bolted hatch doors.

The lights projecting from the helm chased away the bizarre creatures that called these abyssal depths home, and which had already begun to colonise the dead wreck, dining upon the choicest morsels of the brand new banquet the sinking of the *Neptune* had provided for them. Slithering albino ragworms, skittering near-translucent shrimps and warty, black-skinned fish, every one of them as ugly as sin.

The pressure suit having effectively doubled his size, Ulysses could only just squeeze down some of the corridors at these lower levels, making his journey even more challenging. The other factor which made his expedition all the more arduous were the bodies. He had seen death in all its myriad forms more times than he cared to remember, but that didn't make it any easier, seeing the bloated, bulging-eyed corpses that had become trapped within the buckled passageways; crew, passengers, men and women, even children. The place had become a veritable ghost ship.

He also passed the occasional droid-automaton, the drudges non-operational now, the seawater and dreadful hydrostatic pressures having done for their delicate internal workings. But he continued to make steady progress as he negotiated the tortured passageways of the flooded wreck nonetheless, using the cutaway deck plans of the ship located at regular intervals to help check his progress, until he finally made it to the heart of the vessel.

Forcing open the doors bearing the *Neptune's* trident crest, Ulysses pushed through the space between them and entered the AI chamber. Having seen what the sea had done for the ship's automata crew, he only hoped that the significantly more complicated Babbage systems of the AI were better shielded and, as a result, still operational, otherwise they were all doomed.

Apart from obviously being entirely flooded and in utter darkness, Ulysses seeing everything through a particle-suffused murk of chill sea-water, illuminated only by his suit lights, the chamber did not look significantly different to the one and only time Ulysses had been here before.

The green-topped desk stood in the centre of the room before him, although the chair that was normally tucked in behind the control console was floating against the ceiling above him. Ulysses considered the keyboard of the Babbage terminal and then considered the massive pincer claw and Gatling harpoon gun gauntlet of his right hand. This wasn't going to be easy.

Carefully he manoeuvred the gauntlet hand over the control console and depressed the button recessed into the top of the desk. Ulysses held his breath, hoping against hope, not only that the artificial intelligence was still operational but also that the input terminal was working.

He thought he heard a faint bleep and then, with a definite click, the cover on the opposite wall slid open, the screen humming into life.

"Thank God for that," Ulysses said to himself as he let out a pent-up heartfelt sigh. "Or should that be, thank Neptune?"

The start-up image of the trident logo on a calm blue sea glowed into life, bathing the room in ghostly white light. The artificial waves appeared to ripple in the current swirling within the chamber with Ulysses' every movement, magnified by the hulking diving suit.

A prompt appeared on the screen.

USER:

The purser had hopefully provided him with all the information he needed – codenames, passwords and the like. Slowly he entered the late captain's name, keying in each letter with careful movements of the massive gauntlet's index finger.

Another prompt appeared.

PASSWORD:

Ulysses could see that this was going to be slow progress, typing with one finger.

There was a jolt and Ulysses had to steady himself. The ship had moved again. Not very much, but enough to emphasise the point that he didn't have long. And here he was having to type like an imbecilic child.

All he had to do was initiate the link and set the AI's systems to cracking the codes that would open the sub-dock doors and free those still trapped inside the base. But, there was so much more he wanted to do before he had to quit the ship. He had been given unprecedented access to the Neptune AI and all the secrets it contained.

His suspicions about what was going on were stronger than ever now, the possible identity of the culprit at the forefront of his mind. And he hoped that the AI would be able to help him uncover the last pieces of the complex puzzle this mystery had become, and confirm the psychopath's identity.

After all, some still unidentified saboteur had used the *Neptune* itself to initiate the first phase of the sub-liner's destruction. And what was it that Glenda Finch had been trying to tease from the data files of the all-knowing AI?

He entered the last letters of the captain's password and then hit the enter key.

The synthesised voice of the artificial intelligence came to him in a buzz of static, relayed through the intercom speakers built into the helm.

"Hello, Captain McCormack," the AI said in a softly spoken voice that would be forever England. "It is good to hear from you again."

With careful, patient movements, with the ship creaking and shivering around him, Ulysses set to work.

THE SHIP GROANED and shifted once more, the complaining sounds of metal under stress the *Neptune's* death rattle. The hull fissure was before him now. With pounding steps, moving as quickly as the bulky suit would allow, Ulysses powered towards the breach.

And then he was through. He dropped back down to the seabed, only a matter of feet from the precipitous edge of the black maw of the trench, his landing causing impact craters to appear in the silt and sand beneath the heavy weighted boots. Without pausing for a moment's thought, Ulysses kept moving forwards, towards the devastated domes, visible as no more than shadow-shapes in the murk, barely lit from inside. He was abruptly aware of how bright his own suit's spotlights must appear in the torpid darkness. But then, such feelings of conspicuousness and inferiority compared with what awaited him out there in the abyss could not crush the growing sense of excitement and euphoria welling up inside him.

He had risked life and limb but it had all been worth it, he thought with a burgeoning sense of elation. Not only had he been able to initiate the required link to the Marianas Base, and thereby hopefully help save the lives of those trapped inside, he had also been able to wheedle the other information he had wanted from the inner enigmatic workings of the *Neptune's* Babbage brain.

He had accessed the AI's log and had it confirmed for him that someone – and chances were it had been Glenda Finch, using another's identity – had accessed files about the Carcharodon Shipping Company's accounts, just as McCormack had told those at the briefing after her death that now seemed like weeks ago, but which in reality must only have been less than forty-eight hours before. More importantly, he also knew that whoever it was that had initiated the sabotage sub-routine had logged on as 'Father'.

These were indisputable facts, facts that would help him uncover the true villain of this tragedy, the one responsible for the deaths of so many, not only those murdered in the last few hours, but the thousands who had died when the *Neptune* went down.

He felt the seismic tremor of the sea-bed moving uncomfortably beneath him, like some great whale disturbed from its rest. He stumbled, not daring to stop and look back, knowing that time had run out for the *Neptune* at last. He ran on, at least he moved at what approximated to a run, hampered as he was by the grinding servos of the suit. It had been constructed for diver-engineers to work at static points outside the safety of the scientific facility. It had not been designed to win races.

He kept on, pushing the suit as hard as he dared. There was no telling how the ship might go. It might even swing round, slam into him and carry him over the edge with it. So he kept moving forwards, at the same time angling his course so that he was moving further and further away from the edge of the precipice, hearing the scraping of the ship as it grated across the sea-bed, the metal of its hull groaning in protest. Ulysses only hoped that the AI cracked the codes before the link was lost and the ship pitched into the crushing depths.

Then the cacophonous noise of the sliding vessel subsided and ceased, and so did the seismic juddering Ulysses felt through the heavy feet of the suit. Was the sub-liner gone? Had it plummeted over the edge and was it, even now, sinking to its final resting place, far beyond the reach of man?

Ulysses stopped and swung the suit round. The *Neptune* was still there, although in an even more precarious position than it had been before. It was lying along the edge of the abyss now, fully one third of its length suspended over the impossible drop.

He heard a crack as loud as a thunderclap, as if some colossus had broken a giant stone egg against a submerged mountain peak. Alarm bells rang inside his head as blood turned to ice in his veins. He had to keep moving.

The suit pounding across the seabed, ever carrying him towards the beleaguered base, Ulysses saw the fissure appear to his left and race away ahead of him. Rock shifted beneath him, slid sideways, dropping the section of seabed across which he was moving by several feet. His pulse thumped in his chest and in his brain. It seemed undoable now, impossible, but when had that ever stopped him?

An entire shelf of rock at the edge of the precipice had splintered free of the rest of the sea-bed, giving way under the weight and movement of the shifting sub-liner and weakened by the explosive destruction of the vessel's engines.

With a roar like pebbles being ground on a beach by the surf, only a hundred times louder, the cliff gave way, boulders the size of houses tumbling into the hungry darkness, taking Ulysses, helpless now, trapped inside the pressure suit, with it, down into the unfathomable depths of the Marianas Trench.

CHAPTER TWENTY-THREE

The Belly of the Beast

As THE HEAVY suit dropped like a stone, plunging Ulysses into the untold depths on his back, watching the trench wall slide past, the lip of the precipice disappearing from view, he found himself wishing that he had fitted a grappling hook extension before embarking on his mission. Ulysses wondered how long he had before the ever-increasing hydrostatic pressures crushed the suit and his body locked inside.

Now he came to think about it, there was a painful building pressure in his ears. Straining to peer through the bubble of the helm he was certain he saw a depression forming in the casing of the suit's left forearm. A rainbow of fairy lights began to blink on and off across the instrument panel in front of him. A discordant tinny beeping sounded in his ear.

A wave of nauseous panic washed through him and he wondered how many more seconds he had before the reinforced glass in front of his face cracked. With an audible pop, a spotlight imploded, the beam projecting into the gloom from his left shoulder snapping off.

Everything about the suit flashing him hazard indicators and blaring sirens in his ears, Ulysses' own sixth sense screamed loudest of all. But he could see nothing; there was no sign of any approaching threat. At least, not from above.

There was a metallic crunch as something closed around him and suddenly he was hurtling upwards. The trench wall raced past as if

Ulysses were riding an express elevator to the surface. Straining his neck to see every which way he could out of the helmet dome, through the myriad porthole windows Ulysses saw saw-edged teeth, each the size of a man's hand, row upon row of them rolling back into the massive jaw clenched around the suit. He saw pink flesh, his remaining spot-beam revealing flapping gills and a pitch-black cavernous gullet.

Ulysses could hear a cracking, creaking sound, suggesting that the enclosing jaws were trying to close even tighter. The pressure suit had resisted the terrible forces that tons of water pressure per square inch had worked on it, and was now resisting the crushing forces being applied by the massive shark's jaws. But Ulysses couldn't be certain how long the suit could hold out. After all, he had seen with his own eyes what a Megalodon had done to the bio-mechanically engineered marvel that was the Kraken. The huge fish had, like as not, been surprised to find what it had considered to be a tasty morsel dropping into its abyssal home which was then more resistant to its attentions than it had expected, but that sense of surprise wouldn't last for long.

Activate weapon systems, Ulysses told himself, his own imperative helping him to focus his mind on the matter in hand.

With his right hand he pulled hard on the trigger lever built into the suit's right arm. At once the Gatling-style harpoon gun opened up. Short, barbed quarrels tore through the flesh of the monster's jaw, shredding its gills, leaving ragged white flesh in its wake, black blood trailing from the savage wounds Ulysses had dealt the prehistoric fish.

The Megalodon's jaws were enormous, but Ulysses, encased inside the equally impressive pressure suit, was much bigger than a normal man. The giant looked like it could swallow even a Great White whole, but the dandy adventurer was something else. Ulysses fought hard.

A vast shadow passed across his field of view, his remaining spotlight illuminating a circle of grey-green underbelly as the form soared passed.

There was another abrupt lurch, this time as the Megalodon's speeding progress slowed, and another, jolting Ulysses hard within his harness. If it hadn't been for the restraining straps, Ulysses would surely have brained himself against the reinforced glass and steel in front of his face.

The shark's jaws spasmed, opening again, and Ulysses dropped from the huge mouth.

He could see the ruins of Marianas Base directly below him now, the devastated outer domes, the fractured tunnels, the dim lights of the still intact central hub. The Megalodon's attack had carried him right over the facility.

Ulysses dropped feet first, the leaden weights in his boots drawing him back down towards the seabed. It looked like he was going to land within the man-made canyon of rusted steel between two bulkhead domes, all that was left of another gutted laboratory-cum-weapons-testing facility, a mere hundred yards from the airlock access. Lady Luck, or the god of the sea, was certainly smiling on him now.

He was moving before he even touched down on the solid seabed beneath him. That now seemingly ever-present dull throb of his subconscious warning him flared again and, instinctively, Ulysses turned.

He saw the severed head of the Megalodon, jaws open wide, its black pearlescent eyes bulging, dropping through the water.

Above it he saw a demon's maw of even more terribly distended jaws crunch down on the rest of its huge forty-foot long body, devouring it in three economic mouthfuls.

He saw an ensnaring net of boneless arms pull back around the squid's mantle, fanning out around the hideous alien head of the beast, ready to strike, as the dead head of the giant shark bumped against a spar of sheered metal.

"There's always a bigger fish," Ulysses muttered.

Not waiting to see what the Kraken would do next, Ulysses turned and, with thudding steps, pounded towards the relative shelter of the dome wall in front of him. In his mind's eye he could see the creature behind him, as it readied to strike, hooked tentacles whipping forwards, ready to send a thousand volts of electricity through his body, cooking him inside the armoured suit. The thought spurred Ulysses onwards.

He felt the whoosh of the water surging around him, saw the shadow above him, caught a flicker of a tentacle paddle sweeping past him, and then was hurled forwards by the rippling watery shockwave of the monster colliding with something solid, something that was not Ulysses in the pressure suit.

On his hands and knees now, Ulysses risked looking behind him again. An unalloyed whoop of joy broke from his lips as, in his adrenalin-heightened state, he saw the Kraken trying to untangle itself from the skeletal ribs of the ruins, the outer limits of which Ulysses had passed beneath before the monster could seize him.

"The one that got away!" he laughed, punching the wall with the balled fist of his harpooning arm in delight. The open outer pressure gate of the airlock was within reach.

THE BLARING SIREN died, the amber light stopped spinning, and, locking clamps disengaged, Ulysses was able to open the airlock door in front of him. Easing himself through the round hatch, he stepped back inside the Marianas Base, his feet clanging hollowly on the steel-mesh decking.

He was feeling suitably pleased with himself. Not only had he had an encounter with both a Megalodon and the Kraken and lived to tell the tale, he had freed those left inside the facility from Lamprey's legacy and he knew who the murderer was! From this moment on, Jonah Carcharodon was a man with a price on his head.

Ulysses was convinced that it was he who was responsible for the murders. The information ferreted away within the *Neptune*'s Babbage data banks had provided him with the missing link that now made sense of the mystery. The billionaire's shipping line was in trouble, suffering serious financial difficulties. The building of the *Neptune*, which had wiped out Carcharodon's personal fortune, had been a last ditch attempt to improve the company's portfolio and raise the value of its stock again. But construction costs and running costs, with this project more than any other as it had turned out, far outstripped the income that could be derived from selling berths on the cruise-liner. Ulysses supposed that Carcharodon had planned to sink the *Neptune* and claim on the insurance. With the ship lost to the Marianas Trench there would have been no way for anyone to effectively check up on his claim. But discovering that Glenda Finch was onto his fraudulent little scheme, and the subsequent intervention of the Kraken, and then believing Miss Birkin was onto him as well, he had had to ensure that there were no other survivors to contradict his story. Glenda's initial attempt at investigative journalism had turned Jonah Carcharodon into a desperate man, driving him to become a murderer. And who would have thought it of an old man confined to a wheelchair? Who but Ulysses Quicksilver?

But such epithets of self-satisfaction were put to the back of his mind as two facts regarding the reality of the current situation pressed in upon him.

Firstly, Ulysses had expected to be greeted by at least some of the team who had seen him off, Nimrod at least. But there was no one. A nauseous feeling began to creep into his gut, knotting his intestines with the cold, clenching claw of horrified realisation. Had he been wrong to leave his manservant behind, alone? But what else could he have done? There had been no other way of reversing the lock down.

And secondly, there was the countdown.

"T minus nine minutes and counting," the voice of Neptune boomed from speakers set into the roof cavity of the dome-chamber, the voice that had sounded so soft-spoken and gentle when he had heard it in the quiet of the AI chamber now sounded as ominous and echoingly thunderous as might the strident wave-crashing voice of the God of the Deep himself.

But what concerned Ulysses more than the booming presence of the Neptune AI within the Marianas Base, was the fact that he didn't know what it was counting down to.

And then Ulysses noticed a third change that must have occurred within the last hour when he wasn't there. The already dim lights were dimmer than ever before and flickering fitfully. Power relay cables hung from the ceiling like streamers and he wondered what other destruction had been wrought by the Kraken in his absence. He could only hope now that he was not too late, that the Neptune AI would complete its task and crack the necessary codes before the damage wrought by the monster finally overwhelmed the facility and proved the end of them all.

"T minus eight minutes and counting," Neptune spoke again, the coldly detached voice crashing from the steel walls like the sound of the trench shelf collapsing into darkness.

Ulysses turned towards the access way leading to the sub-dock.

Then Neptune spoke again. "Decryption complete. Access codes accepted. Lockdown reprieved. Target achieved. You may now exit Marianas Base at your leisure, Captain McCormack. I wish you a safe and pleasant journey."

Ulysses' momentarily renewed feeling of triumph – that he hadn't been too late after all – was quickly replaced by feelings of confusion and equally compounded feelings of unease.

"T minus seven minutes and counting," Neptune boomed, increasing Ulysses' fears.

If the AI hadn't been counting down to the completion of the task he had set in the guise of the late captain, then what was it counting down to?

Ulysses stomped into the dock, his weighted footsteps clanging from the hard floor. The scene that greeted him rooted him to the spot, leaving him wrestling with a near-overwhelming mix of emotions: feelings of horror, guilt, fear and despair.

By the light of a swinging electric lamp, dislodged from its mounting in the vaulted roof of the dock space and penduluming now back and forth at the end of a length of rubberised cabling, he saw –

– Lady Josephine Denning dead, body stiff as a board, eyes wide open, too much of the whites showing, pupils contracted to pin-pricks, the test tentacle they had found back in the abominable lab lying on the deck beside her, shrivelled and charred, its attached energy source discharged –

– John Schafer, spread-eagled beneath a fallen pillar, groaning as he tried to shift the metal beam from on top of him –

– Nimrod, unmoving, unconscious, a puddle of blood oozing from his scalp –

– Agent Harry Cheng struggling to free himself, pulling at the loops of his handcuffs, rubbing his wrists raw until they bled, trying to use his freely running blood to help lubricate the manacles and allow him to escape –

– two more bodies, this time those of Wates and the purser, bobbing on the surface of the disturbed pressure gate pool, facedown, both of them having been shot –

– bubbles rising to the surface of the choppy waves in the wake of the passing of the *Ahab* as the submersible sank beneath the water and powered out through the blossoming pressure gate and free of the Marianas Base, leaving the rest of them behind, to their fate.

CHAPTER TWENTY-FOUR

Sins of the Father

"T MINUS SIX minutes and counting."

The continuing countdown shook Ulysses from the stunned stupor that had momentarily overcome him. He had been on the verge of being overwhelmed as the shock he felt on seeing the scene of death, devastation and despair before him took hold. To have battled against all the odds to lift the lockdown – risking life and limb aboard the doomed *Neptune*, having to contend with first an attack by a giant prehistoric shark and then confront the Kraken – and to discover it had all been for naught had almost been too much for his exhausted mind to bear. To find Lady Denning murdered and both Nimrod and Schafer apparently left for dead, with the *Ahab* steaming away with, he had to assume, Carcharodon holding Constance, Selby and his poor PA Miss Celeste hostage. What had it all been for if they were to die here now? But he wasn't about to let that happen!

Now, suddenly the passage of time seemed hyper-real to him, as if his strange extrasensory perception was working in a new way, time slowing to accommodate everything that needed to be accomplished in what felt like, on the other hand, no time at all. He could almost feel the individual seconds ticking by.

He activated the controls within the suit again and strode forwards.

In the hulking pressure suit, the armoured exo-skeleton dented and gouged from the attentions of the sea and the monsters that dwelt within it, Ulysses Quicksilver strode across the dock, armoured boots clanging against the metal floor.

"T minus five minutes and counting."

He reached the spot where Schafer lay pinned beneath the fallen pillar, the young man struggling to free himself, desperation writ large across his sweating, contorted features.

Ulysses paused for only a split second to look again at Nimrod's unconscious form lying nearby. Then he reached for the steel beam. Catching the pillar in the pincer-claw of the suit, the notched clasping pads gripping, the metal of the beam crumpling fractionally as they did so, he heaved. The pillar shifted and Schafer groaned, with relief at being freed at such a crucial juncture and with pain, as the injuries he had sustained flared.

Wincing, Schafer struggled to work himself free.

Grasping the other end of the length of steel with the automated right gauntlet hand, Ulysses strained again, heaving on the controls inside the cockpit, as his protective suit struggled to move the beam out of the way. With the beam moved safely away from Schafer, Ulysses let it drop. The steel crashed onto the decking with a resounding clang, bouncing once with the force of its fall.

Ulysses tried to kneel down beside Schafer to help him, but the bulky suit hampered him. The injured Schafer stared at Ulysses through the glass discs of the sturdy helmet dome, the look in his eyes one of hopelessness and intense personal desolation.

"How badly hurt are you?" Ulysses asked.

"I've been better," Schafer replied. "My left leg hurts to buggery but I suppose I'm lucky."

"It could have been worse." Ulysses agreed.

"Although right now, apart from the fact I could be dead already, I can hardly see how it could be worse."

The young man's love of his life was gone and Ulysses knew there was no way that she could have left willingly, after everything else that could have torn them apart during their descent into disaster having failed to do so.

He didn't need to ask what had happened, or where Constance had gone. The answers to such questions wouldn't speed a resolution to their desperate situation and there would be time later, if there was to be a later, if they made it out of there.

Ulysses needed Schafer with him; he needed every able bodied man to play his part, if those left behind by the escaping *Ahab* were going to get out of this alive.

"T minus four minutes and counting."

"John, stay with me. We're going to get Constance back!" Ulysses declared. "But, right now, I need you to see to Nimrod. I need you to tell me the old boy's going to be all right."

Schafer just stared at Ulysses, his face wracked with a mixture of shock and disbelief, fear and grief. He looked like he was about to breakdown and lose all control.

"Come on, John!" Ulysses bawled. "Is he breathing? Does he have a pulse? Is he going to live?"

Schafer blinked as if only just seeing Nimrod lying there for the first time. With tentative fingers he felt for a pulse at the old retainer's throat.

"I-I can feel something. There is a pulse. He's still breathing."

"Destruction imminent. Total destruction of this facility will occur in three minutes. This is your three-minute warning. Evacuate now."

Another seismic rumble juddered through the decking beneath Ulysses' feet.

He swallowed hard. Somehow, someone had initiated a self-destruct sequence that would totally obliterate what was left of the Marianas base. But how? And why now?

He judged that their not-so mysterious killer was to blame, from everything he saw around him. The reason was clear: destroy the evidence, stop anyone – but Ulysses in particular – from coming after him. His calculating mind working nineteen to the dozen he began to see how it had been achieved as well.

In all their time within the facility, they had seen evidence of great difference engines, cogitator banks, analytical calculating machines and Babbage-unit terminals. The macabre chair device had been hooked up to a whole pile of the things. And yet, not once had he seen any of the thinking machines in an operational state. He had assumed that the systems were all dead, but of course he had now received evidence to the contrary. And there was the fact that he had been able to establish a link with the base at all. How stupid could he have been? If it had not been for the restrictive bracings of the suit, Ulysses would have kicked himself.

With Ulysses having established the connection between the Neptune AI and the Marianas Base's cogitator network, waking the sleeping machineries after a quarter of a century's dormancy, someone still within the Marianas Base had utilised the very same link with the sub-liner to terrible effect. They had effectively used the state-of-the-art artificial intelligence to activate long dormant systems, to bring about the destruction of the Marianas Base.

For a moment Ulysses wondered whether the ghost of Felix Lamprey had somehow lived on in the link, everything that made him who he was – his thoughts, his memories, desires, beliefs, disillusionments even – retained within the precision engineered clockwork guts of the chair's difference engine, waiting to be woken when someone turned it on again. Was it possible that perhaps Lamprey was not truly dead at all, those marvellous machineries somehow keeping his mind alive inside the withered husk of his body?

But Ulysses dismissed such hokum as impossible. Surely it wasn't feasible, not after twenty-five lonely years, and it certainly hadn't been a lifeless husk of a man that had done for Miss Birkin, Haugland, the Major or Professor Crichton.

He could only guess at why Felix Lamprey had not used the same method to wipe all trace of the base from the bottom of the ocean. He supposed that, having decided to use the Kraken to bring about the demise of its creators, having strapped himself into the chair, he could not then access the base's difference engines to do anything else, having committed himself. Perhaps access to the difference engines he needed had been compromised. Perhaps there were too many who could have done something to countermand his instructions and prevent the cogitators from making the final countdown, thereby denying him the option of initiating the self-destruct sequence. Ulysses imagined that paranoia had caused the base's architects to include such a system, if the Marianas facility had been erected at the height of the cold war that had been waged between Magna Britannia and its imperial Chinese rival, in case it was in danger of falling into enemy hands. In all likelihood, Lamprey may well have hoped to make his own escape from Marianas before the Kraken wrought too great a level of damage, giving him the precious minutes to get away himself.

However, now, at this allotted time, at this allotted hour, someone had activated that which had being lying dormant within the very foundations of the base, far, far below the ocean waves. Someone insane enough, with their own escape route already planned had used the link to their own advantage, to ensure that any and all loose ends were finally tied up for good.

With a weak groan, Ulysses' faithful manservant, never one to shirk his responsibilities or be accused of dereliction of his duty, stirred at Schafer's touch.

Ulysses felt a surge of relief pass through every fibre of his being. "I knew you wouldn't let me down, old chap," he said quietly, as Schafer helped Nimrod into a sitting position, seeing what he could do for the cut on his head. After all, every able-bodied man would have to play his part, if any of them were going to escape from the base with their lives.

And talking of able-bodied men...

Still encased within the pressure suit, Ulysses cut an imposing figure as he strode towards Cheng's place of confinement.

Harry Cheng physically withered before him, recoiling as much as was possible, given his state of bondage, until Ulysses slammed to an abrupt halt a few feet from him.

For a moment they regarded each other, Ulysses seeing Cheng through the panels of thick glass in the portholes of his helmet, a cowering wretch who had tried to seize control and take over but who had failed, now looking like he was convinced that his time had come.

"T minus two minutes and counting," came the monotonously cheerful voice of the Neptune AI as the countdown continued to echo from the walls of the dock.

Ulysses raised the massive, pincer arm of the mechanised suit above his head.

"Mr Quicksilver, have mercy. I beg your most humble apologies for my impolite actions earlier. It was not my wish that anyone lose their life."

Not a word issued from the speakers of the suit. The heavy claw hung there, motionless in mid-air.

Cheng pulled back as far as he could, exposing the links of the cuffs against the bare metal of the pillar to which he had been chained. There could be no doubt now that he believed Ulysses was going to finish him.

The claw swept down, describing a slow scything arc. There was the sound of impact, the shearing scream of metal on metal, the jingling of shattered links raining down on the deck, and Harry Cheng tumbled backwards onto the floor.

He sat up, looking at Ulysses with equal parts amazement and elated relief, distractedly rubbing at his bloodied wrists.

"Don't make me regret doing that," Ulysses' voice boomed from within the suit.

Cheng scrambled to his feet. Then, body straight, he bowed low. "I am your humble servant," he said.

"So, NIMROD, you think you can pilot this?"

Easing himself into one of the padded leather seats, Ulysses' loyal aide did his best to make himself comfortable, dabbing at the open wound on his head again with his no longer pristine handkerchief.

"Yes, sir. It shouldn't be too difficult."

"It certainly won't be if I take the co-pilot's seat," Cheng offered, smiling weakly and climbing into the seat next to him.

There was a moment's awkward silence. Nimrod looked back to where his master stood, squeezed into the cabin of the *Nemo*, still encased inside the massive pressure suit. Ulysses said nothing.

"Very well, sir," Nimrod said graciously, his aquiline features not betraying any emotion whatsoever. "That would be most kind."

"Take us out then, Nimrod," Ulysses commanded, as John Schafer buckled himself into a seat behind the pilots' position.

"As you wish, sir."

Slowly the *Nemo* powered up, its propeller chopping the water noisily behind it, and then, ballast tanks filling, it sank below the unsettled waters of the sub-dock and glided towards the open pressure gate. And then they were through.

Leaving Marianas Base behind – a strange, haunted place that had on first impressions appeared to be a place of sanctuary – the *Nemo* powered after the *Ahab*, already a good hundred yards ahead of their position.

"It's now or never, Nimrod," Ulysses stated soberly, observing the distant shape of the vessel chugging away from them. "We have to catch up with that sub."

"And then what?" Schafer asked.

Ulysses fixed the young man with a thoughtful look through a side port in the helmet dome.

"Don't worry, I'll think of something."

"Sir, I hope you don't mind me asking," Nimrod said. "But you do know what you're doing, don't you?"

"Oh, you know me, Nimrod. I'm making this up as we go along."

"Very well, sir. It is as I suspected."

Seeing the horrified expression on Schafer's face, Ulysses laid the gauntlet hand of the suit gently upon the young man's shoulder.

"Don't worry, old chap," his voice crackled from the suit speakers. "We'll reunite you with your precious Constance soon enough."

"And what of the Kraken?" It was Cheng who threatened to jinx their enterprise with his talk of the sea monster.

Ulysses turned awkwardly in his suit so that he could see beyond the viewing port at the rear of the *Nemo*'s passenger pod. The Marianas Base was already a shrinking conglomeration of broken domes, like cracked open eggs, overshadowed by the cliff-spur above it. And there, amidst the twisted spars and shattered structures the squid-beast wrestled with a stubbornly resisting hull section, caught up in its own frenzied assault, as if it was determined to bring an end to the place that had spawned it, nature using this most unnatural of tools to eradicate what had been begun here twenty-five years before.

"As I said, Cheng, it's now or never. So let's make the most of now, shall we?"

"T MINUS ONE minute and counting," the sober English voice resounded around the empty dock, but there was no one left alive to hear it.

"Fifty seconds," the AI told the corpse of Lady Josephine Denning, rigor mortis having locked her body into the pose that electrocution by mecha-tentacle arm had forced upon it.

"Forty seconds," it announced to the floating bodies belonging to the two crewmen of the *Neptune*, the purser and Mr Wates, gunned down as they had tried to fulfil their obligations to those they had helped save from drowning.

"Thirty seconds," it addressed the dead Captain Connor 'Mac' McCormack, hands still clasped to the ugly wound in his belly, the late Dr Ogilvy and the deceased engineers Swann and Clements, left behind in the dive preparation chamber.

"Twenty seconds," the voice boomed from the intercom panel in the Marianas archive, where Professor Maxwell Crichton lay, his face locked in a grimace of perpetual agony, the venom having done its work with deadly efficiency.

"Ten seconds," the voice of Neptune boomed from speakers in the workshop-cum-operating theatre, its continuing echoes sounding like the slamming of airlock hatches, Thor Haugland's hanging body swinging in its chains as the sub-seismic shuddering increased in intensity.

Nine.

Major Marmaduke Horsley, head hung low on his chest, the harpoon shaft still pinning his body tight to the chamber wall, stared with sadness into oblivion, a glassy expression in his never closing eyes.

Eight.

The mummified body of Felix Lamprey smiled its rictus grin with good reason now, knowing that the insane genius' final master plan would come to fruition at last, after so long a hiatus.

Seven.

Six.

Five.

Four.

FRAMED WITHIN THE rear view porthole of the *Nemo*, the detonation that enveloped the Marianas Base seemed like such a little thing. Nothing really to write home about, Ulysses thought.

But nervous anticipation did set his heart racing again as he saw the Kraken disappear within the expanding sphere of light that suddenly brought stark luminescence to the abyssal night.

Had the abomination been destroyed, caught up within the sphere of destruction, which came like the wrath of the God of the Sea claiming its own?

TEARS OBSCURING HER vision, mucus running thickly from her nose and into her mouth, she pulled hard at the life-pod hatch. A blubbering moan of despair issued from between her quivering lips, from deep inside her – so heart-rending a sound from one so young – at last, all her weight hanging off the door handle, she felt the clamp depress in her hands and with a slow gasp of compressed air and the creak of complaining hinges, she pulled the hatch open.

She clambered into the bathysphere capsule with ease, pulling the hatch shut again behind her, young muscles straining as she activated the locking clamps, sealing the pod tight.

In a moment of near panic she tried to make sense of the instrument panel above her head, all winking lights, dials and switches. But then she saw what her father had always told her to look for, on those occasions when he had reminded her of the safety protocols active within Marianas Base.

She slammed her open palm against a large red button and then collapsed back into the padded seat behind her, trembling fingers attempting to secure the harness straps over her shoulders and across her waist, as the warning siren blared its discordant wail, alerting the bathysphere's passenger that it was about to blast free of the base, a sinister crimson light filling the pod with its hellish glow.

She tensed in her seat, eyes squeezed tight shut, teeth gritted in terror, desperate hands clutching for the doll that wasn't there, her ever faithful companion who could have seen her through this and made her feel better, but whom she had been forced to leave behind, just like her beloved father.

And then, announced by a deafening *clunk-chsssss*, the locking clamps blew, hurling the bathysphere away from the facility, the tiny escape capsule soaring upwards through the miasmal darkness, heading for the surface and safety thousands of feet above, the child howling in anguish, knowing that she would never see her father again.

HE WAS INSIDE the airlock now, the huge suit barely fitting inside the conning tower airlock of the submersible. The *Nemo* was closing on the *Ahab* at last, the smaller sub apparently the faster of the two.

Ulysses waited, with bated breath, his heart thumping hard against his ribs, every sense heightened by the rush of adrenalin pulsing through his body.

The crackle of static interference that presaged the activation of the radio pick-up in his helm was followed by the measured tones of his manservant's voice.

"We are closing, sir. *Nemo* will be in range in three, two, one. *Ahab* in range. It's now or never, sir."

"Now or never," Ulysses whispered, his mouth suddenly dry, his tongue sticking to the roof of his mouth.

"Good luck, sir."

Ulysses punched the emergency eject and the airlock blasted open in a torrent of bubbles and swirling seawater. The abominable pressures working on the craft at these depths sucked out the air, the pressure suit and Ulysses with it.

CHAPTER TWENTY-FIVE

Sea Change

BUBBLES OF ESCAPING air blinding him, the hull of the *Ahab* nothing but a blur in the whirling confusion of light from the one remaining suit spot and the surrounding hungry darkness of the deep, Ulysses flung out the left arm of the suit. As the pincer touched the second sub, he pulled hard on the closing mechanism built into the arm, the effort of his exertions jarring his shoulder just as much as if it had been his own arm that had grabbed hold of the speeding vessel. The pincer teeth seized a protrusion on the outside of the *Ahab* and snapped shut, biting into the fin they had captured.

For one heart-stopping moment, the two subs touched, the collision barely more than a kiss but one which still sent the two craft reeling away from one another, the *Ahab* spinning on its axis. Ulysses clung on for dear life, but he needn't have worried; the vice-like grip of the steel lobster claw held fast. However, this didn't stop the suited Ulysses from being thrown against the hull of the sub, rebounding with a metallic thud that left him feeling nauseous and disorientated.

He reached out with his other arm, the gauntlet-hand taking hold of another protruding part of the vessel. Heaving on that hand as well, he was able to bring himself under control again. He was now flat against the hull of the *Ahab*, facedown, cinched tight to the curved surface, a tail fin in one pincer and a maintenance ladder rung held tight within his right gauntlet-fist.

To his right he could see a porthole, yellow sodium light washing out of it. He was so close that he could almost see inside the sub, but he wasn't quite close enough.

His curiosity frustrated, instead Ulysses focused on his primary task, that of reaching the *Ahab's* lateral airlock access. Hand over cautious hand he pulled himself along the side of the submersible, first releasing the pincer and then, when that was securely clamped around another handhold, loosening the grip of the suit's over-large robot hand.

And all the while the *Ahab* continued powering through the water, heading inexorably for the surface, forcing Ulysses to battle the drag of the slipstream, which tugged horribly at the unstreamlined pressure suit.

Slowly but surely he traversed the exterior of the *Ahab*, the convoluted construction of the hull providing him with plenty of handholds with which to heave himself up, until eventually he came alongside the entrance to the vessel's airlock.

Where those who had made the journey to Marianas Base from the incapacitated *Neptune* on board the *Nemo* had had to exit through the conning tower airlock – as Ulysses had just done again himself – when they had surfaced in the pressure dock pool, Carcharodon's cronies aboard his private submersible had been able to stride out through the lateral dock and down a gangplank to the deck below.

Ulysses found himself alongside that same hatchway now and, grabbing hold of the door's opening mechanism cranked the manual override. With a shunk the door opened and Ulysses pulled the massive bulk of his suit inside, manually sealing the airlock again from inside.

He realised that one of the things he did not have working for him, given this approach, was the element of surprise. Those on board the *Ahab* already knew that the *Nemo* was on their tail, the two, thankfully unarmed, submersibles having already scraped together. They would also have heard Ulysses' clanking progress as he struggled up the side of the craft and would now be listening to him operating the airlock. But he did have something else on his side. He was, of course, encased inside an armoured suit that made him twice as tall as any other man, and ten times as strong, a suit that had resisted the horrendous pressures exerted upon it down in the ocean depths as well as the attentions of a fully grown Megalodon.

It wouldn't be a matter of what Carcharodon could do to him now that would be the problem, but what he might do to his hostages in desperation, as he stared into the gaping jaws of defeat.

With the hiss and suck of water being drawn out of the chamber, the air inside the airlock equalised with that inside the craft, allowing the inner door to be opened. Spinning the wheel-handle with a flick of his wrist, readying himself – his breathing slow, his heart racing – Ulysses opened the hatch.

He took in the scene that greeted him inside the cabin of the *Ahab* in a second. Constance Pennyroyal was huddled in a corner, tied up and gagged. Her eyes widened first in shock at seeing the bulky mass of the deep sea diving suit crammed into the airlock and then brightened noticeably on seeing who it was inside.

At the other end of the cabin, Chief Engineer Selby stood at the controls, being forced to pilot the vessel with a gun to his head; a gun, which was held in the wobbling hand of Miss Celeste. Next to her, Jonah Carcharodon sat hunched within his wheelchair, his back to Ulysses.

"Quicksilver? Is that you?" Carcharodon challenged.

"Miss Celeste," Ulysses said, speaking through the intercom of the suit. "Put the gun down. It's going to be all right."

"So it is you. I thought so," said Carcharodon, weariness evident in his voice. "Who else would it be?"

"I'm sorry, Mr Quicksilver," the PA said in a quavering voice, "but I can't do that."

"Whatever hold Carcharodon has over you, it's finished. I know what he's done. It's over now. He can't hurt you anymore. I won't let him."

"But, Mr Quicksilver, it would appear you have made a terrible mistake."

Taking the gun off Selby, Miss Celeste turned, spinning Carcharodon's chair around with her free hand at the same time – in which Ulysses now saw she was also holding a moth-eaten rag-doll – and trained her weapon on Ulysses, for all the good bullets would do against the abyss-resistant armour. A look of surprise flickered across her face as she took in the imposing figure of the dandy adventurer sheathed within the massive pressure suit, but only for a moment. A second later, it was replaced by a cruel frown, a dark expression which filled Ulysses with a sense of unaccustomed foreboding.

The passing look of surprise on Miss Celeste's face was nothing compared to the shock which possessed Ulysses' features on coming face-to-face with the ageing shipping magnate once more.

He was wearing a bright yellow, yet deflated lifejacket, tied tight around his neck and waist. The pockets, pouches and ripped open inflation chambers had been loaded with sticks of dynamite, the same explosives the escapees had found in their search of the divers' prep chamber. The cobbled together bomb-jacket was packed with enough dynamite to obliterate the *Ahab* and all on board. Twists of wire protruded from the explosives, connecting them to a black box in Carcharodon's lap, on the front of which was a dialled timer.

"You've been busy," was all Ulysses could think to say.

"Oh, he doesn't know the half of it, does he, Madeleine?" Miss Celeste said, addressing the doll in her hand. The doll she had rescued from the base. The doll Ulysses had seen in a flaking sepia-tint in the hands of –

"The little girl," he said in wonder. "The child in the photograph."

"You recognise me then?"

"Now that you mention it, yes, I do see a resemblance. Your father was Felix Lamprey."

"Little Marie Lamprey?" Carcharodon uttered in disbelief.

"Yes, you doddering old fool." She hissed. "All this time, right under your nose. And you never knew. And not so little now, nor so helpless! The cuckoo in the nest."

"More like the viper in the nest," Ulysses said quietly to himself.

"Well, I..." Carcharodon blustered.

"What? Assumed that I was dead like my father, left behind for the sea to claim? Didn't give me a second thought? Never wondered what happened to that little girl you all left behind? Didn't care what had happened to her? Is that what you're trying to say?"

Ulysses had never heard the young woman say so much during all time they had spent together.

"It all makes sense now," Ulysses said.

"Oh, does it?" she snapped. "I'm so pleased. It took you long enough though, didn't it, Mr Consulting Detective? Had to see it for yourself before you would readily believe it, didn't you? We had to show him, didn't we, Madeleine?" The doll said nothing. "Well perhaps you can explain how I can make sense of it all, tell me why they killed my father and left an innocent little girl behind to die, a sacrifice to the beast, just like my mother, because I don't understand it!"

Ulysses stared deep into her eyes. If the eyes were the windows to the soul, then the soul he could see reflected in these particular orbs was a damaged, tarnished thing. She was wild now, any semblance of the mousey deference she had managed to maintain for so long entirely gone. They were now seeing her true face. The quiet, patient, ever-tolerant, uncomplaining, subservient Miss Celeste had vanished, to be replaced by the wrathful, vengeful, violent and unpredictable Marie Lamprey. And where Miss Celeste had seemed like a perfectly rational and reasonable individual, her alter ego was utterly mad.

The slightest of movements distracted Ulysses for a split second. In that moment his eyes jerked a fraction of an inch, and refocused on the figure of Selby, but only for a moment. But that was all it took for Ulysses to inadvertently betray the engineer.

Marie Lamprey, her own psychotic stare transfixing Ulysses' eyes, as much as his were locked on hers, saw the miniscule change.

She spun round as Selby heroically moved to stop her. There was the concussive retort of a pistol firing and a spray of red, grey and white splashed the viewing port beyond the pilot's position, as a soup of blood, brains and skull plastered the inside of the reinforced cockpit. Selby collapsed, looking like a puppet that had had its strings cut.

Constance gave a muffled scream from behind her gag and even Ulysses, who had seen far too much mindless violence in his life, gave an involuntary cry of shock. But despite that, the second Marie Lamprey moved against Selby, Ulysses took a long step forward in the massive suit.

And then the gun was back on him.

"Don't come another step closer," the insane young woman warned him, "or you know what I'll do."

"That? Against that suit of armour?" Carcharodon pooh-poohed, unable to stop himself, having got away with treating people like inferior beings all his life. "Don't be ridic –"

Carcharodon was silenced by Marie bringing the butt of the gun down hard on the back of his head. The old man gasped in pain, his head dropping onto his chest.

"Shut up, you senile imbecile!" she snapped. "I mean it, I'll start the countdown on that bomb you're wearing. And once it's started, there's no stopping it."

"Why?" Carcharodon slurred, unable to take in everything that had happened in so short a space of time, desperate for some reason to be given to rationalise the irrational.

"Why?" she shrieked. "You want to know why? After all this time, only now do you wonder why all this had to happen? Why you all had to die? Isn't it obvious?"

"Revenge," Ulysses stated bluntly, "pure and simple. It usually is."

"And what's that supposed to mean?" Marie railed, turning on Ulysses. "Don't think for one second that there was anything usual about what happened. Everything happened for a reason, the most important reason of all: for my father's good name! I couldn't have him remembered as a psychopath or worse, forgotten about!"

"Oh no, I can see that. The name of Lamprey is going to be remembered for a very long time," Ulysses said. "You've certainly made sure of that. You'll be infamous after what you've done, but it still won't be your father that people remember, not when the name of Marie Lamprey is plastered across the headlines of broadsheets across the Empire."

"Why, you!" she spluttered, reaching for the timer dial on the hastily-constructed device.

"I understand why you believed Carcharodon here, Lady Denning, the Major and Professor Crichton had to die," he went on. Marie's hand froze, hovering over the dial.

"You do?" Carcharodon bristled.

"The Professor practically gave the game away himself. He actually told us what your motivation for committing this series of cold-blooded crimes was. You wanted revenge on all those you saw as being responsible for your father's death, for driving him to do what he did, once they had turned their backs on him. The other leading figures of the Leviathan project. You even planned to ensnare Josiah Umbridge, the industrialist, in your little trap; only he didn't take the bait. He sent that wretch Sylvester in his stead.

"And it was thanks to you that all the right people just happened to be on board ship for the *Neptune's* maiden voyage, wasn't it?"

Marie Lamprey said nothing but continued to fix Ulysses with her disturbing wild-eyed stare.

"Your own employer's confession should have given you away long ago."

"What confession?" Carcharodon groused, one hand clamped to the rising bump on the back of his head.

"It was over dinner, that first time at the captain's table. You said yourself, Jonah, it hadn't been down to you that any of us had been invited on board for the inaugural round-the-world cruise. You told me that your PA had sent out all the personal invitations. You said that she did everything for you. That way she could make sure that she had everybody here who she needed, or at least that's what you had hoped for," he said, turning back to Marie. "But as we've already established, Umbridge escaped the end you doubtless had cooked up for him, by dint of being at death's door already and being too unwell to travel.

"You must have been plotting this for years," Ulysses went on, only now, as he reasoned through all the salient points, realising the scale of Miss Celeste's – or rather Marie Lamprey's – audaciously planned act of vengeance. "What probably started out as a backlash against the injustice of a world that had taken both your parents from you, fuelled by grief and a dozen other childish insecurities gradually – perhaps inevitably – became an obsession until the desire for revenge was your whole raison d'être. There was nothing left but the desire to be revenged on those you saw as being responsible for Felix Lamprey's death. Quite simply, your obsession drove you mad.

"It must have taken you years to work yourself into a position from where you could put your plan into action, to satisfy your sick irrational need for retribution."

"Don't say that!" Marie screeched.

"What? That you're sick, Marie?" Ulysses reasoned calmly. "But it's the truth. You are: terribly sick."

"They were the ones who were sick, weren't they, Madeleine," she sobbed, tears suddenly streaming down her face, "leaving a child to die having already done away with her father?"

"Ruthless, yes, but sick? I would like to be able to agree with you, but I'm not so sure. Whereas you, my dear, are one hundred per cent certifiably a fruitcake!"

"Stop it!" she screamed. "Stop saying that!" She pushed the muzzle of the gun hard against Carcharodon's head.

"So I suppose it was you who sabotaged the ship as well," Ulysses went on, managing to stay sounding calm, although he didn't feel in anyway calm on the inside. "But how did you manage that, I wonder?"

"You mean you haven't worked that out yet?"

"I thought I had," Ulysses confessed. "But I'm afraid I had this wretch Carcharodon here down as the culprit of our little morality play."

Carcharodon looked up at Ulysses, indignation blazing in his bleary unfocused eyes.

"I saw the log," Ulysses explained. "I know that the person who initiated the sabotage routine buried within the AI's memory core used the ident 'Father' to access the system, and I'm afraid I took that to be you, Jonah. I thought it was an insurance job." He paused as realisation struck. "Oh, yes. Oh, of course. If only I had seen it before. Lady Denning told us all we needed to know about the identity of the one the AI referred to as 'Father'."

"Then I take it I'm exonerated, cleared of all charges?" Carcharodon asked. "For all the good it will do me."

"Lady Denning told us that Lamprey – Felix Lamprey I mean – designed the difference engines that maintained the life support systems for Marianas Base. She also said that these more rudimentary systems were the forerunners of the significantly more complex artificial intelligence created for the *Neptune*. Its father, as far as the AI was concerned, wasn't you, Carcharodon, but Lamprey, the creator of the original AI template. Oh yes, very clever."

Still the quivering woman returned his stare, fire in her eyes, like the hellfire surely crisping her soul even now, in light of what she had done.

"And I'm guessing you used a combination of your cogitator skills and the privileged information you had access to as Carcharodon's personal assistant to sneak into the AI chamber at a time that suited you, access Neptune and activate the programme you must have implanted inside its memory core probably months before."

"Very good, Mr Quicksilver. He thinks he's so clever, doesn't he, Madeleine? But it doesn't matter now, does it? He's still too late to stop us, isn't he?"

"All right Miss Celeste, or Miss Lamprey, or however it is you like to be known nowadays, I understand why, by your twisted logic, Carcharodon and all his cronies from Project Leviathan were doomed to die. But tell me, why did the others have to die? Why did you kill Glenda Finch?"

"Even now, after all we've shown him, all we've told him, he can't see it, can he, Madeleine?"

The tenuous grasp Marie Lamprey had on reality was steadily slipping away.

"No, wait, I see now. I've just given you the reason myself, haven't I? The AI chamber. You planned to set your scheme in motion almost twenty-four hours earlier, that night after the Blackjack marathon at the Casino. But on that occasion you were seen, or at least you thought you were. Of course. Being so bound up in your own scheme, with your own psychotic need for revenge, you were always paranoid about anyone else finding out what you were up to and putting a stop to things before you were done. You must have met Glenda as she was leaving the AI, after she had been doing a little digging of her own into the Carcharodon's finances. And you couldn't risk arousing her suspicions about you as well, could you?"

"Everything had been worked out down to the finest detail. I couldn't let a snooping strumpet like her ruin everything for me before I had even begun."

"But you didn't stop there, did you? You couldn't, not after Miss Birkin revealed that she'd seen the murderer with Glenda, the poor old biddy. What was it the Major said about her? Oh yes, always looking for a conspiracy behind everything. If only she'd known. If only she'd kept her mouth shut!

"Only she hadn't seen you at all, had she? She saw me, escorting Glenda back to my room after the Blackjack game. She didn't need to die, not even by the standards of your twisted logic. And of course, having killed Miss Birkin you had to keep on eliminating all of those who might have overheard her conversation with the captain.

"She wasn't a threat to you, but then you couldn't have known that until later, after Captain McCormack accused me of your crimes! And while people were busy thinking it was me, and added to that when Cheng tried to carry out his ill-timed little coup, it gave you all the distraction you needed to keep killing, hunting down the doomed members of Project Leviathan one by one, making sure they all paid for what they had done to your father. What they had done to you. You even bought yourself some more time by faking that attack on Carcharodon and yourself, when your attack on the Captain failed.

"And each of them died in a manner befitting the part they played in the creation of the Kraken. Horsley the big game hunter, skewered like a shish kebab by a harpoon, Crichton the evolutionary biologist poisoned with a lethally evolved neuro-toxin, Denning the marine biologist, electrocuted with a prototype cybernetic tentacle that she had helped to create. And now you've turned Carcharodon into some kind of living bomb.

"So, what I'm thinking now, having reached something of an impasse, is – where do we go from here?"

"We're not going anywhere," Marie Lamprey said coldly.

Reaching behind her with her free hand, she lifted something from the control console, something Ulysses had failed to notice, so preoccupied had he been with the goings on between Marie, Carcharodon and himself, although he realised now that he had seen it before – they all had, only the last time it was being worn by a dead man.

Carefully, Marie placed the metal-banded helmet on top of her head. The coloured light-emitting diodes that covered its surface were blinking on and off like fairy lights. The wires that trailed from the crown had been bound together into one thick cable which, in turn, had been plugged into the console.

"You were busy while I was away, weren't you? Well, they do say the Devil makes work for idle hands."

Marie said nothing, but continued to press the barrel of her gun roughly against her employer's temple, staring ahead of her at Ulysses. There was something about the look in her eyes that suggested she was seeing something else, that wasn't there with them inside the submersible.

"I'm guessing you're as much a whiz with computers as your father was. It looks like you've also inherited his tendency towards mental instability," Ulysses added. "But what, precisely, are you planning on doing with that, Marie?"

A slow smile spread across the haggard young woman's lips, and at that moment it scared Ulysses far more than the gaping grin of the Megalodon that had tried to make a meal of him.

"Why, don't you know? This is how I'm going break this stalemate we've got ourselves into. This is how I finally put paid to the last of the masterminds behind Project Leviathan, behind my father's murder, and the son of the government representative who allowed such a scheme to continue. All in one easy stroke."

Knowing he had nothing to lose by doing so, Ulysses turned and peered out through the viewing port at the rear of the cabin.

There was something moving out there in the night-blue darkness.

The cold chill of fear slithered down his spine and made itself at home in his gut, turning his bowels to ice water.

He had hoped against hope that they had seen the last of it, that it had been destroyed along with Marianas Base. But deep down he always knew that such a result would simply be too good to be true.

He could see it more clearly now as it slid through the water after the two craft, chasing them to the surface, its grasping arms reaching out ahead of it.

And now Ulysses could see the injuries it had sustained, the damage it had suffered, caught up in the death throes of the dying facility. It had lost parts of several of its arms, sheared metal showing amidst the torn flesh. There were also whole areas where its pallid underbelly, and even pieces of its armoured shell, had been torn asunder to reveal its endo-skeleton beneath. And yet, despite having suffered such extensive damage, the Kraken still looked more than capable of taking down both the *Ahab* and the *Nemo*.

Ulysses turned back to face Marie. She looked very peculiar with the bulbous metal helmet covering her head down to her eyes, almost comical.

"I was wrong in my assumptions about the value the killer placed on their own life."

"What do you mean?" Marie asked, Ulysses having got her attention, piquing her own sense of the curious.

"You would willingly sacrifice yourself to see us all dead."

"With my father's killers brought to justice, my life has no further purpose. This has been my life's work. With it completed, there is no reason for me to keep on living."

"Why? Why? Why?"

Ulysses was slightly surprised when he realised that Carcharodon was sobbing as he repeated the same word over and over through his tears. The man who he had known to show hardly any emotion, other than anger or annoyance, was crying like a baby.

"What do you mean, why?" Marie shrieked, lifting the gun from the old man's head only to bring it down hard again against his skull a second time. "Haven't you been listening? He never listens, does he, Madeleine?" She was screaming now, her words a screeching banshee wail. "Don't you understand? You have to understand why you have to die! He has to, doesn't he, Madeleine, otherwise it's all been for nothing." Tears were streaming down her face again, mucus running from her nose.

"I understand. I understand why I have to die," Carcharodon struggled on, gasping for breath from the pain of the blows to his head. "I drove you to this. I understand that. But why did the others have to die?"

Now it was Marie Lamprey's who suddenly didn't understand. "What?" she said, her voice suddenly quiet. Ulysses thought he preferred it when she had been screaming.

"It was me. It was me who killed your father."

"What?"

"It was me. I shot him."

Marie's attention was now fully on the old man, slumped forward in his wheelchair at her side. He suddenly looked so very small and frail as he quietly confessed his sins, the two of them, employer and psychotic employee, master and servant, frozen in that moment of time in some weird parody of priestly absolution.

Ulysses readied himself. He could feel the moment coming when he would be able to bring this matter to its resolution.

"You killed my father?" Marie stammered, suddenly the uncertain, insecure Miss Celeste surfacing again.

"Yes. And there is another crime of which I am guilty. In doing so I helped create another monster, and this time I'm going to face up to my responsibilities and do away with it!"

With that, Carcharodon flicked the switch on top of the timer in his lap.

With a whirring hum the hand began to turn, the needle on the dial hastening away the seconds until the moment when the bomb would detonate.

"What have you done?" Marie screamed levelling the gun at Carcharodon again, holding the weapon tightly with both shaking hands.

The old man looked her straight in the eye and said with chilling calmness, "I'm bringing an end to this impasse."

The woman pulled the trigger. Ulysses heard the sharp crack of the gunshot even as he saw Jonah Carcharodon's head disintegrate in a spray of blood and bone.

It was now or never. Ulysses took a bounding step forwards. Still screaming, Marie grabbed Carcharodon's wheelchair by its handles and pushed it into his path, the old man's body lolling forwards as she did so.

Catching the chair in the huge gauntlet fist and the pincer-claw, Ulysses pushed back. Caught between the arms of the chair, Marie Lamprey stumbled backwards, the helmet falling from her head. Unbalanced she fell against the chair, skewing it sideways, before she toppled over, falling into the still open airlock.

The timer continued to spin round, speeding towards inescapable oblivion. Ulysses could still hear it over the muffled screams of the bound Constance Pennyroyal.

Without a second thought, Ulysses pushed the dead Carcharodon, in his invalid's chair, in after Marie and punched the control panel beside the airlock. With a satisfying shunk, and the hiss of altering air pressures, the inner door shut. Sirens sounded. Lights flashed. Marie Lamprey's face screamed at Ulysses through the small window in the airlock door. But there was nothing that could be done, not now.

With a sudden violent rush of escaping air the dead Carcharodon and the still living Miss Celeste were jettisoned from the airlock. The *Ahab* hurtled onwards, thanks to Selby's last act before he had died, the engineer having switched on the submersible's autopilot.

Ulysses turned his attention back to the rear viewing port. He could see the Kraken even closer now, grasping limbs outstretched, hideous jaws angling open. And he could see Carcharodon's chair sinking towards it, falling in slow motion through the churning water. And he could see Marie Lamprey kicking against the currents, arms flailing, as if trying to swim free, mouth open wide, silvered bubbles of air escaping her lungs in one last defiant scream, wide staring eyes, piercing Ulysses' own, staring straight into his soul, chilling him to the core.

*   *   *

THE FIRST THING she thought as she peered up through the porthole above her was how blue the sky was. She had almost forgotten, she had been dwelling down there in the ocean depths for so long. Seeing it now she could almost believe that what had happened down there, so far below, had been nothing more than a bad dream.

Only it hadn't been a dream. It had been a nightmare, and one from which she would never – could never – wake up.

The bathysphere bobbed on the rolling waves, making her feel a little queasy. She had stopped crying now, her tears spent, but the pain was still there, an aching hole in her heart, a hole that she knew time could never hope to heal.

She peered up again through the porthole. There were seabirds now, wheeling over the ocean under the porcelain sky, and something else, an iron hull, streaked red with rust, plying its way through the water towards her.

The vessel bumped against the side of the pod with a resounding clang. The bathysphere bell rang again, tolling an arrhythmic tattoo as it knocked repeatedly against the hull of the ship. A death-knell for those lost to her, far, far below the ocean waves.

She could see a ladder now – rungs black with pitch, crusted white with salt – and a man descending it. Ropes slapped against her small round window on the world and she could hear the shouts of sailors as the pod was secured to the side of the ship.

At last a face appeared at the glass above her. It was lined and weather-beaten, having something of a doting aged relative about it that comforted her. And then a kind smile spread across the crab apple features as twinkling eyes caught sight of the little girl inside.

"It's a child," she heard him say, his voice muffled. "A little girl, for God's sake."

Strong hands worked the hatch handle on the outside of the escape capsule and the sailor pulled it open, letting out the musty, stale smell of fear and letting in the rich aromas of brine, fish guts and stale tobacco. It was a heady mix of scents which, in that instance smelt like heavenly perfume to the terrified little girl.

A calloused hand reached into the pod.

"Come on, my little sparrow," the sailor said warmly, his voice thick with the apple orchard accents of the West Country. "Let's be having you."

Tentatively she reached up, putting her small, soft white hand into her liberator's meaty paw. His fingers closed around hers firmly and, in a trice, he had hauled her through the open hatch out of the musty pod.

"Well, well, well. What do we have here?" came a voice from among those crowded at the deck rail above them.

"What's your name, little sparrow?" the kindly sailor asked.

"M-Marie," she stammered, her mind reeling as she tried to take everything in.

"Marie?" the sailor repeated.

"Marie," she said again.

She listened now to the murmurings of the crew on deck. "What's she doing out here, all alone?" someone was saying.

"Who'd abandon a child like that, in the middle of the Pacific Ocean?" asked another.

"Marie, did she say?" said a third. "Would that be Marie Celeste then?"

She looked up, trying to find the face in the crowd, the face of the man who had named her.

Marie Celeste, she thought. She liked the sound of that name. She wondered what sort of a life Marie Celeste would have had so far. With a name like that she had probably had a much happier life than little Marie Lamprey had had to endure until this time.

Yes, Marie Celeste. She liked the sound of that.

AND THEN, JAWS agape, the Kraken swallowed them – chair, Carcharodon, Celeste and all. The massive jaws hinged shut and, for a moment, Ulysses thought that the creature was slowing, pulling back, satisfied at last. But it was not to be.

With a flick of its tail the monster powered forwards again, closing on the *Ahab* once more.

This is it, Ulysses thought. This is the end. There's nowhere left to run now, no aces left to play.

The suckered tentacles reached for the sub, the vessel's autopilot still directing it straight up towards the surface, that hideous angler-fish mouth opening once again, the grotesque limpid jelly-saucer eyes locked on its new prey.

And then the bomb detonated.

The beast's stomach swelled violently, distending horribly. Ulysses could almost believe that there was a look of startled surprise in the leviathan's eyes. And then there was fire in the water, fire and an expanding ball of concussive force.

The Kraken underwent one last appalling transformation as its body – grey-green flesh, cybernetic endo-skeleton, waving tentacles, and crustacean armour plating – was ripped apart by the explosion, destroying it utterly from the inside out.

Marie Lamprey, Jonah Carcharodon and the Kraken were gone. For good.

EPILOGUE

Britannia Rules the Waves

THE *AHAB* SURFACED first, closely followed by the *Nemo*. Within moments, Ulysses was standing in the open air on top of the *Ahab*, drawing in great lungfuls of salt sea air, relishing the freshness of it, delighting in the warmth of the sun beating down on his face. The pressure suit stood unoccupied within the sub. In his hand he held his bloodstone-tipped cane once more, having recovered it from Marie Lamprey's stash that she had carried on board the *Ahab*.

Constance Pennyroyal huddled next to him, anxiously watching the *Nemo* for signs of her beloved fiancé. Her patience was rewarded a moment later when Nimrod popped the hatch of the *Nemo's* conning tower, the equally anxious John Schafer emerging after him. Without even a pause for thought, Schafer took a swan dive off the top of the sub into the Pacific and, with confident strokes, covered the stretch of choppy water between the two vessels to be reunited with his sweetheart once more.

As the elated crying couple renewed their promises of love, Ulysses and Nimrod made use of hawsers to pull the two tubs together.

"Where's Cheng?" Ulysses asked, as he offered his manservant a hand.

"I took the liberty of securing him below, sir," Nimrod said, with a hint of satisfaction in his usually impassive voice.

"Well done, old boy. Good thinking."

Nimrod looked exhausted and unwell. The trials they had all been through, and the wound he had suffered during the Kraken's final attack on the base, were taking their toll, now that the adrenalin rush of the chase and their escape from the beast had passed.

"That was a close call there," Ulysses said, flashing his loyal family retainer a wicked grin, "I don't mind telling you, I thought we were all done for that time."

"I had faith in you, sir," Nimrod said, struggling to maintain his mask of professional detachment.

"Thank you, Nimrod."

"So, am I to take it that the Marianas killer has been brought to book, sir? They have been made to pay for their crimes?"

"Oh yes, there's no doubt about that," Ulysses said, a wry smile on his lips. "Remind me, Nimrod, when we get back to civilisation to send a letter of condolence to Jonah Carcharodon's family."

"Really, sir?"

"Really, Nimrod."

"And what about Miss Celeste's family? Will you be sending them a letter of condolence as well, sir? Or flowers perhaps."

"I don't think so," Ulysses replied, his face suddenly hard as stone.

There was the roar and chop of a propeller starting up, and the water behind the stern of the *Nemo* became a churning spume of white froth. The tiny sub slid forwards, pulling the ropes holding it to the *Ahab* taut, for a moment even dipping the nose of the larger vessel, before, with a sharp crack, they snapped.

"Nimrod, what did you secure Mr Cheng to, I wonder?" the dandy said, his features relaxing again.

"I do apologise, sir," *Nimrod* said, his rigidly maintained façade of indifference suddenly crumbling, his face flushing in embarrassment, "there really wasn't very much else to secure him to. Should we pursue, sir?"

"I don't think so, Nimrod. I don't know about you, old chap, but I've had quite enough of breakneck pursuits for one day. Haven't you? I think we can leave him to his own fate now. After all, he's going to have to face the wrath of his superiors, and I'm sure that whatever they have in mind for him will be much worse than anything our government would dare to implement against an agent of the Chinese Empire. I'm not sure our new Prime Minister is ruthless enough."

"So, if I might be so bold, sir, what now?"

"Now, Nimrod? Now we just have to wait for the Royal Navy to pick us up. We're broadcasting on all bands a general distress call so it shouldn't take too long. A day or two at most."

"Very good, sir."

"And seeing as how the young couple are so bound up in each other, that just leaves you and me, Nimrod."

"Yes, sir."

Ulysses was quiet for a moment as he gazed out over the Pacific, nothing but sea and sky to the horizon in every direction. It was a beautifully calm day, but something was still troubling him, deep down.

"Nimrod," he said after several minutes' silent thought, "there's been something I've been meaning to ask you."

"Go on, sir. You know you can ask me anything."

"Very well then." Ulysses paused again and took a death breath before continuing. "What did you know of my father's involvement in Project Leviathan?"

FAR, FAR BELOW the surface, beneath the spot where the *Ahab* bobbed like a twig on the roiling surface of the Pacific, past the wreck of the *Neptune* and beyond the ravaged remains of the ruined base, beyond the hunting grounds of the Megalodons, deeper even inside the haunted depths of the Marianas Trench, something stirred.

Woken by the seismic disturbances that had followed both the destruction of the *Neptune* and the undersea facility, drawn for a time by the distant signal that had briefly been projected into the abyss, it rose now from those same untold depths. Disturbed from its slumber of ages, active once more, its original programming rebooting, it rose from its resting place within the trench, a gnawing ache deep within its massive gut.

The giant sharks sensed its approach and fled before it, but in moments all were devoured whole.

It swept past the ruined domes of the devastated Marianas base, something like memory recalling its connection with that obscene place, that was now just another watery grave.

It glided over the teetering liner, the backwash of its passing sending the greatest submersible liner the world had ever seen over the edge, to be claimed by the hungry abyss at last.

It pushed on through the sinking cloud of flesh and metal debris, pausing for a moment to taste a few particles, its augmented mind attempting to reconstruct what had happened, what threats it might encounter itself.

Hunger like nothing it had ever known seizing the primitive, instinctive, unadapted portion of its mind, it continued to rise, seeking the surface.

And at its passing, a sturdy sheet of paper, a blueprint plan not yet turned to mush by the water flew and flapped in its wake, on it a schematic image of a bio-weapon twice the size of the Kraken, far more lethally equipped to hunt and kill, and a coded designation: Project Leviathan – 002.

THE END

Canst thou draw out Leviathan with an hook?
Or his tongue with a cord which thou lettest down?...
Canst thou fill his skin with barbed irons?
Or his head with fish spears?
Lay thine hand upon him,
remember the battle, do no more.

– Job, ch.1 v.1

PAX BRITANNIA
VANISHING POINT

JONATHAN GREEN

I

The Haunting of Hardewick Hall

~ October 1997 ~

HARDEWICK HALL WAS definitely haunted, of that there could be no doubt. Madam Garside had declared it was so within only a matter of minutes of entering the crumbling Gothic pile, her nose wrinkling as she was confronted by an atmosphere heavy with beeswax polish and camphor. A séance had to be held, she had informed Emilia, to discover why the spirits were restless. That way they could then discover which ghosts it was that were troubling her and lay those spirits to rest, although Emilia was sure she knew who it was who was trapped within the house, unable to escape to eternal rest in paradise. And of course Madame Garside decreed that the séance had to take place on the night of All Hallows' Eve, which was auspicious for such an undertaking, when the veil between the worlds was at its thinnest and spirits might more freely cross from the other side, into the land of the living.

So it was that on the evening of the 31st October 1997, as dusk was drawing on under a sky bruised purple-black with the promise of a coming storm, a group of disparate individuals gathered at the brooding manse in Warwickshire, at the personal invitation of Emilia Oddfellow, daughter of the late Alexander Oddfellow, scientist, inventor and eccentric.

Seven of them were to take part in the séance itself, with Madam Garside taking the lead, but of course such honoured guests could not be expected to attend without bringing their own staff too.

Emilia Oddfellow paused before the doors to the Library where Caruthers had gathered her guests to await the arrival of the lady of the house.

Lady of the house, she thought. That was a term that would still take some getting used to. Her father had been gone these last three months, but still she couldn't quite believe it, perhaps because of the manner of his passing.

She paused to adjust the cameo brooch that had once been her mother's, pinned at the collar of her high-buttoned mourning dress. Her hands were shaking: she blushed in embarrassment at herself. Then, taking a few controlled breaths to compose herself, she pushed open the doors and stepped into the Library to greet her guests.

All eyes turned to look at her. She in turn scanned the faces around the room, her heart quickening in excited anticipation as she searched for one face in particular.

Four men awaited her, their own servants in attendance with them. To her left, sitting in a large, leather-upholstered armchair – which needed to be large to contain his corpulent bulk – was her honoured guest, Herr Sigmund Faustus. He was dressed in the manner of a country gent, wearing a tweed three piece suit. Standing stiffly beside his chair was his personal aide. He was staring at her expectantly, making no effort to hide the fact, his right eye bulging from behind the lens of a monocle, while his left eye was scrunched almost entirely shut.

Emilia moved on in her observations.

Trying to look casual, leaning an elbow on the mantelpiece above the fire smouldering in the grate, was a handsome, athletically lean man, his dark hair slicked back with lacquer, nonchalantly balancing a cigarette holder between thumb and the first finger of his left hand. On seeing Emilia, a brief smile rested for a moment upon his otherwise dourly aloof countenance. Emilia felt her spirits lift, but his delightfully welcome face wasn't the one she had been hoping for in particular.

The two remaining gentlemen were standing either side of a partially-unfolded card table between the library's two velvet-draped windows that looked out onto the croquet lawn. On becoming aware of her entering the room, the two of them stopped fiddling with the curious device standing on the table and looked up. Mr Smythe, the taller of the two, had a pinched and pale face, and wore round wire-framed spectacles. His companion, Mr Wentworth, was an unattractive specimen, stooped as if his spine was malformed with a feeble growth of spiky whiskers on his upper lip, the pathetic moustache only serving to make him look like some kind of rodent.

Both had attempted to dress smartly for the occasion, although Emilia rather suspected that their stained and moth-eaten suits were what amounted to their Sunday best.

She quickly scanned the room, hoping against hope that she had missed something the first time. Then her heart dropped; he had not come.

"Good evening, gentlemen," she said, doing her best to hide her obvious disappointment. "Have you all been introduced?"

"Herr Dashwood, kindly – how do you say? – did the honourables," the corpulent foreign gentleman replied. His voice was higher than might have been expected, with a fluting tone, curiously at odds with his guttural native accent.

"Thank you, Daniel," she said, addressing the young man at the fireplace, who dismissed the need to be thanked with a wave of his cigarette holder, and then turned back to the German. "Herr Faustus," she said, clasping her hands together in front of her, to prevent herself from nervously fidgeting while she spoke. "Thank you so much for coming such a long way to be here."

"Not at all, my dear," Faustus replied, tapping the arm of his chair with a finger, as if to emphasise the point he was making.

"You were always so generous in your support of my father's work. He spoke very well of you."

"The late lamented Prince Consort was not the only German philanthropist with a desire to help the people of the British Empire, my dear." He spoke to her as if he were an affectionate, although not altogether heterosexual, uncle. "And besides I had a – how do you say? – a vested interest in his work. It shames me greatly that the very project I was funding might have brought about his untimely end."

Emilia's throat went taught – to hear it put so bluntly like that, even after three months – and she swallowed hard.

"If there is anything I can do – anything at all – you only need to ask," Faustus added.

"You are too kind," Emilia replied, blinking away the moisture collecting at the corners of her eyes. "You have done more than enough, already."

She turned to the curious-looking pair at the card table, and their equally curious device.

"And thanks to you both, Mr Smythe. Mr Wentworth." She looked at the machine, all polished teak, glass dials and gnarled brass knobs. It looked not unlike the bastard offspring of a wireless radio set and an ornate clock. "You really think this machine will help?"

"We certainly hope so, Miss Oddfellow," Smythe replied, an excited, slightly manic smile suddenly seizing control of his pinched features. "We still need to carry out a final calibration of the device," he said, a hand straying back to the dials with which he had been fiddling when Emilia entered the room, "but we are highly confident of success."

"Confident of success," the weaselly Wentworth parroted.

The library's wall-lights suddenly flickered and dimmed. All eyes were drawn anxiously to the humming lamps and Emilia's heart missed a beat. A moment later, full power was restored.

"I... I'm very pleased to hear it," Emilia said, feeling that someone needed to say something to dispel the growing sense of unease, but her words didn't seem to make any difference. "I am told that Madam Garside has almost finished her preparations and that we shall soon be able to begin. Please help yourselves to another drink in the meantime."

Her duties as a hostess dispensed with for the moment, Emilia moved swiftly across the room to the dashing Dashwood at the fireplace.

"Daniel, how delightful to see you," she said, clasping the young man's hands in her own. "I am so glad you're here."

"I wouldn't have missed this for the world," he beamed back at her, giving her a wink. He paused, looking around the room. "Any sign of you-know-who?"

"No, not yet," Emilia said, her carefully composed mask of togetherness wilting for a second, threatening to reveal her true feelings.

"Come on, chin up. I hate to say it, cuz, I really do, but... Well, I told you so."

"Yes. Yes, you did, dear Daniel, and I should have listened to you. He's obviously not coming."

"He could have at least replied to your invitation."

"I'm sure he's been very busy. I think I read that he'd been involved in that Carcharodon debacle."

"That was months ago," her cousin chided, good-naturedly. "Stop making excuses for him, Em. He was always letting you down before, and now he's gone and let you down again."

Someone coughed politely behind her.

"Um, excuse me, Miss Oddfellow, but if your guests are all assembled, Madam Garside is ready for you now."

Emilia turned to see the medium's assistant, Renfield, standing behind her. She hadn't heard him approach.

"What? Oh yes, of course," she sighed, feeling her shoulders sag as disappointment deflated her. "We're ready. Caruthers will just have to join in to make up numbers," she said pragmatically, lowering her voice so that only Dashwood heard what she had to say.

She moved to cross the hall to the study where the séance was to take place. "This way, please."

Emilia paused in the hallway – her guests filing past her, led by the moon-faced Renfield into the mahogany-panelled study – and looked longingly in the direction of the front door.

And then she heard it; the faint purr of an engine and the grinding crunch of tyres on the gravel drive at the front of the house.

A moment later the sound of the engine died. A door slammed and leather soles were heard trotting up on the steps to the front door. The strident jangling of the doorbell made everyone pause and look round then, and sent Emilia chasing along the corridor, reaching the door before the hobbling Caruthers could get anywhere near it.

She flung it open.

"Not too late, am I?" Ulysses Quicksilver asked, flashing Emilia a rakish grin.

"Oh, Ulysses, I thought you weren't coming!" Emilia chided, grabbing him and pulling him close to plant a kiss on his cheek.

"You wouldn't believe the traffic coming out of London tonight," he said, pulling away from her. Behind him, his manservant, Nimrod, was extricating his master's luggage from the boot of a Mark IV Rolls Royce Silver Phantom.

Clasping her hands in his Ulysses looked deeply into Emilia's eyes, his expression suddenly serious. "I was so sorry to hear of your loss," he said. "His passing is a great loss to us all."

"Thank you," she said, returning his intense stare.

"How are you?"

"All the better for seeing you," Emilia said, and pulled him close again. There was a moment's silence between the two of them, which said more than words ever could, and then they parted, as if suddenly remembering that they had company.

"Ah, Dashwood," Ulysses said, catching sight of the darkly dressed individual at the other end of the hall. "How long's it been?"

"Not long enough," the other replied, that same aloof glower on his face.

"Well, I'd like to be able to say that it's good to see you again, but..."

"The feeling's mutual," Dashwood said, a false smile contorting his facial muscles for a moment.

"Not now, Daniel," Emilia said with forceful calm.

"But he can't just walk back into your life like this and carry on as if nothing happened."

"Daniel, please."

"Your concern for your cousin is very sweet, Dashwood, but I'm sure Miss Oddfellow can stick up for herself. At least she could when she and I were better acquainted," Ulysses said, flashing her that rakish grin. "Black suits you, by the way."

"Now come along, Ulysses, everyone's waiting. This way."

II

Parlour Tricks

WITH EVERYONE SEATED at the circular table that had been set up in the late Alexander Oddfellow's study expressly for the purpose, the séance began.

"Spirits, can you hear me?" Madam Garside called, her eyes tight shut, her head held high. "I beseech you, dark watchers from beyond the veil, hear my plea, and answer."

Ulysses Quicksilver opened one eye and took in the faces of his fellow attendees. Madam Garside sat at the head of the table, a glass and walnut bookcase behind her, her palms flat on the table cloth in front of her. Her bony fingers were adorned with ostentatious rings but Ulysses seriously doubted that any of them were of any real value, the precious stones set within were no more than cunningly cut-glass copies. Her dress was as vulgar as her jewellery, and about her shoulders was draped a shawl, embroidered with silver stars and crescent moons. But the piece which set it all off for Ulysses was the turban she had seen fit to place on top of her head. The green silk from which it had been wound was fastened together with an apparently gold and lapis lazuli scarab beetle brooch, like those cheap knock-offs sold in their thousands to tourists visiting the Nile kingdom every year. She was certainly keeping her options open with such an array of cosmological symbols.

In the ruddy light of the shuttered Bedouin lamp she had placed on the table in front of her, her overly made-up face took on an appropriately hellish quality.

"Spirits, heed the call of one who knows you, answer the petition of Madam Garside."

Ulysses couldn't stop himself from smirking at hearing that, and snorted as he tried to suppress a laugh. He then had to loudly clear his throat to try to cover up his inappropriate reaction.

One eye suddenly flicked open and fixed on Ulysses. "Spirits!" she said again, her entreaty louder this time, as she tried to bring the séance back under control.

But it didn't change the fact that, as far as Ulysses was concerned, the whole thing was no more than an embarrassing charade.

To the phoney mystic's left sat Daniel Dashwood, hands flat on the table also – as had been dictated for all of them by Madam Garside – eyes closed and head erect, cigarette holder clenched between his teeth. The lazy blue tobacco smoke coiled upwards to join the clouds of incense fugging the room.

Beside Dashwood was Emilia, her eyes screwed tight shut, an expression of earnest desperation knotting her usually soft features. Ulysses seat was next to hers.

He noticed that his former sweetheart had taken to wearing her straw blonde hair plaited into a tight bun at the back of her head. The girl he had once known had worn it down, like a cascade of gold. That same girl would never have been seen dead in a stiff black mourning gown buttoned to the neck. Time and its cruel predations had changed her, he thought. And a broken heart might have had its part to play too, he considered ruefully.

She was so close he could almost touch her, the little fingers of their hands inches apart. The sarcastic smile left his lips, and at that moment he wanted nothing more than to grab hold of her, take her away from this morbid shadow play which was wringing a bitter grief from her.

Instead he turned his attention to the man to his left. Smythe was paying about as much attention to proceedings as Ulysses was himself. He was absorbed in fiddling with his machine. As he played with the knobs and dials on the front panel, the two short aerials that sprouted from the top rotated independently about a hemispherical gimble and the crackle of radio interference came from speakers at either end of the device.

It was a ghost detector, or so Smythe had told him as they had taken their seats at the table. All the fiddling was necessary to focus the signal apparently projected by all supernatural entities, thereby allowing the machine to read the presence of ghosts. Next to him sat his fellow parapsychologist Wentworth, who flicked switches and adjusted dials on his side of the machine from time to time.

Despite being an obvious fraud, as far as Ulysses was concerned, he had to give Madam Garside her due. It was testament to her level of concentration that she was able to keep up the pretence of communing with the souls of the departed with the constant background disturbance of Smythe and Wentworth's box of tricks.

Next around the table, and someone who was trying desperately hard to concentrate, despite the distraction of the apparition manifestation meter, was the rotund Faustus. Eyes closed, his mouth was slightly agape, as if in wonder.

And that completed the circle of seven.

"Spirits of the netherworld, if you can hear me, send me a sign."

The gathered séance-goers variously held their breath in expectation or struggled to keep a straight face. Smythe and Wentworth continued to tinker with their gizmo.

They waited, but if the spirits were there they were not in a talkative mood this particular evening.

Madam Garside stretched out her hands again and decried: "Spirits, I invoke you, by Osiris, by Hades and by Samhain. I command you, answer me!" Her voice had become a savage growl of barely suppressed fury.

An unearthly quiet fell upon the room and Ulysses became aware of the muffled pitter-patter of rain from behind the thick velvet drapes drawn across the one window in the study.

And then, the expectant hush was sharply broken by a loud knock on wood. Emilia gasped and jumped in her seat while Faustus let out a girlish cry of alarm. Ulysses looked at Dashwood, but he remained unmoved, chin in the air, eyes calmly closed.

"Thank you, spirits. Now, you watchers from the shadow world, answer me clearly. Can you hear me?"

The knock came again. In the muted red light of the room Ulysses looked for the medium's assistant but he was nowhere to be seen. He knew that there was some manner of trickery at work here, and Renfield was certainly up to his neck in it.

"Are you ready and willing to answer my questions?"

Again, the knock.

"Very well," Madam Garside said, with the commanding tone of one who believes themselves to be in authority, "who is it that haunts this place, who is lost and cannot find their way to the other side?"

The two parapsychologists made another adjustment to their machine and it began to emit a high-pitched whine, accompanied by a cockroach-like clicking.

"What is that?" Ulysses hissed, leaning towards the fiddling Smythe.

"Just white noise,"the investigator whispered back.

"Bit like her over there then."

The lights flickered. Madam Garside broke off suddenly, opened her eyes momentarily to glance around the room and then, finding Ulysses boldly meeting her gaze, shut them again.

"Dwellers in darkness, if you can hear me, give us a sign."

As Ulysses watched the Bedouin lamp began to rise slowly into the air above the table as, with a fizzing hum, that almost seemed in tune with the noise being made by the strange machine on the table, the lights in the room faded until only a feint dirty glow remained inside each buzzing bulb.

They all heard the mournful voice, despite its eerie distortion, as it came to them through the loud speakers of the wireless box. "Emmiilliiaa!"

Emilia cried out in alarm and gasps came from those around the table. Ulysses looked to the startled woman who returned his gaze imploringly, eyes open now, glistening with tears. "Father!"

"Emmiillliiaa," the voice came again and all looked to the parapsychologists' device.

"Mein gott!" Faustus whispered.

Smythe immediately began twiddling knobs and flicking switches again, in an attempt to fine-tune the signal.

"Come on, man," Dashwood said, although more demanding than encouraging in tone.

"Emilia!" came the plaintive cry, more clearly still.

"Oh, Father! Father?" she returned the call, looking desperately around the room, searching the air above her, as if hoping to see her father as well as hear his voice. "Can you hear me?"

"Emilia? Can you hear me?" the ethereal voice echoed her words. It was becoming chopped with interference.

"Come on, man! Get it back!" Dashwood snarled.

"I'm trying," Smythe threw back, "but the storm's interfering with the signal!"

"Interference," Wentworth added pointlessly.

"Just white noise, eh?" Ulysses muttered darkly, one questioning eyebrow raised.

More concerned by the distressed state of Emilia than the miraculous signal apparently being picked up by the ghost detector, Ulysses looked past her, seeing the strange reaction of the medium, Madam Garside. She was sitting in her chair, staring straight ahead of her, eyes bulging from their sockets, her face slack with an expression of horror, her mouth hanging open.

Ulysses followed her horrified gaze to the far side of the study. Another strangled gasp from Emilia told him that she had done the same and could see what he was seeing. Unbelievable as it might seem, an eerie luminescence was beginning to suffuse the darkened room with its own unearthly light. As Ulysses watched, the light began to take on shape and form. The spectral image was that of a man, of that there could be no doubt. Smythe made another adjustment.

"Emilia..." came the broken voice again, still being heard through the machine. "...ere... the sphere..."

"What was that he said?" Dashwood snapped.

"...ere... the sphere... sphe..."

Ulysses strained to make sense of the unearthly message, but the signal was breaking up and the task was made all the more difficult by another dreadful moaning that now pervaded the study.

"For God's sake, woman," Dashwood turned on Madam Garside, "shut up!"

"Father!" Emilia all but screamed, for if there had ever been any doubt before, there could be none now. The apparition of Alexander Oddfellow had materialized before their very eyes, standing half inside his own book-strewn desk, as if it wasn't there.

"Well, that's a turn up for the books," Ulysses muttered under his breath.

The late Alexander Oddfellow reached towards his daughter and cried her name once more. "Emi..lia... pher.. the sph..ere..."

"Fear the sphere? What's that supposed to mean?" Dashwood exclaimed, in irritation.

The phantasmal image flickered, washed as if with static, and then blinked out of existence, leaving the room in almost utter darkness. The lights on Smythe and Wentworth's machine had winked out too and the falling pitch of the device's power cell running dry could be heard emanating from the speakers.

"What happened?" Dashwood demanded.

"It's no good," Smythe admitted, giving the machine a thump of annoyance. "It's dead."

"Dead," Wentworth echoed, emotionlessly.

"That's not all that's dead," Ulysses said, his tone demanding the attention of all present. All eyes turned to him and thence, from him, to the medium.

Madam Garside sat stock still in her chair, her mouth still agape, her skin white and waxy, glassy eyes bulging from her head, the light of life that should have shone behind them snuffed out.

Ulysses studied the body with clinical interest. So that's what someone looks like when they've been scared to death, he thought.

III

The Late Gladys Garside

MADAM GARSIDE WAS dead, there was no doubt about it. Ulysses had felt for a pulse as had his manservant Nimrod. Consensus of opinion was that her heart had given out on witnessing the appearance of the apparition of Alexander Oddfellow. It had shocked everyone, although they had all reacted in different ways.

Emilia was understandably distressed, and Ulysses had done his best to comfort her. However, he himself had been surprised by something else altogether: he was surprised that the parapsychologists' machine had seemingly worked so well.

Dashwood appeared angry more than anything else, seemingly frustrated that they had lost the phantom Oddfellow so soon after managing to make his ghost materialize before them. Smythe's reaction was one of frustration, with Wentworth seeming to follow where his partner led, as ever.

Sigmund Faustus had retired to the library looking as white as the corpse he had left behind in the study and, once there, poured himself a large scotch. Having downed it, he poured another straight away.

By the time he was onto his third, the philanthropist had calmed down enough for Ulysses to leave Emilia in his care, whilst the dandy returned to the scene of the visitation, and the stiffening body in the study.

Smythe and Wentworth were still there, taking apart their contraption – Ulysses supposed to change its battery – able to see quite clearly now that the lights in the room had returned to normal. And so was Nimrod, standing behind another of the chairs, pulled out now from the table, with Madam Garside's sagging flunkey slouched within it, the butler's hand resting firmly on his shoulder, in case he should get any foolish ideas.

"Tell me about the medium Madam Garside," Ulysses said sternly.

Renfield had revealed himself when he burst from behind the curtains in horror at hearing of his mistress's death, dropping the fishing line with the Bedouin lamp attached in the process. Any theatrical pretension he might have had before was gone now. Sidney Renfield had gone to pieces as soon as he realised Madam Garside really was dead.

He looked up at Ulysses with red-rimmed eyes, cheeks wet with tears of panic and fear.

"She wasn't one, a real medium I mean, but then I think you've worked that out for yourself, haven't you?" he blubbed.

"So she was a con artist. After Miss Oddfellow's inheritance was she?"

"No."

"Then what? All this tonight; was she doing that simply out of the goodness of her heart?"

"No, of course not."

"Then Miss Oddfellow was paying her for her services."

Renfield nodded, dabbing at his eyes with a balled up handkerchief.

"How many séances were there to be? How many tarot readings to help get Emilia's life back on track? What does an exorcism cost these days anyway?"

"I don't know. There'd only been two meetings before today, the second to set up the séance," Renfield said, confessing all he knew. "Gladys had never seen a ghost in all her life, of course. At least, not until... until..." Unable to continue he broke down, sobbing his heart out.

"Until tonight, and the shock killed her." Ulysses finished bluntly. "Didn't see that coming, did she?"

He paced the floor in front of the shaking Renfield as if deep in thought.

"I take it you've heard of karma, Mr Renfield? Well, I'd say that the late Gladys Garside got what was coming to her. How many other poor unfortunate souls – grieving widows and orphans the lot I'm sure – have you conned over the years? I think the authorities would like to hear about what you've been up to, don't you? Well you can contemplate your fate while the rest of us get to the bottom of what's been going on around here."

Turning from the wretched Renfield, Ulysses circled the table to where the two ghost hunting boffins were tinkering with their startlingly effective box of tricks.

"Gentlemen," he said. "How's it going?"

Smythe looked up in irritation while Wentworth continued to take out the screws that held the back plate of the machine in place.

"It's the battery," he confessed, not telling Ulysses anything he hadn't already worked out for himself.

"The battery," Wentworth agreed.

"Can you replace it?"

"We can. But it will take a few minutes."

"A few minutes, then you can have another go," Ulysses said enthusiastically, a devilish grin back on his face.

"Really? You want us to try again?" Smythe said, unable to hide the amazement from his voice.

"Indeed," said Ulysses. "It worked, didn't it?"

"Well, the device was designed to detect the presence of paranormal anomalies but..."

"I'm intrigued by the apparent connection between your gizmo here and the appearance of Oddfellow's ghost," Ulysses explained, without giving the pondering Smythe a chance to finish, a note of glee in his voice. "Like I say, I want you to do whatever's necessary to get that machine ready to have another go."

IV

White Noise

"WE'RE READY WHEN you are, Mr Quicksilver," Smythe announced, sticking his head around the door of the library.

"Ready for what?" Dashwood asked, suspicious and yet intrigued.

"To try again," Ulysses stated, as if that much was obvious.

"Who died and put you in charge?" Dashwood challenged as Ulysses followed Smythe out of the library, but Ulysses did not deign to offer a reply.

Ulysses re-entered Oddfellow's study after the parapsychologist. The machine was there on the table, reassembled with a new battery cell installed, Wentworth waiting patiently for his partner. The late Gladys Garside had been moved to another room at Ulysses' request.

"Well, I'm here now, aren't I? Don't wait any longer. Start it up!"

Smythe and Wentworth went through their well-practised routine and, as soon as the machine hummed into life, Ulysses could hear a high-pitched drone coming from the box. Then the clicking commenced and Smythe began frantically tuning the device once more.

Without looking round, Ulysses sensed the presence of the other house guests at the door to the study. The electric lamps flickered, their luminescence failing yet again. He heard gasps behind him but kept his attention focused on the machine sat in the middle of the table.

Thunder rumbled ominously beyond the walls of the gothic pile.

This time it was only a matter of moments before the clicking tone warped into recognisable speech.

"Emilia?" came the haunting voice. "Can you hear me? Anyone?"

"We can hear you, Oddfellow," Ulysses spoke up excitedly. Smythe continued to focus the signal the ghost detector was receiving from God alone knew where.

A sphere of luminescence glowed into life within the study again, this time above the table. It swelled, flickered and dulled, becoming the spectre of Alexander Oddfellow once more, everything below the waist sunk into and through the table.

"Oh, father, it really is you!"

Ulysses spun round startled. So intently focused had he been on the reappearance of the ghost, he had not realised that Emilia had joined the group of curious onlookers at the door.

The ghost seemed to reach imploringly towards the young woman but the voice coming from the box had become unintelligible static again. The wall lamps glowed into life and, in contrast, the ethereal image of Emilia's late father dulled.

"Father? What is it?" she asked, pushing past Ulysses into the study.

The fading ghost's lips moved in desperate articulation but nothing of what it was trying to say could be heard.

"Ulysses do something, please. I have to know what he's trying to tell me," Emilia gasped.

"Smythe, what's the matter?" the dandy demanded, looking past Emilia, but placing a reassuring hand on her arm. "Why is the image fading? Don't tell me the battery's dead already."

"We're losing the signal," Smythe explained. "The more we try to boost it, the more power it drains from the cell. It's like it's moving out of range."

And then, as Ulysses was looking through Oddfellow's blurring body at the two ghost hunters, the spectre moved, as if making for the door. Then it was gone.

"Quick!" Ulysses exclaimed. "Oddfellow's leading us somewhere!"

Smythe and Wentworth looked at one another in bewilderment, then at Ulysses.

"Well, come on!" Ulysses exclaimed frustratedly, as he leapt for the door, sending the gaggle of gasping onlookers into a scurrying retreat. "We mustn't lose it."

Smythe and Wentworth looked at one another blankly again.

"For a couple of boffins capable of creating such a device, you really can be quite stupid, can't you? Pick up your box of tricks and follow me!"

Cottoning on at last they did as he commanded, Wentworth lugging the heavy metal box in his arms whilst Smythe awkwardly attempted to focus the signal the ghost detector was receiving.

Out in the passageway, the static whooshing from the speakers became a clear tone again and the ghost of Alexander Oddfellow materialized a few yards from them. It seemed to Ulysses that the apparition was looking through him as it beckoned with one hand. It then turned and moved off along the corridor.

"Keep up!" Ulysses darted a glance back at the encumbered parapsychologists. Emilia was at his side, the rest of the curious party following after Smythe and Wentworth.

At the foot of the polished staircase opposite the front door of the house, the ghost turned, following a narrow tiled passageway that ran alongside the stairs. At its end, Ulysses could see an archway, leading under the stairs themselves.

"Where's he taking us?" he asked Emilia as they kept pace with the ghost.

"The cellar," she said, her voice no more than a whisper.

Ducking under the archway, Ulysses found himself at the top of a draughty flight of steps that led down into the damp and cold of Hardewick Hall's cellars. At the bottom of the staircase, the unearthly luminescence of the apparition illuminated a padlocked door. The ghost gave them a melancholic look and placed a hand on the lock.

A shaded wall light behind Ulysses fizzed and faded, then flared magnesium bright. Smythe cursed. There was a fizzing crack, and a burst of sparks erupted from the box of tricks. With an audible pop the detector shorted out and the entrance to the cellar was plunged into darkness as the apparition vanished.

Ulysses swore, punching the plaster beside him. "I really thought we had it then," he said.

He looked at Emilia. The sadness in her eyes was heart-breaking. He looked back at the door, making out the padlock in the gloom, now he knew where to look, the after-image of the apparition remaining as a grey smudge on his retina for a moment until he blinked it away.

"Why's this door padlocked?" he asked. "What's down there?"

"My father's lab," Emilia said plainly, her voice dulled with sorrow. "I've kept it locked since his death."

"Well I think it's about time it was unlocked again, don't you?"

V

Fear the Sphere

THE DODDERING CARUTHERS came with a key, the padlock was removed and, with a confident gesture, Ulysses flung open the door.

The party followed in Ulysses' wake as he led the way, with wary steps, into the darkened cellar. A moment later the gloom was banished as someone managed to switch on the lights. Electric bulbs fizzed into life, illuminating patches of the brick-built cellar, revealing intriguing silhouettes and the hint of unfathomable pieces of equipment, until Alexander Oddfellow's laboratory was revealed in all its glory. The distant grumbling of the storm could be heard, even here.

Between archways of crumbling brick a space the size of a ballroom was filled with the inventor's forgotten, half-finished contraptions, masterpieces in the making left to rust and gather dust in the musty gloom.

Amidst all the cluttered workbenches and abandoned mechanisms, on the far side of the cellar, against a wall all by itself, a waxy tarpaulin lay draped almost haphazardly over something that Ulysses could see was large and roughly spherical.

"And what do we have here?" he asked aloud, approaching the tarpaulin, the excitement of discovery flashing in his eyes. Emilia and her guests followed in a timid, yet morbidly fascinated, huddle.

Boldly he grabbed hold of a corner of the covering, making ready to tug it free.

"Wait! Stop!"

Ulysses was so surprised to hear Emilia utter the command that he immediately halted. "Why, Emilia? What's under here?"

"Don't you understand? This was where it happened. This was where he died." She cast her gaze at the ground, as tears welled in her eyes. "Under there is the sphere; the project he was working on when he died."

"When you believe he died," Ulysses corrected.

"What's that supposed to mean?" Emilia challenged, melancholic sorrow suddenly becoming the anger of the grieving, raging at the injustice of it all.

"Hey, steady on, Quicksilver!" added Dashwood, coming to his cousin's defence.

"I know this is hard for you," Ulysses said, dropping the tarpaulin and taking a step towards Emilia, clasping her shaking arms with his strong comforting hands, "but all along it has been assumed that Alexander Oddfellow died here, working on his latest project, and yet his body was never found."

"There were witnesses, Quicksilver, you fool. My uncle wasn't alone when the last test run of the device back-fired. They saw the explosion. He was atomised – I'm sorry, Em, really I am – but he must have been. There can be no other explanation."

"There, you've said it yourself. These witnesses of ,yours saw a disappearance. They did not necessarily witness Alexander Oddfellow's death."

"Then, if he's not dead, where is he?" Emilia demanded.

"That's what I plan to find out." For a moment Ulysses and Emilia just looked at each other.

"You know, Em," Dashwood said, interrupting their unspoken conversation, "I think Quicksilver might be onto something here."

"Really?" Emilia said in surprise.

"Really?" echoed Ulysses. "You've changed your tune."

"Yes, I think you might actually have something there, old boy." There wasn't even an undercurrent of sarcasm to Dashwood's words. "Tug away."

With a dramatic flourish, Ulysses took hold of the tarpaulin and pulled it free.

As tall as a man and half that again, supported on a claw-footed base, stood the concentric rings of a gyroscope. The broken rings described a void in the shape of a sphere at the heart of the machine. Thick vulcanised rubber sheathed bundles of wires trailed from the strange device to the control panel of a logic engine.

Smythe and Wentworth both immediately approached the machine, placing their own useless device on the floor, running excited hands over the control levers and dials, unable to hide their boyish delight.

"So, Quicksilver," Dashwood said, "what's your theory?"

"What?"

"I was too hasty before. Tell us what you think happened."

"Yes, Herr Quicksilver," Sigmund Faustus joined the discussion, "go on. I would like to hear more about your theories myself. I am intrigued to learn how my learned friend Herr Oddfellow might have survived the accident, and where he went."

Emilia stared at Ulysses in bewilderment, looking like she had been knocked for six.

"Well," Ulysses paused, giving himself time to formulate how he was going to back up his hunch, having been caught off guard by Dashwood's dramatic change of heart towards him. "To be honest, I have no idea what it is that Oddfellow was working on when he vanished, but I am certain that this device, this sphere, was right there at the heart of it. For a start, has anyone else noticed that this thing is still on?"

Everyone looked towards the curious contraption again, and in the silence they all heard the electrical hum coming from the weird mechanical workings. Dusty yellow light glowed behind the glass dials of the controlling logic engine.

"Erstaunlich!"

"That's a good point," Ulysses mused aloud, turning to the German. "Herr Faustus, could you tell us what Oddfellow was working on?"

"I wish that I could," the philanthropist sighed, his expression one of open disappointment. "I am afraid I was only his sponsor, not his confidante."

"Really? You would fund an operation like this," Ulysses said, taking in the contraption with a sweep of his arm, "without having any idea of what he was attempting to do?"

Others among the party were considering the German philanthropist now, Dashwood frowning at him, as if he were trying to read his emotions and judge whether Faustus was telling the truth or not.

"I am a philanthropist, Herr Quicksilver," Faustus replied curtly. "You know what that means? I act – how do you say? – with benevolence towards my fellow men. I do not choose to judge them. I knew enough about Herr Oddfellow's successes in the past to know that it was worth sponsoring his latest project. His word was good enough for me."

His eyes still narrowed in suspicion, Ulysses turned to Emilia. "Can you shed any light on this mystery?"

"What? No. Father was always very secretive about his work."

"But you're his daughter. Surely he would have confided in you?"

"I didn't like to pry," Emilia said, surprised and affronted by Ulysses' challenge. "What are you trying to say?"

"I just find it incredible that nobody here – people who were close enough to your old man that they should be invited to a séance held in the wake of his supposed passing – has any idea what this machine is for, particularly when it's still running three months after it supposedly killed its creator!"

"That might explain the power drains and flickering lights around the house," Smythe threw in, as if someone might be interested to hear his theory.

"Power drains. Lights," Wentworth repeated.

"Then where do you suggest we go from here?" Emilia challenged Ulysses, her voice only one step away from becoming a scream.

"We run it up to speed again and see what it does!" he said, a manic gleam in his eye.

"You can't be serious?" Emilia rebuked him instantly. "Didn't you hear my father's warning? His last words to us were 'fear the sphere'."

"If that was what he was saying. There was a lot of distortion."

"He was warning us away because that was what killed him."

"Supposedly killed him, you mean," Ulysses corrected her.

"What?"

"That has yet to be proven."

"Oh, for pity's sake!" Emilia shrieked. "You're impossible! You haven't changed one bit!"

"I'm sorry, was I supposed to? Only I didn't think I was your problem anymore."

Faustus coughed politely, diverting everyone's attention onto him. "Herr Quicksilver, I think you should listen to Miss Oddfellow. I would also warn against that course of action."

"You would, would you?" Ulysses' voice was almost a snarl as he turned on the quivering German. "And why is that, I wonder?"

"Simply because it was working on that machine that killed Herr Oddfellow as our hostess here was having pains to point out."

"I ask you again, Herr Faustus, what you know about the operation of this machine?"

"And I have already answered that question. Nothing!"

"Gentlemen. Gentlemen, please." It was the usually aloof Dashwood who interrupted the bickering this time, his soothing calm pouring oil on troubled waters. "We're not going to get any closer to solving this mystery if we don't do something."

He looked from the fuming Emilia to the furious Ulysses to the shaken Faustus and back to his flush-faced cousin.

"I have it," he said, an unaccustomed smile brightening his face. "Let's put it to a vote." He glanced round the cellar-cum-laboratory, performing a quick head count. "There are six of us who I would say are eligible to vote," he said, ignoring the servants. "So come on, all those in favour of running the machine up to speed?"

Ulysses confidently put up his hand straight away, although he continued to eye Dashwood with as much suspicion as he had Faustus. Dashwood also raised his hand, as did the two boffins Smythe and Wentworth, managing to tear their attention away from the wonderful machine for a moment.

"Is that everyone? All right, then. All those against."

Emilia defiantly stuck her own hand in the air, Faustus following her example, although rather more tentatively.

"Right you are then," Ulysses said sourly. "Let's get this thing going."

In light of their intensive analysis of the control console, with the excited assistance of both Ulysses and Dashwood, Smythe and Wentworth set about reactivating the sphere.

Emilia retreated almost as far as the cellar door, as if in defiance of the decision taken by the others to power up the machine, but not quite able to leave them entirely to it by themselves. Her father's patron joined her, putting a flabby arm around her slight shoulders to comfort her, but he too was unable to tear his eyes from what Ulysses and the others were doing.

Dials were adjusted, levers cranked and switches thrown. The broken metal circles of the gyroscope began to rotate, slowly at first and then, as the machine drew more power, faster and faster. The spinning rings began to sing, a harmonic whirring hum rising in intensity as the rings hurtled quicker and quicker.

The cellar lights began to pulse and fade as the machine pulled more energy from the house's generator.

In the near darkness of the dusty laboratory, the sphere at the heart of the machine could be seen, delineated by the whirling strands of light, a solid ball of darkness beneath.

Static electricity charged the air. The device was acting like some huge Vander Graf generator. As he stared into the heart of the gyroscope Ulysses could feel every hair on his head stand on end. A glance around the cellar revealed the same had happened to everyone else, making them all look as terrified as many of them were surely feeling. But Ulysses felt only the adrenalin rush of excitement.

He glanced at the control panel next to him. One switch – large and gleaming brass – remained to be thrown. Ulysses seized the handle.

"Well, here goes nothing!" he announced, somewhat recklessly, and flipped the switch.

VI

The Ghost in the Machine

A FUZZY BALL of light glowed into life, like a blown ember, at the heart of the void-sphere. It rapidly began to take on a recognisable shape as Alexander Oddfellow materialized, suspended within the spinning gyroscope.

He appeared more solid than on either of the two previous occasions when he had manifested within the house. Looking through the whirling barrier of light, squinting as if he was struggling to focus through the distortion, he fixed his gaze on Ulysses and Ulysses saw a glimmer of recognition there.

"Ulysses Quicksilver," Oddfellow's voice wafted to him as if he were speaking to the dandy from another room. "What are you doing here?"

"Oddfellow," Ulysses said. "What is this thing? You've caused no end of problems, disappearing like that. There are questions that need answering."

"You can hear me?"

"I can hear you."

"Then listen carefully. I do not know how long we've got. I've been trapped here for... it feels like... I don't know how long."

"Where?"

"Within this damnable machine; inside this wretched containment field," Ulysses heard Oddfellow's strained words a split second after he saw them form on his lips. It was as if image and sound were fractionally out of sync.

"What was it designed to do?"

"What you see before you is the experimental prototype of Oddfellow's Matter Transmitting Device."

"A teleport?"

"That's what it was supposed to be, only something catastrophic occurred." Oddfellow seemed to peer past Ulysses, taking in the others gathered within the cellar-lab, before adding, "A spanner in the works, you might say."

"So where did it teleport you to?"

"Nowhere. Limbo? I don't know. All I do know is that I'm still trapped within it. If the power were to fail, I don't know what would happen; where I might end up. I rather suspect my component atoms would be spread across the ether, never to be reunited."

"Well, Smythe was right, it does explain the power drains and the problem with the lights," Ulysses said, half to himself as he tried to make sense of what the unreal Oddfellow was telling him. "But if you're trapped in there, how come you appeared to us during the séance? And how did you lead us here in this incorporeal form?"

"I have wondered the same thing myself," the floating Oddfellow admitted. "I can only presume that some other device was used to focus my signal and project me to those locations in this wretched form. But I don't know of such a device."

"I can help you there," Ulysses exclaimed excitedly, "Smythe and Wentworth's Patent Paranormal Anomaly Detector! That crazy gizmo of theirs must have inadvertently focused the signal." The lights in the cellar dimmed still further and bulbs on the panel of the sphere's control console flickered and faded. "But I rather suspect that we do not have much time. Just wait there. Don't go anywhere," Ulysses instructed the hovering ghost.

The dandy turned to the two technical whizzes working the logic engine next to him.

"This thing requires massive reserves of energy," Smythe said, looking anxious. He and Wentworth had been listening in on Ulysses' communion with the dead.

"Massive reserves."

"It's soon going to drain everything the house generators have got, and then it will conk out again."

"Never mind that," Ulysses snapped dismissively. "If you could couple your detector to the sphere, do you think you could lock onto Oddfellow's signal again, but this time extract it from the device?"

Smythe stared intently at Ulysses from behind his spectacles, the dying lights of the control panel dancing on the lenses. "It might be possible."

"Then do it," Ulysses commanded.

"But this thing's using up a great deal of power as it is," Smythe countered. "I don't think we'll be able to keep it running like this for much longer."

"We don't have time to think. Just do it."

Without another word, and only a nod to his partner, Smythe did as Ulysses commanded and the two parapsychologists set to work.

And it was then that the machine died. With a gut-wrenching sound of rapid deceleration that set a numbing chill in Ulysses' stomach, the whirling rings slowed, the last Christmas tree lights of the control panel winking out one by one.

Smythe's hypothesis had been all to accurate; running the sphere up to speed had drained Hardewick Hall's power supply, killing the generator.

The rings stopped spinning and the cocoon of light they made evaporated into shadow. The ghostly image of Alexander Oddfellow faded into oblivion too, and the cellar was plunged into total darkness. There were startled gasps from the gathered guests.

"Damn!" Ulysses swore. "Just as we were getting somewhere."

"If this is going to work, we're going to need another source of power," Smythe said his voice loud in the hushed darkness.

"Indeed," Ulysses growled. "But from where?"

Somewhere, far above the crumbling pile, thunder rumbled and lightning bathed the entire estate in a flickering flash of monochrome light.

The storm had broken.

VII

Phase Shift

"Are you quite sure this is a good idea, sir?" Nimrod asked, leaning far out of the garret window, a bulky length of vulcanised rubber-sheathed cable in his hands.

"Don't fuss, old chap," Ulysses chastised his manservant as he danced along the apex of the rain-slicked roof tiles. "It makes you sound like Nanny Fitzgerald. We've been in worse scrapes than this."

"Yes, but you've never been out in the open, practically the highest thing in the vicinity of a thunderstorm with a trunk of copper wire in your hands before, as far as I am aware, sir," Nimrod replied, pointedly.

With a last, half-slipping lunge, Ulysses grabbed hold of the chimney stack and gave an audible sigh of relief.

"There. Made it," he called back over the drumming of the rain. "Should have this fixed up in a jiffy."

Wiping the rain from his eyes with the back of a hand, Ulysses set about the task of securing the cable to Hardewick Hall's lightning conductor. Three floors below in the cellar, Smythe and Wentworth were busily attaching their ghost detecting gizmo to Oddfellow's teleportation sphere, by candlelight. After the generator had failed, Smythe informed Ulysses that they had discovered that the machine's own reserve battery had retained enough energy to keep the sphere running on standby, as it had done for the last three months, and so still retained the teleport-trapped scientist's scrambled signal, but would only be able to do so for an hour at most. Time was once again of the essence.

"There, I'm done!" Ulysses called back to Nimrod as the downpour strengthened.

"Pardon, sir?" his manservant called back, his master's words subsumed by a booming thunderclap.

"Never mind. I'm coming do– "

The flash of prescience struck a split second before the storm did. Sizzling white light exploded around the rooftop and Ulysses felt its heat as he went skidding down the rain-slicked tiles. The garret window shot past and he flung out his right hand, hoping to catch hold of the guttering. His fingertips brushed the mossy lip of a drainpipe and then he was over. His fall was sharply arrested by Nimrod's grasping hand.

Ulysses winced in pain as his shoulder jarred, antagonising the old injury, but despite the white-hot lances of lightning that felt like they were flaring along his arm, Ulysses still managed a knotted smile as he looked up into the aquiline features of his loyal manservant, now leaning bodily out of the attic room window above him. He hung there for a moment, the rain steaming from his clothes in the aftermath of the searing lightning strike. Above him the conductor crackled with the last vestiges of storm-born electricity.

"Told you there was nothing to worry about, Nimrod," he grinned and then gasped as his shoulder pulled again.

"Quite, sir."

"I know they say lightning never strikes twice," Ulysses managed through gritted teeth, "but under the circumstances I wouldn't like to tempt fate, so, when you're ready, if you wouldn't mind reeling me back in, as it were?"

A MATTER OF minutes later, back in the basement laboratory, the sphere was running up to speed again. The vibrating hum of the whirling rings filled the space with its organ-resonating force, the feeble light cast by candles stuck into the necks of empty wine bottles suffused by the lurid glowing shell of light at the centre of the gyroscopic machine. Everyone's hair stood on end like weird halos around their heads.

"Is it working?" Ulysses asked, sprinting over to join the boffins at the control panel. Wentworth was monitoring the sphere while Smythe was concentrating on the dials and switches adorning the front of his own device, now resting on the logic engine console in front of him.

"Let's see, shall we?"

Ulysses watched with baited breath, the ion charged hairs on his head streaming out around his scalp. As before, the image of the struggling

Oddfellow appeared within the coruscating ball of light. It began to gain in opacity and colour, as if the old man were solidifying out of the ether in front of them, the incorporeal becoming corporeal again.

Whatever was happening to the aged inventor, it seemed to be hurting him.

"Father!" Emilia cried out as Oddfellow's features knotted in agony, strangely out-of-sync moans of pain wafting to them through the distorting containment field conjured by the machine.

And then, there he was, solid flesh and blood once more – although he looked pale and drawn – wearing the same clothes he had the day he disappeared, shirt sleeves rolled up, an untied bow tie loose about his neck.

"We've got him!" Smythe exulted.

"Got 'im!" Wentworth echoed.

"By Jove, they've done it," Daniel Dashwood gasped.

Tears running in tiny rivulets down her face, Emilia ran to her father as the circling concentric rings ground to a halt and the cellar was left lit only by the wax-dripping tapers. There was a distinct smell of burnt ozone and singed eyebrows.

"Emilia," the shaking scientist said weakly, his clothes and skin wet with perspiration, and took a faltering step out of the bounds of the matter transmitter. And then he collapsed, unconscious, into his daughters outstretched arms.

VIII

Deal With the Devil

"How's he doing?" Ulysses asked, observing the wan figure lying swamped beneath the sheets and blankets of his own bed.

"All right, I suppose, all things considered," said Emilia as she gently mopped the old man's brow with a flannel. "Anything's an improvement on being dead."

"You've got a point there. And how are you doing?"

Emilia took a moment to answer. "Better," she said simply.

In the soft candlelight of the bedchamber she looked more tired, more overwrought, more resolved, more noble and more beautiful than he had ever seen her.

"I'll leave you two alone," Ulysses said, suddenly feeling like he was intruding.

"No," Emilia said sharply, her voice loud in the pervading stillness of the room. "Stay. Please?"

The old man suddenly stirred under the covers and murmured something.

"What's that, father?" Emilia asked, putting her ear close to his mouth.

"Is he here?" the old man asked again.

"Who?"

"Quicksilver," Oddfellow managed before his efforts to speak gave way to a phlegm-ridden bout of coughing.

"Yes, Ulysses is here."

Half opening rheum-encrusted eyes, Oddfellow turned his head on his pillow to look at Ulysses. A hand appeared from beneath the covers and the old man beckoned him over.

"Hello, old chap," Ulysses said as he approached the bed. "How are you feeling?"

"Never mind that." Oddfellow sounded irritated. "I must speak with you alone."

"Father?" Emilia asked, surprised.

"Please leave us, my dear."

Emilia looked like she was about to protest, tears glistening at the corners of her eyes again. Then she thought better of it. "Very well." She sounded hurt. "I'll be out in the corridor if you need me."

"Understood," Ulysses said, feeling her pain but also keen to hear whatever it was that Oddfellow wanted to share with him.

"What is it, old chap?" Ulysses asked, as soon as he heard the door close softly behind Emilia.

"You know me of old, Quicksilver." Ulysses nodded. "And I know you. I know for example that you're not entirely the dandy playboy you make yourself out to be," he went on. "I know of your government connections, whereas, I believe, Emilia does not know how involved you are with the defence of the realm of Magna Britannia."

"I think you're right," Ulysses confessed. "It was that secrecy that drove a wedge between us in the past."

"But now is not the time to tell her either," Oddfellow warned. "There is still action that must be taken to bring this matter to an end," he wheezed and then coughing consumed him again.

"But it's over, isn't it?" Ulysses pressed.

"Would that it were," the old man managed. "Would that it were. You now know what that thing in the basement is," he growled bitterly.

"Yes, it's incredible – an experimental teleportation device. It's an incredible feat of scientific invention, Oddfellow." Ulysses gushed.

"It was slow progress at first, but then I got myself a sponsor and, with the necessary financial backing, I was really starting to get somewhere. But then certain things came to my attention – nothing major, just niggling doubts – and I began to suspect that, how shall I put this?" He broke off to cough again.

"Go on," Ulysses urged impatiently.

"Well, that certain malign agencies had taken an interest in what I was doing and were funding the project, intent on getting their hands on the fruits of my labours. You know the accident that trapped me inside the transmat's containment field?"

"Of course."

"Well, it wasn't entirely an accident."

"You were set-up? A booby-trap?"

"Something like that. I believe it was the work of..." Oddfellow paused, lowering his voice to a whisper, even though there was no one else present to hear. "An agent of the Nazis."

"Really?" Ulysses was incredulous. He knew that the Nazis were still an underground power in Europe, with their hooks in other parts of the world too, but he hadn't had anything to do with them himself within the British Isles.

"You must believe me!" Oddfellow pressed, his plea loud again. "Because if I'm right, now that I am free of the sphere, it won't be long before they make their move."

"Who is this agent?"

"I don't know – that's the trouble. They could be here, right now, in this house!" He sounded desperate now, close to panicking. "But they cannot be allowed to get their hands on my machine. I got as far as destroying all of my notes associated with the project and was preparing to destroy the machine itself when that so-called 'accident' occurred."

Ulysses fixed Oddfellow with a penetrating stare, the pieces of the puzzle finally beginning to make sense. "What do you want me to do?" he asked, with cold purpose.

"You must destroy the sphere, so that no-one can ever use it as a weapon or to further any evil plan for dominion."

Ulysses didn't need to be told twice. He trusted the old man, and if he had decided that the machine was a danger to the safety of the realm, and needed to be destroyed, that was the course of action that had to be taken.

Outside the room he met Emilia pacing the corridor. "Stay with him, he told her, "and keep the door locked."

Ignoring her protestations and questions, Ulysses raced downstairs to find everyone else gathered in the library.

Something close to precognition sent an icy chill down his spine and turned his skin to gooseflesh even before he saw Sigmund Faustus, sitting in the same leather-upholstered armchair from earlier that evening. Fingers steepled in front of his face, he announced solemnly, "Mr Quicksilver, it would appear that you have walked into – how do you say? – something of a situation."

IX

Vanishing Point

"ODDFELLOW TRULY MADE a deal with the Devil when he fell in with you, didn't he Faustus?" Ulysses riled, his body tensing, ready to deal with whatever the alleged German philanthropist might have in store for him.

"Oh, but you are mistaken," the bloated Faustus railed in response, his double chins wobbling in indignation.

A bark of cruel laughter from the corner of the library caused Ulysses to snap his head round in surprise.

"Not as quick as you thought, are you, Quicksilver?" Dashwood sneered as he emerged from the shadows, the gun in his hand trained on Ulysses.

Ulysses considered his own pistol, feeling the weight of it in the holster under his arm, but he kept his hands down by his sides. Now was not the time to go for his own weapon; Dashwood would shoot first and ask questions later, he was sure of it.

He hurriedly scanned the room. From left to right around the library, either seated or standing in anxious anticipation were the parapsychologist Wentworth, Sigmund Faustus, his aide, Ulysses' own manservant Nimrod, the quaking, all-but-forgotten Renfield, Smythe, Caruthers and then the pistol-wielding Daniel Dashwood.

"But Herr Faustus really hit the nail on the head there. This is what you might call something of a situation."

With a barely perceptible nod to Ulysses Nimrod suddenly leapt at Dashwood, more agilely than his slicked back grey hair and apparent age might suggest. But before he could reach the traitorous gentleman, and before Ulysses could make the most of Nimrod's diversion, Smythe, standing between Nimrod and Dashwood, sprung into life himself and floored the manservant with a vicious punch to the face.

In his shadowy life before finding a position as Ulysses' father's butler and manservant, Nimrod had, for a time, held something of a reputation as a bare-knuckle prize-fighter, but Smythe's attack had been entirely unexpected.

Dashwood's aim didn't waiver for a second. His eyes still fixed upon Ulysses, he gave another bark of harsh laughter and tensed his finger on the trigger.

"I believe you've met my colleagues – partners-in-crime, as it were – Mr Smythe and Mr Wentworth."

Ulysses said nothing but merely continued to watch Dashwood, hardly daring to blink in case he missed the one moment of opportunity he needed.

"Very useful they are too," the gloating Dashwood went on. "Particularly when it comes to cobbling together a containment field focusing device from what little I was able to salvage from my rather ingenious uncle's notes. They're also dab hands at setting up little 'accidents', shall we say.

"Although, of course, they might not have been so hasty to arrange one in particular if they had realised that uncle had already made moves to stop anyone following in his footsteps. But now we have both the inventor and his invention intact, thanks in part to you, Quicksilver, so what need have we now of cremated blueprints?"

Obviously already considering himself victorious, the arrogantly boastful Dashwood saw no reason to keep any element of his schemes secret any longer. He had revealed to Ulysses the how and the why, certain that there was nothing that the dandy could do to stop him. And, unfortunately with Nimrod out of action, he appeared to be right.

"All that remains is for me to tie up a few loose ends."

Dashwood's finger tightened still further on the trigger, easing the mechanism back, the barrel of the gun aimed directly at Ulysses' chest.

With a wailing cry, the flabby Faustus launched himself out of his chair with surprising speed. Startled, Dashwood turned, amazement writ large across his face, as the fat German barrelled into him.

The discharge of the gun was loud in the close confines of the library. Faustus gave a grunt, as if winded, and tumbled forwards onto Dashwood. It was the opportunity Ulysses had been hoping for. He went for Wentworth and sent him smashing to the floor with a well-aimed blow to the stomach, which he followed up with a double-handed blow to the back of the neck.

There was an audible crunch and Ulysses look round as Smythe cried out. Nimrod had had his revenge. Smythe lay howling, curled in a ball on the floor as blood poured from his broken nose.

Dashwood lay motionless, beneath the bulk of Oddfellow's sponsor.

"Nimrod, with me!" Ulysses shouted. "We haven't a moment to lose!"

Ulysses leading the way, the two of them raced back down the cellar steps and into the abandoned laboratory once more.

The sphere squatted there on its claw-footed stand, the machinery glowing faintly with what little power remained in its storm-charged reserve batteries, a malevolent presence in the candle-pierced gloom of the cellar.

The last time it had been activated, to effect the release of the imprisoned Oddfellow from its containment field, had drained the potential energy released by the lightning strike but no-one had thought to actually turn it off afterwards.

"We have to destroy this thing," Ulysses said, finding himself suddenly in awe of the machine.

"I do not mean to sound impertinent, sir," Nimrod said, "but how do you suggest we do that?"

Ulysses scanned the control panels of the device and the stilled rings. "There must be a way to overload it. Sabotage its controls or something."

"But overload it with what?"

"Ahh..." Ulysses was suddenly caught out. The generator was still down. "Don't worry, I'll think of something."

Ulysses hastened over to the control panel, frantic eyes searching for a solution. Then preternatural awareness flared inside his skull and he flung himself down behind the logic engine.

The retort of the pistol was dulled by the damp stone acoustics of the cellar. There was a second crack as the bullet spanged off the control console, shattering a glass dial. A second shot rang out and Ulysses heard it smack into the gyroscope itself.

He dared a glance around the edge of his sturdy shelter. The three scoundrels stood at the bottom of the steps. Smythe had a bloody handkerchief clamped to his nose while both Wentworth and Dashwood were gasping for breath, having been badly winded. But Ulysses couldn't see Nimrod. He had doubtless taken cover when he heard the felons dashing down the steps into the cellar.

However, Ulysses couldn't let their presence halt his mission. It was all the more important now that he destroyed the sphere and stopped the traitorous Dashwood and his lackeys getting their hands on it.

Grasping the thick trunking that connected the control panel to the machine he gave a sharp tug. He heard a tearing metal sound and felt something give at the other end of the cable. Teeth gritted he heaved again and was rewarded by a spray of sparks as a bundle of wires came away from the back of the gyroscopic frame. But other cables still connected the sphere to the logic engine, in some unnatural imitation of the umbilical cord connecting an unborn infant to its mother's womb.

As Ulysses reached for another bundle of wires, another flash of prescience sent him scrabbling away, shuffling backwards on his backside, heels kicking against the floor of the cellar.

Dashwood saw Ulysses as he emerged from behind the sheltering cover of the control console and drew his aim on the dandy once more. Distant thunder rumbled over Hardewick Hall.

"Now I've got you," Dashwood snarled.

Scintillating electric blue light exploded throughout the laboratory as the broken rings of the sphere began to spin again. Dashwood threw a hand up over his eyes against the retina-searing glare.

"Lightning never strikes twice, my arse!" Ulysses exclaimed delightedly to himself as he ran for cover.

Eyes narrowed to slits against the brilliant light pouring from the spinning sphere, Dashwood dropped his shielding hand and searched for his target beyond the edges of the coruscating glare, where the shadows appeared even darker now in contrast to the blinding whiteness. But there was no sign of Ulysses.

"God's teeth!" he swore. Smythe and Wentworth looked at him in confusion. "Turn that thing off!" he commanded, waggling his gun at the machine.

Not wanting to risk the wrath of their employer any further, his lackeys moved cautiously towards the now sparking control console of the matter transmitter.

The machine wasn't running as it had been before. Whether it was as a result of something Ulysses had done to sabotage the sphere, or thanks to one of Dashwood's poorly-aimed shots in the dark, something was most definitely wrong with Oddfellow's invention.

There was something feral and untamed about the arcs of lightning zigzagging between the crazily orbiting rings.

"Hurry up!" Dashwood bellowed, hastening Smythe and Wentworth over to the console with another wave of his pistol.

And that was when Nimrod struck. He caught Dashwood firmly between the shoulder blades with the wine bottle, smashing it across his back and sending him reeling. As the villain stumbled forwards, Ulysses made his move. He flung himself out of the shadows and, catching both Smythe and Wentworth around the side of the head, brought their skulls together sharply.

Smythe reeled sideways, a silent expression of pain on his face. Wentworth slumped onto the control panel, stunned. As he slid down the front of the console, he fumbled for purchase with a flailing hand and caught hold of a large, gleaming brass switch, and pulled.

Ulysses leapt from the control platform, sprinting past the bewildered Dashwood, covering the cellar with long strides, as the sphere activated one last time. There was a sound like a thunderclap, deafening within the cellar. Blinding white light flooded the lab, burning Ulysses' eyes even though they were closed. It was as if they had been caught at the very heart of a violent electrical storm, where the turbulent skies birthed their lightning progeny.

His ears hurt, his eyes hurt, his skin felt like it was on fire.

And then the light was gone, leaving glaring after-images on his abused eyeballs, and the acrid stink of obliterated ozone in its wake.

Ulysses fought to open his eyes despite the pain. He could see nothing. The exposed skin of his hands and face stung.

He cast his gaze around the cellar, blinking all the time, and then he saw Nimrod through the gloom. His faithful retainer's eyes were watering and his exposed skin looked like he was suffering from a bad case of sunburn.

And then Ulysses realised something; he could see Nimrod, he could see the workbenches of the lab behind him, he could see the cloud of smoke left by the lightning explosion. He looked around the cellar space again, hardly able to believe the what he was seeing, or rather, what he wasn't seeing. The reason he had seen nothing when he first opened his eyes, beyond the shadows sliding over his tortured corneas was because there had been nothing to see.

Caught within the matter transmitter's zone of influence, Dashwood, Smythe and Wentworth were gone. And so was the sphere. All of them had disappeared – villains, sphere, logic engine, all – teleported to God alone knew where.

Considering how Oddfellow's machine had failed before, Ulysses wondered darkly whether their final destination had been anywhere within the physical realm at all.

"WON'T YOU STAY, just for a little while?" Emilia beseeched him, practically on the verge of begging. "We have so much to catch up on." She found herself absent-mindedly stroking the material of his waistcoat.

Ulysses noticed that she was wearing her hair down, loose about her shoulders. He put a hand to her chin and raised her head, gazing into her darkly-lidded eyes. The day had dawned bright and clear, the storm having blown itself out in the night. The cold crystal blue sky of the first day of November was now reflected in those dark eyes of hers.

He could have lost himself in those limpid pools at that moment, he thought, but he had to be strong. The way fate and personal preference had dictated how he live his life was no life for a delicate flower like Emilia Oddfellow.

"I'm afraid there are matters awaiting my attention back in London," he said in all honesty, without actually giving away any pertinent details.

"I mourned you once," she said, "when *The Times* reported you lost over the Himalayas. Just as I mourned my father. But now I have you both back. I do not want to mourn you again."

"Which is why I must go," Ulysses stated flatly. "Go to your father now. Be with him. He needs you."

"Don't you need me, Ulysses?" she asked. He looked away to where a sunburnt Nimrod was loading his luggage back into the boot of the Silver Phantom.

Ulysses turned back to her and, a forced smile on his face, said: "It's been a pleasure, as always."

"Oh, I see. It's like that." Now it was Emilia's turn to look away. "So are we to live parallel lives now," she challenged, "never to meet again?"

Ulysses said nothing, but gazed out at the mist rising from the croquet lawn.

"Well, thank you for all you've done," Emilia said, suddenly prim. "Good day to you, Mr Quicksilver. I hope you have a safe journey back to London."

"Good day, Miss Oddfellow."

Feeling lonelier at that moment than he had in a long time, turning his back on Emilia and Hardewick Hall, Ulysses Quicksilver descended the steps to the gravel drive.

Two other vehicles were waiting in the cold crisp morning. A team of horses and adapted carriage sent by the local constabulary were taking Madam Garside's body to the morgue and the broken Renfield for further questioning. The second vehicle was a private ambulance. A pair of medical orderlies was lifting a stretcher-bound Sigmund Faustus into the back, his young aide looking on anxiously. The German still looked pale, unsurprisingly, but at least he was still alive.

"I meant to thank you, and apologise," Ulysses said holding up a hand to the stretcher-bearers to wait as he humbly approached the prone philanthropist. "I was wrong to accuse you. What you did was incredibly brave."

The German smiled weakly. "I was foolish and incredibly lucky, Herr Quicksilver. You, on the other hand, saved the day."

"I couldn't have done it without you," Ulysses admitted.

"Very well then, if you insist, I will – how do you say it? – take my share of the blame." He held Ulysses' gaze for a moment, suddenly serious. "Your father, Hercules, would have been proud of you."

An unsettling chill began to gnaw away within his gut at Faustus' mention of his father, as the injured man was loaded into the ambulance. Ulysses had not realised that Oddfellow's mysterious benefactor had known his father. What else didn't he know, he wondered.

There was a tug on his arm and before he really knew what was going on, Emilia was there in front of him her scent heady in his nostrils, her lips crushed against his. And at that moment their parallel lives seemed to converge and all his doubts and conflicting emotions vanished.

THE END

TEIL EKD

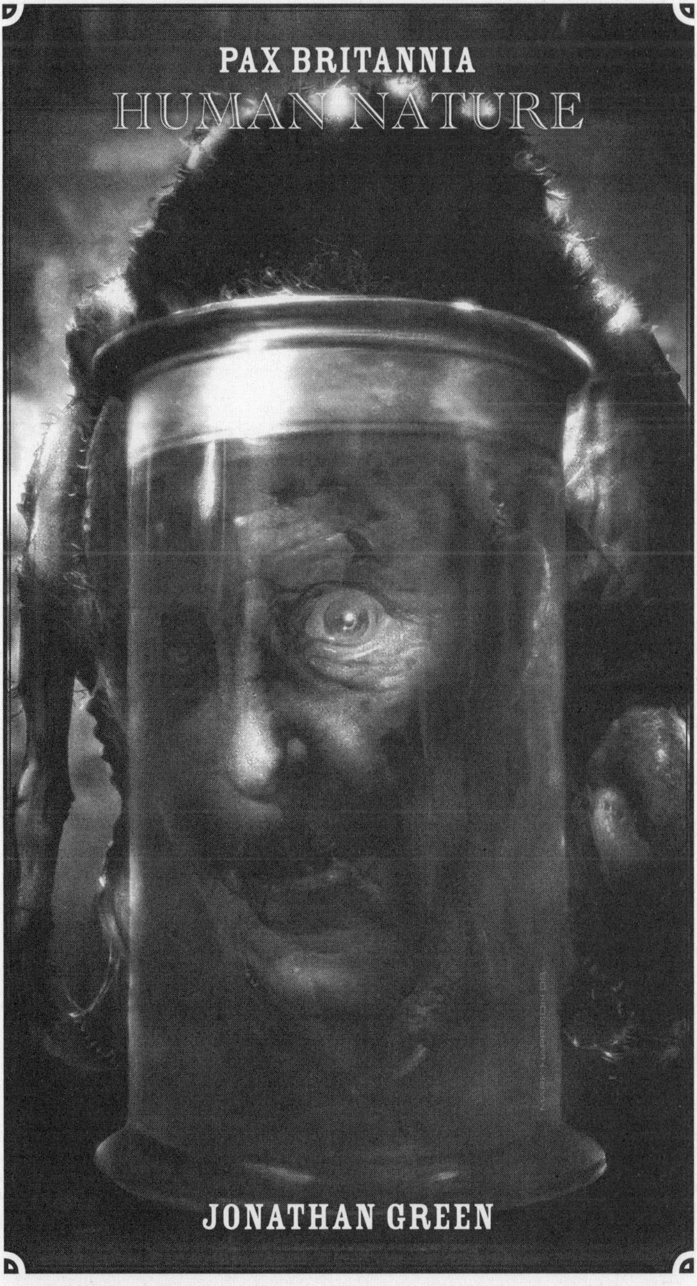
PAX BRITANNIA
HUMAN NATURE
JONATHAN GREEN

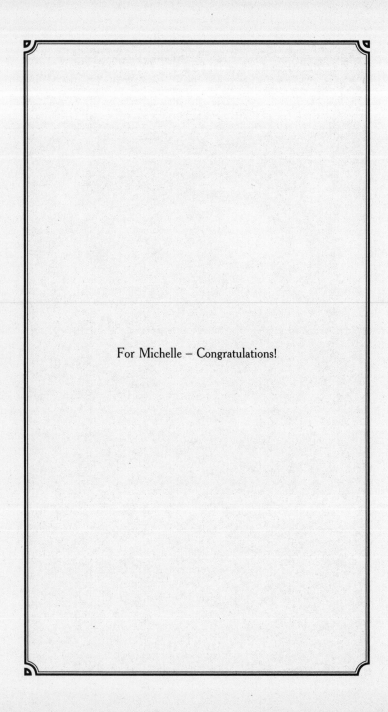

For Michelle – Congratulations!

PROLOGUE

Catch of the Day

THE REVEREND NATHANIEL Creed gazed out across the oily black waves towards the impossible place where sky met sea, and considered what it meant to be a man.

In the unreal twilight that came just before dawn the North Sea appeared as an oily surge – an ocean of bleak blackness that mirrored the darkness slowly gnawing away at his heart.

To be a man was to be a thing divine, was it not?

The night was darkest just before dawn, or so they said. But what about the darkness that was slowly but surely eating away at his soul, that had consumed him from the inside out like the worm in the apple, like a rotten canker, for the last seventeen years? He felt himself tense, every fibre of his body tightening in impotent rage.

His soul had never been more steeped in darkness and malice. Did that mean that redemption was waiting just around the corner? Was it darkest just before the light of revelation showed itself too? Was he on the verge of his own epiphany?

The scales had fallen from Paul's eyes three days after he had been struck down on the road to Damascus. Nathaniel Creed had been struck down seventeen years ago. When would be his moment of enlightenment? When would his revelation come? How long did he have to serve like this before the Lord absolved him of his sins? How long?

"How long?" he demanded of the sky. "How long?"

His scream of frustration was snatched away by the wind sweeping over the hilltops and out to sea, and then it was gone, his desperate plea swallowed up by the turgid polluted clouds, his anger made impotent by the hugeness of the vista before him.

The Reverend Creed's fists bunched in anger, knuckles whitening, nails digging painfully into the palms of his hands. The pain startled him, distracting him from his fury. He blinked, as if on waking from sleep, and looked down at his hands. He could feel that his palms were wet and in the near darkness his fingernails appeared glossily black. Without a moment's thought he wiped his hands on the material of his cassock, the coarse black cloth rough against his lacerated palms.

The Lord is my shepherd; I shall not want. He maketh me lie down in green pastures; He leadeth me beside still waters. He restores my soul. He leadeth me in the paths of righteousness for His name's sake.

What was it to be a man? he wondered. To be a man was to be a creature bound by emotions, at the mercy of one's appetites, to love, to hate, to feel. But he was a priest; he was supposed to be above such transitory, ephemeral concerns. And yet didn't the Bible demand that he love his Lord and Saviour – *Love the Lord your God with all your heart, and with all your soul, and with all your mind, and with all your strength* – hate the Enemy and feel with all the passion of Christ on the cross?

And did not the Bible teach that all men are sinners? Wasn't it Man's fallible nature that had forced God to take human form that he might die for the sins of all? So, then, to be a man was to be a sinner.

Behold, the hour is at hand, and the Son of Man is being betrayed into the hands of sinners.

Well, he was certainly one of those.

He had sinned – O how he had sinned – and he had been repaid ten times over for it.

Eyes narrowed, he fixed the brooding firmament with a gaze as cold and hard as stone, as if he were trying to discern heaven there beyond the clouds.

"My Lord, why have you forsaken me?" he railed at the stormy sky. As if in response, the clouds broiled and distant thunder rumbled across the cold grey surge at the horizon.

How had it all come to this? He had had hopes, dreams, aspirations... once. But they were long gone. He had had to give them up long ago, exchanging them for his penance, for his transgressions of the flesh.

And it came to pass in an eveningtide, that David arose from off his bed, and walked upon the roof of the king's house: and from the roof he saw a woman washing herself; and the woman was very beautiful to look upon.

The surf sucked at the rugged rocks at the foot of the cliff, the greasy waters petroleum-black as an oil slick. As sunrise drew closer the pollutant cloud cover lightened, puffs of magenta and turquoise appearing amidst the otherwise interminable grey.

The Reverend Creed stared down at the exposed rocks one hundred feet below, made rough and ragged by the relentless attentions of the sea. He could end it all now, should he so choose. He had that much power at any rate – the power to end his own life. The Lord had seen fit to give Mankind the gift, and curse, of free will after all.

If any man defile the temple of God, him shall God destroy; for the temple of God is holy, which temple ye are.

The hungry surges roiled and broke to white water on the black rocks, the gaping maw of a sudden hollow in the waves, a whirlpool forming as the surge pulled back out to sea for a moment, beckoning to him. But he ignored its tempting summons, as he had on every other occasion. He would not give the Lord his God the satisfaction of condemning him to an eternity in Hell for taking his own life. No, he would see out his penance to its end, all the while hiding his shame from his parishioners, until God chose to end his life, and release him from his perpetual torment.

To his flock he would ever be the genteel vicar of St Mary's, there to serve their every spiritual need. They would never know of the sin that stained his heart black, as black as the hungry sea.

Look like the innocent flower, but be the serpent under it.

Behind him, back along the cliff path, the squat church hugged the cliff top, as if it feared being uprooted from the exposed spot by the unrelenting wind. But it needn't have worried; behind it, on the wind-swept escarpment above the town stood the black skeletal remains of the Abbey that both raiders and kings had attempted to destroy in the past, and yet still it clung on, its stone pillars and buttresses seeming to grow out of the very ground.

Reverend Creed turned his attention towards the town. Lights were coming on in windows on the other side of the Esk as well as in the nearer buildings that clustered together on the slopes beneath the church in the parish of St Mary's. Whitby was waking up.

But while some were only just beginning their day, others – like the Reverend – had been up for hours already.

Creed was momentarily distracted by a bobbing shape out beyond the coast, riding the rolling waves like a skittish colt. It was a fishing boat, clinker built, nets slipping from its sides. Whoever was on board would doubtless be feeling every rolling surge and sucking tug of the sea. But then, the Reverend considered, it probably wouldn't bother the lone fisherman, when so many of the townsfolk made their living from the sea.

As he watched the fisherman hauling in the dragging nets, he was momentarily distracted from his melancholy as he considered that when it came to the fishermen of Whitby, what it meant to be a man was to be, in fact, half-fish, or so it seemed.

For the briefest moment something like a wry smile twisted the priest's lips, a mouth unused to smiling forming a gargoyle grimace in its place.

"Father?" a voice called from behind him, from the direction of the cramped graveyard.

In an instant the smile was gone and he turned to face the figure standing there amidst the weather-worn gravestones. His penance was still not done.

He closed his eyes and, with a harsh prayer, offered himself to God. *Take me now*, he willed, *if you are done with me.* He swayed there in the pre-dawn light, the wind tugging at the uncombed wisps of hair at the sides of his head.

"Father?"

He opened his eyes again. The Lord was not done with him yet.

God is jealous, and the Lord revengeth; the Lord revengeth, and is furious; the Lord will take vengeance on his adversaries, and He reserveth wrath for his enemies.

Reverend Creed turned back towards the church, preparing to face another day of dealing with past sins made flesh, and cursed inwardly, the cruel scowl now shaping his features looking much more at home there.

GEORGE CRAVEN STARTED, feeling his skin turn to gooseflesh beneath his weather-alls, despite the layers of linen, wool and rubberized fabric.

"Someone must've walked over me grave," he muttered to himself. Still pulling in the net, hand over hand, the rough hemp going unnoticed under the thick calluses covering fingers and palms, he looked back over his shoulder, back towards the black cliffs of Whitby.

He had that uncomfortable feeling that someone was watching him. For a moment, he thought he saw that someone, up there on the cliff, past the church of St Mary's, the squat building silhouetted against the torpid grey-green clouds.

Squinting to perceive any more through the pre-dawn twilight and across such a distance, the fisherman blinked. And then the figure was gone.

"Who was that, I wonder?" he muttered. "Who'd be out at this hour? Apart from you, George Craven," he laughed suddenly, the sensation of being observed passing, his goose pimples diminishing.

Further back, beyond the edge of the grass-tufted cliffs, the ancient, semi-skeletal silhouette of the Abbey rose black out of the gloom. George's goose bumps returned.

"Talking to yerself again, George," he said, hoping the sound of his own voice would shake the renewed feelings of unease, and then stopped, catching himself. "People'll say yer mad if yer not careful," he added.

But he wasn't going mad, not really, and George Craven knew it. Talking to himself while he was out in the *Mabel* was just a habit of his, something he did to while away the monotonous hours. No, he wasn't mad, bored with the monotony of it all maybe, but not mad.

The fishing boat bobbed and rolled beneath his heavy booted feet, the fisherman bobbing and rolling with it, never losing his footing for a moment.

The Cravens had always been fishermen, for as long as anyone in the family could remember. George had followed in his father's footsteps to the sea, like his grandfather before him, and his great-grandfather before that. It probably went all the way back down their family tree to the bottom, where it was rooted in the very sea bed itself.

George's grandmother would cackle like the fish wife she was, through cracked teeth and blistered gums, that Old Man Craven must have married a mermaid, and that their offspring had been trying to get back to the sea ever since.

George smiled as he remembered his grandmother, a cheery soul, and a dab hand with a net needle and a length of twine, as well as with a penknife and a piece of Whitby jet.

Distracted, George's gaze fell to the nets at his feet, now swamping the bottom of the boat. The haul hadn't been great and he would be making a pretty poor showing at the fish market later that morning. By the light of the swaying oil lamp hanging from the mast he could see that there were precious few fish of any worth, meaning he would be back out again tonight after precious little rest. Octopuses and cuttlefish writhed slimily over the wriggling fish as they all suffocated on the deck of the small boat. A spider crab or two crawled over the catch, not large specimens themselves, but worth a bob or two at least. He was almost surprised they weren't bigger though; with the increasing industrialisation of the North of England, the growth in unchecked pollution levels in the sea had gone hand-in-hand with the growth of some of its inhabitants.

"Yer not goin' t'make yer fortune with this little lot," he complained to the salt-sea air. "Yer not ever goin' t'make yer fortune out 'ere," he mused, pensively eyeing the shoreline again. No, he was never going to get rich this way.

And then there was something else... something else that by rights shouldn't even be amongst the catch.

The fisherman squinted again, this time peering at the glistening conglomeration of creatures caught in the net. The catch looked like one grotesque amorphous creature as it pulsed and heaved, all misshapen tentacles, barbed fins, gasping gills, flicking tails, scales and sucker pods.

"Is that hair?" George gasped in surprise.

The catch seethed and moved and there it was again. If it hadn't been right there before his eyes, he wouldn't have believed it. Gasping and choking, the gills at its neck flapping uselessly, the creature was dying, but George just stood there in the rocking boat, staring in dumb amazement.

"Neptune's beard! I don't bloody believe it!" he exclaimed, and dropped the net.

ACT ONE

The Curious Case of the
Whitby Mermaid

November 1997

CHAPTER ONE

Gabriel Wraith Investigates

THE WAITING ROOM was opulent to the point of over-extravagance, Miss Michelle Powell considered, grander and more grandiose than what she was used to certainly, even though her father's legacy had made her independently wealthy. London's foremost consulting detective was obviously doing very well for himself off the back of such a reputation. But then it was also patently clear that he was someone with money and breeding as well. A house in Bloomsbury, no less, only a stone's throw from Russell Square and the austere edifice of the British Museum.

Rising from the chair to which she had been guided on being admitted to the town house, Miss Powell began to pace the room, as one would if enjoying the works of the grand masters on show within the National Gallery.

She admired the Qing dynasty vase above the mantelpiece, the black ebony-wood pedestal bearing a marble bust of the Roman emperor Hadrian and a decorative screen from nineteenth century Japan. She paused before the portrait of a girl in seventeenth century Dutch dress. It was of the Flemish school, she believed, and as a result she strongly doubted that it depicted a distant family member of the house's owner. The oil painting was just another adornment, something of monetary value to be collected and then subsequently shown off.

There was something of the air of an art gallery to this room, in fact, as if everything were on show for appearance's sake, rather than it being there for any reason of emotional attachment or because it spoke to the soul of the house's owner. But then that, in its own way, spoke volumes about the mysterious Mr Wraith.

"Miss Powell?"

The young woman jumped, and gave an involuntary cry of alarm, startled by the sudden reappearance of the manservant. Where a moment before she had been alone, the hawkish butler had suddenly appeared in the doorway, as if he had miraculously materialized out of thin air.

"Are you all right, Miss Powell?" the butler asked, in that forbidding monotone drone of his. It was how she imagined the Grim Reaper would speak, which was an analogy that went well with the manservant's pallid features and hollow cheeks, their gauntness merely serving to highlight the underlying bone structure, giving his features a knife-edge sharpness.

"Y-Yes. Th-Thank you. I'm fine," she stammered, trying to regain her composure. Nervously she adjusted the purple velvet top hat that was already carefully positioned on top of her immaculately coiffeured hair, held in place with half a dozen hat pins, before straightening the bodice of her fitted crushed velvet jacket. She looked – and indeed was – the height of fashion. Only the brass-trimmed velocipede driver's goggles hanging around her neck seemed incongruous when put with the rest of the outfit. But then where was it written that chic young ladies couldn't be budding amateur engineers as well, in this more socially-enlightened Neo Victorian age?

"Very good, ma'am. Then, if you are quite ready, Mr Wraith will see you now."

"Very good," Miss Powell repeated unconsciously, her tone clipped – possibly over-severe she considered, her cheeks reddening at the thought – in an effort to regain her composure.

Why did she feel so intimidated by this place? There was no need to; she wasn't some silly working class girl applying for the position of scullery-maid. She was the client here after all. Then why did she feel so nervous?

"We'd best not keep your employer waiting," she went on. "I'm sure he must be a very busy man."

"Very well, ma'am. If you would like to follow me?"

The butler, dressed in the regulation black, as if he was going to a funeral, turned and marched out of the waiting room with carefully paced strides. Miss Powell followed, the skirts of her dress sweeping the floor as she kept pace with the man, who moved with all the precision of a fish-stalking heron.

He led her back into the just-as-opulent entrance hall of the Bloomsbury house and from there up a mahogany and marble staircase to the first floor. From there they crossed a landing and came to a halt by a pair of grand doors. Seizing the gleaming brass door handles in his white-gloved hands the butler opened the doors and entered the room.

"Miss Powell, sir," the butler announced before promptly backing out of the room again.

Michelle stepped forward, suddenly feeling self-conscious again. There, standing before an unnecessarily large marble fireplace was Maximum Londinium's foremost consulting detective, Gabriel Wraith. He was standing straight as a beanpole, staring disinterestedly out of one of the windows on the opposite side of the ballroom-styled chamber. His profile looked as sharp as a stiletto dagger – hawkish nose, jutting chin and pointed, vespertilian ears – accentuated by the way his boot black hair had been scraped back from a widow's peak and kept in place with so much hair lacquer that it gleamed in the light of the ostentatious crystal chandeliers that lit the room.

The room was almost bare of furniture, other than for a leather-topped desk in the far corner, on which stood a reading lamp and a carefully positioned copy of *The Times*, a large magnifying glass resting conspicuously on top of it. It certainly didn't look like the sort of room where a consulting detective could actually do any work, Michelle thought. Was all this ostentation really just for show?

She cleared her throat nervously, even though she wasn't really sure that she should be so presumptuous as to speak first in the presence of the gentleman detective.

His head snapped round and he studied her with unblinking ophidian eyes. He appeared thin almost to the point of anorexia. Michelle caught her own curve-endowed figure in one of the tall mirrors that stood between the windows on the other side of the room and, unable to help herself, automatically found herself thinking that she was looking rather less than totally stunning that day, even though no right-thinking male would have ever agreed with her.

"You sent word, Mr Wraith," she said, trying to hide the anxious excitement from her voice. "You have, I take it, something to report?"

"I have news, Miss Powell, good news."

"You have recovered it?"

Gabriel Wraith put a tapering white finger to his lips and the young woman was almost surprised to find her words faltering into silence. He had hushed her without saying a word.

The thin man flicked aside a tail of his jacket and dipped long fingers into a waistcoat pocket, pulling out a glittering silver chain, and the pendant that dangled from it.

Wraith stared at the jewel as it spun and sparkled in its setting on the end of the chain. Michelle watched him intently. There was a hungry, almost lascivious, look in his snake-like eyes. She almost expected him to lick his lips in delight at any second, as if the jewel was good enough to eat.

"The Huntingdon Jewel," he said at last, his unblinking eyes never once leaving the faceted face of the gemstone which now swung only inches away from the end of his nose.

"Then I was right," Michelle said with unashamed relief. "You have it!"

"Yes, Miss Powell, I have it. I have it indeed." The consulting detective continued to stare at the gently turning jewel. "A black diamond, is it not?"

"Yes... That's right," she replied, suddenly cautious. "Why do you mention it?"

"Oh, no reason, Miss Powell. No reason. Merely out of professional interest. Worth a fortune, is it not?"

"I told you, Mr Wraith, it is a family heirloom. Its value is beyond reckoning, as far as I am concerned."

"Come, come, Miss Powell, there is no need to be so suspicious," Wraith said, and smiled for the first time since he had begun his audience with Michelle, holding court as a university don might deign to entertain a group of first year students. She had preferred it when he hadn't been smiling. "It is a very rare piece, that is all, and one with a most fascinating history."

"Legend, that is all," Michelle was quick to point out.

"If you say so, Miss Powell, if you say so. Still, all those people who have met untimely and unusual deaths. Some might say it was cursed."

"There is no curse!" Michelle said pointedly, taken aback herself by the vehemence of her own retort.

"No, of course not, Miss Powell. Of course not. Perish the thought. But fascinating nonetheless."

"Mr Wraith," Michelle began, concentrating on controlling her growing anger and impatience – it was as if the man was deliberately goading her – "I appreciate you recovering what I thought had been lost forever – nay, I am delighted – but I would be grateful if you would now fulfil the final part of our agreement by returning the Huntingdon Jewel to me."

Gabriel Wraith snatched the dangling pendant up into his hand again, clenching the piece tightly within his closed fist, and looked at Michelle directly. Once again, she had preferred it when he hadn't been looking at her. She could feel the hairs on the back of her neck standing on end, as her sense of unease grew.

This is getting ridiculous! she scolded herself silently. *Pull yourself together, woman; it is almost within your grasp. Only a minute more and it shall be yours!*

"Mr Wraith?"

The consulting detective smiled again and then, with a sudden movement, tossed the pendant the length of the room into Michelle's waiting hands. She immediately began to inspect the jewel in its setting, looking for any signs of damage, any clue that the original black diamond had been exchanged for a forgery, but there was nothing; as far as she could tell, it was the genuine article, and she should know.

"I'm sorry to say that the other items – the watch, the money, the jewellery – the rest of it had already been fenced on. I am truly very sorry," Wraith said, his words devoid of any real sentiment.

"But you managed to recover the pendant," she said, possibly rather too quickly. "The rest doesn't matter."

"But it was worth a tidy sum, was it not, Miss Powell? A tidy sum indeed."

"The rest of it didn't have the same... sentimental value, Mr Wraith. Let us not speak of it again."

"As you wish, Miss Powell. As you wish."

"Then I believe that our business together is concluded."

The stick thin gentleman detective raised one supercilious eyebrow.

"There is just the small matter of the remainder of my fee, Miss Powell, or had you forgotten?"

"I had *not* forgotten," Michelle said, extracting a slip of paper from within the bosom of her bodice, and proffering it to him. "Your cheque, Mr Wraith."

"Carstairs will take it on your way out," he said, waving her away as if the concept of an exchange of funds for services filled him with disdain, and he hadn't been the one to suggest payment in the first place.

"Ma'am?" And then Carstairs was there at her shoulder again, without having apparently entered and crossed the room to get there.

Michelle could not help letting out an involuntary cry of surprise.

Having recovered herself, she placed the cheque onto the butler's outstretched porcelain palm.

"Good day, Miss Powell," Gabriel Wraith said from his position at the fireplace.

"Good day, Mr Wraith," she responded, and without waiting to be told twice, turned on her heel and strode out of the room, Carstairs swiftly taking his place ahead of her without even having had to speed up to overtake her. "And if I don't see you again, it will be too soon," she added barely under her breath. She didn't want to spend a minute longer than she had to in that house.

TURNING BACK FROM observing his guest's hurried departure, Gabriel Wraith relaxed his affected pose of arrogant supremacy and moved gracefully from his place at the mantelpiece to the reading desk positioned so carefully in the corner of the room. Picking up the folded newspaper he returned to his perusal of its column inches.

Gabriel Wraith loved the smell of newsprint. It was the smell of information, of intrigue and of inscrutability. And he always found *The Times* to be satisfyingly abundant in both.

The front page was laden with pieces about Prime Minister Valentine's war on climate change. Even if their hoped for revolution had not come to pass, the Darwinian Dawn's campaign of terror had certainly raised awareness of ecological issues around the globe. And the new PM was not averse to using such concerns as a means of promoting himself. He had made the subject his own personal project, effectively killing two birds with one stone. On the one hand he was seen to be listening to the general populace's concerns, and thereby helping to avert any further terrorist activity from groups such as the Darwinian Dawn, whilst, on the other hand, doing as much as he could to distance himself from his traitorous predecessor.

Much was being made of Prime Minister Valentine's efforts to make a stand on climate change and industrial pollution here at home, in the capital to be precise. Early next year would see the launch of the *Jupiter* Station, which the popular press had already dubbed the Weather Machine.

It was claimed that the *Jupiter* would be capable of controlling and influencing the weather over London, and ultimately the rest of the South East, the primary intention being to rid the capital of the worsening pall of smog that smothered its streets and clung to its towering skyscrapers with greasy perniciousness.

There were parts of the Upper City that were now almost permanently trapped within the Smog as it was commonly known. The *Jupiter* was being constructed by the factories of the philanthropist millionaire Halcyon Beaufort-Monsoon, apparently as an act of true altruism by the reclusive industrialist, for the paper reported that it wasn't going to cost the tax payer a single brass farthing. Whether this wondrous machine would actually work as was intended was yet to be seen.

Gabriel Wraith turned the page, and let out a disgruntled *harrumph*.

There, taking up a quarter of the page was an over-embellished advertisement for Doctor Feelgood's Tonic Stout.

What was becoming of one of Magna Britannia's greatest institutions, for it to sport such gutter press advertisements, the kind he would have expected to find plastered to the walls of East End slums?

Over-embellished with all manner of curlicues and ornamentations available to the typesetter, the advertisement made much of the supposedly beneficial properties of the fictional doctor's health drink. Wraith had seen their like before – he could hardly miss them and nor could anybody else – they were plastered all over brick walls and billboards from here to the suburbs, while animated, kinema-style versions ran on a loop on broadcast screens across the capital, and had done for some weeks now.

He moved on, scanning the tightly-printed columns, searching for any morsel, any titbit, that might lead him on to his next endeavour.

Apparently Professor Alexander Oddfellow, scientist, inventor and eccentric, who had been missing, presumed dead, for some months had turned up again at his Warwickshire home, while in another part of the country there were still concerns over the health of the industrialist Josiah Umbridge – a rival to the philanthropic Beaufort-

Monsoon – who had now not been seen in public for over a year.

On page seven, as he scanned the lines of densely-printed text, Gabriel homed in on one name, mentioned almost in passing as part of an article about the re-building of the Amaranth House at Kew Gardens, destroyed before it was even officially opened by a terrible fire. Half the page was covered by a photograph of the re-building work in progress, the original exotic glasshouse having been razed to the ground by the blazing inferno.

The passage briefly mentioned that Ulysses Quicksilver had somehow been mixed up in the incident that had seen the glasshouse's destruction, the very morning of its intended opening, much to the chagrin of new Prime Minister Devlin Valentine, who was now focusing his energies on the *Jupiter* project and on building a better Londinium for all.

"Page seven," Wraith chuckled to himself. "He won't like that. He won't like that at all." He turned the page.

The first thing that caught his eye was the hideous photograph. At first he thought it was something from the Royal College of Surgeons Hall in Edinburgh; one of those inhuman aborted foetuses that morbidly curious pathologists seemed to delight in keeping around the place, preserving them in formaldehyde for posterity, as if it was Great Aunt Maud's ashes they were hanging onto so proudly.

Then he looked more closely. The thing was humanoid, at least in part, but rather than being some partially-formed embryo it was in fact disfigured as a result of the chemical process that it had been subjected to, in a crude attempt to preserve the specimen.

The photographic reproduction wasn't the best either. What Gabriel had at first taken to be a malformation of the legs, limbs joined where they shouldn't be (as in cases of *sirenomelia*), he now realised was actually a fish's tail, rapidly losing its scales it appeared, and any doubts he might have still harboured were dispelled as soon as he read the suitably sensationalist headline that accompanied the piece: 'Mermaid stolen from Museum'.

Gabriel Wraith read on with interest, a wry smile spreading across his pinched lips.

A minute later he picked up a small brass bell from its place on the desk, next to the reading lamp, and gave it a short sharp ring. Only a moment later, the doors to the room opened and Wraith's butler returned.

"You rang, sir?"

"I am needed elsewhere, Carstairs. I am needed most urgently. A crime has been committed and an incisive mind will be needed to unravel the mystery."

"Very good, sir."

Wraith examined the photograph of the mermaid in its formaldehyde-flooded glass jar one more time before placing the paper carefully back on the desk.

"Fire up the Bentley, Carstairs. I cannot keep my public waiting. The game is afoot."

CHAPTER TWO

November in Mayfair

"Page seven? Is that all? I risk life and limb for queen and country, *again*, and that's all I get? A passing comment on page seven?"

Bartholomew Quicksilver looked up languidly from his breakfast plate and swallowed his mouthful of scrambled eggs.

"But Ully, big brother, you don't really want the press making a big fuss about your night time exploits do you?"

Ulysses Quicksilver fixed his younger sibling with an icy glare. Barty stabbed a piece of sausage on the tines of his fork and popped it in his mouth, giving Ulysses a broad grin. Ulysses' wintry expression melted a little.

"Well, no," he blustered, "but a little recognition wouldn't go amiss. It's been two months. *Two months*, and still no word of thanks!"

"From whom?" Barty asked distractedly eyeing what was left of his grilled tomato.

"The Ministry, of course, brother dear. Do try to keep up!"

"But I thought your contact at the Ministry was long gone," Barty managed through a mouthful of tomato.

"Of course he is! But that doesn't mean that Department Q has up and left!"

"Oh."

"Oh? Is that all you can say."

"Come on, Ulysses, you've hardly touched your breakfast, and it's one of Mrs Prufrock's finest."

Ulysses eyed Barty, looking him up and down. "Yes, I can see how much you've been enjoying Mrs Prufrock's cooking over the last couple of months. Eating me out of house and home, no doubt.

"You know I have an addictive personality," his brother countered.

"Is that what Doctor Armitage calls it? And better food than the gee-gees, eh?" Ulysses said pointedly. "I don't know, I risk life and limb –"

"Yes, you made that point already," Barty said, making a point himself, ignoring Ulysses' jibe about the few pounds he had put on since moving into the Mayfair residence, and effectively taking the wind out of Ulysses' sails.

"I don't know what's worse," Ulysses fumed, "your lack of interest or the Ministry's."

"Very well, assuming for a moment that I *am* interested, what's happened to Department Q then?"

Ulysses' annoyed expression didn't change but he realised that this was as good as he was going to get so he made the most of the opportunity.

"Word is there's been a shake-up. No more direct ministerial interference. And about time too."

"No more ministerial involvement?" Barty said, putting a piece of black pudding in his mouth and chewing it lugubriously.

"It's been brought in under the wire, along with Prime Minister Valentine's other reforms, in the wake of the terror attacks and Wormwood's attempted coup. About time too. Can't have politicians getting in the way when there are Magna Britannia's national interests to protect."

Barty swallowed and paused in his decimation of the breakfast plate in front of him. "Prime Ministers and political parties come and go, but the Empire endures!"

"Quite so."

A minute passed without either of them saying anything, the only sound in the dining room, other than the ticking of the ormolu clock on the mantelpiece, the scrape of Barty's cutlery on his plate as he chased the last of the fried mushrooms around his plate.

"But just the same. Page *seven*?"

"Anyway, apart from nothing of significance about you," Barty said with strained good humour, "what else is in the news today?"

"Oh, you know, the usual," Ulysses muttered, shaking the paper out in front of him as he finally moved on from his brief mention on page seven. "More about Valentine and his attempts to turn back the tide, or rather, in his case, the Smog."

"Right little Canute, isn't he?"

"You could say that." Ulysses said half under his breath, eyes scanning the newsprint in front of him.

"And?"

"Oh, how wonderful. It says here that Petunia Chase is being considered for the recently vacated post of Director of Kew. Bully for her!"

"Anything else?"

"There's something about Oddfellow's return as well."

"Oh yes?" Barty said, soundly properly interested now. "Any mention of your other lady friend? What was her name again? Emily? Amelia?"

"Emilia, with an 'E'."

"Oh yes, that was it," Barty said locking onto this little nugget, seeing how Ulysses was squirming at his interrogation. There weren't many occasions when Barty had the chance to feel superior to his brother, so when one did come along, he liked to make the most of it. "You never did tell me how the two of you got on."

"No, I didn't," Ulysses snapped.

"How long has it been, now?'

"Listen to this!" Ulysses suddenly exclaimed, behaving as if the last two minutes of conversation had never happened. "A mermaid has been stolen from an exhibition, right here in London!"

Realising that Ulysses wasn't going to be drawn further on the subject of him and his old flame Emilia Oddfellow, no matter how much he badgered, Barty gave in and feigned interest in the article Ulysses was reading.

"What? You mean like the figurehead of some ship, or something."

"No, I mean like a half-human, half-fish hybrid. Comb, mirror, siren song, beloved of sailors. I swear on our mother's grave –"

"There's no need for that," Barty protested.

"– it's the genuine article. A sailor's wet dream, I tell you."

"Oh, you mean like a manatee, or sea cow, or whatever they're called."

There was a suggestion of mania about both Ulysses' tone and his expression now. "No. I mean a mermaid!" he said, delighted.

"You can't be serious. You're having me on."

"No honestly."

"It has to be a hoax."

"No, it's in *The Times*."

"But everyone knows that mermaids don't exist," Barty persisted, even though by the gleam in his brother's eye he already knew he was fighting a losing battle. But he had to persist, for sanity's sake.

"Oh, I wouldn't bet on it." *Not after what I saw, within the rusting chambers of Marianas Base,* he added to himself. "There's a photograph and everything, if you don't believe me."

He roughly folded the broadsheet pages back on themselves and then in half again, proffering the rustling wodge of pages to his brother across the pristine white linen of the tablecloth, exposing the grainy, unbelievable black and white image. Barty took it from him.

"But it's a fake, obviously," he said, taking in the hideous image of what looked like some species of primate melded with the lower half of a large fish – a sturgeon perhaps – with just a hint of doubt entering his voice. Whatever it was made up of, it was a truly repugnant creature.

No matter how much he wanted to hide it, the soupcon of uncertainty was there nonetheless.

"There's no such thing as mermaids," he pronounced again, as if the more times he reiterated that fact, the truer it became.

"You're sure about that are you?" Ulysses challenged, the same manic rictus grin still distorting his features.

Barty looked at the picture again, studying it more closely.

"Look, it's a fake. It's obvious. Look at how the two halves don't match up."

"How do you mean?"

"I mean in terms of scale. The proportions are all wrong. Surely something as skinny as the monkey half would have to have a much more slender lower body – if you believed mermaids really existed, which they don't!"

"Go on."

"And you can practically see where the two halves have been sewn together. It doesn't look so much like a chimpanzee has been bothering a trout, and this was the obscene offspring of the unnatural coupling, as it looks as though someone just chopped a monkey and a fish in half, and then stuck the two together. There's probably a tuna-headed chimp masquerading as some kind of fishman at the same exhibition; part of a matching set."

He thrust the paper back into his brother's hands.

"Well, listen to this," Ulysses said, releasing Barty from his scrutinous gaze and applying it to *The Times* again.

"'The exhibit known as the Whitby Mermaid has been stolen from the Cruickshank's Cabinet of Curiosities exhibition, which has taken up residence within the Holbrook Museum for the duration of the London leg of its nationwide tour,'" Ulysses read.

Bartholomew Quicksilver put down his knife and fork to listen more intently.

"'Mr Mycroft Cruickshank told *The Times* that nothing else was taken from the exhibition of the bizarre and the macabre.'" Ulysses went on. "'Police are baffled' – but then, aren't they always? – 'as there appears to be no sign of a break-in. The question also remains as to why the Whitby Mermaid was singled out by the thieves.'"

"You're telling me," Barty interrupted. "Why would anyone want to steal what is so obviously a fake? Where did it come from anyway?"

Continuing to scan the meat of the article, paraphrasing Ulysses said: "Apparently it was caught off the coast of North Yorkshire, near Whitby, by one," – there was a brief hiatus, as he looked for the name that he had seen earlier – "George Craven. Says it's made him and the freak show's owner, Mycroft Cruickshank, a pretty penny. And the longer the tour continues, the more they'll rake in, but not with their prize exhibit gone."

"Frauds and charlatans," Barty pronounced, imperiously, conveniently forgetting that Ulysses might have said the same thing of him less than six months before.

"Craven claims to have caught the thing whilst out fishing, and he claims that it was alive when he hauled it in, only it suffocated once it was out of the water, before he could do anything to save it."

"Oh, what a shame. How inconvenient," Barty sneered.

"Says he's given up his old job to travel with the tour and see the sights while the exhibition's in London."

"Bully for him."

"Now, don't be like that, Barty," Ulysses chided. "You wouldn't deny a fellow man, who had been down on his luck, a little good fortune, would you?"

"S'pose not," Barty mumbled ungraciously. "Still looks fake to me, though. Don't tell me you think that thing's the genuine article," he said, stabbing an accusing finger at the picture in the paper.

"Perhaps not."

"Perhaps? There's no 'perhaps' about it! Why I'd bet you anything that somewhere in this farce there's someone with a big fat sail needle, a ball of twine and a bloody big knife," Barty finished, a triumphant look in his eyes.

"If you were a gambling man."

Barty suddenly looked sheepish and cast his eyes down at the tablecloth.

"Which you're not."

"No. No anymore."

"Not anymore indeed."

"But it's still fake."

"But if that's the case, why would anyone want to go to all the trouble of stealing this mermaid, and it alone?"

"That one I can't answer," Barty admitted, stumped. "But you're the one with all the deductive reasoning. I'll let you work that one out, Ully."

"Right you are then!" Ulysses said with gleeful delight and jumped to his feet.

"What?"

"I said, right you are then," Ulysses repeated.

"But what are you doing?"

"I'm taking your advice, Barty. I'm going to find out for myself, as you so rightly pointed out, why someone would bother to steal a fake."

"What, now?"

"There's no time like the present. Are you coming?"

"But it's barely ten o'clock. I'm not seen out these days before noon," Barty said, looking at the clock on the mantelpiece. "So, if you don't mind, I think I'll pass. I don't want to ruin my carefully cultivated reputation."

"Heaven forbid," Ulysses scoffed and pulled the cord hanging between the drapes and the door. A moment later a voice crackled over an intercom speaker half-hidden in an aspidistra pot.

"You rang, sir?" came the carefully cultivated tone of disinterest of gentlemen's menservants the world over.

"I did indeed, Nimrod. We're going out."

"Very good, sir." Nimrod continued in the same unemotional manner. "Will you be needing the car?"

"Yes, why not? I like to travel in style. Fire up the Phantom."

"Might I enquire as to where we are going, sir?"

"The Holbrook Museum, old chap. We have an appointment with one Mr Cruickshank who inexplicably finds his freak show short of one freak."

CHAPTER THREE

A Cabinet of Curiosities

"SORRY, SIR. I can't let you in there," the well-meaning yet resolute guard at the door to the museum instructed Ulysses.

"Really?" Ulysses said, exaggeratedly, looking somewhat taken aback.

"'Fraid so. It's a crime scene, see?"

"Yes, I know," Ulysses said, looking the man directly in the eye. "The Whitby Mermaid was stolen from here two nights ago. It was in the paper. That's why I'm here."

"Really, sir?" Now it was the slow-thinking guardsman's turn to look taken aback. He wasn't stupid exactly, just single-minded of purpose and very forward focused in his thinking. He did what he was told.

With one deft movement, Ulysses dipped his hand into an inside pocket of the morning frock coat he was wearing and whipped out a leather card-holder. With an equally assured flick of the wrist he opened it and held it up in the guard's narrow-minded field of vision.

There was a pause as the guard read what was printed on the card inside. Ulysses could see the moment the penny dropped from the way the man's features contorted in, if not confusion, then bewildered understanding.

"Oh. I see, sir. I'm very sorry. If you would like to step this way?"

"Don't mind if I do," Ulysses said breezily and bounded up the last few steps, making for the door to the museum.

As the man's attention moved onto Nimrod on the steps behind him, Ulysses saw the way in which the guard's former steadfastness was regrouping in his features and pre-empted any further delay with a brusque, "He's with me."

Passing through a gloomy walnut-panelled hallway, motes of disturbed dust spinning lazily in the thin beams of autumn sunlight that managed to penetrate the grimy leaded windows, the dandy and his batman followed the signs to the exhibition and came at last to the hallowed hall of ephemera that was Cruickshank's Cabinet of Curiosities.

They had barely crossed the threshold of the equally drear and dusty room in which the exhibition was housed when they were met by an anxiously fidgeting man sporting a startling yellow checked waistcoat under his even more startling crushed green velvet jacket. His clothes made him look like some kind of showman, which, Ulysses considered, was probably precisely what he was. He had an impressive belly – no doubt the product of a strong attraction to ale – and an even more impressive curled handlebar moustache. In fact, this sideshow man appeared to have made a feature of his hair; his moustache was matched by his bushy eyebrows which looked as if they were trying to take flight to join the curly, upstanding knot on the top of his head. Between the eyebrows and the moustache, the man's face was a podgy pink mass of broken veins and purple cheeks, a bulbous, gout-swollen nose and a pair of beady black eyes buried amidst all the flesh.

"And who are you?" Ulysses asked, even though there could be no doubt.

"I, sir, am the curator and owner of this museum of marvels, this assembly of astonishments," the man blustered, going red in the face as he did so. "I, sir, am Cruickshank – Mycroft Cruickshank." It looked to Ulysses like the curator's moustache might unravel itself as he seethed away, his complexion steadily turning to beetroot. "And who, sir, are you?"

"Oh, don't you recognise me? You really don't know?"

"Such arrogance!" Cruickshank bridled. "Why the arrogance of you, sir!"

"It's just that I thought you might have recognised me from the papers or the MBBC newscasts."

From a few feet behind him, Ulysses heard Nimrod sigh in polite impatience. Goading pompous fools might be sport for Ulysses but it was a game others soon tired of, including the Quicksilver family's long-suffering butler.

"No, sir, I do not!"

In a trice Ulysses had whipped out his card-holder again. "Ulysses Quicksilver, at your service."

"Oh," was all the exhibition's proprietor could muster as he read the details of Ulysses' ID. And then, recovering himself again: "I see. But your services are not required, sir."

"Look, I'm sorry if we got off on the wrong foot, but I could be of help here."

Cruickshank looked Ulysses up and down, while Ulysses gave the curator a second once-over.

"You know about the debacle surrounding Her Majesty's 160th jubilee celebrations," Ulysses went on.

"Well, yes, of course," Cruickshank had to admit.

"And the loss of the cruise-liner *Neptune* was widely reportedly in the press I believe."

"What? Yes, I did read of it."

"Well, that was me. I was the one who got everyone out of some rather tight spots."

"Oh, I see."

"So, if you wouldn't mind letting us carry on with our work, I'll make sure we keep out of your way. All right?"

Ulysses took a step forward but Cruickshank moved to block him again.

"It's not that," he said, bushy brows beetling, his face already a much calmer shade of cerise. "It's just that Mr Wraith is already on the case."

"What?" The muscles of Ulysses' face tightened and a bloom of colour now came to *his* cheeks.

"Yes. Mr Wraith is already helping the police solve this mystery."

"Wraith?" Ulysses gasped incredulously. "Gabriel Wraith?"

"The very same, sir. London's foremost consulting detective. We are most fortunate. Perhaps now we'll discover just what's been going on around here." Cruickshank cast his eyes around the panelled room and its many and varied glass display cases.

"When did *he* get here?"

Cruickshank consulted his pocket watch. "Almost an hour ago. It would appear that your services are not required after all."

Ulysses stood there, stunned, not knowing what to say. He glanced back at his manservant who raised his left eyebrow in response; as much of a look of surprise as Nimrod was ever likely to give.

This wasn't getting him anywhere, Ulysses thought, and now that Gabriel Wraith was involved he was even more intrigued. *Time to turn on the old Quicksilver charm.*

"Very well," Ulysses said, relaxing his posture, suddenly aware of how tense he had become at mention of his rival's name. "Fair's fair, I suppose. The early bird, and all that. But it's a personal shame, it really is. A real pity."

"What is?" Cruickshank asked, unable to help himself, wrong-footed by Ulysses' sudden change of temperament.

"I've heard so much about your little exhibition here that I was going to offer my services for free, simply to be able to say that I had some small part to play with the phenomenon of the season."

"Really?" Cruickshank said, his ears pricking up at the mention of 'services for free', Ulysses supposed. "Well, that's very kind of you, Mr Quicksilver. But, as I said, Mr Wraith is already on the case."

Ulysses detected the barely concealed disappointment in Cruickshank's tone, like that of a man who realises he's just missed out on that most elusive of meals – a free lunch. Ulysses also noted that Cruickshank hadn't bothered to question why, if he was so eager to visit the freak show he had waited until after the theft to bother to come at all.

"I've heard tell that it is the finest collection this side of Dusseldorf."

"And so it should be, sir. It has taken me nearly thirty years to gather this most... unique of collections."

Vanity and self-importance had done their bit. He had the proprietor on side now.

"Well, seeing as how we're here now, you don't mind if we take a look around for ourselves, do you?"

"Be my guest, sir."

"We'll be sure to keep out of Mr Wraith's way."

"Very good, sir."

Cruickshank moved aside, and Ulysses strode into the man's inner sanctum, into his chamber of delights, as it were, Nimrod close behind as usual.

Ulysses took in the entirety of the collection laid out around the room, having to turn his head and crane his neck to take in all its wonders. And there was certainly a very great deal crammed into the room, for the benefit of the viewing public.

It seemed to Ulysses' experienced eye that there wasn't a walnut-panel that was free of some manner of exhibit, if not several. Hung from the walls or filling dusty glass display cases were holy relics recovered from the wreck of a Spanish galleon, their gold-leaf and gesso decorations scoured clean by the relentless attentions of the sea; earthenware pitchers and porcelain from China; an icon of Madonna and Child from Russia, the wood dry and cracked; a necklace of monkey teeth; the broken-off top of a Celtic stone cross; the carved dragon-prow of a Viking longship; a Javanese ritual-dance mask, that of a red-eyed, leering demon; Egyptian galibaias – he had worn such a thing himself whilst on secondment to the land of the pharaohs; a snake-charmer's basket and pipes from Bombay; human skulls, their eye-sockets filled with clay and flints; the baubles and bells of King Henry VIII's fool; the Turkish Emperor's gold seal; a pharaoh's death-mask; scrolls of papyrus; an Aztec codex; an intricately worked astrolabe; a Viking lodestone compass; a Neolithic quern-stone; and a morose limestone gargoyle, pilfered from a church in Antwerp.

Or at least that was what the exhibits all claimed to be, each label carefully filled out in a tight copperplate hand.

Ulysses half expected to see the green-eyed monkey god of Sumatra snuck in there, buried amongst the other items, having mysteriously become part of the exhibition.

And the objects – or object d'art, as Mycroft Cruickshank might have preferred it – were not all man-made either; far from it. There were the polished shells of sea turtles and giant tortoises; the horn and tail of a rhinoceros; the scalp and one tusk of a mammoth – although Ulysses didn't understand what was so special about that when one could still see the real thing roaming the tundra of Siberia, if one was lucky.

A number of the exhibits had been stuffed to preserve them but they were not the finest examples of the taxidermist's art. There was an elephant's head, minus its ivory; a still-born two-headed lamb; a stuffed pangolin; a two-tailed lizard; various cases of pin-stuck butterflies, moths, spiders and scorpions; and then there was a large pickling jar containing the knotted form of an octopus, which reminded him far too vividly of his jaunt to the Pacific only a few months before.

He was disappointed not to see much in the way of dinosaurian artefacts. Thought of the terrible lizards then took him back to London Zoo and the breakout from the Challenger Enclosure nearly six months previously, and his rather too close an encounter with a fully-grown megasaur. What had happened to the brute after he brought it down in Parliament Square, he wondered.

And there were plants too; dried vanilla pods; the rump-shaped seed of the Coco-de-Mer palm; and, supposedly, a mandrake root, but which to Ulysses looked more like a prize-winning obscenely shaped vegetable at a village flower show. He had seen the genuine article, and it looked nothing like a cheekily-shaped parsnip.

But none of the plants on show here were as amazing, or as deadly, as the others he had encountered within the Amaranth House at Kew.

Suspended from the ceiling by means of a complicated system of pulleys and wires was a hollowed-out bark canoe that had once belonged to a lost Amazonian tribe; a gaudily-painted totem pole of the Gitxsan Indians of Canada, painted in what would have once been bright, overpowering primary colours; a slice taken out of a Californian giant redwood; and the hull of a Chinese junk.

"It's as if the spirit of Pitt Rivers is alive and well, and residing here in London," Ulysses announced with something like delight in his voice. "Oh, I've got one of those," he said, pointing at a Balinese fetish mask, "or at least I should say I had one of those, before the fire and all."

It amazed Ulysses how many items there were. It seemed that it was not enough merely to own the tusk of a narwhal; Cruickshank needed to possess at least three of the things, each carefully labelled and catalogued with its provenance, including where and when it was acquired, or killed, in the case of the whale tusks.

It a less enlightened age, when the world was a much larger and more mysterious place, such tusks were passed off as the horns of unicorns, and for a suitably unreal price too. Recalling to mind the photograph of the Whitby Mermaid from the paper, Ulysses was almost disappointed not to find one of the horns screwed into the skull of a stuffed antelope or llama with the proud boast that this was the last unicorn to die on British soil. However, his faith in human nature, specifically man's ability and desire to dupe his fellow man, and man's readiness, in turn, to be duped, was restored when he spotted what was purported to be the shed skin of a basilisk – in truth, a cobra's skin with cockerel's wattles sewn on.

The Germans had a wonderful word for collections such as these; they called them *Wunderkammer* – literally "Cabinet of Wonders." But Cabinet of Curiosities seemed to suit this place better. Most of the objects on display weren't wonders; they were tired, faded, deteriorating scrag-ends of dubious provenance, or downright fakes. There wasn't anything wonderful about them although they did make Ulysses wonder as to the obsessive hoarding nature of the man who had gathered this disparate collection together. Yes, curiosities, not wonders.

"Excuse me, constable," Ulysses said, putting a fraternal hand on the shoulder of a young policeman whose misfortune it had been to be put on this case. "But who's the officer in charge?"

There weren't any robots Peelers on the case. Apparently it wasn't deemed important enough to warrant that sort of interest or protection. No, it was going to be up to the Bobby in the street to solve this one.

Ulysses supposed that it was an unimportant matter, when one considered what went on in a city the size of Londinium Maximum on a daily basis. It was only the curious nature of the object that had been stolen, and the public's insatiable appetite for the bizarre and macabre that had meant it had even made it into the papers.

Catching the confident look in Ulysses' eye, the policeman – who looked as though he hadn't even started shaving yet, now Ulysses came to consider it – swallowed nervously before answering. "Inspector Wallace," he said, pointing at an immaculately turned out gentleman standing in the middle of the room, wearing a sharp pin-striped suit with a tailored trench coat over the top.

Not for the first time that morning – the day was still just shy of noon – Ulysses was unable to hide the look of surprise that seized his face, his emotions as readable as an open book.

"Oh, not Inspector Allardyce then? I would have thought this one would be his territory."

"It would normally, sir," the constable agreed, "but Inspector Allardyce is on holiday at present."

"On holiday? Really? I always took him to be the kind of man who ate, drank and slept the job."

"Not this week, sir." The constable gave a wry smile. "Did you want to speak to Inspector Wallace at all?"

"No, no, don't trouble him." Ulysses was looking beyond the constable and the curiosities now to a darkly-attired man in the far corner of the room. "I'm just here to catch up with an old friend."

The early bird that had caught this particular worm was studying an empty glass display case, the front panel of it hanging open.

"Well, well, well. Gabriel Wraith," Ulysses declared, approaching the cabinet in the corner. "Who'd have thought it?"

The man spun round on his heel, otherwise maintaining his carefully poised, and yet ironing board straight, posture and glowered at the beaming Ulysses.

"Quicksilver."

"Fancy meeting you here."

"Fancy indeed."

Ignoring Ulysses, Wraith turned back to his examination of the display case.

Ignoring the rebuff, Ulysses peered over his shoulder none too subtly to get a view of the case for himself. Resting on the black velvet mount at the base of the cabinet, looking rather forlorn now, was a handwritten card bearing the inscription, 'Whitby Mermaid'.

As Wraith picked at pieces of fluff attached to the velvet with a pair of tweezers, Ulysses also saw now that the consulting detective was wearing crisp white cotton gloves, so as not to contaminate any evidence he might find there.

Wraith snorted irritably at Ulysses' continued and obviously unwanted presence. "Is there something I can help you with?" he asked icily, still refusing to actually face the interloper.

"So, any ideas?"

"I am considering a number of alternative hypotheses at the moment."

"Hmm, a mystery, isn't it?"

"No, not really. Not to someone with a logical mind."

"So you have an answer then?"

"There is always an answer, a logical answer, arrived at following careful consideration of the evidence. It just takes a disciplined mind to uncover it."

"So, you think you'll find the answer?" Ulysses pressed, with all the enthusiasm of an eager puppy, much to Wraith's obvious annoyance.

"I have no doubt that I shall solve this – as you put it – 'mystery', although there is nothing mysterious about it. And I certainly don't need your help." A cold smile suddenly appeared on Wraith's pinched lips. "I understand you had something to do with the fire at Kew," he said, brightly. "You're a walking liability, Quicksilver. First the Crystal Palace, then the loss of that cruise-liner and now Kew Gardens has felt the fell hand of the Quicksilver curse upon it. Why, wasn't your own home gutted by fire not so long ago?"

"That incident suffered from gross exaggeration by the press," Ulysses suddenly found himself at pains to point out.

"Yes, I remember the papers reported your death. Pity."

Hearing hurried footsteps tap-tapping their way across the parquet floor of the room, Ulysses turned to see a yet again red-faced Mycroft Cruickshank steaming his way over to where they were inspecting the cabinet together.

"Ah, Mr Cruickshank. Would you like to give us your considered opinion as to who broke in here and how they got away? Perhaps you could fill in a few gaps for me; clarify a few details," Ulysses began.

Cruickshank glared at him with those piggy black eyes of his from out of the doughy arrangement of his face. From the colour of the curator's face, Ulysses just knew that all this stress couldn't be doing his blood pressure any good.

"I'm sorry, Mr Wraith, is this gentlemen bothering you?"

"Yes he is, Mr Cruickshank."

"Mr Quicksilver, you are here thanks to my gracious goodwill, sir. Please don't abuse that generosity of spirit."

"Of course not. So the break-in was two nights ago now?" Ulysses deftly side-stepped the subject, just as he deftly ushered the curator of this weird and wonderful collection of the macabre and downright bizarre away from where Wraith was working, as if it was he who had interrupted the private detective's investigation of the crime scene.

"What? Yes," Cruickshank replied, caught out by Ulysses' abrupt change of conversational direction.

"And you reported it to the police yesterday morning when you discovered that the mermaid was missing, is that right?"

"Er, yes."

Ulysses waited, eyeing Cruickshank expectantly, as if waiting for him to speak. The bewildered proprietor obliging took his cue and began to spill the beans.

"I came in to open up, as it were, as usual and was caught out by the chill draft that was sweeping the room."

"And where was this draft coming from?"

"A window in the one of the – *ahem* – conveniences had been left open."

"The door hadn't been tampered with?"

"No. It was locked, just as I had left it the night before."

"And who else has a key?"

"Only, Mr Gallowglass, the director of the museum. But the police have already questioned him and his alibi stands up to the closest scrutiny. Besides, he's a trustworthy sort of a fellow."

"And where are these – *ahem* – conveniences?"

"Over there," Cruickshank pointed to a door in the adjacent corner half hidden behind the sarcophagus of a ninth dynasty Egyptian king.

"And is there any other way of reaching them?"

"No, only from this room."

"Well then, if it wasn't Mr Gallowglass, and I have to say, why would a man of his standing be interested in stealing a forgery –"

"I'll have you know I have it on the best authority that it is – *was* – the genuine article!" Cruickshank blazed.

"– and unless it was you, planning some insurance scam –"

"What are you trying to say, sir?"

"– which I sincerely doubt, otherwise you'd have taken something of more obvious value that the mermaid. And talking of fakes," Ulysses said, "where did the Whitby Mermaid come from? And don't say 'Whitby'." Cruickshank looked as if he was about to protest again but instead made a face like a goldfish gasping for air. "You don't honestly expect anyone to believe that it was the real deal, do you?"

Cruickshank's manner changed in an instant. He drew Ulysses to one side, an arm around his shoulders and dropped his voice to a conspiratorial hush.

"You're a man of the world, Mr Quicksilver, I can see that, so I won't try to fool you in this regard. If you ask me the thing's a fake. You can even see the stitching if you look closely enough – or at least the scars where the stitches would have been, they're not there now – but old Craven was adamant that when he caught the thing in his nets it was alive, gasping for air on the deck of his little boat as he looked on in disbelief. He swears on the Bible it's the truth, but it hardly seems credible, does it?"

Ulysses gave that thought some consideration for a moment. There were certainly many strange and downright weird things in this world, and he had seen a fair few of them, but mermaids? That just seemed one sea dog's tale too far.

"But nonetheless you saw fit to reveal this abomination, anomaly – call it what you will – to the world."

"Of course. I saw it as my duty, to let the viewing public decide for themselves," Cruickshank said, putting a showman's spin on the subject.

"And you cut Mr Craven in for a share of the proceeds raised from the viewing public?"

"Of course, sir."

"Well, I'm sure that whatever it was you offered him, it was a fair cut, once you take off your, no doubt, not inconsiderable running costs."

"That's right," Cruickshank said, warily. A confidence trickster was always going to be a hard man to play when he was already wise to the tricks played by others.

"Putting that aside for the moment," Ulysses went on, "the fact is that the mermaid was stolen and the only way the felon could have entered was through the open window in the conveniences?"

"But that's impossible. No-one could get in through there; it's hardly bigger than a letterbox!"

"Not impossible, Cruickshank, old boy, only highly improbable."

"What?"

"And once you have ruled out the impossible, what's left, no matter how improbable it might appear, holds the key to the truth!" Ulysses declared triumphantly. "And the cabinet wasn't forced either?"

"No." The cabinet of curiosities' curator was wearing an expression of confusion on his face now.

"Then I would say that the scoundrel we're after is a dab hand with lock picks as well," Ulysses mused, a thoughtful hand supporting his chin. "Good day to you, Mr Cruickshank."

"What? You're going?" Cruickshank exclaimed, as Ulysses strode off, making for the exit, wrong-footed once again. Strangely, he sounded, if not disappointed, then at least annoyed that Ulysses was ready to depart as quickly as he arrived.

"We have all the information we need, haven't we, Nimrod?"

"It would seem so, sir," Nimrod replied in that familiar disinterested tone of his.

"And we wouldn't want to trouble you or Mr Wraith any longer. You don't want us getting under your feet more than is necessary, I'm sure?"

"Well... No?"

"Then good day to you, sir, and I hope Mr Wraith comes up trumps for you, I really do."

And with that, Ulysses left Cruickshank's Cabinet of Curiosities.

As he and Nimrod descended the steps in front of the Holbrook Museum, his ever-faithful manservant asked: "You're not really leaving the matter in the hands of Mr Wraith, are you, sir?"

"You know me better than that, Nimrod," Ulysses replied, unable to hide the look of glee on his face. He was always the same when he was at the beginning of a new adventure. The hunt was all.

"The game is afoot, Nimrod. We have a mystery to solve. And I think it's about time you looked up some of your old acquaintances again."

CHAPTER FOUR

The Whitechapel Irregulars

"WHY IS IT that your 'contacts' always want to meet in such charming places?" Ulysses asked, as he took in the black looming tombs and ivy-clad gravestones of Highgate Cemetery. The skeletal branches of the trees scratched at the night's sky with their talon-like tips, the twigs rattling like dry bones in the chill November wind.

Regardless of the fact that they were still within the bounds of the capital, right at this moment civilisation seemed a long way away. They might as well have been out in the desolate wilds in the middle of nowhere, with only the bodies of the dead for company.

"I understand that they are of the underworld, but do they really need to get so close to the real thing? Does it provide them with some sense of security or something?"

"It goes with the territory, sir, so to speak," Nimrod explained patiently. "No-one else comes to graveyards after dark."

"Indeed. Hardly surprising, is it?"

"The view from the other side, eh, sir?"

"I suppose you could call it that. Although the other side of what?"

Ulysses strained his eyes to peer uneasily between the crypts and iron-speared fences of guarded graves. His edginess didn't arise from a fear of such places, or from being reminded of his mortality. Ulysses

508

had witnessed the death of others and faced death himself more times than he would care to remember in his years as a dandy adventurer and agent of the throne of Magna Britannia.

No, his unease arose from a desire to get a move on with his latest case. If there was something Ulysses Quicksilver didn't like, it was pointlessly hanging around. What he enjoyed – what he craved – was the thrill of the chase, whether it was pursuing a mystery to its conclusion, battling enemies of the state, life and death struggles or, as it had once been, setting about capturing the heart – or at least the libido – of whichever lovely it was that currently caught his eye.

"You did say nine o'clock, didn't you, Nimrod?"

"I did, sir," Nimrod replied in the same indefatigably patient manner. "Then where is he?"

And then he felt it, the hairs on the back of his neck rising, his skin goose-pimpling as that ever reliable sixth sense of his kicked in.

"Oh, don' chou worry," came a voice whose words were distorted by a broad cockney drawl, "I'm 'ere. 'Ave bin for the last ten minutes. 'Eard every word you said, din' I?"

Ulysses' head snapped round and his eyes locked on the empty space between a towering unkempt yew and a long forgotten family's house-sized tomb. Only it wasn't empty. There was a figure there, a silhouette darker still against the already oppressive blackness of another Smog-shrouded London night.

But now that Ulysses knew where the man was, he could see subtle signs of movement as Nimrod's contact approached.

"'Evenin', Mr Nimrod," he said, nodding to Ulysses' manservant.

"Good evening, Rat." Nimrod spoke to the shadow no differently to how he would address his master or even Her Majesty Queen Victoria herself. But it sounded strange to hear him pronounce a name such as Rat in the clipped syllables of that well-bred accent of his. "May I introduce my employer, Mr Quicksilver."

The man said nothing but merely regarded Ulysses with the kind of scowl that implied that he rated the dandy barely above something he might find on the bottom of his shoe. Ulysses put this down to the natural distrust of the criminal for any figure of authority or with a higher social status than himself.

Ulysses in turn regarded Nimrod's contact with a look of intense curiosity. He had a scruffy, worn appearance. Everything he wore from the crumpled cloth cap that barely kept an unruly grey thatch in check, to the scuffed hobnail boots on his feet, even if it hadn't started out as a uniform had nevertheless ended up that way.

The man himself appeared to have worn even less well than his clothes, his jutting, angular features marked with the tell-tale scars of smallpox and other scars acquired through misadventure rather than misfortune. He hadn't shaved for a number of days and he didn't appear to have washed either. But he did have most of his own teeth by the look of things.

As to how old he was, it was anyone's guess. The grey hair with its straw-like texture could put him at as old as fifty, but there was a certain youthful sparkle in his eye that could have made him prematurely grey at thirty.

Deciding that someone needed to do something to progress this meeting, Ulysses held out his hand to the wastrel. "Mr Rat. Delighted to meet you."

"It's just Rat," he said, leaving Ulysses' hand well alone.

"Nimrod's told me so much about you," Ulysses went on, feeling that he wasn't getting anywhere very fast with his current tack.

"Has 'e?" Rat replied suspiciously, taking a wary step backwards, glancing between Ulysses and his manservant, his features knotted into a feral grimace. Ulysses could see now why the name Rat suited this ne'er-do-well so well. Nimrod shook his head, never once taking his eyes off the shady character.

"Well, no, he hasn't," Ulysses admitted, "but he has told me that you're the man who has all the answers."

The man known as Rat appeared to relax, although only ever so slightly. He still looked like he could turn tail and run at any moment. "For a price," he said, by way of confirmation, his own appraising gaze fixed firmly on Ulysses again.

"That's understood. Nimrod has made your terms clear to me."

Rat said nothing but continued to subject Ulysses to uncomfortable scrutiny.

"'Ere, I know you," he said suddenly, with devilish glee.

"Well, I should hope so; we have just been introduced."

"Yeah," Rat continued, as if Ulysses hadn't said anything at all. "I've seen your mug on the cast screens."

"Oh, you know me like that, you mean."

"Yeah. I'm right, aren't I?"

"Well, how privileged you are. You seem to have *me* at something of a disadvantage," Ulysses said, tiring of the grass's cocky swaggering manner.

Ulysses had not taken his eyes off the man's face since the two of them had been introduced. He saw Rat's eyes narrow and could almost hear the *k-ching* of the ringing cash register.

"Is there a problem?" Ulysses asked with icy calm, the hairs on the back of his neck bristling, already knowing what the other was about to say.

"Well that changes things, see?"

"In what way?"

"Information is a valuable commodity, isn't it?" Rat spoke the word commodity as if every syllable was a separate word. "Much more valuable than say, gold, jewels or... a bit of the foldin' stuff. And much more valuable to a man of your... standing, Mr Quicksilver, who, at the present time, if I might say so, one might be so bold as to presume is not short of the latter but sadly lacking in the former."

The grass grinned, revealing the yellow pegs of his teeth. This simple action made him look even more like his namesake.

"Rat," Nimrod spoke up suddenly, "we agreed terms at the same time as we arranged this meeting."

"Ah, but Mr Nimrod, you weren't entirely honest with me, were you?"

"I am scrupulously honest," Nimrod growled.

"Well then, let's just say you weren't entirely... forthcoming regarding all the particulars of this 'ere exchange."

"Don't worry, Nimrod," Ulysses said wearily, still not taking his eyes off the opportunist thief as he reached into his coat. "I'll handle this."

Rat's eyes began to sparkle, as if shining with the reflected shine of the money he was hoping to acquire.

"Will this suffice?"

Ulysses' hand came free of his coat in one sudden sharp movement, but it wasn't as sharp as the rapier blade he was now holding under Rat's chin, the sheaf formed by his black wood cane in his other hand.

His body rigid with fear, Rat swallowed, his Adam's apple sliding against the razor-edge of the blade, which gleamed darkly.

"Let's get one thing clear, Mr Rat," Ulysses said, his voice like steel. "No one rips me off!"

Rat said nothing, his bulging eyes darting from Ulysses' own steely gaze to the steel of his sword-cane and back again.

"Do I make myself perfectly clear?"

Rat gulped again and nodded slowly, anxious not to cut himself on the keenly-honed blade.

"Good. I'm glad we've got that sorted out."

Ulysses waited for a moment, holding his fencer's stance, his blade at the grass's throat, before slowly withdrawing the rapier and sheathing it.

"Now, Mr Rat, I am sure that we both have places we would rather be right now so, let's not waste each other's time any longer. I think the expression is 'spill the beans'. The theft of the Whitby Mermaid – what do you know?"

Rat gulped again and despite the rapier blade being sheathed and safe it still seemed to be hovering there, a metaphorical ghost of itself, just under his chin.

It took him a moment to find his voice. When he did speak, his earlier cocksureness was gone, his voice cracked, his tongue sticking to the roof of his mouth, parched from fear.

"Word is, the Whitechapel Irregulars had something to do with it," he managed at last.

"And who might they be?"

"Gang of thieving street urchins. Conniving little bleeders, if you ask me."

"And where would I find them?"

A momentary look of disbelief knotted the man's face and he opened his mouth as if he was about to make some sarcastic comment.

Ulysses pre-empted any such inappropriateness by arching an eyebrow at the still quivering man.

"Humour me," was all he needed to say to make his point.

"Make your way to Whitechapel and if you don't find them first they'll be sure to find you, I 'ave no doubt." Rat gave Ulysses a bitter smile. "Failin' that, you could look in the Blind Beggar. That's all I know."

Ulysses relaxed a little. "There. That wasn't so bad, was it?"

Rat said nothing but just glowered at him in return.

"Now then, Mr Rat," Ulysses said happily as, beaming, he reached inside his coat again. Rat tensed. But rather than a blade, this time Ulysses brought out his wallet. "The matter of your fee."

"So, this is Whitechapel?" Ulysses declared, as the cab pulled away, a look of child-like wonder on his face.

"Yes, sir."

Ulysses paused, cane in hand, looking all around him and inhaled deeply, absorbing the aroma of the place as much as the sight of the slums. The teeming hordes making their way through the streets of Whitechapel – hawkers, pedlars, navvies, dockers, gong cleaners, street sweepers, whores and scruffy children by the score – milled around and past him, not giving him a second look.

There were few droids present here; it wasn't the sort of place where (a) people could afford them, or (b) where it was safe to send them; within an hour they could be melted down for scrap, or disassembled and their parts cannibalised to make something else or sold on the black market. Neither was it the sort of place Ulysses wanted to risk his Rolls Royce Mark IV Silver Phantom, hence the need for the cab.

Here, the desperate and the destitute laboured under the almost permanent shadow of the Smog as the factories of the industrialised East End belched their foul clouds of toxicants into the atmosphere. It was said that inhaling the lungfuls of dust present in the air here shortened people's lives considerably.

"Incredible, isn't it? All my years living in this teeming metropolis and hunting down villains within its winding streets, and I've never set foot in Whitechapel." He turned and looked at his manservant. "I suppose you've been here many times before, Nimrod. In the past, I mean."

"Oh, I know it well, sir. You might say, far too well."

Ulysses took a step forward. He looked up at the street sign nailed to the crumbling brick of a junction above him, letting the tide of struggling humanity wash past him.

"Old Montague Street," he said. "And where's the Blind Beggar?"

"Up this way." Nimrod pointed, indicating the crowded street ahead of them. The way was packed with all manner of people going about their daily business, minding their own, while other more prying eyes looked on.

"Well, no point in hanging around here. If we're going to do this, we'd best get going."

Beggars and others skulked in the many secreting shadows, small bright eyes watching their every move by the light of crackling electric street lamps and a chestnut seller's brazier.

The night was cold, this close to winter – for all the talk that certain meteorologists and protest groups spoke of the new-fangled phenomenon of 'global warming' – and come the morning a crust of ice would cover the effluent streams running down the street. A bag of hot roast chestnuts wouldn't go amiss on a night such as this, Ulysses thought, pulling his scarf tight at his neck. While he was at it, he pulled the cashmere up over his mouth to filter out the worst of the ripe stench of raw sewage and lung-tarring smoke. The noxious stink seemed to characterise Whitechapel rather too well.

This place had been the haunt of prostitutes, thieves and ne'er-do-wells for centuries. When Covent Garden had been cleared, the scum had ended up here, washed east like the rest of the effluent produced by the city.

Ulysses paused again. That old familiar feeling that was both reassuring and at the same time unnerving, had returned; his near-prescient sixth sense scratching away at the edges of his conscious mind.

"Tell me, Nimrod, do you get the feeling that we're being watched?" he said.

"Indubitably, sir."

"Then we have their attention."

"I should say so, sir."

"Excellent. Then let's be having them, as the Peelers would put it."

The two men continued on their way up Old Montague Street, navigating the bustling crowds, Ulysses looking like a fop out to find some diverting entertainment for the evening, with his fixer-manservant at hand to keep an eye on him; just the sort of image they wanted to portray, in fact.

Ulysses had the manner of a hedonistic cad down pat, quite possibly because that was what he himself had once been. The enticements offered by the ladies of night were not totally unknown to him, as the infamous Queen of Hearts herself could vouch.

But that wasn't what he was looking for tonight as he enjoyed the change of scene from the more conservative streets of Mayfair and Bloomsbury. Whitechapel had a look all of its own, its walls plastered with layer upon layer of bill posters – promoting everything from the Chinese magician Lao Shen's show at the Palace Theatre to the new panacea of the modern age, Dr Feelgood's Tonic Stout – until Ulysses could quite believe that it was these layers of paper and glue that were all that was holding some of these crumbling tenements together.

And then, the dull throb of his subconscious became a white hot flare of awareness, just as Ulysses felt what might have been someone simply brushing past his coat tails, but wasn't.

He spun round, fast as a pouncing panther and grabbed the child by the wrist in a grip of iron. The urchin – his clothes rags, his face a smear of soot, the whites of his eyes almost all that was visible beneath the grime, a mop of filthy, lice-ridden hair contained within a cloth cap that was obviously too big for him – squealed like a stuck pig. Meanwhile, a waist-coated monkey, with an ugly, old man's face, jumped up and down on the boy's shoulder shrieking, tugging at the string the boy was still holding fast in his free hand.

Ulysses bent low, eyes blazing and he looked into the boy's terrified pale face. His devilish gleeful grin only made his aspect all the more terrifying as far as the cowering child was concerned.

A triumphant laugh escaped Ulysses' lips. "Got you!" he growled.

CHAPTER FIVE

The House of Monkeys

"So, Sidney, where do you want to begin?"

The boy put down his tankard, containing a double measure of gin, but did not relinquish his grip on the handle.

"Don't send me back to the spike, sir. Please, sir. Not that, sir."

"No one said anything about the workhouse, did they Nimrod?" Ulysses said calmly, regarding the boy's anxious expression with something somewhere between suspicion and almost paternal concern.

His manservant muttered something under his breath that obviously wasn't really intended for his master's ears, and continued to nurse his hand. The monkey had bitten him when he had tried to wrest it from the boy's grasp, Ulysses having apprehended the would-be pickpocket. That had been the last straw as far as Nimrod was concerned, and if Ulysses hadn't stopped him he would have throttled the simian with its own leash. The creature now sat hiding behind the boy's head, peering at the older man with a malevolent, gargoyle scowl whilst picking the occasional louse out of Sidney's hair to chew on.

Ulysses looked to his companion again. "You all right there, old chap?"

"I've suffered worse, sir." That was true, Ulysses thought. "The whiskey's helping." With that Nimrod dipped his bloodied handkerchief into the glass again and dabbed it onto the bite. He hadn't swallowed a drop of the stuff.

"Soon as we're done here, we'll see about getting you a tetanus jab."

"Very good, sir."

Ulysses turned his attention back to the boy, who was taking another noisy slurp of gin. Ulysses didn't have any children of his own – at least none that he knew of – but if there were any of his bastard progeny out there, then he hoped that they were growing up with people who loved them and who could care for them, and not scraping a living from the streets – if it could be called a living – like the poor wretch in front of him.

The boy was small. Under all the dirt and hand-me-down rags he appeared to be about seven or eight years old. He was pale-faced, like so many who lived under the permanent pall of the Smog and thin through obvious malnutrition. The gin probably didn't help, but it was what the boy had wanted.

He was strong, Ulysses would give him that. There'd been a tussle when the dandy had first seized the young dip-thief. The boy had kicked and screamed and tried to get away, as Nimrod tried to stop the monkey from joining in the fracas, but Ulysses had won in the end, bundling the boy away under one arm, the hand of the other covering his mouth. People in the street had watched the confrontation and resulting abduction with nothing more than passing interest and nobody acted to stop Ulysses or Nimrod. It just went to show that such incidents weren't uncommon in the rougher parts of town. The general consensus of opinion seemed to be that it was best just to avert your gaze and mind your own business. The boy had probably wronged the finely-attired gentleman in some way they figured, or owed him for services paid for but not yet rendered. Best to keep out of it.

If Ulysses had stopped to consider it for a moment, he might have pondered on what manner of life could crush a person's spirit so much that any sense of compassion for one's fellow man had been crushed along with it.

"How old are you, Sidney?" Ulysses asked, lowering his voice so that he came across as unthreatening as possible.

"Eleven years old, sir," the child said proudly. Appearances could be deceiving, Ulysses mused. "At least so's I'm told," he added.

"How do you mean?" Ulysses asked.

"That's what they told me at the workhouse where I's was born. Born in the flood of '86, they said, when the Thames burst its banks. Don't send me back there, sir. Don't send me back to the beadles. Please don't."

"Look, calm down. No one's going anywhere at the moment, Sidney."

The boy looked at him with wide, watery brown eyes. They appeared large in comparison to the rest of his head, doeishly cute and appealing, thanks to his stunted growth.

"You're one of the Irregulars, isn't that right?"

"Irregular what, sir? Don't know whatcha mean." The boy's sudden show of bravado told Ulysses everything he needed to know.

"Best gang in the East End, I heard."

The boy eyed him suspiciously, knocking back the last of the rotgut that passed for gin round these parts.

"Another drink?"

"Don't mind if I do, guv'nor! Seein' as 'ow you're payin'."

Once Ulysses had the boy in his grasp and had carried him away from the main thoroughfare of Old Montague Street, he had dropped him in the archwayed entrance to a blind alley. By that point the boy had realised that it was pointless trying to run, at least for the time being, and so had sat and listened as Ulysses had made his claim that he only wanted to ask him a few questions over a drink. The child had certainly had much worse threatened to be done to him, so he had taken the two high-falutin' gents to a drinking den he knew.

There had been little conversation made over the first round but now the gin was starting to loosen the boy's tongue, as Ulysses had hoped. He did not stop to consider the moral implications of getting the boy drunk so that he might disgorge all that Ulysses' needed to know about the urchin street-gang. If he had done, he might as well have given up on ever solving the case of the missing Whitby Mermaid altogether, and he wasn't prepared to do that, not by a long shot.

Ulysses watched his aide's progress at the bar, through the blue fug of tobacco smoke. The barkeep gave Nimrod what could only be called 'a look' but didn't refuse him his drinks. His money was good and money was all that mattered here. This was Victorian England after all and what rich gentlemen got up to with young waifs and strays wasn't anyone's business but their own. There was always the possibility that the man was a philanthropist who would rescue the boy from poverty and take him away to a better life somewhere else. At least that was what the barkeep tried to tell himself as he looked away from their table again.

"So," Ulysses went on, when the refreshed tankard of gin had been placed in front of the boy, "you were telling me about the Whitechapel Irregulars."

"Was I?" the boy asked, innocently, raising the pewter to his lips.

Ulysses' reply was an arching eyebrow, pregnant with meaning. The monkey glared at him before starting to nuzzle the boy's ear, chattering and chirruping in its shrill simian voice.

And then, seemingly under the influence of the eyebrow, Sidney relented at last. He might have little or no education to speak of, but he wasn't stupid; he knew when he was beaten.

"Like I said, best gang in the East End," Ulysses said.

"Then you 'eard wrong. Best gang in the whole of London more like."

Ulysses smiled in the face of the boy's indefatigable bravado. "Been running with them long?"

"Four years, give or take," Sidney announced proudly, "ever since I hopped spike."

"And how exactly did you get away from there?"

"Got meself taken out with the rest of the shit when the night soil collectors did their round, along with Nobby Clark, didn't I?"

"Very resourceful," was all Ulysses could think to say. He had thought the boy smelt bad before, but now the aroma of unwashed bodies and the street suddenly seemed that much worse.

"Yeah, bin one of thieving Magpie's boys ever since."

Ulysses' ears pricked up at the mention of a name at last – at least at the mention of what was as close to a real name as he felt he was going to get.

"Who's Magpie?"

"That's *Mr* Magpie to you, if you don't mind," the boy said curtly, his former anxiety regarding the workhouse having apparently evaporated.

"So, who is he?"

"You've not heard of the Magpie?" the boy mocked, as if he was as well-known as Queen Victoria herself.

"Humour me," Ulysses continued in the same calm manner but with an edge of steel to his voice now; the same tone in which he had addressed the informant known as Rat.

"Well that's why he's the master, ain't it! He's so good he don't get caught." Sidney took another swig from the tankard in his hands. "I doubt Scotland Yard even knows 'e exists, but 'e's got fingers in all sorts of pies." He was beginning to noticeably slur his words. "But if they ever found out about the thieving Magpie, if they ever *did* catch 'im, they'd probably be able to solve an 'undred cases in one go. Not that they will ever catch 'im though!" The boy suddenly riled, real venom in his voice.

Whatever hold this Magpie had over the boys in his – to put it loosely – employ, it produced a powerful sense of loyalty among the Whitechapel Irregulars. If the rest of the urchins were like Sidney, Ulysses wouldn't be surprised if they would in fact be loyal to their master – the one who had 'rescued' them from the streets, taken them in, given them a home – even unto death. That thought sent a shiver down his spine. The way Sidney spoke, Ulysses could well believe that the Magpie was like some Messianic figure to his boys.

"'Is boys 'e calls us; 'is bonny darlin's. Princes of the street, that's what 'e calls us. 'Is lovely boys." Sidney's mouth was starting to run away with him.

Sidney suddenly looked anxious, a look that suggested that he had only just realised what Ulysses and Nimrod already knew, that he had said too much.

"But they won't catch 'im, will they? Not the Magpie."

"Who won't?"

"The Peelers, Scotland Yard, them robo-Bobbies in blue," Sidney pressed, the anxiety clear in his voice now. "They won't find out about 'im will they?" The boy started to scan the snug nervously, shooting darting glances into the shadows of booths and unlit corners. "You won't tell them, will you, sir? I'll be brown bread if you do!"

Sidney was nothing more than a scared child again. Who was this man, this Magpie, Ulysses wondered, that he could instil a religious fervour in one of his 'lovely boys' one minute and have him fearing for his wretched excuse for a life the next?

"Your Mr Magpie... Do you know if he had anything to do with a certain missing mermaid?"

"I wouldn't know, sir," Sidney said in a small voice, apparently unphased by the mention of an aquatic impossibility. "'E sends us out on all sorts of errands. It's 'ard to keep track sometimes; so many jobs on the go. Like I said, fingers in lots of pies."

The boy was now distractedly rubbing at his ribs, the sparse flesh covering them hidden beneath his ill-fitting attire, a distant look in his watery eyes, as if he were remembering past punishments. But were they ones received at the hands of the beadles or his new messiah?

"But what if the Magpie were to, fly the nest, shall we say? He couldn't hurt you then, could he?" Ulysses stated calmly, letting the implications of what he had said sink in, watching the boy's face intently as he processed what the dandy was suggesting.

The monkey had been watching the exchange with its own intense simian scrutiny. As Sidney considered Ulysses' words, the ape started shrieking and jumping up and down on the boy's shoulder again, attracting the attention of a number of nearby drinkers.

Nimrod glared at the monkey, raising his handkerchief-bound hand, as if he were about to slap the primate from its perch.

The monkey abruptly stopped its screeching, settled down beside the boy's ear and returned to foraging within his messy mop of hair, looking for any choice, wriggling morsels that might be hidden there.

Ulysses watched the creature for a moment as the monkey chattered into the boy's ear. If he hadn't known better he might have said that it was actually talking to the young scallywag.

"I could take you to 'im," the boy suddenly announced, his whole face lighting up under its coating of grime. "I could lead you to 'is lair. 'E's cocky, 'e is, the Magpie. 'E'd never suspect anyone 'e didn't want snooping around could find 'is way into the rookeries." Sidney boasted, his face aglow.

"You'd do that for us, Sidney?"

"Well, you know 'ow it goes. You scratch my back... Deal?" The boy wiped a filthy hand on his even filthier trouser leg and then, hawking a gobbet of phlegm into the back of his throat spat on it noisily, and held it out to Ulysses.

The finely-turned out dandy looked at the boy's palm with obvious discomfort but after only a moment's pause, he took hold of it in a solid grasp.

"We have a deal."

THE BOY LED them through the labyrinthine side-streets and half hidden, built-over alleyways of Whitechapel's slum rookeries. After countless twists and turns, double blinds, cul-de-sacs and doubling back through cellars and under arch-spans, Ulysses didn't know where he was or how far they had actually travelled. He had lost all sense of direction, the sky and its pall of ever-present choking cloud was no longer visible, hidden as it was beyond a roof of timbers and brick archways.

They came at last to an enclosed octagonal space between the crumbling ruins of a huddle of tenement housing. The structures could have been there since the eighteenth century Ulysses supposed, looking at them, only they were so rundown now that there were no discerning features by which to date the basic architecture of the place. A forest of bamboo scaffolding had been raised before the facades of the buildings, strung with rope and timber walkways, ladders leading ever upwards towards the canvas awnings that formed a roof over this place.

These were the rookeries; there could be no doubt. The crumbling square smelt of damp, mould, rotting wood and ammonia. A stream gurgled under the planking at their feet, a steady flow of piss and effluent sloshing its way along the boarded-over drain emptying out of the seemingly lifeless slum around them – an indication that there must be some life here, despite initial appearances – on its way to join the Thames or one of the capital's lost waterways, like the Fleet, or the Effra or the Wallbrook. Ulysses might have had an idea as to which if he had had a better notion of where the boy had led them.

The boy stopped beside a dusty tarpaulin, abandoned on the ground and covered in a dusting of broken plaster. He looked back at Ulysses and Nimrod, who looked the most uncomfortable, picking his way through the dust, filth and wreckage. Ulysses knew, however, that he had put up with much worse in his time.

Perched on the boy's shoulder, the monkey scratched its arse and then nibbled at something it found there. Sidney watched the progress of the other two with a look akin to delight on his face.

"At the risk of sounding trite, are we there yet?" Ulysses asked, suddenly conscious of how loud his voice sounded in the muffled near silence of the octagon. You wouldn't have known you were at the heart of the largest metropolis on Earth, not here.

The quiet unnerved him. There was the steady *drip-drip-drip* of a pipe overflowing somewhere, or a tear in an awning letting in overspill from the Upper City way overhead. There was the distant, inescapable rattle and clatter of the Overground system. There was the creak and groan of the awnings as they were pulled by unseen breezes and changes in air pressure. But the presence of any sound to suggest that anything lived here – even pigeons or rats – was absent.

And yet, even here, there was another of those cheerful advertisements for the latest restorative drink – Dr Feelgood's Tonic Stout.

Ulysses suddenly felt very exposed. This was hardly the way to go about creeping up on such a supposedly elusive criminal mastermind.

"We're nearly there now," Sidney said, pointing through a broken doorway, a network of smashed timbers just about visible in the shadows beyond. "We'll need to be quiet from 'ere on in. We're not exactly goin' in the front door, if you know what I mean – it's not even the tradesmen entrance – but 'e's got eyes and ears everywhere."

"I can well believe it," Ulysses said. "Can't be too careful in his line of business, I'm sure." He turned to his manservant, still a few steps behind him. "As they said in the Boy Scouts, be prepared, and all that, eh, Nimrod?" and he took out the pistol he kept holstered under his left arm and checked the chamber. On cue, Nimrod produced his own weapon and readied it.

Sidney acknowledged the presence of the guns with a widening of those puppy dog eyes of his but said nothing. From here on in, silence was key.

"Sir, if you don't mind me saying so, I don't like this," Nimrod whispered at Ulysses' shoulder.

"Don't worry, old chap," Ulysses blustered, instinctive bravado covering up the doubt he felt on his part. "This is our only lead."

"I'm just saying, sir. That's all."

"Duly noted," Ulysses hissed. "Now, can we be about our business?"

They followed their urchin guide through the doorway, their progress slowing considerably as they clambered over the web of broken beams whilst trying to keep their weapons aimed ahead of them, just in case. The underdeveloped boy had no such trouble, scurrying through the spaces between the beams at their feet, his monkey, loosed from its string-leash, bounding ahead, as if scouting a way through the tangle of fallen floorboards and roof supports.

The two men followed as best they could, as quickly and as quietly as possible, which with stealth being of the utmost importance, meant that their progress was not quick at all.

As they progressed, a soft orange glow grew in intensity ahead of them, the passageway they were following steadily lightening until the three of them stood huddled at the entrance to a wide open atrium within the rookery. They were on the ground floor, which was covered in rough planks, the space opening up to a height of at least three storeys above them.

Daring to peer further around the edge of the door jamb, Ulysses saw a spider's web of wooden walkways, suspended rope bridges and ladders of one sort or another. From somewhere near his waist Sidney whispered: "It's all right, they're not here."

Ulysses looked again. The web of walkways was slung with glowing hurricane lamps and guttering torches, even the occasional caged halogen light. He could see little in the dark spaces between the hazy spheres of light but still his senses told him that the situation hadn't changed and that the potential threat facing them was no different than when they had started on their journey into the rookery

"Are you sure?" he asked, just the same.

"Sure I'm sure. They'll all be out dipping the pockets of the rich."

"So where will we find the Magpie?"

"'E'll be in 'is counting house," Sidney said, his voice a breathy whisper. "Come on, it's this way."

"Feathering his nest, I suppose," Ulysses said, trying to make light of the situation, but it was a poor attempt to hide how he was really feeling.

The boy started out across the middle of the floor beneath the walkways, scampering ahead as before, only something had changed. Halfway across the void Ulysses realised what it was.

He stopped and Nimrod halted too. A moment later, realising Ulysses' footfalls over the boards behind him had come to a halt, the boy stopped and turned.

"Come on, guv'nor!" he hissed. "Whatcha waitin' for? Bleeding Christmas?"

"Where's your monkey?" Ulysses asked, his voice still quiet but nonetheless commanding for all that.

"What?" the boy asked, his face a picture of pure incomprehension.

"Where's your monkey?"

Ulysses could feel the dull throb of his hypothalamus swelling to a subconscious ache. Something wasn't right.

His head snapped back and he looked up into the glowing constellation of lamps suspended above them. There was movement at the corner of his eye. He followed it and saw another scampering shape elsewhere at the periphery of his vision.

Squinting, he began to see shapes forming amidst the contrasting shadows and sunspots.

And then, there on a walkway ten feet above his head, he saw, quite clearly, a lithe black and yellow shape run along a rope stretched taught across the void, seeming to defy gravity with its inverted aerial run. It wasn't Sidney's missing companion, but another simian altogether.

And then there were more. As if he now knew what he was looking for, Ulysses could hardly miss them. There were rhesus monkeys dangling from ropes and walkways, gnawing nuts and bits of fruit; spider monkeys by the dozen, family groups gathered on shelf-like perches attached to the walls; mandrills scaling vertically suspended ropes. He even thought he could make out the squatting shape and orange fur of an orang-utan on one of the higher levels, half-hidden in shadow behind a balcony.

"Don't bother answering that," Ulysses said coldly, his hind-brain hot with alarm, his grip on the gun in his hand tightening to knuckle white. "Where's the Magpie?"

Preternatural awareness flashed through his brain like a migraine.

"Right here!" came a cackle from the rafters above them. "As is you, Mr Quicksilver, as is you. Right where I wants ya!"

CHAPTER SIX

One for Sorrow

"Welcome to the House of Monkeys, my fine gentlemen."

Ulysses peered up at the rows of balconies above them, shielding his eyes with one hand to try to cut out the glare from the myriad lamps hung from the network of walkways.

His whole body was tensed, ready to spring into action, although Ulysses didn't rate their chances; he and Nimrod were like sitting ducks where they stood out in the open.

"Mr Magpie, I presume," he called up to the galleries, trying to locate their welcomer, his own voice bouncing back to him from the crumbling plaster walls.

"You presume right, Mr Quicksilver," the voice confirmed. "At your service, sah."

"I highly doubt that," Ulysses muttered under his breath.

He was struggling to place the accent. The metropolis of Londinium Maximum was a melting pot of cultures and nationalities, even if outwardly it appeared to be British to the core. But in reality there wasn't a more cosmopolitan city on the planet. Off-planet, that was a different matter, but on Earth the empire of Magna Britannia ruled supreme, governed from the seat of power that was old London town.

Ulysses continued to try to penetrate the dark spaces between the swaying lights. He could see that the apes that obviously gave the place its name were everywhere, larger orders of primate, including whey-faced chimps, slouched on the higher walkways or with their over-long arms wrapped around the supporting pillars of the tiered balconies, while the smaller simians scuttled and bounded between swinging rope ladders and branch-like perches with gay abandon. None of them seemed particularly interested in the presence of the two interlopers.

When Ulysses said nothing else, the master of this den of thieves spoke up again instead.

"So, Mr Quicksilver, what can I do for you?"

"I thought you said you had me right where *you* wanted *me*," Ulysses pointed out, scanning for ways out, should the opportunity arise for them to make their escape.

"So I did, Mr Quicksilver. So I did." The Magpie chuckled.

And there he was. A shadow, a silhouette, no more. The Magpie had positioned himself directly in front of a bright electric light, legs apart, hands on hips, surrounded by a suffused angelic glow. It was a stance that screamed confidence. It said, *you are in my domain. I am king here. Here my word is law. Watch your step.*

The master thief's tone only served to enhance the idea that this was an individual you didn't want to mess with. Not here, not anywhere.

Nonetheless, trying to avoid making any obvious sudden movement, Ulysses slowly angled the muzzle of his gun upwards, aiming it at the silhouette.

"I should watch where you're pointing that thing, if I were you, Mr Quicksilver," Magpie warned, his intent as clear and as lethal as arsenic.

As if on cue, a myriad pairs of simian eyes turned and locked on him from out of the darkness, the flickering light of the oil lamps reflecting redly from their corneas, tiny coals in the semi-darkness. A raucous chattering and screeching swelled from every corner of the space, reverberating from the enclosing walls and setting Ulysses' nerves on edge. He took his eyes off Magpie to glance at where his manservant stood tensed behind him; he looked just as perturbed as Ulysses was feeling. There was also the unmistakeable fleshy thumping of simian fists beating their chests.

Ulysses' hand stopped moving.

Gradually the cacophony subsided, but the inhabitants of the House of Monkeys had made their feelings plain.

"Tell me, Mr Quicksilver. What did you hope to achieve by coming here?"

Ulysses realised he had been given an unprecedented opportunity to find out more, to have his theories about this puzzling case confirmed or denied, one way or the other.

"Very well, then," he began. "Word is that you were involved in the theft of the Whitby Mermaid."

"Well now, you heard right." He wasn't even going to make a show of denying it. The flagrant arrogance of the man! It also only went to show how supremely confident he felt within his own petty kingdom.

"So, how did you do it?" Ulysses went on, remaining outwardly cool, calm and collected, despite feeling riled by the man's arrogance on the inside, his words slow with cold anger.

"He can't even see it," Magpie said, as if he was speaking to someone else. "It's right before his eyes, and he can't even see it."

As if in response to his comment the apes started hooting and chattering again, only this time Ulysses could have sworn they were laughing.

It was just as Ulysses had suspected. The Magpie's mastery of his pets must have been unrivalled in all the empire, outside of the Congo.

Loosely holding the pistol in his hand by only a couple of fingers, Ulysses raised both hands and began a slow clap, each slap of palm on palm reverberating loudly, amplified by the acoustics of the strange monkey house.

"I applaud you, Magpie. An incredible example of man's mastery of the lower forms of life on this planet. The window, the picked lock, it all makes sense to me now."

The silhouette shifted as the villain bowed, luxuriating in the chance to boast of his daring exploits before someone who could appreciate his work, even if he could not condone it.

"But why?"

"Ah," the Magpie mused, obviously delighted to have someone with whom he could share the truth of his cunning, "there it is, the unanswerable question. The one for which any answer, no matter what, can still be interpreted with the same question again; why? Why, why, why?"

Trained monkeys, Ulysses thought. Imagine all the places they could go without ever even arousing any suspicions. He wondered how many other unsolved crimes – or even as yet unnoticed thefts – were the work of Magpie and his monkeys.

"So, why?" Ulysses repeated. "What is a fake, such as the Whitby Mermaid, worth to you?"

"Oh, not to me, Mr Quicksilver, not to me," the Magpie chuckled.

"Then who?"

"Ah, Mr Quicksilver. Now that would be telling, wouldn't it?" Magpie teased.

"But what have you got to lose?" Ulysses pressed. "Who's going to know? Who am I going to tell? Something tells me you're not going to let me walk out of here Scot free."

The Magpie chuckled again. "I do have a reputation to uphold."

"And I have a desperate desire to know, having got so close to the answer. What can it hurt? What about granting a condemned man's final wish?"

"But what would life be without a little mystery? Where would be the excitement in that?"

That was what all this was about, Ulysses realised, having a little fun. It was all for the thrill; the chase was everything.

"Indeed."

Ulysses aimed his gun, and fired.

The bulb that had been doing such a good job of silhouetting his target exploded and, as the light died, Ulysses caught a glimpse of the Magpie throwing his arms up to protect his head. And then, he was moving.

"Nimrod, duck and cover!"

At his command, his manservant went for the shelter of the doorway by which they had entered the place.

As Ulysses raced for the shadows the only sound he could hear was the mass intake of breath as the House of Monkeys recoiled at his audacity. He raised his gun and fired a second shot towards the network of aerial walkways.

There was a second explosive crack as his shot exploded a lamp, and an angry, animalistic roar as the resulting shower of oil ignited, even as it rained down on the flammable boards and bindings.

"I would appear that you missed, Mr Quicksilver," the voice came from elsewhere now.

"Did I?"

"You are a fool, Mr Quicksilver. A fool. You won't get a second chance."

The Magpie gave a shrill whistle and, with a cacophony of simian shrieks and near-human cries, it started raining monkeys.

The primates dropped from their perches or swung down from the burning boards and bridges above, all gunning for the gunman... even as, after the initial shower of animals, fire began to rain down within the House of Monkeys.

The screams of the apes increased ten-fold as burning oil splashed their hairy hides, setting them alight.

Something man-like – and yet too strangely proportioned to be a man – launched itself at Ulysses out of the whirling rabble and landed heavily in the middle of his chest. He was thrown backwards by the baboon that now sat astride him as he landed on top of an apple crate, which turned to matchwood beneath them.

The baboon raised its powerful fists above its head and, snarling, bared yellow, predator's fangs. Ulysses bit his own lip as fresh pain shot through his shoulder; an old wound suddenly remembered.

Ulysses heard a gun bark – he knew it wasn't his – and the ape was thrown from him as the bullet punched into it between the eyes.

Ulysses scrambled to his feet, and dusted himself down, testing his flaring shoulder joint. The pain was passing. He assessed that it wasn't going to hamper him.

A gun barked again and another shambling ape fell face down on the boards.

"Nimrod, go!" Ulysses shouted over the shrieks of the terrified animals and hungry roar of the spreading fires. "Get back-up!"

He didn't bother to try to see if his faithful manservant had followed his instructions. They had been in such circumstances too many times, and they both knew the drill. If he were able, Nimrod would be on his way now, re-negotiating the labyrinth of the rookeries to escape their bounds and get help. A cunning criminal mastermind was making his escape and Ulysses wanted him alive – he wasn't done with the Magpie yet!

Moving out from the shelter of the first tier of balconies, Ulysses dared another glance upwards. Somewhere up there, the Magpie was getting away. And there were still questions to be answered, to begin with the one which had been bothering Ulysses ever since he had first read of the theft of the Whitby Mermaid; why anyone would go to so much trouble to steal what was so obviously a fake?

Fire was eating away at the walkway nearest to the oil lamp that Ulysses had exploded with his pistol, the strands of the ropes holding it up burning through and snapping free under tension, one by one. It would be only a matter of seconds before the whole thing came crashing down, Ulysses guessed. He had to get out of there, and fast.

He looked from the burning rope-bridge to the ropes securing it in place, to an iron-cast eyelet punched into the wall high above him which one of the thicker, mooring ropes ran through before descending to a securing bolt in the floor only a few paces away.

Kicking a gambolling monkey aside, Ulysses ran for the rope, holstering his gun as he did so, and grabbed hold with his left hand. With his right he drew his rapier from the sheath of its cane and slashed through the anchoring rope with one strong sweep of the razor-sharp blade.

Its mooring support gone, the bridge went slack and unravelled as the fire did the rest. The walkway dropped, trailing flames, with an animal roar, as it plummeted towards the mass of milling bodies and Ulysses headed skyward.

Ulysses hurtled upwards, pulled through the flames and falling bodies of burning monkeys as the rope ran out through the iron ring in the wall still two floors above him.

Something that was all arms and legs leapt at him as he rocketed upwards, but a sharp thrust of his blade put pay to whatever intentions the ape might have had for him. The rope-bridge crashed to the ground, crushing apes beneath it and sending a rippling blast of air to fan the flames of the other fires that had already taken hold.

And then his ascent came to a sudden stop. Dangling there, twenty feet above the inferno, Ulysses jerked and kicked, attempting to swing closer to the balustrades of a balcony which was tantalizingly out of reach. He had better be quick about it too or the rope would burn through and drop him back into the blaze below.

Ever so slowly, it seemed, the rope began to swing. The tips of his toes scraped against the edge of the balcony. Ulysses put both feet against the wall and pushed off again. Like the weight at the end of a pendulum he swung backwards.

The gulf between him and the balcony cruelly widened. When he was at the apex of his swing, with too much space between him and safety Ulysses felt the rope sag. It was burning through.

And then he was swinging backwards. The rope gave again and he felt himself drop several dangerous inches. Knees bent, feet out flat before him, he connected with the banisters of the balustrade as the rope gave way completely.

Crashing through the timbers, the rope slack in his hands, he rolled across the creaking wooden floor, athletically coming out of the roll and into a fighting stance, rapier blade poised.

There was no sign of anyone who might pass for the villain through the smoke and heat haze. The Magpie had flown.

Picking himself up and taking a moment to dust himself down, sword-cane in hand, Ulysses set off in hot pursuit, into the dancing shadows.

CHAPTER SEVEN

Flight of the Magpie

ULYSSES FOUND HIMSELF running through what appeared to be one large room, sub-divided into smaller areas by temporary partitions, stretches of canvas and old blankets nailed to the wooden pillars that supported the floor of the level above.

Behind him he could hear the jabbering screams of the apes, trapped within the blazing conflagration as the fire took hold. Occasionally a smouldering blackened shape would go knuckling by on all fours, leaving behind a trail of smoke and the stink of singed fur.

Ahead of him he could pick out running footsteps, beating a tattoo of panicked flight on the splintering floorboards. And all around him an anxious hubbub of bewilderment and panic swelled to fill the space between.

As he raced on, through the makeshift partitions he saw them – Magpie's lovely boys, the urchin-thieves that made up the Whitechapel Irregulars. He saw grimy face after grimy face, gap-toothed expressions of curiosity, wide bewildered eyes, the first suggestion of tears of fear in those of the younger members of the gang, children as young as four or five, to look at them, although his experiences with Sidney told him that that didn't mean as much here.

Some had been sleeping, until the growing commotion roused them, bleary eyes blinking from faces half-buried under threadbare blankets and pilfered rag-rugs slung over their hammock-beds. Others appeared to be playing games of chance, some with clay pipes clamped between their teeth, betting for anything that might pass for possessions among the boys – teeth, coloured glass beads, scrag-ends of stale bread, waxy rinds of cheese, cigarette butts. Yet more appeared to have been playing a game that tested the boys' pick-pocketing skills, with a more experienced rogue cast in the role of gentleman-about-town, and acting as their teacher too, as the younger boys tried to relieve him of silk handkerchiefs and a bottle top on the end of a plug-chain, in place of a genuine pocket watch.

Their attire could only be described as haphazard. The boys obviously wore any clothes they could get their hands on, whether they were hand-me-downs from older gang members or stolen from washing lines within the neighbouring streets. There were jackets, dated frock coats, waistcoats, breeches, trews, cloth caps, battered top hats, hobnail boots and wooden clogs. The fashions were worn and dated, patched so many times in some cases that there was practically nothing left of the original item of clothing, and little – if anything – fitted, many of the items being adult's clothing. Amongst the rags was the occasional, much richer item – silk scarves, cravats, gold waistcoat buttons – prizes the boys had won for themselves out on the streets as they ran errands for their master, or simply to pass the time between one meagre meal and the next.

Some of the boys were eating, huddled round small cook-stoves, hunched over mess tins, mismatched pilfered plates and bowls, a thin, grey soup that was unmistakeably gruel, barely covering the bottom of each container.

Most of the children looked startled to see him. One scrawny, whey-faced child stood before the cold iron pot, ladling out portions of the gruel into the wooden bowls and empty food tins that the boys held possessively between thin fingers.

And was it his imagination, or did some of the monkeys look worryingly like boys, whilst some of the boys were beginning to look like apes to him now – all eating the same stuff. What was it doing to them? As he moved in and out of the shadows he tried to convince himself that it was only an optical illusion caused by the changing patterns of light and dark, but nonetheless, to his haggard mind some of the boys were starting to look like monkeys and vice versa.

Ulysses ran on, trying not to look at any of the boys' half-human faces – upper lips distended, noses flattened to simian snouts, arms held awkwardly as if they were longer than they should be, shoeless feet wiggling with toes that were too much like fingers for his liking. He had seen all manner of terrible things in his life, and he had been exposed to the dire predicaments of the destitute and the dispossessed before, but it was those hybrid child-ape faces that would haunt his dreams in the dark watches of the nights to come.

Forcing the disturbing expressions from his mind, he focused again on his sole intent – to halt the Magpie's flight.

Still running, Ulysses tossed his sword-cane into his left hand and unholstered his gun again with his right. As he ran on he recounted how many shots he had already fired. The first shot had broken the light behind the Magpie, the second had shattered the oil lamp that started the fire. He had started the night with a full load which meant that he had four bullets left, before he would have to reload.

And then he saw the villain, flying through another crooked doorway before he disappeared into the shadows of a landing. The Magpie was way ahead of him. If he didn't stop him soon, Ulysses would be lucky to even catch one last sight of him before he lost himself in the tangled rat-runs of the rookeries.

He had one chance, and now was the time to act. As the Magpie disappeared into the darkness Ulysses fired.

The crack of the pistol was loud in the compressed space between the gang's living quarters but, despite that, Ulysses was sure that there had been no cry following the shot before he heard, quite clearly, the dull thud, as of a body dropping onto bare boards. Could it be that he had accidentally killed his quarry?

Ignoring the gaggle of children that seemed to be gravitating towards him, alerted by the flight of their master while others moved to escape from the fire behind them, roused by the smoke and heat approaching from the other end of the house, Ulysses vaulted a tumbled tea chest and made for the doorway and the landing beyond.

But now the press of children was greater, fear of the fire spreading faster than the fire itself. Among them were more of the weird not-quite-human-yet-not-quite-simian creatures, but all of them, no matter what they were, were shouting, hooting and screaming in terror.

He had to push them aside; he could not allow anything to hamper his progress now or he might lose this momentary advantage.

His shoe connected with a child and he kicked the boy aside. The heel of his other shoe crunched down on the splayed fingers of a monkey, a shrill animal scream accompanying the soft crunch of breaking bones.

And then he was through the panicking throng and into the shadows of the landing. Here the air was sharp and cold. Above him a rusting skylight swung in the breeze. Beyond lay access to the rooftops of the rookeries, still in shadow under the pall cast by the Smog and the towering edifices of the Upper City.

Ulysses paused, scanning the darkness. Nimrod should be on his way back to civilisation by now, tracking down the authorities, getting help.

Where could his quarry be, he thought. *Concentrate!* he willed himself.

The skills he had learnt during his brief stay with the monks of Shangri-la, as he recovered at their pagoda-temple, within the jasmine-scented lost valley of the Himalayas, still kept him in good stead. Although not a master like the monks with whom he had stayed as his body healed and his mind was tempered and strengthened, he still had a mastery of his senses that few others possessed.

Shrinking the world around him, straining out the extraneous background noise and the other sensations emitted by the growing conflagration, he held his breath and concentrated on putting the thrumming of his own racing pulse from his mind. He listened instead for the panting breaths of another, the sound of footfalls on wood, or the clatter of feet on the tiles of the rooftops beyond.

Awareness flared in Ulysses' mind. He turned as something at the periphery of his vision detached itself from the darkness, breaking his concentration. A scrawny, spindle-limbed shape launched itself at his face with a savage shrill scream. And then there was movement behind him too.

Ulysses threw up his hands – there was no time to bring sword or gun to bear – grabbing hold of the monkey before it could claw his face. As he grabbed the monkey out of the air he spun on his heel and thrust it towards the man who had tried to come at him from behind, putting all his weight and the momentum of the monkey's leap behind the push.

The monkey gave a strangled cry and tensed momentarily before going limp in Ulysses' hands, a point of metal glistening darkly with the creature's blood, protruding from the middle of its chest.

Then the monkey was pulled savagely from Ulysses' hands as the Magpie shook the dead animal from his blade, and for the first time the dandy got a good look at the robber-king of the Whitechapel Irregulars, the master of the House of Monkeys.

He was both shorter and slighter than Ulysses. A scruffy mess of black hair hid much of his face, but he caught a glimpse, nonetheless of a nose as sharp as a knife. The villain's clothes don't seem to fit him either – just like those of his urchin-sons – a rag-cloak of grey, white, black and blue, making him look like his eponymous magpie! He patently had a taste for the theatrical, as had been evidenced by everything Ulysses had seen of him since entering his lair.

The tiny ape rolled onto the floor and lay limply where it landed, arms, legs and tail all at unnatural angles, blood staining the faded green waistcoat it wore.

Ulysses pressed home his advantage, hoping to wrong-foot the Magpie still further and bring him down. The knife flashed in the near dark. Ulysses yelped in pain as the serrated blade cut into the meat of his wrist. His fingers spasmed open, his gun clattering onto the bare boards at his feet.

Ulysses lurched backwards as the Magpie danced in below his guard with the knife again. He heard the rip and felt the snag as the tip of the blade caught the edge of a buttonhole on his coat and tore through the fabric.

He was dimly aware of the bouncing thuds and bangs of his gun as it continued to tumble down the staircase from the landing, and far out of reach. But for the time being he was more concerned about the dextrous knife-fighting abilities of the rogue in front of him.

As the Magpie bounded forwards again Ulysses took two steps back. The palm of his right hand was wet with blood now but the adrenalin of the moment helped him to put aside the pain in his wrist. Instead, focusing all his energies on the fight, he brought his rapier blade to bear again.

He sensed the Magpie hesitate and knew that he had already turned the tide of battle. Now it was his turn to lunge forward but the Magpie had already made his move. The felon flung himself at the ladder to the skylight and, displaying all the agility of a monkey, scampered up it, heading for the roof.

Ulysses pressed forward again, slashing his sword down onto the ladder, slicing splinters from the wooden rungs. And then his quarry was gone. Without a moment's hesitation Ulysses grabbed the ladder and was up it after the Magpie.

As he pulled himself through the open skylight, the felon's fleeing footfalls carried to him over the roofs of the rookery.

In an instant Ulysses was on his feet. As he took a swaying moment to gain his balance, he took in his surroundings. He was standing on the edge of the roof of the slum building. Only a few feet below him, the slanting lip of the roof dropped into a dark void, many storeys high. Above and to his left, at the apex of the roof, the Magpie was making a run for it, away over the rooftops. He looked like a prancing demon, given a hellish cast, as he was, by the fire and smoke rising up from the centre of the rookery, crackling hungrily in the cold November air. Beyond lay a sparse forest of chimney stacks, aerial masts and cast-iron fire escapes. And above it all loomed the might and magnificence of the Upper City, a spider's web of Overground lines twisting and turning between the towering edifices.

There was no time to lose. Sword still in hand, Ulysses scrambled up the sloping tiles towards the crest of the roof. Several times his feet slipped on the smooth shingle and once a tile came free beneath him as he kicked against it. But then he made the apex and, following the Magpie's example, rose cautiously to his feet. Then, arms outstretched, he began to scamper after the rogue again.

But where the Magpie's movements were like those of a dancer, almost balletic, Ulysses' pursuit of the fleeing felon was a clumsy, stumbling run, as he tried to make the next nearest chimney stack before he lost his balance and went sliding away down the steeply sloping roof to the drop beyond.

As he staggered after the Magpie, he found himself calling to mind his close-quarters combat with the reactionary Jago Kane atop the speeding Overground train, only seven months before. Although he was in a perilous position skittering over the rooftops now, at least they weren't rattling and rumbling beneath him.

He glanced up. Incredibly, he appeared to be closing on the Magpie, who seemed to be pausing for breath as he clung to a chimney stack not ten feet from Ulysses.

Ulysses threw himself towards the chimney, but before he slammed into the tottering brick structure, the Magpie was away again. Gasping for breath, heart racing, Ulysses watched as the man sprinted to the end of the roof and launched himself into space.

A second later, the Magpie landed with a crash of breaking tiles on top of the roof of the next slum tenement. It was only as he let out a pent-up lungful of air that Ulysses realised he'd been holding his breath. And then there was only one thing for it.

He couldn't think about what he was going to do, he simply had to do it. Relinquishing the security of the chimney stack, he sprinted for the gable-end of the building, the void between the slums seeming to widen with every bounding step. And then, with one almighty leap, he threw himself out over the vertiginous void, horrid images of plummeting airships and death-defying leaps from the top of speeding trains returning to haunt him.

The lip of the roof beyond loomed large before him, but then it was directly in his eye-line, and then all he could see before his face were crumbling bricks and mortar. He flung his arms out and up, felt them grab hold of the lip of the roof, braced himself as his body slammed into the wall, knocking the wind from him, and the flesh of the fingertips of his left hand tore as his own body weight pulled them across the rough surface, the skin of the knuckles of his right scraping red raw as he refused to relinquish his hold on his sword, barely managing to cling on. But cling on he did, like a limpet to a rock at low tide.

He hung there for a moment, gasping to get some air back into his empty lungs. But there was no time to delay; right at this moment, the Magpie was making his escape. The muscles of his back and arms straining, the toes of his shoes scuffing as he tried to get a purchase on the wall, Ulysses began to heave himself upwards.

There was the crunch of gravel above him and a face, like that of some leering gargoyle, peered out over the drop. He needn't have worried about his quarry getting away; the Magpie had come to him.

"Well, well, Mr Quicksilver. Not so quick now, are you? It would appear that you need a hand," the thief-lord gloated.

"No, I'm alright thanks," Ulysses managed through gritted teeth.

"Alright then. Here, let me give you a foot."

The felon's boot heel smashed down on Ulysses' sword hand. Bones ground.

With a cry of anguish, Ulysses pulled his hand away and let go of his precious sword at last. Through the agony of his broken fingers, only a second later, he heard the clattering jangle of metal ringing on metal below him. And despite the pain, that instinctive part of his brain that had seen him through so many scrapes before told him what he needed to do.

Before the Magpie could move his foot again, with all the strength he could muster, Ulysses jerked himself up enough with his left arm to release his hold on the parapet and grab hold of the Magpie's ankle instead. With all his weight hanging off the man's leg, he pulled.

With the Magpie already balanced precariously at the edge of the roof, and Ulysses the more heavily built of the two, it did not take much to gain the desired result. The felon lost his footing, falling heavily on his rump on the edge of the wall before the two men fell into the space between the tightly-packed buildings.

Only a matter of a few seconds later – that seemed more like minutes to Ulysses – he and the Magpie crashed down together on the narrow metal walkway of a fire escape bolted to the side of the building, still three storeys above the ground.

Lashing out, the Magpie quickly extricated himself from the tangle of Ulysses' limbs, but Ulysses hadn't been interested in restraining the rogue. In an instant he was on his feet, sword held tightly in his left hand now, the broken fingers of his right clamped tightly under his armpit, still gasping for breath.

The Magpie sprang cat-like to his feet, knife back in his hand, but where the master criminal was agile as a panther, Ulysses had pain and rage on his side.

Bellowing like some injured animal, he charged the Magpie, forcing the man back towards the railings at the end of the walkway, releasing his fury in an unstoppable assault. Their blades rang as the two traded blows but in no time, Ulysses had hacked his way through the best defence the Magpie could offer. With a final lunge he thrust the tip of his rapier blade at the man's eye; although Ulysses still needed the villain alive for interrogation, something small, like being blinded in one eye, seemed like a perfectly valid option, if it meant he could bring the Magpie in for questioning.

Still possessed of all the poise and grace of a puma, The Magpie sidestepped the blow, but Ulysses still felt the briefest resistance in his blade, as if he had made contact.

And then, with one hand on the railing behind him, the Magpie swung himself over the edge and dropped, body held straight as an arrow as he plummeted to the alley below.

Ulysses watched, transfixed by the man's daring, as his quarry escaped him again, landing in a feline crouch amidst the debris and detritus covering the cobbles below.

For a moment Ulysses was rooted to the spot, as he assessed the jump the Magpie had made. But if that felon could make it, then so could he, Ulysses realised. Snapping himself out of his momentary hiatus, the pain in his hand like a distant memory, Ulysses clambered over the railings and then, after a second or two, his pulse pounding in his ears, he took a deep breath, and jumped.

He landed awkwardly among the piles of rotting rubbish, a sack of something soft and mouldering breaking his fall, but he still ended up splayed on his hands and knees on the cold, wet, filthy cobbles.

Even as he picked himself up he knew that he was too late, that the Magpie had flown. He strained his ears, but all he could hear were the sounds of the unsettled city, the ever-present rattle of locomotives above, the crackle and roar of the fire rampaging through the rookeries and the distant wailing sirens of the approaching fire brigade.

What he couldn't hear were the tell-tale footfalls of the fleeing felon.

Ulysses looked around him, at the maze of side-streets, alleyways and dead-ends he now found himself in. This was the Magpie's territory. In the time it would take him to find his way back to a main thoroughfare – any thoroughfare that he could at least read the name of – his quarry would be long gone.

Yet despite the throbbing hurt of his hands and wrist, and all the other injuries he had sustained in his pursuit of the Magpie, a dark smile spread across Ulysses' face, as something clicked inside his head. The thrill of the chase was all, and the chase wasn't over yet.

Extracting his personal communicator from a coat pocket, he began to key in a number.

CHAPTER EIGHT

The Game is Afoot

THE CAB PULLED up outside the Bloomsbury residence with a screech, tyres skidding on the wet leaves clogging the gutter. A door flew open and Ulysses Quicksilver bundled out of the vehicle, quickly followed by his manservant Nimrod.

The street lamps were dim at this late hour – or should it have been classed as early now, Ulysses wondered – and there was no one else around in this part of town.

Ulysses looked up at the imposing facade in front of him. *This is the place*, he thought as he read the name on the brass plate beside the grand columned entrance. And there was a light burning in one of the windows on the first floor.

It had taken him a good half an hour to find his way out of the maze of rookery rat-runs and be reunited with his manservant, who by that point had already managed to procure them a cab to carry them out of Whitechapel. The journey to Bloomsbury had not taken long, but had given Ulysses enough time to order his thoughts and decide on the best course of action to follow next. And that was to not waste time beating about the bush.

He felt for the reassuring presence of the sword-cane currently tucked into the belt of his trousers.

Taking the steps to the front door two at a time, Ulysses went to ring the door bell. He winced in pain, almost crying out, as he tried to close his ruined fingers around the bell-pull and withdrew his hand sharply.

"Let me, sir," Nimrod said, stepping past Ulysses.

A bell clattered and jangled noisily somewhere within the dark house.

"Come on!" Ulysses hissed impatiently, his foot tapping on the step as he listened for any sign of someone coming to answer the door. "Ring it again," he ordered. "And if they don't answer this time, we're breaking the door down!"

Nimrod tugged sharply on the bell-pull again. A renewed jangling disturbed the peace of this exclusive address once more.

As the ringing died away, Ulysses heard the *tap-tap-tapping* of leather soles on floor tiles. A few seconds later the front door opened and a scowling face greeted them, peering gargoyle-like from the gloom beyond.

"Do you know what time it is, sir?" the face demanded crossly.

Ulysses made a show of taking out his pocket watch. "As it happens, I do," he said. "Half past one, as you're asking. And that is relevant, why?"

"Mr Wraith is not used to receiving guests in the middle of the night, sir!" the butler said with some vehemence.

Awkwardly, using his left hand, Ulysses extracted the leather cardholder from his jacket pocket and flipped it open. The butler scanned the details so presented.

"Mr Quicksilver," he said, maintaining the same disapproving tone – like a schoolmaster giving a misbehaving pupil a dressing down – "Mr Wraith is not receiving guests at this hour."

Ulysses was taken aback. He was not used to people challenging the authority referred to on his Department ID, not unless he was already wrestling them on top of a train or negotiating with the use of extreme force.

"Oh, I see. That authority not good enough for you, eh? Then try this. Nimrod?"

Ulysses stepped aside, Nimrod forcing his way past the threshold.

"I must protest!" the butler spluttered, his carefully created demeanour of arrogant correctitude crumbling in an instant.

"Must you?" Ulysses said, wearily.

Before the butler knew what was going on, Nimrod's bunched fist connected with his face. He went down, stunned, falling to his knees as he whimpered in shock and pain, his hands pressed to his bloodied nose.

The two men barged past the stunned retainer and into the house.

"Carstairs? Who is it?" came a man's muffled voice from somewhere above.

Saying nothing, Ulysses grabbed his manservant's sleeve and jerked his head upwards, indicating the floor above.

Trying to tread as lightly as he could on the plush carpet covering the grand staircase, Ulysses dashed up it to the first floor, Nimrod following after. Ahead of him, at the end of a darkened landing, stood a set of double doors, light from the room beyond escaping through the cracks where the doors met the frame.

"Carstairs?" came the voice again, warier now and closer, as if its owner stood just on the other side of the doors.

Without hesitation, Ulysses grabbed a brass handle and forced the door open violently, catching the man who had been standing behind it by surprise.

Gabriel Wraith danced back, hastily trying to regain his composure. He stood there in full evening dress, hair slicked down as smoothly as ever with half a tin of pomade.

"Quicksilver!" he yelped in what Ulysses imagined was a more nervously high-pitched tone than he had intended. "What is the meaning of this?"

"With have things to discuss, Wraith," Ulysses announced as he strode into the room, the other man backing into the corner as far as his reading desk, before his unstoppable, glacial advance.

"Things? What do you mean, man, barging in like this?" he demanded, his voice like cold steel now. "What things?"

"The Whitby Mermaid, the Whitechapel Irregulars, the House of Monkeys," Ulysses reeled off the list. "What do you know of th –"

He stopped abruptly, catching sight of the drop of blood, a single crimson droplet oozing from the otherwise almost indistinguishable nick on the consulting detective's otherwise immaculately pale cheek.

"What happened to your face?" Ulysses asked, eyes narrowing as he pointed an accusing, wrongly-angled finger at Wraith.

"I cut myself shaving," he answered icily, subconsciously feeling for the wound. With an arrogant motion he tossed his head back. "You're raving man. I would be grateful if you would depart these premises immediately!"

But even as the words were out of his mouth it was obvious that Gabriel Wraith knew that it was too late, that he had been rumbled. Even as Ulysses went for his blade, pulling the rapier free of its cane-scabbard, Wraith went for his. And then the heavy knife was in his hand again.

"How did you know?" Wraith demanded as he dropped into a fighting stance more befitting of his criminal alter ego than a respectable Bloomsbury gentleman.

"What, that Gabriel Wraith and the Magpie were one and the same?" Ulysses said. "I didn't know, I only suspected."

"What?" the other man shrieked in angry disbelief.

"But now you've confirmed that fact yourself, the similarities are clear; you're both light on your feet, balletic you might say, face sharp as a blade, mind to match, a propensity for repeating words and phrases. I suppose it would explain your success as a consulting detective as well, if you were the one responsible for the thefts in the first place." Ulysses flashed the icily furious man a devilish grin. "Oh, and you're both arrogant bastards," Ulysses snarled.

"Well then, it would appear we have unfinished business, you and I," Gabriel Wraith declared as he shifted his balance from one foot to the other, preparing himself for the moment when he could duck in under Ulysses' guard and deliver a fatal blow.

"Indeed," Ulysses agreed, hefting the blade in his left hand – not his preferred hand but competent enough, nonetheless. There was the click of a pistol being cocked behind him. "Shame, it appears it's going to have to stay that way, my old fruit. Now drop the knife, or my man here will drop you."

Wraith grimaced and made a sound like an animal snarl. "Idiot!" he hissed.

"What, you or me?"

With a roar born of frustration, rage and despair, Gabriel Wraith sprang at Ulysses, suddenly all semblance of composure gone.

Ulysses raised his own blade just in time to parry the maniac's descending sweep. So angry was the man that, what skill and finesse he might have had was lost as blind rage took over. Ulysses sidestepped and kicked out at the same time, sending his opponent sprawling across the remarkable Turkish carpet that covered the floor of Wraith's consultation chamber.

Before he could recover himself, Nimrod stepped forward, the barrel of the pistol pointed directly at Wraith's face. The rogue's features lost what little colour they still retained as he realised that he had come to the end of the line.

"Go on then – kill me, if that's what you're going to do. Just don't make a damned meal of it."

"Don't be so bloody stupid," Ulysses laughed. "I've not hunted you through Whitechapel and chased you over rooftops simply to kill you now. As you said yourself, Mr Magpie, we have unfinished business you and I."

Wraith looked up into Ulysses' cruelly smiling face and felt his bowels turn to water. He suddenly felt much worse than he had done when he just thought that Ulysses was going to have him killed.

"I hope you have a head for heights," Ulysses hissed as Nimrod delivered a blow to the head with the butt of his pistol.

SLOWLY A BLEARY consciousness returned and Gabriel Wraith opened his eyes. He immediately let out a wail of fear as the street appeared four storeys above him, gently swaying from side to side. His head felt thick, engorged with the blood that seemed to be collecting within his skull. The shock of his situation merely helped to bring him round more completely.

Gradually reality reasserted itself and he realised the seriousness of his predicament. He looked up, straining his neck and could see the cord around his ankle just as he became aware of the dull throb there. Beyond that lay only the dark pall of the Smog, under-lit a satanic red by the blinking lights of the city below, the Overground network a dark spider's web against it. The cord ran up and over a bent aerial mast and back to a window on the fourth floor of the house.

"Ah, you're awake. Had a nice sleep, did you?"

Wraith froze. The familiarity of the voice cut through him like a blade of ice and brought with it sudden remembrance of the night-time chase over the rooftops of Whitechapel and Quicksilver's sudden attack within his own home.

Wraith's lip curled into an angry sneer. "Quicksilver, you bastard," he snarled. "What are you doing? What, precisely, do you think you are doing?"

"I'll give you a clue," Quicksilver said, the same cruel smile still locked on his face. "Nimrod?"

At once the line holding him up went slack and suddenly he was falling. The cord whizzed over the mast, accompanied by the sharp smell of scorched rope.

He cried out in fear as the slabs of the pavement and the points of the railings shot rapidly closer.

He was only vaguely aware of Quicksilver shouting for his manservant to halt his descent.

"You said... you weren't... going to... kill me!" the panicking Wraith protested, as he panted for breath. "That's what you said!"

He could see Quicksilver's manservant now, standing at another window on the top floor of the house, the rope held tightly in his great bunched fists.

"I said I hadn't come all this way to kill you *then*," the other clarified, an expression of cruel delight etched onto his clean cut aristocratic features. "But your fate now depends on whether you answer my questions truthfully. You see, there are things that you know Wraith – or should that be Magpie? – things that I *need* to know."

"And what makes you I'll give you the answers?" Wraith retorted pathetically, making one last ditch attempt at a rebellious front.

"Because I believe you to be a sensible man," Quicksilver said calmly. "Nimrod?"

The cord went loose again and Wraith dropped, another involuntary cry escaping his lips.

It took longer for his fall to be slowed this time and, with a growing sense of dread, Wraith realised that Quicksilver quite possibly was willing to do anything to get the answers he wanted.

As he hung there, swinging from the end of the thin line, upside down, like a fish on a hook, gravity pushing his eyes out of his head, he had a clear view of the spear-tipped railings outside his Bloomsbury residence. Were he to fall he would be lucky if all he ended up with was a fractured skull and a broken neck; at least that way death would be instantaneous. If he was unlucky, he might puncture a kidney, or skewer some other vital internal organ, before bleeding to death in agonising pain, like a stuck pig on the railings.

He felt the cord jerk again, but this time he was being pulled upwards. When he was level with the sadistically-smiling face once more, Quicksilver spoke again. "If you're suspended uncomfortably, then we'll begin."

Wraith nodded slowly; he didn't see that he had any other option.

"You were behind the theft of the Whitby Mermaid, weren't you?" Quicksilver stated calmly.

Wraith paused for a moment. He had determined to be defiant to the end, but the fire had gone from him now. All that stubbornness would achieve, other than saving his pride, was a painful death on the pavement below.

He nodded again. "Yes."

"But why steal a fake? What was it worth to you?"

"A fair amount. It was stolen to order," Wraith stated flatly.

For the first time something other than an absolute conviction in his own arrogant opinion crossed Quicksilver's features. It was the one thing that gave Wraith some small nugget of satisfaction.

"To order?" Quicksilver echoed.

"That's what I said."

"Who for?"

The pedant in Wraith couldn't resist: "I think you mean 'for whom?'"

The cord went slack again. Wraith dropped a floor before the rope pulled taut, tugging sharply on his hip. He almost bit through his tongue with the shock of it.

"Bellerophon," he gasped, blood spraying from his mouth as he spat the name.

"Who is Bellerophon? And don't tell me he's a hero from Greek myth."

"I don't know," Wraith snarled. "It was just a name. There was never any face to face meeting."

"What does Bellerophon want with a fake?" Quicksilver pressed.

"I don't know! I didn't ask!"

"You just took the money."

"As you say," Wraith snarled, "I just took the money."

"So, where is it now? The mermaid."

"There were instructions to send it north, to Whitby."

"Back to Whitby, eh?" Quicksilver pondered. "It keeps coming back to Whitby. But I still don't understand why someone would go to so much trouble to steal what appears to be – what *must* be – a fake." He stepped back from his place by the window and Wraith heard him say to his manservant: "We're not done with this mystery yet, Nimrod. But we're done here."

Disbelieving doubt was soon ousted by cold horror as Wraith awakened to his fate as he watched the one called Nimrod tie off the cord to something inside the room. Quicksilver turned from the window, immediately disappearing into the shadows of the room beyond.

"You can't just leave me here!" Wraith screamed after him, all his fear and anxiety suddenly taking hold.

There was a moment's pause and then his tormentor appeared at the window again.

"Oh, can't I? Goodnight, Mr Wraith." He turned and then was gone, for good this time.

Wraith stared up at the heaving morass of the Smog that hung over the city like a funeral shroud and listened as the distant sounds of police sirens grew louder.

It was the end of the line for the Magpie, and, more importantly, it was the end for Gabriel Wraith as well.

His eyes on the cord cutting into his aching ankle, he reached deep inside a trouser pocket, searching for the pen knife that he always kept there.

This night would see the end of both the master of the House of Monkeys, the Magpie, and Gabriel Wraith, London's finest consulting detective. And all thanks to that smug-faced bastard, Ulysses Quicksilver.

ACT TWO

The Hound of Hanivers

November 1997

CHAPTER NINE

A Word to the Wise

THE JOURNEY NORTH took no time at all, or so it seemed, once the train had left St Pancras and the looming edifices of London. Heavily built-up suburban conurbation gave way – along with the ever-present, tangible tobacco-yellow Smog – to pleasant green countryside beyond the furthest limits of Londinium Maximum as they passed through Hertfordshire, Bedfordshire and Northamptonshire. Stations, villages and towns whipped past in an anonymous blur as the speeding locomotive ate up the miles.

The further north they travelled the darker loomed the sky ahead of them as the clear cerulean blue, drawn with streaks of white cotton clouds, steadily gave way to the polluted skies of the North. The towns of the Midlands had been swallowed by the rampant industrialisation that had continued throughout the twentieth century leaving the conurbations as islands of miserable, second-rate civilisation, separated by great expanses of automated factories and industry-polluted wasteland. At this point in the journey, stewards took care to secure all the windows, least the sulphurous fumes of that region proved disagreeable to those travelling on the ten thirty from St Pancras.

What had started out as a relatively fine day in London – and that had become a clear, chill autumnal day in the farmland beyond – now gave way to the permanently overcast misery of Nottinghamshire. The toxic wasteland gave way at last as the train diverted across the windswept moors of Yorkshire, this natural wilderness seeming almost as desolate as the industry-spoiled wasteland through which they had passed on the way.

Having left London only that morning, that same afternoon saw the huffing and puffing locomotive hissing to a halt amidst a rising cloud of steam at Whitby Station, the end of the line, the tracks coming to a stop less than half a mile from the sea.

It being late in the day, the dandy and his manservant set about finding lodgings for the duration of their stay. After making enquiries at the station master's office, they took a horse-drawn cab to the East Crescent and took rooms at a superior lodging house there that had plenty of vacancies for those few visitors Whitby still received at this time of year; people looking to benefit from the curious properties of the sea air or wishing to follow in the footsteps of Mr Stoker's Dracula.

Determining to begin their search for the mysterious Mr Bellerophon – an assumed name, Ulysses presumed – first thing the following morning, He and Nimrod retired for the night in their suite of rooms on the second floor, Ulysses taking the master bedroom, while Nimrod made for the significantly smaller valet's chamber off the suite's day room-cum-dining room.

"NIMROD, THAT WAS a triumph," Ulysses declared, placing his knife and fork together on the grease-smeared plate before him.

"I shall pass your compliments to Mrs Scoresby, sir," Nimrod replied.

"There's nothing like a full English to set oneself up for the day. And I do like black pudding."

"More coffee, sir?"

"Yes, why not, old chap?"

Ulysses lent back in his chair, putting his arms behind his head. His wrist still hurt, as did the broken fingers of his right hand which were still bound together to aid their healing.

Nimrod dutifully got up from his seat at the breakfast table opposite his master, draped a freshly-pressed napkin over one arm, lifted the cafetiere from its silver-plated salver, walked round the table to where Ulysses sat stretched out in his dressing gown, and carefully re-filled the dandy's coffee cup.

"Thank you, Nimrod," he said as his manservant placed the cafetiere back on the salver in the middle of the table and returned to his seat. Nimrod nodded in polite acknowledgement.

Ulysses deposited a heaped teaspoon of sugar into the dark steaming fluid and began to stir languidly.

"So, where to start?" he mused, not so much asking Nimrod for his advice as simply giving voice to his own thoughts.

His eyes drifted across to the front page of the local paper that had been laid on the pristine white tablecloth next to his place setting.

"Hey, look at this will you, Nimrod?"

Eyebrows arching, Nimrod looked down his nose, concentrating as he read the inverted headline in front of him.

"'Ghestdale Beast claims Tenth Victim'," he read. "Hmm, it sounds... intriguing, sir."

"I'd say!" Ulysses exclaimed excitedly, scanning the column inches beneath the attention-grabbing banner headline.

"Tabloid scare-mongering?" Nimrod queried as Ulysses reached the bottom of the page and looked up again, a delighted grin on his face.

"It says here that the body of some poor sod was found up on the moors yesterday with his throat and intestines torn out."

"Sounds ghastly," Nimrod said dispassionately.

"Apparently he was found by a sheep farmer who's lost a number of his sheep to wild animal attacks over the last few months."

"Wild animals, sir?"

"That's what it says here."

"But the British Isles have very few natural predators left, certainly nothing big enough to take down a man, surely. I must be some kind of feral dog, or perhaps one of those big cats that keep getting loose from private zoos."

"That's what the editor of this local rag thinks too." Ulysses pointed to the editorial comment at the top of the second page. "Local rumour's blaming it on the Barghest, some local legend, a phantom hound said to stalk Ghestdale Moor."

"A phantom hound, sir?"

"According to folklore, those who see the beast don't live to see another day."

"If that's the case, how can anybody have ever reported that that is the case?"

"You can't over-analyse folklore, Nimrod," Ulysses pointed out. "That's what it says here."

"Surely they can't be serious."

"Well, according to this, there have been ten confirmed deaths, supposedly perpetrated by this hobgoblin hound, and just as many people have simply disappeared over the last four months. Most of the bodies were discovered on Ghestdale, the expanse of moorland that lies south-east of Whitby, close to the coast and the notorious Beast Cliff, which is said to be another haunt of the Barghest."

"If you don't mind me saying so, sir, that is nothing but a load of old poppycock."

"But something's responsible for all those deaths."

Nimrod's eyes narrowed as he attempted to assess his employer's true opinion regarding the matter.

"How did the others die?"

"All in a similarly savage manner, from what I can gather. Gutted, throats torn out, internal organs missing; some of the bodies were even partially devoured."

"Delightful. It really is a mystery, sir."

"A mystery indeed. And you know how I feel about mysteries."

"Indeed I do, sir," Nimrod said with what Ulysses hoped was feigned weariness.

"But," Ulysses went on, with what sounded like profound disappointment, "we already have one mystery on our hands; that of the identity of the elusive Mr Bellerophon, which is, I have to assume, an assumed name."

"Quite, sir," Nimrod agreed. "So, if I might be so bold as to ask, how do you suggest we move things forward from here?"

Putting the paper to one side, Ulysses devoted all his attention to the older man seated opposite him, immaculate as ever in his simple self-styled butler's uniform.

"You know what, Nimrod? I think it's about time we played the part of tourists to the full and took in the sights of Whitby, starting with some of those delightful looking ale-quaffing establishments down by the docks."

"Very good, sir. Shall I unpack the pistols, or will the bloodstone suffice?"

BY THE TIME Ulysses was dressed and ready to face the day – wearing a light tweed suit underneath a long check overcoat, finished off with a crimson cravat held in place with a diamond pin – it was already past ten.

Leaving their lodging house on the Crescent, the dandy and his manservant made their way to the East Terrace and the footpath that led down towards the estuary of the Esk, passing through the whale bone arch – a reminder of Whitby's whaling past – to emerge at the harbour end of the great stone West Pier. From there, the two men skirted the Esk, following the river back upstream through the old fishing town. The air was thick with the smell of fish, wood smoke and the ever-present pollution that drifted down off the moors from the vast brick-built factories with the morning mist.

Through the bobbing forest formed by the masts and rigging of the ships moored in the Lower Harbour, Ulysses could just make out the grey ghost of the Abbey, up there on the windswept crown of East Cliff, through shifting spaces between the smoke billowing from chimneys up and down the town.

Whitby was all of a bustle at this time in the day and even though it wasn't the height of the tourist season, there was still plenty for the local populace to do; the fishing and jet industries were still the life-blood of the old town.

Passing the swing bridge that crossed the silt-brown river as it flowed on its inexorable way to the sea, following the smell of bubbling pitch and the echoing clamour of sawing and hammering, Ulysses led the two of them towards the shipyards of Endeavour Wharf and onto New Quay Road.

They stopped at last outside the white painted facade of a large, five storey building that sported a sign declaring that this was 'The Angel Hotel'.

"This looks like just the place to start making our enquiries," he said, looking past the stacks of lobster pots to what had all the appearance of being one of Whitby's principal drinking establishments, "don't you think?"

"If you're sure that this is the best way to go about our business here, sir," Nimrod replied with a hint of wariness in his voice.

"Oh, don't be such a bore," Ulysses chided the older man good-humouredly. "Come on, it'll be fun!"

FIVE DRINKING ESTABLISHMENTS later, and Ulysses Quicksilver and his manservant found themselves in the blue-fugged bar-room of the Black Swan Inn on Baxtergate. It was just like every other. Although it was still only the middle of the day, the taverns in the vicinity of the docks were heaving, the fishermen and many of the stevedores having finished work for the day and made it the few yards to the public houses of Whitby to start spending their wages straight away.

Such was certainly true of the fish-reeking clientele of the Black Swan. For many of them, the working day had finished hours ago, and the men were well into their cups, having been at their seats in the bar since the pub first opened its doors to the desperate drinkers.

Ulysses stepped into the lamp-lit dark of the snug and, blinking against the change in light levels, he casually took in the sprawl of the bar – with its low beams and closeted drinking stalls – which looked just like every other tavern he had entered that morning.

As flamboyantly dressed as he was he would obviously appear out of place no matter how he carried himself, and so Ulysses saw no point in being anything other than the dandy he truly was, striding across the bar-room with a cocky swagger and an all-embracing smile on his face. Such misplaced confidence wrong-footed people, and that gave him the advantage.

He could feel the eyes of everyone on him and couldn't help but allow himself a private smile. Nimrod followed behind, as ever, apparently above it all, whether he was faced with cocky arrogance or disgruntled hostility.

From the furtive glances he kept giving the two of them, it looked as though the barman – his belly swollen from beer, his cheeks jowly, his eyes small black holes amongst the flab – was doing his best to keep a clandestine eye on them. The bar-top looked as if it had been made from the warped timbers of a ship's deck, uneven and stained almost black.

Ulysses tapped three times on the wooden counter with his cane and grinned as he saw the man twitch. With a face as overcast and thundery as the dull November day outside, finally admitting defeat, he looked up at his newest customers.

The man eyed Ulysses and Nimrod uncomfortably from under beetling brows. Sweat covered his face like grease. He started wiping the beer glass he held in one hand vigorously with the grubby rag he held in the other.

"Yes?" he asked, grudgingly.

"Good –" Ulysses paused and made a show of taking out his pocket watch and checking the time, before putting it back. "– afternoon, my good man. I wonder if I might take a moment of your time."

"Case you hadn't noticed, this is a pub."

Ulysses looked almost bewildered for a moment and then said: "Ah, yes, of course. I see. Cognac, please. Nimrod?"

"This, is a *pub*," the barman repeated.

"Oh. Better make it a pint of... What would you recommend?"

"Bitter is what most people drink round these parts."

"Then make it a pint of bitter please, barman."

The sweating barkeep scowled as he filled the glass he had been smearing with the dirty cloth with something the colour and clarity of watered down sewage from an age-worn pump on the bar.

"What'll 'e 'ave?" he asked, jerking his head towards Nimrod who stood impassively, and straight as a lamppost, at Ulysses' shoulder.

"Nimrod?"

"A glass of orange juice will suffice, sir."

"This. Is. A. Pub," the barkeep growled.

Ulysses looked at Nimrod and raised both eyebrows.

"A glass of tap water then."

The barkeep muttered something under his breath along the lines of "Soft, southern poofs," and looked for another glass for Nimrod's water. It was then that Ulysses struck.

"I don't suppose you would have happened to have heard of a Mr Bellerophon, would you?"

"A who?"

"Bellerophon. Mr Bellerophon. After that chap from Greek myth."

"The what?"

"Greek myth," Ulysses persisted in the face of such over-bearing obstinacy and ignorance. "Bellerophon. Chap who tamed Pegasus, the winged-horse, and killed the Chi –"

Ulysses stopped abruptly, in mid-sentence, a split second before he felt the heavy hand come to rest on his arm, his whole body tensing, as his genetically-inherited fight or flight response prepared him for whatever might befall him next. He couldn't help noticing the change in the barkeep's expression either; sullen unhelpfulness had transformed into fearful uncertainty.

Ulysses looked down at the ham-sized hand, the fat, calloused fingers, the scar-tissue knotted knuckles, the doubloon-sized signet ring. He followed the large hand to a ragged coat-sleeve, tufts of wiry black hair sprouting from the wrist beneath, up past the well-worn coarse wool and eventually to the man's face.

To Ulysses he looked not unlike a Toby jug in terms of broadness and his stout shape. He was tall, taller than Ulysses, and broad; 'built like a brick shithouse' was how he would have been described in the vernacular. His face was brown as a nut from exposure to the wind and weather, and he was ugly, although he smiled broadly through his Neanderthal features. His nose looked like it had been broken several times and was now a flattened pug-snout.

He was wearing a pork pie hat on top of a messy mop of matted grey tresses, and a bright mustard yellow neckerchief was tied in a knot at his neck. Under his coat he wore a tatty waistcoat that must once have been red and must also have once had more than the three brass buttons it sported now.

And the man smelt, although it wasn't of fish, like the Black Swan's other customers. He smelt of animals, musty and with an ever-present aroma of ammonia about him. And when he spoke Ulysses almost gagged at the rank smell of stale tobacco that was exhaled his way.

"I'd be careful what you say in here, sir," the man said in a harsh whisper.

Ulysses stared into the ivory whites of the other's eyes, his expression suddenly hard as stone. "And why might that be, I wonder?"

The large man smiled broadly through lumpen features that made him look as though someone had beaten him about the head with a fence post. "What I mean, sir, is that if I were you, a stranger in town and all, I wouldn't be going about asking such questions so – 'ow shall I put it? – so brazenly. That's all."

"Is that right, Mr...?"

"Rudge, sir. Just call me Rudge," the man smiled, his expression as warm as a sunny autumn day, and released his grip on Ulysses' arm. "There are some – 'ow might I put it? – some dodgy characters about, sir. Untrustworthy types," he glowered at the barkeep as the fat man placed Ulysses' pint unceremoniously on the uneven counter, slopping the brown liquid over the bar top as he did so, "that's all."

Ulysses relaxed slightly, picked up his pint and took a sip. His mouth tensed again; the stuff tasted as bad as it looked. Bitter was obviously an acquired taste, and Ulysses didn't think he had the patience or the desire to acquire it.

"So, Mr Rudge, do you know of a Mr Bellerophon?"

The man grimaced, shoulders hunched, hands up in front of him as if to shush Ulysses' prattling mouth. "I told you, sir, not so bold, if you please."

"Then, I take it you do."

"It's not as simple as that, sir. Things are a little – 'ow shall I put it? – a little delicate in that regard."

"But you can help us, Mr Rudge?"

Rudge took up the pint of bitter that the barkeep had pulled for him, apparently without having to be asked, and took a careless gulp from the glass, rivulets of beer coursing down the sides of his chin and into the stubble at his neck, to eventually be soaked up by the neckerchief. Suddenly the pint glass appeared to be half empty.

"I can help you, Mr...?"

"Quicksilver," Ulysses replied.

"Mr Quicksilver. But not here, sir. Not here."

"Where then?"

Rudge shot the blubbery barkeep a look full of meaning and menace, given extra emphasis by his disenchanting features, and the piggy man found something else to do at the other end of the bar.

"Up on the moors, sir, up beyond the town. Follow the cliff path until you reach a lone standing stone of black granite. From there head west onto the moors. You'll find a tumbledown shepherd's shelter. You can't miss it. It's a few miles walk mind. I'll meet you there in a couple of hours. Something I've got to finish here in Whitby first. Then we can talk."

"Very well. Shall we say, three o'clock?"

"Three o'clock it is, sir."

With that, Rudge downed the rest of his pint with a few economical, if noisy, gulps, put the empty glass back on the counter and, with a tip of his hat to Ulysses, he walked out of the Black Swan.

Ulysses watched the large man as he squeezed his huge frame through the door of the pub and then turned to Nimrod, a wry smile on his face.

"We have a lead, Nimrod. A lead at last."

"Indeed, sir," his manservant replied unenthusiastically, taking a sip from his glass of none-too-clean-looking tap water.

"And we have an afternoon on the moors to look forward to. It's not such an awful day. An afternoon's stroll will be bracing. Maybe we'll be able to clear the stink of fish from our nostrils."

"If you say so, sir." Nimrod replied, still stubbornly unenthusiastic at the prospect.

"I do, old chap, I do." Forgetting himself for a moment, Ulysses took a swig of his own drink and instantly regretted it, grimacing at the bitter aftertaste the ale left in his mouth. What he wouldn't do for a decent glass of Rémy Martin right now.

"The game is afoot, Nimrod. The game is most definitely afoot."

CHAPTER TEN

The Circus of Wonders

THE WIND CAME down off the moors in fitful gusts, like the final breaths of a dying asthmatic, rippling the long grass of the cliff top meadow above the town. Ulysses Quicksilver tugged the deerstalker, that he had purchased in the town, down tight over his ears and pulled the tweed cape tighter about his shoulders. If Nimrod felt the cold underneath his funereal black coat, he wasn't showing it.

As the two men strode on their way Ulysses turned to the older man. "What did you make of our friend, Mr Rudge?"

Nimrod took a deep breath of the cold moorland air and, keeping his eyes on the grey horizon, even in the face of the biting breeze, said: "I think you should be careful, sir. I don't think we can trust him."

"Why ever not, Nimrod?" Ulysses asked jovially.

The older man gave him a withering look. "Do I really need to answer that question, sir?"

"I suppose not, old chap," Ulysses laughed.

"But we are obviously going to meet with him anyway."

"Absolutely," Ulysses grinned. "We all need a little risk in our lives to keep us on our toes, to keep us sharp – although possibly not quite as much risk as Barty seems to favour," he added, almost as an aside. "Besides, he's the only lead we've got as far as this Bellerophon fellow is concerned."

"You're certain it's an assumed name, sir?" Nimrod probed.

"Oh yes – a name like that? And, that aside, I don't think anyone who chooses to deal with a reprobate like Magpie, or Wraith, or whatever he wants to call himself, would risk divulging his true identity to a felon like that."

The initial climb up from the town and past the skeletal Abbey ruins had left the two of them a little puffed, but they were getting into their stride now.

Having left the Black Swan Inn and its curmudgeonly barkeep, the two men had crossed the river by the swing bridge that spanned the Esk, turned into Church Street and climbed the one hundred and ninety-nine well-worn steps of the Church Stair to the Abbey ruins at the top of the headland, where they stood like some silent sentinel, a stone bastion guarding the town from the predations of sea and sky. They then set off along the packed earth path that led past the grey-black ruins along the cliff path and to the blasted moors beyond.

"Bellerophon," Nimrod said after a moment, as if he had been pondering the name. "The prince of Corinth who slew the dread Chimera with the aid of Pegasus the winged horse."

"Yes, I've been wondering about the significance of that too," Ulysses admitted. "Bellerophon may well be an assumed name, but there may well be a subtle subconscious reasoning behind that particular choice, or even a significant overt one, which we merely aren't party to yet."

"Where there's a hero, there's usually a monster."

"Yes, there's usually a monster," Ulysses agreed, images of the tentacled Kraken, the serum-warped lizard man, and half a dozen other horrors suddenly surfacing from the dark depths of his memory.

The wind blew sour here over the scraggy grass, rank with the smell of petrochemical pollutants, and redolent with the stink of rotting peat bogs and bitter salt sea spray. As they came over the rise at the crest of the hill, St Hild's abbey now nothing more than a charcoal sketch against the sky behind them, they gained their first glimpse of the Circus of Wonders.

The main tent was a mildewed expanse of tarred canvas, stretched taut by thick, green guy-ropes. In places the faded and peeling remnants of brighter colours were just visible against the flapping fabric of the bedraggled Big Top.

That was the first thing Ulysses noticed. The second thing was the police presence.

"'Ello, 'ello, 'ello! What's going on 'ere then?" he asked with enthusiastic interest.

"It would appear to me that the circus folk are helping the police with their enquiries," his manservant replied.

"Come on, Nimrod," Ulysses went in the same vein of boyish delight. "Let's find out for ourselves!"

As they neared the conglomeration of tents and steam-wagons, Ulysses saw huddles of circus folk and policemen gathered between the sanctuary of the main tent and a cordon of police vehicles. The two groups couldn't be more different. There were the uniformed police officers – not an automaton-drone among them, Ulysses noted – notebooks out, licked pencil stubs scratching away, all with unimpressed, or uncomprehending, expressions on their faces. And then there were the circus folk.

To Ulysses it looked like they had stepped out of another time, and one that had never really existed. It was as if a band of medieval mummers had suddenly found themselves living in a Dickens' novel. They were all attired in a similar manner, in that none of them were wearing what could be described as new clothes. Every costume had been carefully created from an amalgam of hand-me-downs.

The circus performers' uniquely individual costumes actually gave them their own uniform, a sense of identity, marking them out as something not quite of this world; something out of kilter with the rest of the empire of Magna Britannia. It provided them with a sense of belonging. And for many of them, their bizarre costumes only served to enhance the other, more unusual, aspects that some of them possessed – the traits that marked them out as members of a freakshow.

Ulysses began to notice these just as he became aware of the signs and billboards littering the grounds around the main tent, all designed and arranged to lure a macabrely-fascinated public inside the 'Circus of Wonders.'

Without really being conscious of where they were going, the two men now found themselves beyond the ramshackle police cordon, treading between knotty tufts of grass, drawn by the lure of the scene.

Glancing at an anxious huddle of performers, who appeared to be trying to keep the police at arm's length, he saw a dwarf, wearing nothing but a leather waistcoat over his muscular, tattooed torso, his bulging biceps bare, a larger lady, her fuller figure squeezed into a lace and taffeta creation, the curled ringlets of her full beard carefully plaited, and a stick thin, pale-skinned man who was wearing nothing but what appeared to be a loin-cloth and ribboned top hat, despite the November chill, his exposed skin a painted canvas of intricate tattoos and body piercings, copious rings drawn through the scrawny, pinched flesh of his shoulders, arms, neck and knees, as well as having bones and feathers thrust through his ears, nose and eyebrows.

Close by them a tall man, with mantis-like limbs and a skeletally gaunt face – his eyes dramatic white orbs within the shadowed pits of their sockets – wearing scuffed top hat and tails, and wholly inappropriate skin-tight, black leggings, and long-toed pixie boots, giving the impression, once again, of a medieval antecedent – was talking animatedly with an unimaginative constable. Everything about his demeanour and the fact that he was the centre of the police's attention, suggested to Ulysses that this was the freakshow's master of ceremonies and *de facto* leader.

A young woman with ridiculously long straw-blond hair – so long, in fact, that it was tied like a belt at her waist to stop it dragging in the dirt – plaited with pink and purple ribbons, beads and even shells, was huddled nervously beside the master of ceremonies. Her dress might have once been the ball gown of a Versailles courtier, but was now a dusty and faded shadow of the glorious centrepiece costume it had once been. The embroidered bodice was loose upon her skinny frame and her slight chest could not hope to fill it. A knitted shawl about her shoulders added to the impression of the impoverished gypsy lifestyle.

A bald, near giant of a man, with the quizzical expression of a three-year old on his prominently-browed face, was led away docilely by the hand into the main tent, by a girl of no more than eleven or twelve, revealing the trio of policemen, deep in conversation, that his hulking frame had obscured from view.

"I don't bloody believe it!" Ulysses exclaimed, a broad grin spreading across his face.

"Ah," Nimrod said as he caught sight of the tuft of orange hair only a moment after his master.

"Ah, indeed, Nimrod! It's only Inspector sodding Allardyce," Ulysses laughed. "Here, in North Yorkshire!"

Casting his eyes heavenward and letting out a long breathy sigh, Nimrod followed as his master quickened his steps towards the unmistakeable ginger-haired figure of Inspector Allardyce of Scotland Yard, and Ulysses' regular sparring partner.

"Hello, Maurice." The inspector's eyes flashed with furious fire. Allardyce's venomous look came with an accompaniment of spluttering grunts and snorts as the other policemen attempted to suppress their sniggers. "And what brings you here?"

"I don't bloody believe it," the put-upon inspector grumbled. "Quicksilver! What the hell are *you* doing here?"

"Oh, you know, enjoying a little unseasonal sea air. I hear it's very good for one's constitution."

"You're joking, right? Air's as polluted in this godforsaken place as it is back in the Big Smoke. And what do you think you look like in that get up? Get dressed in the dark, did you?"

"And what brings you here?"

Inspector Maurice Allardyce pulled himself up to his full height – all five foot six inches of it – and tugged at the lapels of his grey trench coat. "I'll have you know that I am investigating a series of most foul and savage murders."

"Ah, that's funny, because I'd heard you were on holiday. Although, if that *is* the case, it looks more like a busman's holiday to me."

The policemen exchanged knowing glances at this. Allardyce's face reddened still further.

"Well, yes, I may happen to have been holidaying in the area, visiting the wife's sister."

"But as soon as we heard that Inspector Allardyce of Scotland Yard was staying here, in Whitby," said an enthusiastic young constable, coming to Allardyce's aid, something like hero-worship sparkling in his eyes, "we knew that we just had to get him on the case."

Allardyce smiled, looking half embarrassed and half delighted with the compliment he had just been paid.

"Ah, so it *is* a busman's holiday then."

"You could say that," Allardyce conceded. "Now, Quicksilver, if you wouldn't mind being about your business, then I can be about mine."

Pushing past Ulysses, Allardyce approached the belligerent constable still questioning the increasingly irritated ringmaster.

The near-skeletal MC gave Ulysses the impression that he was an incredibly patient man – having developed his tolerant attitude in the face of society's mistrust and ostracising, coupled with its fascination, nonetheless, for the freaks that inhabited the otherworld of which he was the master – and yet who was now being pushed to his absolute limit.

Allardyce interrupted the constable's ongoing fruitless line of questioning with an abrupt: "Have you finished with this one?" pointing an accusing finger at the ghoulish ringmaster. To his mind, the man had already been tried and convicted, and now he was ready to see sentence passed.

Ulysses sidestepped past the inspector and extended a hand towards the suddenly startled master of the Circus of Wonders. "Ulysses Quicksilver, special investigator of rum goings-on and uncanny occurrences," he said. "And you are?"

Eyeing him like a hawk, the circus-master ignored Ulysses' proffered hand and instead doffed his hat – to expose a few straggly strings of lank grey shoulder-length hair – and took a bow, bending low at the waist.

"They call me Steerpike, and I am indeed master of ceremonies at this Circus of Wonders," he announced, unfolding his body again and returning the hat to his head. "I am also known as the Incredible Eating Man," he said.

With a flourish, he took an Edison bulb from a pocket of his tailcoat, a clockmaker's hammer from another, and then proceeded to break the bulb into a fingerless-mittened hand, and popped one of the larger pieces of glass into his mouth. There followed an uncomfortable crunching sound that set Ulysses' teeth on edge, which was followed by some moments of mastication, that sounded like the man was chewing a mouthful of grit, before Steerpike swallowed noisily and with an exaggerated dip and rise of his head. He opened his mouth wide, sticking out a long pink tongue, to show all assembled that his mouth was now completely empty.

"Very impressive," Ulysses said, offering up a short burst of applause.

"Never mind all that," Inspector Allardyce butted in, his face locked in a grimace that made Ulysses think of a pit-bull chewing a wasp, and demanded of the constable, "what have you found out?"

"Still claims 'e and 'is freaks are innocent," he sighed with frustration.

"Innocent?" Ulysses said, his ears pricking up at the merest hint of any miscarriage of justice taking place here.

"Oh, here we go," Allardyce complained.

"Innocent of what, exactly?" Ulysses asked, visions of local newspaper headlines cramming his head.

"Murder, of course! I thought you had to be clever to go to Eton," the inspector added, giving Ulysses a disparaging look.

"But not to be a policeman, eh? Just blinkered," Ulysses countered.

"Look, if you're not off my patch in the next thirty seconds, I'll have you up before the local magistrate for obstructing police business!" Allardyce snarled. "Or perhaps," he said, suddenly smiling darkly, "you know more than you're letting on, and I should take *you* in for questioning."

"Oh you know me, Inspector; nothing to hide here. In fact I would gladly offer myself up for interrogation, if you feel that it would help you bring this particularly nasty case to a satisfactory conclusion," Ulysses offered magnanimously.

"Not bloody likely," Allardyce snarled. "Now bugger off."

"Gladly, Inspector," Ulysses said, doffing his deerstalker to the red-faced policeman. "We wouldn't want to get in the way of justice now, would we, Nimrod?"

"No, sir. Good day, Inspector."

Without another word, Ulysses turned and began to stride away from the enticing Circus of Wonders and Inspector Allardyce's ham-fisted murder investigation.

He glanced back over his shoulder once and caught the eye of the enigmatic Steerpike, and the waif-like girl now hanging off his arm, as the labouring policeman attempted to wheedle anything that might amount to an admission of guilt from the circus folk. Such a thing would wrap up this case nicely and be a feather in the cap of the disgraced copper as he was no doubt still trying to live down the disaster that had been the Jubilee debacle.

Ulysses was certain that the mysterious master of ceremonies and his cronies had plenty of things to hide – secrets that they didn't want the rest of the world knowing about – but murder? Ulysses wasn't so sure. Why hang around in the wake of ten murders, when they could have packed up and been on their way by dawn the next day, if they were responsible? Travellers like those who made up the Circus of Wonders were good at avoiding unwanted attention by never staying in any one place for too long.

And besides, the paper had recorded that the killings appeared to have been carried out by a wild animal of some kind. Some of the circus performers might be a little wilder than was the norm, but unless the freakshow's star attraction was the Hound of the Baskervilles, Ulysses sincerely doubted that anyone from the circus had anything to do with the mysterious deaths.

"What did you make of that little lot, Nimrod?" he asked when they had left the Circus of Wonders well behind them.

"If you ask me, sir, they're queer coves the lot of them," Nimrod said, his impeccably cultured tones dismissively aloof.

"Hmm, I thought you'd say that," said Ulysses. "Anyway, we'd best not dally here any longer; we have an appointment to keep with our new friend Mr Rudge, do we not?"

FROM BEHIND A grassy hummock, inquisitive eyes watched the man in the deerstalker and his servant leave the circus behind and continue on their way, along the path that would lead them to the blasted expanse of Ghestdale.

The sentience behind those eyes hoped that the men knew what they were letting themselves in for. Surely they had heard about the deaths. They had just been talking with the very policemen who were investigating the Barghest killings after all.

Those same eyes had observed the meeting between the man in the deerstalker and the ginger-haired inspector with interest. There was obviously a history between the two of them and a mutual lack of respect.

And yet still the man in the deerstalker and his companion were leaving to continue on alone to Ghestdale, that most damnable godforsaken place.

Keeping low, out of sight of both the policemen and the circus folk, the watcher left the cover of the hummock and, keeping to the shelter of an ancient ditch, set off after the dandy and his valet.

CHAPTER ELEVEN

A Damsel in Distress

SCUDS OF CLOUD raced across the leaden face of heaven, the greens, yellows and blues of sub-dermal hematomas bruising the corpse-grey epidermis of the sky.

Everything in this wilderness had been shaped by the elements – the wind most of all – from the few gale-bent trees, looking like dowager-stooped witches, and the storm-scoured slabs of sandstone, denuded of any living thing other than the ever tenacious lichen, to the hardy heather and prickly gorse. Springs bubbled up to gurgle their way between the roots of grassy mounds, reshaping the landscape with geological slowness.

With the rock-gnawing wind pricking the exposed skin of hands and faces, Ulysses took out his pocket watch for the umpteenth time since he and his manservant had begun their trek over the blasted heather and gorse-blanketed moors, between the wind-scoured tors of tumbled boulders and skirted the meandering streams and bogs of Ghestdale.

He *harrumphed* and, flicking the case of his father's watch shut again, returned it to his waistcoat pocket.

Nimrod looked at him, raising one expectant eyebrow.

"Three thirty. He's late."

Eyes straining, Ulysses peered at the horizon, where the grey, overcast sky met the blasted moors, seeking the big man's huge silhouette. If it hadn't been for his trusty pocket watch he wouldn't have had any idea as to what time it was; it could have been any time between dawn and dusk, the quality of the light hadn't changed once since sun-up.

Ulysses scanned the horizon again, as he had done every thirty minutes or so since they had come upon the tumbledown shepherd's hut. Rudge might only be half an hour late, but Ulysses had been waiting to meet with him again as soon as he and Nimrod had left the Black Swan three hours before.

"It looks like the mysterious Mr Rudge is going to prove himself to be as untrustworthy as you at first suspected, Nimrod," Ulysses said, with a bitter sigh.

"It would appear so, sir," Nimrod agreed. "If it helps to settle your mind at all, I do so hate it when I'm right."

"Thanks, Nimrod, but don't worry, old chap. We'll give him until four, shall we, before heading back?"

"As you wish, sir."

Ulysses felt irritable, a condition brought on not only by Rudge's failure to make their meeting. It was also exacerbated by the biting cold and the gurgling, churning hunger gnawing away at his belly. He realised now that he hadn't eaten anything since putting away the full English Nimrod had served up that morning back at the guest house. The only sustenance he had had since then was a couple of drinks back in Whitby and the revitalising effects of the alcohol had long since worn off.

It was already beginning to get dark, the texture of the sky becoming still more leaden as the sun sank steadily towards the horizon, behind the ever-present pall of cloud. It was as if North Yorkshire had its own inescapable pall, just like London had its ever-present Smog.

For want of anything better to do, considering the circumstances, and as a means of trying to keep the marrow-numbing cold at bay, Ulysses continued picking his way between the hummocks of knotty, yellowing grass and the peaty bog-holes that could so easily ensnare the unwary.

A hundred yards away he could see the start of a defile among the otherwise near-featureless rolling moorlands of Ghestdale; a stream-cut hollow between scrubby bushes, exposed sandstone stacks. The air was redolent with the peaty smell of standing water and no doubt buzzing with moorland midges. Ulysses turned his steps towards the moorland morass, watchful for rabbit holes and half-hidden sink-holes between the tufts of grass and tangle-stemmed bushes of gorse.

There were worse things than rabbit holes on Ghestdale that might endanger the unwary explorer, of course. First there were the peat-steeped pot holes, sucking hollows of saturated peat-mud, perfectly blended into the surrounding landscape thanks to the rafts of sphagnum moss and grasses that anchored their roots in the rich loam, insubstantial as water and yet with all the lethal clinging might of quicksand. Any who stumbled into one of them had better have some means of getting themselves out again or they would be swallowed up within a matter of minutes, drowning in the soupy mud.

And then there were the abandoned mine-workings that riddled the rocks beneath Ghestdale. Whitby and its immediate environs possessed some of the finest deposits of jet in, not only the British Isles, but the whole of the empire of Magna Britannia and, in fact, the world. A black, fossilized wood, jet could be intricately carved and given a superb polish which made for some fabulous pieces of jewellery and other trinkets. The stuff had been mined in the region for centuries and during the mid-nineteenth Whitby supported a very successful jet industry, the interest from the royal family at the time helping it become highly fashionable.

Although the manufacture of jet jewellery and the like still took place in the town, it was nowhere near the peak it had enjoyed a hundred years before. The mines, however, remained, many of them worked out completely, treacherous tunnels left neglected, pit-props left to rot, galleries becoming water-logged by the run-off that was once pumped out, so that now many tunnels were unsafe, or flooded, or had collapsed under the weight of rock and earth above them.

Ulysses was roused from his distracted musings by the cry of a woman.

"Did you hear that?" he asked, turning to his companion.

"Yes, sir, I did."

"Unless I'm very much mistaken, that sounded like a damsel in distress," Ulysses said, his pace already quickening to a run, forcing Nimrod to lengthen his strides to keep up.

Running as fast as he could, almost entirely heedless now of any potential pitfalls that might catch him out, Ulysses sprinted for the defile hidden between the gorse, from where he was certain the cry had come.

And as he ran, so his mind raced too, as – adrenalin flooding his system – he began to imagine what might await them. The first thought that came into his head was that the woman had been attacked; the next moment his mind was flooded with images of savaged bodies, like those unfortunate wretches that had been found dead here on the moors, carcasses slashed open, gutted by gouging claws, arms and legs bent at unnatural angles, looking like so many discarded ragdolls. Suddenly his comment about there being a damsel in distress seemed in terribly bad taste.

Reaching the top of the defile, he flung himself through a tangled thicket of thorns, tearing the lining of his cape open as he ran, stumbling down over the tumbled stones at his feet. He rounded a spur in the defile, half-expecting to see the body of a young woman lying there, gutted and jointed like a Sunday roast, some monstrous hellhound – all black fur and glowing-coal eyes – standing over its trophy, blood dripping from its cruel jaws; so much so, that he stumbled to an abrupt halt in surprise when that wasn't what confronted him in the hollow at all.

Sitting rather uncomfortably on the damp ground, with her back to him, was indeed a young woman, her taut figure hidden beneath a well-tailored Harris tweed jacket and knickerbockers of the same material, long woollen socks covering the shapely curve of her well-toned calves, with practical walking boots on her feet and her long blonde hair carefully plaited and tied up in a bun beneath her hat. And rather than further cries of pain or terror, Ulysses could hear her berating herself.

"You fool girl," she said, "you've been out on these moors a hundred times and look at you, caught out by a rabbit hole! You can be such an idiot!"

The expectant look of horror on Ulysses' face turning to one of curious delight, he picked his way across the floor of the shallow gorge that he might come to the aid of his damsel in distress.

His highly developed sixth sense flared, shaking him out of his ever-so slightly lecherous reverie, with white hot awareness. He already had his hands up to defend himself as the animal launched itself at him, yapping furiously.

Hearing the noise, the woman's head suddenly snapped round, and for a moment, Ulysses fancied he could see the image of the devil dog reflected in the pupils of her wide brown eyes, behind the lenses of her round, wire-rimmed glasses, as if she too were half-expecting to see the same thing that his imagination had conjured. And then, with a blink, the imagined monster was gone, as was the brief grimace of terror, to be replaced by a pink-cheeked look of embarrassment.

"Rover!" she barked at the terrier now leaping up and down in front of Ulysses. "Leave the poor gentleman alone. Now, Rover! Heel!"

"Oh, don't mind him," Ulysses said, keeping his hands out low at his waist, just in case, "he's only looking out for his mistress."

"That's very gracious of you, Mr...?"

"Quicksilver, Miss, but call me Ulysses, please."

For a moment something like recognition or curiosity flashed across the young woman's features. Her clear complexion and soft, yet firm skin gave her the natural, understated beauty of an English rose. Ulysses judged that she couldn't have been older than thirty and was most likely still in her mid-to late twenties.

"But his mistress should be looking out for herself, the silly thing," she said crossly. It took Ulysses a moment to realise that the 'silly thing' she was referring to was herself and not the terrier, which was now prancing around the young woman, watching Ulysses intently and giving off the occasional small growl to remind this interloper who the alpha male was around here.

Ulysses knelt down beside her, meeting her worried, embarrassed look with a kind smile. "Now, what seems to be the problem, Miss...?"

"Haniver. Jennifer Haniver."

"Haniver," Ulysses repeated. There was something strangely familiar about that name. Now, where had he heard it before?

Ulysses offered her his hand and she took it, surprising him with the firmness of her shake.

"Pleased to meet you, Miss Haniver." Ulysses was unable to be anything other than utterly charming, finding himself in the company of another attractive young woman. There was a tired sigh from Nimrod behind him and Ulysses could imagine his manservant's eyebrows raised in disapproval and exasperation.

"It's my ankle," she explained, rubbing at the joint beneath her sock. "I caught my foot in a rabbit hole – silly old fool – and went over on it. Should've been looking where I was going, rather than for paw-prints, shouldn't I?"

"May I?" Ulysses asked, reaching out towards the young woman's ankle.

"No, please do."

He carefully squeezed the flesh beneath the wool.

"Out doing a bit of hunting, were you?" he asked, innocuously.

"You might say that."

"Partridge? Woodcock, was it?"

The young woman paused for a moment before answering, as if trying to assess how this stranger might take her next remark. "The Barghest Beast, actually."

With a sharp intake of breath Miss Haniver flinched, trying to pull her foot away, which only caused her to actually cry out in pain.

"I'm sorry. I'm being as careful as I can."

"Go on," Jennifer said, holding her leg and biting her lip, in an effort not to jerk her leg away again. "I'll try not to move this time – I promise."

Holding the back of her leg in his right hand, Ulysses tentatively felt the flesh around the ankle itself.

"You say you were following animal tracks," Ulysses commented as he stared into the middle distance, concentrating on his examination.

"Er, yes."

"But I thought you said you were out hunting."

"Well they're one and the same thing really."

"You looking for this Barghest beast of yours?"

"Th-That's right," the young woman replied, tensing again under the ministrations of Ulysses probing fingertips.

"I've never heard of a Barghest before." Ulysses said, remembering full well the reference to the ghostly hound in the newspaper article in which he had read of the recent killings. "Do you mind telling me what it is?"

Jennifer Haniver looked down at the boggy ground, her cheeks flushing pink again.

"You'd probably think me even more foolish than you doubtless already do for having fallen down a rabbit hole."

"Well, when you put it like that," Ulysses said with a grin, "what have you got to lose? You couldn't be any more embarrassed than you already are."

She smiled at him, her warm hazel eyes staring directly into his. And, if anything, the flush in her cheeks deepened.

She came across as so lacking in any kind of egotism or narcissism that her way of not making any effort to draw attention to her own attractiveness simply made her appear all the more appealing.

"I suppose not," she admitted, returning Ulysses' smile for the first time since they had met. "The Barghest is a phantom hound said to haunt the area known as Beast Cliff and the moors beyond."

"Ah, a ghost story," Ulysses said. "I've heard such tales of phantom hounds before."

"Of course, practically every county of the British Isles has its own legends of black dogs or hellhounds as they are also called. East Anglia has its Black Shuck, Cornwall the Shony and even the Channel Island of Jersey has its own Black Dog of Death.

"To most, the Barghest is nothing more than a fanciful phantasm, imagined into existence by less enlightened people from times past who didn't know any better, as they tried to explain away natural phenomena they didn't understand." Jennifer Haniver paused, distracted for a moment by the pain from her ankle.

"To most," Ulysses' attention was fully focused on what the young woman had to say now; he wasn't even examining her ankle any more. "But not, I take it, to you."

"Well, no."

"So what do you know that the rest of us don't?" Ulysses asked with a wry grin.

"I am a cryptozoologist, Mr Quicksilver. Investigating the mysteries of the natural world – the supposedly impossible, the unsubstantiated and the allegedly extinct – is what I do. I take it you're not a local man yourself."

"No."

"Then what brings you to Yorkshire?"

"A little hunting myself, actually."

Jennifer smiled.

"So what are you hunting for, Ulysses?" she asked, trying the informal for a change.

"Mermaids, as it happens."

"Mermaids? Up here, on the moors?"

"Now who's feeling embarrassed?"

"Then, have you heard of the recent attacks?"

"I only know what I read in the paper this morning."

"Well, to my mind, these attacks have all the hallmarks of a large dog."

"And the Barghest is, supposedly, just that. A big dog?"

"Exactly, Mr Quicksilver; the biggest." The fading flush returned to her cheeks for a moment. There was something particularly appealing about that. "You don't think me absurd to talk of such things?"

"Not at all," Ulysses admitted. "I have seen too many weird and wonderful things in my life to dismiss anything too readily."

"You don't know what a relief it is to hear you say that," Jennifer gushed.

"Glad to be of service," Ulysses said, his gaze locking with hers again. This time he felt his own cheeks glowing.

"So, doctor, what's your diagnosis?"

"What?" Ulysses shook himself from his pleasant reverie.

"My ankle, Mr Quicksilver. Is it broken?"

"I'm sorry? Your ankle, of course," he said, stumbling over himself, trying to remember what it was that he was supposed to be doing. "Well, I don't think you've broken it, but I would say that it's sprained."

"Silly dithering idiot!" the young woman chided herself again. "Should have been looking where you were going, shouldn't you?"

"Look, I think your hunt for the Barghest is over for the time being, don't you? You're not going to get very far on that ankle by yourself, so is there somewhere that we can help you to? Where are you staying?"

"That's very chivalrous of you," she said, blushing again. "But I feel as though you've done enough for me already."

"But I don't think you're really in a position to refuse us, are you? I mean, it'll be getting dark soon and I'm sure you don't want to be hobbling around out here on your own, with a monster hound on the loose."

"No, of course not. You're quite right," Miss Haniver agreed. "Hunter's Lodge – my father's house; I've lived with him there, since his... retirement."

"What did he do?"

"You might have heard of him; Hannibal Haniver? He was someone, once. A naturalist; a leader in his field."

"Haniver. Hannibal Haniver," Ulysses repeated. "I knew that name sounded familiar. Yes, I've heard of him."

"Well, like I say, he was someone – *once*."

"Give us a hand will you, Nimrod?" Ulysses said, with one arm already around the young woman's waist.

The terrier still skipping and yapping at their heels, Ulysses and Nimrod helped her stand and then, with one either side, her arms across their shoulders, they set off.

"What sort of signs were you hoping to find?" Ulysses asked, as much as by way of finding something to distract them all – but mostly himself

– from the sudden enforced intimacy the three of them suddenly found themselves sharing.

"Spoor, claw-marks, a paw-print if I was lucky."

"Like this one you mean, ma'am?" Nimrod said in his usual underwhelmed monotone, raising an eyebrow at something on the ground – or rather, an impression in the ground.

And there, in front of them, partially hidden by tufts of grass and moss, was the nonetheless still clear indentation of four claw marks and the pads to match.

"That's it!" Jennifer shrieked in delight. "You've found it!"

"By Jove, old chap! Score one to you, eh? But bloody hell!" Ulysses exclaimed as he studied the mark for himself. "Look at the size of it!"

The single, threatening paw-print was more the size of a horse's hoof than the impression left by a dog, even something as large as a Great Dane. The terrier's feet were dwarfed by it, in comparison.

"It looks like you were right, Jennifer!" he added excitedly.

"Yes, it does rather, doesn't it?" she replied just as excitedly, for the moment the pain in her ankle forgotten. "We should take an impression. I have a mould and some plaster of Paris in my bag. It shouldn't take us more than about –"

"Sir," Nimrod suddenly butted in, eyes turned to the subtly darkening blanket of clouds that covered these desolate moors, "I hate to put a damper on things, but dusk is drawing on and we have just found the very evidence Miss Haniver was looking for to prove that there *is* a ravening beast at large on Ghestdale."

Suddenly realising what he was saying, he looked at the sky again and noted how much greyer and gloomier the moors appeared than when they had first arrived at this spot. Dusk came early this late in the year, frighteningly early.

"Nimrod's right," Ulysses said. "We have to press on. We can come back here again in force, after someone's seen to that ankle of yours. But have no fear, Jennifer, I do believe you've made the discovery of the deca –"

"Ulysses?" the young woman asked, looking anxiously at her knight in shining armour, who was now suddenly doubled up beside her.

"Sir? Are you all right?" Nimrod sounded genuinely concerned, his voice laden with unaccustomed emotion.

A hand pressed to his temple, Ulysses straightened again as the shock of the migraine-flash of awareness began to pass.

"Oh, Nimrod, I do so hate it when you're right."

And then they all heard the deep-throated, guttural growl behind them.

CHAPTER TWELVE

The Barghest

ALL THREE OF them snapped their heads round at the same time, terror-widened eyes staring through the encroaching gloom at the entrance to the narrow defile by which Ulysses and Nimrod had come to find Jennifer Haniver.

There, standing stock still on four thick legs was a black shape, a blot of darkness against the dimming horizon, a threatening shadow charged with menace and power. It seemed to exude an aura of malevolence that hit the three of them with a wave of nausea-inducing fear.

And Ulysses knew that the beast was watching them just as intently. He almost fancied he could see its eyes glowing red in the darkness, and then he chided himself for allowing such fanciful imaginings to subsume all rational thought. He needed to keep his wits about him: now was the time for action, not for macabre, doom-laden fantasies.

The creature stood rigid, apparently simply watching them. Ulysses knew that they had to run, that if they were to survive the surely inevitable attack that was sure to come, they had to give themselves as much of a head-start as possible.

And there was no doubt that it *was* the Barghest beast. Everything about it exuded malign threat, even at this distance. It looked as big as a pony, although there was something about the shape of its silhouette, and the way the creature held itself, that suggested its essence could not be contained by something as ordinary as a dog's hide.

As Ulysses watched, transfixed by the appalling majesty of the animal standing there, the dog-beast threw back its head and howled.

The sound – one long ululating howl of savage animal delight and hunger – echoed from the walls of the enclosing defile, screwing Ulysses' stomach into a knot, an icy chill rippling through every part of him. He felt his skin contract, the hairs of his arms standing on end, and heard the rapid *dub-dub dub-dub* tattoo of his quickening pulse pounding in his ears, as the old adrenalin-fuelled flight or fight response kicked in.

And then – still unable to take his eyes off the ominous black shadow-shape – Ulysses saw the creature drop its head and look straight at the compromised trio. He saw its stance visibly tighten, thick cords of muscle knotting beneath its velvet-black hide. The Barghest was tensing, ready to spring. And then something in Ulysses snapped.

"Come on!" he hissed at his manservant and the girl, muscles moving again now that he was freed of the paralysis of unbridled fear. "We have to get out of here."

"Yes, sir!" Nimrod acknowledged his master emphatically.

Jennifer, however, now that she was faced with the truth of what had so far only been her academic pursuit of the Barghest beast, could only whimper and mutter to herself, her own anxiety overwhelming her.

Ulysses' gut instinct told him that it was now a case of when, not if, the creature would launch an attack. With the deadliest of intent.

"Come on, Jenny, you can do it, I know you can," Ulysses encouraged her, trying to make his words as calm and reassuring as possible, worried as he himself was that the young woman's own fear might prove more crippling than her injured ankle. "We have to keep moving."

"Nimrod," he said, turning to his manservant, his voice hushed but as hard as iron, "arm yourself, just in case."

He heard the click of Nimrod's pistol chamber being closed again, his ever-reliable manservant close to being a mind-reader himself, having already unholstered his gun and checked its load.

"Already done, sir. Just in case."

"Yes, just in case," Ulysses repeated, as if the animal's attack was anything but inevitable, clinging onto the desperate hope that they could all still get out of this alive.

"We're doomed!" Jennifer hissed. Ulysses could feel her body shaking, pressed against his as it was. "Those who hear the Barghest's howl are doomed to die."

"You know what always made me laugh about folk tales like that?" Ulysses said between puffs and sharp intakes of breath as the three of them attempted to quicken their pace, like competitors in some bizarre four-legged race.

"What?" Jennifer found herself replying.

"If all those who hear its howl always die, then who was it who passed on that little titbit of information?"

And then, the adrenalin-high emotion of the moment catching her completely off-guard, a burst of laughter escaped Jennifer's lips, startling herself so much that she suddenly fell silent again.

"That's more like it," Ulysses gasped, as they continued their stumbling run.

But Ulysses' forced good humour was short lived as he looked back over his shoulder and was unable to stifle his own moan of shock and horror.

"What is it?" Jennifer gasped. "It's gaining on us, isn't it?"

"You could say that," Ulysses had to agree.

Jennifer turned her head.

"Hey," Ulysses snapped, "I think we should concentrate our energies on keeping going, don't you?"

Jennifer gave up on her attempted observation and instead re-doubled her own efforts, pushing hard with her good leg, her hops helping the others carry her over the uneven ground.

Ulysses had only had a split-second's look at the beast, but it had been more than enough. In that split-second the monstrous appearance of the creature had indelibly seared itself onto his retinas. Although it roughly resembled a dog in shape and form – hunched shoulders and slavering muscular jaws screaming its canine ancestry – at the same time it was like no dog he had ever seen.

First of all, the thing's head appeared too large for its body, the thick hump of its broadly-muscled shoulders seeming to have to compensate for the extra weight. Its skin appeared to be pulled too tight against its skull, and this aspect of its appearance wasn't down to the creature being malnourished either. It might have a ravenous hunger – Ulysses could well believe it, seeing the thick strings of saliva dripping from its tusk-like teeth – but if so, it was by design rather than due to the fact that the creature hadn't fed well.

The flesh of the dog's head was drawn back from jaws that seemed too large for even its over-sized skull. It was as if a lion's skull had been forced inside the tight sack of the dog's skin. Jutting fangs, far larger than those of any naturally evolved canine, thrust from glistening gums and partially denuded bone, while the skin at the side of the creature's head was pulled back in creased rolls that seemed close to tearing. Its muzzle was practically debrided bone, giving its snout a bat-like appearance. In fact, the stretched nostrils, jutting, over-sized fangs, red eyes and midnight-black pelt gave the beast a sinister, vampiric quality on top of everything else.

The rest of the beast's body, its heaving ribcage, its lithe, muscular flanks – even its thick, heavy, tail that in the half-light appeared to glisten as might a snake's – spoke of strength, savagery and ferocity. A nightmarish terror-dog; the perfectly designed killing machine.

"Nimrod, leave me to it," Ulysses said, indicating Jennifer with a nod of his head. "I want you to concentrate on emptying your gun into that thing as soon as it's close enough, preferably right between its eyes."

"Very good, sir."

Leaving the young woman solely to his master's attentions, Nimrod turned to face the approaching monster, continuing his half-run backwards, parallel to the other two, pistol out straight in front of him, aimed at the beast.

Just for a moment, Ulysses looked Nimrod's way, just to check that his manservant was all right, and then wished he hadn't. He could not remember the last time he had seen such a look of shock and unadulterated terror on his aide's face. And that unsettled him even more than the appearance of the beast closing on their position.

It unsettled him to the point where, his usual indefatigable positivity suddenly crushed, for the first time he dared to allow the possibility to enter his mind that perhaps the three of them weren't going to get out of this one alive; that he had met his nemesis at last, in the form of unbridled, savage nature, blood red in tooth and claw.

And then they were out of the defile, with nothing but open moorland between them and the twinkling lights of a house, visible on the horizon, a postage stamp of shadow against the rapidly darkening, overcast sky.

The fading twilight played tricks on the eyes, as Ulysses was well aware, but the house still appeared to be a long way away; further than they could ever hope to reach before the terror-dog surely caught up with them.

And then the shooting started.

The first shot was loud and close. The pistol-crack caused Ulysses' body to tense automatically, almost as if he had been shot himself. Jennifer gave a gasp of surprise and hugged herself to him even more tightly as he re-doubled his efforts once again.

"If you'll excuse me, Miss Haniver," Ulysses said as he hastily swept Jennifer up in his arms. She, in response, put both arms around his neck and clung on tightly. Momentarily her eyes locked onto his, limpid pools of fear meeting his steely gaze.

Biting his lip against the pain, Ulysses ran on, adrenalin spurring him forward. It felt as if the fingers of his right hand were being broken all over again, while his irksome old shoulder injury was flaring up under the added duress. But he focused his mind on the house on the horizon, compartmentalising the pain, so that it might be dealt with later – if there was to be a later – the cocktail of chemicals being released into the bloodstream by his own body helping to numb the searing agony in his hand.

More shots followed, seeming to mark his own fleeing footsteps.

Then several things happened in close succession that sent Ulysses' world into a whirl.

The first thing he was aware of was the savage snarling of the dog, so close behind them that, his overwrought imagination working overtime, he felt as if the unnatural animal's hot, fetid breath was gusting on the back of his neck.

He heard two more shots. *Five, six.*

He suddenly realised he had been subconsciously counting how many bullets had been fired. And now Nimrod's pistol was empty and Ulysses doubted that he would have any hope of reloading in time.

And then he heard a cry, followed by a sharp, splintering crack, and Nimrod was suddenly no longer gallivanting backwards beside them. His manservant was down, but all Ulysses could do was keep running. He had no choice.

Ulysses did not need his uncanny sixth sense to warn him when the beast was about to strike, as it finally caught up with them. He could hear its slavering, panting snarls, smell its rank breath and the stinking filth of its blood-matted fur.

As the Barghest pounced, Ulysses dropped. He, and the young woman in his arms, had their landing cushioned by a blanket of heather.

A springing ambush that should have knocked the two of them flat on the ground, the dog-beast crushing Ulysses with its massive bulk as it sank its knife-like talons into his spine, instead sent the beast flying over their heads, to land on the uneven ground beyond.

Ulysses' action had been a hastily calculated risk, and it wasn't going to give them much time but hopefully it would be enough.

Snarling in impotent rage, the animal skidded to a halt, arresting its momentum by unsheathing its claws, gouging muddy ruts in the earth as it turned to face them.

The Barghest bared its horribly distended jaws and barked ferociously, only a few feet from them now.

Ulysses' gun barked twice, silencing the monster. He was right; it had been enough time.

But then another, forbidding guttural growl rumbled up from deep inside the dog's ribcage and it was clawing the ground again to gain purchase.

"But I hit it!" Ulysses gasped in dismay and disbelief. "I know I was using my left hand, but I hit it; twice, in the head, from only five feet away. That should have floored it."

Too shocked and stunned to do anything other than stare at the resolutely still standing monster he did not think to raise his gun and try again. Recovering itself, the Barghest began to pace towards them, more warily now, perhaps, but nonetheless its savage bloodlust still driving it towards its goal of their bloody demise.

"Ulysses!" the stricken young woman screamed, as she struggled onto her hands and knees in a futile, yet determined, effort to escape her inevitable end, tears of terror streaming down her cheeks. "Ulysses! Move! We have to get away! Shoot it again!"

Her plaintive, desperate, quavering cry was enough to galvanise Ulysses, and as the beast closed the gap between them, he took aim and fired. Although not enough to halt the monster in its tracks, it was enough to enrage it. The animal leapt again. This time Ulysses was ready for it.

Tugging at the tied lace at his throat with shaking, pain-numbed fingers, Ulysses pulled the cape free and swung it at the Barghest's muzzle, using it like a matador's cloak. The creature baulked, giving Ulysses enough time to scramble to his feet again.

Slowly, backing away from the beast, watching as it worried at the cape – the cloth becoming more and more tangled around its fangs – breathing deeply, trying to slow his racing heartbeat, Ulysses took careful aim once more. He was beginning to doubt that his gun *could* stop the monster – Nimrod's hadn't, nor had the shots he had loosed into the beast so far – but he had little else he could try. His sword-cane was still there, tucked into his belt, but he hadn't even had a chance to draw.

Ulysses knew the rapidly disintegrating cape would only be a temporary distraction, but with every second that passed, Jennifer was able to get a little further away from the savage creature.

One eye still on the enraged monster, the other on Jennifer as she continued to crawl out of reach of the Barghest, Ulysses began to wonder about what had actually happened to his loyal manservant. Was he dead? Was he alive, but terribly injured? Had he somehow managed to escape his encounter with the brute?

And where was Jennifer's terrier, Ambrose?

Ulysses took his eyes from the hulking devil dog and the damsel for only a moment, shooting desperate glances around him at the darkening moor, eyes straining against the failing light. He saw the faint flicker of movement – the white cuff of a shirt waving in the gathering gloom – as his ears picked up the cry of: "Over here, sir!"

Ulysses looked again, not entirely sure he could trust what he had seen the first time. It looked as if half of his manservant was missing; Ulysses couldn't see Nimrod's legs. He looked half buried in the ground, only visible from the waist up. For a split second he wondered if the monster had managed to tear Nimrod in half, but then, if that had been the case, he wouldn't have been in any position to sit up and wave, whilst calling out to his master.

"Quickly, sir. I have an idea."

With one more glance at the Barghest – which was still struggling to free itself from the snare of the cape – Ulysses made a snap decision.

"Nimrod, old chap! I can't tell you how happy I am to see you're still alive!" Ulysses declared, arriving at his companion's side.

"The feeling is mutual, sir. But with all due respect, the pleasantries can wait. I would be most grateful, however, if you could pull me out of this hole."

"Hole?" Ulysses repeated, bewildered, as he offered his manservant his left hand. Nimrod took it gladly and Ulysses heaved him up. As he did so, he saw the mouldering planks half hidden by the growth of unruly grasses.

"Yes, sir. It would appear that in my efforts to escape imminent death at the claws of the beast, I have inadvertently discovered the boarded up entrance to an old mineshaft."

"Have you now?" Ulysses said, a smile creeping across his face in the darkness.

And then, suddenly, there was a way out of their impossible predicament – a faint glimmer of light, no more than a candle-flicker, in the encroaching darkness.

"Are you thinking what I'm thinking."

"I'm way ahead of you, sir."

"Excellent, then let's make some noise."

The two men began hollering and whooping; anything to get the beast's attention.

"Hey! Over here!" Ulysses shouted, waving his hands in the air.

The dog-monster pulled the last shredded remnant of Ulysses' cape from its muzzle – the flesh there criss-crossed with a myriad bloody scratches – and bared its teeth, issuing another menacing challenge, sounding like an angry wolf. The beast looked at Ulysses directly with blood and fury in its eyes.

And yet despite the obvious rage it held in its black heart, just when Ulysses was certain the beast had taken the bait, it turned away from him and, seeing Jennifer still struggling to get away on her hands and knees, for a moment it looked about take its fury out on her.

"Bad dog!" Ulysses shouted, took aim and fired. A chunk of meat flew from the bunching shoulders of the beast in a welter of black blood.

With a snarl the Barghest turned.

"There, that's got your attention again!"

And suddenly it was a bounding blur of darkness as it bore down on Ulysses. There was no way the beast was going to stop now, not until it had torn him limb from limb and left his body as something that was indistinguishable from the offal found at the end of the day on an abattoir floor.

When there was almost no more ground between them, Ulysses saw the creature's muscles bunch as it readied itself to leap, and tensed himself. When it leapt, he dropped.

Only this time the hellhound had learnt from the last time it had been caught out that way. In that split second Ulysses pulled the trigger again. The chamber returned empty.

And then the firearm was knocked from his hand as the beast landed on top of him, the heavy swipe of a paw sending the weapon flying while Ulysses was thrown back onto the ground, the full weight of the creature on top of him forcing the wind from his lungs, the nauseous dead-meat stink of the devil dog's rank breath washing over his face in intolerable waves.

But, even as the monster sent him tumbling backwards, short of the pit shaft, Ulysses boldly grabbed great handfuls of its matted fur, nearly hard enough to pull great clumps of it from the creature's hide.

As he rolled onto his back, with the beast on top of him, those terrible snapping jaws mere inches from his suddenly vulnerable face, he kicked upwards with his feet with all the strength he could muster, even as the breath was violently forced from his lungs.

For a moment something like surprise appeared in the creature's soulless eyes. And then, using its own mass and the momentum of his own fall against it, Ulysses bodily hurled the Barghest over his head. It hit what remained of the boarded-up pit cover and smashed through it as if it were nothing more than plywood.

And then it was gone. All that remained were angry howls and pained yelps, receding into the darkness, accompanied by the occasional scrape of claws, skittering showers of stone and dull thuds.

Ulysses lay where he had fallen, his head hanging over the edge of the pit-shaft, his deerstalker having gone the way of the devil dog – Nimrod on the other side – gasping for breath as he listened to the creature's descent.

And then there was only silence. When at last he felt able to move, broken fingers throbbing with pain, his shoulder feeling nearly as bad, Ulysses cautiously sat up.

"Ulysses!" It was Jennifer, the pale features of her worried face peering at him, ghost-like out of the encroaching dusk. "You're all right. I thought there, for a moment, that..." But she couldn't bring herself to put her imagined horrors into words.

"Yeah, me too," he said, his half-smile turned to a grimace of pain.

"Sir, I would suggest we keep on to Miss Haniver's home, as originally planned. Both of you have injuries that need to be attended to."

"And you, Nimrod?"

Ulysses saw his manservant's usually so rigid aquiline features soften in the presence of an unaccustomed smile at hearing of his master's concern. "There's nothing wrong with me, sir, that a good cup of Earl Grey wouldn't put right."

"Glad to hear it, old boy. Glad to hear it."

Suddenly something bounded into Ulysses' lap, yapping furiously.

"I see you're all right then," he said.

"Ambrose!" Jennifer shrieked in delight. "Come here, you naughty boy. Come here at once!"

Nimrod coughed politely. "I'm sure we don't want to be caught out in the open by the beast again, do we, sir?" he pointed out ominously, Ulysses' body tensing again at the unwelcome thought that the monster might have survived its fall and was even now making its way back to the surface to exact its revenge. "Best to keep moving, just in case."

"Just in case." The echo of Nimrod's words sounded hollow, as the anxiety Ulysses had felt himself, in the face of the monster's attack, returned. "Come on then. You help Miss Haniver and I'll –" He winced again in pain. "I'll do my best to keep up."

IT WAS SO dark now, dusk leading inexorably into night, that the three survivors were nothing more than black paper cut-outs against the horizon-wide blanket of clouds.

He had caught up with them at the same time as the beast. It had been pure luck that the prevailing wind had meant that the creature picked up the scent of the dandy before it had sniffed him out, otherwise he wouldn't have been alive now.

He had wanted to do more to help, dearly wished that there was something he could have done, but he was impotent. He was unarmed and he did not have the obvious physical skills that the other – who had previously been wearing the deerstalker – had. But there had been a moment then, when the monster looked like it was going to turn on the lady, the one he had admired from afar for so many months now, that he had been about to fling himself between the beauty and the beast, ready to sacrifice himself so that she might live. But, thanks to the actions of the other, in the end it hadn't come to that.

At that thought he offered up a prayer to his Lord. Surely it wasn't a sin to sacrifice one's own life for that of another, even if it did mean taking on what was effectively a suicide mission.

But then, of course, it hadn't come to that.

And so he followed them as they continued on their way towards the sanctuary of the house on the crest of the rise, always keeping a respectful distance so that he wouldn't be seen or heard. It wouldn't pay to be seen by them after all. No, not at all.

Making his way onwards, picking his way carefully between hidden sink holes and peaty morasses, he followed them, into the embrace of the forgiving darkness.

CHAPTER THIRTEEN

The Naturalist

THE STURDY FRONT door to the lodge house opened with a groan of protesting hinges and a pale grey, skeletal face appeared out of the semi-darkness of the candle-lit hallway beyond. The old man was completely bald but had apparently tried to make up for his extreme hair loss by growing a bushy white beard on his chin instead.

"Who is it?" the crotchety face demanded. "What do you wan– Oh my god, Jenny!" he suddenly exclaimed, coming to horrified life as his eyes moved from Ulysses' haggard face and that of his weary manservant to the young woman they were supporting between them.

He hurried out, his walking stick clattering to the black and white diamond check tiles of the hall as he crossed the threshold.

"What happened?" he demanded of her, taking her face in his hands, his own visage as white as a sheet. "It's already dark. What have you been doing?"

"I was searching for the beast, Father."

"But out on these moors, with that monster on the loose?"

"That's exactly why, Daddy. That's precisely why I had to go out."

"Sunset came and I began worrying about where you had got to." His tone was chiding, precisely that of a parent punishing a child purely as a result of their own feelings of fear, panic and love.

"I sprained my ankle," Jennifer admitted.

"Where's the dog?" the old man suddenly asked, his over-wrought mind flitting from one thought to the next. "Where's Ambrose?"

At the merest mention of its name, the terrier darted between Ulysses' legs, past the old man and into the warmth of the house.

Ulysses cleared his throat loudly; they needed to get Jennifer inside so that they might examine her ankle more closely. And besides, he felt that he could do with a sit down and a glass of cognac. "Excuse me, sir," he began, "but might we –"

"What are you doing just standing there?" the old man suddenly snapped. "Bring her inside. We need to take a look at that ankle."

With an exasperated *harrumph*, Ulysses helped Jennifer over the doorstep and into the antler-festooned hallway beyond. He noticed that Nimrod wiped his feet on the stiff brush doormat before entering; ever mindful of his place within the social hierarchy.

"Bring her through to the drawing room," the old man instructed, leading them inside the house, one hand on the wall to steady himself. "Make her comfortable. Get her foot up. I'll get some ice from the pantry."

"Your stick, sir," Nimrod said, proffering the handle towards the old man. He took it, barely giving Nimrod a second look.

"Now come on. Chop chop!" he ordered, stopping at the entrance to a corridor.

"Welcome to Hunter's Lodge, gentlemen," Jennifer offered somewhat belatedly, as they entered the warm embrace of the house.

Ulysses followed the old man's pointed directions, passing a dining room to his left, then on through the hall, with the staircase leading to the first floor on the right and a door marked 'LIBRARY' to the left, and finally, through the last door on the left. This led into the drawing room itself, while the old man disappeared along a corridor opposite the dining room his stick *tap-tap*-tapping on the tiles as he went on his way.

On entering the drawing room, Ulysses helped Jennifer onto a sofa facing a roaring fire – a number of logs blazing away within the grate, filling the room with heat and flickering orange light – and made her comfortable. He plumped up a pair of cushions for her to lie against whilst he used another to help him prop up her swollen ankle.

There were two other chairs in the room. The one closest to the fire had a table next to it on which lay a pile of dusty-looking books. The tome on the top of the pile looked to be about botany. Discarded on the rug in front of the chair was a tartan-patterned woollen blanket.

"Your father feels the cold," Ulysses said, as he helped Jennifer remove her walking boots.

"Yes. He's not a well man, hasn't been for a long time."

"I'm sorry to hear that."

He unrolled the long, knee-length sock - revealing the supple, well-toned calf beneath - and Jennifer winced as he pulled it over the bruised and swollen joint. "Yup, it's definitely sprained," he said. "Sorry. Plenty of rest - that's what you need. So, what's the matter with him? Your father, I mean."

"It's not what's the matter," Jennifer tried to explain, "so much as what happened to him."

"Oh?"

Jennifer looked like she was about to say something more but at that moment the old man returned, a bucket of ice and a tea towel in his free hand.

"Here, get that on there. Wrap it up nice and tight too, mind," the girl's father instructed, pointing at his daughter's ankle with his stick.

"Yes, sir," Ulysses replied, unable to negate the sarcastic sneer that entered his voice. He never had responded well to authority, especially when it resulted in someone treating him like an idiot.

Ulysses took the bucket and immediately grimaced in pain as his damaged fingers took the weight. He let go again quickly, the tin bucket dropping to the floor with a clang.

"Can you see to Miss Haniver's leg?" he winced, addressing his manservant. "It's just that I appear to be somewhat incapacitated."

"Of course, sir. You should take a seat yourself. You look as though you could do with a rest."

Ulysses regarded his manservant with unashamed admiration. He had been through just as much as the rest of them as they had fled from the predations of the Ghestdale beast and yet here he was, taking the strain and helping out, carrying on as he would with his usual duties, as if nothing were amiss.

Nimrod was, Ulysses decided, really something else. And he had always been the same, such as when Hercules Quicksilver, Ulysses' father, had been alive.

Not needing to be told twice to take the weight off his feet, Ulysses gratefully collapsed into a chair by the fire. His deerstalker and cape were gone, lost to the moors and the Barghest, but at least that was all that had been taken. Things could have been so much worse.

"So, Jennifer tells me you're a naturalist," Ulysses said, by way of making light conversation.

Hannibal Haniver, his face a wizened mask, but one that still spoke of former glory, looked myopically at Ulysses and then, without saying anything, turned his face to the fire, losing himself in the hypnotic, inconstant flames.

"I've heard your name mentioned before, certainly," Ulysses went on, in an effort to break the uncomfortable silence. He sensed Jennifer tense where she lay on the sofa, now with a cup of hot, sweet tea in her hands, the drink being intended to take away the chill of the moors and the shock that both the accident and the beast had wrought.

Ulysses swirled the cognac in the glass in his hands – a very fine Courvoisier – and then downed the last of it, enjoying the sinus clearing blast of alcoholic vapour as its essence filled his mouth.

"I might have been someone," Haniver replied eventually, with a weary sigh, "once."

"And you still are someone," Jennifer chided him, speaking up in his defence. Ulysses was reminded, however, of the fact that it had not been so long ago that Jennifer had said precisely the same thing of her father. "It's just that my father doesn't enjoy as good health as he once did," she went on.

"She is such a comfort to me, you have no idea," Haniver said. "She is not only my eyes and ears in the world beyond this house. She is so kind and gentle – just like her mother. So beautiful." The old man's eyes hazed over, as if he were looking at something that only he could see, gazing back across the years to a time when he was a younger, stronger man and his wife was still alive.

"Is that her?" Ulysses asked, pointing at a portrait hung above the fireplace.

"That's her," the old man replied wistfully. "So beautiful. I never knew what she saw in an old man like me."

Ulysses studied the painting thoughtfully for a moment. The likeness that Jennifer and her mother shared was clear.

"Yes, I know what you're thinking, and you are right," Haniver suddenly blurted out irascibly. "What is a fool like him doing with a beautiful, young daughter? Well, the truth is, I met Jenny's mother when I was already well on in years, but she made me feel young again. And she gave me some of the happiest years of my life, even though it wasn't to last."

"She died in childbirth," Jennifer said matter-of-factly, gazing into her tea.

"Oh, I'm sorry," Ulysses faltered, feeling that he should say something in acknowledgement of such a personal revelation.

"It's all right, I don't mind talking about it," Jennifer stated. "There are no feelings of guilt there. I do not have any issues to deal with in that regard. You see, I never knew her."

"But you are so like her," her father repeated and Jennifer smiled weakly. The old man turned from the flickering flames in the grate and his memories to Ulysses. "Jennifer is all I have now. I have no career or reputation to speak of, after all. No, she really is all I've got."

"There you go again," Jennifer muttered wearily. "If you would just let me explain..."

"Hush now, Jenny. Quicksilver and his man don't need to learn of all the ins and outs of my shame."

"Your shame? Oh, you're too proud!" Jennifer scolded. "I think they do, Father, because it shouldn't be your shame. We have proof now. You can go back to the Royal Society, as one utterly vindicated!"

"What?" The old man's eyes were suddenly alive with something other than the dancing firelight as he turned to look at his daughter.

"We found it, father!" Jennifer said excitedly, her former fear now replaced by an excited euphoria.

"You found it? The beast itself, not just a sign?" The old man sounded just as excited as his daughter now, and clapped his hands together in delight, his heavily-lined face lighting up with unadulterated glee.

"It was more like it found us," Ulysses added coolly.

"Yes, Daddy, we found it!"

"Oh, my poor Jenny," the old man extolled, looking about to well up with tears. "My poor child. It must have been terrifying for you. You could have been killed! I should never have let you go out on the moor alone."

"I wasn't alone; Ambrose was with me. And besides, I'm not a *child*, Daddy."

"You are!" the old man countered, his rheumy eyes wet with tears. "You're *my* child."

He took out a handkerchief, blew his nose into it, and then looked to his daughter expectantly again, the smile returning to his face.

"But how wonderful for you as well! What was it like?"

"As big as a Shetland pony, covered in a thick, black hide. Half-Rottweiler, half-wolf, half-lion, all nightmare," she gushed excitedly as she described the beast that had tried to kill them all.

"Breath like an unwashed abattoir, claws like kitchen knives," Ulysses put in, remembering the injuries he himself had suffered, "all the wit and charm of a Scotsman."

"So it's *not* just another feral dog, beaten and abused and now living wild on the moors?" Hannibal asked, although, from his tone, it sounded as though he didn't really need to be convinced that Jennifer was telling the truth.

"Oh no, not at all. It's definitely our killer."

"I don't know about you, but I feel like I could eat a horse," Ulysses suddenly threw in, interrupting the conversation. "I've not eaten anything since... since breakfast, in fact!"

Hannibal Haniver broke off from his discussion with his daughter and gave Ulysses a look that revealed exactly how he felt about the dandy and his rude interruptions, regardless of whether he had saved his precious child's life or not.

"I wouldn't mind something to eat myself," Jennifer chipped in, looking at the grandmother clock in the corner of the room. "It's past six o'clock, and I forgot to have that sandwich I made for myself I was so absorbed in my search for the beast."

"Very well, then. But I want to continue this discussion over supper."

"IT'S ONLY COLD cuts, I'm afraid," Hannibal Haniver said as they all took their places at the table in the lodge's dining room. Ulysses helped Jennifer to a place at the table, Nimrod pulling out Haniver's chair for him.

As master of the house, Hannibal Haniver had taken his place at the head of the table while Jennifer sat to his right, where she was able to put her injured leg up on the chair next to her. Ulysses sat opposite. Nimrod had not set a place for himself; Ulysses assumed he would eat by himself in the kitchen after they had finished their meal.

There were another six potential seats at the table, the place opposite Haniver at the foot of the table close to the heavy maroon drapes hiding a set of French windows, firmly shut and locked now against the wind and weather until the spring returned.

The chamber was decorated much like the rest of the house, all oak panelling and dark heavy drapes to keep out the coming winter chill, over-filled with heavy pieces of furniture, making the room appear even darker and more cramped than it really was.

"I would have asked Jennifer to prepare something for us," good manners dictating that the host apologise for any failings in his ability to cater for his dinner guest, "but, under the circumstances... Anyway, I can see your batman has managed to rustle something up," he went on, surveying the epicurean feast that awaited them.

There were slices of ham, tongue and corned beef, all laid out immaculately on china platters, a bowl of pickled onions, a cheese still in its rind and a radish salad.

"Only cold cuts eh, Haniver? Then I'd like to see what Christmas dinner's like at Hunter's Lodge."

"Your man," Hannibal said under his breath, towards Ulysses, "is he, quite, well, you know."

"Oh, absolutely," Ulysses said with a smile at the disparaging expression the older man offered him in response.

Nimrod, wearing a frilly pink pinny over his waistcoat, having dispensed with his coat and butler's tails, placed a jar of piccalilli on a mat in front of Haniver.

"Suits you, old man," Ulysses said, nodding at his valet. "Pink."

Nimrod didn't bat an eyelid. "Thank you, sir. I like to think that it brings out the blue of my eyes," he said, as poker-faced as ever.

"So, Haniver, who usually keeps house for you?"

"A woman from Stainsacre, a village on the edge of the moor, a Mrs Pritchard. I would have got her to concoct us something – cook us one of her venison pies or prepare a pan of her legendary Scotch broth – but her son came to collect her in that infernal jalopy of his," he said as an aside to Jennifer, "before dusk. You know what people are like since the killings began and the Press started their scaremongering. No-one wants to find themselves caught out on the moors after dark."

"Well you can add before dark as well now, in light of our little run in with your phantom hound."

"Oh, it's no phantom, Quicksilver, I can assure you of that," the naturalist said vehemently.

"I know. I can vouch for that fact myself," Ulysses pointed out, riled by the old man's defensive attack. "I only meant that the legend of the Barghest has been perpetuated for centuries and what I saw on the moors today looked nothing like the product of any natural birth."

"What are you saying, sir?" the curmudgeonly Haniver challenged. Before Ulysses had a chance to explain himself, the old man turned to the girl again. "Is that right, Jennifer?"

"Well, Daddy, it was getting dark and we were hardly in the best position to see, but the creature was certainly unlike any dog that I have ever seen before, or any wolf for that matter."

"How do you mean? In what way was it different?"

Jennifer put down her knife and fork and thought for a moment. "In that its various body parts didn't seem to fit together properly, quite as they should, in that... I know this is going to sound ridiculous, but in that it appeared cobbled together. In that it was greater than the sum of its parts."

"Precisely!" Ulysses crowed triumphantly.

"What are you getting at, Mr Quicksilver?"

"Jennifer's just told you! It was greater than the sum of its parts."

"I'm sorry, I don't follow you."

"But, that aside, what I want to know is where did it come from? And why now?"

"What are you saying, Ulysses?"

All eyes were on Ulysses now.

"When did the first death occur?"

"The first Barghest killing, you mean?" Haniver asked.

"Yes," Ulysses nodded.

"Back in September," Jennifer said, "a rambler, not far from here in fact, up on Fencher's Tor, at the edge of the Umbridge estate."

"Not Umbridge as in Josiah Umbridge, famous industrialist who's dropped out of the public eye due to poor health?"

"That's right." The old man was a picture of bewilderment.

"And yet the legend of the Barghest has been around for centuries, hasn't it?"

"There have been reported sightings from as far back as the twelfth century," Haniver proffered the information from his obviously encyclopaedic knowledge of the legend.

"But these deaths are the first that can be properly tied to the beast in, what, a hundred years?"

"There was a report from the seventeenth century that a farm worker witnessed the Barghest carry off a woman accused of witchcraft after it was said she had poisoned her husband."

"But the first substantiated report of a death to occur in this century happened two months or so ago?"

"What are you getting at, Mr Quicksilver?"

"What was it you said just now, Jennifer, about the beast?"

"I think I said that it looked like it had been cobbled together."

"Precisely!" Ulysses put down his knife and fork and, resting his elbows on the starched white tablecloth, gently cupped his injured right hand in his left. "What do you know of the Whitby Mermaid?"

Hannibal Haniver grunted in annoyance. "Is there any danger of you actually giving us a simple answer to a simple question? First we're talking about the Black Dog of Beast Cliff and now you've thrown mermaids into the equation."

"If I might beg your indulgence for a moment? The Whitby Mermaid – have you heard of it?"

"But of course, this isn't the arse end of beyond, you know. I do read *The Times*. And of course it was reported in the local paper – huge furore. I would have liked to have looked into that one more closely myself, but that scoundrel Cruikshank saw to it that the thing was whisked away to London before myself, or Jennifer – or anyone else for that matter – could take a closer look. And now the damn thing's been stolen, hasn't it?" A spark of excitement appeared in the old man's eyes again. "Have you seen it, Quicksilver?"

"Only a photograph. Not in the flesh, as it were. I would have liked to though. For a start it might have made my current investigation a little more straightforward. But I've seen enough to know it's a fake."

"Your investigation?" Jennifer asked.

"Yes, Quicksilver, you haven't told us what brings you to Ghestdale," Haniver said, almost accusingly.

"And you haven't told me why a leader in his field, like yourself, is living as a recluse at the edge of these godforsaken moors."

"The impudent cheek. I'll have you know that this is God's own county!"

"My apologies," Ulysses said hastily, making an instant retraction.

"I find that this is the perfect environment in which to pursue my studies."

"Would that be your studies in natural history or cryptozoology?"

"Mr Quicksilver! I will not be made a mockery of in my own home!" the old man fumed, slamming a fist down on the table. "I am going to have to ask you to leave!"

"Daddy," Jennifer said, stepping in. "I do not believe that Ulysses is trying to mock you."

"No, not at all, sir," Ulysses backed her up, trying to sound as sincere as possible. "Considering how events have escalated recently, I really would appreciate your input in this matter. As you will know from reading *The Times*, the Whitby mermaid was stolen, but what you probably don't know is that it was stolen to order, and sent back to Whitby."

"Do you know *who* it was sent to?" The old man was intrigued now.

"Only that it was stolen on the orders of one Mr Bellerophon."

"Bellerophon? I've never heard of anyone by that name living in these parts."

"No, and I wouldn't have expected you to."

"But back to the mermaid; it was obviously a fake," Haniver said. "You could just about see the stitch marks in the photograph."

"But who's to say that it wasn't stitched together while it was still alive." Ulysses smiled wryly.

"Are you saying that it was a vivisect?" Haniver blustered in wondrous disbelief.

"Are you serious, Ulysses?" Jennifer asked, sounding just as astonished.

"Like the Barghest hound."

For a moment everyone around the table was silent; only the chink of silverware on the finest bone china disturbed the eerily tense atmosphere, as Ulysses dissected a slice of ham on his plate.

"You speak of such things as if you have encountered them before," Haniver pointed out. "Have you seen something like this before, Quicksilver?"

"Yes, actually I have."

The stunned silence returned.

With a deafening crash of breaking glass, the French windows exploded into the room as something huge and terrible hurtled through them, tearing the heavy drapes from their curtain pole to trail the thick velvet hangings.

Shards of broken glass whickered through the air like a crystalline hailstorm as the beast landed in the centre of the table, its varnished surface splintering under its weight.

Jennifer screamed.

The beast roared.

And Ulysses Quicksilver stared death in the face.

CHAPTER FOURTEEN

Red in Tooth and Claw

THE BEAST'S ROAR silenced the screaming Jennifer. Struggling to know what else to do she pushed herself back into her chair, as if somehow that would save her from the slavering jaws and razor talons of the monster.

For a moment the Barghest simply sat there, not looking at any of them. Its nose in the air, the grossly malformed hound sniffed sharply several times while all those present in the room could do was watch in stunned horror.

The monster must have found a way out of the jet mine, Ulysses thought, climbing back above ground before hunting them to the house.

In the brightly-lit dining room, with the beast mere inches from his face again, Ulysses saw the monster clearly for the first time as it squatted there in the centre of the table, panting heavily. The room filled with the stink of its steaming body, its filth-matted hide, a stomach-turning blend of wet dog and spoiled meat.

In that same instant, Ulysses' over-wrought mind took in every hideous detail. The creature's short black pelt glistened wetly in the suffused candle-light, the bristles of its fur standing on end. Ulysses fancied he could see every one of its powerful muscles as they slid and bunched beneath the scabrous skin of its hide.

Up close he could also make out every one of the injuries it had already sustained. There were grazes and lacerations acquired, no doubt, when it fell into the mine shaft. In fact, the creature's right eye had been practically gouged out, no doubt by some outcropping rock. Cuts flecked its shoulders, forelimbs and flanks. Some still had diamond-sharp splinters of glass embedded within them. The beast's blood mixed with the mud its paws had smeared over the tablecloth.

And then there were the gunshot wounds. Ulysses could see the hole he had managed to blast in its shoulder, and one ear was now a ragged mess thanks to where another shot had pulverised half of it. Both he and Nimrod had actually hit the thing then – he had been beginning to wonder if they really had, seeing it there in front of him now – but none of their shots had been killing shots. The beast's resilience and stamina must be incredible, practically any of the other shots would have been enough to floor a lesser animal.

It was bold too, in a way that other dogs weren't. Not even a wolf would have thrown itself through a set of French windows to get at its prey. It must have followed their scent to the house and then, attracted to the noise they had made during dinner, it knew where to attack. But now Ulysses was almost certain that the Barghest was looking for one person in particular. And then he saw the dull metal box sunk into the flesh at the base of its skull, and that was enough to shock him into action: he had seen such a thing before.

He lunged for the carving knife beside the ham, even as the dog turned.

"Get out of here!" he yelled as he slashed at the dog's debrided snout, cutting through the string of flesh that separated its nostrils. Thank goodness the Hanivers' housekeeper liked to keep the knives sharp.

A combination of his natural instinct for survival and a greatly developed subconscious prescience, sent Ulysses leaping from his chair. Spinning round, he grabbed the chair in time to use it to shield himself from the Barghest's attack when it came a split second later.

The creature struck out with a massive paw, claws tearing through the upholstered chair as though it were matchwood. Ulysses' shield was gone, utterly destroyed, having only bought him one second more. Backed up against a heavy sideboard, with two-hundred and fifty pounds of killer dog bearing down on him, looking like it was ready to drive him through the wall, Ulysses tightened his grip on the carving knife. If only he had kept his sword-cane with him, rather than leaving it in the drawing room along with his jacket.

And then Nimrod was at the door, as Hannibal Haniver and his daughter both made for the way out, Jennifer sobbing in pain and fear as she was forced to put weight on her wrecked ankle. Still in his pink pinny and shirt sleeves, Nimrod assumed a marksman's stance, a fresh load in his pistol. The shot came sharp and loud, like a thunderclap in the close confines of the dining-room. It hit the creature's grasping forelimb and punched clean through flesh and bone. The Barghest gave up a surprisingly shrill yelp of pain.

Ulysses suddenly felt very cold, but it wasn't just down to the fact that the creature's destructive entrance had brought the cold night in after it.

The creature snarled and lunged at Nimrod from its perch on the table, muscles shifting as it lashed out at the butler. The swipe knocked the gun from Nimrod's hands, forcing him back towards the door, as Jennifer and her father ducked through it behind him.

Ulysses' manservant had probably just saved his life for the umpteenth time, but in doing so had now brought the monster's ire upon himself. If he didn't do something quickly he had no doubt that Nimrod was going to die.

Ulysses felt impotent against the beast. He had no gun, no sword and no chance of overcoming the beast for as long as he remained trapped in the dining room. He was up against an enemy that could not be placated, that could not be reasoned with and that would not stop, or so it seemed – no matter what they threw at it – until either it or they were dead, and right now, Ulysses didn't fancy their chances much.

But in the height of adrenalin-fuelled desperation, instinct took over.

Ulysses grabbed a chair. Raising it in front of him, as might a lion tamer, with a roar of his own, putting all his weight behind the thrust he pushed forwards.

The chair connected with the side of the monster's over-sized head, clubbing it violently sideways. For a moment the beast was caught off balance and looked like it might slip off the edge of the table. Then it recovered and lunged again, making a swipe for the chair. But Ulysses was already moving for the door, after the retreating Nimrod, letting go of the chair as the monster's jaws shattered it.

Nimrod was safely out of the room and Ulysses was now moving to the open doorway himself.

He felt the flash of prescience even as Nimrod gave a shouted "Sir!" Both told him that there wasn't a hope of him making the door before the beast clawed him to the floor.

He stepped swiftly sideways. The fireplace was next to him, the poker that he himself had used to stoke it before dinner, still protruding from amid the white-hot coals. Ulysses' right hand closed around the hot metal, a welter of scalding pain flared across his palm to join with the breath-catching agony of his broken fingers. At this rate they were never going to heal!

Adrenalin and an instinct for self-preservation helping him to put the pain aside, Ulysses swung the smoking tip of the poker in an arc, smacking the snapping Barghest across the end of its muzzle. The creature gave a piercing scream like a gin-trapped wolf and recoiled, the stink of scorched fur causing Ulysses to do the same, his nose wrinkled in disgust.

And that was enough for him to cover the last few feet left between him and the dining room door, throw himself through, and slam it behind him. He heard the latch bolt catch in the lock plate.

Three ashen faces and sets of anxious eyes stared into his.

With a crash the door shook in its frame as the beast slammed into it from the other side, panels splintering under the force of the impact.

"Move!" Ulysses shouted.

"Where to?" Hannibal Haniver spluttered.

"The kitchen!" Jennifer shouted, already beginning to move herself.

The old man said something but his words were drowned out by the savage barking of the dog behind them and the cruel sound of splintering wood as the Barghest demolished the dining-room door.

With Jennifer leading the way, the four of them stumbled, limped and ran for the kitchen passageway. The creature lunged through the shredded door panels, snagging the tail-end of Ulysses' waistcoat with a sickle-blade claw. Jaws snapping, it came no closer, its great bulk wedged between the ruptured boards.

Tearing free of its grasping paw, Ulysses herded the rest of them into the passageway. He knew that they had only been granted a moment's grace; in no time at all the Barghest would be upon them.

"Come on!" he urged. "We can't stop!"

Old man Haniver was gasping for breath as he managed something close to a run along the narrow tiled passageway. Ulysses wondered how Haniver's ill-health manifested itself. How was the old man's heart, say? He didn't want him dropping dead of a heart attack before he'd had a chance to bring the devil-dog to heel.

Then the animal was through; Ulysses heard the wooden tearing of the door as it came apart, and then the scrabbling of clawed feet on smooth tiles that paved the way to the kitchen.

Re-doubling his own efforts, he spurred them all onwards.

Ulysses was dimly aware of passing a darkened adjoining passageway to the right that ended at a descending staircase, and then he was entering the lamp-lit brightness of an immaculately-kept kitchen.

As he turned to close the door behind him he was faced by the appalling aspect of the brutally deformed Barghest as it bounded down the passageway towards him, its flanks scraping against the walls either side of the corridor as it closed the gap between them.

Ulysses slammed the kitchen door shut and, keeping his hands pressed against the wood, braced his body against it. The Barghest slammed into the door and Ulysses was pushed backwards several inches as the wood around the lock splintered.

Looking down he saw the tips of the predator's tusk-like teeth appear through the gap as the dog pushed against the door. Ulysses kicked out viciously, catching the dog squarely on the nose. There was a yelp of pain which transformed into a snarl of snapping rage. The dog pulled back, Ulysses assumed in readiness to ram the door again.

Desperate eyes scanned the kitchen for some means of barricading the door, and fell upon the tall wooden dresser to his left.

"Quick, Nimrod, the dresser." But his quick-thinking manservant already had his shoulder against the other end of the heavy piece of kitchen furniture, as the dog's second charge met with the sundered door.

With an agonisingly-shrill screech, like fingernails scraping across a blackboard, the dresser shifted, crockery shaken loose from its shelves crashing down onto the terracotta tiles of the kitchen floor, as Nimrod put all his weight behind it. The sliding dresser hit the beast squarely on the muzzle as it tried to push itself further through the widening gap. There was a meaty tearing sound, another protest of pain, and the muzzle was pulled back again, the solid piece of furniture sliding into place across the door, barricading them all inside.

Ulysses took in the strained, uncertain expressions of the others. But there was more to be read in their faces and the way they held themselves than just the heightened emotions they were feeling at present. He could see that Jennifer was in pain, the extra strain she was putting on her ankle obviously taking its toll and giving her a sickening pallor. If Jennifer looked like she was suffering, the old man looked much worse.

Even Nimrod was no longer his usual self, his eyes sunken within dark rings of shadow.

"Now what?" Jennifer asked, her voice almost a shout as the dog crashed against the kitchen door again, sending more of the teetering crockery on the dresser crashing to the floor.

His thoughts awhirl, Ulysses took a moment to consider their options.

"You don't know, do you?" the old man blustered, his words punctuated by great wheezing gasps.

Ignoring Hannibal Haniver, Ulysses focused all of his attention on Jennifer, who was propping herself up against the cold, porcelain basin of the kitchen sink.

"Is there another way out of here? Another door leading outside?"

"No," she replied, her voice betraying that she was on the verge of hysteria.

"We're trapped in here, aren't we?" the old man challenged. Part of Ulysses' brain understood that Hannibal Haniver's anger was born of fear and incomprehension, faced with such a dire predicament, but it didn't make him any easier to put up with.

There was another crash from behind the rocking dresser.

"Think, Jennifer," he pressed, "is there any other way out?"

"There's the scullery window, but that's probably too small." And then enlightenment dawned across her face, and the effect was like the sun appearing from behind the clouds on a rainy day. "But there are the back stairs!"

"That'll do," Ulysses said with relief, a nervous grin taking shape upon his own haggard features. "How do I get to them?"

"Through there," Jennifer pointed to a door on the other side of the kitchen.

"Right, that dresser's not going to hold forever, but just for now I want you to wait here," he commanded. "I'll be as quick as I can."

"What do you plan to do, sir?"

"Plan?" Ulysses laughed. "You know me, Nimrod! Since when did I ever have a plan?"

Then he saw the crestfallen expression on the face of Hannibal Haniver and saw the glimmer of hope fade from Jennifer's eyes and her face sagged in abject despair.

"I'm kidding! I'm kidding," he said, desperately wishing he could retract his last flippant statement. "I'm going to create a distraction."

He turned to Nimrod, meeting the butler's piercing sapphire stare. "As soon as you can get these two somewhere safe." He looked back at Jennifer. "We passed the stairs to a cellar on the way to the kitchen."

"Then what, sir?"

"Well then I'd appreciate it if you could see to giving me a hand with this wayward hound of ours."

"Very good, sir."

Ulysses turned and made for the door.

"Good luck, Ulysses," Jennifer said, the look in her eyes a confused mixture of anxiety, affection and even adoration.

"Yes, good luck, Quicksilver," Hannibal Haniver added.

Once through the door Ulysses entered a servant's passageway, finding the twisting back stairs directly in front of him.

He could still hear the shuddering crashes of the relentless beast throwing itself at the barricaded kitchen door as he made his way up to the first floor of the house. At the top of the stairs a short landing led to a narrow door which, in turn, led into an empty bedroom. Through that he entered a carpeted, oak-panelled passageway that ran past another bedroom, down a couple of steps and finally turned right onto the main landing, at the top of the central staircase of Hunter's Lodge. From here he could hear the scrabbling of the monster's claws tearing up the tiles of the scullery passageway as it tried to gain purchase, so that it might push its way through the kitchen door at last.

And as he had made his way through the house he had desperately tried to formulate some sort of a plan. If he could get back down the main stairs while the dog was still distracted, he could retrieve his sword-cane from where he had left it in the drawing-room and then at least he would have a fighting chance against the beast. Perhaps he could hamstring the thing before plunging his blade into the base of its skull.

He didn't think the beast's heightened sense of smell would detect that he had left the kitchen and was now upstairs, not after the mess he had made of its nose. Probably the only thing the creature could smell now was its own blood.

His heart in his mouth, he took his first step down the staircase. The stair cried out like a creaking coffin lid as he put his weight onto his leading foot, and he froze. Surely the monster would have heard that.

Then he heard the cacophonous crash of the dresser finally toppling over, every last piece of crockery still stored inside smashing to smithereens upon the hard floor of the kitchen. Ulysses realised that if he didn't do something fast, Nimrod and the others would all soon be dead.

"Here doggy-doggy!" he bellowed at the top of his voice.

In the silence that followed, all he could hear was the solemn ticking of the grandfather clock in the hallway below, and the dub-dub dub-dub of his pulse, right at the centre of his head.

And then he heard the savage, wolfish snarling of the Barghest, the scrape of talons clawing up the floorboards of the hall below and his blood turned to ice in his veins.

For a moment he found himself frozen to the spot, two million years of evolution unable to erase the memory that for much of that time man had been the prey and not the hunter.

What have I done? he wondered. The monster was coming for him and he had nothing to defend himself with. He had hoped to have had enough time to descend the staircase, at least retrieve his sword-cane from the drawing room before he had to face the beast again.

Another instinct taking over now, he went for his gun. But it was only when his aching fingers found nothing there in the holster under his arm that he remembered how he had lost it during his first run-in with the beast-dog.

And then it was there, at the bottom of the stairs, ruined muzzle sniffing the air, those massively mishapen jaws now missing more than just a couple of fangs. A moment later it caught sight of Ulysses, the darkly burning pin-pricks of its eyes narrowing with cold animal hatred.

His petrified muscles miraculously unfreezing, Ulysses didn't hang around to find out what the monster would do next. Turning, he threw himself through the door nearest to him, finding himself inside a bedroom – quite possibly Hannibal Haniver's by the look of things. He slammed the door shut behind him, knowing that it would only slow the beast for a second.

Eyes scanning the room for anything that he could turn into a weapon, Ulysses took note of a large, heavy-looking lamp on a bedside table, and even the table itself.

And all the time, at the back of his mind, bubbling away beneath his surface thoughts, he found himself wondering whether Jennifer was all right, and whether Nimrod was leading the girl and her curmudgeonly father to safety in the cellars beneath the house.

"I DON'T BELIEVE it!" the old man fumed as he took in the state of his kitchen, the terracotta tiles buried beneath a porcelain-white snowfall of broken china shards. "This is my home. My *home*!"

"Quickly, sir!" Nimrod hissed. "We have to go now!"

"Daddy, come on!" Jennifer urged, her voice strained with emotion, her eyes red from crying.

Picking his way over the carpet of broken pottery, taking care not to crunch any of it beneath the soles of his shoes – keen not to do anything to attract the monster's attention again – Nimrod led the naturalist and his daughter out of the kitchen, into the passageway beyond, and down to the cellars.

"I mean I've been hunting the thing my whole life and now that pompous idiot has brought it *here*, it's destroying my home! God damn it, its ruining everything!" old man Haniver went on, incensed.

"Hush, father!" Jennifer whimpered, from fear of the monster coming after them again, rather than from the pain of her ankle.

A loud crash reverberated through the house from the floor above: the monster must be hunting his master now, Nimrod considered, which would hopefully give him enough time to discharge his duties towards the old man and his daughter.

Leading the way, Nimrod helped Miss Haniver down the steps to the cellar. At the foot of the stairs she scrabbled with the key that had been left in the lock and opened the door.

"Mind that last step, sir," he said, turning to help the girl's father and then saying nothing more as he realised the old man was no longer with them.

"Mr Haniver, sir!" Nimrod called back up the stairs as loudly as he dared.

"Daddy?" Miss Haniver called out, willing her worst fears to be confounded. "Daddy!"

"Miss Haniver," Nimrod said, his voice stern, his tone commanding, "lock yourself in the cellar and wait for me there. I will not be long."

Jennifer said nothing, the tears running freely now down her cheeks and splashing onto the dusty flags at her feet as she slumped awkwardly against the cold bricks of the wall.

What does the old man think he's doing? Nimrod fretted, his long legs taking the cellar steps two at a time, as he chased back up them after the old man.

ULYSSES BURST OUT of the bathroom and back onto the landing. He could hear the monster's claws scrabbling against the enamelled sides of the bathtub, punctuated by a guttural growling as it tried to extricate itself from the shower curtain.

And then he was at the top of the stairs, staring down the twin barrels of a rifle, held in the hands of a shaking Hannibal Haniver. Ulysses had to grab the roundel at the end of the banister to stop himself careering into the old man and, as a result, lost his footing, his legs sliding out from under him, slipping on the carpeted stair. Falling heavily, he bumped down the first turn of the stairs on his arse towards the gun-toting naturalist.

Feeling a rising sense of panic, Ulysses heard the crash of the bathroom door flying open, the angry shout of the old man and the throaty bellow of the beast.

Lying almost on his back, Ulysses saw the monstrous shape of the Barghest as it leapt over him. He heard the retort of the rifle firing and, ears ringing, closed his eyes against the shower of dust and plaster that fell from the ceiling where the shotgun shells had struck.

The Barghest struck the old man with such force that he bounced off the wall and smashed through the banisters, plunging to the hallway below.

Ulysses got to his feet, stumbling down the stairs in horror as he saw how the old man had landed, limp as a discarded doll, the hunched black form of the devil dog now astride him.

"Get off him! Leave him alone!" Ulysses screamed at the beast, descending the stairs at a run. Its huge, misshapen head jerked from side to side as it burrowed into the old man's meagre flesh.

Pulling a broken baluster from the ruined staircase, Ulysses hurled it at the animal.

"Bad dog!"

The splintered spar struck the monster's flank, finding an open wound there, and remained lodged in the creature's flesh. It was enough to turn the monster's attention back to Ulysses.

Leaving the red ruin of the old man, the Barghest paced its way to the foot of the stairs and began to climb, Hannibal Haniver's blood spraying from its gore-drenched muzzle as it barked and snapped at the dandy hastily retreating back up the stairs.

And then, when it felt as though there was nowhere left to run, Ulysses heard the shout, "Sir!" and glanced back down to the hallway in time to see Nimrod throw something up to him.

The bloodstone-tipped cane spun through the air and over the banisters. Ulysses reached out an arm and plucked it from the air. Grabbing the black wood shaft of the cane with his left hand, he pulled the rapier blade free of its scabbard as the monster leapt.

In the unnatural stillness that followed Ulysses heard an audible pop and blinked against the wet spray that spurted into his face. He felt the blade meet resistance but it held firm. The dead weight of the monster fell on top of him, outstretched claws raking the wood-panelling behind him, tearing great slivers of veneer from the wall.

Ulysses found himself sitting on the stairs, back pressed up against the wall, gasping for air, all two-hundred and fifty pounds of muscle and evil intent crushing his body below the waist.

And there the monster remained, the stink of its foulness strong in Ulysses' nostrils. It died not with a roar or a whimper but with a last gust of bloody breath and with Ulysses' blade sunk up to the hilt in its one remaining eye.

An awareness of his surroundings returned, as if someone had turned up the volume on a radio set and he heard Jennifer's great gulping sobs of shock and grief on seeing the savaged corpse of her father and Nimrod, unable to hide the emotion from his voice himself now, say: "Sir, are you all right?"

And then he felt tears of relief, hot and uncontrollable, welling up in his eyes and running down his cheeks, and when he could speak again he said simply: "Get me out from under here, would you? I'm a little stuck."

CHAPTER FIFTEEN

A Death in the Family

"I MEAN LOOK at it, Nimrod," the dandy said, prodding at the flopping jaw of the dead beast, stretched out on the dining table, with the same silvered serving tongs his manservant had used to serve supper only an hour before. "Have you ever seen anything like it?"

"No, sir. Not since our sojourn at the Marianas Base."

"Precisely what I was thinking," Ulysses said, knocking back the rest of the brandy he held in his other hand, unable to take his eyes from the monstrosity in front of them.

It had taken no small effort to get the cooling carcass of the beast back into the dining room and up onto the table. First they had had to shift the thing from where it had collapsed on top of Ulysses. Between himself and Nimrod they had finally managed to roll the monster off Ulysses' legs and through the broken banisters, letting it fall, loose-limbed, onto the floor of the hallway below.

The thud of meat and muscle hitting the floor had startled the weeping girl, kneeling beside her father's lifeless body, his blood-soaked head in her lap, her freely-running tears splashing onto his gore-reddened face. From the expression on the old man's face, if it hadn't been for the torn out larynx and the opened ribcage, Ulysses could have almost believed that he was just sleeping.

Easing himself up from where he had lain squashed under the bulk of the beast, Ulysses descended the stairs to stand at Jennifer's side. Saying nothing he put a comforting hand on her shoulder. Welcoming contact with another human being, she grasped his hand tightly in hers and he was able to help her to her feet.

Guiding her away from the gutted carcass of her father he half-carried her up the stairs, despite feeling exhausted himself, and escorted her to her room. There were more gasps of horror when she saw first-hand the destruction the monster had wrought to her father's chambers in pursuit of Ulysses.

Leaving her sobbing quietly in her bed, the covers pulled up over her still clothed form, he returned to where he had left Nimrod to clear up the mess downstairs.

The ever-reliable Nimrod had already moved Hannibal Haniver's body to the scullery passageway, but not before wrapping it in one of the destroyed dining-room drapes, as much as to hold it together as to not cause any further distress to the dead man's already distraught daughter.

It took both of them to move the body of the dog-beast into the dining-room and onto the table, so that Ulysses might have a closer look at it, in the hope of finding some clues as to the beast's origins. Someone had been trying to kill one of them – but whether the intended victim had been himself or Jenny, or even the old man, he wasn't sure – and he needed to know, in case the killer tried again. Perhaps the beast's handler – and he was sure that it had a handler – had wanted all of them dead.

As Ulysses poured himself the first of several glasses of cognac, and prepared to make his cursory examination of the Barghest's corpse, Nimrod set about mopping the old man's blood from the floor and walls of the hall.

Ulysses refilled his glass sloppily from the bottle on the sideboard next to him and took another swig.

"Sure I can't get you one?" Ulysses asked, proffering the glass to his manservant.

"No thank you, sir. Not while I'm on duty."

Something of Nimrod's indefatigable demeanour had returned, despite the fact that for the last half an hour he had been clearing corpses and mopping up blood. It was just business as usual as far as his butler was concerned.

"On duty? You're never *off* duty," Ulysses said.

He found the alcohol helped; it was relaxing him after his frantic fight with the Barghest, and the fumes of the cognac swirling in the glass provided the added benefit of going some way to mask the excremental stench of the beast itself.

"So, this is a vivisect too," Nimrod said, "like the missing mermaid?"

"I think so," Ulysses replied, wiping splashes of brandy from his chin with the back of his hand. His broken fingers were just a dull ache now; for the time being residual adrenalin in his system and alcohol were having a pain-numbing effect. "I mean there's no way this thing's natural. So far I haven't found any obvious signs of suturing, where one body part has been grafted onto another, but then we have no idea how long ago it was that this thing left the operating table."

"And I suppose the body's rather badly damaged," Nimrod pointed out, looking down his nose at the thing on the table.

"There is that," Ulysses agreed. "But you only have to look at the thing to see that it wasn't born so much as made. Those are never a dog's jaws. They're not even those of a wolf. They look like they should belong to something the size of a big cat, a tiger or a lion. Its skin doesn't even fit over the skeletal structure beneath. And then there are the claws."

"And the creature's musculature," Nimrod added as he ran an appraising eye over the dead brute. "It definitely looks like it's been added to, particularly around the shoulders."

"To support the extra weight that's been added to its skull," Ulysses conjectured. "It would have helped the beast climb out of that mineshaft we dropped it into no doubt."

"And would go some way to explaining how it seemed to shrug off the damage caused by our shots," Nimrod mused.

"Yes, that and an enlarged medulla oblongata, no doubt. I bet if we cut it open we'd find its bones are thicker than they should be, perhaps even reinforced with metal rods."

Ulysses stared into the ruined eyes of the creature, one practically gouged out, the other popped by the tip of his own rapier blade. His gaze moved from the creature's ugly bifurcated face to the top of its thickened skull to the hunched, muscle-bound shoulders, slashed and grazed, and with pieces missing from the flesh there.

He gave the small metal box sunk into the thick flesh at the base of the creature's skull a tap with the serving tongs. "What do you make of that, Nimrod? Look familiar, does it?"

Before Nimrod could offer a reply, Ulysses turned to face the ruined doorway of the dining room, the unmistakeable sensation of someone watching him causing the hairs on the back of his neck to stand on end.

Jennifer Haniver stood there, leaning against the ruptured wood, her grime-smeared face streaked with tears, her blouse red with her father's blood, the eyes of both Ulysses and his manservant heavy upon her.

"Jenny," Ulysses said, somewhat surprised to see the wretched girl again so soon. "You should be resting."

"No," she said firmly, in a voice that brooked no discussion. "I want to know what killed him – what killed my father. I need to... understand why he died." There were no tears, no wailing, no hysterical recriminations or shrieks of protest, just a resolute determination to discover some answers.

Ulysses saw the implacable look in her eyes as she kept them locked firmly on the creature in front of her. "So be it," he said, equally determined, equally resolute.

"What is it?" she demanded. "The Barghest, I mean. What is it really?"

"It's man-made, the work of a skilled vivisectionist," Ulysses explained.

"Where did it come from?" was her next straightforward question. "Who was responsible for its ungodly creation," she hissed, her voice replete with quiet rage.

"You mean, what leads do we have as to who set this thing on us?"

"I think you mean on *me*, Ulysses," Jennifer corrected him coldly.

"We can't be certain which of us the dog was after, but I'm convinced that it was set on us, to hunt one of us down and get us out of the way."

"But I was the one who was out on the moors searching for it and knowing what sort of reputation my father has..." – she broke off, catching herself – "my father *had*, I wouldn't be surprised if people in certain quarters would have known that too. He never made a secret of his quest to uncover the truth, even though it forced his retirement to this godforsaken place!"

"Well, let's just say that I had been making enquiries of my own, regarding the missing mermaid, that were probably just as poorly received in those same quarters."

"Then what of the Barghest's other victims, sir? The ones whose deaths were reported in the local press?" Nimrod asked, challenging Ulysses' hypothesis, as only one completely loyal to his master could. "Were they all hunted down as part of some nefarious master-plan?"

Ulysses was quiet for a moment, another swig of the honey-coloured alcohol helping lubricate the grinding gears relentlessly turning his thoughts over inside his head.

"I wouldn't be surprised that if Allardyce and his cronies had half a mind to look beyond the obvious they would find something connecting them all. Remind me to look into it when we get back to the guest house will you, old boy?"

"As you wish, sir."

Ulysses looked from his manservant to the dog's carcass and then back again at Nimrod. "You think I'm looking for Machiavellian machinations where there are none?"

"Not at all, sir, I was merely playing devil's advocate. Is it not possible that all of the beast's victims have merely been the terribly unlucky?"

"Maybe so, in the case of the others, but not tonight. I don't believe the beast would have gone to all the trouble off tracking us here simply for revenge. An animal that had already survived a beating like the one we dealt out would have gone back to its lair whimpering, with its tail between its legs, not tracked us for miles across Ghestdale to then leap through a plate glass window to teach us a lesson!

"No, the Barghest was merely a puppet; there's someone pulling the strings, someone behind the scenes," he said, his eyes returning to the metal box clamped to the back of its neck.

"Besides there was someone who knew where we would be this afternoon as well, Nimrod, someone other than Inspector Maurice Allardyce of Scotland Yard and the North Yorkshire constabulary."

"I was just thinking the same thing myself, sir."

"Who? Who knew?" Jennifer said.

"A man called Rudge. We ran into him whilst pursuing our investigations down in the town. In fact, now I come to think of it, he made his entrance as I was asking a barkeep if he knew the name Bellerophon."

"Rudge?" Jennifer said, surprise raising her voice an octave.

"You know him?"

"Tall as he is broad? Built like a brick... well, you know how that saying goes."

"You *do* know him then!"

"Oh yes, I know him. I suppose you could describe him as a nasty piece of work, a cruel man. No time or regard for his animals, let alone his fellow man."

Nimrod gave Ulysses a look heavy with meaning.

"Really? He was really turning on the charm when he spoke to us then."

Ulysses put his the brandy balloon to his lips but then paused.

"We come to Whitby looking for Mr Bellerophon but run into Rudge instead. Rudge arranges to meet us on the moors but rather than Rudge, the Barghest turns up..." With a swift jerk of his head, he knocked back the remainder of the brandy.

"So where would we find this Rudge?"

"He's gamekeeper to the Umbridge Estate."

"That name again," Ulysses pondered. "Then we have the lead we need. Come the morning we shall pay a visit to the reclusive Josiah Umbridge."

Putting the empty glass down on the table beside the dead dog-beast Ulysses turned to Jennifer, put both his hands on her shoulders and gazed into her grief-stricken face.

"But for now, let's get some rest. We're all in need of a good night's sleep."

MORNING CAME, IT seemed, all too soon, the watery grey light of a dreary dawn oozing across the moors along with the stagnant mists that rose from the peat bogs and waterlogged hollows. Hunter's Lodge having once been precisely that, it had not been a problem finding accommodation for both Ulysses and his manservant, so that each of them was able to have his own room.

Before the three of them had retired for what remained of the night, Jennifer had told both of her gentlemen house guests to feel free to help themselves to anything from her father's wardrobe, to replace that which had been either soiled or ruined during their battles with the Barghest. But she wouldn't enter the old man's room herself. It was all too soon, his death too recent, her loss still too raw. It would take her some time to come to terms with the old man's death, if she could at all.

On rising, Ulysses washed at the basin in the guest room. Peering at himself through bleary, half-closed eyes, he took in all the little nicks and scratches he had sustained battling the beast. There was even a bruise blossoming, like a blue-black carnation, on his cheek under his left eye, but he couldn't actually remember how he had come to sustain such an injury.

He decided that he would look a whole lot better if he shaved and so, finding soap and a brush, set to work, careful not to give himself any further injuries. One last dousing with chill water removed the last of the lather from his face and helped to bring him fully to his senses.

Sleep had come easily to him – exhaustion and alcohol both playing their part – but his slumber had been punctuated by dark dreams of savage dogs and desperate flights across the moors. The moors had given way to the sea and he had found himself at the edge of a cliff, white spume crashing on the black rocks below, like the distended open jaws of a predator. He heard the grunting panting of the black dog bearing down on him and yet he had been unable to take his eyes off the churning, corpse-grey surge of the sea. For there, visible between the rise and fall of the dark waves was a beautiful woman, her naked torso draped with the seaweed that tangled her hair, her pert breasts glistening milky-white against the black waters. He looked from her nakedness to her face and saw Jennifer Haniver staring back at him with anxious eyes, calling to him, her words subsumed beneath the crash of the breakers and the rattling suck of the sea as it retreated, preparing for its next assault on the jagged rocks. And then he could hear her and she was laughing. He watched as Jennifer's skin shrivelled and her hair receded until he was staring into the eyeless face of a mummified monkey. And then, with a flick of its fishy tail, the mermaid was gone.

Ulysses blinked sharply, chasing the last fading images of his disturbing dream from his waking mind. He dressed, Nimrod having already chosen him an appropriate outfit – and one in his size, no less – from the old man's wardrobe. He still felt slightly muzzy-headed, and as he dressed he had to sit down on the bed to put on his spotlessly clean shoes. But that wasn't down to a lack of sleep, but the result of an excess of medicinal cognac the night before.

Attired in a green-check suit and starched white shirt, the whole arrangement set off with a bold paisley-patterned bow-tie, Ulysses descended the stairs to be greeted by Nimrod who had a steaming cafetiere in one hand and a white napkin draped over his other arm.

The ever resourceful manservant appeared to be wearing the same set of clothes in which he had fought off the beast on the moors, cleared away corpses and cleaned up after them. And yet there didn't appear to be a mark on it. With perhaps the exception of a clean shirt from Hannibal Haniver's wardrobe, he must have been up most of the night doing the laundry.

"Good morning, sir. I take it you slept well," he enquired politely.

"As much as might be expected, under the circumstances." Ulysses looked around him in dazed confusion and then realised what it was that had surprised him. Nimrod had already cleared away the detritus from their final showdown with the beast the night before.

"You will find breakfast served in the drawing room this morning, sir."

"Ah yes, breakfast," Ulysses said, eyeing the coffee pot in Nimrod's hand. "A capital idea!"

Ulysses turned at the bottom of the stairs and made his way across the hall to the drawing room. Jennifer was already there and her appearance took Ulysses aback somewhat. He had been preparing himself to have to deal with a puffy-eyed, grief-stricken girl constantly dabbing at her tears with the scrunched up ball of a damp handkerchief and not the resolute young woman stood before him instead.

She looked better than he had ever seen her since they had first met on the moors the previous afternoon. For then she had just sprained her ankle and was suffering from the cold shock brought on by the trauma of the injury.

But now she appeared fresh-faced and with a rosy glow he had not seen before. She had washed and dried her hair, tying it up in a practical bun, and she was wearing an open-necked shirt and a new pair of Harris tweed knickerbockers. He could see from the way the knee-length sock on her right foot bulged that she must have strapped up her ankle well – it certainly didn't appear to be troubling her unduly – and had managed to put on another pair of walking shoes.

Ulysses found himself struck dumb by her simple, natural beauty – his English Rose had blossomed – and so it was Jennifer who initiated their first exchange of the day.

"Good morning, Ulysses. Is something the matter?"

"What? No. No, nothing." He realised he had stopped dead in the doorway of the drawing room on catching sight of Jennifer. Crossing the room, he sat down in an armchair next to the windows through which wan sunlight was streaming. "You're looking well," he said cautiously. "Are you feeling –"

"Yes, quite well, thank you."

"There's nothing quite like the smell of grilling bacon, is there?" he said, by way of making light conversation, anxious not to say anything that might upset Jennifer's seemingly cheerful mood, which he was sure must be balanced on a knife edge.

Nimrod returned and placed a plate laden with bacon, scrambled eggs and black pudding in front of Ulysses. Not only had he managed to rustle up a filling breakfast amidst the devastation of the kitchen, he had even found enough intact plates to serve it on.

"Looks wonderful, old boy," he beamed, inhaling deeply, savouring the succulent aromas of the hot food.

"Thank you, sir."

Having made himself scarce the night before when the much bigger dog had invaded his home, the smell of bacon and other such delights had drawn Ambrose the terrier out from his hiding place under the sofa. The dog squatted down beside Ulysses, hopeful eyes watching every forkful of food with expectant relish, but he wasn't even going to get a look in.

The dandy tucked in straight away, but, as far as he was concerned, the pot of coffee that Nimrod had produced was by far his greatest achievement.

"I'm sure you must ravenous after all your exertions last night," Jennifer said, placing her own knife and fork delicately together on her empty plate.

"What? Oh, yes," he admitted, still somewhat unsettled by her oh-so positive tone.

"Well, come on then, eat up. We're all going to need our strength for what lies ahead of us today, aren't we?"

There was something disconcerting about the way she was speaking so freely, a dark, disquieting edge to her strikingly cheerful tone. As far as she was concerned, there would be time enough to grieve later. For now, determination and a resolution to find her father's true killer was paramount.

"Um, yes," Ulysses managed through a mouthful of black pudding. "I'm looking forward to meeting Mr Umbridge."

LESS THAN HALF an hour later, with breakfast finished and everyone suitably attired for a clear, cold day on Ghestdale, the trio, made up of the cryptozoologist, the dandy and his manservant, set off west, following the stony track that led across the moors in the direction of the Umbridge estate, Miss Haniver taking the gentleman detective's arm for support.

It had been cold out the night before, but certain that the beast would not be troubling him, he had made a bed of heather and bracken for himself in the lea of a rocky outcrop that sheltered him from the warmth-stealing winds that seemed to constantly scour the moors.

He had risen at first light, as the fragile light of the sun struggled to penetrate the cloying November mists and made his way back to the lodge. From his hiding place behind a dry-stone wall he saw a tattered curtain flapping in the breeze, tugged through the shattered remains of the French windows and wet with dew.

When he had reached the house after the others, the night before, all had seemed well. He too had thought the beast dead, or at least trapped within the warren of mine-workings underground. It was only as he was making his way home, scampering back towards the distant lights of the town, that he heard the blood-curdling howls and the woman's screams.

He had returned to the lodge at a run, but by the time he got there it was all over. It took some minutes for him to realise what had happened. It had been then that he had resolved to wait close by until morning, just in case she needed his help again.

It wasn't until the party were a good two hundred yards along the track – Miss Haniver making confident progress despite her injured ankle – that he left his hiding place and, careful as ever not to be seen, set off after them.

HEAVY HOBNAIL BOOTS kicked away the wreckage of the devastated French windows, crunched over broken glass and entered the dining room. There on the table, lying under a blood-soaked tablecloth, was the dog. Yanking the cloth free of the animal's body the man turned his face away; the combination of blood, shit and putrefaction was too revolting to stomach even for him.

Hearing the sound of more heavy footsteps in the hall beyond, the man looked up to see his companion standing there, behind the splintered remains of the dining room door.

"Did ya find 'em?" the first asked gruffly, not bothering to remove the stub of the cigar he was smoking from between his teeth as he spoke.

"Only the old man," the second replied, "wrapped up in a curtain in the scullery."

"Bloody 'ell!" The man kicked at the remains of a shredded upholstered chair.

"The boss isn't going to be happy," the second offered unhelpfully.

"No, 'e's bloody not," the first scowled. He looked down at the corpse stretched out on the table next to him. "Come on, we'd better get on and shift this. We don't want anyone else coming round here and finding the bloody thing, do we? Come on, give me an 'and will ya?"

None too willingly his partner joined him at the end of the tables and took hold of one of the creature's back legs.

"And what do we do when we've moved the bugger?" the second asked.

The first took the cigar from between his teeth and smiled, the few yellow pegs of what teeth he had left looking like a row of discoloured headstones planted within the blood red cemetery of his gums. "What do we do then? Why, then we burn the place," he said, with obvious delight. "To the ground."

CHAPTER SIXTEEN

The Industrialist

ULYSSES STOOD AT the top of the flight of broad white stone steps, Jenny waiting nervously beside him, both of them looking up at the awesome facade of the mansion.

Umbridge house had been constructed in the Neo-Classical style. To either side of them stood great columns of white stone which in turn supported a grand pediment which was itself decorated with carved figures from Greek and Roman myth. The whole place looked more like a temple of antiquity, than someone's home.

Considering the imposing edifice in front of him, for a moment Ulysses felt butterflies of nervousness take flight within his stomach.

'Well, here goes nothing,' he said giving the bell-pull a tug.

A moment later a distant bell tolled ominously somewhere away within the vast complex of the building.

They had been able to approach the mansion unhindered, having not seen another human soul since arriving at the main gates half a mile away, down the gravel drive that snaked up to the main house through an acre of sparse woodland. For someone so keen on his privacy, Ulysses would have expected Josiah Umbridge to have had someone on the gate to monitor the approach of strangers.

For not only was Umbridge a recluse, he was also one of the richest, most successful men in the empire and, hence, the world. Umbridge's factories had proliferated across the North York moors, polluting the surrounding environment, in the process making him a very rich man. It was Umbridge Industries that provided other factory-owners with the factory structures themselves and internal machinery they needed to produce the automobiles, automata, steam engines, printing presses, traffic control systems, dirigibles, kinema cameras and scores of other mechanisms that kept every major city from Edinburgh to Calcutta running.

And of course Ulysses now knew that Josiah Umbridge had had his own part to play in Project Leviathan. He might be an ill man, as was reported in the papers, but ironically, if it hadn't been for his deteriorating state of health he would like as not have been a dead man by now.

Ulysses was roused from the recollection of his last fateful sea voyage by footsteps coming from beyond the closed double doors. There was the rattle of bolts being loosened, a handle being turned and then one of the doors opened a crack. An ancient face peered out at them through the gap, the sagging jowls, the bags of skin under the eyes and scraggy wattles of the butler's neck wobbling loosely as he looked from Ulysses to his female companion and back again.

"Yes?" the butler asked, managing to sound both imperious and irritated at the same time.

"Good morning," Ulysses said brightly. "We're here to see Mr Umbridge."

The butler looked down his nose first at Ulysses and then, even more disdainfully, at Jennifer.

"Mr Umbridge is not receiving visitors."

"He'll see us," Ulysses said confidently, his jaunty tone shot through with steel. Reaching into a jacket pocket he extracted his leather card-holder with his left hand and then almost dropped it as he attempted to flick it open. The butler could not help but be unimpressed by Ulysses' clumsiness.

The butler took a moment or two to read the information presented there on the ID – a moment or two longer than was really necessary, Ulysses thought – all the while looking as though he was being expected to survey the contents of a gutter press publication.

"This way please, sir. Madam," the Umbridge Estate's ancient retainer said, stepping aside and ushering them into the cavernous, echoing entrance hall beyond. Everything was cold and white and palatial, like some eccentric aristocrat's mausoleum, an edifice built to honour the memory of a dead man.

The butler was a good head shorter than Ulysses' own manservant – and even Jennifer was a good few inches taller, and able to see the top of his balding pate – but he still managed to look down at the two of them.

As soon as Ulysses and Jennifer were over the threshold, the butler assiduously closed the door again, shutting out the morning light, returning the white-stoned hall to its previous state of grey shadow, and then, as the two visitors waited for him to show them to his master, simply held out a white-gloved hand.

"I'm sorry," Ulysses said, confused. "Aren't you going to take us to see Mr Umbridge?"

"Your ID, sir," the butler said unsmilingly, "if you would be so kind."

"Oh, I see." Ulysses hesitated for a moment before handing it over.

"Wait here," he said, and then, turning on his spatted heel, strode slowly away into the depths of the house, leaving the two of them alone in the sepulchral atrium.

IN THE SHELTER of a sparse stand of beech, Nimrod paused in front of a high stone wall. It extended away from him on both sides. He had approached it from the right, where, one hundred yards away, it turned a sharp corner and headed off northwards across the moors.

Nimrod had parted company with his master and the young Miss Haniver as they made their way along the rough dirt road that skirted the edge of Ghestdale as it tracked its way towards the Umbridge estate. The estate, with its Neo-Classical style mansion set at the north-east corner, came into view when they were still two or three miles away, the house itself framed by formal gardens. The high wall which was blocking Nimrod's own approach to the house, appeared to encompass the entire estate.

It was at this point that Nimrod split from the other two, taking a divergent path which headed back across the undulating acres of bracken and heather towards the rear of the estate. While his master and the naturalist's daughter sought an audience with the industrialist himself, Nimrod's remit had been to try to locate the gamekeeper Rudge – assuming he wasn't ensconced within some Whitby drinking house, or out on the moors – without attracting undue attention to himself. But Master Ulysses had a feeling that the thug wouldn't be too far away, and Nimrod tended to agree. And of course, even if he didn't find the man himself, who knew what other clues or dark secrets he might uncover? Under the circumstances, a little, clandestine exploration could pay dividends.

Nimrod wasn't blessed with the near prescient powers that his master seemed to have acquired during his sojourn with the monks of Shangri-La, but he still had the sudden and uneasy feeling that someone was watching him, right now.

One hand on the butt of the fully loaded pistol in its underarm holster, Nimrod turned, half-expecting to see the burly gamekeeper, pork pie hat pulled down hard on top of his head, bearing down on him, ham-sized fists bunched, ready to give him a pummelling.

For a split second he thought he saw movement, as if somebody had just ducked down out of sight, but then there was nothing. One tussock of coarse, sun-bleached grass looking just like another.

Who was it? Who was out there? Was it the gamekeeper, returning to the estate after unleashing the monstrous hound on the Hanivers?

And then the uneasy feeling was gone.

He turned back to the wall. After making a quick assessment of the arrangement of the stones, Nimrod started to climb, his black leather gloves helping him secure a confident grip. As soon as he could see over the top – the stones there arranged so that their jagged points might cause anyone trying to scale the wall no small discomfort – he scanned the grounds beyond, his gloves protecting his palms and fingertips.

He could see Umbridge house at the top of the hill, a good mile from his current position. Beneath the house and its clinically symmetrical formal gardens, carefully tended lawns stretched down to a babbling stream, the lush green sward a stark contrast to the sombre, almost spectral palette, of Ghestdale itself. The stream itself had clearly been re-engineered to produce a series of pleasantly descending and carefully sculpted cascades that eventually emptied into a lake at the bottom of the valley. Around the man-made mere, a carefully-managed strip of woodland was nestled, protected from the moor-scouring winds by the steeply-rising slopes and the estate wall itself.

Seeing no one within the fastidiously-kept gardens, Nimrod scrambled over the parapet and dropped down on the other side, landing lightly on his feet among the drifts of autumnal leaves that had collected there. Keeping to the shadows on this side of the wall, Nimrod moved as quickly and as quietly as he could towards the leafless wood. For if the gamekeeper had a hovel anywhere within the estate, it would be there.

AFTER WHAT SEEMED like an eternity, Umbridge's butler returned. He made no apology for keeping them waiting but simply said: "Follow me."

"I told you he'd see us," Ulysses said in a forced whisper, offering Jennifer his arm again.

"But what are you actually going to say to him?" Jennifer whispered back.

"Don't worry, I do this sort of thing all the time."

"Really?" She looked at him with genuine astonishment.

"Really. And usually I just make something up on the spot."

"You're not serious?"

"No," Ulysses said with a forced grin, "of course I'm not. Not really. Do you think I'd walk in here to confront the man we suspect of masterminding the theft of the Whitby mermaid and the Barghest killings without having some sort of a plan?"

Ulysses wondered if all the white lies he told would catch up with him one day.

The butler led them from the funereal white entrance hall into a wood-panelled corridor – clinical and dustless – through another room, another hallway, just like those before, and so on. Many of the rooms they passed seemed more like museum pieces, as if the stately home was open for public viewings, the rooms and their contents trapped in time, like galleries in a museum of antiquities. The place certainly didn't feel lived in. It was almost as if the fading Umbridge had actually died long ago.

That was until the diminutive manservant led them into a fire-lit study at the back of the house, and the warmest room in the place they had so far experienced.

The study was small compared with the palatial, columned chambers they had passed – sterile ballrooms, libraries, dining chambers and galleries, all unoccupied – but it was still easily as big as the largest room in Ulysses' own Mayfair residence. Much of one wall was taken up by a huge stone-carved fireplace, the fire that had been set within it blazing away, keeping out the wintry chill that seemed to pervade the rest of the house. Two massive leather armchairs, upholstered in a deep red, had been arranged so as to face the fire.

"Mr Quicksilver and Miss Haniver, sir," the butler announced to someone sitting in the chair with its back to the door, and so still out of sight.

"Show them in," came a reedy, age-cracked voice.

The unsmiling manservant signalled for Ulysses and Jennifer to approach.

As they rounded the side of the unnecessarily large chair, the voice said: "That will be all, Molesworth," and waved the butler away with a skeletally-thin hand, veins visible beneath the parchment-like skin.

Where Hannibal Haniver had appeared aged and withered by ill-health, the older Josiah Umbridge appeared even more so. He looked like little more than a skeleton. There was almost no flesh on the bones beneath his waxy, liver-spotted skin and his out-dated black suit hung off his sparse frame as if he were no more than a glorified coat-hanger. As well as liver spots, his pallid skin was covered with crusted black pressure sores. From the waist down he was buried beneath a bundle of blankets so that his feet and legs couldn't be seen at all. There was barely a hair left on his head, other than for the occasional, intermittently sprouting strand of grey, which only served to give his head a truly skull-like appearance.

The dying man – and he certainly smelt as if he were dying, the air around him already heavy with the smell of decay – regarded the two of them from the abyssal pits of his sunken eye-sockets and his thin lips parted in a deaths-head grimace.

"Miss Haniver; what a pleasure it is to meet you at last."

"Mr Umbridge." Jennifer hesitated, having not expected to be the one to have to speak. "Thank you for agreeing to see us at such short notice, um, without an appointment," she said, as if feeling under pressure to give some sort of explanation as to their presence within his home. "I hope that we are not keeping you from anything important."

"Well, I could hardly refuse now, could I?" Umbridge replied, turning his deathly gaze on Ulysses. "Not when you come bearing such auspicious authority." Still without having actually addressed his other guest directly, Umbridge turned his gaze and his smile back onto Jennifer. "You're dear old Hannibal's daughter, aren't you?"

"Yes."

The atmosphere within the study suddenly became thick with expectation.

"And how is your father?" he asked softly, regarding her closely from beneath beetling eyebrows. "I trust he is well."

"Actually, he's dead."

Ulysses watched Jennifer closely. She made the announcement without any hint of emotion. *She must still be in a state of shock,* he thought.

In the awkward silence that followed Jennifer's revelation, Ulysses became uncomfortably aware of the inescapable ticking of a clock on the mantelpiece above the fire. Its steady clockwork heartbeat seemed to draw attention to his own mortality, the way it moved on from one second to the next, unceasingly, with never a single one to be reclaimed, to be lived again.

"As am I," Umbridge said at last, his words doing nothing to alleviate the atmosphere of tension and despair.

Ulysses looked at him askance, one cynical eyebrow raised. "Really, Mr Umbridge. Then I must congratulate you on your most excellent impression of a living being."

"I am as good as dead!" the old man suddenly snapped, turning on Ulysses like a tiger cornered by hunters, knowing that its time has come, but determined to fight to the last. "I have a death sentence hanging over me. It's cancer, you know? Whole damn body's riddled with it. There is no cure, hence I am a dead man."

He stared at Ulysses, his caustic gaze intended to strip away the younger man's resolve, but Ulysses Quicksilver was made of sterner stuff than that and simply stared right back.

"I know what you're thinking," Umbridge snarled.

"Oh? And what's that?" Ulysses challenged, calling the old man's bluff.

"You think I deserve everything that's coming to me. You think I'm an old man who's lived beyond his time anyway, getting rich at the expense of the poor downtrodden working classes. I know what people like you are like – like that damned Darwinian Dawn – eco-terrorist sympathisers. You despise me."

"Do any of *us* look like we have much in common with the working classes?" Ulysses pointed out. "And I don't mind telling you, there is little love lost between myself and the Darwinian Dawn."

"But I can see it in your eyes, just the same," Umbridge persisted. It seemed that Ulysses' one chance remark had awoken the lion in the old man's heart. "You claim to care about the empire, about the legacy we are leaving future generations, as custodians of this planet. You think that industry has ruined this green and pleasant land. Well I'll tell you; without those dark satanic mills, your world would not exist. That is the reality we live in, and there is no going back."

Ulysses opened his mouth to speak, but then, for once, thought better of it. At this rate, the old man would have them thrown out before they managed to find out anything.

When he was certain that he had silenced Ulysses with his tirade, Umbridge turned his attention back to the young woman again. "You must excuse me, my dear," he said, his tongue darting out from his mouth to moisten the dry, peeling skin of his lips, "what is it that I can do for you?"

Jenny hesitated, looking to Ulysses for support.

"Go on," he said, encouraging her to speak with a nod of his head.

"Well, it's like this. Last night..."

Jenny broke off abruptly. Taking a deep breath, to calm herself, she started again. "Last night my father was killed, while yesterday afternoon Mr Quicksilver, his manservant, and myself were attacked whilst out on the moors."

"I am very sorry to hear that, my dear. Truly I am. Very sorry to hear of your loss, my dear, very sorry," the old man suddenly looked crestfallen. "Your father was a great man. If there is anything I can do to help at what must be a very difficult time..." he said, his corpse-smile returning, "please do not hesitate to ask, and I will do all I can to assist you. All I can."

"We have reason to believe that your man Rudge might have had something to do with the attacks," Ulysses put in forcefully.

"What, the gamekeeper?"

"I don't know of any other."

"I'm sorry, but do I know you, Mr Quicksilver? Have we met before?"

"No, but I met your man Sylvester last year, on the first and last voyage of the *Neptune*."

"Ah, yes. A most unfortunate business."

"You go in for understatement, do you, Mr Umbridge?"

"I see no point in being melodramatic about these things."

"But do you know why the world's most sophisticated submersible cruise-liner ended up at the bottom of the Pacific Ocean?"

"Perhaps you could enlighten me on another occasion. I'm sure you understand, Mr Quicksilver," – the man's breath was a rattling wheeze in his chest – "that my time is precious; more so now than ever. It takes no little amount of time and effort to keep a ship like Umbridge Industries on course, and I am not blessed with much of either."

"You met my father once though, didn't you?"

"Really? Quicksilver, Quicksilver," the old man mused, as if trawling the fathomless depths of his memory for any recollection that might help make sense of things.

"His name was Hercules. Hercules Quicksilver."

"I must apologise," Umbridge said, the same fixed smile on his face but now full of sinister intent. "I am an old man. My body's riddled with cancer. I'm afraid that my memory is not what it once was."

"But I bet you remember the name Project Leviathan."

"I'm sorry, Mr Quicksilver, but I thought you came here to talk to me about yesterday's dreadful occurrences."

"Indeed."

"And you believe someone in my employ had something to do with this poor young woman's father?"

"I would appreciate the opportunity to discuss the matter with him."

"And on what do you base such a ludicrous supposition?"

"On the fact that I was supposed to meet him at the edge of Ghestdale yesterday, only he didn't turn up and instead I had a run in with the Barghest beast!"

"The Barghest? Will you listen to yourself, man? You sound as bad as those melodramatic gossip-pedlars at the paper. Phantom dogs roaming Ghestdale, taking the lives of all and sundry? You'll be telling me that the Whitby Mermaid was the real deal and not a poorly-conceived fake next."

"Mr Umbridge, I saw the creature with my own eyes, I watched as it tore my father's... my father..." And then, unable to hold back the tears any longer, Jennifer dissolving into a fit of silent sobbing. Ulysses put a comforting arm around her shoulders and pulled her close.

"I am sorry, my dear, really I am, and I don't doubt the veracity of your words for a moment," Umbridge said, leaning forward in his chair, as if this gave his words an added sense of sincerity. "This is indeed a most distressing matter. I don't believe that Mr Rudge is on estate land at present, but I am very concerned by what you have told me. Leave the matter with me and I promise that I *will* look into it."

The old man slumped back into the chair and closed his eyes, a long rattling breath escaping from his cancerous lungs. For a moment

Ulysses wondered if he had actually passed away, there and then, right in front of them. Then his rheumy eyes flicked open and the darting tongue reappeared from between the pale drawn lips.

"Now, if you will excuse me, I am very tired. It's the cancer, you know? A little bit more of me dies every day. So, if you will excuse me, our meeting has quite taken it out of me. I would ask that you leave now." He looked at Jennifer again, with hooded, half-closed eyes. "And have no fear, I *shall* give this matter my utmost attention."

He closed his eyes.

Sensing another presence in the room, Ulysses looked up. Molesworth was standing there, regarding them with that familiar disdainful frown. "This way," the butler said abruptly, ushering them out of the study.

As Molesworth was about to follow after them, Umbridge's eyes flicked open once more, like a corpse waking from its eternal rest, and a wave of his long fingers halted the butler in his tracks. Molesworth looked at his master.

"Sir?"

"They know too much," Umbridge said darkly, his voice a sinister, serpentine hiss. "Get Rudge up here. Miss Haniver and Mr Quicksilver are going to be staying after all."

CHAPTER SEVENTEEN

The Freak

NIMROD LOOKED AT his watch for the umpteenth time and then back at where the sky was purpling like a bruise on the horizon. The persistent cloud cover had not let up all day, keeping everything beneath its foggy clutches in a state of permanent cloying dampness.

There was no point lying to himself; he was becoming concerned. Dusk was falling and after four hours neither Master Ulysses nor the young Miss Haniver had returned to the rendezvous point. And he had been waiting at the south-east corner of the estate, back on the Ghestdale side of the wall, since three o'clock that afternoon.

It was perfectly possible that Josiah Umbridge had been the perfect host and had invited the gentleman and his lady friend to stay for supper, but knowing that they had arranged to meet over an hour ago at the latest, Nimrod was now convinced that something untoward had happened to them. He had already tried calling his master using his own personal communicator, and there had been no response.

His own search of the estate grounds had born fruit, up to a point. He had found the gamekeeper's cottage at last – a stone-built refuge, that was not much more than a single-roomed hovel, various ill-kept vicious steel traps hung from nails on the wall, a clutch of dead vermin strung up on a line between two trees outside – not far from a rusted gate that led onto sheep grazing land on the far side of the walled grounds.

But he had not found the gamekeeper himself. A cursory search of the roughly-furnished cottage had turned up nothing that linked Rudge, the Umbridge estate, or even Josiah Umbridge himself, to the Barghest or the late Hannibal Haniver in anyway. The one thing he had noted in particular was the cudgel hung up in pride of place on the plain whitewashed wall above the cold grate of the fire.

Nimrod was starting to wonder what Master Ulysses and Miss Haniver had uncovered. Whatever it was, it was preventing them from making the rendezvous as planned.

He had promised Ulysses' father that he would look out for his eldest son, no matter what. It was a vow that he took very seriously – even more so after Ulysses' return after an absence of eighteen months, in April that year, having been declared dead after his hot-air balloon went down over the Himalayas – one that he had sworn to uphold with his very life, if necessary. After all, it came, in part, as his repayment of a debt that he could never repay to the late Hercules Quicksilver for having saved his own life, in more ways than one, all those years ago.

For a moment he considered contacting Inspector Allardyce and the local police – he even got as far as taking out his emergency personal communicator – but had then dropped the brass, teak and enamel device back into his pocket. Until he had a better idea of what sort of trouble Master Ulysses had got himself into, Nimrod didn't want to do anything that might make what was already doubtless a dangerous situation even worse. After all, so far they knew that a crazed vivisectionist was involved, a brute of a man who wasn't averse to dishing out a good beating and, possibly, a powerful industrialist.

No, the police would only turn up in a whirlwind of flashing blue lights and wailing sirens, barrelling in there in their clumsy size elevens, and God alone knew what a man who revelled in cutting up living things, a desperate thug, or a man whose position of power and affluence made him believe that he could do anything he wanted, might do.

Leaving the police to their investigations into the Ghestdale killings – even though he already knew who, or rather so far, *what* was responsible – remembering the old adage that if you want something done properly, you'd best do it yourself, Nimrod set off west, following the wall where it demarcated the perimeter of the Umbridge estate.

This time, to avoid drawing attention to himself, Nimrod took the longer, and yet less exposed route, around the outside of the estate wall until he reached the rusted gate, close to where Rudge's hideaway lay.

The decorative ironwork of the gate made it an easy thing to climb, and dropping down on the other side Nimrod re-entered the estate wood. Still unseen, he made his furtive way back to the gamekeeper's cottage through the rapidly encroaching gloom.

Creeping through stands of elm and ash he saw the hovel as now nothing more than a shadowy construction growing out of the murk of the darkening woods. There were no lights shining from the windows and so it seemed likely that there was no one at home.

Placing his feet with care, and moving at a cautious pace – so as not to trip over an exposed tree root or catch his foot in the mouth of an animal burrow – remaining as vigilant as possible in the encroaching dark, Nimrod made his way to the door.

Earlier that afternoon, when he had first explored the estate, he had kept half an eye open for any signs that the Barghest had been there – oversized paw prints, the animal's spoor, claw marks in the trunks of trees – but he had found nothing. But then he hadn't approached the gamekeeper's domain from this direction before: he wondered what he was missing now in the dark, unable to even make out the ground beneath his feet.

Cautiously, one hand on the pistol underneath his arm, Nimrod eased open the door. The hinges complained loudly in the twilight stillness, the protesting metal seeming to scream into the November night. But, when no one shouted in surprise or leapt at him from the darkness, Nimrod stepped inside, closing the door carefully behind him.

Inside, the cottage was just as he had left it before, only now it was in utter darkness. Nimrod knew that if he was going to find anything else here he was going to need to light a lamp, despite the risk that it would alert anyone nearby to his presence within. However, that one slight risk was nothing compared to the terrible fate that could befall his master the more time he wasted here, blundering about in the dark.

He could see a hurricane lamp on a window sill, silhouetted against the window behind it: that would do. With the lamp lit, its warm amber glow suffusing the cottage, playing a game of cat and mouse with the shadows at the corners of the single room, Nimrod took another, closer look around.

Last time he had only really been looking for the gamekeeper, or any sign of a connection to the Barghest beast. Now he was looking for anything, *anything* that might give him a clue as to what might have happened to his master. And it wasn't as if he could just walk in through the front door of Umbridge House. That was how Master Ulysses had made his move and, chances were, that was what had got him into trouble. No, he had the certain growing suspicion that he had missed something the last time he had been here and that he was missing it all over again.

Standing in the middle of the room, he held the lamp high and looked all around him, peering into every darkened corner, at every piece of furniture.

There was a simple sink and a stove next to the small hearth built into the chimney breast. In one corner stood the gamekeeper's rough, unmade bed, a chamber pot underneath. In the opposite corner was a rocking chair with a knitted blanket thrown over one arm.

There were other seemingly incongruous homely touches – the rag rug on the floor, a picture of an old mop-capped woman, that might have been the man's mother, over the range, an anonymous brass trinket of some kind – but on the whole it looked like precisely what it was, the simple home of a middle-aged man with few, if any, attachments in the world, a man with simple needs, the torture of defenceless creatures being one of them.

Nimrod turned around to look at the other side of the room and felt something shift beneath him, heard the subtle creak of wood giving under his weight.

He stopped and looked down at the rug on which he was standing. Shifting his weight from one foot to the other he heard the creak again. Stepping off the rug, he took hold of a corner and lifted it up. Pulling the rug away completely, there, revealed in the middle of the flagstoned floor of the hut, was a trapdoor.

Nimrod's pulse began to quicken. He took hold of the iron ring recessed into it at one end and pulled it open. A waft of cold, earthy air hit him full in the face. He could see a set of worn stone steps leading down into the dank darkness below.

Laying the open trapdoor carefully down on the discarded rug, so as not to alert anyone who might be down there already, Nimrod crouched down, lowering the hurricane lamp into the hole.

Six feet or so down, the steps met with the floor of a rough-hewn tunnel, cut from the rock and earth that lay beneath the foundations of the cottage. Here and there he could see where tree-roots penetrated the underground passageway. He breathed deeply and caught the aroma of peaty soil and mould.

Who knew how far down the tunnel went or where it led, other than that, to begin with at least, it appeared to lead in the direction of the house? The steps certainly didn't lead down to a cellar – after all, why would such a small dwelling even have one – and it seemed as likely that the tunnel would connect it to the house, as anywhere.

There was nothing else for it. If Nimrod was to find out where the tunnel led for sure, he was going to have to follow it.

Lantern held high to illuminate his way, eyes peering into the darkness at the limit of the lantern's sphere of radiance, ears listening for any indication that he might not be alone down there, Nimrod descended the steps and set off along the tunnel. Taking care to place his feet lightly on the dirt floor, he had to crouch to keep from grazing his scalp on the low ceiling of the passageway.

The tunnel proceeded in a straight line for some forty yards until it reached another set of steps. These had been cut from the bedrock itself, rather than being laid stones, like the first flight, and were slick with water. Steadying himself against the sides of the rock-cut passageway, Nimrod descended still further, the uneven steps twisting this way and that down through a chimney in the rock, a natural formation in part created by the erosive action of water seeping through from the moors above and into the fissure-riven sandstone on which Ghestdale rested.

Reaching the bottom of this haphazard flight, Nimrod found himself on one side of a wide gallery, the roof of which ascended out of reach of the lantern's circle of light, and knew exactly where he was. He could make out the marks left by digging tools on the rocks around him quite clearly. The air was moist down here and Nimrod found himself pulling his coat tighter about him against the bone-numbing chill that permeated the tunnels.

He was inside the hollowed-out innards of an abandoned mine, any deposits of jet it might once have had having been stripped out long ago, possibly as far back as the end of the nineteenth century. It had since become absorbed into the Umbridge estate, providing a network of secret tunnels that connected the gamekeeper's cottage to the main house, Nimrod expected, and who knew where else? Nimrod surmised that there were half a dozen hidden entrance points up on the moors and possibly as far away as the coast and Beast Cliff itself that led into and out of the Umbridge estate.

One of them could even have been the shaft into which Master Ulysses had first bundled the Barghest. And if the beast had originated from somewhere within the estate, it may well have already been familiar with the tunnels, using its enhanced sense of smell to sniff its way out again, and back onto their trail.

The Barghest may well have known its way around these tunnels, but that did not change the fact that Nimrod did not. And so, although he might know in principle where he was, he didn't know where he needed to go next. And so the question remained: which way should he go now?

Hearing the skitter of stone on stone he held his breath. In the eerie stillness he listened for the sound again. And then, there it was; the sandpaper scrape of grit on stone. It had come from his right.

Nimrod set off. There was no point dousing his light – without it he would be utterly lost. Instead he reached for his holstered pistol.

He could hear the footfalls ahead of him quite clearly now, their pace quickening, any pretence at stealth rejected in favour of flight. His quarry was on the run.

Picking up the pace, Nimrod hurried on through the worked-out mine. The tunnel twisted and turned, the ceiling of bedrock undulating above him, so that from time to time he found himself having to duck again to avoid knocking himself out on the downward pointing rocks.

For a moment he saw the bobbing will-o'-the-wisp flicker of another light source ahead of him. But then it was gone. He came to a halt. The running footsteps were gone too.

Slowly, ever so warily, Nimrod continued his advance, trying to tread as lightly as he could on the sandy floor of the tunnel, avoiding the noisy ripple and splash of stepping into puddles. Gun in hand, he kept going, trying to judge at what location the second light had disappeared.

Ten yards. Nine yards.

He kept going at the same steady pace, pistol tight in his hand, muzzle pointing forwards.

Five yards. Four.

His steps slowed, footfalls near silent in the smothering darkness, the only other sounds disturbing the oppressive stillness the *drip-drip-drip* of water elsewhere within the mine, the sound carried as hollow echoes by the eerie acoustics of the place, and –

Two. One.

– nervous, panting breaths.

Nimrod spun round, shining his light into the natural cleft within the rock face in front of him, taking aim with his pistol.

Something hideous and misshapen – a lumpen body, uncoordinated limbs, a face that was only human thanks to it having the requisite features – surfaced from the thickly-cast shadows like a phantasm walking through a wall.

Its equally misshapen mouth agape, fists like cudgels raised before it, pin-pricks of eyes amidst the mass of deformities that was its face glittering in the light of the hurricane lamp, strangled vocal cords giving voice to a terrible wailing howl, the horror threw itself at Nimrod.

CHAPTER EIGHTEEN

An Appointment with Doktor Seziermesser

Ulysses half-opened his eyes and then shut them again tightly, against the brilliant fury of the lights in front of his face. Aware of them now, he tried again, still blinking against the harsh glare. He could feel the raw heat of the bulbs against the skin of his face, hot as sunburn.

He tried to raise a hand to shield his face from the incandescent glare. It was only then that he realised his arms had been restrained at the wrists. And now he was also aware that he was lying prostrate on his back. That certain knowledge didn't help how he was feeling right that moment, not when he considered what had almost happened to him the last time he had come to lying on his back and restrained.

He tried his legs but these too had been strapped down, restrained by what felt like a leather strap around his ankles. Somebody didn't want him going anywhere in a hurry.

He turned his head as he tugged against the restraint binding his left arm. The old injury his shoulder had suffered nearly two years ago now – as his hot air balloon plummeted groundwards amid the snow-capped peaks of the Himalayas, the basket locked in a spiralling, deathly embrace with the Black Mamba's gondola – grumbled in protest.

He understood now: he had been strapped to some kind of operating table. His arms had been restrained so that they were at right angles to his torso. They were held tightly at the wrists by buckled leather straps and Ulysses could also feel a tightness just below the ball and socket joints of both his shoulders. And he was shirtless.

In frustration Ulysses pulled and kicked and attempted to arch his back, but all to no avail. There was another belt strap around his middle.

He still felt muzzy-headed, his recollections of what had happened to him prior to ending up in this most undignified and uncomfortable of predicaments a jumble of sepia-blurred images, like out of focus photographs.

Focusing all his mental energies on recollection, Ulysses tried to piece together what had happened. If he could re-order his dream-like recollections perhaps he then might remember who it was that had done this to him and why? And if he could understand his enemy's motivations, then he might yet talk his way out of this predicament.

He remembered the meeting with the industrialist. He remembered being escorted to the front door by the dour-faced butler. Then he remembered the first itch of prescience at the back of his skull, a moment before the butler opened the door and a hulking silhouette appeared there, quickly resolving into the outline of the elusive Mr Rudge.

Ulysses was already going for his sword-cane and pushing Jennifer aside as the brute came at them, cosh raised. And there had been someone else with him, a snivelling weasel of a man. Ulysses remembered thinking that two against one weren't such bad odds but then his tingling sixth sense screamed a warning and he turned to see that it wasn't two against one at all, but three. As the butler came at him with the chloroform-soaked handkerchief, Rudge barrelled in too.

Distracted, suddenly forced to defend himself on two fronts, with Jennifer's screams filling his ears, he took on none of his attackers particularly effectively. His broken fingers didn't help. Rudge's cosh descended, black stars going supernova inside Ulysses' brain, and then the butler's doping cloth finished what the thug's beating had started.

Cold panic gripped his heart and squeezed, as Ulysses' mind turned to thoughts of Jennifer. What had happened to the girl?

Violently twisting his head from one side to the other, Ulysses struggled to see if she was anywhere nearby. He tried calling her name but his tongue felt thick and heavy inside his mouth, and all that came out was an incomprehensible splutter.

'Ah, I see you are awake.'

Ulysses turned his head in the same direction that the voice had come from. It took his addled mind a moment to realise that the words he had heard had been spoken with a clipped German accent.

An indistinct shape moved between him and the punishing lights. His eyes taking a moment to adjust to the sudden change in light levels, Ulysses peered at the features now sharpening into focus from the man-shaped shadow before him.

There was something unsettlingly familiar about the man's appearance, as he regarded Ulysses from behind curiously protruding, telescopic spectacles, a haughty expression on his time-worn face. It felt to Ulysses as if he must have once run into the man's son, or the man himself, only when he was younger. He was wearing what must have once been a white lab coat, but was now a faded grey, interspersed with patches of rusty brown.

And he could see other things now behind the man, beyond the glare of the lights – walls of crumbling red brick, metal work surfaces, a range of wheeled stands and gurneys bearing all manner of surgical instruments and devices.

The cold knot of nausea took hold of his guts and twisted. He tried to speak again, but panic and his sluggish tongue conspired to ensure that nothing comprehensible came out.

"I shouldn't try to speak," the other suggested. "I would just relax if I were you. It's better that way." The man wasn't looking at Ulysses as he spoke but was busying himself with laying out the tools of his trade, ready to set to work.

Ulysses swallowed, grimacing at the taste of stale saliva and old blood in his mouth.

He tried to speak again. "Where's Jenny?" he managed.

"Jenny? Who is this Jenny?"

"She was with me," he struggled, slurring his words with the effort of speech.

"Ah, I understand now," the German said, as he continued to prepare for whatever was to come next. "All in good time, Herr Quicksilver. All in good time."

Ulysses craned his head forward in an attempt to see what the man was doing. For a moment, in the reflecting glare of the lights, he saw quite clearly the serrated blade of a bone-saw.

Ulysses felt sick. With a sudden shout of frustration he kicked and bucked, a part of him knowing that it wouldn't make any difference, but the fighter in him knowing that he had to do something, that he couldn't just lie there and wait for this strangely bespectacled other to decide his fate for him.

"Now, now, Herr Quicksilver. Struggling will only make it worse."

With one last muscle-tearing convulsion of effort, Ulysses relented and fell back on the table. His skin was cold against the bare metal, as the sweat of his exertions began to evaporate.

"Who are you?" Ulysses hissed through gritted teeth.

The man turned to face him again and this time Ulysses realised that his spectacles had been fitted with decreasing sizes of magnifying lenses, that could be flicked down in front of the main lens as and when required. They gave the impression that his eyes were too big to fit within the orbits of his skull.

"I am sorry, Herr Quicksilver, how rude of me. Where are my manners? You must forgive me. I was so caught up in my preparations... But, that is not important. I am Doktor Seziermesser and I will be your surgeon for the duration of this procedure."

Ulysses' mind raced. *Procedure? What procedure?*

"You!" he gasped. "You're Mr Bellerophon."

"I am sorry, but you are mistaken, Herr Quicksilver. No, I assure you, I am Doktor Seziermesser." Ulysses could hear the 'k' in doktor quite clearly.

Seziermesser. Seziermesser. Where had he heard that name before?

"I thought you had already met my employer."

"What?"

"I am afraid that it was because of me that he had to create the alternative persona of Herr Bellerophon. The mermaid's escape was the result of carelessness on my part. But do not worry, I have been suitably punished."

He held up his left hand – or at least the stump of where his left hand had been. In its place a prosthetic metal claw had been strapped to the knot of pink scar tissue that covered the nub of his wrist. The claw itself looked as if it had been cobbled together from whatever had been lying around the lab that day.

"I am a surgeon, a master craftsman," Seziermesser continued, gazing at the stump and the artificial claw, a glazed expression on his face. "In fact, I like to think of myself as a sculptor, but one that works in flesh. My hands are my tools. That was why it was only right that I should lose one in payment for my recklessness. But have no fear, I have become quite adept at using this replacement."

The surgeon's voice belied no sense of malice or sarcasm. Instead he appeared suitably chastened, and seemed to bear his master no resentment for what had been done to him.

"It was only right that Herr Umbridge have his man show me the error of my ways. I was becoming distracted from the great work, my life's greatest accomplishment. Indeed, the greatest accomplishment in the history of vivisection!

"And perhaps, if I do a good job on you, when the great work is finished, perhaps Herr Umbridge will deign to let me replace it with something more... appropriate."

Ulysses watched as the man's eyes fell on his own hand, but was only half aware of the fact that it was his right hand which he was regarding with such lascivious intent. There was nothing else for it, nothing else he could do, and although he had tried the self-same thing already, he couldn't let this madman take him apart like a Sunday roast, and so struggled against his bonds again.

"Here, this should help you relax."

Ulysses felt the stab of a needle being thrust into his arm and gasped involuntarily. He was dimly aware of a curious sensation of cold spreading along his arm as the injection was delivered directly into his bloodstream.

The surgeon returned to laying out his scalpels, clamps and bone-saws. Ulysses felt the effect of the drug almost immediately, a strangely welcome warmth taking hold of his aching muscles and easing him back down onto the table, taking him to the very edge of unconsciousness.

But still that name haunted him. *Seziermesser* – where *had* he heard it before?

Heard it, or read it?

"Very good. I think we are ready to begin," the surgeon said, turning back to the operating table and Ulysses' prone form.

"Such a fine specimen," he said, starting to run the fingers of his right hand over the flesh of his arms and torso. His dancing fingertips felt like spiders scuttling over his exposed body. Inside Ulysses raged and riled in frustration but on the outside there was nothing he could do now to resist Seziermesser's probing touch.

Seziermesser. Seziermesser.

And then the memory surfaced from the depths of his subconscious like some great Biblical leviathan. Dark, forgotten domes, tanks of something like rancid primordial soup, indistinct shapes suspended in the slime – arms and legs, webs of skin between their digits, gills where necks should be – faded parchment labels and a name, written in a spidery copperplate; *Seziermesser.*

"Marianas," Ulysses hissed.

"Ah, yes. I understand now. I was still a young man then, a protégé of the late Doktor Waldman, a leader in my field; a trail-blazer, you might say. Just defected from the Frankenstein Corps – with your father's help, as it happens – with wonderful new opportunities ahead of me. And then it all went wrong, but not as a result of *my* work, I can assure you!"

"But that is all in the past. What we are concerned with today is the future, Herr Quicksilver; the future of the human race. So, let us begin."

Ulysses tried to say something else, but his thoughts were becoming clouded. It was as if he were sinking into himself, his mind wandering in a world of its own, as if mind and body were no longer quite one.

A piercing scream cut through the fastidious quiet of the operating theatre, rebounding from the broken brick walls.

"Ah, such sweet music," Seziermesser said distractedly, as if savouring the agonised sound of a body in torment, and then, flicking another lens down in front of his glasses, returned to his work.

Dreamily Ulysses turned his head in another attempt to see what the doktor was doing. Eyes struggling to focus, he saw the crimson tip of the scalpel blade and then watched as it entered the meat of his arm again, as the surgeon made a neat incision right around his arm, just below the ball and socket joint of his shoulder, the man apparently unperturbed by the screaming that now filled the dank chamber.

And in the split second before he lost consciousness, lost in a world of shock and pain, Ulysses realised that the screams were his own.

ACT THREE

The Fall of the
House of Umbridge

November 1997

CHAPTER NINETEEN

The Menagerie

"There. There it is again," the creature slurred, angling its chin upwards and putting its head on one side, as if that, in some way, helped it to hear more clearly. But there certainly wasn't anything wrong with its hearing – despite everything else that appeared to be physically wrong with it – for Nimrod could hear the sound now too, a gaggle of mewling voices, yammering cries and woeful wails.

Nimrod found it hard to think of the creature as a man: it was the deformities that did it. He looked at the poor wretch again as they moved through the semi-darkness together. Nimrod was no medical man, but it occurred to him that the creature was nothing more than a collection of tumours, his wretched body hung with a conglomeration of abnormal growths. Most noticeable, of course, were those that disfigured his face, giving it a grotesquely asymmetrical structure. The right side of his visage was swollen with sub-dermal growths, that made his ear protrude far from the side of his skull and pulled his mouth into a perpetually open maw.

But the left side of his face hadn't been saved by whatever disfiguring condition it was that he was undoubtedly suffering from. His forehead above his left eye jutted a good two inches from his brow. Hair covered only some parts of his head, the rest bare areas of warty grey scalp.

In fact, in the suffused light of the lantern, all of the creature's skin appeared to have the same rough texture and grey tone.

And his disfigurement wasn't just restricted to his head. Even through the rumpled suit of coarse grey cloth, Nimrod could see the lumps and bumps that afflicted the rest of his body. Again, the right hand side appeared to suffer from this condition the most. Certainly the creature's right paw was a twisted, swollen thing with fingers entwined into a club-like fist.

His semblance was more monster than man. It was little wonder that Nimrod had almost killed him on first sight, although he had soon discovered that it was not, in fact, the first time they had met. The wretch had been following he and his master ever since their run in with Inspector Allardyce of Scotland Yard.

Nimrod had not stopped to ask the deformed young man, but he would not have been surprised to learn that his condition was incredibly painful. The stress on his neck alone, in having to support the over-sized head, must have put a great strain on his whole body.

But for all that, he moved agilely and without drawing undue attention to himself, even though he was wearing a battered pair of mismatched boots. And then he stopped, head tilted to one side again.

"Creature, what is it?"

"I heard a scream."

"A man or a woman?" Nimrod pressed. He hadn't heard anything other than the distant background noise of plaintive cries and slack-jawed moans. Certainly nothing as clear and chilling as the cry of a traumatised soul.

"A man. And I would prefer it if you called me Jacob."

"I'm sorry?"

"I would prefer that you not call me 'creature'. My father saw fit to give me a name and I would rather you addressed me by that name."

Knowing that the thing had a name only served to trouble Nimrod's mind further; that something so inhuman should have such a human name.

"Very well, Jacob," Nimrod said uncomfortably. Something approximating a smile formed on the creature's blistered lips. "The scream: from which direction did it come?"

"The way we are heading."

Nimrod's heart went cold.

"Then let us press on."

As they wended their way onward through the dark Nimrod considered what a sudden reversal of fate he had witnessed. One minute the monstrous freak had seemed intent on smashing out his brains on the rock wall behind him, and then, in the next instant, Nimrod had found himself faced with a cowering wretch, as monstrous and as malformed as anything he would have expected to see stuffed and mounted in a glass display case as part of Cruickshanks' Cabinet of Curiosities.

"Don't shoot! Don't shoot!" the thing had wailed. Nimrod had been almost as surprised by the fact that the creature could speak as he had been by its appearance.

With his gun levelled at the creature, he had carried out his interrogation.

"What are you doing here?"

"I am here to save her."

"Who? Who are you here to save?"

"Miss Jennifer."

"You mean Miss Haniver."

"Yes."

"But how do you know she is here?"

"I followed her – I followed you all – from the lodge."

"You saw what happened there?"

"I have worked it out."

"You worked it out?"

"I was not there."

"You didn't witness the attack?"

"No."

"The beast had nothing to do with you?"

"Nothing, I swear on the Holy Cross – on my mother's grave – I had nothing to do with it!"

"Then how did you know to come to the house?"

"I... I followed *you* there."

"You followed me?"

"You and your master."

"How long had you been trailing us?"

"Since... since you left the town. Since the circus."

"Why?"

"You... intrigued me. And I thought you might be heading into danger."

"Danger?"

"On the moors, what with the Barghest killings and all. You were obviously strangers to these parts. I was concerned that you might fall foul of the beast yourselves."

"Well we did, didn't we? But you already know that. So why didn't you step in to help us then? Why didn't you intervene when Miss Haniver's life was in danger then?"

"I... was scared. It is to my great shame. It is why I have come here now, to make amends. Miss Jennifer is still in danger."

"She's not the only one."

The second revelation, as far as Nimrod was concerned, had been how gentle and well-spoken the creature was. But good manners and a pleasant speaking manner did not an innocent man make. So Nimrod kept his gun on the young man, just in case. He had no reason to believe that this Jacob was truly on his side at all. He had not had the chance to back up his bold words with actions yet, and until that time came, Nimrod judged that it was better to keep him at arm's length, and right where he could see him, with a gun trained on his back at all times.

And, in this manner, they had proceeded together further into the abandoned mine, following the snaking network of tunnels that led them ever onwards under the Umbridge estate.

"Look. Up there," the creature – this Jacob – said, suddenly stopping as he emerged from another low-roofed section of tunnel.

Nimrod quickly followed, and looked. There was a light ahead of them, an electric light.

Jacob turned his misshapen face towards Nimrod. "We're almost there."

There was a skittering of legs upon the uneven rocky floor at his feet and Nimrod nearly jumped as he felt something squeeze past him, its pliable body rubbing against his legs.

He lowered the lantern and looked at the floor. Beetles scuttled away from the light, long-bodied centipedes snapping at one another with nutcracker mandibles, fighting to claim a fissure in the rock for protection. Only they weren't beetles, Nimrod realised, or centipedes, they were both and yet neither, at the same time grotesque man-made creations that were all legs, chitin and mandibles.

He swept his lantern over the undulating mass at his feet. He saw things with the bodies of crabs, propelled across the floor with writhing starfish limbs. He saw something with the body of a snake scuttle past on half a dozen lobster legs. There were many-legged things, things with the bristling limbs of spiders, with the amorphous, oozing bodies of slugs, while something scampered across the wall, nearly brushing Nimrod's ear, before disappearing into the shadows again, that left him with the enduring, unpleasant image of a rat engulfed by an octopus.

"Abominations," the creature that called itself Jacob declared. "Blasphemies against both God and Nature!"

"Vivisects," Nimrod muttered.

"I beg your pardon, sir?"

"I rather feel that these are the work of another Creator entirely."

Placing his feet carefully, so as not to tread on any of the creatures if he could at all help it – not because he cared about the fate of the vivisects but simply because he found the idea of squashed slug-bodies beneath his feet abhorrent – Nimrod took the lead now, the light from his lamp helping to clear a path through the seething mass of bodies in front of them.

And then they were on the other side of the glistening black cavern, Nimrod and his unexpected companion. Ahead, the mined out cave gradually gave way to an obviously man-made tunnel, this one faced with stone. Its damp, moss-covered walls suggested great age to Nimrod. He wondered how long ago the passageway had been created, how old the foundations of the Umbridge House really were.

Had this tunnel been in regular use during the smugglers' heyday of the eighteenth century? He thought it likely. Who knew what had been brought into the country without the revenue men being party to it. Whiskey, tobacco, slaves? Or perhaps this tunnel had been used for more altruistic purposes, as an escape route, to get persecuted men to safety, following the network of caves beyond perhaps as far as the sea.

"We are beneath the house, I think," Jacob said, studying the tunnel with his head still on one side.

"I think you're right," Nimrod agreed. "Keep your wits about you. We don't want to be discovered now."

The way ahead was lit by dully pulsing caged bulbs, positioned at regular intervals as far as the eye could see. Nimrod placed the hurricane lantern on the floor, at the mouth of the cave, causing a momentary commotion among the encroaching abominations, which slithered back across the rocky floor behind them into the oily darkness. He then set off again with renewed vigour, quickening his pace, now that the surface on which he ran was packed earth rather than moisture-slick, uneven stone. Jacob loped after him.

The passageway gave way to more stone steps, which this time took Nimrod and his companion back up into the bedrock, on which the Umbridge estate stood, he assumed towards the cellars of the house. The further they climbed, the more recent the building work appeared to be.

Reaching the top of the flight Nimrod came to a halt. Jacob stopped below him and looked up quizzically, his head tipped to the right. "What is it?" he asked.

Nimrod silenced the freak with a "Shhh!", a finger on his lips and a wave of his hand. Ahead of him was a network of rooms and corridors, vaulted cellars and storerooms that led off from one central sanded passageway. He could see the brickwork of other walls and further doorways through the archways opening off both sides of this passage. He did not need Jacob's heightened sense of hearing now to make out the pitiful moaning voices, the dragging of feet – or other body parts – on the sandy floor. And the smell – the smell was indescribable.

Nimrod's grip on the gun in his hand tightened, one gloved finger tensed against the trigger. With his free hand he signalled for Jacob to follow him.

Placing his feet carefully again – this time to avoid grinding the grains of sand beneath his heels as much as he was able – Nimrod led the way through the cellar-dungeon.

He had only gone five yards when he came upon the first of the dungeon's prisoners. He surprised the thing, lying there in the near darkness, and cursed inwardly as it let out a yelp of surprise. Nimrod pointed his gun at the thing's face, his finger tightening on the trigger.

It had been human once – at least part of it had – that much he could tell from its face. But it could hardly be described as human now. It looked more like a human face had somehow become attached to a seal's body. The thing still had one arm – although the elbow seemed to bend the wrong way – but on the other side of its body it had a flipper. Its hide glistened wetly.

On seeing Nimrod the inhuman thing tried to pull itself out of the way, dragging its great body along by its one crooked arm.

Hearing a hiss of aggression from his right, Nimrod spun round, gun raised.

The seal-thing's cry of alarm had attracted more inhuman things. A figure emerged from the shadows contained within an archway. A head shorter than Nimrod, it walked on two legs, like a man, but its features were something wholly other. The roughness of the skin and the jaundiced yellow of its eyes reminded Nimrod of the lizard-creature he and Master Ulysses had run into in the sewers beneath Southwark, while the thin red sliver of a forked tongue darted in and out of its toothless mouth.

Where the seal-thing was naked, this creature wore a basic sackcloth shirt and trews, like someone incarcerated in the poorhouse.

And there were still more abominations crowding in on them; things that were half-men and half sea-creature, the head of one – entirely hairless, its porcelain pale skin shot through with blue veins – swelled and then deflated again with its own pulsating rhythm, where there should have been a mouth there was nothing but the fronds of a sea anemone.

One squatted like a toad, its mouth forced open by a set of anglerfish jaws that were far too big for it. Another was only human from the trunk down; its arms were writhing octopoidal tentacles while the beaked head of some large fish sat directly on top of its shoulders. They were like something out of a Hieronymus Bosch painting he had once lifted from an art gallery, the denizens of some macabre garden of unearthly delights.

Nimrod tried to count how many of them there were, moving towards he and Jacob from out of the dank shadows. He reached twenty before another movement to his left distracted him from the task. Certainly there were more than he had bullets for. Perhaps he would only need to kill a few of them before the others gave up the fight.

Another peered around the corner of an archway, and for a moment Nimrod felt relief that there was another normal human being down there with them. The young woman looked at him with puppyish curiosity and then moved into the light cast by the flickering fizzing bulbs. Nimrod took an involuntary step backwards as he realised that the entire left-hand side of her body – the side that had been hidden behind the arch – was in no way human at all.

Half of her head was that of some overgrown insect, a lone mandible clacking uselessly from within the woman's distended mouth. Her torso writhed with unidentifiable pseudopods and she supported the weight of her albino body on a pair of crustacean limbs, as long as a man's arm and with one too many joints.

He bumped into something soft and pliable and spun on his heel again. The slug-like body, the size of a child with the face to match shifting and sliding across the inconstant, rippling flesh of the gastropod mollusc flinched, recoiling into its own mucusy mass.

Nimrod gagged. He was not one to have his stomach turned so easily, but what he and the freak had found down here, dwelling in near darkness under the Umbridge estate was something of another magnitude of appalling horror altogether.

Who would do such a thing? And how, against all the odds, had it been achieved?

As he was so ready to decry, Nimrod was not a medical man, but he knew enough about physiology to understand that any attempt to marry human flesh with that of another species should have resulted in failure and, like as not, death, as a result of tissue rejection.

In his moment of shocked hesitation, the things moved in closer again. He swallowed hard. It was time to take decisive action.

"Take care, Jacob," Nimrod said clearly, so that the other things present might hear him just as well. "They may be hostile."

Nimrod swept his pistol round in an arc in front of him. Instinctively, it seemed, the creatures moved back, as if they were fully aware of the danger the weapon presented. They must have seen such a thing before.

Nimrod set his eyes on the door he could see now at the end of the passageway; solid steel, with a small barred grille at face height.

He took a confident step forward and the gathered pack backed away before him. He poked his gun at a slavering, dog-faced creature and the horde moved away further still. Nimrod took another step forward into the space left by the retreating abominations. He glanced back over his shoulder and saw Jacob still close behind him, the pack moving in to block the way back behind them.

Apart from the occasional discomforting mewling whimper, snake-like hiss or epileptic tapping of chitinous claws, none of the cellar's inhabitants moved to attack them, or to halt their progress. It seemed as though the half-human things were letting Nimrod and his companion pass, almost as if they were keen for them to make it to the door and leave. It was almost as if the creatures were showing them the way out.

As he passed the abominations he looked at them more closely. The things looked back at him with pleading watery eyes. And there was fear there too. He became aware of inflamed knots of scar tissue, where one unnatural body part was joined to another.

There were other marks too, that were not the result of some abominable surgery; burns, grazes, contusions. And there was something about the condition of their skin, the way it clung so closely to whatever passed for a skeleton in each individual case – if they even had such a thing – sunken eyes and bony joints that suggested malnutrition in many cases.

The longer he observed them the more certain he became. These were wretched specimens indeed, but what made their already abominable condition even worse was that they were scared and abused, both mentally and physically. They had been half-starved and beaten into submission. Nimrod was almost amazed that hunger hadn't driven them to fall upon each other. Perhaps they were more human than he had at first realised.

But who could do such a thing to creatures that must once have been human, no matter how unlikely that seemed now.

The rough, broken-nosed face of one individual came to mind immediately: Rudge, the gamekeeper.

The last of the surgical subjects hauled its massive bulk out of the way – a creature with the pallid, hairless physique of a great ape topped off with the head of a child, a languid expression in its eyes, and strings of saliva dangling from its stroke-twisted mouth – and then there was the door in front of them.

Nimrod tried the handle.

"I might have known it," he said gravely, finding himself talking in a whisper, feeling suddenly self-conscious in the expectant stillness that hung over the pack. "It's locked."

"Then where do we go from here?" Jacob asked. The half-human, half-animal things – like the inmates of some macabre and grotesque menagerie – watched them with expectant eyes, as if hoping against hope that Nimrod and his companion would find a way to open the door. "Miss Jennifer needs us."

"As, I suspect, does Master Ulysses," Nimrod said, boldly putting away his gun and taking something else from one of his coat pockets. "But do not worry, I have yet to encounter a lock that I could not pick."

Having chosen a pick from the set on the hoop of metal he had taken from his pocket, Nimrod set to work. Pushing the shaped metal rod into the keyhole, he twisted and turned it, staring blankly ahead of him as he did so, tongue sticking out of the corner of his mouth, visualising in his mind's eye what he could determine from his probing.

He gave one last twist, and a sharp metal click echoed through the stillness of the cellar.

Nimrod remained exactly where he was. Had his release of the lock sounded as loud in the passageway beyond? Was there someone approaching their position even now, armed and dangerous and ready to deal with them once and for all?

He waited; one second, two seconds, five, ten...

Slowly, Nimrod tried the handle again. This time the door opened a crack.

Not one of the creatures moved: Nimrod had half expected them to make a break for freedom, but they remained where they were, all eyes on him and Jacob as first one, and then the other, passed through the open door and into the corridor beyond.

Nimrod looked back at the gathered pack, as if giving them one last chance to escape, waiting for them to make their move. But no move came. It was as if by some silent consensus the creatures had decided that they had played their part, that they had done enough.

The fear was there in their eyes again, clearer than ever, as if they knew what it was that lay beyond the door and could not bear to confront it again.

Nimrod closed the door, but left it unlocked. He scanned the corridor ahead, lit again by strings of caged electric lights, and wondered what it was that the inhabitants of the bizarre menagerie knew, that he did not.

"What do we do now?" Jacob asked, looking at Nimrod with imploring, anxious eyes from beneath the lumpen growths of his face.

Nimrod put away the lock picks and took out his pistol.

"Now we face our fears," he said.

CHAPTER TWENTY

Last Supper

THE SNAP AND crunch of the crab cracker breaking open the cooked crustacean's claw cut sharply through the stillness of the vast dining room. The only sound other than the crunch and clatter of specialised cutlery was the crack and pop of the fire blazing within the vast fireplace.

The polished mahogany table that ran the length of the formal dining chamber was easily large enough to seat thirty, but only two places had been laid this evening. At the head of the table, sat in a wheeled wicker bath chair, was Josiah Umbridge, terminally-ill industrialist, host and kidnapper. Opposite him, at the far end of the table, was Jennifer Haniver, cryptozoologist, orphan and now reluctant dinner guest.

Umbridge scooped fibres of white meat from the crab claw with a fork and stuffed them into his mouth. He ate ravenously, like a condemned man relishing his last meal.

Hands gripping the arms of her chair tightly, Jenny stared down at her plate, having no desire to look her incarcerator in the face.

"It'll get cold," Umbridge pointed out, gesticulating with his fork. "Aren't you hungry?"

"Funnily enough, no," Jenny spat, continuing to stare at the plate in front of her.

There was half a crab, some lobster in there too, and the coils of an octopus's tentacles, some squid and chunks of eel, by the looks of things, but not one of the dead sea creatures that had been served up for the meal was wholly intact. It had all been presented with care and, Jenny had to admit that it smelt delicious, but none of it had been presented in the conventional manner. And besides, no matter how much the aroma of the fish might cause her to salivate, she wouldn't be able to stomach a single mouthful, considering how this little supper for two had come about.

"What is it?" she said, disgust in her voice. "It looks like leftovers."

"I suppose it is, after a manner of speaking. But it is also the finest food that a man could ever hope to feast upon. The fruits of the sea. Surely you would not deny a dying man the chance to be a little extravagant and spoil himself when it came to his last supper."

Jenny looked up, startled. "Your *last* supper?" What did the old man know that she didn't? Was he planning to kill himself, end his agony now?

"That's right, my dear. And so I am sure that you would not deny me only the finest company also for such a meal."

Despite herself, Jenny felt her cheeks redden at the old man's compliment. Perhaps she had judged him too harshly. But that didn't change the fact that she and Ulysses had effectively been abducted against their will. Ulysses himself had received a vicious beating at the hands of the vile gamekeeper Rudge, and she had been taken away by another, a snivelling weasel of a man who looked like his ancestry included a whole host of other vermin as well. Her steely resolve returned in an instant.

She looked at the butler standing patiently beside the door at the other end of the room. He looked back at her, his face impassive, and she knew precisely what would happen if she tried anything.

For a moment she thought about taking her knife and making a run for Umbridge, holding him hostage until she was able to get out of there, perhaps even rescue Ulysses too. She considered the possibility for a moment and then dismissed the idea. There was no way she would be able to get away with it. The butler would have Umbridge's heavies there in an instant and then who knew what might happen to her. She had no idea how long the old man's tolerance of her might last, how deep his feelings for her ran; she doubted deep enough to stop him killing her. No, he had something else in mind, she was sure of it, something far more important than the imagined romance with a girl more than a third of his own age.

"Perhaps you would like some wine?" her host and abductor suggested, as he champed away at a mouthful of rubbery octopus flesh. "Molesworth, wine for our guest."

Jenny gazed at Umbridge in disbelief. How could he be so relaxed, carrying on as if she were a willing participant in this fiasco?

"I know," Umbridge laughed, catching her eye. "Chardonnay is not to your liking; you would prefer the claret. Well, hang convention! This is a special occasion. Have what you want."

"What I want?" Jenny seethed, no longer able to contain her frustration and despair in the face of the man's unwarranted good humour. "What I want? What I want is to not be forced to remain in this house a moment longer against my will. What I want is to know what you have done with Mr Quicksilver. What I want is to know why my father had to die!"

"That was a most unfortunate... accident." Umbridge stated flatly.

"An unfortunate accident?" Jenny screamed at him down the length of the table. "He was torn apart by some monstrous dog that, we believe, was under the control of your man Rudge!"

"Please, my dear," Umbridge said, picking up his wine glass and taking a sip. "You are disturbing the ambience. I am trying to enjoy my last meal as a human being."

"Oh, I'm sorry!" Jenny shrieked. "Perhaps you would prefer it if I ate up my food like a good little girl?"

Picking up her plate she hurled it towards the fireplace, the fine bone china smashing to smithereens against the cast iron grate. Crab meat and squid sizzled and popped on the white-hot logs.

For a moment her eyes alighted upon the hideous shrivelled thing that had been mounted in a glass display case on the mantelpiece above the fire. Something not quite fish and yet not quite mammal.

"You really should drink something," Umbridge said, carefully placing his cutlery on the table, his hands bunching to fists, knuckles whitening, his voice suddenly steel.

"Well, here's to you!" Raising her glass to the seething old man at the other end of the table, standing she shot him a grim smile through the tears now streaming down her cheeks and made her toast. "Up yours!" she said and tossed the wineglass into the fire after the plate.

"That was foolish," he said icily, taking another swig of wine from his own glass. "I am told that it will help make the experience that much easier to bear."

"What? What experience?"

He regarded her with an intense, gimlet gaze, all signs of good humour gone from his face.

"The world is changing, my dear, and I, for one, do not intend to be left behind."

"Left behind? But you're dying, you said so yourself," Jenny sobbed, confused and upset, trying to make sense of the madness unfolding around her and into which she felt she was falling, deeper and deeper.

"This body is dying," he stated matter-of-factly, "but I do not intend to die with it."

"What are you talking about?" she screamed.

"I am going to ascend this pathetic mortal frame of mine. I have spent too long building my company, lived through too much to lose it all now... to cancer! The inheritors of Darwin's legacy will have to create a new classification for me, for I shall be the first of a new species. I shall become *homo superior*. The textbooks will have to be re-written in my honour."

"What?" she gasped, cruel realisation slowly dawning on her.

"You were right, Miss Haniver," Umbridge said, his voice calm again. "The creature that killed your father was just one step on the way to achieving perfection and the accomplishment of my dream – every man's dream – the desire for immortality. I do not intend to die today or tomorrow, or whenever fate and the cancer consuming my body choose." A dark smile crept across his face. "I do not intend to die at all."

Jenny collapsed back into her chair as she realised that she was at the mercy of a madman, the sheer level of insanity on display too much to cope with.

"Our planet is sick," Umbridge went on. "This country, the empire, the whole world, is sickening, is changing. Every day it becomes ever more polluted and no matter what Prime Minister Valentine and his toadies might say, we are long past the point of no return. No, this is what our world has become, and we should embrace that change, as failed custodians of planet Earth.

"I shall be the first of this wondrous new species. But if I am to be father to a new race, I shall need a consort," Jenny stared at him in horror, mouth open in a silent scream, body frozen rigid with terror, "which is where you come in. A much preferable choice than the scullery maid I had marked down for that purpose, I must say, my dear, to your credit. You know, you really should drink something."

"You're mad," Jenny spluttered, finding her voice again, and, with it, the ability to move. She began to lift herself out of the chair, keeping her eyes on Umbridge's right-hand man all the time.

There was nothing else for it now. She grabbed the knife with her right hand. She had to get out of there now. She had to try, no matter what they might do to her, no matter how hard she had to fight. Anything, even death, had to be better than the horrific fate Umbridge had in mind for her.

Umbridge nodded to someone over Jenny's shoulder. She glanced back to see Rudge and his weasely accomplice closing on her position, having entered by some disguised doorway at the back of the room.

Jenny was still half out of her chair when the two rogues made a grab for her.

She spun round, lashing out with the knife in her hand as she did so. For a moment she felt resistance as the serrated edge made contact with something and then froze in shocked surprise as she saw blood beading across the burly gamekeeper's cheek and the bridge of his nose. He put a hand to his face and then looked at the blood now painting his fingertips.

"Bitch!" Rudge snapped and struck out with the flat of his ham-sized hand, slapping her hard across the face.

Stunned, Jenny lost coordination, making it all the more easy for the two ruffians to restrain her and drag her from the room.

The heels of her walking boots kicked against the polished floorboards as she tried to do something – anything – in the hope of breaking free and somehow, against all the odds, getting away. The pain in her ankle was as nothing compared to her fear of what Umbridge had in store for her.

"You're insane!" she screamed as she was hauled from the room. "Insane!"

THE YOUNG WOMAN'S cries echoing back to him along the sepulchral halls and passageways of the great house, Josiah Umbridge continued his meal – alone.

How will food taste after I have ascended? he wondered, as he tucked into a platter of roast pheasant, honey-roast parsnips, rosti potatoes and shallots. Indeed, how would he experience any of his senses through his new body?

Would he still only be able to see in the conventional optical spectrum? Would he touch, taste and hear in the same way, smell in the same way? Surely not; not when his new body offered him so many more ways in which to experience the world around him. One thing was for certain, it would be far superior to the cancer-riddled, corpse-in-waiting he inhabited at present. As far as Umbridge was concerned, his longed-for transformation could not come quickly enough.

After the pheasant there came a magnificent dessert of crème brule and chocolate chestnut truffles, and after that the cheese platter, the crackers and grapes as well.

Just as he was savouring his last mouthful, a telephone rang in an adjacent room.

"If you'll excuse me, sir," Molesworth mumbled before departing the dining room to take the call on his master's behalf. He returned only a few minutes later.

The butler approached the table and coughed politely.

"Yes, Molesworth?"

"Doktor Seziermesser is ready for you now, sir."

"Excellent," Umbridge said, dabbing at the corners of his mouth with his napkin before laying it beside his empty plate. "Excellent! The time has come, Molesworth. The time has come at last!"

"Yes, sir."

Umbridge let out an almost girlish giggle. "Tonight I say farewell to this feeble flesh, this mortal coil. Tonight I become immortal. Tonight I shall ascend to godhood!"

"Yes, sir," Molesworth said impassively and wheeled the wizened old man, hunched in his bath chair, from the room.

CHAPTER TWENTY-ONE

The Doktor Will See You Now

CAUTIOUSLY, PISTOL CINCHED close to his waist, Nimrod peered around the cracked plaster corner of another bend in the passageway. "This is more like it," he said to himself.

The corridor ahead of him was the most modern-seeming and clearly the most regularly used of any they had come across so far. The lights were brighter here, gently humming fluorescent tubes placed at regular intervals so that nothing was left in darkness. The floor, rather than being made of compacted earth, or sand-dusted brick, was tiled. Tiles also covered the lower half of the walls, while above that they were painted a dull hospital blue.

Not that there was much blue to be seen. The place still didn't look like it had been cleaned recently, a thin veneer of grease and grime covering everything. One beneficent consequence of this was that Nimrod could clearly see the footprints of those who had passed along here most recently as smeary marks on the sticky floor tiles.

Three doors led off from the clinical corridor to the left, another to the right, and at the end of the brightly-lit passageway, a flight of steps led up to, what Nimrod imagined must be, the ground floor of the house.

Jacob waiting patiently behind Nimrod, happy for the more experienced man to lead the way into whatever danger might await them here.

Nimrod listened. He could hear unsettling sounds, a muffled sobbing from behind one of the doors, the rattling purr and rumble of an engine somewhere and, clearly audible above them all, the insidious dentist-drill whirr of an electrical cutting tool being put to use.

Nimrod took a step forward – feeling suddenly very exposed under the neon glare of the lights – feeling the adhesive resistance of whatever it was that covered the tiled floor with its sticky residue. He decided not to spend too long dwelling on what it might be; it had a greasy sheen and when he moved the smell of rancid fat rose from the floor.

He paused at the first door on his left. Over the other noises coming to him down the passageway he could hear a plaintive moaning.

He tried the handle. It wasn't locked.

He opened the door a crack. Dirty yellow light spilled out. The moaning voice became louder. Pistol at the ready, Nimrod pushed the door open fully.

The sight that met his eyes shocked him far more than anything he had so far witnessed within this den of vivisection and madness.

Master Ulysses lay huddled on the sparse straw mattress of a pallet bed. He was rocking from side to side, his eyes tight shut, hair plastered to his head with sweat, his abused body wet with it.

From the waist up he was naked – his jacket and blood-stained shirt had been laid carefully over a wooden stool. The dark blooms of bruises were visible over his ribs, his chest, his back. His face was pale, his eyes grey-ringed hollows, the bandages bound around the stump of his left arm crimson with blood.

Without pausing to check whether the coast was clear, Nimrod ran to his master's side, and fell on his knees beside the shabby cot. Encircling him with both his arms, Nimrod hugged him close, rocking backwards and forwards in time with the deliriously moaning man, tears streaming down his face.

"It's alright, sir. I'm here now. It's alright," he whispered softly, into Ulysses' ear. "It's alright. They can't hurt you anymore. I wouldn't let them hurt you anymore."

He manoeuvred his right hand and examined the stump of his master's arm by touch alone. He could feel the nub of clean-cut bone beneath the folds of skin that had been roughly-stitched together over the severed humerus.

Ulysses flinched at Nimrod's touch, his constant moaning becoming more pained, but still his eyes remained closed.

"It's alright now," Nimrod repeated, stroking the delirious man's sweat-slick hair out of his face, his own freely-flowing tears splashing onto Ulysses' eyelids. "It's going to be alright."

Hearing the scraping drag of clubfeet on the tiled floor of the cell, Nimrod looked up and for a moment appeared almost surprised to see the lumpen-headed Jacob standing there.

The lips of the man's sagging mouth moved, as if he was about to speak, and then he seemed to think better of it. He had no words for what had happened here.

Nimrod stared at the other plaintively, with an expression of desperation, as if pleading with the malformed young man to help, to do something – anything. And then his features took on a terrifying aspect, tightening into a look of unadulterated hatred, the eyes hardening to diamond, cold and piercing, the tears blinked away in a moment.

"Someone is going to pay for this," he hissed with barely restrained fury. "Someone will pay!"

Jacob took a nervous step backwards in the face of Nimrod's rage.

Carefully laying his master back onto the sweat-drenched mattress and pulling a discarded grey blanket from the foot of the bed over his shivering form, Nimrod sprang to his feet.

"Watch him," he instructed Jacob, in a voice that brooked no debate, and strode from the room.

Pistol in hand, Nimrod proceeded along the empty passageway and stopped outside the second door. Putting his ear to the unsmoothed wooden planks, he listened.

The sound of sobbing came from beyond. Nimrod had little doubt who it was making them, although as to her current condition, that was another matter altogether.

And there was something else. Mingled with the smells of stale disinfectant and unwashed bodies wafting through the corridor, another aroma seemed to ooze from under the door, the ammonia and dung of terrified animals.

He tried the handle. The door was unlocked, like the last.

Eschewing stealth for urgency now, he stepped boldly into the room. In was much like the last, except that a matted mess of rotten straw and faeces covered the floor here. It looked as though it had been used as a holding pen for animals – before they were subjected to the incomprehensible whims of an over-eager surgeon. Another door in the far corner of the room connected the stinking cell to the room beyond, from which came the unmistakeable rattling whirr and squeal of mechanical cutting blades.

It was as he had expected; Miss Haniver sat sprawled against the wall on the other side of the dimly-lit cell, hands pulled up above her head, bound together with cord at the wrists which had then been tied again to a rusted iron ring hammered into the wall. The young woman's ankles had been bound as well, the cord cutting into the puffy flesh of her sprained right ankle in particular. And she had been gagged, but that didn't stop her sobs and couldn't hold back her tears of terror.

At first she pulled back, seeing Nimrod silhouetted there within the doorway, the brighter light of the passageway behind him, turning him into a shadow whose body language spoke of deadly intent. But then, as he entered the room, terror was replaced by a surge of relief and her sobs of resigned despair became gasping sobs of delight.

Unsheathing a pocketknife, Nimrod cut through the cords binding her wrists and her ankles. He helped her to her feet and then, putting a finger to his lips, he helped her pull the gag free.

The two of them stood there for a moment in the stinking cell, listening to the sound of the powered cutting blade, the young woman attempting to read Nimrod's intentions from his steely expression. Placing the knife into her shaking hands, he guided her back towards the door, from there into the corridor, and then to the cell where he had left his master. Before opening the second cell door, he fixed her with his sapphire stare and put a finger to his lips. Only then did he direct her through it.

Ignoring the involuntary sobbing gasp he heard, Nimrod re-entered the holding pen and approached the door in the far corner. With a dying whine, he heard the mechanical cutter come to a stop.

Pressing himself against the damp brickwork beside the door, he tested the handle. It turned with a click.

He froze. Had whoever was on the other side heard it too?

He waited, his breath shallow, his heart beating a tattoo of adrenalin-heightened anticipation against his ribcage.

He heard voices, and they were coming his way. Pistol at the ready once more, he prepared to meet whoever was approaching. Rubbing his eyes with the back of a sleeve he pulled at the handle and opened the door just a fraction, trying to get a glimpse of who, or what, awaited him on the other side.

From what Nimrod could see, the room beyond was decorated in the same way as the neon-lit corridor outside – all white tiles and blue paint – but here they were stained with the rust-red traces of dried blood.

The sour smell of disinfectant, the strong iron reek of blood, and something else – something strangely familiar, like aniseed mixed in with the rancid meat smell of the laboratory – permeated the place.

"Take him back to the cell," he heard someone say in a clipped German accent. "The anaesthetic will start to wear off soon." Nimrod didn't recognise the voice.

"Right you are, doc," he heard another man say. This voice he knew; it belonged to Rudge the gamekeeper. He had tracked him down at last.

"And if I were you, I'd make sure I wasn't in the same room as Mr Umbridge when he comes round," the German went on. "It might take him a little time to... adjust."

"Don't worry, I wasn't planning on being," Rudge replied, his voice receding.

Someone walked right past the door – grubby, once-white lab-coat, shock of untidy grey hair, long vulcanised rubber gloves, and strangely-lensed spectacles – their sudden appearance startling Nimrod.

He pressed himself flat against the wall, holding his breath. For a moment he considered simply bursting into the room and taking on the peculiar scientist. But whatever thoughts of vengeance he might now harbour in his heart – and he was not a man to let a trespass go unpunished – acting on them would have to wait. What was of prime importance now was finding a way of putting right the wrong that had been done to Ulysses Quicksilver.

He was going to have to choose his moment carefully. Someone had amputated Master Ulysses' arm with surgical precision and Nimrod planned to make that same someone undo the damage he had caused, ideally reversing the procedure, if he could. If not, then the faithful retainer's wrath would know no bounds.

There was the sound of movement, like something large – something very large – moving sluggishly around inside the room. There was a sudden crash as a tray of metal tools was sent cascading onto the tiled floor.

"Please be careful, Mr Rudge," the German's voice came again.

"I can't 'elp it, like. Its legs are 'alf asleep as well. How much of the knock-out juice did you give it?"

"Do I tell you how to do your job, Mr Rudge?"

Nimrod did not hear the gamekeeper's answer as the sluggish thing he was trying to shift bashed into a cabinet. But he heard the doctor's response.

"Then kindly do not tell me how to do mine. The rest of the subject should be anaesthetised enough that it can be guided but remains docile until Mr Umbridge can exert his will and take control of the body."

There was another crash.

"But I would not take too long about it. Anaesthesia is not an exact science in a case such as this."

"I thought you said you knew what you were doing," Rudge's complaining voice came again.

Nimrod heard the other reply with a *harrumph* of annoyance.

"Don't worry, doc. I know how to handle this thing."

The doctor sighed. "I know you do, and I do wish you would refrain from tormenting it so. I would prefer not to have to perform another skin graft."

"I thought you weren't going to tell me how to do my job."

"But you have Mr Umbridge in your tender care now. You would do well to remember that, Mr Rudge."

The gamekeeper muttered something in return that was subsumed by more grating scrapes as whatever it was that Rudge was trying to manoeuvre dragged a steel gurney after it.

"I shall just check on our other guest," Nimrod heard the surgeon say as Rudge, and whatever it was he had with him, left the operating theatre, the German's voice getting louder as he approached the door to the holding cell.

The unkempt surgeon opened the door without a second thought and entered the pen. Before he had even clocked that his guest was gone, Nimrod grabbed him, twisting one arm up behind the man's back. With his other hand he seized doctor around the neck, putting pressure on his windpipe, so that the surgeon couldn't cry out and yet, at the same time, could see the gun in his hand.

"And who might you be?" Nimrod hissed into his hostage's ear.

Nimrod continued to squeeze the man's throat, pressing the muzzle of his pistol into the soft flesh under his jaw.

"And, before I let you answer, just remember that I can carry out a little operation of my own in a split second – a craniotomy, if you like. I can transplant your brain from inside your skull to the wall behind us with one simple incision. So, your name."

"Seziermesser," the German croaked as Nimrod eased the pressure on his windpipe slightly. At the same time he increased the pressure on the arm he had forced behind the man's back.

"Well done, Doktor Seziermesser. Very good. Now I take it that you are the one who removed Mr Quicksilver's arm, are you not?"

The surgeon did not answer immediately, as if weighing up the merits of trying to pass the blame onto someone else, but then obviously thought better of it. He nodded.

"Excellent. Excellent."

The pressure on Seziermesser's arm increased, almost to the point where his wrist was ready to snap. The surgeon's cry of pain was stifled by Nimrod's arm tightening around his neck again.

"Why?" Nimrod hissed sharply in his ear.

"For... For the great work," the doktor replied, as if that was all the explanation that was needed.

"But that was a mistake, wasn't it?"

Nimrod felt the man's Adam's apple bob as he swallowed hard.

"And now you have the opportunity to correct your little mistake, because you're going to put it back."

Nimrod eased the tightness of his hold on the surgeon's arm. After all, he didn't want to break his arm when Seziermesser needed his hands to operate on Master Ulysses again.

The doktor craned his head round, trying to look Nimrod in the eye. "But I can't."

"What?" Nimrod snarled, his anger bubbling to boiling point. "Why not?"

"Because it has become part of the great work. I no longer have it."

"Then you are of no further use to me."

Nimrod pushed the doktor away from him violently, hooking one foot around the man's ankles and pulling his feet out from under him. The surgeon went sprawling in the muck and mouldering straw that covered the cell floor.

Gripping his pistol firmly in two hands, Nimrod took aim and began to squeeze the trigger.

"Wait!" the other screeched, turning desperate lens-magnified eyes on his would-be executioner, holding up his hands as if in surrender. It was then that, for the first time, Nimrod saw that the surgeon's own left hand was missing, a two-pronged metal claw poking out of the sleeve of his filthy coat.

"Why?" Nimrod said coldly. "You no longer have the arm, ergo you cannot make amends for your crime, hence you are of no further use to me. You have seen my face, you know I'm here. I cannot allow you to live."

"No, I-I said I don't have *his* arm," the doktor stammered, desperate for his plea to be heard before Nimrod shot him. "But I do have another. Please, just don't shoot me!"

Nimrod slowly lowered the gun. The surgeon continued to regard him with wide, anxious eyes.

"Another arm?"

Tentatively, never once taking his eyes off Nimrod, the man struggled to his feet, pushing at the stones of the floor with his crude claw.

"It's this way," he said, indicating the door to the operating theatre. "Come this way."

CHAPTER TWENTY-TWO

A Fate Worse Than Death

HE WOKE TO the sound of distant roaring. It was a terrible, savage sound, a sound like fury, a sound like bloodlust, a sound like nothing he had ever heard before – the bellow of a bull, the roar of a lion and the scream of a man all rolled into one. It spoke of rage, frustration, horror and madness. Such a sound could surely only be made by a creature from his nightmares, not by any actual living thing.

Perhaps, Ulysses Quicksilver considered, he was delirious or trapped in some waking nightmare.

He blinked his eyes and saw three figures standing there looking down at him, outlined by grimy yellow light. There, to his right, was Jennifer, holding his hand tightly, and that knowledge and her touch were enough to make him want to smile.

He raised his head. Pain rolled around his skull, as if a heavy metal ball was trapped in there, forcing him to lie back and making him close his eyes. But before he did so, he saw that there was someone else standing by the door, beyond the three, someone who looked as if his head should be too heavy for his neck to support.

He lay still for a moment before opening his eyes again, and found Jennifer's tear-stained face once more. As he gazed into the young woman's glistening eyes he couldn't quite shake the feeling that there was something he had forgotten, something that he really should try to remember. It was like a memory-shaped hole inside his head, a fading thought like a dream that, on waking, refuses to be forgotten, wanting to be remembered.

But as he struggled to recall what it was that he really should have remembered, a dull ache grew within his mind, as if the effort of recollection was too much, an ache that began to permeate every part of his body, from his arms to his legs.

His arms... It was something about his arms...

Ulysses moved his gaze from his dear, sweet Jenny to the tall, lean figure, standing at the foot of the cot he was lying on. There stood Nimrod, looking like some grim-faced guardian angel, as stern as Ulysses had ever seen him look. He had his arms folded in front of him, his gun in his right hand, cocked and ready.

And then suddenly he was seeing Nimrod in his mind's eye, tears streaming down his face – which was most unlike the old, emotional cold fish that he was – and he heard his manservant's voice in his ear again, as if from far away: *"It's alright now. It's going to be alright."*

He turned from Nimrod to the figure to his left, the one who was monitoring a drip that had been set up next to his bed.

And then the memories came flooding back, in a torrent of unmitigated horror and excruciating agony.

"No!" Ulysses screamed, suddenly finding his voice, drawing himself up at the head of the bed, anything to get away from the maniac surgeon.

"He is awake," Doktor Seziermesser said with unbelievable calm.

"It's alright, Ulysses," he could hear Jenny saying, but his mind refused to believe that it could be, not with that scalpel-wielding madman there in the room.

"No! Get him out of here!" he bawled. His desperate eyes fixed on Jennifer, his imploring gaze transfixing her own. "You don't know what he did to me!"

"But it's alright now, Ulysses."

This had to be a dream; some sick nightmare. Jennifer didn't know what she was saying! It couldn't be real, because the reality of the situation was too terrible to bear.

Recalling what the unbearable truth was now, remembered pain lancing his body, Ulysses pulled his hand from her desperate grasp and felt for the stump of his left arm. But before his fingers reached the bony nub he felt them come into contact with a covering of coarse hair.

Surprise seizing hold of him again, he looked at what his hand had found.

Black fur covered leathery grey skin, stretched taut over a pronounced and unusual musculature.

The agitated Ulysses traced the shape of the arm from the overly-long fingers and the grey leather palm of the hand to where stitching formed the boundary where his own shoulder ended and the primate's arm began.

"What have you done?" he shrieked at the vivisectionist.

"What had to be done," Nimrod said frankly.

Ulysses' turned back to his most trusted companion.

"Nimrod," he gasped, "he's given me a monkey's arm!"

"It is that of a chimpanzee, actually," Seziermesser corrected him, "not a monkey."

Ulysses' appalled stare returned to the surgeon.

"You did this to me!" he screamed, rising from what he now realised was the operating table, as shock turned to anger and anger swiftly blackened to hatred.

Jenny clutched her hands together in anxiety, as if waiting for someone else to make the move to stop him. Nimrod didn't move a muscle but watched the furious Ulysses advance on the maleficent Seziermesser, a grim smile playing about his lips.

Seziermesser took a shuffling step backwards, looking from Ulysses to Jennifer and Nimrod and back again, as if somehow hoping against all hope that one of them might intervene.

"*You did this to me!*" Ulysses screamed directly into Seziermesser's face, spittle flying from his lips. He seized the doktor by the lapels of his filthy lab-coat, with both his one human hand and the chimp substitute. The drip-stand rattled as the tube in his arm pulled taut. Releasing the doktor for a moment, Ulysses yanked the tube from his simian arm, a yellowish liquid dribbling onto the floor of the operating theatre. His nose curled as his nostrils were assailed by the acrid stink of aniseed and spoiled beef.

He grabbed hold of the doktor again and slammed him into a counter, sending a tray of tools flying.

"Where is my arm? *Where is my arm?*"

And just when everyone in the room thought that Ulysses was going to crack the vivisectionist's skull open, to everyone's surprise, including his own, he released his hold on the surgeon. Seziermesser dropped onto the metal counter with a crash, glass bottles tinkling together in reply.

Ulysses turned away in disgust, his whole body suddenly sagging as if the trauma of what had happened to him was at last starting to sink in.

Despite that fact that he had been either unconscious or delirious for God knows how many hours, his unerring sixth sense still played its part, awareness blooming hotly in his hindbrain. He turned in time to see Seziermesser, scalpel gripped tightly in his right hand, pushing himself off from the counter, using his blunt steel claw to give himself extra leverage.

Acting virtually on instinct alone, Ulysses lashed out. The bunched fingers of the simian hand struck the man, connecting with the side of his head before the surgeon could land his own poorly-judged attack.

The blow lifted Seziermesser off his feet and sent him crashing into the operating table, the drip-stand clattering to the floor beneath him. He lay sprawled where he fell, the scalpel slipping from slack fingers, a dazed groan of pain escaping his lips. His magnifying spectacles skittered across the floor to come to rest several feet away.

And then Ulysses was leaning over him again, pulling the dazed Seziermesser up by the lapels of his coat, until he was practically nose to nose with the surgeon.

"How did you do it, eh, doktor?" Ulysses growled. "How did you do this?" He glanced sharply at the ape arm clutching a handful of the surgeon's lab-coat. "*How did you do it?*"

Blinking myopically, Seziermesser craned his head backwards. Ulysses followed his gaze as the surgeon tried to see what was on top of the counter behind him. Ulysses peered at the collection of bottles, flasks and other vessels, eyes darting from one container to the next, desperately trying to see what must be right there, staring him in the face.

And then, there it was; an unassuming flask, with no label or other distinguishing marks whatsoever, other than for the yellow-green liquid that half-filled it.

Dropping the wretched physician again, Ulysses stepped over him and grabbed the container. He sniffed at the neck of the flask. The heady scent of fennel and spoiled steak rose from the liquid within. Ulysses' quizzical frown became a gargoyle grimace of utter hatred.

"We have the Alchemist to thank for that," Seziermesser said mysteriously.

Ignoring him, stepping back over the prone surgeon, not even giving him a second glance, Ulysses walked over to Nimrod.

"Get him out of my sight," he snarled.

"Yes, sir. With pleasure, sir."

Hauling Seziermesser to his feet by the scruff of his neck, without another word Nimrod dragged the unnervingly quiet surgeon from the room.

NIMROD LED THE slouching surgeon along the tiled corridor and into the dungeon-like cellars beyond. They stopped at last in front of a large steel door with a barred grille set into it at head height.

"What are you going to do to me?" the doktor asked at last, as if resigned to the fact that there was no hope for him now.

"Oh, it's not what *I'm* going to do to you."

A cold shiver coursing down his spine and into his stomach, Seziermesser turned and saw the other's dark, shark-like smile, revealed as they passed through the dirty cylinders of sodium light cast by the crackling nicotine-brown bulbs. Fear of the uncertain fate that awaited him consumed him completely now.

His despair deepened when he looked back at the door and a chill realisation seeped into his brain, as cold as glacial melt-water. He had not been here himself for some time – care of the test subjects had always been one of Rudge's responsibilities – but Seziermesser recognised it now, faced with the ominous, rust-streaked door again.

In the quiet of the corridor, Seziermesser listened. He could hear slavering sounds, pitiful mewling cries and a noise like an old woman weeping. And there were other, more sinister – more threatening – sounds too, animalistic grunts and guttural growls.

"No, please no," he begged, knowing in his heart that it wouldn't make any difference anyway, that they had passed the point of no return.

Nimrod raised a sarcastic eyebrow at the doktor, checked the load in his gun and then promptly shot the man through the left kneecap.

Seziermesser cried out in shock and pain, and fell to the floor. Nimrod roughly hauled him to his feet and opened the door. The sounds became louder and a pungent, vile odour assailed their nostrils – an acrid mix of rank, unwashed bodies, like fish guts and faeces. Shapes moved in the gloom beyond.

"Goodbye, doktor," Nimrod said calmly, before throwing him through the opening and slamming the door shut after him.

NIMROD RETURNED A few minutes later, alone, by which time Ulysses had put on his borrowed shirt and jacket again, and introductions, of a sort, had been made.

The dandy looked almost like his old self again, other than for the fact that his shirt was stained with blood, his face was the colour and texture of a candle, and the incongruous grey chimp's hand protruding from the end of one sleeve.

"Nimrod," he said. "Give me your gloves."

Nimrod obediently took them off and handed them to his master. Without saying anything, Ulysses pulled them on, struggling a little to get the left glove on over his differently-proportioned ape hand.

And all the while the bestial howls and bellowing continued.

"What is that?" Ulysses asked finally having managed to put on both of the black leather gloves.

"I can't be certain, sir, but –" Nimrod began, before Jennifer interrupted him.

"I know what it is," she said. "It's Umbridge."

"It's what?"

"Before I ended up down here, before all this," she said, taking in the cell, and, by extension, all that had befallen them in the dungeons beneath Umbridge House, with a wave of her arm, "he shared his plans with me."

"So what you're telling me is that the sick old man we met earlier, the old bastard dying of cancer, has since become... *that*?" Ulysses challenged as another bellow rattled the light fittings of the room.

The reticent Jacob said nothing, listening intently to the exchange taking place between the dandy, his servant and Jennifer.

"But that's insane!"

"I know it is!" Jennifer answered shrilly. "I know it's insane, but he told me that he was going to ascend... be the first of a new species, that the doktor was building him a brand new body, and that I was to be his bride." She broke up in another fit of sobbing.

The poor girl had been pushed to the limit, Ulysses considered, thinking about someone else for the first time since he had come round from his traumatised delirious half-sleep. But then he too had been pushed to the edge and then right over it. As far as he was concerned, somebody still had to pay for what had been done to him.

"Then our work is not yet done here," he stated coldly. "I think it's time we put the poor bastard out of his misery, don't you?"

He took in the faces of those around him: the darkly smiling Nimrod; the puffy-eyed Jennifer; the anxious freak.

"But before we do, there is one last thing I have to do here."

Choosing a bottle from among those lined up on the metal counter, labelled 'Ethanol,' he pulled out the glass stopper – his nose wrinkling as the whiff of industrial alcohol hit him hard in the face – and then started sloshing its contents liberally around the room; over the operating table, over the tiled and stainless steel surfaces. He threw the empty bottle onto the floor, apparently uncaring of the fact that he might alert other servants of the insane industrialist to what he was doing.

"Nimrod, a light."

Without hesitation, his manservant reached into another well-resourced coat pocket and took out something square and silver, that gleamed dully in the bright lights of the operating theatre. Ulysses took the lighter and flicked it open, spinning the flint-wheel as he did so.

Without a second thought, He tossed the lighter into the middle of the room. The alcohol ignited with a satisfying *whoomph*, orange and blue flames rising right across the room, licking up the walls and embracing everything within its fiery clutches.

"That's better," Ulysses said, a cruel smile on his face, and turned to exit the operating theatre.

Out in the corridor, Jacob turned to Nimrod. "What did you do with the doktor?" he asked.

At that moment, a high-pitched scream echoed through the cellar-dungeons beneath the house, briefly even drowning out the bellows of the beast that lurked, unseen, elsewhere.

"As the saying goes," Nimrod said sagely, "ask me no questions and I'll tell you no lies."

Leaving the door open behind him, Ulysses followed the others as they hurried towards the steps at the end of the tarnished corridor. At least someone seemed to know where they were going, and it was Jenny who was leading the way, closely followed by Nimrod and the stray he appeared to have picked up along the way.

Giving the vivisectionist's burning lair one last lingering look, satisfied that nothing would ever be tortured and diced up there again, he stumbled after the others.

He could hear a voice now, coming from behind the lone door to the right, the last one that led off from the corridor, before the cellar steps. He would have known that traitorous voice anywhere. "Get away, yer bastard!" it barked, before adding. "I mean, sir. Keep back! Or you'll be gettin' another taste of the lash."

Ulysses quickened his steps.

When he was only a few feet away from the start of the staircase, the door opened, and Rudge stepped through.

"What the bloody 'ell's goin' on out 'ere?" he asked of no-one in particular. Then he saw Ulysses, his startled gaze moving quickly from the dandy's unsmiling face, to his left arm, his look of surprise becoming all the more pronounced.

As the two of them stood, frozen to the spot, staring at each other in bewildered surprise, something massive began to squeeze itself through the open doorway behind Rudge.

A huge hand, its skin grey leather, thick with black hair, grabbed the doorframe. Huge fingers dug into the mouldering wall on one side of the door, while on the other, a chitinous talon appeared – just as large as the hand – plaster cracking and crumbling beneath its indelicate touch as the claw sank into the brickwork beneath. And then another grasping forelimb appeared, and another, and lastly a startlingly human hand – compared to all the others – and one that Ulysses recognised.

Muscles bunching, crustacean claws levered the appalling bulk of the creature half through the door. The thing straightened, attempting to draw itself upright and its hulking shoulders, at least six feet across, scraped the ceiling of the passageway.

Atop the massive, multiple-armed torso – which appeared to be not one thing but created from parts of many different specimens – between the muscled mass of its unbalanced shoulders, Ulysses saw the face of Josiah Umbridge staring down at him.

The old man's eyes latched onto Ulysses, looking down at where he stood, isolated from his companions, his own appalled expression a mixture of revulsion, contempt and disbelief. Seeing who it was, cowering there before its grotesque majesty, the eyes narrowed as they continued to bore into Ulysses' own horror-widened gaze.

And then the abomination spoke, its voice a booming guttural growl, that wasn't quite a bullish roar and yet wasn't entirely human either.

"*Quiiick-siiil-verrr,*" it rasped.

CHAPTER TWENTY-THREE

The Chimera

ULYSSES STARED AT the monstrous thing as it continued to heave its malformed mass out of the door, the flickering firelight behind him and the neon strip lights above illuminating it all the more clearly now.

It was clear to Ulysses that the old man's head had been transplanted onto a hideous, man-made body, created by the insane vivisectionist Seziermesser. And what a piece of work it was – the great work that the surgeon had spoken of – a true chimera, stitched together from pieces of a plethora of other creatures. The torso in particular was criss-crossed with livid pink and purple scarring, demonstrating quite clearly where one body part had been connected to another, as the vivisectionist had pieced it together like some monstrous flesh-puzzle.

It looked as though the torso had been created around that of a large silverback gorilla, that had also provided the chimera with one of its left arms, but much had been added to both the ape's skeletal structure as well as its musculature, judging by the curious contours of its patchy hide. Externally it looked like there might even be some bull or bear in there, while smooth grey seal skin had been used to fill some of the gaps where the monster's skin had split under pressure from the shifting musculature beneath.

There had obviously been a need to add additional muscle groups to support the vivisect's unbalanced and wholly unnatural physique.

The creature's right shoulder was noticeably larger than the left, and in places heaving red wet muscles could be seen moving through further rents in the chimera's patchwork hide. But then the thing needed all that muscle to provide support and movement for three upper arms – if they could be called arms – on the right-hand side of its body.

Uppermost there was a long crustacean-like claw that must have been made from more than one creature, judging by its length and the unnatural number of joints it possessed. Close to the body was what appeared to be the hairy orange-furred arm of an orang-utan. Between these two was an arm that was more human in appearance, except that this one had two elbows and the vivid scarring where one bicep had been sewn onto the second elbow was clearly visible.

It was this one appendage that Ulysses recognised. Slowly a spark of anger reignited the ire deep inside him. Well he should recognise it. Admittedly, it appeared to have been inverted and now possessed a hideous purple hue, but nonetheless, it was still his arm!

A deep rage taking hold, Ulysses took in the rest of the abomination. It only had two limbs protruding from the left side of its upper body. The dominant limb was that of the gorilla, having been severed from the torso only to be stitched back on again but now with a slick-skinned protrusion beneath it, that didn't seem to have any bone structure at all, but writhed and twisted like a cephalopod's tentacle, although it ended in a huge, crushing crab's claw.

Even the old man's swaying head was not as it should be. While he had been putting the finishing touches to his last masterpiece, the mad doktor had added a little something here. The mouth was no longer able to shut properly as it looked like Seziermesser had managed to cram the teeth of another predatory killer in there, the skin around the hinging joint of the jawbone appearing stretched and more elastic.

Having used its arms to pull itself through the restricted opening of the doorway, the creature reared up before the incredulous dandy, its head nearly scraping the ceiling a good four feet above Ulysses' head. And it still wasn't fully out of the door.

The thing cantered forwards on a host of legs that could only have belonged to a giant spider crab – one of the monstrous twenty foot specimens that trawlers occasionally dragged up from rocky holes at the bottom of the North sea. The eight shell-encased limbs knocked hollowly on the tiled floor of the corridor.

And now Ulysses could see the monster in all its terrible glory. From the waist down its mammalian characteristics gave way to the mid-section of a crocodile – no doubt one of those century old monsters that could still be found lurking in the fetid jungle rivers at the heart of the Dark Continent – with its rough grey-green scale-armour and softer white underbelly. It was to this part that the giant spider crab legs had been attached. Reptilian flesh in turn gave way to the thick, fleshy grey tail of a shark, made up of almost nothing but the dagger-like rudder of the caudal fin.

Ulysses backed away from the monstrosity blocking their path to freedom.

"So, you wanted to become a new species, did you?" Ulysses asked the beast quietly, looking into the old man's unblinking eyes. "Well, as they say, you should be careful what you wish for, or you might just get it."

Unable to tear his gaze from Umbridge's tiny head, swaying hypnotically like a cobra between the brutish, adapted shoulders, he slowly became aware of another sound over the laboured snorting of the chimera, and the crackle and pop of the fire spreading behind him. It was a filthy, repugnant sound, like a boarish snorting. It was the sound of Rudge laughing.

There was no doubt about it: with the fire licking at the doorframe of the laboratory behind him, feeling its incandescent heat on his back, and with Rudge and the Umbridge-chimera in front of him, Ulysses was trapped.

Rudge's howls of laughter increased in volume as the Umbridge-chimera towered over him, the old man's distorted features peering at Ulysses with malign intent. Lips rolled back, exposing a double row of teeth, everything from canine fangs to the serrated triangular tips of shark's teeth. A thick, grey tongue slipped between them and the chimera hissed at Ulysses.

As he stared into the bloodshot eyes of the insane industrialist, transfixed by the old man's unblinking gaze – he was dimly aware that the thing's jaws were stretching open, far wider than was humanly possible. But then what had once been Josiah Umbridge wasn't truly human anymore. Their eyes still locked together, the old man's head glided closer on its twisting neck, as if Umbridge somehow intended to bite off his head.

The Umbridge-chimera opened its mouth and a reptilian bark emerged as smoke began to fill the passageway. Ulysses coughed and instinctively put a hand to his mouth as he suddenly came to his senses.

There was the cracking pop and shatter of glass breaking as the fire inside the laboratory grew in intensity. The chimera barked again, its head darting from side to side in distress.

It's afraid of the fire, Ulysses realised. And then he saw the burn marks – the scorched patches of fur, the shiny pink scar tissue on its flanks. Ulysses could only guess at their origins, but to look at the cruelly laughing Rudge, it wasn't hard to imagine that the gamekeeper had caused those injuries, long before Josiah Umbridge's head had been transplanted onto the vivisect body. The abuse had probably taken place over a period of some months, judging by the way some of the burns had healed; a means of keeping the growing abomination under control.

God alone knew what kind of primitive brain had been used to keep the vivisect's autonomic processes working until it was ready to receive the old man's head. Perhaps that rudimentary collection of ganglia had never been removed, left in to aid the old man in controlling all the disparate body parts. And what the chimerical body remembered, from the time before it had become the Umbridge-chimera, was that fire was to be feared.

And the primal fear of fire was now coupled with the old man's desperate desire to survive.

Ulysses wished he had his sword-cane with him as he watched the monster and its handler's every move, in case they unwittingly provided him with an opportunity to escape.

Then he saw it, tucked into the gamekeeper's trousers. He had obviously decided to keep that particular trinket for himself.

"Not so fast," Rudge growled, seeing where Ulysses' gaze had fallen, and put a possessive calloused hand over the end of it. "It's mine now."

Behind Rudge the chimera reared up on its spider-crab legs and let out a shriek. Flames were licking the ceiling now, the smoke thickening, accompanied by the acrid stink of boiling chemicals. It wouldn't be long before all of them were overcome by the smoke.

The creature was becoming more and more agitated. It skittered backwards and forwards, its great armoured limbs fidgeting restlessly beneath it. Its thick shark's tail lashed in alarm, sending Rudge suddenly stumbling towards Ulysses.

As Ulysses readied himself to make a grab for the exposed sword-cane at the big man's belt, Rudge turned sharply on the beast and, without a second thought, smacked it across the torso with the heavy cosh in his hands.

"Watch it, yer big bastard!" he shouted at the vivisect and the huge monstrosity retreated before the gamekeeper's blows, as its body-memory was reminded who the master was here.

Smoke billowed along the corridor, carried forward by the currents created in the air as the cold cellar was heated by the fire.

Ulysses edged forwards, closer to the gamekeeper and his monstrous charge, closer to his one hope of getting out of there.

And then he saw a change come over the Umbridge-chimera's expression. Where at first there had been only fear of Rudge's beatings, now there was full-blown desperate panic. The old man's eyes glared down at Rudge as he rained blow after blow onto the vivisect's massive body. The blows themselves didn't particularly hurt the beast, but they reminded it of pain the cruel man had inflicted in the past.

"Get back! Get back!" the gamekeeper shouted, trying to force the chimera back into the chamber from which it had come. "Come on! Move!"

And then its rheumy human eyes narrowed with a vicious intent all of its own. Rudge was the one thing stopping it from escaping from the hungry flames.

When the attack came, it came fast. The chimera lashed out with its crustacean claw and double-jointed arm at the same time, seizing hold of the huge man and lifting him off the ground. Before Rudge really understood what was going on, the tentacle, squid-like, whipped forwards, the huge crab's claw closing around the gamekeeper's kicking legs.

Rudge cried out. His yelp of pain became an agonised scream as the three limbs began to pull in different directions, the horrible high-pitched shriek filling the corridor for a moment before Rudge was suddenly and savagely silenced as the chimera tore him in half.

Loops of steaming intestine splashed to the floor as the gamekeeper gave one last gargling death rattle and a spray of hot, red blood bathed the walls, the floor, the chimera and Ulysses in a ruddy shower.

There was never going to be a better chance than this, Ulysses decided, as he made a break for it. The Umbridge-chimera distracted as it continued to dismember the gamekeeper's corpse, Ulysses pushed past the creature's scrabbling crab's legs.

And then he was through, only cool air and the cellar steps ahead of him.

AT THE TOP of the stairs Ulysses caught up with Nimrod and the others.

"It's this way," Jenny said breathlessly, as she led the party back through the palatial stately home at a run, heading for the entrance hall and a way out of the house.

Entering the dimly lit atrium, Ulysses became aware of several things all at once. The front door was already open and voices raised in argument echoed from the marble columns.

Umbridge's butler was there, valiantly trying to prevent a helmeted policeman from entering the premises. The dulcet tones of another irate officer reached Ulysses' ears, and for the first time in his life he felt pleased to hear Inspector Maurice Allardyce's voice raised in anger.

"Get out of the bloody way!" he heard Allardyce shout as two burly constables barged their way past the startled butler and into the house.

And then Ulysses heard the sound he had been dreading, booming from the passageway behind them.

"And who might you be, sir?" one of the constables asked as he was suddenly confronted by a wild-eyed Ulysses, trailing the smell of smoke with him into the atrium, accompanied by an agitated-looking older man in a long black cloak, a desperate, bedraggled young woman, and what could only be described as a sideshow freak.

"Never mind that!" Ulysses snapped as he pushed past the policeman. "You have to get out of here!"

"Now hang on a minute, sir," the constable said, putting out his arms as if to stop Ulysses' flight from the house. "We've had a report about this place –"

"Quicksilver!" Inspector Allardyce exclaimed as he too pushed his way into the entrance hall. "You look terrible. What have you got yourself mixed up in this time?"

"Allardyce, we all have to get out of here now!"

"What? But we've only just got here!"

"Are your men armed?" Ulysses said, half over his shoulder, as he continued to make for the door, Nimrod and the others close behind him.

"No."

"Then get them out of here now. You have to withdraw!"

"Now look here, Quicksilver! You can't just charge in here and start ordering me around like this, I'll have you know."

"Allardyce!" Ulysses roared in frustration. And then his face fell, as he caught sight of what had entered the hallway after them. "Just run," he said, his voice suddenly horribly quiet.

"What?" The confused inspector turned from the ashen-faced Ulysses to see what it was that had caused what little colour there was to drain from his waxy cheeks. "You're shitting me," he gasped.

The first to fall foul of the chimera was the policeman who had tried to stop Ulysses. The monster picked the constable up with one claw and then merely tossed him aside. He collided with the top of a column and then dropped fifteen feet to the floor, landing face first on the cold marble tiles without making a sound, other than the sickening crunch of his skull breaking.

Ulysses paused at the doorway and stared at the monster in appalled horror. The wretched butler Molesworth stood beside him staring aghast at the creature that now bore only the vaguest similarity to his master Josiah Umbridge.

Screeching, the vivisect reached for another wretched policeman who was already scrabbling to get away, feet slipping on the highly-polished floor. The Umbridge-chimera lunged forwards, bringing the man down with the point of one crustacean leg. The man screamed as the great weight of the monster pressed down on that one clawed crab's leg, puncturing the flesh of his thigh, and pinning him to the ground.

The chimera regarded the policeman curiously for a moment. Absently-mindedly tossing the gamekeeper's lower body aside – which it had still been holding in the vice-like grip of its monstrous claw – the creature closed its pincer around the constable's head and, with one neat twist, removed it from his shoulders.

"Quick! Get out!" Ulysses screamed as he hurried his friends through the door, hoping that Jenny would not look back and witness any of the carnage consuming the atrium behind them.

Unable to tear his own gaze away, he looked from the twitching corpse of the decapitated policeman to the white-faced Allardyce staring transfixed at the vivisect-beast and the remains of the gamekeeper. Beside the oozing remains was Ulysses' cane.

Scrambling back into the hall, he pulled the black wood cane free, feeling its reassuring weight as he held it in his hand again, and then turned for the door, dragging the dumbfounded Allardyce after him.

Shoving the bewildered inspector ahead of him, Ulysses paused in front of the frozen Molesworth, paralysed now that he was faced with the reality of what his master had become.

Ulysses drew back his left hand and hit the butler full in the face, his new simian arm delivering a powerful punch. Molesworth's head hit an alabaster pedestal behind him and he crumpled to the floor, out cold.

"That's for the knockout drops," Ulysses declared with indignant self-righteousness, and then dashed through the door, after the dazed Allardyce.

Once outside in the biting cold of the November night, he paused again, this time to slam the double doors shut behind him; anything to slow the creature down, even if only for a second.

With the beast and its enraged bellows trapped inside the house for the time being, Ulysses caught up with Allardyce as the inspector was making for the gleaming black police car pulled up on the gravel drive.

"This your car?" Ulysses asked.

"Y-Yes," the inspector stammered.

"Everyone, get in!" Ulysses commanded, pulling open a door. "Keys?"

"In the ignition."

"Good. I'll drive. Now, get in!"

CHAPTER TWENTY-FOUR

Fight or Flight

ULYSSES PUSHED THE accelerator pedal to the floor, and the car took off, throwing up a spray of gravel behind it. Almost as an afterthought he found the right switch on the dashboard and flicked on the headlights. Two powerful white beams cut through the dark, illuminating the driveway ahead and reaching as far as the boundary wall of the estate.

For a few moments, the only sounds inside the car – other than the rising and falling tone of the engine – were the gasping pants of its occupants as they all tried to recover their breath and make sense of what had happened to them back at the house.

Ulysses tore up the driveway, accelerating into the gentle curve of the gravel road as it pulled round parallel with the Neo-Classical facade of the stately home.

"What *was* that?" Allardyce demanded, turning in his seat to face Ulysses. Ulysses' eyes remained firmly on the drive ahead, a manic gleam ablaze there.

"By *that* I take it you mean the monster that just tore apart your friends from the North Yorks constabulary."

"Of course that's what I bloody mean!" Allardyce shrieked.

"Didn't you recognise him? That was the renowned industrialist billionaire recluse Josiah Umbridge. Although it looks like he's not such a recluse any more, doesn't it?"

Allardyce gawped at the dandy, hunched over the steering wheel, a haunted expression on his face as he peered beyond the windscreen of the car. Details flashed into existence out of the darkness as the beams of the police car's headlights briefly illuminated trees and topiary before the night swallowed them up again.

"Nimrod, any sign?" Ulysses asked his manservant, who had bundled into the back of the car with Jenny and Jacob.

Nimrod peered out of the window next to him, trying to discern anything through the darkness. Behind them the great house was aglow, the fire having spread.

"I see it, sir!" he suddenly shouted. "Approaching from the right!"

Holding the steering wheel straight, Ulysses dared a glance. The chimera was moving towards them at speed across the carefully tended lawns, galloping through the water of an ornamental pool in its rush to catch up with them.

The landscape designer who had laid out the estate and the approach to it along the drive had planned it so that visitors might enjoy unprecedented views of the whole of the carefully constructed Neo-Classical facade of the house as they entered the grounds.

However, the curve of the drive, provided the thing, of which Josiah Umbridge had become a part, with a shortcut by which to intercept the escaping police car and its passengers.

Teeth gritted, knuckles white around the steering wheel – his left arm aching right down to the bone – Ulysses watched as the chimera hove into view, galloping over the last rise of turf to reach the road.

The only way out was the private estate road that cut across Ghestdale, but to make it they were first going to have to pass through the stone-pillared gates and, right now, that meant confronting the chimera head-on.

Ulysses pushed his right foot down as hard as he could, as if trying to ram the pedal beneath through the floor.

"Look out!" Allardyce yelled, and pulled hard on the steering wheel, as the creature skidded onto the road, its hideousness revealed again by the wildly swinging headlights.

"Get off!" Ulysses shouted, fighting to get the car under control as it bounced off the gravel drive, its tyres gouging ruts in the perfectly-manicured lawn.

The car swung back onto the road with a squeal of tyres.

There was a resounding crash and the car lurched sideways. Jennifer screamed and Jacob moaned in terror as well.

"Bloody hell!" was all the inspector could think to say.

Allardyce looked out of the driver's window. He saw the dark mass of the chimera moving alongside the car, galloping to keep pace with the speeding vehicle. And then he cried out in unintelligible dread as the chimera's old man's face appeared, craning forwards over the top of the car on its elongated neck.

There was another crash and the police car's passengers were shaken out of their seats, Jennifer falling into Jacob's lap.

"What's he trying to do?" Jenny wailed.

"My guess would be that Umbridge is attempting to ram us off the road." Ulysses glanced back over his shoulder at Jenny. "To get to you. You were to be his bride, after all."

Jennifer's face in reaction to this statement said it all.

"But don't worry, that's not going to happen. I'm going to get you out of here. We're all getting out of here!"

And then the stone pillars of the estate entrance stood ahead of them. Desperately willing the car towards them as it powered up the drive, Ulysses aimed right for the middle of the open gateway.

With another resounding crash, the chimera collided with the car again, denting the driver's door and crazing the window, such was the force of its attack. The wheels on the nearside left the ground and the car scraped against a gate post as it hurtled through, this second collision righting the vehicle again.

Ulysses was sure he heard a squeal of pain and thought he saw the Umbridge-chimera run headlong into the opposite pillar, out of the corner of his eye.

With the road across the moors clear ahead of them, Ulysses risked looking in the car's rear-view mirror. He could see the house, flames dancing high into the sky, the brilliant orange blaze lighting up the estate like a beacon. Visible against the burning house was the malformed shadow of the vivisect-beast. Ulysses thought he saw the creature shaking its head – as if the old man was trying to recover his senses – and then the monster was on the move again, dogged in its pursuit of them. But they had the advantage; on a straight run, Ulysses sincerely doubted that the beast would be able to keep up with the car.

"So, what now?" Allardyce asked, turning back to Ulysses.

"Now?" Ulysses said, as if this was genuinely the first time he had considered where they should go from here. "Now, we head in to town for reinforcements and then head back up here to run down the beast and put an end to it!"

"Reinforcements?" Allardyce screeched. "Where do you think we are? This isn't London, you know. There are no automata-Peeler grunts here."

"Call ahead!" Ulysses demanded, thinking on his feet. "Tell your friends at the Whitby constabulary that you need them up here now, with everything they've got!"

"I don't bloody believe this," Allardyce muttered under his breath as he took out his police-issue personal communicator.

"What don't you bloody believe?" Ulysses challenged, his dander up.

"Any of this. Is your life always like this?" Allardyce demanded. "Is it always this mad?"

"Not all of the time," Ulysses muttered, taking his right hand off the wheel to massage the place where the ape's arm had been attached to his body. "What were you and your men doing at Umbridge House anyway?"

"We had an anonymous tip-off that something was up."

"I took the liberty of calling for back-up, sir, when I became fully aware of the seriousness of our situation," Nimrod explained.

"So it was you?" the policeman railed.

"Yes, inspector."

"I don't believe it! *You* called me for back-up?"

"I know. I couldn't believe it either, as I was making the call, sir."

The car's occupants fell silent.

Ulysses returned to massaging his arm. It still pained him, but then he had undergone major surgery only a few hours ago.

How had Seziermesser done it? he wondered. How long had he taken to perfect his technique and test the properties of his secret formula? And where had he got the animals from? He and Umbridge must have been planning this for months, if not longer; two madmen sharing the same twisted vision but with entirely different motives.

Ulysses had to admire the vivisectionist on one level, to have accomplished such a feat of creation. But for the most part it appalled him. If it hadn't been for the good doktor, then Ulysses would still have his arm. But then, if it hadn't been for the surgeon's skill with a needle and nerve-splicer he wouldn't have been in any fit state to fight back against the crazed beast that old man Umbridge had become.

And it must have been quite some cocktail of drugs that Seziermesser had plied him with, (a) to overcome his body's natural defences to stop it rejecting the chimp's arm, (b) for him not to be doubled up in agony, gibbering like a moron on the laboratory floor, and (c) for him to have come round so quickly, without feeling any extreme ill-effects. He wondered how long he had until their effects wore off.

Or was it something else that was keeping him going? Had the doktor in fact attached additional adrenal glands to his body while he was poking around inside him, reattaching his shoulder? Was that what was keeping his body stimulated to the point of euphoria?

His mind starting to wander, as he tried to make sense of all that had happened to him in the last twelve hours or so, Ulysses did not see the dip in the rutted moorland road. The car flew into it, its bumper impacting into the road surface on the other side, before bouncing out again. For a split second Ulysses lost control of the vehicle and, breaking, spun it on the loose dirt surface of the track, sending it off the road.

Shouts of panic and surprise filled the police car as it slid to a halt facing the wrong way amidst a knot of gorsy tussocks. The engine died.

"What the hell are you playing at, Quicksilver?" Allardyce shouted.

Slowly Ulysses released his white-knuckled grip on the steering wheel.

"Look, get this ruddy thing started, you bloody idiot!"

"Are you alright, sir?" Nimrod asked from the backseat. "Would you like me to drive?"

In a daze Ulysses reached for the ignition key and turned it.

"Yeah, that's it. Get your man to drive. Or here's a better idea. Swap seats and I'll drive."

The engine rattled into life again.

"I'm alright," Ulysses said, coming out of his stupor.

"No, let me drive!" the agitated inspector demanded.

"I'm alright! I – *Hnnn!*" Ulysses winced and threw up a hand to his temple.

"Look, Quicksilver, you're obviously in no fit state... Bloody hell! You've got to be frigging joking!"

The look in the inspector's eyes demanded that Ulysses follow it, although his screaming sixth sense had already told him all he needed to know.

Leaping over the tussocks and trenches, the uneven ground not hindering its progress in any way, the chimera galloped towards them out of the night.

Slamming his foot to the floor, his heart racing, Ulysses willed the car to start moving as the monster bore down on them. The car's wheels spun, churning the damp moorland to mud, and then incredibly they found purchase again. The automobile shot forwards, throwing the passengers around inside the car as it bounced over the rough heath and back onto the rutted track.

But the beast had caught up with them again now. As Ulysses pulled hard on the wheel, spinning the car to the left and onto the moorland road, the chimera made contact. The police car lurched as its rear end briefly left the road. There was a second crash as the monster reared and brought almost its full weight down on the back of the car. The rear window shattered, showering Nimrod, Jenny and Jacob with glass fragments as the monster's crab-claw smashed its way inside.

Tyres gripping the road again, the police car shot forwards, leaving the lethal pincer snapping at thin air.

Giving voice to a booming bellow of frustration the chimera powered after them. The small part of the increasingly feral creature – the primitive part of Umbridge's brain that lusted after Jenny Haniver – was determined not to let her get away, not when she was practically within its clutches.

It hurled its elastic octopus limb at the car again. This time the pincer snapped shut around the rear nearside-wheel of the car. There was another part of the old Umbridge intelligence at work here, the part that demonstrated the old man's cunning that had helped to make him one of the richest men in the Empire.

Those inside the police car heard the loud bang of the tyre bursting as the crushing claw punctured it and proceeded to tear its rubbery remains from the wheel.

Ulysses felt the effects immediately as the car jolted and bounced on the road. He had to fight the steering wheel as it pulled to the left, and the vehicle veered dangerously close to the edge of the road.

Again the car slewed sideways, as the vivisect hit it side on.

"Hold on!" Ulysses shouted, although whether he was addressing himself or his passengers wasn't clear.

He pulled the car sharply to the right and then left again, as the road swerved sharply to avoid an outcropping of rock. He was dimly aware of the monster charging past and thought he heard the clatter of its armoured limbs as it scrabbled over the rocky summit of the obstacle.

And then it was down the other side and the road was leading the police car back into the path of the persistent beast.

Understanding the limits of his new body better now, or rather the lack of them, the vivisect threw its full weight at the left-hand side of the car.

Wrong-footed, Ulysses overcompensated as the road took them over the crest of a sloping stretch of moorland, the rugged landscape dropping away to Ulysses' right in a sudden incline. The car's right-hand wheels left the road, skidding through the mud and wet grass at its edge.

The inhuman creature's grotesquely human head appeared beside the wailing Allardyce as the beast put all its weight behind its enormous right shoulder. The window beside Allardyce cracked and the metal pillar between the door and the body of the car buckled inwards.

Ulysses' view of the world rolled sideways, as the car left the road. The world began to spin before his eyes and he threw up his hands to shield his face as the windscreen shattered.

Tiny shards of glass filled the air around the five of them as they rolled with the car, the vehicle tumbling down the slope of the hill. The roof dented, window glass popped and shattered, the beams of the headlights spun wildly, illuminating inverted trees, then scrubby moorland, then nothing as the impenetrable darkness passed overhead and then back to moorland again.

With a dull *crump*, the car rolled to a stop against a sandstone boulder.

Ulysses opened his eyes and blinked. He was in darkness, lying on his side, with the befuddled moans of his companions close by.

"Is... Is everyone alright?" he said, desperately trying to shake the clouds of concussion from his mind.

He tried to look round but a sharp pain in his neck stopped him from trying any more. He slouched even further over to the right as the door beside him was wrenched open.

"This way, sir," he heard Nimrod say from beside him and felt himself being hauled from the battered vehicle. Finding his feet he stumbled after Nimrod as his manservant led him further into the shelter of the rocky outcroppings beside which the car had come to rest.

He was aware of Allardyce running ahead of them and, looking back, saw the freak Jacob assisting Jennifer as she stumbled after them.

His wits felt addled, as if he was having some kind of out of body experience. Was this the effects of the doktor's drug therapy wearing off or a result of the crash, he wondered as his mind began to stray again.

He almost blacked out as preternatural awareness threatened to overwhelm his traumatised mind. A second later he heard the screeching, primeval cry of the triumphant chimera as it bore down on them, having stopped briefly at the crash site to inspected the wreckage of the car for bodies.

His vision swimming into focus again, Ulysses saw the rocky defile ahead of them as Nimrod half-dragged him towards a tight crevice between the sandstone walls. The exposed cleft ran a good ten yards into the feature which towered above them to a height of twenty feet or more. Once they were in there, there would be no way the creature would be able to prise them out again. Then it would simply be a matter of waiting for Allardyce's back-up to reach them.

The scream cut through Ulysses like Seziermesser's scalpel, finally bringing him fully to his senses. There could be no mistaking that cry; it was Jennifer. He pulled free of Nimrod, his feet slipping on the mud and stones, already scrambling back out of the defile towards Jenny.

Jacob lay sprawled on the ground, moaning in pain. And there was Jenny, suspended in mid-air, her feet high off the ground, her body held tight in the clutches of the monster's claw. Her cry was cut short as the chimera squeezed her in its pincer grip, leaving her gasping for air as she struggled.

"Jennifer! Jenny!" he screamed in impotent rage as the Umbridge-chimera, having got what it wanted, turned and began to ascend the slope again, turning back to the road.

And then she was gone, swallowed by the darkness as the creature carried her into the bitter night.

CHAPTER TWENTY-FIVE

The Abbey

Jennifer Haniver opened her eyes. The world swung past her in dull greys and purples in the pre-dawn twilight. She felt dizzy, her senses reeling from the galloping motion of the beast. She closed her eyes again.

Her chest felt tight. She tried to breathe, but when her lungs were only half-full, she felt the crushing pressure of the claw across her midriff again and let her breath out in a gasp.

Her head felt thick. She half-opened her eyes and craned her whiplash-sore neck, trying to focus on one point on the swaying horizon. Somewhere, far off, she thought she saw stars, until she realised that the yellow-orange pinpricks were lights coming on in the wakening town below the cliff tops.

She blinked, forcing wakefulness upon herself. And as awareness came to her, so did a plethora of other sensations. There was the salt-smell of the wind blowing in off the sea; the cold, damp touch of the wind on her face; the breath of the breeze rippling the long grass of the moors; the looming shadows of a building ahead of her; the stomach-turning mammalian musk and fish-stink of the creature filling her nose; the grunt and snort of the thing, as it galloped on, loud in her ears.

They appeared to be heading towards a dark structure on the horizon, shot through with arch-holes of sky, two pinnacles and a pointed triangular pediment, thrusting up towards heaven. Even from the curious angle from which Jennifer was viewing it, it looked familiar.

With a tremendous splashing, the vivisect galloped through the boggy waters of a reed-edged pool. The water splashed up into her face, drenching her hair. And then they were through, the beast clearing the shallow bank on the other side and entering the shadowy sanctuary of the ruined Abbey.

"Come on!" Ulysses urged, maintaining his stumbling run through the wind-blown grass.

They had been in pursuit of the beast for the last hour, ever since it had run the police car off the road and made its escape with Jenny in its clutches. The thought that any harm might come to her cut Ulysses to the quick. He had not known her for long, but in the short, dramatic time they had spent together he had come to feel hugely responsible for her, as if, with her father's death, her welfare had become his concern.

So, ignoring the cuts and bruises he had sustained in the car crash Ulysses kept up his dogged pursuit of the Umbridge-chimera and Jenny Haniver.

"And where are we heading, exactly?" Inspector Allardyce puffed.

Ulysses glanced at the ground. It was not hard to follow the chimera's path, the flattened grass, the stab marks in the mud from its arthropod legs, the occasional gouged area of turf. He looked from the ground and the trail across the heath towards the crest of the cliff, beneath which lay the fishing port of Whitby.

"There!" he panted, pointing.

"It's heading towards the town?" Allardyce exclaimed.

"Not the town, you idiot. *There.*"

Ulysses pointed again, towards the remnants of walls and buttresses that were all that was left of the Benedictine monastery of St Peter and St Hilda.

"That old ruin? But what good's that?"

Ulysses paused, considering his answer carefully for a moment.

"Perhaps the creature is seeking sanctuary." Nimrod suggested, coming alongside his master.

"Or absolution."

All turned. It was the freak that had spoken.

"Who knows what the bugger wants. But if that's where it's hiding out, then we have it," Allardyce said with conviction. He was a man who liked to deal in hard facts – not metaphysical musings on man's state of original sin.

Ulysses could see the lights of torch-beams piercing the early morning gloom now as well. The Yorkshire constabulary had arrived.

"Our back-up's here."

The policemen were approaching the ruins from the other side of the East Cliff, a line of ten men.

"It's not going to be enough," Jacob said in a worried tone.

Ulysses looked at him, although it made his skin crawl to do so. But nonetheless, the boy's eyes were human, windows to a troubled soul.

And perhaps the boy was right, Ulysses thought, as he set his eyes on the ruins ahead of them. They had all witnessed what the chimera had done to the policemen back at the house, without even batting an eyelid. Then there had been the resilience it had demonstrated in running a police car off the road. Ulysses doubted that anything the Whitby police could throw at it would do the beast much harm. For a start, they probably weren't even armed.

"You could be right," Ulysses said as he jogged on. He turned back to the boy, only to see him haring away over the grass, back the way they had come.

"I don't bloody believe it!" Allardyce swore. "The coward! I should have him arrested for dereliction of duty!"

"Leave him," Ulysses said coldly. "We don't have the time."

"And to think I thought he had a soft spot for the girl," Nimrod mused behind Ulysses. "After all that he's been through already, I would not have expected this."

Umbridge's pursuers – now numbering only three – helped each other scale the boundary wall of the Abbey's grounds.

The trail left by the beast, more clearly visible as the sky lightened in expectation of the coming dawn, led directly into the abbey's ancient fishpond and then cleared the bank on the other side.

Skirting the pond, lungs aching now – every breath like fire in his throat – Ulysses led Nimrod and the inspector over the undulating mounds of the grassy field in which the ruins stood.

There was no point trying to be subtle now. Time was of the essence and, besides, there wasn't anywhere to hide. Until they reached the sanctuary of the Abbey itself, they remained totally exposed. And besides, Ulysses pondered, God alone knew what other senses Umbridge had acquired since becoming a part of the chimera. It wouldn't surprise him to learn that the thing had heightened hearing, or that it could see by the heat-trace left by their bodies in the infra-red spectrum.

Ahead of them and a little to the left stood the black oblong of Cholmley House. To the right stood the silhouette of the Abbey. The policemen, more than just sweeping spots of light in the darkness now, were moving towards them on an intercept course between the two structures, having caught sight of the inspector from Scotland Yard and his dishevelled companions.

And then they were standing in the shadows of the once-great Abbey, all dark pillars and empty archways. As Allardyce got his second wind and strode off to make contact with the approaching policemen, Ulysses hung back, keeping one eye firmly on the ruined edifice rising up beside him.

The chimera was here; he was sure of it. Such conviction came from the nagging voice of his subconscious, like an itch at the back of his brain.

He stared up at the ruins – his chest heaving as his lungs dragged air into his body – desperately trying to penetrate the shadow of the Abbey, hoping to see anything – anything at all – that might reveal to him where the creature was lurking.

A little way away from Ulysses and Nimrod now, Allardyce and the policemen were entering the nave of the Abbey through a gaping rift in a ruined wall.

Ulysses followed, Nimrod at his heel, like some faithful hound.

"How many of you are armed?" he heard Allardyce hiss in annoyance.

Ulysses couldn't make out the policeman's reply but he heard the inspector's heartfelt, angry response.

"I don't bloody believe it! And you came on foot?"

"Yes, sir," a bleary-voiced sergeant replied. "Up St Mary's steps."

"You're more out of breath than I am," Ulysses heard Allardyce chide the officer, "and I feel like I've just run halfway across Yorkshire, *and* having just walked away from a car crash, I'll have you know!"

Part of him, annoyed at their lack of professionalism, he supposed, wanted to tell them to be quiet. But there seemed little point. He was sure Umbridge – or whatever passed for Umbridge now – was already well aware of their arrival.

They were standing amidst the grass-covered mounds of rubble that had once been the Choir of the church. In front of them stood what remained of the north transept, one of the more intact parts of the ruin.

"What are we looking for, sir?" a constable asked, looking up at the jagged spurs of broken walls above them.

"You'll know when you see it," Allardyce said, his eyes on the surrounding walls.

Awareness crackled through Ulysses like a bolt of electricity and he ducked, shooting darting glances upwards at the looming columns.

A split second later, there was movement in the darkness, a scraping sound – as of hardened carapace grating against stone – and the whip-crack of a snapping pincer. The curious constable knew what they were looking for now, as the chimera's claw closed around his neck and shoulders and the vivisect pulled him violently off his feet.

All eyes followed the policeman's struggling form as he was dragged into the air, feet kicking uselessly. As horrified eyes caught sight of the vivisect-chimera the constable's struggles became nerveless spasms and a shower of hot, viscous rain fell on those assembled below.

The chimera was peering down at them from its perch, halfway up one of the thick pillars that rose like petrified tree trunks from the earth.

Gasps of horror and revulsion added to the sense of panic, but the bloody shower was as nothing compared to what came thudding down around the party next. The constable's head thudded to the ground only a few feet away from Ulysses, his dismembered torso and legs landing in two entirely different places altogether, but the dandy couldn't have cared less. He had only one thing on his mind and nothing was going to distract him from that over-arching purpose now.

Ulysses peered into the darkness as excited voices began shouting around him, taking a chance to scan the walls nearby. There was the glint of light on a trailing tress of wet hair, and he saw what he was looking for. He had found Jennifer.

She was lying within the crook of an archway above the Choir. The monster must have put her there for safe keeping. Ulysses was certain she was still alive, but also unconscious – thankfully, for her sake!

A shot rang out, the echo of its retort as loud as the crack of doom itself, within the confines of the church.

A bellow of pain or rage – Ulysses wasn't sure which – shook the crumbling structure to its foundations and the crab-claw came sweeping down out of the darkness.

Ulysses followed the sound of the gun shot to its source: Allardyce had been the one to fire on the chimera. His shot had obviously had little impact – if the inspector had hit the thing at all – but now he had made himself the creature's prime target.

Ulysses was already running towards the inspector before his conscious mind had realised that he had decided to move. The rapier-blade slid from the sheath of the black wood cane with a zinging hum of reverberating metal.

He and the chimera landed their blows at the same time. Allardyce was sent flying as the heavy pincer smacked into him, and Ulysses' trusty blade made contact with boneless flesh.

With all his weight behind it, the tempered blade sliced cleanly through the cephalopod limb. The full weight of the unnaturally large claw landed on top of Allardyce, knocking the wind from his lungs, the pincer twitching as lifeless muscles relaxed.

Howling in agony, black inky fluid dripping from the severed limb, the chimera scuttled backwards further up the pillar and out of harm's way. Ulysses could just make out the old man's face snarling and spitting at him from the darkness.

Umbridge was definitely becoming more feral, the bestial body-memory of the vivisect corrupting what was left of his barely human mind.

Another figure was moving among the ruins now, but this one appeared to be scampering up the corner of the north transept, as if it were a monkey climbing a tree. It was a young woman, he could see that much, and the silhouette bore the suggestion of damask and lacy skirts. And she wasn't the only one; there were other figures like her, all bizarrely dressed, scaling the walls of the north transept as if it was the sort of thing they did every day.

Ulysses could see that they were carrying something between them, something that was almost invisible against the twilight sky, but something which each of them had a hand upon as they hauled it up after them. He took in the rest of the transept above him and saw more figures doing the same on two outer sides of the transept. Some had already reached the top now, running along the walls, drawing the net over the apex of the ruin, so that soon the only side not covered was that which opened onto the main body of the church. But give them long enough, Ulysses thought, and they would probably have that covered too.

Where had they got the net from, he wondered, and then realised that it was probably the same net they used to ensure the safety of the high-wire and trapeze artists in the Big Top.

A few moments more and the acrobats of the Circus of Wonders would have the beast trapped within the ruins. What Ulysses needed to do now was keep the chimera there long enough for the circus folk to bring their plan to fruition.

"What's the matter, Umbridge?" Ulysses shouted at the inhuman monster. "Are you scared? Is this all that the world can expect from *homo superior*? What's the matter, did I hurt you?"

His words resounded around the cold dead vault of the Abbey, as did the monster's bellowed response.

"*Quuiiick-siiill-veerrr!*" it snarled, the name of its nemesis becoming a howl of bloodthirsty intent. The creature began to descend the pillar.

"I must be mad," Ulysses said to himself, seeing the monstrosity bearing down on him, its four remaining arms open wide, ready to seize him in its deadly, crushing embrace.

"Yes, I am mad!" he decided, shouting the fact to the world, as he felt the adrenalin quicken the blood in his veins, his pulse thrumming in his ears, nerves tingling, muscles tightening. "In fact I'm utterly furious!' he raged at the beast. 'Because that's my arm you've got there!"

With a roar the creature leapt the last ten feet, aiming to crush Ulysses beneath its spider-crab legs. But Ulysses was too quick for it. Spinning out of the creature's way, his blade scored a cut across its crocodilian midriff. It was not enough to debilitate the vivisect, but it was enough to keep its attention as the circus folk swarmed overhead, pulling their net to the limit of the chancel.

Turning again to deliver a two-handed strike at one of the crustacean limbs, Ulysses saw two of the scrambling figures take a run up and, the edge of the net in their hands, take a leap of faith that reminded him of his own death-defying leap from the top of the Bakerloo Line train as it sped on its way over Trafalgar Square. They fell gracefully through the air in an arcing curve, the cords of the net making a whizzing sound as they were pulled sharply over the broken mortar and weathered stones at the top of the tower.

Momentarily distracted by the acrobats bold act of circus fearlessness, Ulysses only just brought his blade to bear in time as the vivisect stamped down with one stabbing claw-foot and swung at him with its scything talon at the same time. He parried the swipe whilst dodging the claw, but that put him on the wrong foot and left him vulnerable to the sudden tail-lash that came his way.

Ulysses was sent flying into the rough stones of the transept wall, adding another graze to his already cut face. For someone who was so proud of his good looks, he wasn't looking so good anymore. But the injury was nothing more than a superficial abrasion of the cheek and so, with his wits still about him, Ulysses double-bluffed the creature, running straight for it as it cantered towards him, so that it mistimed its next strike as the dandy threw himself under its crocodilian underbelly.

Rolling over on the turf he leapt to his feet again and let out a gasp of surprise as he almost ran slap-bang into the elephantine freak.

"You!" was all he could manage. But it was all he needed to say.

Jacob stared back at him with open, apologetic eyes.

"You brought back-up!" Ulysses suddenly laughed. The boy was no coward after all, and here he was again, ready to do his part.

The Umbridge-chimera turned, the old man's head swaying on its grotesquely elongated neck, frantically searching for its prey. And then its savage gaze – any semblance of humanity gone from those feral eyes now – found them both and a guttural screech issued from somewhere deep inside its Seziermesser-made chest.

"Help! Somebody?" came a distraught wail from above them. "I'm up here!" Ulysses did not dare take his eyes off the beast again, not for a moment. But then he didn't need to; he knew who the voice belonged to and where the desperate pleas were coming from. It was none other than his poor, traumatised Jenny.

"Jacob," Ulysses said, addressing the deformed young man by his name for the first time since they had met. He spoke with a clarity of mind and purpose, as the chimera took a rhythmic, many-legged step towards them; there wasn't time for any misunderstandings or mistakes. "Get Jenny down and get her out of here!"

The boy didn't need telling twice. "Yes, sir!"

And then he was gone from Ulysses' side as the acrobats landed behind him and closed the net on both the vivisect and the desperate dandy.

CHAPTER TWENTY-SIX

Gods & Monsters

"THIS WAY!" JACOB called over the furious berserker screams of the cornered beast. Taking the young woman's hand in his – her long, delicate fingers swamped by his fat, misshapen paw – he made for the cleft in the chancel wall, pulling Jenny after him.

Leaving the desecrated sanctuary of the Abbey, the still standing north wall of the nave to their left, Jenny and the wretched young man stumbled over the undulating turf, past unearthed Saxon tombstones, past the arch of the west door and through the visitor's turnstile, making for the crenulated nave and tower of another church – the parish church of St Mary's.

Their feet pounding over cobbles now, they could both hear the bellows of the beast reverberating from the broken columns of the ruin behind them, the raised voices of the circus folk as they relayed instructions backwards and forwards between themselves, the disorganised shouts of the policemen and the visiting inspector.

Then they were through another gate, pounding down a flagstone path that ran between serried ranks of stone crosses and headstones, the solid walls of the church of St Mary's and the sanctuary they offered directly in front of them.

And now a new and terrible sound reached their ears, a shrill half-human scream of rage, pain and will-shattering insanity, that turned the blood in Jenny's veins to ice-water.

Then a part of her realised what the sound signified. The Umbridge-chimera had discovered that its mate-to-be had been stolen away, and it was angry; angry like they had never seen it before.

Shots were fired. People cried out and there was an ominous tearing sound, as of ropes being ripped apart.

"It's coming!" she spluttered, allowing Jacob to pull her towards the church door.

Jacob fumbled clumsily at the latch until the door creaked open and they tumbled down the cold stone steps into the church.

"What is the meaning of this?" a grim voice demanded. Jenny looked up, wincing as her eyes adjusted to the dusty, candle-pierced gloom of the church. The instantly recognisable smell of musty hymnals, burnt beeswax and cold stone hit her full in the face, mixed, in this place, with the stale aroma of the fishy faithful.

"I demand to know the meaning of this intrusion."

A figure wearing the severe black cassock of a priest was watching them from the steps leading up to the sanctuary, a dully gleaming metal cross hanging around his neck, smoking taper in hand. He was an austere man, standing as straight as one of the pillars supporting the church roof. The wisps of grey hair that tufted the sides of his head only served to make him appear even more sinister. He looked down his nose at the two bloodied and filthy creatures that had fallen through the church door, regarding them through severe wire-framed spectacles.

On seeing the priest, the exhausted Jacob assumed a fawning stance, the boy casting his eyes down at the stone flags as he approached the vicar, as might a sinful petitioner seeking absolution.

"I am sorry, Father, but we have come seeking the sanctuary of God's holy church. For we are in danger – terrible danger."

The austere priest descended the steps from the sanctuary, the slow, deliberate manner of his approach only enhancing the menacing atmosphere, and making Jenny feel more unwelcome by the second. The vicar was scowling, the corner of his top lip flexed upward in a sneer.

Too exhausted to do anything else, Jenny lay where she had fallen, taking in her surroundings with weary, aching eyes, the cold stones leeching what little warmth was left in her body.

The smell of the place might be familiar to Jenny, but the interior layout of the church was not. Everything about it suggested that the original building had since been modified and refurnished by generations of parishioners, giving this particular place of worship a remarkable and entirely idiosyncratic appearance.

The interior was a hotchpotch of styles and eras. As well as box pews there was an incredible pulpit that ascended through three distinct levels.

Behind the pulpit, and astride the chancel arch, a large gallery ran around the walls, supported by twisted columns. There was even what appeared to be a charcoal stove in the middle of the church, its flue rising to the ceiling.

And through the chancel arch could be found the candle-lit sanctuary – that seemed more like a side chapel in its size and design. The painted panes of a stained glass window were already colouring the sanctuary floor with muted tones as the firmament beyond began to lighten in anticipation of the coming dawn.

"Where have you been?" the priest demanded of Jacob, coming to a halt in front of him.

Jacob was practically on his knees now.

"Father, I will explain everything later, but first, lock the door, I beseech you."

Jenny saw the heavy ring of keys at the priest's belt, that jangled together as he moved.

"Have you been out all night?" The priest's tone was cold, like a strict parent chastising a miscreant child. But that was the way of priests the world over, Jenny thought.

Father: it was a term of respect, an honorific. But as Jenny looked from the freak to the priest there was something darkly similar about the two of them.

"Father," Jacob pleaded, his voice sounding as though he was close to tears, "please lock the door. There is something after us, an abomination straight from the darkest pits of hell."

"You do not need to lecture me on abominations," the man said, making no attempt to hide the spite belying his words.

"Please father. Lock the door. Before it's too late."

Jacob's blubbering plea had barely left his lips when, with a crash that shook the building like an earthquake, the door flew open.

For a moment it almost looked as if Josiah Umbridge had regained his natural, human form, as his face peered around the edge of the door, as if he had come to the church seeking absolution. Umbridge stopped, sniffing the air sharply, and then slowly his head turned and his unblinking gaze fell on Jenny. Blood ran from a head-wound obscuring the vision of one bloodshot eye and as Jenny watched in horror, too tired to do anything else, a cruel smile curled the old man's mouth. As his lips parted, the points of arrow-tip teeth became visible.

"*Jeenn-eeee!*" the creature exhaled.

And then all she could hear was the thudding of her heart within her chest; all she could see was the old man's hideous face as it extended into the church on the end of that horrific, vertebrae-ridged neck.

But somehow she found the means to move again, pushing herself backwards, using her hands and heels to put herself out of the reach of the monstrosity.

"Miss Jennifer! Run!"

She felt Jacob's hand grab hold of hers, felt him pulling her further out of harm's way. Without being fully aware of what she was doing, the animal instinct to survive seizing hold, she scrambled to her feet and stumbled after her malformed saviour.

ACCOMPANIED BY THE wet crack of wood, and the scraping clatter of crustacean claws, the Umbridge-chimera pulled itself through the door and into the church.

The Reverend Nathaniel Creed stared at the abomination in abject horror. What unholy visitation had his monster of a son summoned from the depths of hell? What new atrocity was this that had been sent to test him?

They had as king over them the angel of the Abyss, whose name in Hebrew is Abaddon.

Was this the living embodiment of God's judgement that came to claim the souls of those who had sinned in his eyes? Had the day of doom come at last, and with it an end to his own hell-on-earth existence?

How long, Sovereign Lord, holy and true until you judge the inhabitants of the earth and avenge our blood?

A cacophony of splintering pews, tumbling candelabra and scraped stone filled the church, the acoustics of the nave amplifying the hellish roars and bellows of the dread beast bearing down on him as the usurper of his life and his whore fled through the vestry door. The creature cast shattered pews before it, crushing them to matchwood beneath its impossibly large body.

And I saw a beast coming out of the sea. He had ten horns and seven heads, and on each head a blasphemous name. The beast I saw resembled a leopard, but had feet like those of a bear and a mouth like that of a lion.

And then the blasphemy was swaying there before him, a huge shark-like tail lashing the air angrily behind it.

The creature peered down at Creed from its lofty position and the tormented priest responded in the only way he knew how.

"Begone, Satan!" the Reverend Creed roared, with all the conviction of his best fire and brimstone preaching voice.

For a moment the abomination paused, cocking its head to one side as it regarded the priest, an almost quizzical look in its inhuman eyes. A breathless snorting noise escaping its flaring nostrils as its patchwork-flesh chest heaved. The stink that came off the beast – of blood and rot and death – could only be described as hellish.

The thing raised its multitude of limbs – one scythe-like claw held high above its head, some vile secretion oozing from the stump of another abominable limb – and the Reverend Creed knew that his time had come.

As the talon descended, Creed took a stumbling step backwards, the natural instinct for survival hard to deny. The tip of the claw caught the cloth of his cassock as he went down hard on his back, the lighted taper falling from his hands, the cast-iron candlestick beside him crashing to the floor, spilling hot wax across the stone flags and trailing fire.

The monster loomed over him, its hideous form a dark stain against the backdrop of the white-emulsion ceiling above, an evil shadow blocking out God's light. The musty, oily stink of its heaving flanks was hot in his nose and made him want to gag.

A human head supported on an elongated, snake-like neck descended, jaws dislocating as the mouth of hell itself yawned open.

Nathaniel Creed closed his eyes; his longed for end had come. The Lord God had seen fit to send his angel of death to take him from this world. And if he were to reside in hell for all eternity, then so be it; it could not be any worse than the living hell he had put himself through these last seventeen years.

Seventeen years since the boy's mother – the street girl whose path had first crossed his when she was barely past her eighteenth year, the same age the wretched boy was now – had turned up at his door again, the TB already too far gone for him to do anything for her other than hear her last confession, give her the last rites, and acknowledge the boy as his own, the result of his one transgression of the flesh.

He was dimly aware of a dull *whommph* and then he felt the fires of hell against his back.

Sudden scorching pain made Creed open his eyes. He found himself staring right into the gullet of the beast. But then, suddenly, the jaws snapped shut, mere inches from the end of his nose, and the old man's face of the blasphemy recoiled. Creed could see the fires of hell reflected in the eyes of the demon now, and something else too. If he had not known better he would have named it terror. But what did an angel of the Abyss have to fear from a sinner like him?

Intense burning pain suddenly consumed him, and with it, the priest's addled senses returned. Screaming in pain and panic, Creed leapt to his feet, but he was already too late. His cassock was alight.

Screeching in fear – yes, it was fear that he had seen in the old man's eyes – the monster retreated, all eight legs taking a step backwards as it shrank from the preacher.

Creed took an agonised, shuffling step forwards, arms outstretched towards the beast. "'The Lord your God is a jealous god!'" he screamed, as fire clawed its way up his body with flickering fingers, the hair on his head curling and blackening before the advance of the flames. "'*The Lord revengeth, and is furious; the Lord will take vengeance on his adversaries, and he reserveth wrath for his enemies!*'"

Creed's shambling steps became more urgent as the fire spread. Eyelids burned, melting flesh sealing them shut, his tongue cooking in his mouth, his voice nothing but incoherent screams now, he half-ran and half-fell towards the beast, seeking its awful embrace.

And fire consumed his soul.

Free of the remnants of the net at last Ulysses pounded down the path to the church no more than a minute behind the beast.

He reached the sundered door to be greeted by a chorus of unholy screams, bestial roars, and the snarl of hungry flames, the church's stained glass lit up in a brilliant rainbow of flickering light from inside. Ulysses grabbed the splintered door jamb to arrest his flight and stop himself falling headfirst over the threshold, rapier blade still in hand, adrenalin and Seziermesser's cocktail of miracle-drugs numbing his broken fingers.

The warning scream of his subconscious had Ulysses throwing himself aside, so that he saved himself from being trampled underfoot by the fleeing monster. Trailing the charcoal-stink of the church's burning furnishings behind it, back in the chill embrace of another dull November morning, the Umbridge-chimera raised its face to the sky, the gyrating head performing a peculiar cobra-dance of its own, and sniffed the air. Then with a triumphant howl it set off at a gallop, back across the churchyard.

Ulysses hauled himself to his feet. He felt exhausted. He didn't know how much longer he could maintain the chase. But then if he didn't, who would? And besides, he could not – *would* not – let the beast to escape him again.

Turning away from the fire-lit interior of the church, Ulysses stumbled back along the path. But rather than return to the Abbey and the mob of policemen and circus folk awaiting it there, the chimera turned left past the east end of the church, heading out across the stone-planted field of St Mary's cemetery.

Ulysses rounded the end of the building after it and ran on, his lungs feeling like they were on fire, the monster galloping over the weathered tombstones and monuments that littered the graveyard.

And there, even further ahead, Ulysses could make out the running figures of Jennifer and the freak as they followed the cliff-top path towards the eastern extremity of the cemetery and its perimeter wall.

The creature was closing on them.

The intensity of the moment helping him to focus his mind on tapping the last reserves of energy his body possessed, Ulysses bounded along the well-trodden grass path between the gravestones, towards the crumbling cliff path.

The chimera was only a few lolloping strides from its quarry, its pounding footfalls sending shudders through the turf at Ulysses' feet. For Jacob and Jennifer it was only a matter of another ten yards to the cemetery wall. Soon there would be nowhere else for them to run, nowhere left to hide.

As the chimera bore down on them Jacob turned in a display of astonishing bravery, and with nothing but his bare hands, prepared to make a good account of himself in the face of the vivisect's attack.

The move obviously surprised the tiny part of the old man's mind that remained his own and the creature stumbled to a halt, in a confused flurry of lurching legs. As the creature reared up before them, preparing to make its mantis-like strike at last, Jacob took a bold step forwards, looked directly into the old man's leering face and let out a pained roar of anger, frustration and desperation.

For a moment, the bewildered beast withdrew its head. Then slowly its face came level with the boy's again. The chimera opened its gaping mouth and roared in animal fury, meeting the young man's challenge.

And Ulysses' blade fell.

The monster's roar of fury became a howl of pain as the razor-edged rapier sliced through one arthropod leg.

The howl became a scream as Ulysses pushed against the blade to prise the leg apart. With a horrible sucking sound and a popping crack, the lower part of the crab limb came away from the thigh-like merus. The shorn limb fell uselessly to the ground, trailing stringy white meat from the horny-joint, a watery grey fluid dribbling into the grass at Ulysses' feet.

The chimera wheeled round. Ulysses had its attention again. He took a wary step backwards.

He had faced the impossible hybrid three times now, and on every occasion so far the outcome had been inconclusive. However, they shared a mutual understanding now that this time neither would desist until one, or both of them, was dead.

Its old man's face contorting into a bellow, the chimera charged at Ulysses, hampered by the fact that it had lost one of its eight legs. This incapacitation gave Ulysses all the time he needed to prepare his next move.

The monster rushed in, gorilla-fist drawn back ready to take a swipe at the dandy while the long, disembowelling claw unfolded, ready to tear the man open from sternum to groin.

At the last possible moment, Ulysses launched himself at the beast, sprinting from a standing start to charge in under attack-raised arms. He slammed into the solid wall of muscle that was the vivisect's broad crocodilian midriff, forcing the tip of his sword-cane through the leathery epidermis and into the coils of viscera behind. Umbridge screamed again.

Only Doktor Seziermesser had known what manner of internal organs actually lay buried inside the fleshy shell of the monster's body. For all Ulysses knew his blade might have punctured a kidney, a lung, a stomach, the monster's heart – and who was to say that it only had the one? – or maybe he had even managed to sever a major artery.

Bullets might not have had much of an impact against the unnatural creature but good old-fashioned, tempered British steel – that was quite another matter!

Ulysses kept his hold on the pommel of the blade firm as the monster writhed and kicked, pushing him backwards, but the beast was unable to dislodge him despite its frenzied efforts. But then Ulysses felt strong hands grasp his shoulders, blunt fingers digging into his flesh, worrying at his old shoulder wound and threatening to tear the stitches where the ape's arm had been attached to his other shoulder.

Now it was Ulysses' turn to cry out, moaning through gritted teeth as he desperately tried to keep hold of his sword. He might have managed to escape the reach of the chimera's larger limbs, but he had still been within reach of its smaller secondary arms.

And then his fingers slipped from the blood-slicked bloodstone-tip of his sword-cane and he suddenly found himself unable to defend himself against the monster's onslaught.

Ulysses had thought that nothing could top the horrors he had witnessed and experienced first-hand, the personal abuses he had suffered. But as his eyes snapped open, excruciating pain lancing through his aching body as the monster tugged at his left arm, he realised how wrong he had been.

For there, right in front of his eyes, the amalgamated flesh of the chimera was starting to bubble and blister. Ulysses watched as the patches of exposed skin began to sizzle and pop, as if its flesh had been subjected to a chemical attack – or as if something was moving beneath the skin. And then, as he peered closer, unable to tear his eyes away, despite the agonies he was suffering, he saw that there *was* something there beneath the shiny, translucent skin, a tiny something inside each and every blister.

Ulysses cried out again as the stitches securing the chimpanzee's arm to his shoulder began to tear and his eyes swivelled round to see for himself what was happening. What he saw filled him first with horror, then revulsion until that feeling too changed to become furious resolve. Seeing his own left arm worrying at the surgery that had been carried out as a result of its amputation gave him the strength and the determination to fight back.

Using the chimera's hold on him to support himself, Ulysses tucked his legs up to his chest and planted both feet firmly against the monster's reptilian abdomen. Tensing his thighs, he pushed with all the strength he had left. His body skewed to the left as the monster maintained its hold on his ape arm, the pain in his shoulder easing immediately, his right arm pulling free of the chimera's own blood-wet hand.

At once he reached for the beast again, swinging precariously from the stubborn grip of his own left hand. The shattered fingers of his right hand clutched at the old man's face and, making a paralytic claw of his maimed digits, he dug in.

The chimera gave voice to another scream – pain and fury indistinguishable now – and Ulysses felt something, soft and pliable as jelly, pop under pressure. With a sharp, spasmodic jerk, the abomination hurled Ulysses away.

For a moment Ulysses sailed through the cold air, both his left arm and shoulder feeling like they were on fire. He landed hard on his back, sliding over the dew-wet grass. He came to a halt – eyes shut tight against whatever terrible disaster might befall him next – and lay there for a moment, listening to the screams of the girl, the shouts of the boy and the incessant roaring of the beast. The salt sea breeze ruffled his hair and stung his face with cold.

Utterly exhausted, as he was, part of him felt like just lying there and doing nothing, waiting for the inevitable end to come, for the beast to take him. But he had hurt the creature now; he had it on the back foot. The advantage was his.

Ulysses tried to push himself up into a seated position and would have gone off the cliff backwards and into the sea, had it not been for the precarious fence that leaned out over the drop. He had come to a stop right on the very edge of the crumbling precipice, and when he had tried to put his hand down under the wire, to find some purchase, he had put all his weight on thin air.

He sluggishly staggered to his feet once more as the chimera bore down on him. With the creature filling his entire field of vision, Ulysses saw the blistering flesh again, great red wheals forming in other places now.

For a moment, he almost believed that the monster's charging run was going to take it off the edge of the cliff, the abomination unable to slow itself in time before hurling both Ulysses and itself over the precipice and into the sea.

Barely on his feet, he bowled himself clear of the great talon-scythe.

As the monster dug all of its remaining arthropod limbs into the soft turf before the fence, Ulysses suddenly found himself caught in the cage it had made of its claws. He was trapped.

He looked up at the pallid underbelly of the beast. There, sticking out of its reptilian flesh, was the glinting pommel of his sword. Reaching up, he grabbed the bloodstone hilt and pulled. The blade came free with an obscenely wet sucking gasp.

Pulling himself upright within the embrace of the abomination, the swelling blisters mere inches from his face now – the embryonic forms of something horribly familiar squirming within the iridescent mother-of-pearl fluid of their birthing sacs – Ulysses brought the blade up cleanly and parried the panicked thrusting of the creature's own chitin blade.

As the monster's talon slid free of his sword, Ulysses twisted his wrist sharply to deliver a downward cutting stroke of his own. His old left arm flopped onto the windswept grass at the cliff's edge.

"Let's see how you like it!" Ulysses said, a look of grim satisfaction on his face.

The dreadful raging screams of the beast suddenly ceased, replaced by a single, breathless cry. The Umbridge-chimera reeled backwards as gouts of thick black blood pumped from the severed brachial artery at the distended limb's second joint. The creature struck the fence, two of its claw-tipped limbs thrusting through the metal mesh, while others pushed against the wire netting on the near side.

Ulysses stepped in again, bringing his blade back up in a sweeping arc. The tip of the bloodied weapon made contact again, denying the old man any memorable last words, even if Umbridge had been able to articulate them. Ulysses' final blow had half cut through the fibrous muscles of the snaking neck, shearing through the creature's oesophagus and windpipe.

The severed stem writhing like a salted slug, the old man's head flopped impossibly to the right. For a moment the thing's staring eyes locked onto his and, in that one look Ulysses thought he saw something that might have passed for a trace of humanity within the dead-eyed fish stare he found there.

And then the creature's body began to fall, toppling almost languidly off the edge of the windswept cliff. First went the heavy shark's tail, the cancroid legs tearing the tangled fence from its roots under the great weight of the body, then the mish-mash of a torso, its flesh bubbling like boiling mud, then the trailing primate and crustacean limbs, and lastly the snake-like neck and the half-human head, gasping for air like a landed fish.

Ulysses staggered to the edge of the cliff, dropping to his hands and knees at the spot where the monster had fallen. He felt almost ready to go off the edge after it.

Beneath him the monster somersaulted through the air, blood spilling from a multitude of wounds to stomach, limb-stumps, face and neck.

The splash of the abomination entering the sea was lost amidst the white-water torrent of the breakers crashing against the black rocks. And then the abomination was claimed by the hungry waves, the dark surge drawing the vivisect's twitching body down into the freezing, stygian depths.

The roiling waves released the rocks again, pulling back from the rugged coastline, but the creature's carcass was gone. And with the creature gone, Ulysses' body gave in at last.

He collapsed onto the cold, wet grass at the edge of the cliff – the North Sea wind pulling at his clothes and pain-wracked body, stinging his face with cold – and let blissful unconsciousness claim him.

EPILOGUE

Plenty More Fish in the Sea

"So, THIS IS goodbye," Jennifer said, smiling despite the tears welling up at the corners of her eyes. Steam gushed around them as the train prepared to depart.

Standing there, face to face on the platform, Ulysses gently took her hands in his. He caressed her fingers with the soft black leather of his gloves, although inside he was wincing as his right hand throbbed with pain. Plenty of rest, the doctor who had treated him after his wild night on the moors had said.

But Ulysses felt that he had rested enough. He had slept for the whole of the following day, after his battle with the Umbridge-chimera, and had not woken again until well past nine on the morning after that. He had stirred to find Jennifer waiting anxiously at his bedside. He soon discovered that she too was staying at Mrs Scoresby's guesthouse now, as apparently Hunter's Lodge had also suffered the ravages of fire. "Well, they do say these things come in threes," Ulysses had remarked to Nimrod later, in private.

For a moment he had not known where he was or what the girl was doing there. As he came to wakefulness, the events of the previous forty-eight hours had seemed like nothing more than some hideous nightmare. But any such wishful thinking, on Ulysses' part had been banished by the reality of the pain he felt when he tried to move. Every muscle in his body felt either stiff or as if it had been damaged in some way. When eventually he pulled back the sheet, persisting in his struggle to rise, he found his body was a patchwork of bandages and plasters that covered a myriad cuts and bruises. Nimrod had done a good job of taking care of him – as always.

But there had been one thing that his skilled manservant could do nothing about, not now, and that was his replacement left arm. The limb that he had reclaimed from the vivisect had been packed in ice and kept in the guesthouse's cold cellar – unbeknownst to Mrs Scoresby – but Ulysses feared that the flesh would have begun to necrotise before they could get it to a surgeon with the skill to graft it back onto his body. No, it looked like the chimpanzee's arm was there to stay.

And despite having been prescribed three days of bed rest by the local doctor, if not a whole week, Ulysses had insisted in not only getting out of bed, but of also getting dressed – although it took him rather longer than usual – and going about his business as if nothing untoward had happened at all. The rest of that day had been spent sifting through the smouldering embers of Jennifer's home and trying to make sense of all that had happened over the past few days, while Inspector Allardyce led the local police in an investigation of the burnt-out ruins of Umbridge House.

It crossed Ulysses' mind that the inspector didn't seem overly bothered that his visit to his wife's family had turned into a busman's holiday.

Rest was what the doctor had ordered for Ulysses, but in his own expert medical opinion there would be time to rest later. The curious case of the Whitby Mermaid was not yet closed.

"Yes. Goodbye, for now," Ulysses said softly. "There are matters regarding this case that I need to tie up back in London."

"So, you're going after the one who supplied Doktor Seziermesser with his flesh-melding potion? This Alchemist?"

"Indeed I am."

"There's more to this than you're telling me, isn't there?"

Ulysses stared into Jennifer's eyes remembering the distinctive aniseed and rancid meat smell of the serum, as well as the nifty box of tricks they had found embedded in the flesh at the base of the Barghest's skull. He had encountered both before, when they had been used in conjunction by certain elements attempting to bring about the end of the British Empire.

"What will you do now?" he asked.

Jennifer sighed. If that was how it had to be, then so be it. "I'm going back to the Umbridge estate."

"After all that happened there?" Ulysses said, somewhat taken aback.

"The police have cleared the house, rounded up those who were in on Umbridge's scheme, those that he didn't kill in the end or that weren't burnt to a crisp by the fire," she added. "But when they came to the cellars they found them empty, apart from what was left of the good doktor, apparently."

Jennifer broke off and cast her gaze from the waiting train, the platform and the station buildings, to the headland on the other side of the Esk valley and the borders of the blasted moorland beyond.

"They're still out there," she said. "Seziermesser's experiments; his other victims. They've probably gone to ground in the caves and mines. Some might have made it to the coast. Others, who knows. But they need to be tracked down and found, so that they can be helped. And I have the expertise... to help."

Ulysses smiled. "Good for you." The girl was more resilient that he had given her credit for. It just went to prove the old adage of that which doesn't kill you only makes you stronger. "If anyone can make sure that those poor wretches get the help they need, it's you," he said warmly.

"Besides," she went on, blushing, "I feel that it will go some way towards vindicating my father's work."

"He'd be proud of you, to hear you say that. Good for you."

Ulysses lent forward and kissed Jennifer softly on the lips. She pulled away, her blush deepening, but did not remove her hands from his.

A sharp whistle cut through the background hubbub of the station, informing those gathered on the platform that the twelve forty-one to London was ready to depart. It was time for last fond farewells to be shared, for passengers to board and for well-wishers to allow them to do so.

Ulysses and Jennifer remained where they were.

"Sir, I hate to intrude," Nimrod interrupted as politely as he could, "but it's time to go. The train is ready to depart."

"One minute, eh, Nimrod old chap?"

"Very good, sir," Nimrod replied with just the slightest hint of annoyance in his voice.

"Jennifer... Jenny," Ulysses began. "There's something I need to say to you, something that I don't think I've said to you once in all this."

"Yes?" she said expectantly, her face drawing close to his again.

"And that's thank you."

"I'm sorry?"

"Thank you for everything you've done. You have been, quite simply, incredible. And if there's anything I can ever do for you, whatever it is –"

"There is one thing," she said, before he could finish – the flush of colour still there in her cheeks but her eyes now staring confidently into his – and with one hand on the back of his neck pulling him close, her warm lips parted to meet his unprotesting mouth.

* * *

WITH THE TRAIN underway, and the memory of their last lingering kiss still warm on his lips, Ulysses Quicksilver distractedly picked up that morning's copy of *The Times*. The headline read:

AILING INDUSTRIALIST DIES IN HOUSE FIRE

"We made the front page," he said, smiling grimly at Nimrod. It had taken a while for the news to filter down to London, but Umbridge Industries was one of the cornerstones on which the modern British Empire of Magna Britannia was built, so his passing had made headline news – even if all of the facts surrounding the case had not.

The morning after the incident, the local paper had gone with news of another fire, the one that had gutted St Mary's Church and resulted in the death of the Reverend Nathaniel Creed. The fire at Umbridge House and the death therein of the cancer-stricken industrialist Josiah Umbridge had only made page seven.

THE BOY WATCHED the train as it rattled its way along the track, hugging the banks of the Esk as it first headed south before turning west and starting on its way across the moors. He heard the distant *clickety-clack* of its wheels on the rails and the *peep-peep* of its steam-whistle, softened almost into melody by the distance and the muffling wind sweeping across the headland above the town.

"So, are you coming or what?" a skeletally gaunt man wearing scuffed top hat and tails, and tight black leggings, called from the cavalcade of steam-wagons and horse-drawn carts.

"I'm coming!" Jacob called back as he hefted his own meagre pack onto his shoulder. He hadn't had much that he could call his own to begin with, and thanks to the fire and his father's death, he had even less. The fire and brimstone priest might not have loved him, but he had still cared for him after a manner of speaking for the last seventeen years, and Jacob would miss him, even if the recalcitrant sinner had given him a name that summed up how he felt about the impact he had had on his life, a name that translated from the Hebrew as 'usurper'.

And now that his father was gone, it was time for Jacob Creed to make his own way in the world, and not as a boy but as a man, as part of new family, one that accepted him as he was.

"I'm coming!" he called again.

Throwing the blackened shell of the church one last mournful glance, Jacob trotted after the departing wagon-train as the Circus of Wonders went on its way.

*　　*　　*

DAWN WAS STILL two hours off as George Craven started hauling in his nets after another night's fishing. He had slipped back into the old routine as easily as he had slipped into his old galoshes and sou'wester, as easily as Mrs Craven had taken on the mantle of nagging fish wife again – although now she had something else entirely to complain about.

His life of luxury had not lasted for long, as ephemeral as the fame Mycroft Cruickshank had promised him. What had been headline news a month ago was today's fish and chip papers. And George should know; he had been tucking into a portion of deep-fried haddock only the day before when he had come across the words 'Mermaid Stolen' half-obscured by grease at the bottom of the packet.

He was still considering how quickly fame could turn to notoriety and, in turn, to derision when the glistening, writhing mass of his catch began to spill into the bottom of his boat, the *Mabel*, and it took him a moment to realise that something wasn't quite as it should be.

Amidst the wriggling mass of writhing tentacles, flapping fins and scuttling crustaceans there seemed to be some commotion. There was something in there with the catch, something that was voracious and evil-minded, something that was attacking the sea's bounty that lay suffocating in the bottom of the boat; several somethings in fact.

George Craven peered closer, trying to get a proper look at what it was that was molesting the fish, by the swaying inconstant light of the hurricane lantern secured to the mast.

They were hideous, impossible things, like some unholy cross between a crab, a fish and... and something like the mermaid – something almost human. In fact, in comparison, they made the mermaid seem like a perfectly plausible natural hybrid. But there was nothing natural about these things.

Boldly, George reached down with a thick gloved hand and plucked one of the creatures from the writhing mass of bodies sloshing around his feet. It was bright red in colour and only six or seven inches long from head to tail. Parts of it were covered in shell, but the shell itself was still soft and pliable, as if the thing were newly hatched. As George peered at it in disbelieving wonder it hissed and twisted in the grip of his thumb and forefinger, snapping at him with one over-sized pincer-claw.

For a moment he considered taking the specimen back to shore alive. He still had Cruikshank's details. Perhaps this could be the start of something big.

"Now hang on there, George," he announced to the sea and the wind. He peered at the impossible amalgam again, with its asymmetrical physiology, seemingly part mammal, part fish and part crab, and saw nothing but trouble. "They'd never believe you!" he said with a sigh.

And with that he tossed it overboard, back into the cold surge of the sea. Snatching the others from among the morning's catch, one by one, he sent them over the side after the first. The squirming creatures plopped into the water, quickly sinking from view into the black depths of the North Sea.

"How'd you do this morning, George?" the fisherman said aloud, playing all the parts in some imagined conversation he might have later that morning, back at the docks.

"Not bad, not bad."

"No mermaids today?"

"No, not today."

"A good catch then?"

"Yeah, a good catch. But you should've seen the one that got away."

THE END

PAX BRITANNIA
CHRISTMAS PAST

JONATHAN GREEN

I

Whom the Gods Would Destroy

~ December 1997 ~

THE ATMOSPHERE WITHIN the doctor's study was one of quiet, studious application, the only sounds the crackling of the fire in the grate, the scratching of the pen across the sheet of headed notepaper he had placed on his blotter, and the deathly ticking of the clock as it marked the man's last moments on this earth.

The pre-printed heading on the top of the crisp sheet of vellum notepaper read:

Dr Lockwood Lacey, Doctor of Psychiatry

Beneath it the doctor had written the date – 1st December 1997 – and then, in a meticulous hand, had proceeded to set down his written confession.

It was snug within the study: the curtains had been drawn against the encroaching night outside and the doctor had ensured that he had locked the door before he set about his night's business.

He put down his pen and, having re-read the last paragraph of the letter, took up the bundle of crumpled papers again. Shuffling through them one by one he read each again in turn. It did not take him long. Each was a letter, written on significantly poorer quality paper, torn from a child's jotter. Each was written in bright crayon colours, in the same childish hand, was decorated with simplistic illustrations, and each began in just the same way:

Dear Farthr Krissmus

There were thirty-seven of them in total.

With a sigh the doctor put them back on the desk, shuffling the papers together into a neat pile as he did so. Taking off his glasses he rubbed at his eyes. He felt tired, exhausted in fact. He hadn't slept for days; but he would have his rest soon enough.

Replacing his glasses, he re-read the last paragraph of his own letter. Taking up his pen once more he signed his name with a flourish, and then carefully replaced the lid. He folded the sheet of notepaper and slipped it into the envelope that he had addressed before commencing his act of confession and, licking the gummed strip, sealed it. Having tidied the other papers on his desk, the doctor laid the envelope carefully on top of the small pile in his out tray, his eyes alighting on the name of the addressee once more: The Reverend L. G. Havelock.

Calmly, the doctor rose from his chair, took off his shoes and padded across the carpeted floor of the study, the black dog that no-one else could see but which he knew was there – that was always there – trotting at his side. He stopped before the chair, which he had already had the forethought to place under the light fitting in the middle of the room.

Climbing onto the chair he slipped the noose over his head – the noose that he had also seen fit to prepare before he commenced on the rest of his endeavour, while his mind was still clear, his resolve firm. Kicking the chair away from under him, the doctor hanged himself.

A choking gargling sound disturbed the peace of the room, the spasming body sending jerking shadows dancing about the study in the flickering firelight.

And the black dog wagged its tail in approval.

II

The Dead of Jericho

Night fell as the Sunday faithful attended evensong, and with it, the first snows of winter drifted down upon the dreaming spires of Oxford. Feathery flakes descended right across the city from the blanket of clouds above.

The snow fell on the streets of Jericho, and the red-brick homes of the employees of the Oxford University Press, as much as it fell on the domiciles of dons and scholars, swirls of white confetti spiralling down between the terraces to form fractal icing sugar patterns on the roofs and roads and pavements.

But such beauty went unappreciated by Noah Hackett who, in his rotgut-induced alcoholic stupor was, for the time being, only concerned with finding a place to sleep. The snow only made things worse. Tonight it would be both cold *and* wet.

The prospect of sleeping rough on the streets of Oxford, amidst all the wealth and splendour of the complacent colleges, even among the less than salubrious warren of streets of Jericho, was never a pleasant one. But the knowledge that the cold and damp would leech what little warmth the last bottle of cheap gin had left in his bones, only made it seem all the more unappealing.

But he knew Jericho well – it was a favoured haunt of his, the memories of better days dragging him back to the area time after time, and there were always the boathouses and lock-ups down by the canal that were worth trying before hunkering down to wait out the night, the snow and the inevitable hangover.

He turned onto Canal Street, hoping to find an appropriately unlocked coach house in which to shelter. It was then that he heard the jingling sound for the first time, although in the drunken haze through which he lived much of his life these days he barely registered it.

The sound provoked in him nothing more than mild amusement, and into his mind, blown like the whirling inconstant snow, came memories of childhood Christmases, twee carol-rhymes rising from his subconscious like the bubbles in a glass of champagne. Not that he got to drink champagne these days.

There was nothing worth celebrating nowadays; it was enough for him that he managed to beg enough pennies from the guilty worthies of the city to furnish himself with another bottle of cheap gin and a bull scrotum pie, if he was lucky.

The tramp stumbled on along Canal Street, pulling the layers of scavenged shirts, cardigans, waistcoats and his heavy coat closer about him. He tugged his woollen cap down tight over his ears and for once was glad of his lice-ridden beard, which helped keep his face warm under its week's accumulation of grime.

Jingle-jingle.

There it was again, the tinkling of Christmas bells.

Noah trudged on through the slushy first fall.

Jingle-jingle.

And again.

This time the tramp turned. He peered through the snow and the night, and his own ever-present alcoholic fog, and glimpsed movement in a patch of shadow beyond the pool of light of the nearest guttering streetlamp. Something crimson swirled in the light escaping from a first floor window of one of the houses.

Jingle-jingle.

And then it was gone.

Confused by what he had seen and heard, but more irritated at still having nowhere to sleep, the tramp continued on his stumbling way, grumbling to himself through his beard.

Reaching the entrance to one of the alleyways that ran down to the Oxford Canal, Noah ducked into it, fervently hoping to give whoever it was that was following him the slip. He had had enough of the police harassing him and of the do-gooders from the Temperance Society sticking their interfering noses into his private business.

Untended weeds clogged the alleyway, poking out from underneath the ill-fitting doors of lock-ups and boathouses. Surely there had to be somewhere suitable round here?

Rattling the doors of the padlocked outhouses, Noah was only dimly aware of the footsteps approaching him. The renewed jingling, however, was enough to alert him to the presence of the stranger behind him.

He shuffled close to the red-brick structure to his right. He had learnt long ago that it was sometimes best just to blend into the background and not draw attention to oneself, especially when you were creeping round behind people's houses. Accusations of theft and trespass sat all too easily on the shoulders of a vagrant, as far as the authorities were concerned.

The thumping footfalls came nearer.

Jingle-jingle.

Noah froze, his weak heart suddenly racing with fretful apprehension. But still he turned round, to see who was following him.

A huge shadow stepped out of the night and into the middle of the alleyway in front of him and stopped abruptly. Noah's gasp of alarm surprised even himself. Cowering before the figure, he peered up into the hood of the crimson cloak that was pulled up over the stranger's head.

He half-expected to see a jolly, rosy-cheeked face with a bushy white beard. The bifurcated brutish face he saw there instead turned his guts to ice-water colder than the snow, and caused him to blurt out another blubbing cry of dismayed disbelief.

"You?" he gasped, recognition coming to him, despite the mind-fogging effects of the gin.

There was a sudden flurry of movement that sent eddying snowflakes spinning into the air, the reflected flash of the streetlamp on finely-honed steel and Noah gasped again as the air was forced from his body by a crippling punch to the stomach.

The figure pulled back. Noah's gaze was drawn to the fist with which the savage blow had been delivered. Four claw-like appendages glistened wetly, speckles of holly-red dripping onto the ground amidst the smattering of snow.

Noah instinctively put a hand to his belly. It came away painted red. In a state of shock the tramp found himself thinking how hot his lifeblood was, when he himself felt so cold.

With a feral wail of its own the red-cloaked figure moved in again with the gutting blades, and the jingling of Christmas bells accompanied the chorus of savage howls and agonised screams that suddenly filled the winter's night.

And all the time the snow fell.

III

The Body in the Library

"NOT ANOTHER ONE," Chief Inspector Thaw muttered grumpily.

"I'm afraid so, sir," his loyal sidekick Detective Sergeant Whately replied, holding the door for his superior to enter the archive ahead of him.

There, between the rows and rows of shelves lay the crumpled body of the Chief Librarian. From his posture and the rigour-set expression on his face, the Chief Inspector could have believed that Everett Willoughby was only sleeping, if it hadn't been for the blood-sodden mass of papers and irreplaceable archive documents on which he was lying.

The air of the archive was redolent with the smell of old books, mildew and the bitter-iron aroma of blood, and there was lots of it.

"Dear God," Thaw uttered in dismay.

"Ah, you're here at last, Chief Inspector," a young woman wearing blood-stained white coveralls said, rising from where she had been crouched beside the corpse.

"And good morning to you too, Doctor Lavish," Thaw replied, absentmindedly combing a hand through the swirls of white-grey hair on his head, in the presence of the attractive younger woman. "You're looking radiant as ever, if I might be permitted to say so?"

"Well compared to our friend the Chief Librarian here, I suppose I am," she smirked, looking down at the dead man's puffy, fish-white face. His eyes were sunken within blotchy purpling hollows.

"Is it our killer?" Thaw asked, returning to the matter in hand.

"That's for you to find out, isn't it Chief Inspector?" Doctor Lavish said, a twinkle in her eyes.

"Well, yes. Of course, but —"

"But if you mean, is it the same M.O., then yes. Knifed in the stomach with what looks like a fistful of kitchen knives. He was stabbed multiple times. Position and pattern of the wounds suggest that the victim was struck repeatedly with an instrument made up of several long blades."

"You're sure, doctor?"

"Either that, or our killer took the time to meticulously measure the space between each stab wound before administering the next."

The Chief Inspector expressed his irritation by breathing out loudly through his nose. "Point taken."

He turned to his Detective Sergeant. "First it was Higgins, wealthy banker, out for a walk with his dog along Brewer Street, two nights ago. And now this poor bugger."

"Yes, sir," Whately confirmed.

"Two men, two murders, two nights. But what was it that connected the victims? Why were they the targets that our killer chose?"

There was the creak and bang of a door opening and closing, accompanied by the *tap-tap-tap* of footsteps on the polished archive floor.

"And what have we here?" came a cheery voice from behind the Chief Inspector. Thaw turned and came face-to-face with a smartly-dressed man, in his mid-to-late thirties judging by the streaks of grey present at the temples of his thick head of hair. He was handsome, with a well-defined jaw-line, and tall, and the Chief Inspector could see that beneath his long coat and tweed suit he had the physique of an athlete. Behind him, at his shoulder, stood an older man, dressed in the traditional attire of a butler. He was tall like his master and broad across the shoulders, his grey hair swept back from a clearly-defined widow's peak

"Who the bloody hell are you?" Chief Inspector Thaw demanded.

The interloper fixed the policeman with sparkling brown eyes and grinned. "Ulysses Quicksilver, at your service," he said, holding out a black-gloved hand. "You might have heard of me."

"Might I?" the Chief Inspector returned. "Should I have heard of him, Whately?"

"Oh yes, sir," the Detective Sergeant blurted excitedly. "Mr Quicksilver saved her Majesty's life, sir, during the Wormwood Debacle. Don't you remember?"

The Chief Inspector muttered something as undoubtedly unflattering as it was unintelligible.

"It's a pleasure to meet you, sir," the Detective Sergeant said, with all the enthusiasm of an over-excited puppy, taking the proffered handshake where his superior had not.

"Thank you...?"

"Whately. Detective Sergeant Whately."

"Sergeant Whately. A pleasure!"

"Who let you in here anyway?" Thaw snapped.

"Does that matter? I'm here now, and I'm here to help."

"What brings you to Oxford, Mr Quicksilver?" Whately asked, patently awestruck finding himself in the presence of a genuine Hero of the Empire.

"Looking up an old friend," Quicksilver replied. "Or at least I will be when we're done here. Saw all the commotion in the street as we were driving over to Boriel."

"Well, you'll be pleased to hear that we are all done here," the Chief Inspector declared. "Isn't that right, doctor?"

"Yes, Chief Inspector. It's over to you now."

"So thank you for the offer of your help, but we won't need to keep you from renewing your old acquaintance after all."

"What happened to the poor fellow?" Quicksilver pressed, craning to peer past the Chief Inspector at the body lying between the stacks. "Stabbed was he?"

"Yes," Whately replied helpfully, "several times. Just like the other one."

"The other one?"

"Whately!" the irascible Thaw growled.

"Sorry, sir." The Detective Sergeant turned an embarrassed shade of beetroot.

"So, Mr Quicksilver, as we like to say in the Force, there really is nothing to see here. We have everything under control."

"Oh, I'm sure you do, Inspector."

"That's *Chief* Inspector."

"Oh, I *do* beg your pardon, *Chief* Inspector. We wouldn't want to be getting in your way now would we, Nimrod?"

"Indeed not, sir," the dandy's manservant replied in a tone that matched the severity of his expression of aloof disdain as he regarded the two policemen with a stony, sapphire gaze.

"But if you would like my help at all, I'll be in Oxford for the rest of the day, so don't hesitate to get in touch."

He pulled a leather wallet from a jacket pocket and from that extracted a printed calling card, passing it to the still-grinning Sergeant.

"Thank you for your time, *Chief* Inspector. Merry Christmas."

And with that he turned, and left the library.

* * *

"Nimrod, I do believe we have tarried here long enough," Ulysses Quicksilver announced as he and his manservant left the crime scene that the Bodleian Library had become. "I rather feel we've kept old Monty waiting far too long already."

"Very good, sir," Nimrod replied matter-of-factly. "Would you like to take the car, sir?"

The two of them ducked under the police line at the arched entrance to the Bodleian Square and turned left, making for where Nimrod had parked the Mark IV Silver Phantom at the entrance to Catte Street.

"Let's leave the car," Ulysses said, buttoning his coat against the cold. "A walk in this bracing air will help clear the remains of last night's excesses from my head, I hope."

"Very good, sir."

A young woman, wearing a woollen beret and full-length coat against the cold, emerged from the throng of curious onlookers collected outside the Bodleian and hurried to intercept them.

"Mr Quicksilver?" she called.

"Who wants to know?" was Ulysses' sharp rebuttal.

"Lucy Gudrun, *Oxford Echo*. What is that brings you to Oxford on Christmas Eve, when only last night you were seen gallivanting at Lord and Lady Rothschild's Christmas Ball?" The young woman suddenly seemed very confident as to Ulysses' identity.

"Personal business."

"And would that same personal business include the investigation of the Christmas Killings?"

Ulysses' carefully-composed grimace of passive indifference slipped and he turned to look at the girl directly. "Killings plural, you say?"

He was caught by her obvious attractiveness, which she seemed at pains to cover up. But even without the application of any obvious make-up, her cheeks still had an appealing rosy glow and her rosebud lips were none the less appealing.

"Everett Willoughby's death is the second in as many days that match the same M.O. within the city."

"How do you know...?" Ulysses broke off. He wasn't that naive. His comment had been a knee jerk reaction. He knew how the press worked. They always 'had their sources'.

"I have my sources," the young woman said with a mixture of smugness and pride.

"I knew you were going to say that," Ulysses said raising a wry eyebrow. She was young and eager, barely into her twenties, if he was any judge, and he was. "Look, Miss Gudrun, I have tarried too long already and have places I need to be, as I'm sure do you. Now if you'll excuse me."

"Just one comment for the *Oxford Echo*?" the plucky reporter pressed, tireless in her efforts.

Ulysses stopped. "Alright, here's a comment for you. *No comment!*" With that he turned on his heel and strode on his way.

"Can I have a comment from you, sir?" the young woman asked, thrusting the hand-held recorder under Nimrod's nose before he even had a chance to follow his master. The young woman almost wilted under his withering sapphire stare.

"Good day, Miss Gudrun," he intoned sonorously, but the look in his eyes said so much more, and none of it pleasant.

She watched them leave.

Lucy Gudrun knew a good story when she stumbled on one, like a chalk-outlined body on the floor of the Bodleian library, but she also knew when she was pushing her luck and when to admit defeat. Besides, she might have lost this particular battle, but she hadn't lost the war. Not yet.

She turned back to the Great Gate that led from Catte Street into the School's quadrangle and from there into the Bodleian itself. She was just in time to see the curmudgeonly Chief Inspector Thaw and his sidekick Sergeant Whately emerge from beneath the stone gateway and cross the police line.

Ensuring that her hand-held recorder was still running, she trotted towards the pair of policemen. "Chief Inspector!" she shouted. "A word for the *Oxford Echo*?"

IV

The Damocles Club

HE KNEW THAT something was wrong before the porter even opened the door to the old man's rooms. It was the smell. The iron-rich tang of blood at the back of his throat again, the rancid ammonia smell of voided bowels, the unpleasant and wholly unmistakeable smell of death.

"Bloody 'ell!" the porter swore, his hand slipping from the doorknob as he stood there dumbfounded, the door swinging open to reveal the scene of devastation and death beyond.

"Monty!" Ulysses Quicksilver gasped, pushing past the porter – his bowler hat held tight in his shaking hands now – and into the room.

It had obviously been a mess to begin with. A proliferation of books and manuscripts, along with empty tea cups, half-eaten plates of food, and the skull of an Australopithecus, were scattered over desks and bookcases. The half-expected scholarly clutter of an absent-minded professor even littered the tops of glass-fronted cabinets containing stuffed animals and Neolithic tools, cracked leather chairs, and the Persian rugs on the floor as well. The attack on Professor Montgomery Summerson, had obviously left the study in an even greater state of chaos and confusion.

Ulysses stood there, amidst the disorder and disarray, staring down at the cold carcass of his old tutor. Honeyed sunlight pierced the leadlights of the room's windows, revealing the full horror of the scene in intense, sun-washed colours, predominantly red.

Summerson had called him at home only the evening before, but Ulysses had been out on the town, enjoying the company of tipsy and compliant young socialites at the Rothschild's Christmas Ball, held at his Lordship' Gunnersbury Park estate, west of the capital. Ulysses had missed the call then and hadn't even been aware of it until Nimrod woke him that morning, having checked the calls logged to the house the night before.

"I should have come sooner," he said, his voice barely more than a whisper of regret.

"You were out, sir," Nimrod replied. "You weren't to know that Professor Summerson would call. After all, you have not heard from him in some time."

"I know, but if hadn't been out gallivanting about the place, like the self-indulgent idiot I was in my youth, I wouldn't have missed his call."

"You've had a lot on your mind, sir."

Ulysses swore under his breath. "He was onto something, Nimrod," he said, nudging a pile of papers at his foot. "He wanted my help and because I wasn't there for him he's dead."

Ulysses looked at the body again. It was a mess. He didn't need to be a coroner to pronounce the cause of death. He had been knifed like Willoughby the librarian. His face had been carved up by four slashing knife strokes, while his shirt had been turned wholly red by his own blood.

Ulysses knelt down beside the body. Summerson had died in agony, his body curled into an agonised question mark, as if in death every part of him had wanted to know why he had to die in this manner. As far as Ulysses could tell, he had bled to death, having been stabbed so many times that the blood-sodden fabric of his clothes now lay in tatters over the mangled meat of his chest.

There was blood on his face, on his chest, his arms, blood had pooled on the floor around him, soaking fallen papers, the threadbare Persian rug on which he lay, contorted in his death-agonies, it covered his hands... Only it didn't. Ulysses paused and looked more closely.

The dead man only had blood on the rigoured claw of his right hand, and no signs of any wounds there. The hand was stretched out from the professor's body, his fingers partially obscured by a bloodied document that must have fallen across him as he lay dying on the floor of his study.

Suddenly aware of the rapid beating of his heart, caged within his chest, carefully Ulysses moved the papers aside. His breath caught in his throat. There, formed of bloody finger-strokes, was one semi-congealed word: Damocles.

Monty Summerson had sent Ulysses a final message, written in his own blood.

"I-I'd better call the-the police," the porter stammered, backing out of the room, leaving the door open behind him.

"Just give us half an hour," Ulysses said, without looking at the man, but flashing him the contents of his leather card-holder again just in case he needed reminding who's authority they were working under.

For a moment neither Ulysses nor Nimrod moved. Neither of them said anything, the only sound that broke the stillness of the study the insistent ticking of the clock on the mantelpiece on the other side of the room.

As Ulysses continued to take in every detail of the murder scene, a shadow fell across him from the doorway to the study behind him.

He heard a startled gasp and turned.

In a moment the young woman had composed herself again. "Perhaps you would like to make a comment now, Mr Quicksilver," Lucy Gudrun suggested, recording device pointing towards him.

"ANYTHING THAT HAS the name Damocles on it. Anything that might give us any kind of a clue. Anything at all." Ulysses said, frustrated at his own failure to so far discover what it was that his former tutor had been trying to tell him through his last, dying act.

Heedless to what Chief Inspector Thaw might have to say about them disturbing a crime scene, Nimrod set about bringing some semblance of order back to the professor's study – although he made sure that he left the body just as it was – so that Ulysses' search for clues might be made all the easier, while the reporter began going through the papers on the dead man's desk.

Ulysses had taken the attitude that her arrival at Boriel College, having obviously followed them from the Bodleian, had been opportune. She obviously already had a handle on what was going on, and she had seen too much of the scene of Summerson's murder already to be fobbed off, and so he had decided to treat her presence as an asset rather than a hindrance. He had put her to work, promising her the scoop of her career as he set about solving the Christmas Killings. She was tough too, not seeming to mind that the professor's body was still there in the room.

And yet, here they were, with the half hour's grace granted them by the porter almost up, half-expecting the police to turn up at any moment, and still without any answers.

"Here, take a look at this!" Lucy suddenly piped up. Ulysses joined her at the professor's desk. She was poring over a pile of newspapers, among them copies of the *Oxford Echo*. Ulysses peered over her shoulder to see what it was that had caused her outburst.

She had a copy of *The Times* in front of her, folded so as to expose the obituaries page. Circled in red pen was the obituary of Dr Lockwood Lacey, doctor of psychiatry. Ulysses scanned the piece.

"Fifty-seven years old... worked at the Saint Ophelia Sanatorium for the Mentally Infirm," he read. "Very interesting, but what does this have to do with Damocles, or the other killings, for that matter?"

"Well, your professor friend circled it for a reason and then there's this." She moved the paper to reveal another, with another article circled, this time reporting the murder of one Aloysius Higgins, a banker. "This one just made yesterday's *Echo*."

"When's the obituary from?"

"The eighth of December. It says Lacey died on the first of December."

"And when did Higgins die?"

"The night of the twenty-second."

"So how does this one fit in?" Ulysses asked, lifting another folded newspaper from a pile of books on a chair beside him and placing it on the desk. In this case, Summerson appeared to have circled a few lines at the bottom of an inside page of the local paper, that reported the killing of a tramp well-known in the Jericho area, who went by the name of Noah.

"That's news to me," Lucy admitted. "When did that happen?"

"On..." Ulysses paused, searching for a date at the top of the page. "On the twenty-first. Sunday night."

"And then the Chief Librarian was killed last night, which was the twenty-third," Lucy pondered, gazing thoughtfully into the middle distance.

"Along with Summerson. So, what could possibly connect the Professor of Social Anthropology, the Chief Librarian of the Bodleian, a successful banker, and a homeless tramp?"

"You think something does connect them then?"

"Well, apart from the manner of their deaths? It seems likely, doesn't it to you?"

"Well yes, but a couple of academics, a banker and a tramp?"

"And let's not forget the suicidal doctor of psychiatry." Ulysses' face twisted into a knot of concentration. "Physician, heal thyself," he said quietly to himself.

"Excuse me, sir," Nimrod said interrupting his master's musings, "but I think this might be of interest." He was holding up a framed photograph. The glass was cracked right across the middle, no doubt having been damaged at the same time that Summerson was attacked.

Ulysses crossed the room in a series of excited, leaping strides. "Good show, old chap!"

The photograph showed seven young men, undoubtedly undergraduates, by their dress and apparent age. The picture had been taken within the Boriel College quad. Although the pose was formal, their attitude was anything but. All of them were wearing expressions of smug arrogance or feigned aloof indifference.

"Obnoxious arrogant bastards, convinced of their own superiority over the rest of the human race the lot of them," Ulysses muttered under his breath.

"I couldn't possibly comment, sir," was Nimrod's tactful reply, his gaze lingering on Ulysses.

The sepia-tint photograph was mounted within a card frame, at the bottom of which had been written, in an exaggerated Gothic hand:

The Damocles Club, Michaelmas Term, 1960.

Underneath that were recorded the names of the individuals in the picture.

"Well, there are a few familiar names here," he stated with glee. Her reporter's sense of curiosity piqued, Lucy rose from her place behind the desk and joined the two men in their inspection of the image. "There's Higgins, the banker, second from the left, and L. Lacey next to him, the suicidal doctor. Two along from him again is poor old Monty, of all people, and next to him, second from the right, is Willoughby."

"You think this is the connection then?" Lucy asked.

"Well, considering that we have the word 'Damocles' written over there on the floor in Monty's blood, and three of the men from this photograph have been murdered within as many days, I can hardly see how it can be anything other," Ulysses declared.

"It's four, actually," Lucy said.

"I beg your pardon?"

"Four men from that list have been found dead since Monday morning."

"Really?"

"If you include old Noah. N. Hackett?"

"Of course!" Ulysses exclaimed, flashing the girl a delighted smile. "The tramp! Oh how the mighty have fallen."

He turned back to the photograph.

"So, one dead by his own hand. Four dead by the hand of another in the last three nights. That just leaves two names on this list, neither of which mean anything to me. But we have to find them, that is most imperative."

"You think they are in danger, sir?" Nimrod asked.

"Indeed I do. One of them could even be our killer. Either way, we have to find them as quickly as possible. Which is where you come in, Miss Gudrun."

"It is?" the young woman met Ulysses intense gaze.

"Indeed it is! I want you to use the immense resources of that local rag you work for to find out who S. Fitzmaurice and V. Ashton-Griffiths are and where they might be found. I have a feeling that it will be somewhere not a million miles from here."

"Very well, but what's in it for me?"

Ulysses' look of childish excitement darkened to become one of bitter disdain. Reporters the world over; they were all the same.

"Do this, for me," he said, "and I'll give you the exclusive of your career. I'll hand you Oxford's Christmas Killer on a platter."

V

Slay Bells

"Mr Fitzmaurice?" Ulysses tried, as he entered the fusty darkness of the glasshouse. "Saintjohn Fitzmaurice?" he called a little louder. Eyes straining to see anything through the failing twilight, his manservant cautiously followed him into the building.

The place seemed to be entirely deserted – there wasn't a light on anywhere – but that didn't put pay to the uncomfortable feeling Ulysses' had, like a persistent itch on the inside of his skull, that something wasn't right. There was danger here.

It had been several hours since they had made their hasty exit from the Professor's study, leaving as Chief Inspector Thaw and his attendant officers were making their way into Boriel College by the Longwall Street entrance.

As the reporter returned to the *Oxford Echo's* newsroom and its difference engine database, Ulysses and Nimrod retired to the backroom of the Turf Tavern, Ulysses muttering something about the hair of the dog that had bitten him the night before.

In time, Lucy's scouring of her Babbage engine's reader screen had come up trumps and she had contacted Ulysses, furnishing him with the current whereabouts of Saintjohn Fitzmaurice, formerly of the Damocles Club, now Director of Oxford's Botanic Gardens.

"Mr Fitzmaurice!" Ulysses called again into the gathering gloom between the potted plants, louder this time.

Still no reply.

They had tried the man's home already, only to be told by his housekeeper that he had left earlier that evening in a state of high dudgeon, having taken a handwritten missive at the door, saying something about having to go back to the Gardens.

Ulysses edged forwards slowly. The insistent subconscious scratching on the inside of his skull grew in intensity. Was Fitzmaurice waiting for them, just around the corner, garden fork in hand, ready to do them in? Or had the killer struck already, and the Director was, right now, lying dead, half buried in a compost heap somewhere?

And then Ulysses heard the incongruous sound for the first time, the jingling of bells.

"Come on, Nimrod!" he hissed. "This way!"

And then the two of them were running through the glasshouse. Ahead of them the insistent jingle-jingle of the bells continued, leading them on.

Ulysses reached a glazed divide and pushed through the unlatched door swinging on its hinges, almost tripping over the body lying in the darkness between the trestles of the potting shed.

Ulysses guessed that the figure curled in an expanding pool of his own blood, that glistened black in the darkness, was Saintjohn Fitzmaurice, but there wasn't time to stop and check.

The body groaned weakly.

"Nimrod, stay with him," Ulysses instructed his manservant, hopping over the fatally wounded man and charging on his way in pursuit of the bells.

There was a cacophonous crash of breaking glass and splintering glazing struts from the far end of the glasshouse. Ulysses ran on.

He emerged from the end of the glasshouse through the wreck of another glazed door that it looked like his quarry had run straight through without bothering to open, into the oily darkness of the formal gardens.

He ran on, between carefully-manicured black lawns, along gravel paths, always chasing the steady jingle of the Christmas bells. Sleigh bells.

Shrubs and the dark skeletal shapes of trees loomed ahead of him. There was a change in the rhythm of the jingling, as if, Ulysses imagined, the killer had taken a running jump at the walled boundary of the Gardens. A moment later he heard the thud of someone landing heavily in the street on the other side.

He reached the wall himself only a matter of moments later. Using his unnaturally muscled left arm in particular to help with his ascent, Ulysses pulled himself to the top of the wall that marked the western boundary of the Botanic Gardens.

He peered down into the poorly-lit lane beyond. He couldn't see anybody, either running up or down the road, and, he now realised after his own desperate scramble up the wall, he couldn't hear anything in the way of pounding footfalls or jingling sleigh bells either.

A hissed expletive escaped Ulysses' gritted teeth. They had been so close. If only they had got there sooner, he might have had the Christmas Killer in his clutches right at that very moment. Instead he was no closer to catching the murderer of his old friend and tutor, and all those other men. In fact his failure to act in time had led to another man's death. Not for the first time that day, Ulysses berated himself for not answering his tutor's plea sooner.

It was at that moment that his personal communicator buzzed inside his pocket. Straddling the top of the wall, Ulysses took out the device and pressed the enamelled answer key.

"Yes?" he snapped sharply into the mouthpiece.

"It's Lucy," the woman's voice at the other end of the line said. "Did you get to Fitzmaurice in time?"

"No. We were too late. The killer got here first and now he's got away. I lost him!" he snarled, the rancour evident in his voice.

"Well I think I know where you might find him," Lucy said.

"Really?"

"I've identified the last man in the photograph. Get yourself back to Boriel, it's the Master. It's Virgil Ashton-Griffiths! Either he's the killer or he's the next victim!"

VI

The Ghost of Christmas Past

"So, TELL ME about the Damocles Club, Master," Ulysses said, regarding the gargoyle-faced man opposite from over steepled, black-gloved fingers, "and, more specifically, why somebody would want every last member dead."

Ulysses Quicksilver was impressed. The Master had maintained the same stony facade ever since they had invaded his private sanctuary.

The porter – still shaken by his discovery of Montgomery Summerson's eviscerated body – had reluctantly led Ulysses, Nimrod and Lucy through the college buildings to the Master's apartments, as if he half expected to stumble upon another corpse. It had been with some obvious relief that he had opened the door, hearing the Master's voice command them to "Come!" Ulysses' 'by Appointment to Her Majesty' ID had done the rest.

Ulysses and Virgil Ashton-Griffiths met each other's unblinking eyes, each regarding the other by the ruddy glow of the fire crackling in the hearth. For a moment, all that could be heard within the Master's study was the insistent ticking of a clock and the snap and crackle of the fire smouldering in the grate.

And then the older man's expression of steely resolution slowly began to crumble, the hard lines of his hawkish face becoming sagging lines heavy with worry.

"We were undergraduates at the time, here at Boriel College," the Master said quietly. "We were young, we were arrogant –"

"I could see that for myself," Ulysses threw in.

"And we were bored. The idle rich, if you like," Ashton-Griffiths went on.

"So, apart from looking down on everyone else and your Daddies having more money than you had things to fill your days with, what did you do that would make someone wish you all dead?"

"From what I remember of your own background, Mr Quicksilver, you were not left exactly destitute by your parents when they died." The Master's previous steel had started to return in the face of Ulysses' brusque manner.

"But my name isn't the one that's at the bottom of a list of dead men," Ulysses pointed out darkly.

The Master sighed. "To be honest, it will be a relief to be able to tell someone about it after all these years."

"How many years, precisely?"

"Thirty-seven."

"So, around the time the photograph was taken, when the Damocles Club was at its height."

The Master reached for his cup of tea and took a sip before continuing.

"It was the product of the recklessness of youth, I suppose, a group of like-minded individuals, cast free of boarding school and our mothers' apron strings for the first time, with enough money and status to do pretty much as we pleased. Such youthful exuberance manifested itself at first in terms of ridiculous drinking games at various pubs around the town, but they didn't really appeal to our thrill-seeking natures. It was adrenalin that motivated us, the need to face impossible odds and triumph.

"We began to partake in various gambling pursuits, but when money is no object, when you are not really risking anything in a real sense, it takes away the element of risk and saps the excitement from it. So we started gambling with things that were more precious to us than money. We took up some of the rather more extreme sports, rock-climbing, white-water rafting and the like."

"But we've all done that sort of thing haven't we?" Ulysses said, recalling the time in his own life when he had frittered his life away in idle pursuits. He had held the Paris-Dakar rally record for eight years running, for a start. And it could be argued that his life now was even more dangerous, and satisfying as a result. Well, most of the time, he thought, rubbing at the shoulder joint of his left arm.

"We fashioned ourselves into the Damocles Club, named after the infamous sword, of course," the Master went on, as if he hadn't heard a word Ulysses had said. "But, unlike Damocles, we liked that feeling of imminent danger, that everything about our position of privilege could be over-turned in an instant."

He paused, returning the teacup and its saucer to the table.

"And then we met Marley."

"Go on."

"Lacey brought him along, I think he had a bit of thing for him to be honest. Lockwood always did go for those rugger types, the old poof. But Marley wasn't one of us. He didn't fit in. He didn't come from the right background."

"What do you mean?" Lucy asked.

"His father was a churchman. They didn't have money." Ashton-Griffiths gave her a disparaging look. Something of the arrogant youth was still there, just beneath the veneer of social responsibility. "Anyway, it was Higgins who suggested the initiation. Hackett provided the gun. His family were of the huntin', shootin' and fishin' variety."

"So you shot him?" Lucy asked, shocked.

"Don't be ridiculous, my dear," Ulysses rebutted her. "I'm guessing that after a bout of heavy drinking the idea of the initiation was raised with this Marley – a game of Russian roulette was it, Master?"

The older man nodded. He suddenly appeared to have aged ten years, the inconstant shadows cast by the fire giving him a haunted appearance.

"And Marley lost."

"I didn't know Higgins had actually loaded the damn thing! Marley's death shocked us all out of our youthful arrogance and taught us to value what we had more carefully. The Damocles Club was disbanded. We all went our separate ways."

"And yet, almost all of you ended up back in Oxford thirty-seven years later," Ulysses pointed out. "I wonder why that was. A sense of guilt? Unable to completely leave the past behind? Having discovered that you couldn't run from yourselves you all decided to confront your past in some pathetic, subconscious way?"

"So, what do we do now?" The Master raised his head and looked at Ulysses, his eyes glistening in the flickering firelight. "Are you going to have me arrested?"

"Arrested?" Ulysses laughed humourlessly. "But you're not the murderer, are you?"

"But..." Lucy suddenly put in, looking bewildered. "But he's the only one left on the list."

"Yes, but Nimrod and I came straight here, having just chased the killer out of the Botanic Gardens. The Master here is some years older than me and, if you don't mind me saying so Master, he's carrying a few more pounds and he wasn't even out of breath when we arrived. If he had been the killer I wouldn't have expected him to be waiting in his rooms when we arrived and, if by some miracle he was, I would certainly have expected him to be out of breath!"

"But I've just confessed our crime to you," the Master pressed. "I need to pay for the part I played, for being an accessory after the fact."

"If I didn't know any better, I would have to say that I thought you wanted to be arrested, to be put into protective custody and save your own sorry skin."

For a moment the Master was speechless.

"So who's the Christmas Killer?" Lucy asked, completely confused.

"That is, what I suspect, we will all discover before this night is through," Ulysses said, brimful of the sort of arrogant confidence that would have seen him fit quite well with the rest of the Damocles Club where the wretched Marley had not.

"So, what are we going to do now?"

"Now?" Ulysses said, a dark smile forming on his lips. "Now we wait."

VII

Santa Claws is Coming to Town

THE CLOCK IN the Master's study was just striking the tenth bell of eleven when Father Christmas paid a call. He broke down the door on the second attempt, but by that time Ulysses' prescient sixth sense had already alerted him to the assailant's approach.

Lucy screamed as the doorjamb splintered and a hulking figure burst into the room. He was shrouded by a deep red cloak and hood, trimmed with white fur, and as he lurched into the study steel claws gleamed in the dying ember-glow emanating from the grate.

With a startled grunt the hulk hesitated, surprised to discover that the Master had company. But his hesitation lasted only a moment. Dogged in his determination, and apparently unconcerned as to the presence of potential witnesses to the crime he was about to commit, the ogre lunged for the Master with a savage roar.

But Ulysses and Nimrod were ready.

The brute was almost as broad as he was tall, built from slabs of muscle, as Ulysses soon learnt to his cost, the man-mountain hurling him across the room by one swipe of his arm, sending the sleigh bells ringing again.

The killer turned his attention back onto the Master who had backed away as far as he could behind his desk, until he was stopped from going any further by a wall of bookshelves.

"Sir!" Nimrod shouted over the furious bellows of the brute, casting an anxious glance Ulysses' way.

"Don't worry about me!" he shouted back, picking himself out of the remains of the side table on which he had landed. "Take him down!"

Nimrod's pistol was in his hands in an instant. Ulysses looked from the muzzle of the gun to the ogre, batting Lucy aside, claws extended, as he tried to reach the mewling Master. Apart from the fact that there was a mad killer on the loose in the room with them, something wasn't right.

"I want him alive!" Ulysses shouted.

Nimrod's gun fired.

With a howl the brute slumped against the Master's desk as his right leg gave way beneath him, his kneecap a bloody mess.

Seizing the opportunity, Nimrod and Ulysses moved in together, Ulysses disarming the killer with a flick of his own rapier-blade. With the two of them pinning the thrashing attacker to the ground, Lucy pulled down one of the velvet drapes covering the windows with which to bind the captured killer, as the Master looked on in amazement.

"But I mean, Father Christmas?" Lucy repeated.

"Who else were you expecting?" Ulysses said. "After all, it is Christmas Eve. And from the look of the gift he was bringing you, Master, it looks like you've most definitely been a bad boy this year."

The Master said nothing, but continued to stare into the shadows beneath the obscuring hood of the cloak

"But what kind of a disguise is that?" the reporter persisted.

"One that's kept his identity a secret and allowed him to kill four – possibly five – men," Ulysses stated grimly. "So," he said, approaching the chair to which they had bound the moaning brute with the curtain, "shall we see who it is before we inform Chief Inspector Thaw that we've caught his Christmas Killer for him?"

Taking hold of the hood in one black-gloved hand he threw it back.

Lucy gasped in horror. As did the Master.

"Marley!" was all he could say, his voice a strained whisper.

Ulysses studied the face of the killer with clinical interest, as a lepidopterist might examine a moth pinned beneath a microscope.

The brute appeared to be a similar age to the Master – in his late fifties – but that was where the similarity ended. His head was entirely hairless and where the Master's eyes sparkled with a ferocious intelligence, behind the killer's eyes there resided a brutal and imbecilic child.

The reason for the former Oxford undergraduate's reversion to a state of moronic childishness was clear. It was as if his face had been sliced down the middle, from the top of his head to his cleft palette. A livid sunken scar had pulled the man's features into the middle of his face, pulling his eyes closer together, making him appear almost permanently cross-eyed. Saliva drooled continually from his gaping toothless mouth soaking the collar of the cloak with its stinking residue.

"The gunshot wound," Ulysses said. "The one that you thought had killed him, Master, all those years ago did this to him."

"I-I had n-no idea," Ashton-Griffiths stammered.

"Looks like your 'victim' is not as dead as you thought he was. By the way," he added, "what time of year did this" – Ulysses indicated Marley's face with a waving finger – "happen?"

"A few days before Christmas 1960," the Master replied, a distant look in his eyes.

"Well, Ulysses, you promised me an exclusive," Lucy said, turning to the dandy, her own shock passing as her reporter's instinct for a good story took over again, "but I never expected anything like this. The Christmas Killer unmasked before my very eyes. Congratulations!" She put out her hand to shake his.

"Oh, it's not case closed yet, my dear," Ulysses remarked, somewhat condescendingly.

"It's not? But you've caught the killer."

"Yes, but look at him," Ulysses said, "he's an imbecile. Severely brain-damaged as a result of his attempt to become a member of the Damocles Club all those years ago. There's no way that he could have masterminded the murders himself, tracking down the perpetrators of something that took place thirty-seven years ago."

Lucy looked again at the pathetic creature bound to the chair before them. Ulysses was right. Marley was a blunt instrument, nothing more.

"No," Ulysses went on, "this poor wretch is merely the puppet. Someone else has been pulling the strings all along. And when we have this puppet-master, then we can consider the case closed."

"So, who's that then?" Lucy was feeling exasperated now. Ulysses flashed her a devilish grin. "You do know, don't you?"

"No – not at all!" he declared gleefully. His devil-may-care attitude was starting to grate on Lucy's nerves.

"But you know where to start looking," the Master suddenly said.

"I do indeed."

"It's the knife-fist, isn't it?" Ashton-Griffiths went on, focusing all his attention on the murder weapon that now lay on the blotting pad on his desk.

It was a rusted metal affair, not unlike a knuckleduster, with a bar that was held in the palm, and four sharp blades that effectively formed claws in place of the wearer's fingers when it was gripped in the hand.

Ulysses nodded. "And I have my old alma mater to thank for that morsel of useful knowledge. After all, it was at those times when I was actually working towards my degree in Social Anthropology that

I visited the Pitt Rivers Museum and saw this particular item for the first time."

Ulysses turned on his heel and made for the door. "Miss Gudrun, I would appreciate it if you would wait here for the police with the Master."

"But–" Lucy tried to protest.

"Don't worry, you've still got your exclusive, but you've done enough. Nimrod, you're with me."

As the dandy and his butler exited the Master's study in a whirl of coat tails and well-bred arrogance, Lucy was left mouthing 'O's like a goldfish.

"Quicksilver's wasting his time," the Master said from the other side of the room, teacup and saucer in hand again.

"What do you mean?" Lucy asked intrigued.

"I mean, they won't find the killer's manipulator at the museum. They don't know who they're looking for."

"And you do?"

"I've a pretty good idea," the Master said, the steel back in his voice. Ignoring the curious gaze of the drooling idiot still bound to the chair in the middle of his study, Ashton-Griffiths moved for the door. "Wouldn't you rather come with me, now, and find out if I'm right, rather than wait here for the police with... with that?"

A moment later, Lucy Gudrun ran out of the study on the heels of the darkly determined Master.

VIII

Sins of the Fathers

"This is most irregular," the curator complained as Ulysses barged past him and into the echoing hall that housed the Pitt Rivers collection. Nimrod shot the man a look that silenced him and followed his master into the museum annexe.

Their insistent knocking had alerted a night watchman – saving Nimrod the bother of having to pick the locks – who had then fetched the curator from his attic apartment. The curator answered the night watchman's summons in his pyjamas and slippers. He had not been best pleased.

The cavernous space of the museum rose for three floors above them in the darkness. Ulysses was aware of bizarre shadow-shapes looming out of the darkness all around him. As the curator trotted anxiously after the invaders of this sanctuary, Ulysses and Nimrod turned on their torches.

Ulysses gasped in delight as his sweeping beam illuminated the leering faces of a totem pole, suspended Eskimo kayaks and luridly-painted Balinese ritual masks. The place never failed to evoke a familiar thrill of wonder and joy.

Ulysses had been a regular visitor to the University Museum of Natural History and its Pitt Rivers' extension, when he had been a student at Boriel College, sometimes for purposes of study, at other times simply to luxuriate in the eccentric, jingoistic glory of it all.

It was a magical place, a monument to the attitudes and explorers – like Captain James Cook – who had helped to make Magna Britannia great.

It was rumoured that the collection contained half a million objects, displayed according to type – everything from masks and musical instruments, to fetishes, jewellery and weaponry. And it was the last of those things that had brought him back here on this dark Christmas Eve.

His own collection of esoteric and exotic pieces from around the world were almost a homage to this wonderful relic of the nineteenth century, but it couldn't compare to this collection gathered during Cook's expedition to the South Pacific and since donated by Lieutenant General Augustus Henry Lane Fox Pitt Rivers.

"Most irregular, you say," Ulysses announced, suddenly turning on the thin-faced curator, shining his torch beam directly into the startled man's face. The curator threw up a hand to save himself from being blinded.

"So is murder, Mr...?"

"It's Doctor, actually," the curator bit back. "Doctor Brierley."

"Would you happen to know if there was such a thing as a Hootoo Clan fighting-fist in the museum collection?" Ulysses asked, turning his torch back onto the display cases full of shrunken heads and flint axes that surrounded him.

"Wh-What? W-Well, yes," the flustered curator flapped, "as it happens."

"Ah, I knew it! I was sure there was." He turned back to the curator who was still trying to knot the belt of his dressing gown about his waist. "Can I see it?"

"Er, yes... I-I mean no."

"Ah! And why not?" Ulysses pressed, leaning towards the curator, breaking the invisible barrier of Doctor Brierley's own personal space. Brierley took a nervous step backwards, only to find Nimrod there, looming over his shoulder, watching him with eagle-intensity. "Lost it, have you?

"Oh, no. It's out on loan."

"On loan?"

"Yes, along with a number of other items, to the college."

"Which one?" Ulysses said, his voice low and intense.

"Christ Church."

Ulysses' look of diffident arrogance began to weaken and his face began to pale. Things were not working out quite as he had expected them to.

"And in whose name was the agreement made?" he asked, his throat suddenly tight.

"The Reverend Havelock of the cathedral."

IX

Murder in the Cathedral

"THIS IS HARDLY the time, or the place," the old priest chided, keeping his voice low as the lilting strains of the choir soared into the vaulted roof of the cathedral. "Can't you see that we are in the middle of celebrating Midnight Mass?"

"Tell me then, Reverend," Virgil Ashton-Griffiths rallied, "when *would* be a good time to discuss your son?"

Lucy looked from the Master to the old priest and back again, her mouth agape in appalled amazement.

The old man hesitated before answering the Master's challenge. "What are you talking about? What is this talk of a son? I have no son!"

But he had hesitated too long before responding to the Master's accusation.

"You and I both know that you do have a son, Reverend, and that he's alive and – although I wouldn't go so far as to say well – abroad in Oxford!"

"This is outrageous!" the old man hissed. He had to be in his eighties – his late seventies at least – Lucy thought as she studied the quivering wattles of the old man's neck and the liver-spotted scalp visible beneath the few wisps of white hair. He was turning an extraordinary shade of purple. "How dare you come in here, on today of all days, making such wild claims!" he fumed.

"I dare because it's the truth!" the Master snarled. His steely gaze locked with the rheumy eyes of the old man. "We all knew even when we were at University, the first time we met Marley – the priest's bastard!"

Fire leapt in the Reverend's eyes at that but it seemed that the Master's brow-beating persistence had paid off; the old man was no longer able to avoid the younger man's glaring gaze.

"I feel like I have the blood of enough men on my hands as it is," Ashton-Griffiths went on. "I need absolution, I'm fully aware of that, but your need is greater than mine."

The Reverend seemed to visibly shrink before Lucy's eyes, his shoulders sagging, his stick-thin scarecrow frame shrouded by his plain black cassock.

"Very well, he said," his voice softer now. "Come with me."

The old man turned and led them back towards the entrance of the cathedral, away from the candle-lit nave and the host of the Christmas faithful.

Oxford's cathedral was packed. The building was small by the standards of other cathedrals, no bigger in reality than many ordinary churches, and it was never fuller than at Midnight Mass. It was only a matter of minutes now until Great Tom tolled twelve and welcomed in Christmas Day.

Her heart thumping in her chest, Lucy followed the Master as the Reverend Lemuel Havelock led them with faltering steps towards the shadows beneath the raised organ loft.

The choir concluded its anthem and there was the rustle of carol sheets as the congregation rose to their feet, with an accompaniment of coughs and throat-clearing. Then the strident tones of the organ began to sing out, breaking into the tune of 'O Come All Ye Faithful'.

"Here, there's something I should show you," the old man said, still with his back to them. Lucy couldn't be certain in the gloom at the back of the church but it looked like the priest was fumbling for something within the sleeve of his cassock.

He spun round with surprising speed, the carved wooden blowpipe already to his lips and gave one short sharp puff.

The tiny thorn lodged in the Master's neck. Ashton-Griffiths gave a brief cry of surprise and fell to his knees, one hand to where the thorn had entered his flesh. A second later, he fell face first onto the cold stone-flagged floor.

Lucy froze, a stifled scream caught in her throat, as the old man turned to her, a second thorn ready between his lips.

Some of those at the back of the congregation turned and looked back, peering over their shoulders into the shadows beneath the organ loft, uncertain as to what they had heard over the stirring refrain of the carol.

The west door banged opened, the resounding crash reverberating throughout the cathedral. The organist played on, but by now many among the congregation had stopped singing and were exchanging comments and glances instead, as they craned their necks to see who had invaded the sanctity of their Christmas celebration.

"Reverend Havelock! Stop right there!" Ulysses Quicksilver bellowed.

The old man darted a glance the dandy's way, caught completely off-guard by his arrival. The blowpipe still to his lips, the old man puffed again and Ulysses – reacting to the sudden lightning burst of his heightened sixth sense – ducked in time to avoid the dart that came propelled by the breath. He fancied he felt, or heard, the thorn-dart whistle past his ear before being stopped by the door of the church swinging shut behind him.

And then, as Lucy stood rooted to the spot in terror, standing over the body of the Master of Boriel College, with a surprising turn of speed, the priest was away, up the cast-iron spiral staircase to the organ loft.

Ulysses followed, scaling the twisting staircase as quickly as he could. He reached the loft only a moment after the old man and came face-to-face with the priest's puff-cheeked face.

The merry playing of the organ broke off in a cacophonous crash of registers and pedals as Ulysses threw himself sideways onto the startled man, barely avoiding a second poison-tipped missile.

By now, even the choir had realised that something was wrong. All had ceased their singing and were craning their heads to follow the progress of the two combatants above them.

Having untangled himself from the shrieking organist, Ulysses turned to find the old man gone.

"He went that way, sir!" Nimrod called from below, pointing to a narrow stone archway and the tight spiral stair that lay beyond it.

"Give yourself up, man!" Ulysses shouted across the void of the tower. "There's nowhere for you to run!"

He glanced from the withered form of the Reverend Havelock, scrambling unsteadily between the arches of the colonnade beneath the high stained glass windows of the cathedral tower, to the body of the church far below them. He could see pale faces peering up at them from between the myriad nimbuses of candlelight that formed their own constellation of Christmas stars below.

"Never!" Havelock shrieked back at him. "You really think I'm going to give myself up now?"

Distracted, the old man lost his footing. The congregation below them gasped in horror as one. The Reverend Havelock lurched forwards, making a grab for the next stone column as his right foot slipped off the precarious ledge he was attempting to negotiate. Ulysses' breath caught in his throat.

"But you're going to get yourself killed!"

"What do I care? I'm an old man. I might die in my sleep this very night! And my son's life ended thirty-seven years ago. What have I to live for?"

Deciding that actions, in this case were definitely going to speak louder than words, Ulysses gave up attempting to talk the old man down and instead set off in pursuit, swinging from one columned archway to the next, using his unnaturally strong left arm to aid him in his gymnastic endeavour.

Havelock might think he had nothing to live for, but Ulysses wasn't going to let him get off that lightly; he wanted to see him brought to book for what he had engineered. He wanted to see justice served.

With one last death-defying swing, Ulysses cut the last corner of the tower and threw himself into the colonnade opposite the spot from where he had commenced his approach on the old man.

Preternatural senses flared and Ulysses doubled up as the warning bolt of prescience shot right into the middle of his brain. The old man was ready for him. A vicious kick to the shin brought Ulysses down hard and he almost lost his grip on the stone pillar he was still holding with his primate hand. The priest bore down on him, blowpipe to his lips once more, and this time, if he threw himself out of the way Ulysses would be throwing himself to his death on the stone-flagged floor at the bottom of the tower.

Grabbing the other open end of the carved wooden blowpipe, Ulysses tugged it forwards and put it to his own lips – and blew.

The old man dropped the primitive weapon immediately. He stumbled backwards, palsied hands reaching for his throat, a choking rasp escaping his gaping mouth, his failing eyes wide with the shock of it. As Ulysses pulled himself to safety between the arches, the priest's faltering steps carried him to the edge of the ledge – and beyond.

Screams rose from the appalled watchers below, but the old man made no sound as he plummeted to his death. He was dead even before his skull cracked like an egg on the stones below.

X

It's a Wonderful Life

"SO, YOU'RE DONE here, are you?" Lucy asked Ulysses as he walked out of the police station. His shoes crunched on the ice-crusted snow covering the ground.

"Yes, we're done here," he said, pulling up the collar of his coat against the cold and adjusting the scarf at his neck. He had a wide-brimmed hat pulled down firmly over his ears as well.

The Silver Phantom was pulled up next to the kerb, Nimrod at the wheel, the engine ticking over to warm the interior of the car.

"So, what's the story? Why did this all come to pass at this moment in time?"

"You mean, when the wrong done to the Reverend Havelock and his son occurred thirty-seven years ago?"

"Yes."

"It was all down to Doctor Lacey."

"Really?"

"Yes. It all started when he took up a new post at the Saint Ophelia Sanatorium for the Mentally Infirm. Marley was one of the residents there."

"That's something else, I don't understand," Lucy said, interrupting Ulysses' explanation of the events surrounding the Christmas Killings. "Why did Reverend Havelock let everyone think that his son was dead?"

"I would have thought that was obvious."

"Humour me," she said, nudging Ulysses in the ribs.

"Embarrassment. Marley had been a scholar, accepted to study at Boriel College, Oxford. It was all about intelligence, as far as the old man was concerned. And then his boy went and shot himself. He didn't know it had been part of some ridiculous college club initiation. The Damocles Club members covered that bit up, remember?

"Havelock thought his son had attempted suicide, and suicide is a sin against God. As if that wasn't embarrassing enough he didn't have the common decency to die but instead survived, with the mental state of an idiot child, and with a Father Christmas fixation to boot. As far as the Reverend was concerned it was better that he kept his son hidden from the world, and let the world think his son was dead."

"But that's terrible."

"That's as maybe but then of course the Reverend didn't know that his son's condition wasn't a direct consequence of a suicide attempt."

"Yes, how did he find out?"

"Lacey wrote to him. The police found the letter at the Reverend's place. It was effectively a confession and suicide note all rolled into one. Lacey was manic depressive, you see, which meant that he understood what it was like to be mentally ill and so wanted to help others in a similar condition. But when he discovered that his one-time paramour was a dribbling infantile retard he was overcome with guilt and remorse, and started on a downward spiral of depression from which he never recovered.

"Somehow, the letter came to be posted after Lacey's death and when Havelock read it, it brought back all the memories – the hurt, the guilt – which soon turned to anger. And so he planned his revenge more for his own benefit than for his wretched son. But he was old, he couldn't accomplish what he wanted to himself and so we come to his crowning achievement; he used his own brain-damaged son as the instrument of his vengeance.

"He checked Marley out of the asylum, equipping him to fulfil his own dark designs, while he tracked down the surviving members of the Damocles Club, who Lacey had so helpfully listed in his confession. Chief Inspector Thaw and Sergeant Whately found evidence that Marley had been living with the Reverend Havelock in his quarters at the cathedral."

"Incredible," Lucy said, dumbfounded by the immensity of the reverend's plan. "So what will happen to Marley now?"

"I believe he's been returned to the asylum where he has spent the last thirty-seven years of his life, to live out the rest of it, in the maximum security wing."

Ulysses looked thoughtful for a moment as he studied the patterns the snow had made on the toecaps of his shoes. "It's ironic really."

"What is?"

"This all began because Marley wanted to join the Damocles Club but failed the initiation. And in the end, all the Damocles Club members are dead, and Marley's the only one left alive."

Ulysses turned from his musings to his waiting car.

"I can't tempt you to spend what's left of Christmas Day here, in Oxford?" the young woman asked, looking up at him from beneath the brim of her beret.

"Aren't you spending Christmas with friends or family already? Surely your life isn't all work, work, work. It's not good for you. You must have plans."

"Nothing that couldn't be changed," she said, her cheeks reddening in embarrassment. "I don't know about you but I could quite happily spend the rest of the day in bed, catching up, having not slept at all last night."

Ulysses grinned.

"Thank you for the invitation, my dear," he said, smiling wryly, "but Mrs Prufrock's coming in especially and will doubtless already have the turkey on the go. And besides, my brother Barty would cut a very pathetic figure if I wasn't there. You can't pull a cracker by yourself, can you?"

"You've managed," the young woman smiled coyly.

Ulysses took a deep breath. He gazed up at the clear cerulean sky, savouring the honeyed sunlight and the crisp cold air on his face. And then he turned from the car and returned to Lucy's side.

"Tempting as your offer is, and I may well live to regret this, but if I have learnt anything from the Case of the Christmas Killer it is that the rash actions of your youth will inevitably come back to haunt you one day, so, Merry Christmas, Miss Gudrun."

He lent forward and kissed her on her heat-flushed cheek.

"Well, you can't blame a girl for trying," she said, returning the kiss. "Merry Christmas, Mr Quicksilver."

BACK IN THE security of his own cushion-walled room, he opened the jotter on the table in front of him and creased it flat at a clean page.

For the first time in as long as he could remember, he hadn't written a letter this year, but he hoped it wouldn't matter. Father Christmas would understand.

Pulling a bright red crayon from the box beside the jotter, clenching it tightly in the fist of his right hand, the tip of his tongue protruding from between his lips, he began to write.

Dear Farthr Krissmus,

I'm sorry I not wrote my letter in time this year but I was on holiday with my Dad. It was a lot of fun. I haven't seen my Dad in ages. And I was a good boy, like he said I had to be. I always did as I was told and ate up all my greens, even though I don't like greens.

So now you know I bin good this year and said sorry for not writin in time can I have my present anyway?

I really liked seeing my Dad again so this year for Krissmus I dont want any more crayons or a puppy or nothin like that. I would like to go and stay with my Dad again. Do you think I could do that? I hope so.

Happy Krissmus

Love Marley

THE END

Cruickshank's

CABINET OF CURIOSITIES

Featuring the astonishing aquatic marvel
that is the Whitby Mermaid.

Presented by the
distinguished Curator
of the Grotesque and
Collector of the Macabre,
*Mr. Mycroft
Cruickshank, Esq.*
See it for yourself at The
Holbrook Museum now!

(It is recommended
that ladies of uncertain
constitutions be
accompanied by gentlemen
of resolute fortitude, due
to the wholly unseating
nature of some of the
exhibits therein.)

JONATHAN GREEN lives and works in West London. He is well known for his contributions to the *Fighting Fantasy* range of adventure gamebooks, as well as his novels set within Games Workshop's worlds of *Warhammer* and *Warhammer 40,000*. He has written fiction for such diverse properties as *Sonic the Hedgehog* and *Doctor Who*, and non-fiction books including the titles *Match Wits with the Kids* and *What is Myrrh Anyway?* The co-creator of the world of Pax Britannia, *Human Nature* is his third novel for Abaddon Books and the fourth in the series. To find out more about the world of Pax Britannia, set your Babbage engine's ether-relay to www.paxbritanniablog. blogspot.com